THE NORTON BOOK OF
GHOST STORIES

THE NORTON BOOK OF GHOST STORIES

 Edited by BRAD LEITHAUSER

W · W · NORTON & COMPANY · NEW YORK · LONDON

The text of this book is composed in Avanta Electra,
with the display set in Bernhard Modern.
Composition and manufacturing by the Haddon Craftsmen, Inc.
Book design by Antonina Krass adapted by Jack Meserole.

Since this page cannot legibly accommodate all the copyright notices the Copyright
Acknowledgments on pages 429–30 constitute an extension of the copyright page.

Library of Congress Cataloging-in-Publication Data
The Norton book of ghost stories / edited by Brad Leithauser.
p.   cm.
1. Ghost stories, English. 2. Ghost stories, American.
I. Leithauser, Brad.
PR1309.G5N67   1994
823'.0873308—dc20   94-17383

ISBN 0-393-03564-6

W.W. Norton & Company, Inc., 500 Fifth Avenue, New York, N.Y. 10110
W.W. Norton & Company Ltd., 10 Coptic Street, London WC1A 1PU

1 2 3 4 5 6 7 8 9 0

FOR DAVID MOHNEY—

Friend of the Year
and of the years

CONTENTS

INTRODUCTION

In one of M. R. James's most celebrated ghost stories, "Count Magnus," a moment arises that, for me, strikes at the thrillingly cold heart of this peculiar genre. An innkeeper re-creates an evening in which his grandfather nervously awaits the return of two men who have trespassed into what some consider a haunted wood:

> My grandfather was sitting here in this room. It was the summer, and a light night. With the window open, he could see out to the wood, and hear.
> So he sat there, and two or three men with him, and they listened. At first they hear nothing at all; then they hear someone—you know how far away it is—they hear someone scream, just as if the most inside part of his soul was twisted out of him. All of them in the room caught hold of each other, and they sat so for three-quarters of an hour. Then they hear someone else, only about three hundred ells off. They hear him laugh out loud: it was not one of those two men that laughed, and, indeed, they have all of them said that it was not any man at all.

The scream is a simple but pitiful thing, a cry of pure animal terror, but the laughter's a good deal more complex. Just why are they so effectively unnerving—these final, gloating explosions of merriment from a supernatural agent (whether ghost, vampire, genie, or the Devil himself)? Most of us have heard the sound so often—in films, in television skits, in written stories, in oral childhood tales—that we ought by now to be immune to it. Yet it still lays an arresting hand upon us.

Surely, such laughter is chilling in part because of the rich range of messages it manages so compactly—wordlessly—to convey. It speaks volumes. In "Count Magnus," as in many ghost stories, laughter first of all evokes for us an adversary of striking self-possession; this is somebody who not only snares his human prey, but all the while has the distance and detachment, the diabolical *leisure,* to draw amusement from doing so. The laughter also implies that all human calamities—even the loss of

9

one's life, sanity, or immortal soul—are trifling affairs; its eruption abruptly, viciously transforms tragedy into comedy. In this transformation, the doomed is denied what seems the final entitlement of any doomed soul: a lingering moment of pity before his headlong tumble into hell. The laughter usually carries, in addition, an echo of self-satisfaction, of vindication, as though the protagonist's fall were inevitable, his stratagems and evasions foreseen and forfended from the outset. Finally, the laughter may seek to prompt in us an altogether different show of mirth—the reader's nervous chuckle at having himself survived the tale.

One might say, in comparing the ghost story to a sibling genre, that science fiction typically seeks to elicit from the reader a "Wow" of surprise and wonderment, while the ghost story aspires to a "Whew . . ." We are meant at the denouement of most supernatural tales to feel relief. Ghost stories reflect a variety of aims, of course, but in its essential form the tale undertakes a careful sortie into a landscape of terrors—a cyclical journey (from the natural world to the supernatural and back again) that promises to release us, chastened but intact, at its close.

With this prototype in mind I've put together the following anthology, which would have been called "The Norton Book of Modern Supernatural Fiction in English, with an Emphasis on the Two Main Branches of the Ghost Story, as Epitomized by M. R. James and Henry James" had that title not somehow lacked a certain ring. Anyone who would compile a ghost story anthology faces a number of stiff tasks (chief among them, the wretchedness of so much of the material—for is there any other genre whose failures are quite so impossibly god-awful?), but by rights he ought to enjoy one considerable boon: Since this genre is a sort of back lot, a comparatively minor literary form, he surely needn't be overly respectful—need not make inclusions based upon a tale's date of origin, or its historical sway, or the repute of its author. Had I instead been putting together an anthology of nineteenth-century American poetry, say, I might dutifully have included various mediocrities in acknowledgment of their former influence or representative tone. In dealing with the ghost story, though, I felt entitled to uphold merit as my single criterion of selection. Hence, a number of elevated names—staples of other anthologies—will not be found here. Having spoken of the ghost story as a back lot, I should add that I have long found it a particularly lush and verdant site, and therefore have felt no need to "legitimate" the genre by accepting second-rate tales by first-rate figures. Many an illustrious writer, justly renowned for accomplishments in mainstream genres, has stumbled when attempting a ghost story; not surprisingly, it calls for talents that are exacting, narrow, and quirky. It may well be the case, for instance, that Sir Walter Scott invented the modern ghost story in English, and duly deserves a place of preeminence in histories of the genre, but to my mind all the ghosts in his tales have, long ago, shifted from a sleepless to a tranquil grave. They're twice—doubly—dead. The reader will find no Scott here—nor any Brontë, Dickens, Gaskell, Cather, Bierce, Hardy, Wells, or De la Mare. Although I treasure many of these writers, I don't consider most of them best—or even well—represented by their ghost stories. If the tales in this anthology enclose a number of strange "animals," my hope is that the book will feel less like a museum than a zoo: I've tried to avoid the once splendid but now dusty stuffed beast in its glass case, in favor of the restive creature that even yet breathes and eats and watches.

Any discussion of the classic English-language ghost story will likely revolve around a pair of names—or, one might say, around paired branches of a single name, since the form's two acknowledged masters, though unrelated by blood or nationality, happen to be namesakes (a coincidence all the more pleasing for having arisen in a genre much given to musings upon chance similarities and flukes of fate). I am speaking, of course, of Henry James and M. R. James. (The initials stand for Montague Rhodes. He was "Montie" among friends, and thus shall be identified here; the shared surname, with all its possibilities for confusion, seems to invite us to take, toward both of the "James brothers," the liberty of a first-name address.) Henry—whose accomplishments in the field I will turn to shortly—took a lifelong interest in the ghost story. He wrote his first tale, "The Romance of Certain Old Clothes," when he was twenty-four, and the novel he was working on when he died, at the age of seventy-two, had a ghostly premise. His *Stories of the Supernatural*, edited by Leon Edel, encompasses some eighteen stories and more than seven hundred pages. His novella *The Turn of the Screw* has almost certainly sparked more academic debate and exegesis than any other piece of modern supernatural fiction.

If the ghost stories of M. R. James have never fired anything like comparable critical interest, they have not lacked for devotees among either writers of genius (including Housman and Hardy) or the general reading public. While Edel's edition has dropped from print, leaving those readers drawn to Henry's supernatural fiction with the task of piecemeal and fragmentary compilation, Montie's books continue to emerge in fresh editions. Since 1904, when his first collection, *Ghost Stories of an Antiquary*, was published, his stories have been constantly available. His ongoing fame has about it an appealingly haphazard and improbable air. Ghost stories were for him a mere sidelight. The son of an Evangelical clergyman, he was a medievalist and paleographer and biblical scholar of formidable accomplishment, who dedicated nearly two decades of his life to cataloging the manuscript collections at Cambridge University. His stories tended to be composed in a rush in late December—just in time to be narrated aloud, by candlelight, to a Christmas Eve assembly of friends and fellow dons at King's College. If Monte is an ancillary literary figure, he looks to be a durable one, and surely few writers have ever won a portion of immortality with such quick, light-handed ease.

However hasty their production, the stories are brilliant—a truth patent to anyone who explores the genre thoroughly enough to fix Montie beside his numerous imitators. He is as indisputably the master of what might be termed the "plot ghost story" as Henry is of the psychological ghost tale. While Henry's people are marvels of depth—personalities as many-layered as a slab of fossiliferous limestone—Montie's cast of characters consists almost exclusively of stick figures: timid bachelor dons, malapropism-spouting rustics, sinister landholders. Still he manages, repeatedly, to inject his stick figures into a landscape sufficiently realized, and a plot sufficiently skillful and compelling, that we nonetheless fret over the tale's outcome. His stories are brief but densely detailed, and for all their civility and erudition, Montie time and again demonstrates a great flair for what he called the "crescendo": a moment of raw, head-paralyzing grotesquerie.

Montie spent little time analyzing the literary form in which his enduring fame was won. What he left us by way of prefaces and introductions is modest, casual, unreflective. Apparently, it never occurred to him that the ghost story as he constructed it is an especially problem-ridden form.

In embracing those bookish bachelor dons as heroes, he barred himself from many of the most reliably fruitful devices of the genre. Ghost stories commonly strike at us "where we live." In many—perhaps most—tales, the ghost takes on the role of an intimate: One's spouse or betrothed is revealed as a "demon lover"—a theme exemplified in this anthology by, among others, Cheever's "Torch Song," Jackson's "The Tooth," Bowen's "The Cat Jumps" (as well as, of course, her "Demon Lover"), and Henry James's "The Friends of the Friends." In other cases, ghosts infiltrate one's family, incarnating themselves as parents or, more unnerving still, as children (the most celebrated example being *The Turn of the Screw*). But Montie's heroes are likely to have no lovers (and to meet no temptresses), and to be without close family (or distant family either). They are solitary men, whose pared lives offer supernatural agents precious little purchase.

It was Montie's instinctive genius to understand that such men are most productively haunted—are most exquisitely vulnerable—within the two institutions toward which any upright turn-of-the-century English don might reasonably look for impregnable sanctuary: the library and the Anglican Church. Wherever books are gathered in his stories, there's a risk of infernal subterfuge—frequently taking the form of some craftily coded message that only the most adroit scholar might decipher. And wherever a church stands, there's the danger of some kind of satanic interloping, sometimes in the form of a stealthily evil clergyman (like Archdeacon Haynes of "The Stalls of Barchester Cathedral," who arranges to send headlong down a flight of stairs a ninety-two-year-old rival) and sometimes in the form of the various residues—pagan rites, Hebrew texts, or, most threateningly, "papist" designs—of some stubbornly unexpunged faith. His ghosts may trespass simultaneously into both realms, as is presaged in the first sentence of "An Episode of Cathedral History": "There was once a learned gentleman who was deputed to examine and report upon the archives of the cathedral of Southminster."

Haunted archives? Well, they turn out to be a natural lair for ghosts . . . What is a library, after all, but a place where the dead, neatly coffined in their separate volumes, continue to speak? Montie's stock hero is likely to be culpable of no crime more venial than that of scholarly inquisitiveness. Libraries are irresistible to him. He desires merely to *know*, and yet in so desiring may lure catastrophe to himself. The title of one of Montie's stories, "A Warning to the Curious," cuts to the core of the matter. He was forever informing his original audience—that group of dons whose Christmas Eves were consecrated not to families but to colleagues—that their solitary, sedentary livelihood was strewn with hazards. It's a risky business, this process of extracting information from dusty old tomes! Montie's bespectacled heroes are, willy-nilly, intrepid voyagers into the unknown.

He was also advising his colleagues to keep their skills honed, for if perils lurk in the library, one's salvation is likely to be situated there as well. His heroes are forever finessing their way out of a jam by decoding a garbled message, tracking down a rogue citation, locating an obscure medieval document. His tales are part detective story and part brain-teaser. It would not be enough for the reader merely to crack the cryptogram in "Abbot Thomas"; he or she must also know some Latin *and* French to make it out. Montie's are Sherlock Holmesian stories in which Moriarty (a nebulous figure, anyway, in the Conan Doyle series) has been transformed into a wind from the crypt.

In the supernatural world of Henry James, by contrast, the intellect solves nothing. Rather, it engenders its own family of difficulties. His ghost stories repeatedly point out the danger of reason's ascendancy in the mind that has divorced itself from feeling—his characteristic preoccupation with the unlived or unintegrated life. Often the intellect has become derailed; there is a hint of madness in the air. The stories traffic concurrently in apparitions and pathology.

The Edel collection, in its persuasive bulk, leads us to suspect that for Henry this may have been the chief reward of the genre: the opportunities it presented for radically bifurcated discourse. Many of his stories are two-tiered. On one level, the workaday world that most people commonly regard as "real" is shown to be starkly dismissible, for ghosts are afoot in its shadowed purlieus and byways. On another, any reports that we're given concerning supernatural doings are themselves to be dismissed, for they can only be delusional ravings; since the ghosts aren't genuine, the madness has to be. Either way, the reader is unmoored. This is the state of affairs in Henry's most famous ghostly tale, *The Turn of the Screw,* and in the near-century since its publication hundreds of critical pages have been devoted to "proving" either the authenticity of the ghosts or the insanity of the governess who is the tale's primary narrator. It was Edmund Wilson, writing in the twenties, who most prominently advanced the insanity thesis, and his essay might still serve as a prime illustration of how on occasion even the most brilliant thinker can become, in the fervent pursuit of a half-truth, a half-wit. His was the folly of trying to "solve" what was left intentionally ambiguous—a pitfall unlikely to trip up anyone acquainted with both the full range of Henry's supernatural fiction and a healthy assortment of more traditional ghostly tales. No one has written odder supernatural fiction than Henry's, but his stories nonetheless are genre pieces and partake of a good many of the genre's distinguishing characteristics—including a penchant for open-ended mysteries. To find a solution to *The Turn of the Screw* is to miss what is perhaps its principal gratification: that of watching its author deftly mediate between the plausible and the fantastic.

Henry's stratified narration (in this anthology, best exemplified by "The Friends of the Friends") creates problems for two kinds of readers. In one camp are those (frequently undergraduates, my teaching experience tells me) who come to a ghost story looking for tangible spirits; they have little patience with the coy dancing of Henry's shades. In the other camp are those readers and critics for whom the ghostly is instantly reducible to psychological components. For them it is a truism that one's demons are always internal, that the "other" afloat out there represents only some form of ourselves. Neither type of reader is temperamentally adapted to a two-tiered tale—although, since the underpinnings of the entire ghost story genre are inherently primitive and superstitious, a naive undergraduate reader probably does less violence to Henry's stories than an overly sophisticated critic.

This sort of critic often lacks that mobility of imagination needed to understand that what individuates the genre is precisely the fear that our nervous forebodings are *not* all reducible to inner trauma and turmoil. To conceive of the ghost story purely as a battle with inner demons, however terrifying such may be, is to denature it. Henry took his ghosts seriously. (One thinks of his long attendance on posthumous communications from his brother William.) Ghostly horror hinges upon this issue of *ex*ternality—the fear of something out there that is *not* oneself, something wholly independent of one's wishes and feelings. It's the suspicion that, to rephrase Roosevelt, we have more to fear than fear itself.

My bisection of the genre into ghost stories of plot and of psychology unfortunately may work to conceal many of the traits that subtend and unify the form. Whatever their subspecies, ghost stories tend to share many resemblances. In their restless unease, their dissatisfaction with the provable, they constantly hunger for the infinite. They extend toward a vastness that—so they tacitly suggest—we lose sight of in daily life; the supernatural seeks to rescue us from the blinkered vistas of the natural world. Tokens of a wider universe often appear before any visitant actually arrives. One thinks of that timorous "old hen" Parkins in Montie's " 'Oh, Whistle, and I'll Come to You, My Lad' " as he first releases a note from the queer whistle he'd found earlier that day in a pagan ruin:

> He blew tentatively and stopped suddenly, startled and yet pleased at the note he had elicited. It had a quality of infinite distance in it, and, soft as it was, he somehow felt it must be audible for miles round.

Or of the unnamed narrator in Henry's "Sir Edmund Orme" on his way to church, minutes before his initial glimpse of the ghost that stalks his beloved: "We were a straggling procession in the mild damp air—which, as always at that season, gave one the feeling that after the trees were bare there was more of it, a larger sky . . ." Though the ghost story writer's primary currency may be the grotesque, he is, just like the lyric poet, forever urging us to commune with the immeasurable.

Both sorts of ghost story are equally bound up with notions of justice. It is rare for ghosts to prey upon the wholly blameless. Most of the time, one must infract a rule or injunction in order to provoke them. However heartless a ghost may be, he or she will likely respect any sort of compact or bargain. Justice is blind in the next world, too—it binds the living and dead alike. Often the ghost story can be seen as a bizarre gloss on English contract law, in which what lawyers call "consideration" has been expanded to encompass one's sanity or immortal soul. What is so harrowing about ghostly justice is that it appears at once fair and ferocious. True, we have the security of knowing that some transgression is usually required in order to bring down a ghostly reprisal, and yet punishments are brutally disproportionate to offenses. It takes so little to summon up one's doom! Montie's characters typically go astray through peccadilloes: Somebody kicks open a lock on his own property, or, while seeking hidden treasure, reaches into a niche he has been warned against, or ignores a servant's misgivings about the placement of a rose garden. The reader protests, with a shudder, *But I would have done the same thing . . .*

Finally, both sorts of ghost story gradually concretize: They progress from the vaporous to the palpable. Ghosts are wont to announce their arrival first through a scent, or perhaps a distant cry. Gradually, they impinge on senses that we consider more reliable—sight and, culminatingly, touch. They are immaterial entities who are forever solidifying, and the climax of a story often arrives when flesh at last encounters something not quite flesh—something simultaneously human and inhuman. Their ultimate objective is, time and again, an "unnatural" physical contact.

It makes sense, then, that both Henry and Montie apparently were nonpracticing homosexuals: men who might be expected to show an especially keen sensitivity—compounded of fear, desire, and a need for dual outlets of expression and suppression—to the images and implications of "unnatural" contact. These are stories in which, over and over, a self-contained, fastidious narrator suffers some sort of unexpected and unmanning embrace. When these meetings are lifted from their ambience of terror and set down in isolation, it is striking how frequently they suggest an amorous encounter, as in these climactic moments from Montie's stories:

> It hung for an instant on the edge of the hole, then slipped forward on to my chest and *put its arms round my neck.*

> One body had the arms tight round the other.

> . . . two arms enclosing a mass of blackness came before Eldred's face and covered his head and neck. His legs and arms were wildly flourished, but no sound came.

> I was pursued by the very vivid impression that wet lips were whispering into my ear with great rapidity and emphasis for some time together.

The ghost story has innate attractions to the sensibility that inwardly yearns, despite itself, for a touch so overmastering that one's scruples or inhibitions are as nothing, so sweeping that one cannot help succumbing. Who among us, after all, is equipped to reject the advances of the dead?

Probably it is no coincidence that Montie rigorously objected to the insertion into the ghost story of anything overtly sexual ("a fatal mistake"). Nonetheless, I don't see how we can possibly read " 'Oh, Whistle, and I'll Come to You' " as anything but, on one level, a tale of profound homosexual anxiety. When we're introduced to Parkins (who is "hen-like" and "something of an old woman"), he quivers and blushes at the prospect of sharing a room at the seaside with his "bluff" younger colleague Rogers. Parkins reaches the inn a few days before his friend, and his vacation begins auspiciously. Walking on the beach he finds the pagan whistle, and excitedly vows on the morrow to undertake a little archeology.

Yet as he awaits his friend's arrival, he is repeatedly visited by a waking nightmare. He beholds a man on the seashore running from a "figure in pale, fluttering draperies." The pursued takes shelter in the lee of a groyne. When he is eventually discovered, his pursuer darts "straight forward towards the groyne" (a pun of such flagrancy that one marvels its author could have overlooked it), at which point "Parkins always failed in his resolution to keep his eyes shut." The next morning he discovers that the sheets in the neighboring bed are twisted as if someone had "passed a very poor night" (or, the reader wryly observes, a very wanton one). In the story's culminating scene, the hapless Parkins is attacked by—what else?—the sheets of the bed his friend is meant to occupy. He screams. Fortunately, a fellow vacationer (ideally suited to play the dual paternal role of protector and disciplinarian—he's a retired military man, no less) bursts into the room and disentangles Parkins from the sheets.

By sober morning light, the military man ensures that the whistle is tossed into the sea and the offending sheets burned. Significantly, although Parkins is undone by his experience, the author himself recognizes that "it is not so evident what more the creature that came in answer to the whistle could have done than frighten." The ghost had, after all, "nothing material about it save the bed-clothes of which it had made itself a body." At some level, anyway, Montie recognized that the dread of the encounter he could not bring himself to visualize was a greater threat than the encounter itself.

Although some supernatural tales offer no release from their eager-handed spirits, most of the time—as in " 'Whistle' "—the hero breaks from their clutches. In archetype, the ghost story offers the opportunity to contemplate a forbidden embrace and to detach ourselves from it. The form is at once licentious and chaste; it caters to both the libertine and the ascetic in all of us.

The ghost story typically employs a number of hierarchies. Just as ghostly contacts tend to move "upward" physiologically, from smell to sight and touch, they likewise ascend a biological and social pyramid. The lower your position, the quicker you're likely to be about sensing a ghost's arrival. Animals, the lowest beings in the pyramid, will dependably recognize a supernatural visitant long before their owners do. Higher up are children (like the susceptible squabbling boy and girl in "The Cat Jumps") and servants. Still further up are women (feminine intuition) and the Irish (that mystical Celtic blood!). Generally, at the apex stands an upper-class man—a rational being who "knows better" than to believe in spooks. But in the domain of the ghost story, those who know better are usually the last to know.

One of the genre's great charms is its way of regularly reaffirming and upending orthodox social arrangements. (This might help to explain why women have so often and so strikingly found the form congenial. The ghost story is slyly insurgent.) In Montie's world, one never doubts that the world properly revolves around comfortably situated dons and gentlemen scholars. Almost everyone else—loquacious rustics, struggling civil servants, solecism-prone foreigners, shrieking children, occasional domineering aunts and wives—is an amiable joke. But if Montie's oeuvre flatters his colleagues, it also reprimands them. The men he writes about are lacking in a kind of native wit or mother wit; their strict rationality will cost them. In the main, ghost stories rebuke and admonish those at the top of the pyramid, who are warned to pay closer heed to their pets, servants, wives, children.

Whomever a ghost chooses to pursue, the genre can hardly help being subversive of established religions. Its mere existence testifies to the emotional inadequacy of divine justice. In theory, any faith that pledges fairness on an eternal scale—with the wicked consigned to hell and the virtuous ensconced in heaven—ought to be enough for us. Yet it seems that the prospect of justice in the next world is insufficient. We summon up supernatural agents in order to ensure that retribution is effected on earth. Human courts of law are fallible, and too often allow the wicked to disport with impunity; divine justice is presumably unerring, but takes too long. We need something else, something faster, and this is where the supernatural obliges us.

Ghosts are a sort of proto-religion ("Do you believe . . . ," we ask each other), and, as such, they play an uneasy, interstitial role beside any larger, more fixed faith. Their long association with Christmas Eve—a final flurrying of spirits before the advent of the Christ Child—reminds us that they are kin to those minor deities and idols that monotheistic religions insist we abjure. If, individually, ghosts symbolize the lingering potency of a particular deceased, collectively they stand for the deathless power of the pagan. They particularly like to materialize when and where they are least welcome—on Sunday, in churches. Religion has suppressed them and they are resentful. They are always on the lookout for a recrudescence.

Academe's curious disregard of the ghost story suggests that the image of a pyramid might usefully be applied here as well. At a time when English departments throughout the land are bent on rattling orthodoxies and reworking critical assumptions, it is interesting—if sometimes a little alarming—to observe how certain wayworn assumptions persist. If one contrasts the multitudes of critical studies focused on the English gothic novel, as exemplified by Horace Walpole, Ann Radcliffe, and M. G. Lewis, to the few spare examinations of the supernatural fiction of M. R. James or Edith Wharton or Elizabeth Bowen, the conclusion is inarguable that novels continue to be regarded as "higher"—further up the pyramid of genres—than short stories. Because there are so few modern ghost novels of note (the list thins precipitously after Kingsley Amis's *The Green Man* and Shirley Jackson's *The Haunting of Hill House*), ghost fiction can hardly be taken seriously by anyone not first willing to take the short story seriously. Having immersed myself for some time in the literature of the supernatural, I frankly can't imagine anyone who wouldn't trade away a shelf of sagging old gothic novels for the sharp-angled brilliance of Henry's "Maud-Evelyn" or Montie's "Casting the Runes"—or Elizabeth Bowen's "The Cat Jumps" or Muriel Spark's "Portobello Road" or John Cheever's "Torch Song." This is "small" art only in terms of size. The strength of these last three stories, all of relatively recent vintage, attests to the form's ongoing vitality.

The late Roald Dahl was expressing a widespread opinion when, in the introduction to his *Roald Dahl's Book of Ghost Stories*, he wrote, "Spookiness is, after all, the real purpose of the ghost story. It should give you the creeps and disturb your thoughts." He espoused a somewhat narrower view of the genre than I do. If mere spookiness is one's objective, a ghost story anthology may not be the best place to look. While I consider most of the stories assembled here unnerving, a few of them deeply so, I can't help thinking that if the virtue of any artwork that deals with the supernatural is to be directly correlated to adrenaline production—if its aesthetic value could be tabulated by wiring up its audience in a laboratory—one would be better off looking to film rather than typescript. When it comes to the sort of fear that thumps the heart and dampens the temples, horror movies are hard to beat.

My hypothetical laboratory, of course, raises a host of qualifications. The measuring of any audience response, even one as purely primal as terror, is a problematic undertaking. Spookiness might be evaluated not merely by intensity but by duration. In the long run, no horror film I've ever seen has unsettled me as *The Turn of the Screw* has. On the other hand, no ghost story has ever made me literally jump from my seat, as George Romero's low-budget black-and-white cult classic *The Night of the Living Dead* once did.

For many of us who, like me, have little taste for horror films but a bottomless appetite for ghost stories, the written tale offers various pleasures only loosely linked to terror. In the first place, we relish those delights that are innately literary: the author's ability to dart in and out of a character's head; an employment of language's inherent ambiguity in order to shift artfully back and forth between revelation and conceal-ment; the gradual warming of diction as a crescendo nears; the odd aesthetic tuggings inherent in an art form that is at once unsettling in its aims and comfortingly old-fashioned in its conventions; and the playful, often ironic refurbishing of those conventions.

These pleasures are varied and wide-ranging: The cumulative effect is one of rich intricacy. I would take as axiomatic—indeed, as the driving modus of this anthology—the notion that the capital strength of the ghost story over the last century has lain in its diversified renderings of our ambivalence about our mortality. It has proved to be one of the best media we have for exploring our most primitive, irrational attitudes to-ward the dead. Every literary genre, obviously, negotiates with death, but the ghost story elevates precisely those moments in which, distorted by yearnings or misgivings so potent as to be well-nigh uncontainable, our reason attenuates: We enter a realm in which no insurmountable barrier obtains between the living and the deceased. Death traumatizes us all, and wherever in the psyche trauma resides, there also will be located projections of alternate or modified realities. The wounded soul is forever saying *Suppose* . . . and in this case it says, *Suppose the dead are not dead* . . . Although I hope this anthology reflects a deep sympathy with both types of ghost story, any devotee of the genre will immediately see, with a glance at my table of contents, that my allegiance lies with the psychological tale. Hence, I have a good deal of patience with ghosts that are other than malign—with benign ghosts and forgetful ghosts and needy ghosts and ghosts that may or may not be ghosts. I feel the genre ought to mirror the whole outflung gamut of our feelings about the dead.

I've occasionally been asked, by someone who has heard that I was assembling this anthology, whether I myself believe in ghosts—to which I've replied, less facetiously than might first appear, "Everybody does." I can't believe any of us, if we dig deep enough in our psyches, is utterly free of a suspicion that the dead continually attend the living. Where is the person who has not resurrected them in dreams? At *this* level of the psyche—where dreams are bred and cultivated—there are no dead. Similarly, who among us hasn't on some occasion recoiled at one of those tricks of the light by which an inanimate object suddenly is informed with movement and volition? I remember once walking a country road on a viciously cold winter night. There was a car parked some ways ahead, and, my eyes teary with the cold, I didn't immediately notice the human shape behind the steering wheel.

When I did, my step faltered. It *spooked* me, having thought myself alone, to have to accommodate myself so unexpectedly to a night in which I had company. But moments later, my vision clearing, I had a second surprise. The human shape was merely the driver's-side headrest.

The second jolt was stronger than the first, for this time around, a sort of death had unfolded: Where there had been life, there now was none. In a few seconds I'd been twice uncentered. It was an experience famil-iar to devotees of the ghost story. In their bones they know that the universe is unsettling whether it is inhabited by spirits or whether we— lone walkers on a bitter night—are alone in the windy darkness.

THE NORTON BOOK OF
GHOST STORIES

HENRY JAMES

The Romance of Certain Old Clothes

1

Towards the middle of the eighteenth century there lived in the Province of Massachusetts a widowed gentlewoman, the mother of three children, by name Mrs. Veronica Wingrave. She had lost her husband early in life, and had devoted herself to the care of her progeny. These young persons grew up in a manner to reward her tenderness and to gratify her highest hopes. The first-born was a son, whom she had called Bernard, after his father. The others were daughters—born at an interval of three years apart. Good looks were traditional in the family, and this youthful trio were not likely to allow the tradition to perish. The boy was of that fair and ruddy complexion and that athletic structure which in those days (as in these) were the sign of good English descent—a frank, affectionate young fellow, a deferential son, a patronising brother, a steadfast friend. Clever, however, he was not; the wit of the family had been apportioned chiefly to his sisters. The late Mr. Wingrave had been a great reader of Shakespeare, at a time when this pursuit implied more freedom of thought than at the present day, and in a community where it required much courage to patronise the drama even in the closet; and he had wished to call attention to his admiration of the great poet by calling his daughters out of his favourite plays. Upon the elder he had bestowed the romantic name of Rosalind, and the younger he had called Perdita, in memory of a little girl born between them, who had lived but a few weeks.

When Bernard Wingrave came to his sixteenth year his mother put a brave face upon it and prepared to execute her husband's last injunction. This had been a formal command that, at the proper age, his son should be sent out to England, to complete his education at the university of Oxford, where he himself had acquired his taste for elegant literature. It was Mrs. Wingrave's belief that the lad's equal was not to be found in the two hemispheres, but she had the old traditions of literal obedience.

She swallowed her sobs, and made up her boy's trunk and his simple provincial outfit, and sent him on his way across the seas. Bernard presented himself at his father's college, and spent five years in England, without great honour, indeed, but with a vast deal of pleasure and no discredit. On leaving the university he made the journey to France. In his twenty-fourth year he took ship for home, prepared to find poor little New England (New England was very small in those days) a very dull, unfashionable residence. But there had been changes at home, as well as in Mr. Bernard's opinions. He found his mother's house quite habitable, and his sisters grown into two very charming young ladies, with all the accomplishments and graces of the young women of Britain, and a certain native-grown originality and wildness, which, if it was not an accomplishment, was certainly a grace the more. Bernard privately assured his mother that his sisters were fully a match for the most genteel young women in the old country; whereupon poor Mrs. Wingrave, you may be sure, bade them hold up their heads. Such was Bernard's opinion, and such, in a tenfold higher degree, was the opinion of Mr. Arthur Lloyd. This gentleman was a college-mate of Mr. Bernard, a young man of reputable family, of a good person and a handsome inheritance; which latter appurtenance he proposed to invest in trade in the flourishing colony. He and Bernard were sworn friends; they had crossed the ocean together, and the young American had lost no time in presenting him at his mother's house, where he had made quite as good an impression as that which he had received and of which I have just given a hint.

The two sisters were at this time in all the freshness of their youthful bloom; each wearing, of course, this natural brilliancy in the manner that became her best. They were equally dissimilar in appearance and character. Rosalind, the elder—now in her twenty-second year—was tall and white, with calm gray eyes and auburn tresses; a very faint likeness to the Rosalind of Shakespeare's comedy, whom I imagine a brunette (if you will), but a slender, airy creature, full of the softest, quickest impulses. Miss Wingrave, with her slightly lymphatic fairness, her fine arms, her majestic height, her slow utterance, was not cut out for adventures. She would never have put on a man's jacket and hose; and, indeed, being a very plump beauty, she may have had reasons apart from her natural dignity. Perdita, too, might very well have exchanged the sweet melancholy of her name against something more in consonance with her aspect and disposition. She had the cheek of a gipsy and the eye of an eager child, as well as the smallest waist and lightest foot in all the country of the Puritans. When you spoke to her she never made you wait, as her handsome sister was wont to do (while she looked at you with a cold fine eye), but gave you your choice of a dozen answers before you had uttered half your thought.

The young girls were very glad to see their brother once more; but they found themselves quite able to spare part of their attention for their brother's friend. Among the young men their friends and neighbours, the *belle jeunesse* of the Colony, there were many excellent fellows, several devoted swains, and some two or three who enjoyed the reputation of universal charmers and conquerors. But the homebred arts and somewhat boisterous gallantry of these honest colonists were completely eclipsed by the good looks, the fine clothes, the punctilious courtesy, the perfect elegance, the immense information, of Mr. Arthur Lloyd. He was in reality no paragon; he was a capable, honourable, civil youth, rich in pounds sterling, in his health and complacency and his little capital of uninvested affections. But he was a gentleman; he had a handsome person; he had studied and travelled; he spoke French, he played the flute, and he read verses aloud with very great taste. There were a dozen reasons why Miss Wingrave and her sister should have thought their other male acquaintance made but a poor figure before such a perfect man of the world. Mr. Lloyd's anecdotes told our little New England maidens a great deal more of the ways and means of people of fashion in European capitals than he had any idea of doing. It was delightful to sit by and hear him and Bernard talk about the fine people and fine things they had seen. They would all gather round the fire after tea, in the little wainscoted parlour, and the two young men would remind each other, across the rug, of this, that and the other adventure. Rosalind and Perdita would often have given their ears to know exactly what adventure it was, and where it happened, and who was there, and what the ladies had on; but in those days a well-bred young woman was not expected to break into the conversation of her elders, or to ask too many questions; and the poor girls used therefore to sit fluttering behind the more languid—or more discreet—curiosity of their mother.

2

That they were both very fine girls Arthur Lloyd was not slow to discover; but it took him some time to make up his mind whether he liked the big sister or the little sister best. He had a strong presentiment—an emotion of a nature entirely too cheerful to be called a foreboding—that he was destined to stand up before the parson with one of them; yet he was unable to arrive at a preference, and for such a consummation a preference was certainly necessary, for Lloyd had too much young blood in his veins to make a choice by lot and be cheated of the satisfaction of falling in love. He resolved to take things as they came—to let his heart speak. Meanwhile he was on a very pleasant footing. Mrs. Wingrave showed a dignified indifference to his "intentions," equally remote from a carelessness of her daughter's honour and from that sharp alacrity to make him come to the point, which, in his quality of young man of property, he had too often encountered in the worldly matrons of his native islands. As for Bernard, all that he asked was that his friend should treat his sisters as his own; and as for the poor girls themselves, however each may have secretly longed that their visitor should do or say something "marked," they kept a very modest and contented demeanour.

Towards each other, however, they were somewhat more on the offensive. They were good friends enough, and accommodating bedfellows (they shared the same four-poster), betwixt whom it would take more than a day for the seeds of jealousy to sprout and bear fruit; but they felt that the seeds had been sown on the day that Mr. Lloyd came into the house. Each made up her mind that, if she should be slighted, she would bear her grief in silence, and that no one should be any the wiser; for if they had a great deal of ambition, they had also a large share of pride. But each prayed in secret, nevertheless, that upon *her* the selection, the distinction, might fall. They had need of a vast deal of patience, of self-control, of dissimulation. In those days a young girl of decent breeding could make no advances whatever, and barely respond, indeed, to those that were made. She was expected to sit still in her chair, with her eyes on the carpet, watching the spot where the mystic handkerchief should fall. Poor Arthur Lloyd was obliged to carry on his wooing in the little wainscoted parlour, before the eyes of Mrs. Wingrave, her son, and his prospective sister-in-law. But youth and love are so cunning that a hundred signs and tokens might travel to and fro, and not one of these three pairs of eyes detect them in their passage. The two maidens were almost always together, and had plenty of chances to betray themselves. That each knew she was being watched, however, made not a grain of difference in the little offices they mutually rendered, or in the various household tasks they performed in common. Neither flinched nor fluttered beneath the silent battery of her sister's eyes. The only apparent change in their habits was that they had less to say to each other. It was impossible to talk about Mr. Lloyd, and it was ridiculous to talk about anything else. By tacit agreement they began to wear all their choice finery, and to devise such little implements of conquest, in the way of ribbons and top-knots and kerchiefs, as were sanctioned by indubitable modesty. They executed in the same inarticulate fashion a contract of fair play in this exciting game. "Is it better so?" Rosalind would ask, tying a bunch of ribbons on her bosom, and turning about from her glass to her sister. Perdita would look up gravely from her work and examine the decoration. "I think you had better give it another loop," she would say, with great solemnity, looking hard at her sister with eyes that added, "upon my honour!" So they were for ever stitching and trimming their petticoats, and pressing out their muslins, and contriving washes and ointments and cosmetics, like the ladies in the household of the vicar of Wakefield. Some three or four months went by; it grew to be midwinter, and as yet Rosalind knew that if Perdita had nothing more to boast of than she, there was not much to be feared from her rivalry. But Perdita by this time—the charming Perdita—felt that her secret had grown to be tenfold more precious than her sister's.

One afternoon Miss Wingrave sat alone—that was a rare accident—before her toilet-glass, combing out her long hair. It was getting too dark to see; she lit the two candles in their sockets, on the frame of her mirror, and then went to the window to draw her curtains. It was a gray December evening; the landscape was bare and bleak, and the sky heavy with snow-clouds. At the end of the large garden into which her window looked was a wall with a little postern door, opening into a lane. The door stood ajar, as she could vaguely see in the gathering darkness, and moved slowly to and fro, as if some one were swaying it from the lane without. It was doubtless a servant-maid who had been having a tryst with her sweetheart. But as she was about to drop her curtain Rosalind saw her sister step into the garden and hurry along the path which led to the house. She dropped the curtain, all save a little crevice for her eyes. As Perdita came up the path she seemed to be examining something in her hand, holding it close to her eyes. When she reached the house she stopped a moment, looked intently at the object, and pressed it to her lips.

Poor Rosalind slowly came back to her chair and sat down before her glass, where, if she had looked at it less abstractedly, she would have seen her handsome features sadly disfigured by jealousy. A moment afterwards the door opened behind her and her sister came into the room, out of breath, her cheeks aglow with the chilly air.

Perdita started. "Ah," said she, "I thought you were with our mother." The ladies were to go to a tea-party, and on such occasions it was the habit of one of the girls to help their mother to dress. Instead of coming in, Perdita lingered at the door.

"Come in, come in," said Rosalind. "We have more than an hour yet. I should like you very much to give a few strokes to my hair." She knew that her sister wished to retreat, and that she could see in the glass all her movements in the room. "Nay, just help me with my hair," she said, "and I will go to mamma."

Perdita came reluctantly, and took the brush. She saw her sister's eyes, in the glass, fastened hard upon her hands. She had not made three passes when Rosalind clapped her own right hand upon her sister's left, and started out of her chair. "Whose ring is that?" she cried, passionately, drawing her towards the light.

On the young girl's third finger glistened a little gold ring, adorned with a very small sapphire. Perdita felt that she need no longer keep her secret, yet that she must put a bold face on her avowal. "It's mine," she said proudly.

"Who gave it to you?" cried the other.

Perdita hesitated a moment. "Mr. Lloyd."

"Mr. Lloyd is generous, all of a sudden."

"Ah no," cried Perdita, with spirit, "not all of a sudden! He offered it to me a month ago."

"And you needed a month's begging to take it?" said Rosalind, looking at the little trinket, which indeed was not especially elegant, although it was the best that the jeweller of the Province could furnish. "I wouldn't have taken it in less than two."

"It isn't the ring," Perdita answered, "it's what it means!"

"It means that you are not a modest girl!" cried Rosalind. "Pray, does your mother know of your intrigue? does Bernard?"

"My mother has approved my 'intrigue,' as you call it. Mr. Lloyd has asked for my hand, and mamma has given it. Would you have had him apply to you, dearest sister?"

Rosalind gave her companion a long look, full of passionate envy and sorrow. Then she dropped her lashes on her pale cheeks and turned away. Perdita felt that it had not been a pretty scene; but it was her sister's fault. However, the elder girl rapidly called back her pride, and turned herself about again. "You have my very best wishes," she said, with a low curtsey. "I wish you every happiness, and a very long life."

Perdita gave a bitter laugh. "Don't speak in that tone!" she cried. "I would rather you should curse me outright. Come, Rosy," she added, "he couldn't marry both of us."

"I wish you very great joy," Rosalind repeated, mechanically, sitting down to her glass again, "and a very long life, and plenty of children."

There was something in the sound of these words not at all to Perdita's taste. "Will you give me a year to live at least?" she said. "In a year I can have one little boy—or one little girl at least. If you will give me your brush again I will do your hair."

"Thank you," said Rosalind. "You had better go to mamma. It isn't becoming that a young lady with a promised husband should wait on a girl with none."

"Nay," said Perdita, good-humouredly, "I have Arthur to wait upon me. You need my service more than I need yours."

But her sister motioned her away, and she left the room. When she had gone poor Rosalind fell on her knees before her dressing-table, buried her head in her arms, and poured out a flood of tears and sobs. She felt very much the better for this effusion of sorrow. When her sister came back she insisted on helping her to dress—on her wearing her prettiest things. She forced upon her acceptance a bit of lace of her own, and declared that now that she was to be married she should do her best to appear worthy of her lover's choice. She discharged these offices in stern silence; but, such as they were, they had to do duty as an apology and an atonement; she never made any other.

Now that Lloyd was received by the family as an accepted suitor nothing remained but to fix the wedding-day. It was appointed for the following April, and in the interval preparations were diligently made for the marriage. Lloyd, on his side, was busy with his commercial arrangements, and with establishing a correspondence with the great mercantile house to which he had attached himself in England. He was therefore not so frequent a visitor at Mrs. Wingrave's as during the months of his diffidence and irresolution, and poor Rosalind had less to suffer than she had feared from the sight of the mutual endearments of the young lovers. Touching his future sister-in-law Lloyd had a perfectly clear conscience. There had not been a particle of love-making between them, and he had not the slightest suspicion that he had dealt her a terrible blow. He was quite at his ease; life promised so well, both domestically and financially. The great revolt of the Colonies was not yet in the air, and that his connubial felicity should take a tragic turn it was absurd, it was blasphemous, to apprehend. Meanwhile, at Mrs. Wingrave's, there was a greater rustling of silks, a more rapid clicking of scissors and flying of needles, than ever. The good lady had determined that her daughter should carry from home the genteelest outfit that her money could buy or that the country could furnish. All the sage women in the Province were convened, and their united taste was brought to bear on Perdita's wardrobe. Rosalind's situation, at this moment, was assuredly not to be envied. The poor girl had an inordinate love of dress, and the very best taste in the world, as her sister perfectly well knew. Rosalind was tall, she was stately and sweeping, she was made to carry stiff brocade and masses of heavy lace, such as belong to the toilet of a rich man's wife. But Rosalind sat aloof, with her beautiful arms folded and her head averted, while her mother and sister and the venerable women aforesaid worried and wondered over their materials, oppressed by the multitude of their resources. One day there came in a beautiful piece of white silk, brocaded with heavenly blue and silver, sent by the bridegroom himself—it not being thought amiss in those days that the husband-elect should contribute to the bride's trousseau. Perdita could think of no form or fashion which would do sufficient honour to the splendour of the material.

"Blue's your colour, sister, more than mine," she said, with appealing eyes. "It's a pity it's not for you. You would know what to do with it."

Rosalind got up from her place and looked at the great shining fabric, as it lay spread over the back of a chair. Then she took it up in her hands and felt it—lovingly, as Perdita could see—and turned about toward the mirror with it. She let it roll down to her feet, and flung the other end over her shoulder, gathering it in about her waist with her white arm, which was bare to the elbow. She threw back her head, and looked at her image, and a hanging tress of her auburn hair fell upon the gorgeous surface of the silk. It made a dazzling picture. The women standing about uttered a little "Look, look!" of admiration. "Yes, indeed," said Rosalind, quietly, "blue is my colour." But Perdita could see that her fancy had been stirred, and that she would now fall to work and solve all their silken riddles. And indeed she behaved very well, as Perdita, knowing her insatiable love of millinery, was quite ready to declare. Innumerable yards of lustrous silk and satin, of muslin, velvet and lace, passed through her cunning hands, without a jealous word coming from her lips. Thanks to her industry, when the wedding-day came Perdita was prepared to espouse more of the vanities of life than any fluttering young bride who had yet received the sacramental blessing of a New England divine.

It had been arranged that the young couple should go out and spend the first days of their wedded life at the country-house of an English gentleman—a man of rank and a very kind friend to Arthur Lloyd. He was a bachelor; he declared he should be delighted to give up the place to the influence of Hymen. After the ceremony at church—it had been performed by an English clergyman—young Mrs. Lloyd hastened back to her mother's house to change her nuptial robes for a riding-dress. Rosalind helped her to effect the change, in the little homely room in which they had spent their undivided younger years. Perdita then hurried off to bid farewell to her mother, leaving Rosalind to follow. The parting was short; the horses were at the door, and Arthur was impatient to start. But Rosalind had not followed, and Perdita hastened back to her room, opening the door abruptly. Rosalind, as usual, was before the glass, but in a position which caused the other to stand still, amazed. She had dressed herself in Perdita's cast-off wedding veil and wreath, and on her neck she had hung the full string of pearls which the young girl had received from her husband as a wedding-gift. These things had been hastily laid aside, to await their possessor's disposal on her return from the country. Bedizened in this unnatural garb Rosalind stood before the mirror, plunging a long look into its depths and reading heaven knows what audacious visions. Perdita was horrified. It was a hideous image of their old rivalry come to life again. She made a step toward her sister, as if to pull off the veil and the flowers. But catching her eyes in the glass, she stopped.

"Farewell, sweetheart," she said. "You might at least have waited till I had got out of the house!" And she hurried away from the room.

Mr. Lloyd had purchased in Boston a house which to the taste of those days appeared as elegant as it was commodious; and here he very soon established himself with his young wife. He was thus separated by a distance of twenty miles from the residence of his mother-in-law. Twenty miles, in that primitive era of roads and conveyances, were as serious a matter as a hundred at the present day, and Mrs. Wingrave saw but little of her daughter during the first twelvemonth of her marriage. She suffered in no small degree from Perdita's absence; and her affliction was not diminished by the fact that Rosalind had fallen into terribly low spirits and was not to be roused or cheered but by change of air and company. The real cause of the young lady's dejection the reader will not be slow to suspect. Mrs. Wingrave and her gossips, however, deemed her complaint a mere bodily ill, and doubted not that she would obtain relief from the remedy just mentioned. Her mother accordingly proposed, on her behalf, a visit to certain relatives on the paternal side, established in New York, who had long complained that they were able to see so little of their New England cousins. Rosalind was despatched to these good people, under a suitable escort, and remained with them for several months. In the interval her brother Bernard, who had begun the practice of the law, made up his mind to take a wife. Rosalind came home to the wedding, apparently cured of her heartache, with bright roses and lilies in her face and a proud smile on her lips. Arthur Lloyd came over from Boston to see his brother-in-law married, but without his wife, who was expecting very soon to present him with an heir. It was nearly a year since Rosalind had seen him. She was glad—she hardly knew why—that Perdita had stayed at home. Arthur looked happy, but he was more grave and important than before his marriage. She thought he looked "interesting,"—for although the word, in its modern sense, was not then invented, we may be sure that the idea was. The truth is, he was simply anxious about his wife and her coming ordeal. Nevertheless, he by no means failed to observe Rosalind's beauty and splendour, and to note how she effaced the poor little bride. The allowance that Perdita had enjoyed for her dress had now been transferred to her sister, who turned it to wonderful account. On the morning after the wedding he had a lady's saddle put on the horse of the servant who had come with him from town, and went out with the young girl for a ride. It was a keen, clear morning in January; the ground was bare and hard, and the horses in good condition—to say nothing of Rosalind, who was charming in her hat and plume, and her dark blue riding coat, trimmed with fur. They rode all the morning, they lost their way, and were obliged to stop for dinner at a farm-house. The early winter dusk had fallen when they got

home. Mrs. Wingrave met them with a long face. A messenger had
arrived at noon from Mrs. Lloyd; she was beginning to be ill, she desired
her husband's immediate return. The young man, at the thought that he
had lost several hours, and that by hard riding he might already have
been with his wife, uttered a passionate oath. He barely consented to
stop for a mouthful of supper, but mounted the messenger's horse and
started off at a gallop.

He reached home at midnight. His wife had been delivered of a little
girl. "Ah, why weren't you with me?" she said, as he came to her bed-
side.

"I was out of the house when the man came. I was with Rosalind,"
said Lloyd, innocently.

Mrs. Lloyd made a little moan, and turned away. But she continued to
do very well, and for a week her improvement was uninterrupted. Finally, however, through some indiscretion in the way of diet or exposure,
it was checked, and the poor lady grew rapidly worse. Lloyd was in
despair. It very soon became evident that she was breathing her last.
Mrs. Lloyd came to a sense of her approaching end, and declared that
she was reconciled with death. On the third evening after the change
took place she told her husband that she felt she should not get through
the night. She dismissed her servants, and also requested her mother to
withdraw—Mrs. Wingrave having arrived on the preceding day. She
had had her infant placed on the bed beside her, and she lay on her side,
with the child against her breast, holding her husband's hands. The
night-lamp was hidden behind the heavy curtains of the bed, but the
room was illumined with a red glow from the immense fire of logs on the
hearth.

"It seems strange not to be warmed into life by such a fire as that," the
young woman said, feebly trying to smile. "If I had but a little of it in my
veins! But I have given all *my* fire to this little spark of mortality." And
she dropped her eyes on her child. Then raising them she looked at her
husband with a long, penetrating gaze. The last feeling which lingered in
her heart was one of suspicion. She had not recovered from the shock
which Arthur had given her by telling her that in the hour of her agony
he had been with Rosalind. She trusted her husband very nearly as well
as she loved him; but now that she was called away forever she felt a cold
horror of her sister. She felt in her soul that Rosalind had never ceased to
be jealous of her good fortune; and a year of happy security had not
effaced the young girl's image, dressed in her wedding-garments, and
smiling with simulated triumph. Now that Arthur was to be alone, what
might not Rosalind attempt? She was beautiful, she was engaging; what
arts might she not use, what impression might she not make upon the
young man's saddened heart? Mrs. Lloyd looked at her husband in si-

lence. It seemed hard, after all, to doubt of his constancy. His fine eyes were filled with tears; his face was convulsed with weeping; the clasp of his hands was warm and passionate. How noble he looked, how tender, how faithful and devoted! "Nay," thought Perdita, "he's not for such a one as Rosalind. He'll never forget me. Nor does Rosalind truly care for him; she cares only for vanities and finery and jewels." And she lowered her eyes on her white hands, which her husband's liberality had covered with rings, and on the lace ruffles which trimmed the edge of her night-dress. "She covets my rings and my laces more than she covets my husband."

At this moment the thought of her sister's rapacity seemed to cast a dark shadow between her and the helpless figure of her little girl. "Arthur," she said, "you must take off my rings. I shall not be buried in them. One of these days my daughter shall wear them—my rings and my laces and silks. I had them all brought out and shown me today. It's a great wardrobe—there's not such another in the Province; I can say it without vanity, now that I have done with it. It will be a great inheritance for my daughter when she grows into a young woman. There are things there that a man never buys twice, and if they are lost you will never again see the like. So you will watch them well. Some dozen things I have left to Rosalind; I have named them to my mother. I have given her that blue and silver; it was meant for her; I wore it only once, I looked ill in it. But the rest are to be sacredly kept for this little innocent. It's such a providence that she should be my colour; she can wear my gowns; she has her mother's eyes. You know the same fashions come back every twenty years. She can wear my gowns as they are. They will lie there quietly waiting till she grows into them—wrapped in camphor and rose-leaves, and keeping their colours in the sweet-scented darkness. She shall have black hair, she shall wear my carnation satin. Do you promise me, Arthur?"

"Promise you what, dearest?"

"Promise me to keep your poor little wife's old gowns."

"Are you afraid I shall sell them?"

"No, but that they may get scattered. My mother will have them properly wrapped up, and you shall lay them away under a double-lock. Do you know the great chest in the attic, with the iron bands? There is no end to what it will hold. You can put them all there. My mother and the housekeeper will do it, and give you the key. And you will keep the key in your secretary, and never give it to any one but your child. Do you promise me?"

"Ah, yes, I promise you," said Lloyd, puzzled at the intensity with which his wife appeared to cling to this idea.

"Will you swear?" repeated Perdita.

"Yes, I swear."

"Well—I trust you—I trust you," said the poor lady, looking into his eyes with eyes in which, if he had suspected her vague apprehensions, he might have read an appeal quite as much as an assurance.

Lloyd bore his bereavement rationally and manfully. A month after his wife's death, in the course of business, circumstances arose which offered him an opportunity of going to England. He took advantage of it, to change the current of his thoughts. He was absent nearly a year, during which his little girl was tenderly nursed and guarded by her grandmother. On his return he had his house again thrown open, and announced his intention of keeping the same state as during his wife's lifetime. It very soon came to be predicted that he would marry again, and there were at least a dozen young women of whom one may say that it was by no fault of theirs that, for six months after his return, the prediction did not come true. During this interval he still left his little daughter in Mrs. Wingrave's hands, the latter assuring him that a change of residence at so tender an age would be full of danger for her health. Finally, however, he declared that his heart longed for his daughter's presence and that she must be brought up to town. He sent his coach and his housekeeper to fetch her home. Mrs. Wingrave was in terror lest something should befall her on the road; and, in accordance with this feeling, Rosalind offered to accompany her. She could return the next day. So she went up to town with her little niece, and Mr. Lloyd met her on the threshold of his house, overcome with her kindness and with paternal joy. Instead of returning the next day Rosalind stayed out the week; and when at last she reappeared, she had only come for her clothes. Arthur would not hear of her coming home, nor would the baby. That little person cried and choked if Rosalind left her; and at the sight of her grief Arthur lost his wits, and swore that she was going to die. In fine, nothing would suit them but that the aunt should remain until the little niece had grown used to strange faces.

It took two months to bring this consummation about; for it was not until this period had elapsed that Rosalind took leave of her brother-in-law. Mrs. Wingrave had shaken her head over her daughter's absence; she had declared that it was not becoming, that it was the talk of the whole country. She had reconciled herself to it only because, during the girl's visit, the household enjoyed an unwonted term of peace. Bernard Wingrave had brought his wife home to live, between whom and her sister-in-law there was as little love as you please. Rosalind was perhaps no angel; but in the daily practice of life she was a sufficiently good-natured girl, and if she quarrelled with Mrs. Bernard, it was not without provocation. Quarrel, however, she did, to the great annoyance not only of her antagonist, but of the two spectators of these constant altercations. Her stay in the household of her brother-in-law, therefore, would have been delightful, if only because it removed her from contact with the object of her antipathy at home. It was doubly—it was ten times—delightful, in that it kept her near the object of her early passion. Mrs. Lloyd's sharp suspicions had fallen very far short of the truth. Rosalind's sentiment had been a passion at first, and a passion it remained—a passion of whose radiant heat, tempered to the delicate state of his feelings, Mr. Lloyd very soon felt the influence. Lloyd, as I have hinted, was not a modern Petrarch; it was not in his nature to practice an ideal constancy. He had not been many days in the house with his sister-in-law before he began to assure himself that she was, in the language of that day, a devilish fine woman. Whether Rosalind really practised those insidious arts that her sister had been tempted to impute to her it is needless to inquire. It is enough to say that she found means to appear to the very best advantage. She used to seat herself every morning before the big fireplace in the dining room, at work upon a piece of tapestry, with her little niece disporting herself on the carpet at her feet, or on the train of her dress, and playing with her woollen balls. Lloyd would have been a very stupid fellow if he had remained insensible to the rich suggestions of this charming picture. He was exceedingly fond of his little girl, and was never weary of taking her in his arms and tossing her up and down, and making her crow with delight. Very often, however, he would venture upon greater liberties than the young lady was yet prepared to allow, and then she would suddenly vociferate her displeasure. Rosalind, at this, would drop her tapestry, and put out her handsome hands with the serious smile of the young girl whose virgin fancy has revealed to her all a mother's healing arts. Lloyd would give up the child, their eyes would meet, their hands would touch, and Rosalind would extinguish the little girl's sobs upon the snowy folds of the kerchief that crossed her bosom. Her dignity was perfect, and nothing could be more discreet than the manner in which she accepted her brother-in-law's hospitality. It may almost be said, perhaps, that there was something harsh in her reserve. Lloyd had a provoking feeling that she was in the house and yet was unapproachable. Half-an-hour after supper, at the very outset of the long winter evenings, she would light her candle, make the young man a most respectful curtsey, and march off to bed. If these were arts, Rosalind was a great artist. But their effect was so gentle, so gradual, they were calculated to work upon the young widower's fancy with a *crescendo* so finely shaded, that, as the reader has seen, several weeks elapsed before Rosalind began to feel sure that her returns would cover her outlay. When this became morally certain she packed up her trunk and returned to her mother's house. For three days she waited; on the fourth Mr. Lloyd made his appearance—a respectful but pressing suitor. Rosalind heard him to the end, with great humility, and accepted him with infinite modesty. It is hard to imagine that Mrs. Lloyd would have forgiven her husband; but if anything might have disarmed her resentment it would have been the ceremonious continence of this interview. Rosalind imposed upon her lover but a short probation. They were married, as was becoming, with great privacy—almost with secrecy—in the hope perhaps, as was waggishly remarked at the time, that the late Mrs. Lloyd wouldn't hear of it.

The marriage was to all appearance a happy one, and each party obtained what each had desired—Lloyd "a devilish fine woman," and Rosalind—but Rosalind's desires, as the reader will have observed, had remained a good deal of a mystery. There were, indeed, two blots upon their felicity, but time would perhaps efface them. During the first three years of her marriage Mrs. Lloyd failed to become a mother, and her husband on his side suffered heavy losses of money. This latter circumstance compelled a material retrenchment in his expenditure, and Rosalind was perforce less of a fine lady than her sister had been. She contrived, however, to carry it like a woman of considerable fashion. She had long since ascertained that her sister's copious wardrobe had been sequestrated for the benefit of her daughter, and that it lay languishing in thankless gloom in the dusty attic. It was a revolting thought that these exquisite fabrics should await the good pleasure of a little girl who sat in a high chair and ate bread-and-milk with a wooden spoon. Rosalind had the good taste, however, to say nothing about the matter until several months had expired. Then, at last, she timidly broached it to her husband. Was it not a pity that so much finery should be lost?—for lost it would be, what with colours fading, and moths eating it up, and the change of fashions. But Lloyd gave her so abrupt and peremptory a refusal, that she saw, for the present, her attempt was vain. Six months went by, however, and brought with them new needs and new visions. Rosalind's thoughts hovered lovingly about her sister's relics. She went up and looked at the chest in which they lay imprisoned. There was a sullen defiance in its three great padlocks and its iron bands which only quickened her cupidity. There was something exasperating in its incorruptible immobility. It was like a grim and grizzled old household servant, who locks his jaws over a family secret. And then there was a look of capacity in its vast extent, and a sound as of dense fulness, when Rosalind knocked its side with the toe of her little shoe, which caused her to flush with baffled longing. "It's absurd," she cried; "it's improper, it's wicked"; and she forthwith resolved upon another attack upon her husband. On the following day, after dinner, when he had had his wine, she boldly began it. But he cut her short with great sternness.

"Once for all, Rosalind," said he, "it's out of the question. I shall be gravely displeased if you return to the matter."

"Very good," said Rosalind. "I am glad to learn the esteem in which I am held. Gracious heaven," she cried, "I am a very happy woman! It's an agreeable thing to feel one's self sacrificed to a caprice!" And her eyes filled with tears of anger and disappointment.

Lloyd had a good-natured man's horror of a woman's sobs, and he attempted—I may say he condescended—to explain. "It's not a caprice, dear, it's a promise," he said—"an oath."

"An oath? It's a pretty matter for oaths! and to whom, pray?"

"To Perdita," said the young man, raising his eyes for an instant, but immediately dropping them.

"Perdita—ah, Perdita!" and Rosalind's tears broke forth. Her bosom heaved with stormy sobs—sobs which were the long-deferred sequel of the violent fit of weeping in which she had indulged herself on the night when she discovered her sister's betrothal. She had hoped, in her better moments, that she had done with her jealousy; but her temper, on that occasion, had taken an ineffaceable fold. "And pray, what right had Perdita to dispose of my future?" she cried. "What right had she to bind you to meanness and cruelty? Ah, I occupy a dignified place, and I make a very fine figure! I am welcome to what Perdita has left! And what has she left? I never knew till now how little! Nothing, nothing, nothing."

This was very poor logic, but it was very good as a "scene." Lloyd put his arm around his wife's waist and tried to kiss her, but she shook him off with magnificent scorn. Poor fellow! he had coveted a "devilish fine woman," and he had got one. Her scorn was intolerable. He walked away with his ears tingling—irresolute, distracted. Before him was his secretary, and in it the sacred key which with his own hand he had turned in the triple lock. He marched up and opened it, and took the key from a secret drawer, wrapped in a little packet which he had sealed with his own honest bit of blazonry. *Je garde*, said the motto—"I keep." But he was ashamed to put it back. He flung it upon the table beside his wife.

"Put it back!" she cried. "I want it not. I hate it!"

"I wash my hands of it," cried her husband. "God forgive me!"

Mrs. Lloyd gave an indignant shrug of her shoulders, and swept out of the room, while the young man retreated by another door. Ten minutes later Mrs. Lloyd returned, and found the room occupied by her little step-daughter and the nursery-maid. The key was not on the table. She glanced at the child. Her little niece was perched on a chair, with the packet in her hands. She had broken the seal with her own small fingers. Mrs. Lloyd hastily took possession of the key.

At the habitual supper-hour Arthur Lloyd came back from his

counting-room. It was the month of June, and supper was served by daylight. The meal was placed on the table, but Mrs. Lloyd failed to make her appearance. The servant whom his master sent to call her came back with the assurance that her room was empty, and that the women informed him that she had not been seen since dinner. They had, in truth, observed her to have been in tears, and, supposing her to be shut up in her chamber, had not disturbed her. Her husband called her name in various parts of the house, but without response. At last it occurred to him that he might find her by taking the way to the attic. The thought gave him a strange feeling of discomfort, and he bade his servants remain behind, wishing no witness in his quest. He reached the foot of the staircase leading to the topmost flat, and stood with his hand on the banisters, pronouncing his wife's name. His voice trembled. He called again louder and more firmly. The only sound which disturbed the absolute silence was a faint echo of his own tones, repeating his question under the great eaves. He nevertheless felt irresistibly moved to ascend the staircase. It opened upon a wide hall, lined with wooden closets, and terminating in a window which looked westward, and admitted the last rays of the sun. Before the window stood the great chest. Before the chest, on her knees, the young man saw with amazement and horror the figure of his wife. In an instant he crossed the interval between them, bereft of utterance. The lid of the chest stood open, exposing, amid their perfumed napkins, its treasure of stuffs and jewels. Rosalind had fallen backward from a kneeling posture, with one hand supporting her on the floor and the other pressed to her heart. On her limbs was the stiffness of death, and on her face, in the fading light of the sun, the terror of something more than death. Her lips were parted in entreaty, in dismay, in agony; and on her blanched brow and cheeks there glowed the marks of ten hideous wounds from two vengeful ghostly hands.   1868

THE FRIENDS OF THE FRIENDS

I find, as you prophesied, much that's interesting, but little that helps the delicate question—the possibility of publication. Her diaries are less systematic than I hoped; she only had a blessed habit of noting and narrating. She summarized, she saved; she appears seldom indeed to have let a good story pass without catching it on the wing. I allude of course not so much to things she heard as to things she saw and felt. She writes sometimes of herself, sometimes of others, sometimes of the combination. It's under this last rubric that she's usually most vivid. But it's not, you'll understand, when she's most vivid that she's always most publishable. To tell the truth she's fearfully indiscreet, or has at least all the material for making *me* so. Take as an instance the fragment I send you after dividing it for your convenience into several small chapters. It's the contents of a thin blank-book which I've had copied out and which has the merit of being nearly enough a rounded thing, an intelligible whole. These pages evidently date from years ago. I've read with the liveliest wonder the statement they so circumstantially make and done my best to swallow the prodigy they leave to be inferred. These things would be striking, wouldn't they? to any reader; but can you imagine for a moment my placing such a document before the world, even though, as if she herself had desired the world should have the benefit of it, she has given her friends neither name nor initials? Have you any sort of clue to their identity? I leave her the floor.

I

I know perfectly of course that I brought it upon myself; but that doesn't make it any better. I was the first to speak of her to him—he had never even heard her mentioned. Even if I had happened not to speak some one else would have made up for it: I tried afterwards to find comfort in that reflexion. But the comfort of reflexions is thin: the only comfort that counts in life is not to have been a fool. That's a beatitude I shall doubtless never enjoy. "Why you ought to meet her and talk it over" is what I immediately said. "Birds of a feather flock together." I told him who she was and that they were birds of a feather because if he had had in youth a strange adventure she had had about the same time just such another. It was well known to her friends—an incident she was constantly called on to describe. She was charming clever pretty unhappy; but it was none the less the thing to which she had originally owed her reputation.

Being at the age of eighteen somewhere abroad with an aunt she had had a vision of one of her parents at the moment of death. The parent was in England hundreds of miles away and so far as she knew neither dying nor dead. It was by day, in the museum of some great foreign town. She had passed alone, in advance of her companions, into a small room containing some famous work of art and occupied at that moment by two other persons. One of these was an old custodian; the second, before observing him, she took for a stranger, a tourist. She was merely conscious that he was bareheaded and seated on a bench. The instant her eyes rested on him however she beheld to her amazement her father, who, as if he had long waited for her, looked at her in singular distress and an impatience that was akin to reproach. She rushed to him with a bewildered cry, "Papa, what *is* it?" but this was followed by an exhibition of still livelier feeling when on her movement he simply vanished, leaving the custodian and her relations, who were by that time at her heels, to gather round her in dismay. These persons, the official, the aunt, the cousins, were therefore in a manner witnesses of the fact—the fact at least of the impression made on her; and there was the further testimony of a doctor who was attending one of the party and to whom it was immediately afterwards communicated. He gave her a remedy for hysterics, but said to the aunt privately: "Wait and see if something doesn't happen at home." Something *had* happened—the poor father, suddenly and violently seized, had died that morning. The aunt, the mother's sister, received before the day was out a telegram announcing the event and requesting her to prepare her niece for it. Her niece was already prepared, and the girl's sense of this visitation remained of course indelible. We had all, as her friends, had it conveyed to us and had conveyed it creepily to each other. Twelve years had elapsed, and as a woman who had made an unhappy marriage and lived apart from her husband she had become interesting from other sources; but since the name she now bore was a name frequently borne, and since moreover her judicial separation, as things were going, could hardly count as a distinction, it was usual to qualify her as "the one, you know, who saw her father's ghost."

As for him, dear man, he had seen his mother's—so there you are! I had never heard of that till this occasion on which our closer, our pleasanter acquaintance led him, through some turn of the subject of our talk, to mention it and to inspire me in so doing with the impulse to let him know that he had a rival in the field—a person with whom he could compare notes. Later on his story became for him, perhaps because of my unduly repeating it, likewise a convenient worldly label; but it hadn't a year before been the ground on which he was introduced to me. He had other merits, just as she, poor thing, had others. I can honestly say that I was quite aware of them from the first—I discovered them sooner than he discovered mine. I remember how it struck me even at the time that his sense of mine was quickened by my having been able to match, though not indeed straight from my own experience, his curious anecdote. It dated, this anecdote, as hers did, from some dozen years before—a year in which, at Oxford, he had for some reason of his own been staying on into the "Long." He had been in the August afternoon on the river. Coming back into his room while it was still distinct daylight he found his mother standing there as if her eyes had been fixed on the door. He had had a letter from her that morning out of Wales, where she was staying with her father. At the sight of him she smiled with extraordinary radiance and extended her arms to him, and then as he sprang forward and joyfully opened his own she vanished from the place.

He wrote to her that night, telling her what had happened; the letter had been carefully preserved. The next morning he heard of her death. He was through this chance of our talk extremely struck with the little prodigy I was able to produce for him. He had never encountered another case. Certainly they ought to meet, my friend and he; certainly they would have something in common. I would arrange this, wouldn't I?—if *she* didn't mind; for himself he didn't mind in the least. I had promised to speak to her of the matter as soon as possible, and within the week I was able to do so. She "minded" as little as he; she was perfectly willing to see him. And yet no meeting was to occur—as meetings are commonly understood.

II

That's just half my tale—the extraordinary way it was hindered. This was the fault of a series of accidents; but the accidents, persisting for years, became, to me and to others, a subject of mirth with either party. They were droll enough at first, then they grew rather a bore. The odd thing was that both parties were amenable: it wasn't a case of their being indifferent, much less of their being indisposed. It was one of the caprices of chance, aided I suppose by some rather settled opposition of their interests and habits. His were centred in his office, his eternal inspectorship, which left him small leisure, constantly calling him away and making him break engagements. He liked society, but he found it everywhere and took it at a run. I never knew at a given moment where he was, and there were times when for months together I never saw him. She was on her side practically suburban: she lived at Richmond and never went "out." She was a woman of distinction, but not of fashion, and felt, as people said, her situation. Decidedly proud and rather whimsical, she lived her life as she had planned it. There were things one could do with her, but one couldn't make her come to one's parties. One went indeed a little more than seemed quite convenient to hers, which consisted of her cousin, a cup of tea and the view. The tea was good; but the view was familiar, though perhaps not, like the cousin—a disagreeable old maid who had been of the group at the museum and with whom she now lived—offensively so. This connexion with an inferior relative, which had partly an economic motive—she proclaimed her companion a marvellous manager—was one of the little perversities we had to forgive her. Another was her estimate of the proprieties created by her rupture with her husband. That was extreme—many persons called it even morbid. She made no advances; she cultivated scruples; she suspected, or I should perhaps rather say she remembered, slights: she was one of the few women I've known whom that particular predicament had rendered modest rather than bold. Dear thing, she had some delicacy! Especially marked were the limits she had set to possible attentions from men: it was always her thought that her husband only waited to pounce on her. She discouraged if she didn't forbid the visits of male persons not senile: she said she could never be too careful.

When I first mentioned to her that I had a friend whom fate had distinguished in the same weird way as herself I put her quite at liberty to say "Oh bring him out to see me!" I should probably have been able to bring him, and a situation perfectly innocent or at any rate comparatively simple would have been created. But she uttered no such word; she only said: "I must meet him certainly; yes, I shall look out for him!" That caused the first delay, and meanwhile various things happened. One of them was that as time went on she made, charming as she was, more and more friends, and that it regularly befell that these friends were sufficiently also friends of his to bring him up in conversation. It was odd that without belonging, as it were, to the same world or, according to the horrid term, the same set, my baffled pair should have happened in so many cases to fall in with the same people and make them join in the droll chorus. She had friends who didn't know each other but who inevitably and punctually recommended *him*. She had also the sort of originality, the intrinsic interest, that led her to be kept by each of us as a private resource, cultivated jealously, more or less in secret, as a person whom one didn't meet in society, whom it was not for every one—whom it was not for the vulgar—to approach, and with whom therefore acquaintance was particularly difficult and particularly precious. We saw her separately, with appointments and conditions, and found it made on the whole for harmony not to tell each other. Somebody had always had a note from her still later than somebody else. There was some silly woman who for a long time, among the unprivileged, owed to three simple visits to Richmond a reputation for being intimate with "lots of awfully clever out-of-the-way people."

Every one has had friends it has seemed a happy thought to bring together, and every one remembers that his happiest thoughts have not been his greatest successes; but I doubt if there was ever a case in which the failure was in such direct proportion to the quantity of influence set in motion. It's really perhaps here the quantity of influence that was most remarkable. My lady and my gentleman each pronounced it to me and others quite a subject for a roaring farce. The reason first given had with time dropped out of sight and fifty better ones flourished on top of it. They were so awfully alike: they had the same ideas and tricks and tastes, the same prejudices and superstitions and heresies; they said the same things and sometimes did them; they liked and disliked the same persons and places, the same books, authors and styles; there were touches of resemblance even in their looks and features. It established much of a propriety that they were in common parlance equally "nice" and almost equally handsome. But the great sameness, for wonder and chatter, was their rare perversity in regard to being photographed. They were the only persons ever heard of who had never been "taken" and who had a passionate objection to it. They just *wouldn't* be—no, not for anything any one could say. I had loudly complained of this; him in particular I had so vainly desired to be able to show on my drawing-room chimney-piece in a Bond Street frame. It was at any rate the very liveliest of all the reasons why they ought to know each other—all the lively reasons reduced to naught by the strange law that had made them bang so many doors in each other's face, made them the buckets in the well, the two ends of the see-saw, the two parties in the State, so that when one was up the other was down, when one was out the other was in; neither by any possibility entering a house till the other had left it or leaving it all unawares till the other was at hand. They only arrived when they had been given up, which was precisely also when they departed. They were in a word alternate and incompatible; they missed each other with an inveteracy that could be explained only by its being precon-certed. It was however so far from preconcerted that it had ended—literally after several years—by disappointing and annoying them. I don't think their curiosity was lively till it had been proved utterly vain. A great deal was of course done to help them, but it merely laid wires for them to trip. To give examples I should have to have taken notes; but I happen to remember that neither had ever been able to dine on the right occasion. The right occasion for each was the occasion that would be wrong for the other. On the wrong one they were most punctual, and there were never any but wrong ones. The very elements conspired and the constitution of man reenforced them. A cold, a headache, a bereave-ment, a storm, a fog, an earthquake, a cataclysm, infallibly intervened. The whole business was beyond a joke.

Yet as a joke it had still to be taken, though one couldn't help feeling that the joke had made the situation serious, had produced on the part of each a consciousness, an awkwardness, a positive dread of the last acci-dent of all, the only one with any freshness left, the accident that *would* bring them together. The final effect of its predecessors had been to kindle this instinct. They were quite ashamed—perhaps even a little of each other. So much preparation, so much frustration: what indeed could be good enough for it all to lead up to? A mere meeting would be mere flatness. Did I see them at the end of years, they often asked, just stupidly confronted? If they were bored by the joke they might be worse bored by something else. They made exactly the same reflexions, and each in some manner was sure to hear of the other's. I really think it was this peculiar diffidence that finally controlled the situation. I mean that if they had failed for the first year or two because they couldn't help it, they kept up the habit because they had—what shall I call it?—grown nervous. It really took some lurking volition to account for anything both so regular and so ridiculous.

III

When to crown our long acquaintance I accepted his renewed offer of marriage it was humorously said, I know, that I had made the gift of his photograph a condition. This was so far true that I had refused to give him mine without it. At any rate I had him at last, in his high distinction, on the chimney-piece, where the day she called to congratulate me she came nearer than she had ever done to seeing him. He had in being taken set her an example that I invited her to follow; he had sacrificed his perversity—wouldn't she sacrifice hers? She too must give me something on my engagement—wouldn't she give me the companion-piece? She laughed and shook her head; she had headshakes whose impulse seemed to come from as far away as the breeze that stirs a flower. The companion-piece to the portrait of my future husband was the portrait of his future wife. She had taken her stand—she could depart from it as little as she could explain it. It was a prejudice, an *entêtement*, a vow—she would live and die unphotographed. Now too she was alone in that state: this was what she liked; it made her so much more original. She rejoiced in the fall of her late associate and looked a long time at his picture, about which she made no memorable remark, though she even turned it over to see the back. About our engagement she was charming—full of cordiality and sympathy. "You've known him even longer than I've *not*," she said, "and that seems a very long time." She understood how we had jogged together over hill and dale and how inevitable it was that we should now rest together. I'm definite about all this because what followed is so strange that it's a kind of relief to me to mark the point up to which our relations were as natural as ever. It was I myself who in a sudden madness altered and destroyed them. I see now that she gave me no pretext and that I only found one in the way she looked at the fine face in the Bond Street frame. How then would I have had her look at it? What I had wanted from the first was to make her care for him. Well, that was what I still wanted—up to the moment of her having promised me she would on this occasion really aid me to break the silly spell that had kept them asunder. I had arranged with him to do his part if she would as triumphantly do hers. I was on a different footing now—I was on a footing to answer for him. I would positively engage that at five on the following Saturday he should be on that spot. He was out of town on pressing business, but, pledged to keep his promise to the letter, would return on purpose and in abundant time. "Are you perfectly sure?" I remember she asked, looking grave and considering: I thought she had turned a little pale. She was tired, she was indisposed: it was a pity he was to see her after all at so poor a moment. If he only *could* have seen her five years before! However, I replied that this time I was sure and that success therefore depended simply on herself. At five o'clock on the Saturday she would find him in a particular chair I pointed out, the one in which he usually sat and in which—though this I didn't mention—he had been sitting when, the week before, he put the question of our future to me in the way that had brought me round. She looked at it in silence, just as she had looked at the photograph, while I repeated for the twentieth time that it was too preposterous one shouldn't somehow succeed in introducing to one's dearest friend one's second self. "*Am* I your dearest friend?" she asked with a smile that for a moment brought back her beauty. I replied by pressing her to my bosom; after which she said: "Well, I'll come. I'm extraordinarily afraid, but you may count on me."

When she had left me I began to wonder what she was afraid of, for she had spoken as if she fully meant it. The next day, late in the afternoon, I had three lines from her: she found on getting home the announcement of her husband's death. She hadn't seen him for seven years, but she wished me to know it in this way before I should hear of it in another. It made however in her life, strange and sad to say, so little difference that she would scrupulously keep her appointment. I rejoiced for her—I supposed it would make at least the difference of her having more money; but even in this diversion, far from forgetting she had said she was afraid, I seemed to catch sight of a reason for her being so. Her fear, as the evening went on, became contagious, and the contagion took in my breast the form of a sudden panic. It wasn't jealousy—it just was the dread of jealousy. I called myself a fool for not having been quiet till we were man and wife. After that I should somehow feel secure. It was only a question of waiting another month—a trifle surely for people who had waited so long. It had been plain enough she was nervous, and now she was free her nervousness wouldn't be less. What was it therefore but a sharp foreboding? She had been hitherto the victim of interference, but it was quite possible she would henceforth be the source of it. The victim in that case would be my simple self. What had the interference been but the finger of Providence pointing out a danger? The danger was of course for poor *me*. It had been kept at bay by a series of accidents unexampled in their frequency; but the reign of accident was now visibly at an end. I had an intimate conviction that both parties would keep the tryst. It was more and more impressed on me that they were approach-

ing, converging. They were like the seekers for the hidden object in the
game of blindfold; they had one and the other begun to "burn." We had
talked about breaking the spell; well, it would be effectually broken—
unless indeed it should merely take another form and overdo their encounters as it had overdone their escapes. This was something I couldn't
sit still for thinking of; it kept me awake—at midnight I was full of
unrest. At last I felt there was only one way of laying the ghost. If the
reign of accident was over I must just take up the succession. I sat down
and wrote a hurried note which would meet him on his return and which
as the servants had gone to bed I sallied forth bareheaded into the empty
gusty street to drop into the nearest pillar-box. It was to tell him that I
shouldn't be able to be at home in the afternoon as I had hoped and that
he must postpone his visit till dinner-time. This was an implication that
he would find me alone.

IV

When accordingly at five she presented herself I naturally felt false and
base. My act had been a momentary madness, but I had at least, as they
say, to live up to it. She remained an hour; he of course never came; and
I could only persist in my perfidy. I had thought it best to let her come;
singular as this now seems to me I held it diminished my guilt. Yet as she
sat there so visibly white and weary, stricken with a sense of everything
her husband's death had opened up, I felt a really piercing pang of pity
and remorse. If I didn't tell her on the spot what I had done it was
because I was too ashamed. I feigned astonishment—I feigned it to the
end; I protested that if ever I had had confidence I had had it that day. I
blush as I tell my story—I take it as my penance. There was nothing
indignant I didn't say about him; I invented suppositions, attenuations; I
admitted in stupefaction, as the hands of the clock travelled, that their
luck hadn't turned. She smiled at this vision of their "luck," but she
looked anxious—she looked unusual: the only thing that kept me up was
the fact that, oddly enough, she wore mourning—no great depths of
crape, but simple and scrupulous black. She had in her bonnet three
small black feathers. She carried a little muff of astrachan. This put me,
by the aid of some acute reflexion, a little in the right. She had written to
me that the sudden event made no difference for her, but apparently it
made as much difference as that. If she was inclined to the usual forms
why didn't she observe that of not going the first day or two out to tea?
There was some one she wanted so much to see that she couldn't wait till
her husband was buried. Such a betrayal of eagerness made me hard and
cruel enough to practise my odious deceit, though at the same time, as
the hour waxed and waned, I suspected in her something deeper still

than disappointment and somewhat less successfully concealed. I mean a strange underlying relief, the soft low emission of the breath that comes when a danger is past. What happened as she spent her barren hour with me was that at last she gave him up. She let him go for ever. She made the most graceful joke of it that I've ever seen made of anything; but it was for all that a great date in her life. She spoke with her mild gaiety of all the other vain times, the long game of hide-and-seek, the unprecedented queerness of such a relation. For it *was,* or had been, a relation, wasn't it, hadn't it? That was just the absurd part of it. When she got up to go I said to her that it was more a relation than ever, but that I hadn't the face after what had occurred to propose to her for the present another opportunity. It was plain that the only valid opportunity would be my accomplished marriage. Of course she would be at my wedding? It was even to be hoped that *he* would.

"If *I* am, he won't be!"—I remember the high quaver and the little break of her laugh. I admitted there might be something in that. The thing was therefore to get us safely married first. "That won't help us. Nothing will help us!" she said as she kissed me farewell. "I shall never, never see him!" It was with those words she left me.

I could bear her disappointment as I've called it; but when a couple of hours later I received him at dinner I discovered I couldn't bear his. The way my manoeuvre might have affected him hadn't been particularly present to me; but the result of it was the first word of reproach that had ever yet dropped from him. I say "reproach" because that expression is scarcely too strong for the terms in which he conveyed to me his surprise that under the extraordinary circumstances I shouldn't have found some means not to deprive him of such an occasion. I might really have managed either not to be obliged to go out or to let their meeting take place all the same. They would probably have got on, in my drawing-room, well enough without me. At this I quite broke down—I confessed my iniquity and the miserable reason of it. I hadn't put her off and I hadn't gone out; she had been there and, after waiting for him an hour, had departed in the belief that he had been absent by his own fault.

"She must think me a precious brute!" he exclaimed. "Did she say of me"—and I remember the just perceptible catch of breath in his pause—"what she had a right to say?"

"I assure you she said nothing that showed the least feeling. She looked at your photograph, she even turned round the back of it, on which your address happens to be inscribed. Yet it provoked her to no demonstration. She doesn't care so much as all that."

"Then why are you afraid of her?"

"It wasn't of her I was afraid. It was of you."

"Did you think I'd be so sure to fall in love with her? You never alluded to such a possibility before," he went on as I remained silent. "Admirable person as you pronounced her, that wasn't the light in which you showed her to me."

"Do you mean that if it *had* been you'd have managed by this time to catch a glimpse of her? I didn't fear things then," I added. "I hadn't the same reason."

He kissed me at this, and when I remembered that she had done so an hour or two before I felt for an instant as if he were taking from my lips the very pressure of hers. In spite of kisses the incident had shed a certain chill, and I suffered horribly from the sense that he had seen me guilty of a fraud. He had seen it only through my frank avowal, but I was as unhappy as if I had a stain to efface. I couldn't get over the manner of his looking at me when I spoke of her apparent indifference to his not having come. For the first time since I had known him he seemed to have expressed a doubt of my word. Before we parted I told him that I'd undeceive her—start the first thing in the morning for Richmond and there let her know he had been blameless. At this he kissed me again. I'd expiate my sin, I said; I'd humble myself in the dust; I'd confess and ask to be forgiven. At this he kissed me once more.

V

In the train the next day this struck me as a good deal for him to have consented to; but my purpose was firm enough to carry me on. I mounted the long hill to where the view begins, and then I knocked at her door. I was a trifle mystified by the fact that her blinds were still drawn, reflecting that if in the stress of my compunction I had come early I had certainly yet allowed people time to get up.

"At home, mum? She has left home for ever."

I was extraordinarily startled by this announcement of the elderly parlour-maid. "She has gone away?"

"She's dead, mum, please." Then as I gasped at the horrible word: "She died last night."

The loud cry that escaped me sounded even in my own ears like some harsh violation of the hour. I felt for the moment as if I had killed her; I turned faint and saw through a vagueness that woman hold out her arms to me. Of what next happened I've no recollection, nor of anything but my friend's poor stupid cousin, in a darkened room, after an interval that I suppose very brief, sobbing at me in a smothered accusatory way. I can't say how long it took me to understand, to believe and then to press back with an immense effort that pang of responsibility which, superstitiously, insanely, had been at first almost all I was conscious of. The doctor, after the fact, had been superlatively wise and clear: he was satisfied of a long-latent weakness of the heart, determined probably years before by the agitations and terrors to which her marriage had introduced her. She had had in those days cruel scenes with her husband, she had been in fear of her life. All emotion, everything in the nature of anxiety and suspense had been after that to be strongly deprecated, as in her marked cultivation of a quiet life she was evidently well aware; but who could say that any one, especially a "real lady," might be successfully protected from *every* little rub? She had had one a day or two before in the news of her husband's death—since there were shocks of all kinds, not only those of grief and surprise. For that matter she had never dreamed of so near a release: it had looked uncommonly as if he would live as long as herself. Then in the evening, in town, she had manifestly had some misadventure: something must have happened there that it would be imperative to clear up. She had come back very late—it was past eleven o'clock, and on being met in the hall by her cousin, who was extremely anxious, had allowed she was tired and must rest a moment before mounting the stairs. They had passed together into the dining-room, her companion proposing a glass of wine and bustling to the sideboard to pour it out. This took but a moment, and when my informant turned round our poor friend had not had time to seat herself. Suddenly, with a small moan that was barely audible, she dropped upon the sofa. She was dead. What unknown "little rub" had dealt her the blow? What concussion, in the name of wonder, *had* awaited her in town? I mentioned immediately the one thinkable ground of disturbance—her having failed to meet at my house, to which by invitation for the purpose she had come at five o'clock, the gentleman I was to be married to, who had been accidentally kept away and with whom she had no acquaintance whatever. This obviously counted for little; but something else might easily have occurred: nothing in the London streets was more possible than an accident, especially an accident in those desperate cabs. What had she done, where had she gone on leaving my house? I had taken for granted she had gone straight home. We both presently remembered that in her excursions to town she sometimes, for convenience, for refreshment, spent an hour or two at the "Gentlewomen," the quiet little ladies' club, and I promised that it should be my first care to make at that establishment an earnest appeal. Then we entered the dim and dreadful chamber where she lay locked up in death and where, asking after a little to be left alone with her, I remained for half an hour. Death had made her, had kept her beautiful; but I felt above all, as I knelt at her bed, that it had made her, had kept her silent. It had turned the key on something I was concerned to know.

On my return from Richmond and after another duty had been performed I drove to his chambers. It was the first time, but I had often wanted to see them. On the staircase, which, as the house contained twenty sets of rooms, was unrestrictedly public, I met his servant, who went back with me and ushered me in. At the sound of my entrance he appeared in the doorway of a further room, and the instant we were alone I produced my news: "She's dead!"

"Dead?" He was tremendously struck, and I noticed he had no need to ask whom, in this abruptness, I meant.

"She died last evening—just after leaving me."

He stared with the strangest expression, his eyes searching mine as for a trap. "Last evening—after leaving you?" He repeated my words in stupefaction. Then he brought out, so that it was in stupefaction I heard, "Impossible! I saw her."

"You 'saw' her?"

"On that spot—where you stand."

This called back to me after an instant, as if to help me to take it in, the great wonder of the warning of his youth. "In the hour of death—I understand: as you so beautifully saw your mother."

"Ah *not* as I saw my mother—not that way, not that way!" He was deeply moved by my news—far more moved, it was plain, than he would have been the day before: it gave me a vivid sense that, as I had then said to myself, there was indeed a relation between them and that he had actually been face to face with her. Such an idea, by its reassertion of his extraordinary privilege, would have suddenly presented him as painfully abnormal hadn't he vehemently insisted on the difference. "I saw her living. I saw her to speak to her. I saw her as I see you now."

It's remarkable that for a moment, though only for a moment, I found relief in the more personal, as it were, but also the more natural, of the two odd facts. The next, as I embraced this image of her having come to him on leaving me and of just what it accounted for in the disposal of her time, I demanded with a shade of harshness of which I was aware: "What on earth did she come for?"

He had now had a minute to think—to recover himself and judge of effects, so that if it was still with excited eyes he spoke he showed a conscious redness and made an inconsequent attempt to smile away the gravity of his words. "She came just to see me. She came—after what had passed at your house—so that we *should*, nevertheless at last meet. The impulse seemed to me exquisite, and that was the way I took it."

I looked round the room where she had been—where *she* had been and I never had till now. "And was the way you took it the way she expressed it?"

"She only expressed it by being here and by letting me look at her.

That was enough!" he cried with an extraordinary laugh.

I wondered more and more. "You mean she didn't speak to you?"

"She said nothing. She only looked at me as I looked at her."

"And you didn't speak either?"

He gave me again his painful smile. "I thought of *you*. The situation was every way delicate. I used the finest tact. But she saw she had pleased me." He even repeated his dissonant laugh.

"She evidently 'pleased' you!" Then I thought a moment. "How long did she stay?"

"How can I say? It seemed twenty minutes, but it was probably a good deal less."

"Twenty minutes of silence!" I began to have my definite view and now in fact quite to clutch at it. "Do you know you're telling me a thing positively monstrous?"

He had been standing with his back to the fire; at this, with a pleading look, he came to me. "I beseech you, dearest, to take it kindly."

I could take it kindly, and I signified as much; but I couldn't somehow, as he rather awkwardly opened his arms, let him draw me to him. So there fell between us for an appreciable time the discomfort of a great silence.

VI

He broke it by presently saying: "There's absolutely no doubt of her death?"

"Unfortunately none. I've just risen from my knees by the bed where they've laid her out."

He fixed his eyes hard on the floor; then he raised them to mine. "How does she look?"

"She looks—at peace."

He turned away again while I watched him; but after a moment he began: "At what hour then——?"

"It must have been near midnight. She dropped as she reached her house—from an affection of the heart which she knew herself and her physician knew her to have, but of which, patiently, bravely, she had never spoken to me."

He listened intently and for a minute was unable to speak. At last he broke out with an accent of which the almost boyish confidence, the really sublime simplicity, rings in my ears as I write: "Wasn't she *wonderful!*" Even at the time I was able to do it justice enough to answer that I had always told him so; but the next minute, as if after speaking he had caught a glimpse of what he might have made me feel, he went on quickly: "You can easily understand that if she didn't get home till midnight——"

I instantly took him up. "There was plenty of time for you to have seen her? How so," I asked, "when you didn't leave my house till late? I don't remember the very moment—I was preoccupied. But you know that though you said you had lots to do you sat for some time after dinner. She, on her side, was all the evening at the 'Gentlewomen,' I've just come from there—I've ascertained. She had tea there; she remained a long long time."

"What was she doing all the long long time?"

I saw him eager to challenge at every step my account of the matter; and the more he showed this the more I was moved to emphasise that version, to prefer with apparently perversity an explanation which only deepened the marvel and the mystery, but which, of the two prodigies it had to choose from, my reviving jealousy found easiest to accept. He stood there pleading with a candour that now seems to me beautiful for the privilege of having in spite of supreme defeat known the living woman; while I, with a passion I wonder at to-day, though it still smoulders in a manner in its ashes, could only reply that, through a strange gift shared by her with his mother and on her own side likewise hereditary, the miracle of his youth had been renewed for him, the miracle of hers for her. She had been to him—yes, and by an impulse as charming as he liked; but oh she hadn't been in the body! It was a simple question of evidence. I had had, I maintained, a definite statement of what she had done—most of the time—at the little club. The place was almost empty, but the servants had noticed her. She had sat motionless in a deep chair by the drawing-room fire; she had leaned back her head, she had closed her eyes, she had seemed softly to sleep.

"I see. But till what o'clock?"

"There," I was obliged to answer, "the servants fail me a little. The portress in particular is unfortunately a fool, even though she too is supposed to be a Gentlewoman. She was evidently at that period of the evening, without a substitute and against regulations, absent for some little time from the cage in which it's her business to watch the comings and goings. She's muddled, she palpably prevaricates; so I can't positively, from her observation, give you an hour. But it was remarked toward half-past ten that our poor friend was no longer in the club."

It suited him down to the ground. "She came straight here, and from here she went straight to the train."

"She couldn't have run it so close," I declared. "That was a thing she particularly never did."

"There was no need of running it close, my dear—she had plenty of time. Your memory's at fault about my having left you late: I left you, as it happens, unusually early. I'm sorry my stay with you seemed long, for I was back here by ten."

"To put yourself into your slippers," I retorted, "and fall asleep in your chair. You slept till morning—you saw her in a dream!" He looked at me in silence and with sombre eyes—eyes that showed me he had some irritation to repress. Presently I went on: "You had a visit, at an extraordinary hour, from a lady—*soit:* nothing in the world's more probable. But there are ladies and ladies. How in the name of goodness, if she was unannounced and dumb and you had into the bargain never seen the least portrait of her—how could you identify the person we're talking of?"

"Haven't I to absolute satiety heard her described? I'll describe her for you in every particular."

"Don't!" I cried with a promptness that made him laugh once more. I coloured at this, but I continued: "Did your servant introduce her?"

"He wasn't here—he's always away when he's wanted. One of the features of this big house is that from the street-door the different floors are accessible practically without challenge. My servant makes love to a young person employed in the rooms above these, and he had a long bout of it last evening. When he's out on that job he leaves my outer door, on the staircase, so much ajar as to enable him to slip back without a sound. The door then only requires a push. She pushed it—that simply took a little courage."

"A little? It took tons! And it took all sorts of impossible calculations."

"Well, she had them—she made them. Mind you, I don't deny for a moment," he added "that it was very very wonderful!"

Something in his tone kept me a time from trusting myself to speak. At last I said: "How did she come to know where you live?"

"By remembering the address on the little label the shop-people happily left sticking to the frame I had had made for my photograph."

"And how was she dressed?"

"In mourning, my own dear. No great depths of crape, but simple and scrupulous black. She had in her bonnet three small black feathers. She carried a little muff of astrachan. She has near the left eye," he continued, "a tiny vertical scar—"

I stopped him short. "The mark of a caress from her husband." Then I added: "How close you must have been to her!" He made no answer to this, and I thought he blushed, observing which I broke straight off. "Well, good-bye."

"You won't stay a little?" He came to me again tenderly, and this time I suffered him. "Her visit had its beauty," he murmured as he held me, "but yours has a greater one."

I let him kiss me, but I remembered, as I had remembered the day before, that the last kiss she had given, as I supposed, in this world had been for the lips he touched. "I'm life, you see," I answered. "What you saw last night was death."

"It was life—it was life!"

He spoke with a soft stubbornness—I disengaged myself. We stood looking at each other hard. "You describe the scene—so far as you describe it at all—in terms that are incomprehensible. She was in the room before you knew it?"

"I looked up from my letter-writing—at that table under the lamp I had been wholly absorbed in it—and she stood before me."

"Then what did you do?"

"I sprang up with an ejaculation, and she, with a smile, laid her finger, ever so warningly, yet with a sort of delicate dignity, to her lips. I knew it meant silence, but the strange thing was that it seemed immediately to explain and to justify her. We at any rate stood for a time that, as I've told you, I can't calculate, face to face. It was just as you and I stand now."

"Simply staring?"

He shook an impatient head. "Ah! *we're* not staring!"

"Yes, but we're talking."

"Well, *we* were—after a fashion." He lost himself in the memory of it. "It was as friendly as this." I had on my tongue's end to ask if that was saying much for it, but I made the point instead that what they had evidently done was to gaze in mutual admiration. Then I asked if his recognition of her had been immediate. "Not quite," he replied, "for of course I didn't expect her; but it came to me long before she went who she was—who only she could be."

I thought a little. "And how did she at last go?"

"Just as she arrived. The door was open behind her and she passed out."

"Was she rapid—slow?"

"Rather quick. But looking behind her," he smiled to add. "I let her go, for I perfectly knew I was to take it as she wished."

I was conscious of exhaling a long vague sigh. "Well, you must take it now as *I* wish—you must let *me* go."

At this he drew near me again, detaining and persuading me, declaring with all due gallantry that I was a very different matter. I'd have given anything to have been able to ask him if he had touched her, but the words refused to form themselves: I knew to the last tenth of a tone how horrid and vulgar they'd sound. I said something else—I forget exactly what; it was feebly tortuous and intended, meanly enough, to make him tell me without my putting the question. But he didn't tell me; he only repeated, as from a glimpse of the propriety of soothing and consoling me, the sense of his declaration of some minutes before—the assurance that she was indeed exquisite, as I had always insisted, but that I was his "real" friend and his very own for ever. This led me to reassert, in the spirit of my previous rejoinder, that I had at least the merit of being alive; which in turn drew from him again the flash of contradiction I dreaded. "Oh *she* was alive! She was, she was!"

"She was dead, she was dead!" I asseverated with an energy, a determination it should *be* so, which comes back to me now almost as grotesque. But the sound of the word as it rang out filled me suddenly with horror, and all the natural emotion the meaning of it might have evoked in other conditions gathered and broke in a flood. It rolled over me that here was a great affection quenched and how much I had loved and trusted her. I had a vision at the same time of the lonely beauty of her end. "She's gone—she's lost to us for ever!" I burst into sobs.

"That's exactly what I feel," he exclaimed, speaking with extreme kindness and pressing me to him for comfort. "She's gone; she's lost to us for ever: so what does it matter now?" He bent over me, and when his face had touched mine I scarcely knew if it were wet with my tears or with his own.

VII

It was my theory, my conviction, it became, as I may say, my attitude, that they had still never "met"; and it was just on this ground I felt it generous to ask him to stand with me at her grave. He did so very modestly and tenderly, and I assumed, though he himself clearly cared nothing for the danger, that the solemnity of the occasion, largely made up of persons who had known them both and had a sense of the long joke, would sufficiently deprive his presence of all light association. On the question of what had happened the evening of her death little more passed between us; I had been taken by a horror of the element of evidence. On either hypothesis it was gross and prying. He on his side lacked producible corroboration—everything, that is, but a statement of his house-porter, on his own admission a most casual and intermittent personage—that between the hours of ten o'clock and midnight no less than three ladies in deep black had flitted in and out of the place. This proved far too much; we had neither of us any use for three. He knew I considered I had accounted for every fragment of her time, and we dropped the matter as settled; we abstained from further discussion. What *I* knew however was that he abstained to please me rather than because he yielded to my reasons. He didn't yield—he was only indulgent; he clung to his interpretation because he liked it better. He liked it better, I held, because it had more to say to his vanity. That, in a similar position, wouldn't have been its effect on me, though I had doubtless quite as much; but these are things of individual humour and as to which no person can judge for another. I should have supposed it more gratifying to be the subject of one of those inexplicable occurrences that are chronicled in thrilling books and disputed about at learned meetings; I could conceive, on the part of a being just engulfed in the infinite and still vibrating with human emotion, of nothing more fine and pure, more high and august, than such an impulse of reparation, of admonition, or even of curiosity. *That* was beautiful, if one would, and I should in his place have thought more of myself for being so distinguished and so selected. It was public that he had already, that he had long figured in that light, and what was such a fact in itself but almost a proof? Each of the strange visitations contributed to establish the other. He had a different feeling; but he had also, I hasten to add, an unmistakable desire not to make a stand or, as they say, a fuss about it. I might believe what I liked—the more so that the whole thing was in a manner a mystery of my producing. It was an event of my history, a puzzle of my consciousness, not of his; therefore he would take about it any tone that struck me as convenient. We had both at all events other business on hand; we were pressed with preparations for our marriage.

Mine were assuredly urgent, but I found as the days went on that to believe what I "liked" was to believe what I was more and more intimately convinced of. I found also that I didn't like it so much as that came to, or that the pleasure at all events was far from being the cause of my conviction. My obsession, as I may really call it and as I began to perceive, refused to be elbowed away, as I had hoped, by my sense of paramount duties. If I had a great deal to do I had still more to think of, and the moment came when my occupations were gravely menaced by my thoughts. I see it all now, I feel it, I live it over. It's terribly void of joy, it's full indeed to overflowing of bitterness; and yet I must do myself justice—I couldn't have been other than I was. The same strange impressions, had I to meet them again, would produce the same deep anguish, the same sharp doubts, the same still sharper certainties. Oh it's all easier to remember than to write, but even could I retrace the business hour by hour, could I find terms for the inexpressible, the ugliness and the pain would quickly stay my hand. Let me then note very simply and briefly that a week before our wedding-day, three weeks after her death, I knew in all my fibres that I had something very serious to look in the face and that if I was to make this effort I must make it on the spot and before another hour should elapse. My unextinguished jealousy— that was the Medusamask. It hadn't died with her death, it had lividly survived, and it was fed by suspicions unspeakable. They *would* be unspeakable to-day, that is, if I hadn't felt the sharp need of uttering them at the time. This need took possession of me—to save me, as it seemed, from my fate. When once it had done so I saw—in the urgency of the case, the diminishing hours and shrinking interval—only one issue, that of absolute promptness and frankness. I could at least not do him the wrong of delaying another day; I could at least treat my difficulty as too fine for a subterfuge. Therefore very quietly, but none the less abruptly and hideously, I put it before him on a certain evening that we must reconsider our situation and recognise that it had completely altered.

He stared bravely. "How in the world altered?"

"Another person has come between us."

He took but an instant to think. "I won't pretend not to know whom you mean." He smiled in pity for my aberration, but he meant to be kind. "A woman dead and buried!"

"She's buried, but she's not dead. She's dead for the world—she's dead for me. But she's not dead for you."

"You hark back to the different construction we put on her appearance that evening?"

"No," I answered, "I hark back to nothing. I've no need of it. I've more than enough with what's before me."

"And pray, darling, what may that be?"

"You're completely changed."

"By that absurdity?" he laughed.

"Not so much by that one as by other absurdities that have followed it."

"And what may *they* have been?"

We had faced each other fairly, with eyes that didn't flinch; but his had a dim strange light, and my certitude triumphed in his perceptible paleness. "Do you really pretend," I asked, "not to know what they are?"

"My dear child," he replied, "you describe them too sketchily!"

I considered a moment. "One may well be embarrassed to finish the picture! But from that point of view—and from the beginning—what was ever more embarrassing than your idiosyncrasy?"

He invoked his vagueness—a thing he always did beautifully. "My idiosyncrasy?"

"Your notorious, your peculiar power."

He gave a great shrug of impatience, a groan of overdone disdain. "Oh my peculiar power!"

"Your accessibility to forms of life," I coldly went on, "your command of impressions, appearances, contacts, closed—for our gain or our loss—to the rest of us. That was originally a part of the deep interest with which you inspired me—one of the reasons I was amused, I was indeed positively proud, to know you. It was a magnificent distinction; it's a magnificent distinction still. But of course I had no prevision then of the

way it would operate now; and even had that been the case I should have
had none of the extraordinary way of which its action would affect me."

"To what in the name of goodness," he pleadingly enquired, "are you
fantastically alluding?" Then as I remained silent, gathering a tone for
my charge, "How in the world *does* it operate?" he went on; "and how
in the world are you affected?"

"She missed you for five years," I said, "but she never misses you now.
You're making it up!"

"Making it up?" He had begun to turn from white to red.

"You see her—you see her: you see her every night!" He gave a loud
sound of derision, but I felt it ring false. "She comes to you as she came
that evening," I declared; "having tried it she found she liked it!" I was
able, with God's help, to speak without blind passion or vulgar violence;
but those were the exact words—and far from "sketchy" they then
appeared to me—that I uttered. He had turned away in his laughter,
clapping his hands at my folly, but in an instant he faced me again with a
change of expression that struck me. "Do you dare to deny," I then
asked, "that you habitually see her?"

He had taken the line of indulgence, of meeting me halfway and
kindly humouring me. At all events he to my astonishment suddenly
said: "Well, my dear, what if I do?"

"It's your natural right: it belongs to your constitution and to your
wonderful if not perhaps quite enviable fortune. But you'll easily understand that it separates us. I unconditionally release you."

"Release me?"

"You must choose between me and her."

He looked at me hard. "I see." Then he walked away a little, as if
grasping what I had said and thinking how he had best treat it. At last he
turned on me afresh. "How on earth do you know such an awfully
private thing?"

"You mean because you've tried so hard to hide it? It *is* awfully
private, and you may believe I shall never betray you. You've done your
best, you've acted your part, you've behaved, poor dear! loyally and
admirably. Therefore I've watched you in silence, playing my part too;
I've noted every drop in your voice, every absence in your eyes, every
effort in your indifferent hand: I've waited till I was utterly sure and
miserably unhappy. How *can* you hide it when you're abjectly in love
with her, when you're sick almost to death with the joy of what she gives
you?" I checked his quick protest with a quicker gesture. "You love her
as you've *never* loved, and, passion for passion, she gives it straight back!
She rules you, she holds you, she has you all! A woman, in such a case as
mine, divines and feels and sees; she's not a dull dunce who has to be
'credibly informed.' You come to me mechanically, compunctiously,

with the dregs of your tenderness and the remnant of your life. I can renounce you, but I can't share you: the best of you is hers, I know what it is and freely give you up to her for ever!"

He made a gallant fight, but it couldn't be patched up; he repeated his denial, he retracted his admission, he ridiculed my charge, of which I freely granted him moreover the indefensible extravagance. I didn't pretend for a moment that we were talking of common things; I didn't pretend for a moment that he and she were common people. Pray, if they *had* been, how should I ever have cared for them? They had enjoyed a rare extension of being and they had caught me up in their flight; only I couldn't breathe in such air and I promptly asked to be set down. Everything in the facts was monstrous, and most of all my lucid perception of them; the only thing allied to nature and truth was my having to act on that perception. I felt after I had spoken in this sense that my assurance was complete; nothing had been wanting to it but the sight of my effect on him. He disguised indeed the effect in a cloud of chaff, a diversion that gained him time and covered his retreat. He challenged my sincerity, my sanity, almost my humanity, and that of course widened our breach and confirmed our rupture. He did everything in short but convince me either that I was wrong or that he was unhappy: we separated and I left him to his inconceivable communion.

He never married, any more than I've done. When six years later, in solitude and silence, I heard of his death I hailed it as a direct contribution to my theory. It was sudden, it was never properly accounted for, it was surrounded by circumstances in which—for oh I took them to pieces!—I distinctly read an intention, the mark of his own hidden hand. It was the result of a long necessity, of an unquenchable desire. To say exactly what I mean, it was a response to an irresistible call.

1896

MAUD-EVELYN

On some allusion to a lady who, though unknown to myself, was known to two or three of the company it was asked by one of these if we had heard the odd circumstance of what she had just "come in for"—the piece of luck suddenly overtaking, in the grey afternoon of her career, so obscure and lonely a personage. We were at first, in our ignorance, mainly reduced to crude envy; but old Lady Emma, who for a while had said nothing, scarcely even appearing to listen, and letting the chatter, which was indeed plainly beside the mark, subside of itself, came back from a mental absence to observe that if what had happened to Lavinia was wonderful, certainly what had for years gone before it, led up to it, had likewise not been without some singular features. From this we perceived that Lady Emma had a story—a story, moreover, out of the ken even of those of her listeners acquainted with the quiet person who was the subject of it. Almost the oddest thing—as came out afterwards—was that such a situation should for the world have remained so in the background of this person's life. By "afterwards" I mean simply before we separated; for what came out came on the spot, under encouragement and pressure, our common, eager solicitation. Lady Emma, who always reminded me of a fine old instrument that has first to be tuned, agreed, after a few of our scrapings and fingerings, that, having said so much, she couldn't without wantonly tormenting us, forbear to say all. She had known Lavinia, whom she mentioned throughout only by that name, from far away, and she had also known— But what she had known I must give as nearly as possible as she herself gave it. She talked to us from her corner of the sofa, and the flicker of the firelight in her face was like the glow of memory, the play of fancy from within.

I

"Then why on earth don't you take him?" I asked. I think that was the way that, one day when she was about twenty—before some of you perhaps were born—the affair, for me, must have begun. I put the question because I knew she had had a chance, though I didn't know how great a mistake her failure to embrace it was to prove. I took an interest because I liked them both—you see how I like young people still—and because, as they had originally met at my house, I had in a manner to answer to each for the other. I'm afraid I'm thrown baldly back on the fact that if the girl was the daughter of my earliest, almost my only governess, to whom I had remained much attached and who, after leaving me, had married—for a governess—"well," Marmaduke (it isn't *his* real name!) was the son of one of the clever men who had—I was charming then, I assure you I was—wanted, years before, and this one as a widower, to marry me. I hadn't cared, somehow, for widowers, but even after I had taken somebody else I was conscious of a pleasant link with the boy whose stepmother it had been open to me to become and to whom it was perhaps a little a matter of vanity with me to show that I should have been for him one of the kindest. This was what the woman his father eventually did marry was not, and that threw him upon me the more.

Lavinia was one of nine, and her brothers and sisters, who had never done anything for her, help, actually, in different countries and on something, I believe, of that same scale, to people the globe. There were mixed in her then, in a puzzling way, two qualities that mostly exclude each other—an extreme timidity and, as the smallest fault that could qualify a harmless creature for a world of wickedness, a self-complacency hard in tiny, unexpected spots, for which I used sometimes to take her up, but which, I subsequently saw, would have done something for the flatness of her life had they not evaporated with everything else. She was at any rate one of those persons as to whom you don't know whether they might have been attractive if they had been happy, or might have been happy if they had been attractive. If I was a trifle vexed at her not jumping at Marmaduke, it was probably rather less because I expected wonders of him than because I thought she took her own prospect too much for granted. She had made a mistake and, before long, admitted it; yet I remember that when she expressed to me a conviction that he would ask her again, I also thought this highly probable, for in the meantime I had spoken to him. "She does care for you," I declared; and I can see at this moment, long ago though it be, his handsome empty young face look, on the words, as if, in spite of itself for a little, it really thought. I didn't press the matter, for he had, after all, no great things to offer; yet my conscience was easier, later on, for having not said less. He had three hundred and fifty a year from his mother, and one of his uncles had promised him something—I don't mean an allowance, but a place, if I recollect, in a business. He assured me that he loved as a man loves—a man of twenty-two!—but once. He said it, at all events, as a man says it but once.

"Well, then," I replied, "your course is clear."

"To speak to her again, you mean?"

"Yes—try it."

He seemed to try it a moment in imagination; after which, a little to my surprise, he asked: "Would it be very awful if she should speak to *me?*"

I stared. "Do you mean pursue you—overtake you? Ah, if you're running away—"

"I'm not running away!"—he was positive as to that. "But when a fellow has gone so far—"

"He can't go any further? Perhaps," I replied dryly. "But in that case he shouldn't talk of 'caring.' "

"Oh, but I do, I do."

I shook my head. "Not if you're too proud!" On which I turned away, looking round at him again, however, after he had surprised me by a silence that seemed to accept my judgment. Then I saw he had not accepted it; I perceived it indeed to be essentially absurd. He expressed more, on this, than I had yet seen him do—had the queerest, frankest, and, for a young man of his conditions, saddest smile.

"I'm *not* proud. It isn't *in* me. If you're not, you're not, you know. I don't think I'm proud enough."

It came over me that this was, after all, probable; yet somehow I didn't at the moment like him the less for it, though I spoke with some sharpness. "Then what's the matter with you?"

He took a turn or two about the room, as if what he had just said had made him a little happier. "Well, how can a man say more?" Then, just as I was on the point of assuring him that I didn't know what he had said, he went on: "I swore to her that I would never marry. Oughtn't that to be enough?"

"To make her come after you?"

"No—I suppose scarcely that; but to make her feel sure of me—to make her wait."

"Wait for what?"

"Well, till I come back."

"Back from where?"

"From Switzerland—haven't I told you? I go there next month with my aunt and my cousin."

He was quite right about not being proud—this was an alternative distinctly humble.

II

And yet see what it brought forth—the beginning of which was something that, early in the autumn, I learned from poor Lavinia. He had written to her, they were still such friends; and thus it was that she knew his aunt and his cousin to have come back without him. He had stayed on—stayed much longer and travelled much further: he had been to the Italian lakes and to Venice; he was now in Paris. At this I vaguely wondered, knowing that he was always short of funds and that he must, by his uncle's beneficence, have started on the journey on a basis of expenses paid. "Then whom has he picked up?" I asked; but feeling sorry, as soon as I had spoken, to have made Lavinia blush. It was almost as if he had picked up some improper lady, though in this case he wouldn't have told her, and it wouldn't have saved him money.

"Oh, he makes acquaintance so quickly, knows people in two minutes," the girl said. "And every one always wants to be nice to him."

This was perfectly true, and I saw what she saw in it. "Ah, my dear, he will have an immense circle ready for you!"

"Well," she replied, "if they do run after us I'm not likely to suppose it will ever be for me. It will be for *him*, and they may do to me what they like. My pleasure will be—but you'll see." I already saw—saw at least what she supposed she herself saw: her drawing-room crowded with female fashion and her attitude angelic. "Do you know what he said to me again before he went?" she continued.

I wondered; he *had* then spoken to her. "That he will never, never marry—"

"Any one but *me!*" She ingenuously took me up. "Then you knew?"

It might be. "I guessed."

"And don't you believe it?"

Again I hesitated. "Yes." Yet all this didn't tell me why she had changed colour. "Is it a secret—whom he's with?"

"Oh no, they seem so nice. I was only struck with the way you know him—your seeing immediately that it must be a new friendship that has kept him over. It's the devotion of the Dedricks," Lavinia said. "He's travelling with them."

Once more I wondered. "Do you mean they're taking him about?"

"Yes—they've invited him."

No, indeed, I reflected—he wasn't proud. But what I said was: "Who in the world are the Dedricks?"

"Kind, good people whom, last month he accidentally met. He was walking some Swiss pass—a long, rather stupid one, I believe, without his aunt and his cousin, who had gone round some other way and were to meet him somewhere. It came on to rain in torrents, and while he was huddling under a shelter he was overtaken by some people in a carriage, who kindly made him get in. They drove him, I gather, for several hours; it began an intimacy, and they've continued to be charming to him."

I thought a moment. "Are they ladies?"

Her own imagination meanwhile had also strayed a little. "I think about forty."

"Forty ladies?"

She quickly came back. "Oh no; I mean Mrs. Dedrick is."

"About forty? Then Miss Dedrick——"

"There isn't any Miss Dedrick."

"No daughter?"

"Not with them, at any rate. No one but the husband."

I thought again. "And how old is *he?*"

Lavinia followed my example. "Well, about forty, too."

"About forty-two?" We laughed, but "That's all right!" I said; and so, for the time, it seemed.

He continued absent, none the less, and I saw Lavinia repeatedly, and we always talked of him, though this represented a greater concern with his affairs than I had really supposed myself committed to. I had never sought the acquaintance of his father's people, nor seen either his aunt or his cousin, so that the account given by these relatives of the circumstances of their separation reached me at last only through the girl, to whom, also—for she knew them as little,—it had circuitously come. They considered, it appeared, the poor ladies he had started with, that he had treated them ill and thrown them over, sacrificing them selfishly to company picked up on the road—a reproach deeply resented by Lavinia, though about the company too I could see she was not much more at her ease. "How can he help it if he's so taking?" she asked; and to be properly indignant in one quarter she had to pretend to be delighted in the other. Marmaduke *was* "taking"; yet it also came out between us at last that the Dedricks must certainly be extraordinary. We had scant added evidence, for his letters stopped, and that naturally was one of our signs. I had meanwhile leisure to reflect—it was a sort of study of the human scene I always liked—on what to be taking consisted of. The upshot of my meditations, which experience has only confirmed, was that it consisted simply of itself. It was a quality implying no others. Marmaduke *had* no others. What indeed was his need of any?

III

He at last, however, turned up; but then it happened that if, on his coming to see me, his immediate picture of his charming new friends quickened even more than I had expected my sense of the variety of the human species, my curiosity about them failed to make me respond when he suggested I should go to see them. It's a difficult thing to explain, and I don't pretend to put it successfully, but doesn't it often happen that one may think well enough of a person without being in-flamed with the desire to meet—on the ground of any such sentiment—other persons who think still better? Somehow—little harm as there was in Marmaduke—it was but half a recommendation of the Dedricks that they were crazy about him. I didn't say this—I was careful to say little; which didn't prevent his presently asking if he mightn't then bring them to *me*. "If not, why not?" he laughed. He laughed about everything.

"Why not? Because it strikes me that your surrender doesn't require any backing. Since you've done it you must take care of yourself."

"Oh, but they're as safe," he returned, "as the Bank of England. They're wonderful—for respectability and goodness."

"Those are precisely qualities to which my poor intercourse can contribute nothing." He hadn't, I observed, gone so far as to tell me they would be "fun," and he *had*, on the other hand, promptly mentioned that they lived in Westbourne Terrace. They were not forty—they were forty-five; but Mr. Dedrick had already, on considerable gains, retired from some primitive profession. They were the simplest, kindest, yet most original and unusual people, and nothing could exceed, frankly, the fancy they had taken to him. Marmaduke spoke of it with a placidity of resignation that was almost irritating. I suppose I should have despised him if, after benefits accepted, he had said they bored him; yet their not boring him vexed me even more than it puzzled. "Whom do they know?"

"No one but me. There are people in London like that."

"Who know no one but you?"

"No—I mean no one at all. There are extraordinary people in London, and awfully nice. You haven't an idea. You people don't know every one. They lead their lives—they go their way. One finds—what do you call it?—refinement, books, cleverness, don't you know, and music, and pictures, and religion, and an excellent table—all sorts of pleasant things. You only come across them by chance; but it's all perpetually going on."

I assented to this: the world was very wonderful, and one must certainly see what one could. In my own quarter too I found wonders enough. "But are you," I asked, "as fond of them—"

"As they are of *me?*" He took me up promptly, and his eyes were quite unclouded. "I'm quite sure I shall become so."

"Then are you taking Lavinia—?"

"Not to see them—no." I saw, myself, the next minute, of course, that I had made a mistake. "On what footing *can* I?"

I bethought myself. "I keep forgetting you're not engaged."

"Well," he said after a moment, "I shall never marry another."

It somehow, repeated again, gave on my nerves. "Ah, but what good will that do her, or me either, if you don't marry *her?*"

He made no answer to this—only turned away to look at something in the room; after which, when he next faced me, he had a heightened colour. "She ought to have taken me that day," he said gravely and gently, fixing me also as if he wished to say more.

I remember that his very mildness irritated me; some show of resentment would have been a promise that the case might still be righted. But I dropped it, the silly case, without letting him say more, and, coming back to Mr. and Mrs. Dedrick, asked him how in the world, without either occupation or society, they passed so much of their time. My question appeared for a moment to leave him at a loss, but he presently found light; which, at the same time, I saw on my side, really suited him better than further talk about Lavinia. "Oh, they live for Maud-Evelyn."

"And who's Maud-Evelyn?"

"Why, their daughter."

"Their daughter?" I had supposed them childless.

He partly explained. "Unfortunately they've lost her."

"Lost her?" I required more.

He hesitated again. "I mean that a great many people would take it that way. But *they* don't—they won't."

I speculated. "Do you mean other people would have given her up?"

"Yes—perhaps even tried to forget her. But the Dedricks can't."

I wondered what she had done: had it been anything very bad? However, it was none of my business, and I only said: "They communicate with her?"

"Oh, all the while."

"Then why isn't she with them?"

Marmaduke thought. "She *is*—now."

" 'Now'? Since when?"

"Well, this last year."

"Then why do you say they've lost her?"

"Ah," he said, smiling sadly, "*I* should call it that. I, at any rate," he went on, "don't see her."

Still more I wondered. "They keep her apart?"

He thought again. "No, it's not that. As I say, they live for her."

"But they don't want *you* to—is that it?"

At this he looked at me for the first time, as I thought, a little strangely. "How *can* I?"

He put it to me as if it were bad of him, somehow, that he shouldn't; but I made, to the best of my ability, a quick end of that. "You can't. Why in the world *should* you? Live for *my* girl. Live for Lavinia."

IV

I had unfortunately run the risk of boring him again with that idea, and, though he had not repudiated it at the time, I felt in my having returned to it the reason why he never reappeared for weeks. I saw "my girl," as I had called her, in the interval, but we avoided with much intensity the subject of Marmaduke. It was just this that gave me my perspective for finding her constantly full of him. It determined me, in all the circumstances, not to rectify her mistake about the childlessness of the Dedricks. But whatever I left unsaid, her naming the young man was only a question of time, for at the end of a month she told me he had been twice to her mother's and that she had seen him on each of these occasions.

"Well then?"

"Well then, he's very happy."

"And still taken up—"

"As much as ever, yes, with those people. He didn't tell me so, but I could see it."

I could too, and her own view of it. "What, in that case, did he tell you?"

"Nothing—but I think there's something he wants to. Only not what *you* think," she added.

I wondered then if it were what I had had from him the last time. "Well, what prevents him?" I asked.

"From bringing it out? I don't know."

It was in the tone of this that she struck, to my ear, the first note of an acceptance so deep and a patience so strange that they gave me, at the end, even more food for wonderment than the rest of the business. "If he can't speak, why does he come?"

She almost smiled. "Well, I think I *shall* know."

I looked at her; I remember that I kissed her. "You're admirable; but it's very ugly."

"Ah," she replied, "he only wants to be kind!"

"To *them?* Then he should let others alone. But what I call ugly is his being content to be so 'beholden'—"

"To Mr. and Mrs. Dedrick?" She considered as if there might be many sides to it. "But mayn't he do them some good?"

The idea failed to appeal to me. "What good can Marmaduke do? There's one thing," I went on, "in case he should want you to know them. Will you promise me to refuse?"

She only looked helpless and blank. "Making their acquaintance?"

"Seeing them, going near them—ever, ever."

Again she brooded. "Do you mean *you* won't?"

"Never, never."

"Well, then, I don't think I want to."

"Ah, but that's not a promise." I kept her up to it. "I want your word."

She demurred a little. "But why?"

"So that at least he shan't make use of you," I said with energy.

My energy overbore her, though I saw how she would really have given herself. "I promise, but it's only because it's something I know he will never ask."

I differed from her at the time, believing the proposal in question to have been exactly the subject she had supposed him to be wishing to broach; but on our very next meeting I heard from her of quite another matter, upon which, as soon as she came in, I saw her to be much excited.

"You know then about the daughter without having told me? He called again yesterday," she explained as she met my stare at her unconnected plunge, "and now I know that he *has* wanted to speak to me. He at last brought it out."

I continued to stare. "Brought what?"

"Why, everything." She looked surprised at my face. "Didn't he tell you about Maud-Evelyn?"

I perfectly recollected, but I momentarily wondered. "He spoke of there being a daughter, but only to say that there's something the matter with her. What is it?"

The girl echoed my words. "What 'is' it?—you dear, strange thing! The matter with her is simply that she's dead."

"Dead?" I was naturally mystified. "When then did she die?"

"Why, years and years ago—fifteen, I believe. As a little girl. Didn't you understand it so?"

"How *should* I?—when he spoke of her as 'with' them and said that they lived for her!"

"Well," my young friend explained, "that's just what he meant—they live for her memory. She *is* with them in the sense that they think of nothing else."

I found matter for surprise in this correction, but also, at first, matter for relief. At the same time it left, as I turned it over, a fresh ambiguity. "If they think of nothing else, how can they think so much of Marmaduke?"

The difficulty struck her, though she gave me even then a dim impression of being already, as it were, rather on Marmaduke's side, or, at any rate—almost as against herself—in sympathy with the Dedricks. But her answer was prompt: "Why, that's just their reason—that they can talk to him so much about her."

"I see." Yet still I wondered. "But what's *his* interest—?"

"In being drawn into it?" Again Lavinia met her difficulty. "Well, that she was so interesting! It appears she was lovely."

I doubtless fairly gaped. "A little girl in a pinafore?"

"She was out of pinafores; she was, I believe, when she died, about fourteen. Unless it was sixteen! She was at all events wonderful for beauty."

"That's the rule. But what good does it do him if he has never seen her?"

She thought a moment, but this time she had no answer. "Well, you must ask him!"

I determined without delay to do so; but I had before me meanwhile other contradictions. "Hadn't I better ask him on the same occasion what he means by their 'communicating'?"

Oh, this was simple. "They go in for 'mediums,' don't you know, and raps, and sittings. They began a year or two ago."

"Ah, the idiots!" I remember, at this, narrow-mindedly exclaiming. "Do they want to drag *him* in—?"

"Not in the least; they don't desire it, and he has nothing to do with it."

"Then where does his fun come in?"

Lavinia turned away; again she seemed at a loss. At last she brought out: "Make him show you her little photograph."

But I remained unenlightened. "Is her little photograph his fun?"

Once more she coloured for him. "Well, it represents a young loveliness!"

"That he goes about showing?"

She hesitated. "I think he has only shown it to *me*."

"Ah, you're just the last one!" I permitted myself to observe.

"Why so, if I'm also struck?"

There was something about her that began to escape me, and I must have looked at her hard. "It's very good of you to be struck!"

"I don't only mean by the beauty of the face," she went on; "I mean by the whole thing—by that also of the attitude of the parents, their extraordinary fidelity, and the way that, as he says, they have made of her memory a real religion. That was what, above all, he came to tell me about."

I turned away from her now, and she soon afterwards left me; but I couldn't help its dropping from me before we parted that I had never supposed him to be *that* sort of fool.

V

If I were really the perfect cynic you probably think me, I should frankly say that the main interest of the rest of this matter lay for me in fixing the sort of fool I *did* suppose him. But I'm afraid, after all, that my anecdote amounts mainly to a presentation of my own folly. I shouldn't be so in possession of the whole spectacle had I not ended by accepting it, and I shouldn't have accepted it had it not, for my imagination, been saved somehow from grotesqueness. Let me say at once, however, that grotesqueness, and even indeed something worse, did at first appear to me strongly to season it. After that talk with Lavinia I immediately addressed to our friend a request that he would come to see me; when I took the liberty of challenging him outright on everything she had told me. There was one point in particular that I desired to clear up and that seemed to me much more important even than the colour of Maud-Evelyn's hair or the length of her pinafores: the question, I of course mean, of my young man's good faith. Was he altogether silly or was he only altogether mercenary? I felt my choice restricted for the moment to these alternatives.

After he had said to me "It's as ridiculous as you please, but they've simply adopted me," I had it out with him, on the spot, on the issue of common honesty, the question of what he was conscious, so that his self-respect should be saved, of being able to give such benefactors in return for such bounty. I'm obliged to say that to a person so inclined at the start to quarrel with him his amiability could yet prove persuasive. His contention was that the equivalent he represented was something for his friends alone to measure. He didn't for a moment pretend to sound deeper than the fancy they had taken to him. He had not, from the first, made up to them in any way: it was all their own doing, their own insistence, their own eccentricity, no doubt, and even, if I liked, their own insanity. Wasn't it enough that he was ready to declare to me, looking me straight in the eye, that he was "really and truly" fond of them and that they didn't bore him a mite? I had evidently—didn't I see?—an ideal for him that he wasn't at all, if I didn't mind, the fellow to live up to. It was he himself who put it so, and it drew from me the pronouncement that there *was* something irresistible in the refinement of his impudence. "I don't go near Mrs. Jex," he said—Mrs. Jex was their favourite medium: "I do find *her* ugly and vulgar and tiresome, and I hate that part of the business. Besides," he added in words that I afterwards remembered, "I don't require it: I do beautifully without it. But my friends themselves," he pursued, "though they're of a type you've never come within miles of, are not ugly, are not vulgar, are not in any degree whatever any sort of a 'dose.' They're, on the contrary, in their own unconventional way, the very best company. They're endlessly amusing. They're delightfully queer and quaint and kind—they're like people in some old story or of some old time. It's at any rate our own affair—mine and theirs—and I beg you to believe that I should make short work of a remonstrance on the subject from any one but you."

I remember saying to him three months later: "You've never yet told me what they really want of you"; but I'm afraid this was a form of criticism that occurred to me precisely because I had already begun to guess. By that time indeed I had had great initiations, and poor Lavinia had had them as well—hers in fact throughout went further than mine—and we had shared them together, and I had settled down to a tolerably exact sense of what I was to see. It was what Lavinia added to it that really made the picture. The portrait of the little dead girl had evoked something attractive, though one had not lived so long in the world without hearing of plenty of little dead girls; and the day came when I felt as if I had actually sat with Marmaduke in each of the rooms converted by her parents—with the aid not only of the few small, cherished relics, but that of the fondest figments and fictions, ingenious imaginary mementoes and tokens, the unexposed make-believes of the sorrow that broods and the passion that clings—into a temple of grief and worship. The child, incontestably beautiful, had evidently been passionately loved, and in the absence from their lives—I suppose originally a mere accident—of such other elements, either new pleasures or new pains, as abound for most people, their feeling had drawn to itself their whole consciousness: it had become mildly maniacal. The idea was fixed, and it kept others out. The world, for the most part, allows no leisure for such a ritual, but the world had consistently neglected this plain, shy couple, who were sensitive to the wrong things and whose sincerity and fidelity, as well as their tameness and twaddle, were of a rigid, antique pattern.

I must not represent that either of these objects of interest, or my care for their concerns, took up all my leisure; for I had many claims to meet and many complications to handle, a hundred preoccupations and much deeper anxieties. My young woman, on her side, had other contacts and contingencies—other troubles too, poor girl; and there were stretches of time in which I neither saw Marmaduke nor heard a word of the Dedricks. Once, only once, abroad, in Germany at a railway station, I met him in their company. They were colourless, commonplace, elderly Britons, of the kind you identify by the livery of their footman or the labels of their luggage, and the mere sight of them justified me to my conscience in having avoided, from the first, the stiff problem of conversation with them. Marmaduke saw me on the spot and came over to me. There was no doubt whatever of *his* vivid bloom. He had grown fat—or almost, but not with grossness—and might perfectly have passed for the handsome, happy, full-blown son of doting parents who couldn't let him out of view and to whom he was a model of respect and solicitude. They followed him with placid, pleased eyes when he joined me, but asking nothing at all for themselves and quite fitting into his own manner of saying nothing about them. It had its charm, I confess, the way he could be natural and easy, and yet intensely conscious, too, on such a basis. What he was conscious of was that there were things I by this time knew; just as, while we stood there and good-humouredly sounded each other's faces—for, having accepted everything at last, I was only a little curious—I knew that he measured my insight. When he returned again to his doting parents I had to admit that, doting as they were, I felt him not to have been spoiled. It was incongruous in such a career, but he was rather more of a man. There came back to me with a shade of regret after I had got on this occasion into my train, which was not theirs, a memory of some words that, a couple of years before, I had uttered to poor Lavinia. She had said to me, speaking in reference to what was then our frequent topic and on some fresh evidence that I have forgotten: "He feels now, you know, about Maud-Evelyn quite as the old people themselves do."

"Well," I had replied, "it's only a pity he's paid for it!"

"Paid?" She had looked very blank.

"By all the luxuries and conveniences," I had explained, "that he comes in for through living with them. For that's what he practically does."

At present I saw how wrong I had been. He was paid, but paid differently, and the mastered wonder of that was really what had been between us in the waiting-room of the station. Step by step, after this, I followed.

VI

I can see Lavinia, for instance, in her ugly new mourning immediately after her mother's death. There had been long anxieties connected with this event, and she was already faded, already almost old. But Marmaduke, on her bereavement, had been to her, and she came straightway to me.

"Do you know what he thinks now?" she soon began. "He thinks he knew her."

"Knew the child?" It came to me as if I had half expected it.

"He speaks of her now as if she hadn't been a child." My visitor gave me the strangest fixed smile. "It appears that she wasn't so young—it appears she had grown up."

I stared. "How can it 'appear'? They *know*, at least! There were the facts."

"Yes," said Lavinia, "but they seem to have come to take a different view of them. He talked to me a long time, and all about *her*. He told me things."

"What kind of things? Not trumpery stuff, I hope, about 'communicating'—about his seeing or hearing her?"

"Oh no, he doesn't go in for that; he leaves it to the old couple, who, I believe, cling to their mediums, keep up their sittings and their rappings and find in it all a comfort, an amusement, that he doesn't grudge them and that he regards as harmless. I mean anecdotes—memories of his own. I mean things she said to him and that they did together—places they went to. His mind is full of them."

I turned it over. "Do you think he's decidedly mad?"

She shook her head with her bleached patience. "Oh no, it's too beautiful!"

"Then are *you* taking it up? I mean the preposterous theory—"

"It *is* a theory," she broke in, "but it isn't necessarily preposterous. Any theory has to suppose something," she sagely pursued, "and it depends at any rate on what it's a theory *of.* It's wonderful to see this one work."

"Wonderful always to see the growth of a legend!" I laughed. "This is a rare chance to watch one in formation. They're all three in good faith building it up. Isn't that what you made out from him?"

Her tired face fairly lighted. "Yes—you understand it; and you put it better than I. It's the gradual effect of brooding over the past; the past, that way, grows and grows. They make it and make it. They've persuaded each other—the parents—of so many things that they've at last also persuaded *him.* It has been contagious."

"It's you who put it well," I returned. "It's the oddest thing I ever heard of, but it is, in its way, a reality. Only we mustn't speak of it to others."

She quite accepted that precaution. "No—to nobody. *He* doesn't. He keeps it only for me."

"Conferring on you thus," I again laughed, "such a precious privilege!"

She was silent a moment, looking away from me. "Well, he has kept his vow."

"You mean of not marrying? Are you very sure?" I asked. "Didn't he perhaps—?" But I faltered at the boldness of my joke.

The next moment I saw I needn't. "He *was* in love with her," Lavinia brought out.

I broke now into a peal which, however provoked, struck even my own ear at the moment as rude almost to profanity. "He literally tells you outright that he's making believe?"

She met me effectively enough. "I don't think he *knows* he is. He's just completely in the current."

"The current of the old people's twaddle?"

Again my companion hesitated; but she knew what she thought. "Well, whatever we call it, I like it. It isn't so common, as the world goes, for any one—let alone for two or three—to feel and to care for the dead as much as that. It's self-deception, no doubt, but it comes from something that—well," she faltered again, "is beautiful when one does hear of it. They make her out older, so as to imagine they had her longer; and they make out that certain things really happened to her, so that she shall have had more life. They've invented a whole experience for her, and Marmaduke has become a part of it. There's one thing, above all, they want her to have had." My young friend's face, as she analysed the mystery, fairly grew bright with her vision. It came to me with a faint dawn of awe that the attitude of the Dedricks *was* contagious. "And she did have it!" Lavinia declared.

I positively admired her, and if I could yet perfectly be rational without being ridiculous, it was really, more than anything else, to draw from her the whole image. "She had the bliss of knowing Marmaduke? Let us agree to it, then, since she's not here to contradict us. But what I don't get over is the scant material for *him!*" It may easily be conceived how little, for the moment, I could get over it. It was the last time my impatience was to be too much for me, but I remember how it broke out. "A man who might have had *you!*"

For an instant I feared I had upset her—thought I saw in her face the tremor of a wild wail. But poor Lavinia was magnificent. "It wasn't that he might have had 'me'—that's nothing: it was, at the most, that I might have had *him.* Well, isn't that just what has happened? He's mine from the moment no one else has him. I give up the past, but don't you see what it does for the rest of life? I'm surer than ever that he won't marry."

"Of course, he won't—to quarrel, with those people!"

For a minute she answered nothing; then, "Well, for whatever reason!" she simply said. Now, however, I had gouged out of her a couple of still tears, and I pushed away the whole obscure comedy.

VII

I might push it away, but I couldn't really get rid of it; nor, on the whole, doubtless, did I want to, for to have in one's life, year after year, a particular question or two that one couldn't comfortably and imposingly make up one's mind about was just the sort of thing to keep one from turning stupid. There had been little need of my enjoining reserve upon Lavinia: she obeyed, in respect to impenetrable silence save with myself, an instinct, an interest of her own. We never therefore gave poor Marmaduke, as you call it, "away"; we were much too tender, let alone that she was also too proud; and, for himself, evidently, there was not, to the end, in London, another person in his confidence. No echo of the queer part he played ever came back to us; and I can't tell you how this fact, just by itself, brought home to me little by little a sense of the charm he was under. I met him "out" at long intervals—met him usually at dinner. He had grown like a person with a position and a history. Rosy and rich-looking, fat, moreover, distinctly fat at last, there was almost in him something of the bland—yet not too bland—young head of an hereditary business. If the Dedricks had been bankers he might have constituted the future of the house. There was none the less a long middle stretch during which, though we were all so much in London, he dropped out of my talks with Lavinia. We were conscious, she and I, of his absence from them; but we clearly felt in each quarter that there are things after all unspeakable, and the fact, in any case, had nothing to do with her seeing or not seeing our friend. I was sure, as it happened, that she did see him. But there were moments that for myself still stand out.

One of these was a certain Sunday afternoon when it was so dismally wet that, taking for granted I should have no visitors, I had drawn up to the fire with a book—a successful novel of the day—that I promised myself comfortably to finish. Suddenly, in my absorption, I heard a firm rat-tat-tat; on which I remember giving a groan of inhospitality. But my visitor proved in due course Marmaduke, and Marmaduke proved—in a manner even less, at the point we had reached, to have been counted on—still more attaching than my novel. I think it was only an accident that he became so; it would have been the turn of a hair either way. He hadn't come to speak—he had only come to talk, to show once more that we could continue good old friends without his speaking. But somehow there were the circumstances: the insidious fireside, the things in the room, with their reminders of his younger time; perhaps even too the open face of my book, looking at him from where I had laid it down for him and giving him a chance to feel that he could supersede Wilkie Collins. There was at all events a promise of intimacy, of opportunity for him in the cold lash of the windows by the storm. We should be alone; it was cosy; it was safe.

The action of these impressions was the more marked that what was touched by them, I afterwards saw, was not at all a desire for an effect— was just simply a spirit of happiness that needed to overflow. It had finally become too much for him. His past, rolling up year after year, had grown too interesting. But he was, all the same, directly stupefying. I forget what turn of our preliminary gossip brought it out, but it came, in explanation of something or other, as it had not yet come: "When a man has had for a few months what *I* had, you know!" The moral appeared to be that nothing in the way of human experience of the exquisite could again particularly matter. He saw, however, that I failed immediately to fit his reflection to a definite case, and he went on with the frankest smile: "You look as bewildered as if you suspected me of alluding to some sort of thing that isn't usually spoken of; but I assure you I mean nothing more reprehensible than our blessed engagement itself."

"Your blessed engagement?" I couldn't help the tone in which I took · him up; but the way he disposed of that was something of which I feel to this hour the influence. It was only a look, but it put an end to my tone forever. It made me, on my side, after an instant, look at the fire—look hard and even turn a little red. During this moment I saw my alternatives and I chose; so that when I met his eyes again I was fairly ready. "You still feel," I asked with sympathy, "how much it did for you?"

I had no sooner spoken than I saw that that would be from that moment the right way. It instantly made all the difference. The main question would be whether I could keep it up. I remember that only a few minutes later, for instance, this question gave a flare. His reply had been abundant and imperturbable—had included some glance at the way death brings into relief even the faintest things that have preceded it; on which I felt myself suddenly as restless as if I had grown afraid of him. I got up to ring for tea; he went on talking—talking about Maud-Evelyn and what she had been for him; and when the servant had come up I prolonged, nervously, on purpose, the order I had wished to give. It made time, and I could speak to the footman sufficiently without thinking: what I thought of really was the risk of turning right round with a little outbreak. The temptation was strong; the same influences that had worked for my companion just worked, in their way, during that minute or two, for me. *Should* I, taking him unaware, flash at him a plain "I say, just settle it for me once for all. *Are* you the boldest and basest of fortune-hunters, or have you only, more innocently and perhaps more pleasantly, suffered your brain slightly to soften?" But I missed the chance—which I didn't in fact afterwards regret. My servant went out, and I faced again to my visitor, who continued to converse. I met his eyes once more, and their effect was repeated. If anything had happened to his brain this effect was perhaps the domination of the madman's stare. Well, he was the easiest and gentlest of madmen. By the time the footman came back with tea I was in for it; I was in for everything. By "everything" I mean my whole subsequent treatment of the case. It *was*—the case was—really beautiful. So, like all the rest, the hour comes back to me: the sound of the wind and the rain; the look of the empty, ugly, cabless square and of the stormy spring light; the way that, uninterrupted and absorbed, we had tea together by my fire. So it was that he found me receptive and that I found myself able to look merely grave and kind when he said, for example: "Her father and mother, you know, really, that first day—the day they picked me up on the Splügen—recognised me as the proper one."

"The proper one?"

"To make their son-in-law. They wanted her so," he went on, "to have had, don't you know, just everything."

"Well, if she did have it"—I tried to be cheerful—"isn't the whole thing then all right?"

"Oh, it's all right *now,*" he replied—"now that we've got it all there before us. You see, they couldn't like me so much"—he wished me thoroughly to understand—"without wanting me to have been the man."

"I see—that was natural."

"Well," said Marmaduke, "it prevented the possibility of any one else."

"Ah, that would never have done!" I laughed.

His own pleasure at it was impenetrable, splendid. "You see, they couldn't do much, the old people—and they can do still less now—with the future; so they had to do what they could with the past."

"And they seem to have done," I concurred, "remarkably much."

"Everything, simply. Everything," he repeated. Then he had an idea, though without insistence or importunity—I noticed it just flicker in his face. "If you *were* to come to Westbourne Terrace—"

"Oh, don't speak of that!" I broke in. "It wouldn't be decent now. I should have come, if at all, ten years ago."

But he saw, with his good humour, further than this. "I see what you mean. But there's much more in the place now than then."

"I dare say. People get new things. All the same——!" I was at bottom but resisting my curiosity.

Marmaduke didn't press me, but he wanted me to know. "There are our rooms—the whole set; and I don't believe you ever saw anything more charming, for *her* taste was extraordinary. I'm afraid, too, that I myself have had much to say to them." Then as he made out that I was again a little at sea, "I'm talking," he went on, "of the suite prepared for her marriage." He "talked" like a crown prince. "They were ready, to the last touch—there was nothing more to be done. And they're just as they were—not an object moved, not an arrangement altered, not a person but ourselves coming in: they're only exquisitely kept. All our presents are there—I should have liked you to see them."

It had become a torment by this time—I saw that I had made a mistake. But I carried it off. "Oh, I couldn't have borne it!"

"They're not sad," he smiled—"they're too lovely to be sad. They're happy—and the things—!" He seemed, in the excitement of our talk, to have them before him.

"They're so very wonderful?"

"Oh, selected with a patience that makes them almost priceless. It's really a museum. There was nothing they thought too good for her."

I had lost the museum, but I reflected that it could contain no object so rare as my visitor. "Well, you've helped them—you could do *that.*"

He quite eagerly assented. "I could do that, thank God—I could do that! I felt it from the first, and it's what I *have* done." Then as if the connexion were direct: "All *my* things are there."

I thought a moment. "Your presents?"

"Those I made her. She loved each one, and I remember about each the particular thing she said. Though I do say it," he continued, "none of the others, as a matter of fact, come near mine. I look at them every day, and I assure you I'm not ashamed." Evidently, in short, he had spared nothing, and he talked on and on. He really quite swaggered.

VIII

In relation to times and intervals I can only recall that if this visit of his to me had been in the early spring it was one day in the late autumn—a day, which couldn't have been in the same year, with the difference of hazy, drowsy sunshine and brown and yellow leaves—that, taking a short cut across Kensington Gardens, I came, among the untrodden ways, upon a couple occupying chairs under a tree, who immediately rose at the sight of me. I had been behind them at recognition, the fact that Marmaduke was in deep mourning having perhaps, so far as I had observed it, misled me. In my desire both not to look flustered at meeting them and to spare their own confusion I bade them again be seated and asked leave, as a third chair was at hand, to share a little their rest. Thus it befell that after a minute Lavinia and I had sat down, while our friend, who had looked at his watch, stood before us among the fallen foliage and remarked that he was sorry to have to leave us. Lavinia said nothing, but I expressed regret; I couldn't, however, as it struck me, without a false or a vulgar note speak as if I had interrupted a tender passage or separated a pair of lovers. But I could look him up and down, take in his deep mourning. He had not made, for going off, any other pretext than that his time was up and that he was due at home. "Home," with him now, had but one meaning: I knew him to be completely quartered in Westbourne Terrace. "I hope nothing has happened," I said—"that you've lost no one whom *I* know."

Marmaduke looked at my companion, and she looked at Marmaduke. "He has lost his wife," she then observed.

Oh, this time, I fear, I had a small quaver of brutality; but it was at him I directed it. "Your wife? I didn't know you *had* a wife!"

"Well," he replied, positively gay in his black suit, his black gloves, his high hatband, "the more we live in the past, the more things we find in it. That's a literal fact. You would see the truth of it if your life had taken such a turn."

"*I* live in the past," Lavinia put in gently as if to help us both.

"But with the result, my dear," I returned, "of not making, I hope, such extraordinary discoveries!" It seemed absurd to be afraid to be light.

"May none of her discoveries be more fatal than mine!" Marmaduke wasn't uproarious, but his treatment of the matter had the good taste of simplicity. "They've wanted it so for her," he continued to me wonderfully, "that we've at last seen our way to it—I mean to what Lavinia has mentioned." He hesitated but three seconds—he brought it brightly out. "Maud-Evelyn had *all* her young happiness."

I stared, but Lavinia was, in her peculiar manner, as brilliant. "The marriage *did* take place," she quietly, stupendously explained to me. Well, I was determined not to be left. "So you're a widower," I gravely asked, "and these are the signs?"

"Yes; I shall wear them always now."

"But isn't it late to have begun?"

My question had been stupid, I felt the next instant; but it didn't matter—he was quite equal to the occasion. "Oh, I had to wait, you know, till all the facts about my marriage had given me the right." And he looked at his watch again. "Excuse me—I *am* due. Good-bye, good-bye." He shook hands with each of us, and as we sat there together watching him walk away I was struck with his admirable manner of looking the character. I felt indeed as our eyes followed him that we were at one on this, and I said nothing till he was out of sight. Then by the same impulse we turned to each other.

"I thought he was never to marry!" I exclaimed to my friend.

Her fine wasted face met me gravely. "He isn't—ever. He'll be still more faithful."

"Faithful this time to whom?"

"Why, to Maud-Evelyn." I said nothing—I only checked an ejaculation; but I put out a hand and took one of hers, and for a minute we kept silence. "Of course it's only an idea," she began again at last, "but it seems to me a beautiful one." Then she continued resignedly and remarkably: "And now *they* can die."

"Mr. and Mrs. Dedrick?" I pricked up my ears. "Are they dying?"

"Not quite, but the old lady, it appears, is failing, steadily weakening; less, as I understand it, from any definite ailment than because she just feels her work done and her little sum of passion, as Marmaduke calls it, spent. Fancy, with her convictions, all her reasons for wanting to die! And if she goes, he says, Mr. Dedrick won't long linger. It will be quite 'John Anderson my jo.'"

"Keeping her company down the hill, to lie beside her at the foot?"

"Yes, having settled all things."

I turned these things over as we walked away, and how they had settled them—for Maud-Evelyn's dignity and Marmaduke's high advantage; and before we parted that afternoon—we had taken a cab in the Bayswater Road and she had come home with me—I remember saying to her: "Well then, when they die won't he be free?"

She seemed scarce to understand. "Free?"

"To do what he likes."

She wondered. "But he does what he likes now."

"Well then, what *you* like!"

"Oh, you know what *I* like—!"

Ah, I closed her mouth! "You like to tell horrid fibs—yes, I know it!" What she had then put before me, however, came in time to pass: I heard in the course of the next year of Mrs. Dedrick's extinction, and some months later, without, during the interval, having seen a sign of Marmaduke, wholly taken up with his bereaved patron, learned that her husband had touchingly followed her. I was out of England at the time; we had had to put into practice great economies and let our little place; so that, spending three winters successively in Italy, I devoted the periods between, at home, altogether to visits among people, mainly relatives, to whom these friends of mine were not known. Lavinia of course wrote to me—wrote, among many things, that Marmaduke was ill and had not seemed at all himself since the loss of his "family," and this in spite of the circumstance, which she had already promptly communicated, that they had left him, by will, "almost everything." I knew before I came back to remain that she now saw him often and, to the extent of the change that had overtaken his strength and his spirits, greatly ministered to him. As soon as we at last met I asked for news of him; to which she replied: "He's gradually going." Then on my surprise: "He has had his life."

"You mean that, as he said of Mrs. Dedrick, his sum of passion is spent?"

At this she turned away. "You've never understood."

I *had*, I conceived; and when I went subsequently to see him I was moreover sure. But I only said to Lavinia on this first occasion that I would immediately go; which was precisely what brought out the climax, as I feel it to be, of my story. "He's not now, you know,"—she turned round to admonish me, "in Westbourne Terrace. He has taken a little old house in Kensington."

"Then he hasn't kept the things?"

"He has kept everything." She looked at me still more as if I had never understood.

"You mean he has moved them?"

She was patient with me. "He has moved nothing. Everything is as it was, and kept with the same perfection."

I wondered. "But if he doesn't live there?"

"It's just what he does."

"Then how can he be in Kensington?"

She hesitated, but she had still more than her old grasp of it. "He's in Kensington—without living."

"You mean that at the other place—!"

"Yes, he spends most of his time. He's driven over there every day—

he remains there for hours. He keeps it for that."

"I see—it's still the museum."

"It's still the temple!" Lavinia replied with positive austerity.

"Then why did he move?"

"Because, you see, there"—she faltered again—"I could come to him. And he wants me," she said, with admirable simplicity.

Little by little I took it in. "After the death of the parents, even, you never went?"

"Never."

"So you haven't seen anything?"

"Anything of hers? Nothing."

I understood, oh perfectly; but I won't deny that I was disappointed: I had hoped for an account of his wonders, and I immediately felt that it wouldn't be for me to take a step that she had declined. When, a short time later, I saw them together in Kensington Square—there were certain hours of the day that she regularly spent with him—I observed that everything about him was new, handsome and simple. They were, in their strange, final union—if union it could be called—very natural and very touching; but he was visibly stricken—he had his ailment in his eyes. She moved about him like a sister of charity—at all events like a sister. He was neither robust nor rosy now, nor was his attention visibly very present, and I privately and fancifully asked myself where it wandered and waited. But poor Marmaduke was a gentleman to the end—he wasted away with an excellent manner. He died twelve days ago; the will was opened; and last week, having meanwhile heard from her of its contents, I saw Lavinia. He leaves her everything that he himself had inherited. But she spoke of it all in a way that caused me to say in surprise: "You haven't yet been to the house?"

"Not yet. I've only seen the solicitors, who tell me there will be no complications."

There was something in her tone that made me ask more. "Then you're not curious to see what's there?"

She looked at me with a troubled—almost a pleading—sense, which I understood; and presently she said: "Will you go with me?"

"Some day, with pleasure—but not the first time. You must go alone then. The 'relics' that you'll find there," I added—for I had read her look—"you must think of now not as hers—"

"But as his?"

"Isn't that what his death—with his so close relation to them—has made them for you?"

Her face lighted—I saw it was a view she could thank me for putting into words. "I see—I see. They *are* his. I'll go."

She went, and three days ago she came to me. They're really marvels, it appears, treasures extraordinary, and she has them all. Next week I go with her—I shall see them at last. Tell *you* about them, you say? My dear man, everything.   1900

SIR EDMUND ORME

The statement appears to have been written, though the fragment is undated, long after the death of his wife, whom I take to have been one of the persons referred to. There is however nothing in the strange story to establish this point, now perhaps not of importance. When I took possession of his effects I found these pages, in a locked drawer, among papers relating to the unfortunate lady's too brief career—she died in childbirth a year after her marriage: letters, memoranda, accounts, faded photographs, cards of invitation. That's the only connexion I can point to, and you may easily, and will probably, think it too extravagant to have had a palpable basis. I can't, I allow, vouch for his having intended it as a report of real occurrence—I can only vouch for his general veracity. In any case it was written for himself, not for others. I offer it to others— having full option—precisely because of its oddity. Let them, in respect to the form of the thing, bear in mind that it was written quite for himself. I've altered nothing but the names.

If there's a story in the matter I recognise the exact moment at which it began. This was on a soft still Sunday noon in November, just after church, on the sunny Parade. Brighton was full of people; it was the height of the season and the day was even more respectable than lovely—which helped to account for the multitude of walkers. The blue sea itself was decorous; it seemed to doze with a gentle snore—if that *be* decorum—while nature preached a sermon. After writing letters all the morning I had come out to take a look at it before luncheon. I leaned over the rail dividing the King's Road from the beach, and I think I had smoked a cigarette, when I became conscious of an intended joke in the shape of a light walking-stick laid across my shoulders. The idea, I found, had been thrown off by Teddy Bostwick of the Rifles and was intended as a contribution to talk. Our talk came off as we strolled together—he always took your arm to show you he forgave your obtuseness about his humour—and looked at the people, and bowed to some of them, and wondered who others were, and differed in opinion as to the prettiness of girls. About Charlotte Marden we agreed, however, as we saw her come toward us with her mother; and there surely could have been no one who wouldn't have concurred. The Brighton air used of old to make plain girls pretty and pretty girls prettier still—I don't know whether it works the spell now. The place was at any rate rare for complexions, and Miss Marden's was one that made people turn round. It made *us* stop, heaven knows—at least it was one of the things, for we already knew the ladies.

We turned with them, we joined them, we went where they were going. They were only going to the end and back—they had just come out of church. It was another manifestation of Teddy's humour that he got immediate possession of Charlotte, leaving me to walk with her mother. However, I wasn't unhappy; the girl was before me and I had her to talk about. We prolonged our walk; Mrs. Marden kept me and presently said she was tired and must rest. We found a place on a sheltered bench—we gossiped as the people passed. It had already struck me, in this pair, that the resemblance between mother and daughter was wonderful even among such resemblances, all the more that it took so little account of a difference of nature. One often hears mature mothers spoken of as warnings—sign-posts, more or less discouraging, of the way daughters may go. But there was nothing deterrent in the idea that Charlotte should at fifty-five be as beautiful, even though it were conditioned on her being as pale and preoccupied, as Mrs. Marden. At twenty-two she had a rosy blankness and was admirably handsome. Her head had the charming shape of her mother's, and her features the same fine order. Then there were looks and movements and tones—moments when you could scarce say if it were aspect or sound—which, between the two appearances, referred and reminded.

These ladies had a small fortune and a cheerful little house at Brighton, full of portraits and tokens and trophies—stuffed animals on the top of bookcases and sallow varnished fish under glass—to which Mrs. Marden professed herself attached by pious memories. Her husband had been "ordered" there in ill health, to spend the last years of his life, and she had already mentioned to me that it was a place in which she felt herself still under the protection of his goodness. His goodness appeared to have been great, and she sometimes seemed to defend it from vague innuendo. Some sense of protection, of an influence invoked and cherished, was evidently necessary to her; she had a dim wistfulness, a longing for security. She wanted friends and had a good many. She was kind to me on our first meeting, and I never suspected her of the vulgar purpose of "making up" to me—a suspicion of course unduly frequent in conceited young men. It never struck me that she wanted me for her daughter, nor yet, like some unnatural mammas, for herself. It was as if they had had a common deep shy need and had been ready to say: "Oh be friendly to us and be trustful! Don't be afraid—you won't be expected to marry us." "Of course there's something about mamma: that's really what makes her such a dear!" Charlotte said to me, confidentially, at an early stage of our acquaintance. She worshipped her mother's appearance. It was the only thing she was vain of; she accepted the raised eyebrows as a charming ultimate fact. "She looks as if she were waiting for the doctor, dear mamma," she said on another occasion. "Perhaps *you're* the doctor; do you think you are?" It appeared in the event that I had some healing power. At any rate when I learned, for she once dropped the remark, that Mrs. Marden also held there was something "awfully strange" about Charlotte, the relation of the two ladies couldn't but be interesting. It was happy enough, at bottom; each had the other so on her mind.

On the Parade the stream of strollers held its course and Charlotte presently went by with Teddy Bostwick. She smiled and nodded and continued, but when she came back she stopped and spoke to us. Captain Bostwick positively declined to go in—he pronounced the occasion too jolly: might they therefore take another turn? Her mother dropped a "Do as you like," and the girl gave me an impertinent smile over her shoulder as they quitted us. Teddy looked at me with his glass in one eye, but I didn't mind that: it was only of Miss Marden I was thinking as I laughed to my companion. "She's a bit of a coquette, you know."

"Don't say that—don't say that!" Mrs. Marden murmured.

"The nicest girls always are—just a little," I was magnanimous enough to plead.

"Then why are they always punished?"

The intensity of the question startled me—it had come out in a vivid flash. Therefore I had to think a moment before I put to her: "What do you know of their punishment?"

"Well—I was a bad girl myself."

"And were you punished?"

"I carry it through life," she said as she looked away from me. "Ah!" she suddenly panted in the next breath, rising to her feet and staring at her daughter, who had reappeared again with Captain Bostwick. She stood a few seconds, the queerest expression in her face; then she sank on the seat again and I saw she had blushed crimson. Charlotte, who had noticed it all, came straight up to her and, taking her hand with quick tenderness, seated herself at her other side. The girl had turned pale—she gave her mother a fixed scared look. Mrs. Marden, who had had some shock that escaped our detection, recovered herself; that is she sat quiet and inexpressive, gazing at the indifferent crowd, the sunny air, the slumbering sea. My eye happened to fall nevertheless on the interlocked hands of the two ladies, and I quickly guessed the grasp of the elder to be violent. Bostwick stood before them, wondering what was the matter and asking me from his little vacant disk if *I* knew; which led Charlotte to say to him after a moment and with a certain irritation: "Don't stand there that way, Captain Bostwick. Go away—*please* go away."

I got up at this, hoping Mrs. Marden wasn't ill; but she at once begged we wouldn't leave them, that we would particularly stay and that we would presently come home to luncheon. She drew me down beside her and for a moment I felt her hand press my arm in a way that might have been an involuntary betrayal of distress and might have been a private signal. What she should have wished to point out to me I couldn't divine: perhaps she had seen in the crowd somebody or something abnormal. She explained to us in a few minutes that she was all right, that she was only liable to palpitations: they came as quickly as they went. It was time to move—a truth on which we acted. The incident was felt to be closed. Bostwick and I lunched with our sociable friends, and when I walked away with him he professed he had never seen creatures more completely to his taste.

Mrs. Marden had made us promise to come back the next day to tea, and had exhorted us in general to come as often as we could. Yet the next day when, at five o'clock, I knocked at the door of the pretty house it was but to learn that the ladies had gone up to town. They had left a message for us with the butler: he was to say they had suddenly been called and much regretted it. They would be absent a few days. This was all I could extract from the dumb domestic. I went again three days later, but they were still away; and it was not till the end of a week that I got a note from Mrs. Marden. "We're back," she wrote: "do come and forgive us." It was on this occasion, I remember—the occasion of my going just after getting the note—that she told me she had distinct intuitions. I don't know how many people there were in England at that time in that predicament, but there were very few who would have mentioned it; so that the announcement struck me as original, especially as her point was that some of these uncanny promptings were connected with myself. There were other people present—idle Brighton folk, old women with frightened eyes and irrelevant interjections—and I had too few minutes' talk with Charlotte; but the day after this I met them both at dinner and had the satisfaction of sitting next to Miss Marden. I recall this passage as the hour of its first fully coming over me that she was a beautiful liberal creature. I had seen her personality in glimpses and gleams, like a song sung in snatches, but now it was before me in a large rosy glow, as if it had been a full volume of sound. I heard the whole of the air, and it was sweet fresh music, which I was often to hum over.

After dinner I had a few words with Mrs. Marden; it was at the time, late in the evening, when tea was handed about. A servant passed near us with a tray, I asked her if she would have a cup, and, on her assenting, took one and offered it to her. She put out her hand for it and I gave it to her, safely as I supposed; but as her fingers were about to secure it she started and faltered, so that both my frail vessel and its fine recipient dropped with a crash of porcelain and without, on the part of my companion, the usual woman's motion to save her dress. I stopped to pick up the fragments and when I raised myself Mrs. Marden was looking across the room at her daughter, who returned it with lips of cheer but anxious eyes. "Dear mamma, what on earth *is* the matter with you?" The silent question seemed to say. Mrs. Marden coloured just as she had done after her strange movement on the Parade the other week, and I was therefore surprised when she said to me with unexpected assurance: "You should really have a steadier hand!" I had begun to stammer a defence of my hand when I noticed her eyes fixed on me with an intense appeal. It was ambiguous at first and only added to my confusion; then suddenly I understood as plainly as if she had murmured "Make believe it was you—make believe it was you." The servant came back to take the morsels of the cup and wipe up the spilt tea, and while I was in the midst of making believe Mrs. Marden abruptly brushed away from me and from her daughter's attention and went into another room. She gave no heed to the state of her dress.

I saw nothing more of either that evening, but the next morning, in the King's Road, I met the younger lady with a roll of music in her muff. She told me she had been a little way alone, to practise duets with a friend, and I asked her if she would go a little way further in company. She gave me leave to attend her to her door, and as we stood before it I inquired if I might go in. "No, not to-day—I don't want you," she said very straight, though not unamiably; while the words caused me to direct a wistful disconcerted gaze at one of the windows of the house. It fell on the white face of Mrs. Marden, turned out at us from the drawing-room. She stood long enough to show it *was* she and not the apparition I had come near taking it for, and then she vanished before her daughter had observed her. The girl, during our walk, had said nothing about her. As I had been told they didn't want me I left them alone a little, after which certain hazards kept us still longer apart. I finally went up to London, and while there received a pressing invitation to come immediately down to Tranton, a pretty old place in Sussex belonging to a couple whose acquaintance I had lately made.

I went to Tranton from town, and on arriving found the Mardens, with a dozen other people, in the house. The first thing Mrs. Marden said was "Will you forgive me?" and when I asked what I had to forgive she answered "My throwing my tea over you." I replied that it had gone over herself; whereupon she said "At any rate I was very rude—but some day I think you'll understand, and then you'll make allowances for me." The first day I was there she dropped two or three of these references— she had already indulged in more than one—to the mystic initiation in store for me; so that I began, as the phrase is, to chaff her about it, to say I'd rather it were less wonderful and take it out at once. She answered that when it should come to me I'd have indeed to take it out—there would be little enough option. That it *would* come was privately clear to her, a deep presentiment, which was the only reason she had ever mentioned the matter. Didn't I remember she had spoken to me of intuitions? From the first of her seeing me she had been sure there were things I shouldn't escape knowing. Meanwhile there was nothing to do but wait and keep cool, not to be precipitate. She particularly wished not to become extravagantly nervous. And I was above all not to be nervous myself—one got used to everything. I returned that though I couldn't make out what she was talking of I was terribly frightened; the absence of a clue gave such a range to one's imagination. I exaggerated on purpose; for if Mrs. Marden was mystifying I can scarcely say she was alarming. I couldn't imagine what she meant, but I wondered more than I shuddered. I might have said to myself that she was a little wrong in the upper storey; but that never occurred to me. She struck me as hopelessly right.

There were other girls in the house, but Charlotte the most charming; which was so generally allowed that she almost interfered with the slaughter of ground game. There were two or three men, and I was of the number, who actually preferred her to the society of the beaters. In short she was recognised as a form of sport superior and exquisite. She was kind to all of us—she made us go out late and come in early. I don't know whether she flirted, but several other members of the party thought *they* did. Indeed as regards himself Teddy Bostwick, who had come over from Brighton, was visibly sure.

The third of these days was a Sunday, which determined a pretty walk to morning service over the fields. It was grey windless weather, and the bell of the little old church that nestled in the hollow of the Sussex down sounded near and domestic. We were a straggling procession in the mild damp air—which, as always at that season, gave one the feeling that after the trees were bare there was more of it, a larger sky—and I managed to fall a good way behind with Miss Marden. I remember entertaining, as we moved together over the turf, a strong impulse to say something intensely personal, something violent and important, important for *me*—such as that I had never seen her so lovely or that that particular moment was the sweetest of my life. But always, in youth, such words have been on the lips many times before they're spoken to any effect; and I had the sense, not that I didn't know her well enough—I cared little for that—but that she didn't sufficiently know *me*. In the church, a museum of old Tranton tombs and brasses, the big Tranton pew was full. Several of us were scattered, and I found a seat for

Miss Marden, and another for myself beside it, at a distance from her mother and from most of our friends. There were two or three decent rustics on the bench, who moved in further to make room for us, and I took my place first, to cut off my companion from our neighbours. After she was seated there was still a space left, which remained empty till service was about half over.

This at least was the moment of my noting that another person had entered and had taken the seat. When I remarked him he had apparently been for some minutes in the pew—had settled himself and put down his hat beside him and, with his hands crossed on the knob of his cane, was gazing before him at the altar. He was a pale young man in black and with the air of a gentleman. His presence slightly startled me, for Miss Marden hadn't attracted my attention to it by moving to make room for him. After a few minutes, observing that he had no prayer-book, I reached across my neighbour and placed mine before him, on the ledge of the pew; a manœuvre the motive of which was not unconnected with the possibility that, in my own destitution, Miss Marden would give me one side of *her* velvet volume to hold. The pretext however was destined to fail, for at the moment I offered him the book the intruder—whose intrusion I had so condoned—rose from his place without thanking me, stepped noiselessly out of the pew, which had no door, and, so discreetly as to attract no attention, passed down the centre of the church. A few minutes had sufficed for his devotions. His behaviour was unbecoming, his early departure even more than his late arrival; but he managed so quietly that we were not incommoded, and I found, on turning a little to glance after him, that nobody was disturbed by his withdrawal. I only noticed, and with surprise, that Mrs. Marden had been so affected by it as to rise, all involuntarily, in her place. She stared at him as he passed, but he passed very quickly, and she as quickly dropped down again, though not too soon to catch my eye across the church. Five minutes later I asked her daughter, in a low voice, if she would kindly pass me back my prayer-book—I had waited to see if she would spontaneously perform the act. The girl restored this aid to devotion, but had been so far from troubling herself about it that she could say to me as she did so: "Why on earth did you put it there?" I was on the point of answering her when she dropped on her knees, and at this I held my tongue. I had only been going to say: "To be decently civil."

After the benediction, as we were leaving our places, I was slightly surprised again to see that Mrs. Marden, instead of going out with her companions, had come up the aisle to join us, having apparently something to say to her daughter. She said it, but in an instant I saw it had been a pretext—her real business was with me. She pushed Charlotte forward and suddenly breathed to me: "Did you see him?"

"The gentleman who sat down here? How could I help seeing him?"

"Hush!" she said with the intensest excitement; "don't *speak* to her—don't tell her!" She slipped her hand into my arm, to keep me near her, to keep me, it seemed, away from her daughter. The precaution was unnecessary, for Teddy Bostwick had already taken possession of Miss Marden, and as they passed out of church in front of me I saw one of the other men close up on her other hand. It appeared to be felt that I had had my turn. Mrs. Marden released me as soon as we got out, but not before I saw she had needed my support. "Don't speak to any one— don't tell any one!" she went on.

"I don't understand. Tell any one what?"

"Why that you saw him."

"Surely they saw him for themselves."

"Not one of them, not one of them." She spoke with such passionate decision that I glanced at her—she was staring straight before her. But she felt the challenge of my eyes and stopped short, in the old brown timber porch of the church, with the others well in advance of us; where, looking at me now and in quite an extraordinary manner, "You're the only person" she said; "the only person in the world."

"But *you*, dear madam?"

"Oh me—of course. That's my curse!" And with this she moved rapidly off to join the rest of our group. I hovered at its outskirts on the way home—I had such food for rumination. Whom had I seen and why was the apparition—it rose before my mind's eye all clear again—invisible to the others? If an exception had been made for Mrs. Marden why did it constitute a curse, and why was I to share so questionable a boon? This appeal, carried on in my own locked breast, kept me doubtless quiet enough at luncheon. After that repast I went out on the old terrace to smoke a cigarette, but had only taken a turn or two when I caught Mrs. Marden's moulded mask at the window of one of the rooms open to the crooked flags. It reminded me of he same flitting presence behind the pane at Brighton the day I met Charlotte and walked home with her. But this time my ambiguous friend didn't vanish; she tapped on the pane and motioned me to come in. She was in a queer little apartment, one of the many reception-rooms of which the ground-floor at Tranton consisted; it was known as the Indian room and had a style denominated Eastern—bamboo lounges, lacquered screens, lanterns with long fringes and strange idols in cabinets, objects not held to conduce to sociability. The place was little used, and when I went round to her we had it to ourselves. As soon as I appeared she said to me: "Please tell me this—are you in love with my daughter?"

I really had a little to take my time. "Before I answer your question will you kindly tell me what gives you the idea? I don't consider I've been very forward."

Mrs. Marden, contradicting me with her beautiful anxious eyes, gave me no satisfaction on the point I mentioned; she only went on strenuously: "Did you say nothing to her on the way to church?"

"What makes you think I said anything?"

"Why the fact that you saw him."

"Saw whom, dear Mrs. Marden?"

"Oh you know," she answered, gravely, even a little reproachfully, as if I were trying to humiliate her by making her name the unnameable.

"Do you mean the gentleman who formed the subject of your strange statement in church—the one who came into the pew?"

"You saw him, you saw him!" she panted with a strange mixture of dismay and relief.

"Of course I saw him, and so did you."

"It didn't follow. Did you feel it to be inevitable?"

I was puzzled again. "Inevitable?"

"That you *should* see him?"

"Certainly, since I'm not blind."

"You might have been. Every one else is." I was wonderfully at sea and I frankly confessed it to my questioner, but the case wasn't improved by her presently exclaiming: "I knew you would, from the moment you should be really in love with her! I knew it would be the test—what do I mean?—the proof."

"Are there such strange bewilderments attached to that high state?" I smiled to ask.

"You can judge for yourself. You see him, you see him!"—she quite exulted in it. "You'll see him again."

"I've no objection, but I shall take more interest in him if you'll kindly tell me who he is."

She avoided my eyes—then consciously met them. "I'll tell you if you'll tell me first what you said to her on the way to church."

"Has she told you I said anything?"

"Do I need that?" she asked with expression.

"Oh yes, I remember—your intuitions! But I'm sorry to see they're at fault this time; because I really said nothing to your daughter that was the least out of the way."

"Are you very very sure?"

"On my honour, Mrs. Marden."

"Then you consider that you're not in love with her?"

"That's another affair!" I laughed.

""You are—you *are!* You wouldn't have seen him if you hadn't been."

"Then who the deuce *is* he, madam?"—I pressed it with some irritation.

Yet she would still only question me back. "Didn't you at least *want* to say something to her—didn't you come very near it?"

Well, this was more to the point; it justified the famous intuitions. "Ah 'near' it as much as you like—call it the turn of a hair. I don't know what kept me quiet."

"That was quite enough," said Mrs. Marden. "It isn't what you say that makes the difference; it's what you feel. *That's* what he goes by."

I was annoyed at last by her reiterated reference to an identity yet to be established, and I clasped my hands with an air of supplication which covered much real impatience, a sharper curiosity and even the first short throbs of a certain sacred dread. "I entreat you to tell me whom you're talking about."

She threw up her arms, looking away from me, as if to shake off both reserve and responsibility. "Sir Edmund Orme."

"And who may Sir Edmund Orme be?"

At the moment I spoke she gave a start. "Hush—here they come." Then as, following the direction of her eyes, I saw Charlotte, out on the terrace, by our own window, she added, with an intensity of warning: "Don't notice him—*never!*"

The girl, who now had had her hands beside her eyes, peering into the room and smiling, signed to us, through the glass to admit her; on which I went and opened the long window. Her mother turned away and she came in with a laughing challenge: "What plot in the world are you two hatching here?" Some plan—I forget what—was in prospect for the afternoon, as to which Mrs. Marden's participation or consent was solicited, my own adhesion being taken for granted; and she had been half over the place in her quest. I was flurried, seeing the elder woman was—when she turned round to meet her daughter she disguised it to extravagance, throwing herself on the girl's neck and embracing her—so that, to pass it off, I overdid my gallantry.

"I've been asking your mother for your hand."

"Oh indeed, and has she given it?" Miss Marden gaily returned.

"She was just going to when you appeared there."

"Well, it's only for a moment—I'll leave you free."

"Do you like him, Charlotte?" Mrs. Marden asked with a candour I scarcely expected.

"It's difficult to say *before* him, isn't it?" the charming creature went on, entering into the humour of the thing, but looking at me as if she scarce liked me at all.

She would have had to say it before another person as well, for at that moment there stepped into the room from the terrace—the window had been left open—a gentleman who had come into sight, at least into mine, only within the instant. Mrs. Marden had said "Here *they* come," but he appeared to have followed her daughter at a certain distance. I recognised him at once as the personage who had sat beside us in church. This time I saw him better, saw his face and his carriage were strange. I speak of him as a personage, because one felt, indescribably, as if a reigning prince had come into the room. He held himself with something of the grand air and as if he were different from his company. Yet he looked fixedly and gravely at me, till I wondered what he expected. Did he consider that I should bend my knee or kiss his hand? He turned his eyes in the same way on Mrs. Marden, but she knew what to do. After the first agitation produced by his approach she took no notice of him whatever; it made me remember her passionate adjuration to me. I had to achieve a great effort to imitate her, for though I knew nothing about him but that he was Sir Edmund Orme his presence acted as a strong appeal, almost as an oppression. He stood there without speaking—young pale handsome clean-shaven decorous, with extraordinary light blue eyes and something old-fashioned, like a portrait of years ago, in his head and in his manner of wearing his hair. He was in complete mourning—one immediately took him for very well dressed—and he carried his hat in his hand. He looked again strangely hard at me, harder than any one in the world had ever looked before; and I remember feeling rather cold and wishing he would say something. No silence had ever seemed to me so soundless. All this was of course an impression intensely rapid; but that it had consumed some instants was proved to me suddenly by the expression of countenance of Charlotte Marden, who stared from one of us to the other—he never looked at her, and she had no appearance of looking at him—and then broke out with: "What on earth is the matter with you? You've such odd faces!" I felt the colour come back to mine, and when she went on in the same tone: "One would think you had seen a ghost!" I was conscious I had turned very red. Sir Edmund Orme never blushed, and I was sure no embarrassment touched him. One had met people of that sort, but never any one with so high an indifference.

"Don't be impertinent, and go and tell them all that I'll join them," said Mrs. Marden with much dignity but with a tremor of voice that I caught.

"And will you come—*you?*" the girl asked, turning away. I made no answer, taking the question somehow as meant for her companion. But he was more silent than I, and when she reached the door—she was going out that way—she stopped, her hand on the knob, and looked at me, repeating it. I assented, springing forward to open the door for her, and as she passed out she exclaimed to me mockingly: "You haven't got your wits about you—you shan't have my hand!"

I closed the door and turned round to find that Sir Edmund Orme had during the moment my back was presented to him retired by the window. Mrs. Marden stood there and we looked at each other long. It had only then—as the girl flitted away—come home to me that her daughter was unconscious of what had happened. It was *that*, oddly enough, that gave me a sudden sharp shake—not my own perception of our visitor, which felt quite natural. It made the fact vivid to me that she had been equally unaware of him in church, and the two facts together—now that they were over—set my heart more sensibly beating. I wiped my forehead, and Mrs. Marden broke out with a low distressful wail: "Now you know my life—now you know my life!"

"In God's name who is he—*what* is he?"

"He's a man I wronged."

"How did you wrong him?"

"Oh awfully—years ago."

"Years ago? Why, he's very young."

"Young—young?" cried Mrs. Marden. "He was born before *I* was!"

"Then why does he look so?"

She came nearer to me, she laid her hand on my arm, and there was something in her face that made me shrink a little. "Don't you understand—don't you *feel?*" she intensely put to me.

"I feel very queer!" I laughed; and I was conscious that my note betrayed it.

"He's dead!" said Mrs. Marden, from her white face.

"Dead?" I panted. "Then that gentleman was—?" I couldn't even say a word.

"Call him what you like—there are twenty vulgar names. He's a perfect presence."

"He's a splendid presence!" I cried. "The place is haunted, *haunted!*" I exulted in the word as if it stood for all I had ever dreamt of.

"It isn't the place—more's the pity!" she instantly returned. "That has nothing to do with it!"

"Then it's you, dear lady?" I said as if this were still better.

"No, nor me either—I wish it were!"

"Perhaps it's me," I suggested with a sickly smile.

"It's nobody but my child—my innocent, innocent child!" And with this Mrs. Marden broke down—she dropped into a chair and burst into tears. I stammered some question—I pressed on her some bewildered appeal, but she waved me off, unexpectedly and passionately. I persisted—couldn't I help her, couldn't I intervene? "You *have* intervened," she sobbed; "you're *in* it, you're *in* it."

"I'm very glad to be in anything so extraordinary," I boldly declared.

"Glad or not, you can't get out of it."

"I don't want to get out of it—it's too interesting."

"I'm glad you like it!" She had turned from me, making haste to dry her eyes. "And now go away."

"But I want to know more about it."

"You'll see all you want. Go away!"

"But I want to understand what I see."

"How can you—when I don't understand myself?" she helplessly cried.

"We'll do so together—we'll make it out."

At this she got up, doing what more she could to obliterate her tears. "Yes, it will be better together—that's why I've liked you."

"Oh we'll see it through!" I returned.

"Then you must control yourself better."

"I will, I will—with practice."

"You'll get used to it," said my friend in a tone I never forgot. "But go and join them—I'll come in a moment."

I passed out to the terrace and felt I had a part to play. So far from dreading another encounter with the "perfect presence," as she had called it, I was affected altogether in the sense of pleasure. I desired a renewal of my luck: I opened myself wide to the impression; I went round the house as quickly as if I expected to overtake Sir Edmund Orme. I didn't overtake him just then, but the day wasn't to close without my recognising that, as Mrs. Marden had said, I should see all I wanted of him.

We took, or most of us took, the collective sociable walk which, in the English country-house, is—or was at that time—the consecrated pastime of Sunday afternoons. We were restricted to such a regulated ramble as the ladies were good for; the afternoons moreover were short, and by five o'clock we were restored to the fireside in the hall with a sense, on my part at least, that we might have done a little more for our tea. Mrs. Marden had said she would join us, but she hadn't appeared; her daughter, who had seen her again before we went out, only explained that she was tired. She remained invisible all the afternoon, but this was a detail to which I gave as little heed as I had given to the circumstance of my not having Charlotte to myself, even for five minutes, during all our walk. I was too much taken up with another interest to care; I felt beneath my feet the threshold of the strange door, in my life, which had suddenly been thrown open and out of which came an air of a keenness I had never breathed and of a taste stronger than wine. I had heard all my days of apparitions, but it was a different thing to have seen one and to know that I should in all likelihood see it familiarly, as I might say, again.

I was on the look-out for it as a pilot for the flash of a revolving light, and ready to generalise on the sinister subject, to answer for it to all and sundry that ghosts were much less alarming and much more amusing than was commonly supposed. There's no doubt that I was much uplifted. I couldn't get over the distinction conferred on me, the exception—in the way of mystic enlargement of vision—made in my favour. At the same time I think I did justice to Mrs. Marden's absence—a commentary, when I came to think, on what she had said to me: "Now you know my life." She had probably been exposed to our hoverer for years, and, not having my firm fibre, had broken down under it. Her nerve was gone, though she had also been able to attest that, in a degree, one got used to it. She had got used to breaking down.

Afternoon tea, when the dusk fell early, was a friendly hour at Tranton; the firelight played into the wide white last-century hall; sympathies almost confessed themselves, lingering together, before dressing, on deep sofas, in muddy boots, for last words after walks; and even solitary absorption in the third volume of a novel that was wanted by some one else seemed a form of geniality. I watched my moment and went over to Charlotte when I saw her about to withdraw. The ladies had left the place one by one, and after I had addressed myself to her particularly the three men who had been near gradually dispersed. We had a little vague talk—she might have been a good deal preoccupied, and heaven knows *I* was—after which she said she must go: she should be late for dinner. I proved to her by book that she had plenty of time, and she objected that she must at any rate go up to see her mother, who, she feared, was unwell.

"On the contrary, she's better than she has been for a long time—I'll guarantee that," I said. "She has found out she can have confidence in me, and that has done her good." Miss Marden had dropped into her chair again, I was standing before her, and she looked up at me without a smile, with a dim distress in her beautiful eyes: not exactly as if I were hurting her, but as if she were no longer disposed to treat as a joke what had passed—whatever it was, it would give at the same time no ground for the extreme of solemnity—between her mother and myself. But I could answer her enquiry in all kindness and candour, for I was really conscious that the poor lady had put off a part of her burden on me and was proportionately relieved and eased. "I'm sure she has slept all the afternoon as she hasn't slept for years," I went on. "You've only to ask her."

Charlotte got up again. "You make yourself out very useful."

"You've a good quarter of an hour," I said. "Haven't I a right to talk to you a little this way, alone, when your mother has given me your hand?"

"And is it *your* mother who has given me yours? I'm much obliged to her, but I don't want it. I think our hands are not our mothers'—they happen to be our own!" laughed the girl.

"Sit down, sit down and let me tell you!" I pleaded.

I still stood there, urgently, to see if she wouldn't oblige me. She cast about, looking vaguely this way and that, as if under a compulsion that was slightly painful. The empty hall was quiet—we heard the loud ticking of the great clock. Then she slowly sank down and I drew a chair close to her. This made me face round to the fire again, and with the movement I saw disconcertedly that we weren't alone. The next instant, more strangely than I can say, my discomposure, instead of increasing, dropped, for the person before the fire was Sir Edmund Orme. He stood there as I had seen him in the Indian room, looking at me with the expressionless attention that borrowed gravity from his sombre distinction. I knew so much more about him now that I had to check a movement of recognition, an acknowledgement of his presence. When once I was aware of it, and that it lasted, the sense that we had company, Charlotte and I, quitted me: it was impressed on me on the contrary that we were but the more markedly thrown together. No influence from our companion reached her, and I made a tremendous and very nearly successful effort to hide from her that my own sensibility was other and my nerves as tense as harp-strings. I say "very nearly," because she watched me an instant—while my words were arrested—in a way that made me fear she was going to say again, as she had said in the Indian room: "What on earth is the matter with you?"

What the matter with me was I quickly told her, for the full knowledge of it rolled over me with the touching sight of her unconsciousness. It was touching that she became, in the presence of this extraordinary portent. What was portended, danger or sorrow, bliss or bane, was a minor question; all I saw, as she sat there, was that, innocent and charming, she was close to a horror, as she might have thought it, that happened to be veiled from her but that might at any moment be disclosed. I didn't mind it now, as I found—at least more than I could bear; but nothing was more possible than she should, and if it wasn't curious and interesting it might easily be appalling. If I didn't mind it for myself, I afterwards made out, this was largely because I was so taken up with the idea of protecting her. My heart, all at once, beat high with this view; I determined to do everything I could to keep her sense sealed. What I could do might have been obscure to me if I hadn't, as the minutes lapsed, become more aware than of anything else that I loved her. The way to save her was to love her, and the way to love her was to tell her, now and here, that I did so. Sir Edmund Orme didn't prevent me, especially as after a moment he turned his back to us and stood looking discreetly at the fire. At the end of another moment he leaned his head on his arm, against the chimney-piece, with an air of gradual dejection, like a spirit still more weary than discreet. Charlotte Marden rose with a start at what I said to her—she jumped up to escape it; but she took no offence: the feeling I expressed was too real. She only moved about the room with a deprecating murmur, and I was so busy following up any little advantage I might have obtained that I didn't notice in what manner Sir Edmund Orme disappeared. I only found his place presently vacant. This made no difference—he had been so small a hindrance; I only remember being suddenly struck with something inexorable in the sweet sad headshake Charlotte gave me.

"I don't ask for an answer now," I said; "I only want you to be sure—to know how much depends on it."

"Oh I don't want to give it to you now or ever!" she replied. "I hate the subject, please—I wish one could be let alone." And then, since I might have found something harsh in this irrepressible artless cry of beauty beset, she added, quickly vaguely kindly, as she left the room: "Thank you, thank you—thank you so very much!"

At dinner I was generous enough to be glad for her that, on the same side of the table with me, she hadn't me in range. Her mother was nearly opposite me, and just after we had sat down Mrs. Marden gave me a long deep look, that expressed, and to the utmost, our strange communion. It meant of course "She has told me," but it meant other things beside. At any rate I know what my mute response to her conveyed: "I've seen him again—I've seen him again!" This didn't prevent Mrs. Marden from treating her neighbours with her usual scrupulous blandness. After dinner, when, in the drawing-room, the men joined the ladies and I went straight up to her to tell her how I wished we might have some quiet words, she said at once, in a low tone, looking down at her fan while she opened and shut it: "He's here—he's here."

"Here?" I looked round the room, but was disappointed.

"Look where *she* is," said Mrs. Marden, just with the faintest asperity. Charlotte was in fact not in the main saloon, but in a smaller into which it opened and which was known as the morning-room. I took a few steps and saw her, through a doorway, upright in the middle of the room, talking with three gentlemen whose backs were practically turned to me. For a moment my quest seemed vain; then I knew one of the gentlemen—the middle one—could but be Sir Edmund Orme. This time it *was* surprising that the others didn't see him. Charlotte might have seemed absolutely to have her eyes on him and to be addressing him straight. She saw me after an instant, however, and immediately averted herself. I returned to her mother with a sharpened fear the girl might think I was watching *her*, which would be unjust. Mrs. Marden had found a small sofa—a little apart—and I sat down beside her. There were some questions I had so wanted to go into that I wished we were once more in the Indian room. I presently gathered however that our privacy quite sufficed. We communicated so closely and completely now, and with such silent reciprocities, that it would in every circumstance be adequate.

"Oh yes, he's there," I said; "and at about a quarter-past seven he was in the hall."

"I knew it at the time—and I was so glad!" she answered straight.

"So glad?"

"That it was your affair this time and not mine. It's a rest for me."

"Did you sleep all the afternoon?" I then asked.

"As I haven't done for months. But how did you know that?"

"As *you* knew, I take it, that Sir Edmund was in the hall. We shall evidently each of us know things now—where the other's concerned."

"Where *he's* concerned," Mrs. Marden amended. "It's a blessing, the way you take it," she added with a long mild sigh.

"I take it," I at once returned, "as a man who's in love with your daughter."

"Of course—of course." Intense as I now felt my desire for the girl to be I couldn't help laughing a little at the tone of these words; and it led my companion immediately to say: "Otherwise you wouldn't have seen him."

Well, I esteemed my privilege, but I saw an objection to this. "Does every one see him who's in love with her? If so there would be dozens."

"They're not in love with her as you are."

I took this in and couldn't but accept it. "I can of course only speak for myself—and I found a moment before dinner to do so."

"She told me as soon as she saw me," Mrs. Marden replied.

"And have I any hope—any chance?"

"That you may have is what I long for, what I pray for."

The sore sincerity of this touched me. "Ah how can I thank you enough?" I murmured.

"I believe it will all pass—if she only loves you," the poor woman pursued.

"It will all pass?" I was a little at a loss.

"I mean we shall then be rid of him—shall never see him again."

"Oh if she loves me I don't care how often I see him!" I roundly returned.

"Ah you take it better than *I* could," said my companion. "You've the happiness not to know—not to understand."

"I don't indeed. What on earth does he want?"

"He wants to make me suffer." She turned her wan face upon me with it, and I saw now for the first time, and saw well, how perfectly, if this had been our visitant's design he had done his work. "For what I did to him," she explained.

"And what did you do to him?"

She gave me an unforgettable look. "I killed him." As I had seen him fifty yards off only five minutes before, the words gave me a start. "Yes, I make you jump; be careful. He's there still, but he killed himself. I broke his heart—he thought me awfully bad. We were to have been married, but I broke it off—just at the last. I saw some one I liked better; I had no reason but that. It wasn't for interest or money or position or any of that baseness. All the good things were his. It was simply that I fell in love with Major Marden. When I saw *him* I felt I couldn't marry any one else. I wasn't in love with Edmund Orme; my mother and my elder, my married, sister had brought it about. But he did love me and I knew— that is almost knew!—how much! But I told him I didn't care—that I couldn't, that I wouldn't ever. I threw him over, and he took something, some abominable drug or draught that proved fatal. It was dreadful, it was horrible, he was found that way—he died in agony. I married Major Marden, but not for five years. I was happy, perfectly happy—time obliterates. But when my husband died I began to see him."

I had listened intently, wondering. "To see your husband?"

"Never, never—*that* way, thank God! To see *him*—and with Chartie, always with Chartie. The first time it nearly killed me—about seven years ago, when she first came out. Never when I'm by myself—only with her. Sometimes not for months, then every day for a week. I've tried everything to break the spell—doctors and *régimes* and climates; I've prayed to God on my knees. That day at Brighton, on the Parade with you, when you thought I was ill, that was the first for an age. And then in the evening, when I knocked my tea over you, and the day you were at the door with her and I saw you from the window—each time he was there."

"I see, I see." I was more thrilled than I could say. "It's an apparition like another."

"Like another? Have you ever seen another?" she cried.

"No, I mean the sort of thing one has heard of. It's tremendously interesting to encounter a case."

"Do you call me a 'case'?" my friend cried with exquisite resentment.

"I was thinking of myself."

"Oh you're the right one!" she went on. "I was right when I trusted you."

"I'm devoutly grateful you did; but what made you do it?" I asked.

"I had thought the whole thing out. I had had time to in those dreadful years while he was punishing me in my daughter."

"Hardly that," I objected, "if Miss Marden never knew."

"That has been my terror, that she *will*, from one occasion to another. I've an unspeakable dread of the effect on her."

"She shan't, she shan't!" I engaged in such a tone that several people looked round. Mrs. Marden made me rise, and our talk dropped for that evening. The next day I told her I must leave Tranton—it was neither comfortable nor considerate to remain as a rejected suitor. She was disconcerted, but accepted my reasons, only appealing to me with mournful eyes: "You'll leave me alone then with my burden?" It was of course understood between us that for many weeks to come there would be no discretion in "worrying poor Charlotte": such were the terms in which, with odd feminine and maternal inconsistency, she alluded to an attitude on my part that she favoured. I was prepared to be heroically considerate, but I held that even this delicacy permitted me to say a word to Miss Marden before I went. I begged her after breakfast to take a turn with me on the terrace, and as she hesitated, looking at me distantly, I let her know it was only to ask her a question and to say good-bye—I was going away for *her*.

She came out with me and we passed slowly round the house three or four times. Nothing is finer than this great airy platform, from which every glance is a sweep of the country with the sea on the furthest edge. It might have been that as we passed the windows we were conspicuous to our friends in the house, who would make out sarcastically why I was so significantly bolting. But I didn't care; I only wondered if they mightn't really this time receive the impression of Sir Edmund Orme, who joined us on one of our turns and strolled slowly on the other side of Charlotte. Of what odd essence he was made I know now; I've no theory about him—leaving that to others—any more than about such or such another of my fellow mortals (and *his* law of being) as I have elbowed in life. He was as positive, as individual and ultimate a fact as any of these. Above all he was, by every seeming, of as fine and as sensitive, of as thoroughly honourable, a mixture; so that I should no more have thought of taking a liberty, of practising an experiment, with him, of touching him, for instance, or of addressing him, since he set the example of silence, than I should have thought of committing any other social grossness. He had always, as I saw more fully later, the perfect propriety of his position—looked always arrayed and anointed, and carried himself ever, in each particular, exactly as the occasion demanded. He struck me as strange, incontestably, but somehow always struck me as right. I very soon came to attach an idea of beauty to his unrecognised presence, the beauty of an old story, of love and pain and death. What I ended by feeling was that he was on my side, watching over my interest, looking to it that no trick should be played me and that my heart at least shouldn't be broken. Oh he had taken them seriously, his own wound and his own loss—he had certainly proved this in his day. If poor Mrs. Marden, responsible for these things, had, as she told me, thought the case out, I also treated it to the finest analysis I could bring to bear. It was a case of retributive justice, of the visiting on the children of the sins of the mothers, since not of the fathers. This wretched mother was to pay, in suffering, for the suffering she had inflicted, and as the disposition to trifle with an honest man's just expectations might crop up again, to my detriment, in the child, the latter young person was to be studied and watched, so that *she* might be made to suffer should she do an equal wrong. She might emulate her parent by some play of characteristic perversity not less than she resembled her in charm; and if that impulse should be determined in her, if she should be caught, that is to say, in some breach of faith or some heartless act, her eyes would on the spot, by an insidious logic, be opened suddenly and unpitiedly to the "perfect presence," which she would then have to work as she could into her conception of a young lady's universe. I had no great fear for her, because I hadn't felt her lead me on from vanity, and I knew that if I was disconcerted it was because I had myself gone too fast. We should have a good deal of ground to get over at least before I should be in a position to be sacrificed by her. She couldn't take back what she had given before she had given rather more. Whether I asked for more was indeed another matter, and the question I put to her on the terrace that morning was whether I might continue during the winter to come to Mrs. Marden's house. I promised not to come too often and not to speak to her for three months of the issue I had raised the day before. She replied that I might do as I liked, and on this we parted.

I carried out the vow I had made her; I held my tongue for my three months. Unexpectedly to myself there were moments of this time when she did strike me as capable of missing my homage even though she might be indifferent to my happiness. I wanted so to make her like me that I became subtle and ingenious, wonderfully alert, patiently diplomatic. Sometimes I thought I had earned my reward, brought her to the point of saying: "Well, well, you're the best of them all—you may speak to me now." Then there was a greater blankness than ever in her beauty and on certain days a mocking light in her eyes, a light of which the meaning seemed to be: "If you don't take care I *will* accept you, to have done with you the more effectually." Mrs. Marden was a great help to me simply by believing in me, and I valued her faith all the more that it continued even through a sudden intermission of the miracle that had been wrought for me. After our visit to Tranton Sir Edmund Orme gave us a holiday, and I confess it was at first a disappointment to me. I felt myself by so much less designated, less involved and connected—all with

Charlotte I mean to say. "Oh, don't cry till you're out of the wood," was her mother's comment; "he has let me off sometimes for six months. He'll break out again when you least expect it—he understands his game." For her these weeks were happy, and she was wise enough not to talk about me to the girl. She was so good as to assure me I was taking the right line, that I looked as if I felt secure and that in the long run women give way to this. She had known them do it even when the man was a fool for that appearance, for that confidence—a fool indeed on any terms. For herself she felt it a good time, almost her best, a Saint Martin's summer of the soul. She was better than she had been for years, and had me to thank for it. The sense of visitation was light on her—she wasn't in anguish every time she looked round. Charlotte contradicted me repeatedly, but contradicted herself still more. That winter by the old Sussex sea was a wonder of mildness, and we often sat out in the sun. I walked up and down with my young woman, and Mrs. Marden, sometimes on a bench, sometimes in a Bath-chair, waited for us and smiled at us as we passed. I always looked out for a sign in her face—"He's with you, he's with you" (she would see him before I should) but nothing came; the season had brought us as well a sort of spiritual softness. Toward the end of April the air was so like June that, meeting my two friends one night at some Brighton sociability—an evening party with amateur music—I drew the younger unresistingly out upon a balcony to which a window in one of the rooms stood open. The night was close and thick, the stars dim, and below us under the cliff we heard the deep rumble of the tide. We listened to it a little and there came to us, mixed with it from within the house, the sound of a violin accompanied by a piano—a performance that had been our pretext for escaping.

"Do you like me a little better?" I broke out after a minute. "Could you listen to me again?"

I had no sooner spoken than she laid her hand quickly, with a certain force, on my arm. "Hush!—isn't there some one there?" She was looking into the gloom of the far end of the balcony. This balcony ran the whole width of the house, a width very great in the best of the old houses at Brighton. We were to some extent lighted by the open window behind us, but the other windows, curtained within, left the darkness undiminished, so that I made out but dimly the figure of a gentleman standing there and looking at us. He was in evening dress, like a guest—I saw the vague sheen of his white shirt and the pale oval of his face—and he might perfectly have been a guest who had stepped out in advance of us to take the air. Charlotte took him for one at first—then evidently, even in a few seconds, saw that the intensity of his gaze was unconventional. What else she saw I couldn't determine; I was too occupied with my own impression to do more than feel the quick contact of her uneasiness.

My own impression was in fact the strongest of sensations, a sensation of horror; for what could the thing mean but that the girl at last *saw?* I heard her give a sudden, gasping "Ah!" and move quickly into the house. It was only afterwards I knew that I myself had had a totally new emotion—my horror passing into anger and my anger into a stride along the balcony with a gesture of reprobation. The case was simplified to the vision of an adorable girl menaced and terrified. I advanced to vindicate her security, but I found nothing there to meet me. It was either all a mistake or Sir Edmund Orme had vanished.

I followed her at once, but there were symptoms of confusion in the drawing-room when I passed in. A lady had fainted, the music had stopped; there was a shuffling of chairs and a pressing forward. The lady was not Charlotte, as I feared, but Mrs. Marden, who had suddenly been taken ill. I remember the relief with which I learned this, for to see Charlotte stricken would have been anguish, and her mother's condition gave a channel to her agitation. It was of course all a matter for the people of the house and for the ladies, and I could have no share in attending to my friends or in conducting them to their carriage. Mrs. Marden revived and insisted on going home, after which I uneasily withdrew.

I called the next morning for better news and I learnt she was more at ease, but on my asking if Charlotte would see me the message sent down was an excuse. There was nothing for me to do all day but roam with a beating heart. Toward evening however I received a line in pencil, brought by hand—"Please come; mother wishes you." Five minutes later I was at the door again and ushered into the drawing-room. Mrs. Marden lay on the sofa, and as soon as I looked at her I saw the shadow of death in her face. But the first thing she said was that she was better, ever so much better; her poor old fluttered heart had misbehaved again, but now was decently quiet. She gave me her hand and I bent over her, my eyes on her eyes, and in this way was able to read what she didn't speak—"I'm really very ill, but appear to take what I say exactly as I say it." Charlotte stood there beside her, looking not frightened now, but intensely grave, and meeting no look of my own. "She has told me—she has told me!" her mother went on.

"She has told you?" I stared from one of them to the other, wondering if my friend meant that the girl had named to her the unexplained appearance on the balcony.

"That you spoke to her again—that you're admirably faithful."

I felt a thrill of joy at this; it showed me that that memory was uppermost, and also that her daughter had wished to say the thing that would most soothe her, not the thing that would alarm her. Yet I was myself now sure, as sure as if Mrs. Marden had told me, that she knew and had known at the moment what her daughter had seen. "I spoke—I spoke, but she gave me no answer," I said.

"She will now, won't you, Chartie? I want it so, I want it!" our companion murmured with ineffable wistfulness.

"You're very good to me"—Charlotte addressed me, seriously and sweetly, but with her eyes fixed on the carpet. There was something different in her, different from all the past. She had recognised something, she felt a coercion. I could see her uncontrollably tremble.

"Ah if you would let me show you *how* good I can be!" I cried as I held out my hands to her. As I uttered the words I was touched with the knowledge that something had happened. A form had constituted itself on the other side of the couch, and the form leaned over Mrs. Marden. My whole being went forth into a mute prayer that Charlotte shouldn't see it and that I should be able to betray nothing. The impulse to glance toward her mother was even stronger than the involuntary movement of taking in Sir Edmund Orme; but I could resist even that, and Mrs. Marden was perfectly still. Charlotte got up to give me her hand, and then—with the definite act—she dreadfully saw. She gave, with a shriek, one stare of dismay, and another sound, the wail of one of the lost, fell at the same instant on my ear. But I had already sprung toward the creature I loved, to cover her, to veil her face, and she had as passionately thrown herself into my arms. I held her there a moment—pressing her close, given up to her, feeling each of her throbs with my own and not knowing which was which; then all of a sudden, coldly, I was sure we were alone. She released herself. The figure beside the sofa had vanished, but Mrs. Marden lay in her place with closed eyes, with something in her stillness that gave us both a fresh terror. Charlotte expressed it in the cry of "Mother, mother!" with which she flung herself down. I fell on my knees beside her—Mrs. Marden had passed away.

Was the sound I heard when Chartie shrieked—the other and still more tragic sound I mean—the despairing cry of the poor lady's death-shock or the articulate sob (it was like a waft from a great storm) of the exorcised and pacified spirit? Possibly the latter, for that was mercifully the last of Sir Edmund Orme.   1891

M. R. JAMES

Casting the Runes

April 15th, 190–

Dear Sir,

I am requested by the Council of the——Association to return to you the draft of a paper on *The Truth of Alchemy,* which you have been good enough to offer to read at our forthcoming meeting, and to inform you that the Council do not see their way to including it in the programme.

I am,

Yours faithfully,

——Secretary.

April 18th

Dear Sir,

I am sorry to say that my engagements do not permit of my affording you an interview on the subject of your proposed paper. Nor do our laws allow of your discussing the matter with a Committee of our Council, as you suggest. Please allow me to assure you that the fullest consideration was given to the draft which you submitted, and that it was not declined without having been referred to the judgment of a most competent authority. No personal question (it can hardly be necessary for me to add) can have had the slightest influence on the decision of the Council.

Believe me (*ut supra.*)

April 20th

The Secretary of the——Association begs respectfully to inform Mr Karswell that it is impossible for him to communicate the name of any person or persons to whom the draft of Mr Karswell's paper may have been submitted; and further desires to intimate that he cannot undertake to reply to any further letters on this subject.

"And who *is* Mr Karswell?" inquired the Secretary's wife. She had called at his office and (perhaps unwarrantably) had picked up the last of these three letters, which the typist had just brought in.

"Why, my dear, just at present Mr Karswell is a very angry man. But I don't know much about him otherwise, except that he is a person of wealth, his address is Lufford Abbey, Warwickshire, and he's an alchemist, apparently, and wants to tell us all about it; and that's about all—except that I don't want to meet him for the next week or two. Now, if you're ready to leave this place, I am."

"What have you been doing to make him angry?" asked Mrs Secretary.

"The usual thing, my dear, the usual thing: he sent in a draft of a paper he wanted to read at the next meeting, and we referred it to Edward Dunning—almost the only man in England who knows about these things—and he said it was perfectly hopeless, so we declined it. So Karswell has been pelting me with letters ever since. The last thing he wanted was the name of the man we referred his nonsense to: you saw my answer to that. But don't you say anything about it, for goodness' sake."

"I should think not indeed. Did I ever do such a thing? I do hope, though, he won't get to know that it was poor Mr Dunning."

"Poor Mr Dunning? I don't know why you call him that; he's a very happy man, is Dunning. Lots of hobbies and a comfortable home, and all his time to himself."

"I only meant I should be sorry for him if this man got hold of his name, and came and bothered him."

"Oh, ah! yes. I dare say he would be poor Mr Dunning then."

The Secretary and his wife were lunching out, and the friends to whose house they were bound were Warwickshire people. So Mrs Secretary had already settled it in her own mind that she would question them judiciously about Mr Karswell. But she was saved the trouble of leading up to the subject, for the hostess said to the host before many minutes had passed, "I saw the Abbot of Lufford this morning." The host whistled. "*Did* you? What in the world brings him up to town?" "Goodness knows; he was coming out of the British Museum gate as I drove past." It was not unnatural that Mrs Secretary should inquire whether this was a real Abbot who was being spoken of. "Oh no, my dear: only a neighbour of ours in the country who bought Lufford Abbey a few years ago. His real name is Karswell." "Is he a friend of yours?" asked Mr Secretary with a private wink to his wife. The question let loose a torrent of declamation. There was really nothing to be said for Mr Karswell. Nobody knew what he did with himself: his servants were a horrible set of people; he had invented a new religion for himself, and practised no one could tell what appalling rites; he was very easily offended, and never forgave anybody: he had a dreadful face (so the lady insisted, her husband somewhat demurring); he never did a kind action, and whatever influence he did exert was mischievous. "Do the poor man justice, dear," the husband interrupted. "You forget the treat he gave the school children." "Forget it, indeed! But I'm glad you mentioned it because it gives an idea of the man. Now, Florence, listen to this. The first winter he was at Lufford this delightful neighbour of ours wrote to the clergyman of his parish (he's not ours, but we know him very well) and offered to show the school children some magic-lantern slides. He said he had some new kinds which he thought would interest them. Well the clergyman was rather surprised because Mr Karswell had shown himself inclined to be unpleasant to the children—complaining of their trespassing or something of the sort; but of course he accepted, and the evening was fixed and our friend went himself to see that everything went right. He said he never had been so thankful for anything as that his own children were all prevented from being there: they were at a children's party at our house as a matter of fact. Because this Mr. Karswell had evidently set out with the intention of frightening these poor village children out of their wits, and I do believe if he had been allowed to go on he would actually have done so. He began with some comparatively mild things—Red Riding Hood was one, and even then Mr Farrer said the wolf was so dreadful that several of the smaller children had to be taken out: and he said Mr Karswell began the story by producing a noise like a wolf howling in the distance which was the most gruesome thing he had ever heard. All the slides he showed, Mr Farrer said, were most clever; they were absolutely realistic and where he had got them or how he worked them he could not imagine. Well the show went on, and the stories kept on becoming a little more terrifying each time, and the children were mesmerized into complete silence. At last he produced a series which represented a little boy passing through his own park—Lufford, I mean—in the evening. Every child in the room could recognize the place from the pictures. And this poor boy was followed, and at last pursued and overtaken and either torn in pieces or somehow made away with by a horrible hopping creature in white, which you saw first dodging about among the trees and gradually it appeared more and more plainly. Mr Farrer said it gave him one of the worst nightmares he ever remembered, and what it must have meant to the children doesn't bear thinking of. Of course this was too much, and he spoke very sharply indeed to Mr Karswell and said it couldn't go on. All *he* said was: 'Oh, you think it's time to bring our little show to an end and send them home to their beds? *Very* well!' And then, if you please, he switched on another slide which showed a great mass of snakes, centipedes, and disgusting creatures with wings and somehow or other he made it seem as if they were climbing out of the picture and getting in amongst the audience; and this was accompanied by a sort of dry rustling noise which sent the children nearly mad, and of course they stampeded. A good many of them were rather hurt in getting out of the room, and I don't suppose one of them closed an eye that night. There was the most dreadful trouble in the village afterwards. Of course the mothers threw a good part of the blame on poor Mr Farrer, and if they could have got past the gates I believe the fathers would have broken every window in the Abbey. Well, now, that's Mr Karswell: that's the Abbot of Lufford, my dear, and you can imagine how we covet *his* society."

"Yes, I think he has *all* the possibilities of a distinguished criminal, has Karswell," said the host. "I should be sorry for anyone who got into his bad books."

"Is he the man—or am I mixing him up with someone else—" asked the Secretary (who for some minutes had been wearing the frown of the man who is trying to recollect something). "Is he the man who brought out a *History of Witchcraft* some time back—ten years or more?"

"That's the man: do you remember the reviews of it?"

"Certainly I do; and what's equally to the point, I knew the author of the most incisive of the lot. So did you: you must remember John Harrington; he was at John's in our time."

"Oh, very well indeed, though I don't think I saw or heard anything of him between the time I went down and the day I read the account of the inquest on him."

"Inquest?" said one of the ladies. "What has happened to him?"

"Why, what happened was that he fell out of a tree and broke his neck. But the puzzle was what could have induced him to get up there. It was a mysterious business, I must say. Here was this man, not an athletic fellow—was he?—and with no eccentric twist about him that was ever noticed, walking home along a country road late in the evening: no tramps about—well known and liked in the place—and he suddenly begins to run like mad, loses his hat and stick, and finally shins up a tree—quite a difficult tree—growing in the hedgerow: a dead branch gives way and he comes down with it and breaks his neck, and there he's found next morning with the most dreadful face of fear on him that could be imagined. It was pretty evident, of course, that he had been chased by something, and people talked of savage dogs, and beasts escaped out of menageries; but there was nothing to be made of that. That was in '89, and I believe his brother Henry (whom I remember as well at Cambridge, but *you* probably don't) has been trying to get on the track of an explanation ever since. He, of course, insists there was malice in it, but I don't know. It's difficult to see how it could have come in."

After a time the talk reverted to the *History of Witchcraft.* "Did you ever look into it?" asked the host.

"Yes, I did," said the Secretary. "I went so far as to read it."

"Was it as bad as it was made out to be?"

"Oh, in point of style and form, quite hopeless. It deserved all the pulverizing it got. But, besides that, it was an evil book. The man believed every word of what he was saying, and I'm very much mistaken if he hadn't tried the greater part of his receipts."

"Well, I only remember Harrington's review of it, and I must say if I'd been the author it would have quenched my literary ambition for good. I should never have held up my head again."

"It hasn't had that effect in the present case. But come, it's half-past three; I must be off."

On the way home the Secretary's wife said, "I do hope that horrible man won't find out that Mr Dunning had anything to do with the rejection of his paper." "I don't think there's much chance of that," said the Secretary. "Dunning won't mention it himself, for these matters are confidential, and none of us will for the same reason. Karswell won't know his name, for Dunning hasn't published anything on the same subject yet. The only danger is that Karswell might find out if he was to ask the British Museum people who was in the habit of consulting alchemical manuscripts: I can't very well tell them not to mention Dunning, can I? It would set them talking at once. Let's hope it won't occur to him."

However, Mr Karswell was an astute man.

This much is in the way of prologue. On an evening rather later in the same week, Mr Edward Dunning was returning from the British Museum, where he had been engaged in Research, to the comfortable house in a suburb where he lived alone, tended by two excellent women who had been long with him. There is nothing to be added by way of description of him to what we have heard already. Let us follow him as he takes his sober course homewards.

A train took him to within a mile or two of his house, and an electric tram a stage farther. The line ended at a point some three hundred yards from his front door. He had had enough of reading when he got into the car, and indeed the light was not such as to allow him to do more than study the advertisements on the panes of glass that faced him as he sat. As was not unnatural, the advertisements in this particular line of cars were objects of his frequent contemplation, and, with the possible exception of the brilliant and convincing dialogue between Mr Lamplough and an eminent K.C. on the subject of Pyretic Saline, none of them afforded much scope to his imagination. I am wrong: there was one at the corner of the car farthest from him which did not seem familiar. It was in blue letters on a yellow ground, and all that he could read of it was a name—John Harrington—and something like a date. It could be of no interest to him to know more; but for all that, as the car emptied, he was just curious enough to move along the seat until he could read it well. He felt to a slight extent repaid for his trouble; the advertisement was *not* of the usual type. It ran thus: "In memory of John Harrington, F.S.A., of The Laurels, Ashbrooke. Died Sept. 18th, 1889. Three months were allowed."

The car stopped. Mr Dunning, still contemplating the blue letters on the yellow ground, had to be stimulated to rise by a word from the conductor. "I beg your pardon," he said, "I was looking at that advertisement: it's a very odd one, isn't it?" The conductor read it slowly. "Well, my word," he said, "I never see that one before. Well, that is a cure, ain't it? Someone bin up to their jokes 'ere, I should think." He got out a duster and applied it, not without saliva, to the pane and then to the outside. "No," he said, returning, "that ain't no transfer: seems to me as if it was reg'lar *in* the glass, what I mean in the substance, as you may say. Don't you think so, sir?" Mr Dunning examined it and rubbed it with his glove, and agreed. "Who looks after these advertisements and gives leave for them to be put up? I wish you would inquire. I will just take a note of the words." At this moment there came a call from the driver: "Look alive, George, time's up." "All right, all right; there's somethink else what's up at this end. You come and look at this 'ere glass." "What's gorn with the glass?" said the driver, approaching. "Well, and oo's 'Arrington? What's it all about?" "I was just asking who was responsible for putting the advertisements up in your cars and saying it would be as well to make some inquiry about this one." "Well, sir, that's all done at the Company's orfice that work is: it's our Mr Timms I believe looks into that. When we put up tonight I'll leave word and per'aps I'll be able to tell you tomorrer if you 'appen to be coming this way."

This was all that passed that evening. Mr Dunning did just go to the trouble of looking up Ashbrooke and found that it was in Warwickshire.

Next day he went to town again. The car (it was the same car) was too full in the morning to allow of his getting a word with the conductor: he could only be sure that the curious advertisement had been made away with. The close of the day brought a further element of mystery into the transaction. He had missed the tram, or else preferred walking home, but at a rather late hour, while he was at work in his study, one of the maids came to say that two men from the tramways was very anxious to speak to him. This was a reminder of the advertisement, which he had— he says—nearly forgotten. He had the men in—they were the conductor and driver of the car—and when the matter of refreshment had been attended to, asked what Mr Timms had had to say about the advertisement. "Well, sir, that's what we took the liberty to step round about," said the conductor. "Mr Timm's 'e give William and me the rough side of his tongue about that: 'cordin' to 'im there warn't no advertisement of that description sent in nor ordered nor paid for nor put up nor nothink, let alone not bein' there, and we was playing the fool takin' up his time. 'Well,' I says, 'if that's the case, all I ask of you, Mr Timms,' I says, 'is to take and look at it for yourself,' I says. 'Of course if it ain't there,' I says, 'you may take and call me what you like.' 'Right,' he says, 'I will': and we went straight off. Now I leave it to you, sir, if that ad., as we term 'em, with 'Arrington on it warn't as plain as ever you see anythink—blue letters on yeller glass, and as I says at the time, and you borne me out, reg'lar *in* the glass, because if you remember you recollect of me swabbing it with my duster." "To be sure I do, quite clearly—well?" "You may say well, I don't think. Mr Timms he gets in that car with a light— no, he telled William to 'old the light outside. 'Now,' he says, 'where's your precious ad. what we've 'eard so much about?' ' 'Ere it is,' I says, 'Mr Timms,' and I laid my 'and on it." The conductor paused.

"Well," said Mr Dunning, "it was gone, I suppose. Broken?"

"Broke!—not it. There warn't, if you'll believe me, no more trace of them letters—blue letters they was—on that piece o' glass, than—well, it's no good *me* talkin'. I never see such a thing. I leave it to William here if—but there, as I says, where's the benefit in me going on about it?"

"And what did Mr Timms say?"

"Why 'e did what I give 'im leave to—called us pretty much anything he liked, and I don't know as I blame him so much neither. But what we thought, William and me did, was as we seen you take down a bit of a note about that—well, that letterin'—"

"I certainly did that, and I have it now. Did you wish me to speak to Mr Timms myself, and show it to him? Was that what you came in about?"

"There, didn't I say as much?" said William. "Deal with a gent if you can get on the track of one, that's my word. Now perhaps, George, you'll allow as I ain't took you very far wrong tonight."

"Very well, William, very well; no need for you to go on as if you'd 'ad to frog's-march me 'ere. I come quiet, didn't I? All the same for that, we 'adn't ought to take up your time this way, sir; but if it so 'appended you could find time to step round to the Company's orfice in the morning and tell Mr Timms what you seen for yourself, we should lay under a very 'igh obligation to you for the trouble. You see it ain't bin' called— well, one thing and another, as we mind, but if they got it into their 'ead

at the orfice as we seen things as warn't there, why, one thing leads to
another and where we should be a twelvemunce 'ence—well, you can
understand what I mean."

Amid further elucidations of the proposition, George, conducted by
William, left the room.

The incredulity of Mr Timms (who had a nodding acquaintance with
Mr Dunning) was greatly modified on the following day by what the
latter could tell and show him; and any bad mark that might have been
attached to the names of William and George was not suffered to remain on the Company's books; but explanation there was none.

Mr Dunning's interest in the matter was kept alive by an incident of
the following afternoon. He was walking from his club to the train, and
he noticed some way ahead a man with a handful of leaflets such as are
distributed to passers-by by agents of enterprising firms. This agent had
not chosen a very crowded street for his operations: in fact Mr Dunning
did not see him get rid of a single leaflet before he himself reached the
spot. One was thrust into his hand as he passed: the hand that gave it
touched his, and he experienced a sort of little shock as it did so. It
seemed unnaturally rough and hot. He looked in passing at the giver, but
the impression he got was so unclear that however much he tried to
reckon it up subsequently nothing would come. He was walking quickly
and, as he went on, glanced at the paper. It was a blue one. The name of
Harrington in large capitals caught his eye. He stopped, startled, and felt
for his glasses. The next instant the leaflet was twitched out of his hand
by a man who hurried past, and was irrecoverably gone. He ran back a
few paces, but where was the passer-by? and where the distributor?

It was in a somewhat pensive frame of mind that Mr Dunning passed
on the following day into the Select Manuscript Room of the British
Museum, and filled up tickets for Harley 3586 and some other volumes.
After a few minutes they were brought to him and he was settling the
one he wanted first upon the desk when he thought he heard his own
name whispered behind him. He turned round hastily, and, in doing so,
brushed his little portfolio of loose papers on to the floor. He saw no one
he recognized except one of the staff in charge of the room, who nodded
to him, and he proceeded to pick up his papers. He thought he had them
all and was turning to begin work when a stout gentleman at the table
behind him, who was just rising to leave and had collected his own
belongings, touched him on the shoulder, saying: "May I give you this? I
think it should be yours," and handed him a missing quire. "It is mine,
thank you," said Mr Dunning. In another moment the man had left the
room.

Upon finishing his work for the afternoon Mr Dunning had some
conversation with the assistant in charge and took occasion to ask who

the stout gentleman was. "Oh, he's a man named Karswell," said the assistant; "he was asking me a week ago who were the great authorities on alchemy, and of course I told him you were the only one in the country. I'll see if I can't catch him: he'd like to meet you, I'm sure."

"For heaven's sake don't dream of it!" said Mr Dunning, "I'm particularly anxious to avoid him."

"Oh, very well," said the assistant, "he doesn't come here often: I dare say you won't meet him."

More than once on the way home that day Mr Dunning confessed to himself that he did not look forward with his usual cheerfulness to a solitary evening. It seemed to him that something ill-defined and impalpable had stepped in between him and his fellow-men—had taken him in charge, as it were. He wanted to sit close up to his neighbours in the train and in the tram, but as luck would have it both train and car were markedly empty. The conductor George was thoughtful and appeared to be absorbed in calculations as to the number of passengers. On arriving at his house, he found Dr Watson, his medical man, on his doorstep. "I've had to upset your household arrangements, I'm sorry to say, Dunning. Both your servants *hors de combat.* In fact, I've had to send them to the Nursing Home."

"Good heavens! What's the matter?"

"It's something like ptomaine poisoning, I should think: you've not suffered yourself, I can see, or you wouldn't be walking about. I think they'll pull through all right."

"Dear, dear! Have you any idea what brought it on?"

"Well, they tell me they bought some shellfish from a hawker at their dinner-time. It's odd. I've made inquiries, but I can't find that any hawker has been to other houses in the street. I couldn't send word to you—they won't be back for a bit yet. You come and dine with me tonight, anyhow, and we can make arrangements for going on. Eight o'clock. Don't be too anxious."

The solitary evening was thus obviated; at the expense of some distress and inconvenience, it is true. Mr Dunning spent the time pleasantly enough with the doctor (a rather recent settler) and returned to his lonely home at about 11.30. The night he passed is not one on which he looks back with any satisfaction. He was in bed, and the light was out. He was wondering if the charwoman would come early enough to get him hot water next morning when he heard the unmistakable sound of his study door opening. No step followed it on the passage floor, but the sound must mean mischief, for he knew that he had shut the door that evening after putting his papers away in his desk. It was rather shame than courage that induced him to slip out into the passage and lean over the banister in his nightgown, listening. No light was visible; no further sound came: only a gust of warm or even hot air played for an instant round his shins. He went back and decided to lock himself into his room. There was more unpleasantness, however. Either an economical suburban company had decided that their light would not be required in the small hours, and had stopped working, or else something was wrong with the meter: the effect was in any case that the electric light was off. The obvious course was to find a match and also to consult his watch: he might as well know how many hours of discomfort awaited him. So he put his hand into the well-known nook under the pillow: only, it did not get so far. What he touched was, according to his account, a mouth, with teeth and with hair about it, and, he declares, not the mouth of a human being. I do not think it is any use to guess what he said or did: but he was in a spare room with the door locked and his ear to it before he was clearly conscious again. And there he spent the rest of a most miserable night, looking every moment for some fumbling at the door: but nothing came.

The venturing back to his own room in the morning was attended with many listenings and quiverings. The door stood open, fortunately, and the blinds were up (the servants had been out of the house before the hour of drawing them down). There was, to be short, no trace of an inhabitant. The watch, too, was in its usual place: nothing was disturbed, only the wardrobe door had swung open, in accordance with its confirmed habit. A ring at the back door now announced the charwoman, who had been ordered the night before, and nerved Mr Dunning after letting her in to continue his search in other parts of the house. It was equally fruitless.

The day thus begun went on dismally enough. He dared not go to the Museum: in spite of what the assistant had said, Karswell might turn up there, and Dunning felt he could not cope with a probably hostile stranger. His own house was odious; he hated sponging on the doctor. He spent some little time in a call at the Nursing Home, where he was slightly cheered by a good report of his housekeeper and maid. Towards lunch-time he betook himself to his club, again experiencing a gleam of satisfaction at seeing the Secretary of the Association. At luncheon Dunning told his friend the more material of his woes, but could not bring himself to speak of those that weighed most heavily on his spirits. "My poor dear man," said the Secretary, "what an upset! Look here: we're alone at home, absolutely. You must put up with us. Yes! no excuse: send your things in this afternoon." Dunning was unable to stand out: he was, in truth, becoming acutely anxious, as the hours went on, as to what that night might have waiting for him. He was almost happy as he hurried home to pack up.

His friends, when they had time to take stock of him, were rather shocked at his lorn appearance, and did their best to keep him up to the mark. Not altogether without success: but when the two men were smoking alone later Dunning became dull again. Suddenly he said, "Gayton, I believe that alchemist man knows it was I who got his paper rejected." Gayton whistled. "What makes you think that?" he said. Dunning told of his conversation with the Museum assistant, and Gayton could only agree that the guess seemed likely to be correct. "Not that I care much," Dunning went on, "only it might be a nuisance if we were to meet. He's a bad-tempered party, I imagine." Conversation dropped again; Gayton became more and more strongly impressed with the desolateness that came over Dunning's face and bearing, and finally— though with a considerable effort—he asked him point-blank whether something serious was not bothering him. Dunning gave an exclamation of relief. "I was perishing to get it off my mind," he said. "Do you know anything about a man named John Harrington?" Gayton was thoroughly startled and at the moment could only ask why. Then the complete story of Dunning's experiences came out—what had happened in the tram-car, in his own house, and in the street, the troubling of spirit that had crept over him, and still held him; and he ended with the question he had begun with. Gayton was at a loss how to answer him. To tell the story of Harrington's end would perhaps be right; only, Dunning was in a nervous state, the story was a grim one, and he could not help asking himself whether there were not a connecting link between these two cases, in the person of Karswell. It was a difficult concession for a scientific man, but it could be eased by the phrase "hypnotic suggestion." In the end he decided that his answer tonight should be guarded: he would talk the situation over with his wife. So he said that he had known Harrington at Cambridge and believed he had died suddenly in 1889, adding a few details about the man and his published work. He did talk over the matter with Mrs Gayton, and as he had anticipated she leapt at once to the conclusion which had been hovering before him. It was she who reminded him of the surviving brother, Henry Harrington, and she also who suggested that he might be got hold of by means of their hosts of the day before. "He might be a hopeless crank," objected Gayton. "That could be ascertained from the Bennetts, who knew him," Mrs Gayton retorted; and she undertook to see the Bennetts the very next day.

It is not necessary to tell in further detail the steps by which Henry Harrington and Dunning were brought together.

The next scene that does require to be narrated is a conversation that took place between the two. Dunning had told Harrington of the strange ways in which the dead man's name had been brought before him, and had said something, besides, of his own subsequent experiences. Then he had asked if Harrington was disposed, in return, to recall any of the circumstances connected with his brother's death. Harrington's surprise at what he heard can be imagined: but his reply was readily given.

"John," he said, "was in a very odd state undeniably from time to time during some weeks before, though not immediately before the catastrophe. There were several things—the principal notion he had was that he thought he was being followed. No doubt he was an impressionable man but he never had had such fancies as this before. I cannot get it out of my mind that there was ill-will at work, and what you tell me about yourself reminds me very much of my brother. Can you think of any possible connecting link?"

"There is just one that has been taking shape vaguely in my mind. I've been told that your brother reviewed a book very severely not long before he died, and just lately I have happened to cross the path of the man who wrote that book in a way he would resent."

"Don't tell me the man was called Karswell."

"Why not? that is exactly his name."

Henry Harrington leant back. "That is final—to my mind. Now I must explain further. From something he said, I feel sure that my brother John was beginning to believe—very much against his will—that Karswell was at the bottom of his trouble. I want to tell you what seems to me to have a bearing on the situation. My brother was a great musician, and used to run up to concerts in town. He came back, three months before he died, from one of these and gave me his programme to look at—an analytical programme: he always kept them. 'I nearly missed this one,' he said. 'I suppose I must have dropped it: anyhow I was looking for it under my seat and in my pockets and so on and my neighbour offered me his: said might he give it me, he had no further use for it, and he went away just afterwards. I don't know who he was—a stout, clean-shaven man. I should have been sorry to miss it: of course I could have bought another, but this cost me nothing.' At another time he told me that he had been very uncomfortable both on the way to his hotel and during the night. I piece things together now in thinking it over. Then not very long after, he was going over these programmes, putting them in order to have them bound up, and in this particular one (which by the way I had hardly glanced at) he found quite near the beginning a strip of paper with some very odd writing on it in red and black—most carefully done—it looked to me more like Runic letters than anything else. 'Why,' he said, 'this must belong to my fat neighbour. It looks as if it might be worth returning to him; it may be a copy of something;

evidently someone has taken trouble over it. How can I find his address?'
We talked it over for a little and agreed that it wasn't worth advertising
about, and that my brother had better look out for the man at the next
concert, to which he was going very soon. The paper was lying on the
book and we were both by the fire; it was a cold, windy summer evening.
I suppose the door blew open, though I didn't notice it: at any rate a
gust—a warm gust it was—came quite suddenly between us, took the
paper and blew it straight into the fire: it was light, thin paper and flared
and went up the chimney in a single ash. 'Well,' I said, 'you can't give it
back now.' He said nothing for a minute: then rather crossly, 'No, I
can't; but why you should keep on saying so I don't know.' I remarked
that I didn't say it more than once. 'Not more than four times, you
mean,' was all he said. I remember all that very clearly, without any good
reason. And now to come to the point. I don't know if you looked at that
book of Karswell's which my unfortunate brother reviewed. It's not
likely that you should: but I did, both before his death and after it. The
first time we made game of it together. It was written in no style at
all—split infinitives, and every sort of thing that makes an Oxford gorge
rise. Then there was nothing that the man didn't swallow: mixing up
classical myths, and stories out of the *Golden Legend* with reports of
savage customs of today—all very proper, no doubt, if you know how to
use them, but he didn't: he seemed to put the *Golden Legend* and the
Golden Bough exactly on a par and to believe both: a pitiable exhibition,
in short. Well, after the misfortune, I looked over the book again. It was
no better than before, but the impression which it left this time on my
mind was different. I suspected—as I told you—that Karswell had borne
ill-will to my brother, even that he was in some way responsible for what
had happened; and now his book seemed to me to be a very sinister
performance indeed. One chapter in particular struck me, in which he
spoke of 'casting the Runes' on people, either for the purpose of gaining
their affection, or of getting them out of the way—perhaps more especially the latter: he spoke of all this in a way that really seemed to me to
imply actual knowledge. I've not time to go into details; but the upshot is
that I am pretty sure from information received that the civil man at the
concert was Karswell. I suspect—more than suspect—that the paper was
of importance: and I do believe that if my brother had been able to give
it back, he might have been alive now. Therefore, it occurs to me to ask
you whether you have anything to put beside what I have told you."

By way of answer Dunning had the episode in the Manuscript Room
at the British Museum to relate. "Then he did actually hand you some
papers; have you examined them? No? because we must, if you'll allow it,
look at them at once, and very carefully."

They went to the still empty house—empty, for the two servants were not yet able to return to work. Dunning's portfolio of papers was gathering dust on the writing-table. In it were the quires of small-sized scribbling paper which he used for his transcripts: and from one of these, as he took it up, there slipped and fluttered out into the room with uncanny quickness a strip of thin light paper. The window was open, but Harrington slammed it to just in time to intercept the paper, which he caught. "I thought so," he said; "it might be the identical thing that was given to my brother. You'll have to look out, Dunning. This may mean something quite serious for you."

A long consultation took place. The paper was narrowly examined. As Harrington had said, the characters on it were more like Runes than anything else, but not decipherable by either man, and both hesitated to copy them for fear, as they confessed, of perpetuating whatever evil purpose they might conceal. So it has remained impossible (if I may anticipate a little) to ascertain what was conveyed in this curious message or commission: both Dunning and Harrington are firmly convinced that it had the effect of bringing its possessors into very undesirable company. That it must be returned to the source whence it came they were agreed, and further that the only safe and certain way was that of personal service: and here contrivance would be necessary, for Dunning was known by sight to Karswell. He must for one thing alter his appearance by shaving his beard. But then might not the blow fall first? Harrington thought they could time it. He knew the date of the concert at which the "black spot" had been put on his brother: it was June 18th. The death had followed on September 18th. Dunning reminded him that three months had been mentioned on the inscription on the car-window. "Perhaps," he added with a cheerless laugh, "mine may be a bill at three months too. I believe I can fix it by my diary. Yes, April 23rd was the day at the Museum—that brings me to July 23rd. Now, you know, it becomes extremely important to me to know anything you will tell me about the progress of your brother's trouble, if it is possible for you to speak of it." "Of course. Well, the sense of being watched whenever he was alone was the most distressing thing to him. After a time I took to sleeping in his room, and he was the better for that: still, he talked a great deal in his sleep. What about? Is it wise to dwell on that, at least before things are straightened out? I think not, but I can tell you this: two things came for him by post during those weeks—both with a London postmark and addressed in a commercial hand. One was a wood-cut of Bewick's roughly torn out of the page—one which shows a moon-lit road and a man walking along it, followed by an awful demon creature. Under it were written the lines out of the 'Ancient Mariner' (which I suppose the cut illustrates) about one who, having once looked round—

> walks on,
> And turns no more his head;
> Because he knows, a frightful fiend
> Doth close behind him tread.

The other was a calendar such as tradesmen often send. My brother paid no attention to this but I looked at it after his death, and found that everything after September 18 had been torn out. You may be surprised at his having gone out alone the evening he was killed, but the fact is that during the last ten days or so of his life he had been quite free from the sense of being followed or watched."

The end of the consultation was this. Harrington, who knew a neighbour of Karswell's, thought he saw a way of keeping a watch on his movements. It would be Dunning's part to be in readiness to try to cross Karswell's path at any moment, to keep the paper safe, and in a place of ready access.

They parted. The next weeks were no doubt a severe strain upon Dunning's nerves: the intangible barrier which had seemed to rise about him on the day when he received the paper gradually developed into a brooding blackness that cut him off from the means of escape to which one might have thought he might resort. No one was at hand who was likely to suggest them to him, and he seemed robbed of all initiative. He waited with inexpressible anxiety as May, June, and early July passed on for a mandate from Harrington. But all this time Karswell remained immovable at Lufford.

At last, in less than a week before the date he had come to look upon as the end of his earthly activities, came a telegram: "Leaves Victoria by boat train Thursday night. Do not miss. I come to you tonight. Harrington."

He arrived accordingly, and they concocted plans. The train left Victoria at nine and its last stop before Dover was Croydon West. Harrington would mark down Karswell at Victoria and look out for Dunning at Croydon, calling to him if need were by a name agreed upon. Dunning, disguised as far as might be, was to have no label or initials on any hand luggage, and must at all costs have the paper with him.

Dunning's suspense as he waited on the Croydon platform I need not attempt to describe. His sense of danger during the last days had only been sharpened by the fact that the cloud about him had perceptibly been lighter; but relief was an ominous symptom, and, if Karswell eluded him now, hope was gone: and there were so many chances of that. The rumour of the journey might be itself a device. The twenty minutes in which he paced the platform and persecuted every porter with inquiries as to the boat train were as bitter as any he had spent. Still, the train came, and Harrington was at the window. It was important, of course, that there should be no recognition: so Dunning got in at the farther end of the corridor carriage and only gradually made his way to the compartment where Harrington and Karswell were. He was pleased on the whole to see that the train was far from full.

Karswell was on the alert but gave no sign of recognition. Dunning took the seat not immediately facing him and attempted, vainly at first, then with increasing command of his faculties, to reckon the possibilities of making the desired transfer. Opposite to Karswell and next to Dunning was a heap of Karswell's coats on the seat. It would be of no use to slip the paper into these—he would not be safe, or would not feel so, unless in some way it could be proffered by him and accepted by the other. There was a handbag, open, and with papers in it. Could he manage to conceal this (so that perhaps Karswell might leave the carriage without it), and then find and give it to him? This was the plan that suggested itself. If he could only have counselled with Harrington! but that could not be. The minutes went on. More than once Karswell rose and went out into the corridor. The second time Dunning was on the point of attempting to make the bag fall off the seat, but he caught Harrington's eye, and read in it a warning. Karswell, from the corridor, was watching: probably to see if the two men recognized each other. He returned, but was evidently restless: and when he rose the third time, hope dawned: for something did slip off his seat and fall with hardly a sound to the floor. Karswell went out once more and passed out of range of the corridor window. Dunning picked up what had fallen and saw that the key was in his hands in the form of one of Cook's ticket-cases, with tickets in it. These cases have a pocket in the cover, and within very few seconds the paper of which we have heard was in the pocket of this one. To make the operation more secure, Harrington stood in the doorway of the compartment and fiddled with the blind. It was done, and done at the right time, for the train was now slowing down towards Dover.

In a moment more Karswell re-entered the compartment. As he did so Dunning, managing, he knew not how, to suppress the tremble in his voice, handed him the ticket-case, saying, "May I give you this, sir? I believe it is yours." After a brief glance at the ticket inside, Karswell uttered the hoped-for response, "Yes, it is; much obliged to you, sir," and he placed it in his breast pocket.

Even in the few moments that remained—moments of tense anxiety, for they knew not to what a premature finding of the paper might lead—both men noticed that the carriage seemed to darken about them and to grow warmer; that Karswell was fidgety and oppressed; that he drew the heap of loose coats near to him and cast it back as if it repelled him; and that he then sat upright and glanced anxiously at both. They, with sickening anxiety, busied themselves in collecting their belongings: but they both thought that Karswell was on the point of speaking when the train stopped at Dover Town. It was natural that in the short space between town and pier they should both go into the corridor.

At the pier they got out: but so empty was the train that they were forced to linger on the platform until Karswell should have passed ahead of them with his porter on the way to the boat, and only then was it safe for them to exchange a pressure of the hand and a word of concentrated congratulation. The effect upon Dunning was to make him almost faint. Harrington made him lean up against the wall while he himself went forward a few yards within sight of the gangway to the boat, at which Karswell had now arrived. The man at the head of it examined his ticket, and laden with coats he passed down into the boat. Suddenly the official called after him, "You, sir, beg pardon, did the other gentleman show his ticket?" "What the devil do you mean by the other gentleman?" Karswell's snarling voice called back from the deck. The man bent over and looked at him. "The devil? Well, I don't know, I'm sure," Harrington heard him say to himself, and then aloud, "My mistake, sir; must have been your rugs! ask your pardon." And then, to a subordinate near him, "'Ad he got a dog with him, or what? Funny thing: I could 'a' swore 'e wasn't alone. Well, whatever it was, they'll 'ave to see to it aboard. She's off now. Another week and we shall be gettin' the 'oliday customers." In five minutes more there was nothing but the lessening lights of the boat, the long line of the Dover lamps, the night breeze, and the moon.

Long and long the two sat in their room at the Lord Warden. In spite of the removal of their greatest anxiety, they were oppressed with a doubt, not of the lightest. Had they been justified in sending a man to his death, as they believed they had? Ought they not to warn him, at least? "No," said Harrington; "if he is the murderer I think him, we have done no more than is just. Still, if you think it better—but how and where can you warn him?" "He was booked to Abbeville only," said Dunning. "I saw that. If I wired to the hotels there in Joanne's guide, 'Examine your ticket-case, Dunning,' I should feel happier. This is the 21st: he will have a day. But I am afraid he has gone into the dark." So telegrams were left at the hotel office.

It is not clear whether these reached their destination, or whether, if they did, they were understood. All that is known is that on the afternoon of the 23rd an English traveller examining the front of St Wulfram's Church at Abbeville, then under extensive repair, was struck on the head and instantly killed by a stone falling from the scaffold erected round the north-western tower, there being, as was clearly proved, no workman on the scaffold at that moment: and the traveller's papers identified him as Mr Karswell.

Only one detail shall be added. At Karswell's sale a set of Bewick, sold with all faults, was acquired by Harrington. The page with the woodcut of the traveller and the demon was, as he had expected, mutilated. Also, after a judicious interval, Harrington repeated to Dunning something of what he had heard his brother say in his sleep: but it was not long before Dunning stopped him. 1911

"Oh, Whistle, and I'll Come to You, My Lad"

"I suppose you will be getting away pretty soon, now Full term is over, Professor," said a person not in the story to the Professor of Ontography, soon after they had sat down next to each other at a feast in the hospitable hall of St James's College.

The Professor was young, neat, and precise in speech.

"Yes," he said; "my friends have been making me take up golf this term, and I mean to go to the East Coast—in point of fact to Burnstow—(I dare say you know it) for a week or ten days, to improve my game. I hope to get off tomorrow."

"Oh, Parkins," said his neighbour on the other side, "if you are going to Burnstow, I wish you would look at the site of the Templars' preceptory, and let me know if you think it would be any good to have a dig there in the summer."

It was, as you might suppose, a person of antiquarian pursuits who said this, but, since he merely appears in this prologue, there is no need to give his entitlements.

"Certainly," said Parkins, the Professor: "if you will describe to me whereabouts the site is, I will do my best to give you an idea of the lie of the land when I get back; or I could write to you about it, if you would tell me where you are likely to be."

"Don't trouble to do that, thanks. It's only that I'm thinking of taking my family in that direction in the Long, and it occurred to me that, as very few of the English preceptories have ever been properly planned, I might have an opportunity of doing something useful on off-days."

The Professor rather sniffed at the idea that planning out a preceptory could be described as useful. His neighbour continued:

"The site—I doubt if there is anything showing above ground—must be down quite close to the beach now. The sea has encroached tremendously, as you know, all along that bit of coast. I should think, from the map, that it must be about three-quarters of a mile from the Globe Inn, at the north end of the town. Where are you going to stay?"

"Well, *at* the Globe Inn, as a matter of fact," said Parkins; "I have engaged a room there. I couldn't get in anywhere else; most of the lodging-houses are shut up in winter, it seems; and, as it is, they tell me that the only room of any size I can have is really a double-bedded one, and that they haven't a corner in which to store the other bed, and so on. But I must have a fairly large room, for I am taking some books down, and mean to do a bit of work; and though I don't quite fancy having an empty bed—not to speak of two—in what I may call for the time being my study, I suppose I can manage to rough it for the short time I shall be there."

"Do you call having an extra bed in your room roughing it, Parkins?" said a bluff person opposite. "Look here, I shall come down and occupy it for a bit; it'll be company for you."

The Professor quivered, but managed to laugh in a courteous manner.

"By all means, Rogers; there's nothing I should like better. But I'm afraid you would find it rather dull; you don't play golf, do you?"

"No, thank Heaven!" said rude Mr Rogers.

"Well, you see, when I'm not writing I shall most likely be out on the links, and that, as I say, would be rather dull for you, I'm afraid."

"Oh, I don't know! There's certain to be somebody I know in the place; but, of course, if you don't want me, speak the word, Parkins; I shan't be offended. Truth, as you always tell us, is never offensive."

Parkins was, indeed, scrupulously polite and strictly truthful. It is to be feared that Mr Rogers sometimes practised upon his knowledge of these characteristics. In Parkins's breast there was a conflict now raging, which for a moment or two did not allow him to answer. That interval being over, he said:

"Well, if you want the exact truth, Rogers, I was considering whether the room I speak of would really be large enough to accommodate us both comfortably; and also whether (mind, I shouldn't have said this if you hadn't pressed me) you would not constitute something in the nature of a hindrance to my work."

Rogers laughed loudly.

"Well done, Parkins!" he said. "It's all right. I promise not to interrupt your work; don't you disturb yourself about that. No, I won't come if you don't want me; but I thought I should do so nicely to keep the ghosts off." Here he might have been seen to wink and to nudge his next neighbour. Parkins might also have been seen to become pink. "I beg pardon, Parkins," Rogers continued; "I oughtn't to have said that. I forgot you didn't like levity on these topics."

"Well," Parkins said, "as you have mentioned the matter, I freely own that I do *not* like careless talk about what you call ghosts. A man in my position," he went on, raising his voice a little, "cannot, I find, be too careful about appearing to sanction the current beliefs on such subjects.

As you know, Rogers, or as you ought to know; for I think I have never concealed my views—"

"No, you certainly have not, old man," put in Rogers *sotto voce.*

"—I hold that any semblance, any appearance of concession to the view that such things might exist is equivalent to a renunciation of all that I hold most sacred. But I'm afraid I have not succeeded in securing your attention."

"Your *undivided* attention, was what Dr Blimber actually *said,*"[1] Rogers interrupted, with every appearance of an earnest desire for accuracy. "But I beg your pardon, Parkins: I'm stopping you."

"No, not at all," said Parkins. "I don't remember Blimber; perhaps he was before my time. But I needn't go on. I'm sure you know what I mean."

"Yes, yes," said Rogers, rather hastily—"just so. We'll go into it fully at Burnstow, or somewhere."

In repeating the above dialogue I have tried to give the impression which it made on me, that Parkins was something of an old woman—rather hen-like, perhaps, in his little ways; totally destitute, alas! of the sense of humour, but at the same time dauntless and sincere in his convictions, and a man deserving of the greatest respect. Whether or not the reader has gathered so much, that was the character which Parkins had.

On the following day Parkins did, as he had hoped, succeed in getting away from his college, and in arriving at Burnstow. He was made welcome at the Globe Inn, was safely installed in the large double-bedded room of which we have heard, and was able before retiring to rest to arrange his materials for work in apple-pie order upon a commodious table which occupied the outer end of the room, and was surrounded on three sides by windows looking out seaward; that is to say, the central window looked straight out to sea, and those on the left and right commanded prospects along the shore to the north and south respectively. On the south you saw the village of Burnstow. On the north no houses were to be seen, but only the beach and the low cliff backing it. Immediately in front was a strip—not considerable—of rough grass, dotted with old anchors, capstans, and so forth; then a broad path; then the beach. Whatever may have been the original distance between the Globe Inn and the sea, not more than sixty yards now separated them.

The rest of the population of the inn was, of course, a golfing one, and included few elements that call for a special description. The most conspicuous figure was, perhaps, that of an *ancien militaire*, secretary of a

[1]Mr Rogers was wrong, *vide Dombey and Son,* Chapter XII.

London club, and possessed of a voice of incredible strength, and of views of a pronouncedly Protestant type. These were apt to find utterance after his attendance upon the ministrations of the Vicar, an estimable man with inclinations towards a picturesque ritual, which he gallantly kept down as far as he could out of deference to East Anglian tradition.

Professor Parkins, one of whose principal characteristics was pluck, spent the greater part of the day following his arrival at Burnstow in what he had called improving his game, in company with this Colonel Wilson: and during the afternoon—whether the process of improvement were to blame or not, I am not sure—the Colonel's demeanour assumed a colouring so lurid that even Parkins jibbed at the thought of walking home with him from the links. He determined, after a short and furtive look at that bristling moustache and those incarnadined features, that it would be wiser to allow the influences of tea and tobacco to do what they could with the Colonel before the dinner-hour should render a meeting inevitable.

"I might walk home tonight along the beach," he reflected—"yes, and take a look—there will be light enough for that—at the ruins of which Disney was talking. I don't exactly know where they are, by the way; but I expect I can hardly help stumbling on them."

This he accomplished, I may say, in the most literal sense, for in picking his way from the links to the shingle beach his foot caught, partly in a gorse-root and partly in a biggish stone, and over he went. When he got up and surveyed his surroundings, he found himself in a patch of somewhat broken ground covered with small depressions and mounds. These latter, when he came to examine them, proved to be simply masses of flints embedded in mortar and grown over with turf. He must, he quite rightly concluded, be on the site of the preceptory he had promised to look at. It seemed not unlikely to reward the spade of the explorer; enough of the foundations was probably left at no great depth to throw a good deal of light on the general plan. He remembered vaguely that the Templars, to whom this site had belonged, were in the habit of building round churches, and he thought a particular series of the humps or mounds near him did appear to be arranged in something of a circular form. Few people can resist the temptation to try a little amateur research in a department quite outside their own, if only for the satisfaction of showing how successful they would have been had they only taken it up seriously. Our Professor, however, if he felt something of this mean desire, was also truly anxious to oblige Mr Disney. So he paced with care the circular area he had noticed, and wrote down its rough dimensions in his pocket-book. Then he proceeded to examine an oblong eminence which lay east of the centre of the circle, and seemed to his thinking likely to be the base of a platform or altar. At one end of it, the northern, a patch of the turf was gone—removed by some boy or other creature *ferae naturae*. It might, he thought, be as well to probe the soil here for evidences of masonry, and he took out his knife and began scraping away the earth. And now followed another little discovery: a portion of soil fell inward as he scraped, and disclosed a small cavity. He lighted one match after another to help him to see of what nature the hole was, but the wind was too strong for them all. By tapping and scratching the sides with his knife, however, he was able to make out that it must be an artificial hole in masonry. It was rectangular, and the sides, top, and bottom, if not actually plastered, were smooth and regular. Of course it was empty. No! As he withdrew the knife he heard a metallic clink, and when he introduced his hand it met with a cylindrical object lying on the floor of the hole. Naturally enough, he picked it up, and when he brought it into the light, now fast fading, he could see that it, too, was of man's making—a metal tube about four inches long, and evidently of some considerable age.

By the time Parkins had made sure that there was nothing else in this odd receptacle, it was too late and too dark for him to think of undertaking any further search. What he had done had proved so unexpectedly interesting that he determined to sacrifice a little more of the daylight on the morrow to archaeology. The object which he now had safe in his pocket was bound to be of some slight value at least, he felt sure.

Bleak and solemn was the view on which he took a last look before starting homeward. A faint yellow light in the west showed the links, on which a few figures moving towards the club-house were still visible, the squat martello tower, the lights of Aldsey village, the pale ribbon of sands intersected at intervals by black wooden groynes, the dim and murmuring sea. The wind was bitter from the north, but was at his back when he set out for the Globe. He quickly rattled and clashed through the shingle and gained the sand, upon which, but for the groynes which had to be got over every few yards, the going was both good and quiet. One last look behind, to measure the distance he had made since leaving the ruined Templars' church, showed him a prospect of company on his walk, in the shape of a rather indistinct personage, who seemed to be making great efforts to catch up with him, but made little, if any, progress. I mean that there was an appearance of running about his movements, but that the distance between him and Parkins did not seem materially to lessen. So, at least, Parkins thought, and decided that he almost certainly did not know him, and that it would be absurd to wait until he came up. For all that, company, he began to think, would really be very welcome on that lonely shore, if only you could choose your companion. In his unenlightened days he had read of meetings in such

places which even now would hardly bear thinking of. He went on thinking of them, however, until he reached home, and particularly of one
which catches most people's fancy at some time of their childhood.
"Now I saw in my dream that Christian had gone but a very little way
when he saw a foul fiend coming over the field to meet him." "What
should I do now," he thought, "if I looked back and caught sight of a
black figure sharply defined against the yellow sky, and saw that it had
horns and wings? I wonder whether I should stand or run for it. Luckily,
the gentleman behind is not of that kind, and he seems to be about as far
off now as when I saw him first. Well, at this rate he won't get his dinner
as soon as I shall; and, dear me! it's within a quarter of an hour of the
time now. I must run!"

Parkins had, in fact, very little time for dressing. When he met the
Colonel at dinner, Peace—or as much of her as that gentleman could
manage—reigned once more in the military bosom; nor was she put to
flight in the hours of bridge that followed dinner, for Parkins was a more
than respectable player. When, therefore, he retired towards twelve
o'clock, he felt that he had spent his evening in quite a satisfactory way,
and that, even for so long as a fortnight or three weeks, life at the Globe
would be supportable under similar conditions—"especially," thought
he, "if I go on improving my game."

As he went along the passages he met the boots of the Globe, who
stopped and said:

"Beg your pardon, sir, but as I was a-brushing your coat just now there
was somethink fell out of the pocket. I put it on your chest of drawers,
sir, in your room, sir—a piece of a pipe or somethink of that, sir. Thank
you, sir. You'll find it on your chest of drawers, sir—yes, sir. Good night,
sir."

The speech served to remind Parkins of his little discovery of that
afternoon. It was with some considerable curiosity that he turned it over
by the light of his candles. It was of bronze, he now saw, and was shaped
very much after the manner of the modern dog-whistle; in fact it was—
yes, certainly it was—actually no more nor less than a whistle. He put it
to his lips, but it was quite full of a fine, caked-up sand or earth, which
would not yield to knocking, but must be loosened with a knife. Tidy as
ever in his habits, Parkins cleared out the earth on to a piece of paper,
and took the latter to the window to empty it out. The night was clear
and bright, as he saw when he had opened the casement, and he stopped
for an instant to look at the sea and note a belated wanderer stationed on
the shore in front of the inn. Then he shut the window, a little surprised
at the late hours people kept at Burnstow, and took his whistle to the
light again. Why, surely there were marks on it, and not merely marks,
but letters! A very little rubbing rendered the deeply-cut inscription

quite legible, but the Professor had to confess, after some earnest thought, that the meaning of it was as obscure to him as the writing on the wall to Belshazzar. There were legends both on the front and on the back of the whistle. The one read thus:

FLA

FUR   BIS

FLE

The other:

QUIS EST ISTE QUI UENIT

"I ought to be able to make it out," he thought; "but I suppose I am a little rusty in my Latin. When I come to think of it, I don't believe I even know the word for a whistle. The long one does seem simple enough. It ought to mean, 'Who is this who is coming?' Well, the best way to find out is evidently to whistle for him."

He blew tentatively and stopped suddenly, startled and yet pleased at the note he had elicited. It had a quality of infinite distance in it, and, soft as it was, he somehow felt it must be audible for miles round. It was a sound, too, that seemed to have the power (which many scents possess) of forming pictures in the brain. He saw quite clearly for a moment a vision of a wide, dark expanse at night, with a fresh wind blowing, and in the midst a lonely figure—how employed, he could not tell. Perhaps he would have seen more had not the picture been broken by the sudden surge of a gust of wind against his casement, so sudden that it made him look up, just in time to see the white glint of a sea-bird's wing somewhere outside the dark panes.

The sound of the whistle had so fascinated him that he could not help trying it once more, this time more boldly. The note was little, if at all, louder than before, and repetition broke the illusion—no picture followed, as he had half hoped it might. "But what is this? Goodness! what force the wind can get up in a few minutes! What a tremendous gust! There! I knew that window-fastening was no use! Ah! I thought so— both candles out. It's enough to tear the room to pieces."

The first thing was to get the window shut. While you might count twenty Parkins was struggling with the small casement, and felt almost as if he were pushing back a sturdy burglar, so strong was the pressure. It slackened all at once, and the window banged to and latched itself. Now to relight the candles and see what damage, if any, had been done. No, nothing seemed amiss; no glass even was broken in the casement. But the noise had evidently roused at least one member of the household: the

Colonel was to be heard stumping in his stockinged feet on the floor above, and growling.

Quickly as it had risen, the wind did not fall at once. On it went, moaning and rushing past the house, at times rising to a cry so desolate that, as Parkins disinterestedly said, it might have made fanciful people feel quite uncomfortable; even the unimaginative, he thought after a quarter of an hour, might be happier without it.

Whether it was the wind, or the excitement of golf, or of the researches in the preceptory that kept Parkins awake, he was not sure. Awake he remained, in any case, long enough to fancy (as I am afraid I often do myself under such conditions) that he was the victim of all manner of fatal disorders: he would lie counting the beats of his heart, convinced that it was going to stop work every moment, and would entertain grave suspicions of his lungs, brain, liver, etc.—suspicions which he was sure would be dispelled by the return of daylight, but which until then refused to be put aside. He found a little vicarious comfort in the idea that someone else was in the same boat. A near neighbour (in the darkness it was not easy to tell his direction) was tossing and rustling in his bed, too.

The next stage was that Parkins shut his eyes and determined to give sleep every chance. Here again over-excitement asserted itself in another form—that of making pictures. *Experto crede,* pictures do come to the closed eyes of one trying to sleep, and are often so little to his taste that he must open his eyes and disperse them.

Parkins's experience on this occasion was a very distressing one. He found that the picture which presented itself to him was continuous. When he opened his eyes, of course, it went; but when he shut them once more it framed itself afresh, and acted itself out again, neither quicker nor slower than before. What he saw was this:

A long stretch of shore—shingle edged by sand, and intersected at short intervals with black groynes running down to the water—a scene, in fact, so like that of his afternoon's walk that, in the absence of any landmark, it could not be distinguished therefrom. The light was obscure, conveying an impression of gathering storm, late winter evening, and slight cold rain. On this bleak stage at first no actor was visible. Then, in the distance, a bobbing black object appeared; a moment more, and it was a man running, jumping, clambering over the groynes, and every few seconds looking eagerly back. The nearer he came the more obvious it was that he was not only anxious, but even terribly frightened, though his face was not to be distinguished. He was, moreover, almost at the end of his strength. On he came; each successive obstacle seemed to cause him more difficulty than the last. "Will he get over this next one?"

thought Parkins; "it seems a little higher than the others." Yes; half climbing, half throwing himself, he did get over, and fell all in a heap on the other side (the side nearest to the spectator). There, as if really unable to get up again, he remained crouching under the groyne, looking up in an attitude of painful anxiety.

So far no cause whatever for the fear of the runner had been shown; but now there began to be seen, far up the shore, a little flicker of something light-coloured moving to and fro with great swiftness and irregularity. Rapidly growing larger, it, too, declared itself as a figure in pale, fluttering draperies, ill-defined. There was something about its motion which made Parkins very unwilling to see it at close quarters. It would stop, raise arms, bow itself toward the sand, then run stooping across the beach to the water-edge and back again; and then, rising upright, once more continue its course forward at a speed that was startling and terrifying. The moment came when the pursuer was hovering about from left to right only a few yards beyond the groyne where the runner lay in hiding. After two or three ineffectual castings hither and thither it came to a stop, stood upright, with arms raised high, and then darted straight forward towards the groyne.

It was at this point that Parkins always failed in his resolution to keep his eyes shut. With many misgivings as to incipient failure of eyesight, over-worked brain, excessive smoking, and so on, he finally resigned himself to light his candle, get out a book, and pass the night waking, rather than be tormented by this persistent panorama, which he saw clearly enough could only be a morbid reflection of his walk and his thoughts on that very day.

The scraping of match on box and the glare of light must have startled some creatures of the night—rats or what not—which he heard scurry across the floor from the side of his bed with much rustling. Dear, dear! the match is out! Fool that it is! But the second one burnt better, and a candle and book were duly procured, over which Parkins pored till sleep of a wholesome kind came upon him, and that in no long space. For about the first time in his orderly and prudent life he forgot to blow out the candle, and when he was called next morning at eight there was still a flicker in the socket and a sad mess of guttered grease on top of the little table.

After breakfast he was in his room, putting the finishing touches to his golfing costume—fortune had again allotted the Colonel to him for a partner—when one of the maids came in.

"Oh, if you please," she said, "would you like any extra blankets on your bed, sir?"

"Ah! thank you," said Parkins. "Yes, I think I should like one. It seems likely to turn rather colder."

In a very short time the maid was back with the blanket.

"Which bed should I put it on, sir?" she asked.

"What? Why, that one—the one I slept in last night," he said, pointing to it.

"Oh yes! I beg your pardon, sir, but you seemed to have tried both of 'em; leastways, we had to make 'em both up this morning."

"Really? How very absurd!" said Parkins. "I certainly never touched the other, except to lay some things on it. Did it actually seem to have been slept in?"

"Oh yes, sir!" said the maid. "Why, all the things was crumpled and throwed about all ways, if you'll excuse me, sir—quite as if anyone 'adn't passed but a very poor night, sir."

"Dear me," said Parkins. "Well, I may have disordered it more than I thought when I unpacked my things. I'm very sorry to have given you the extra trouble, I'm sure. I expect a friend of mine soon, by the way—a gentleman from Cambridge—to come and occupy it for a night or two. That will be all right, I suppose, won't it?"

"Oh yes, to be sure, sir. Thank you, sir. It's no trouble, I'm sure," said the maid, and departed to giggle with her colleagues.

Parkins set forth, with a stern determination to improve his game.

I am glad to be able to report that he succeeded so far in this enterprise that the Colonel, who had been rather repining at the prospect of a second day's play in his company, became quite chatty as the morning advanced; and his voice boomed out over the flats, as certain also of our own minor poets have said, "like some great bourdon in a minster tower."

"Extraordinary wind, that, we had last night," he said. "In my old home we should have said someone had been whistling for it."

"Should you, indeed!" said Parkins. "Is there a superstition of that kind still current in your part of the country?"

"I don't know about superstition," said the Colonel. "They believe in it all over Denmark and Norway, as well as on the Yorkshire coast; and my experience is, mind you, that there's generally something at the bottom of what these country-folk hold to, and have held to for generations. But it's your drive" (or whatever it might have been: the golfing reader will have to imagine appropriate digressions at the proper intervals).

When conversation was resumed, Parkins said, with a slight hesitancy:

"Apropos of what you were saying just now, Colonel, I think I ought to tell you that my own views on such subjects are very strong. I am, in fact, a convinced disbeliever in what is called the 'supernatural.' "

"What!" said the Colonel, "do you mean to tell me you don't believe in second-sight, or ghosts, or anything of that kind?"

"In nothing whatever of that kind," returned Parkins firmly.

"Well," said the Colonel, "but it appears to me at that rate, sir, that you must be little better than a Sadducee."

Parkins was on the point of answering that, in his opinion, the Sadducees were the most sensible persons he had ever read of in the Old Testament; but, feeling some doubt as to whether much mention of them was to be found in that work, he preferred to laugh the accusation off.

"Perhaps I am," he said; "but—— Here, give me my cleek, boy!— Excuse me one moment, Colonel." A short interval. "Now, as to whistling for the wind, let me give you my theory about it. The laws which govern winds are really not at all perfectly known—to fisher-folk and such, of course, not known at all. A man or woman of eccentric habits, perhaps, or a stranger, is seen repeatedly on the beach at some unusual hour, and is heard whistling. Soon afterwards a violent wind rises; a man who could read the sky perfectly or who possessed a barometer could have foretold that it would. The simple people of a fishing-village have no barometers, and only a few rough rules for prophesying weather. What more natural than that the eccentric personage I postulated should be regarded as having raised the wind, or that he or she should clutch eagerly at the reputation of being able to do so? Now, take last night's wind: as it happens, I myself was whistling. I blew a whistle twice, and the wind seemed to come absolutely in answer to my call. If anyone had seen me——"

The audience had been a little restive under this harangue, and Parkins had, I fear, fallen somewhat into the tone of a lecturer; but at the last sentence the Colonel stopped.

"Whistling, were you?" he said. "And what sort of whistle did you use? Play this stroke first." Interval.

"About that whistle you were asking, Colonel. It's rather a curious one. I have it in my—— No; I see I've left it in my room. As a matter of fact, I found it yesterday."

And then Parkins narrated the manner of his discovery of the whistle, upon hearing which the Colonel grunted, and opined that, in Parkins's place, he should himself be careful about using a thing that had belonged to a set of Papists, of whom, speaking generally, it might be affirmed that you never knew what they might not have been up to. From this topic he diverged to the enormities of the Vicar, who had given notice on the previous Sunday that Friday would be the Feast of St Thomas the Apostle, and that there would be service at eleven o'clock in the church. This and other similar proceedings constituted in the Colonel's view a strong presumption that the Vicar was a concealed Papist, if not a Jesuit; and

Parkins, who could not very readily follow the Colonel in this region, did not disagree with him. In fact, they got on so well together in the morning that there was no talk on either side of their separating after lunch.

Both continued to play well during the afternoon, or, at least, well enough to make them forget everything else until the light began to fail them. Not until then did Parkins remember that he had meant to do some more investigating at the preceptory; but it was of no great importance, he reflected. One day was as good as another; he might as well go home with the Colonel.

As they turned the corner of the house, the Colonel was almost knocked down by a boy who rushed into him at the very top of his speed, and then, instead of running away, remained hanging on to him and panting. The first words of the warrior were naturally those of reproof and objurgation, but he very quickly discerned that the boy was almost speechless with fright. Inquiries were useless at first. When the boy got his breath he began to howl, and still clung to the Colonel's legs. He was at last detached, but continued to howl.

"What in the world *is* the matter with you? What have you been up to? What have you seen?" said the two men.

"Ow, I seen it wive at me out of the winder," wailed the boy, "and I don't like it."

"What window?" said the irritated Colonel. "Come, pull yourself together, my boy."

"The front winder it was, at the 'otel," said the boy.

At this point Parkins was in favour of sending the boy home, but the Colonel refused; he wanted to get to the bottom of it, he said; it was most dangerous to give a boy such a fright as this one had had, and if it turned out that people had been playing jokes, they should suffer for it in some way. And by a series of questions he made out this story: The boy had been playing about on the grass in front of the Globe with some others; then they had gone home to their teas, and he was just going, when he happened to look up at the front winder and see it a-wiving at him. *It* seemed to be a figure of some sort, in white as far as he knew—couldn't see its face; but it wived at him, and it warn't a right thing—not to say not a right person. Was there a light in the room? No, he didn't think to look if there was a light. Which was the window? Was it the top one or the second one? The seckind one it was—the big winder what got two little uns at the sides.

"Very well, my boy," said the Colonel, after a few more questions. "You run away home now. I expect it was some person trying to give you a start. Another time, like a brave English boy, you just throw a stone—well, no, not that exactly, but you go and speak to the waiter, or to Mr

Simpson, the landlord, and—yes—and say that I advised you to do so."

The boy's face expressed some of the doubt he felt as to the likelihood of Mr Simpson's lending a favourable ear to his complaint, but the Colonel did not appear to perceive this, and went on:

"And here's a sixpence—no, I see it's a shilling—and you be off home, and don't think any more about it."

The youth hurried off with agitated thanks, and the Colonel and Parkins went round to the front of the Globe and reconnoitred. There was only one window answering to the description they had been hearing.

"Well, that's curious," said Parkins; "it's evidently my window the lad was talking about. Will you come up for a moment, Colonel Wilson? We ought to be able to see if anyone has been taking liberties in my room."

They were soon in the passage, and Parkins made as if to open the door. Then he stopped and felt in his pockets.

"This is more serious than I thought," was his next remark. "I remember now that before I started this morning I locked the door. It is locked now, and, what is more, here is the key." And he held it up. "Now," he went on, "if the servants are in the habit of going into one's room during the day when one is away, I can only say that—well, that I don't approve of it at all." Conscious of a somewhat weak climax, he busied himself in opening the door (which was indeed locked) and in lighting candles. "No," he said, "nothing seems disturbed."

"Except your bed," put in the Colonel.

"Excuse me, that isn't my bed," said Parkins. "I don't use that one. But it does look as if someone had been playing tricks with it."

It certainly did: the clothes were bundled up and twisted together in a most tortuous confusion. Parkins pondered.

"That must be it," he said at last: "I disordered the clothes last night in unpacking, and they haven't made it since. Perhaps they came in to make it, and that boy saw them through the window; and then they were called away and locked the door after them. Yes, I think that must be it."

"Well, ring and ask," said the Colonel, and this appealed to Parkins as practical.

The maid appeared, and, to make a long story short, deposed that she had made the bed in the morning when the gentleman was in the room, and hadn't been there since. No, she hadn't no other key. Mr Simpson he kep' the keys; he'd be able to tell the gentleman if anyone had been up.

This was a puzzle. Investigation showed that nothing of value had been taken, and Parkins remembered the disposition of the small objects on tables and so forth well enough to be pretty sure that no pranks had been played with them. Mr and Mrs Simpson furthermore agreed that neither of them had given the duplicate key of the room to any person whatever during the day. Nor could Parkins, fair-minded man as he was, detect anything in the demeanour of master, mistress, or maid that indicated guilt. He was much more inclined to think that the boy had been imposing on the Colonel.

The latter was unwontedly silent and pensive at dinner and throughout the evening. When he bade good night to Parkins, he murmured in a gruff undertone:

"You know where I am if you want me during the night."

"Why, yes, thank you, Colonel Wilson, I think I do; but there isn't much prospect of my disturbing you, I hope. By the way," he added, "did I show you that old whistle I spoke of? I think not. Well, here it is."

The Colonel turned it over gingerly in the light of the candle.

"Can you make anything of the inscription?" asked Parkins, as he took it back.

"No, not in this light. What do you mean to do with it?"

"Oh, well, when I get back to Cambridge I shall submit it to some of the archaeologists there, and see what they think of it; and very likely, if they consider it worth having, I may present it to one of the museums."

"M!" said the Colonel. "Well, you may be right. All I know is that, if it were mine, I should chuck it straight into the sea. It's no use talking, I'm well aware, but I expect that with you it's a case of live and learn. I hope so, I'm sure, and I wish you a good night."

He turned away, leaving Parkins in act to speak at the bottom of the stair, and soon each was in his own bedroom.

By some unfortunate accident, there were neither blinds nor curtains to the windows of the Professor's room. The previous night he had thought little of this, but tonight there seemed every prospect of a bright moon rising to shine directly on his bed, and probably wake him later on. When he noticed this he was a good deal annoyed, but, with an ingenuity which I can only envy, he succeeded in rigging up, with the help of a railway-rug, some safety-pins, and a stick and umbrella, a screen which, if it only held together, would completely keep the moonlight off his bed. And shortly afterwards he was comfortably in that bed. When he had read a somewhat solid work long enough to produce a decided wish for sleep, he cast a drowsy glance round the room, blew out the candle, and fell back upon the pillow.

He must have slept soundly for an hour or more, when a sudden clatter shook him up in a most unwelcome manner. In a moment he realized what had happened: his carefully-constructed screen had given way, and a very bright frosty moon was shining directly on his face. This was highly annoying. Could he possibly get up and reconstruct the screen? or could he manage to sleep if he did not?

For some minutes he lay and pondered over the possibilities; then he turned over sharply, and with all his eyes open lay breathlessly listening. There had been a movement, he was sure, in the empty bed on the opposite side of the room. Tomorrow he would have it moved, for there must be rats or something playing about in it. It was quiet now. No! the commotion began again. There was a rustling and shaking: surely more than any rat could cause.

I can figure to myself something of the Professor's bewilderment and horror, for I have in a dream thirty years back seen the same thing happen; but the reader will hardly, perhaps, imagine how dreadful it was to him to see a figure suddenly sit up in what he had known was an empty bed. He was out of his own bed in one bound, and made a dash towards the window, where lay his only weapon, the stick with which he had propped his screen. This was, as it turned out, the worst thing he could have done, because the personage in the empty bed, with a sudden smooth motion, slipped from the bed and took up a position, with out-spread arms, between the two beds, and in front of the door. Parkins watched it in a horrid perplexity. Somehow, the idea of getting past it and escaping through the door was intolerable to him; he could not have borne—he didn't known why—to touch it; and as for its touching him, he would sooner dash himself through the window than have that happen. It stood for the moment in a band of dark shadow, and he had not seen what its face was like. Now it began to move, in a stooping posture, and all at once the spectator realized, with some horror and some relief, that it must be blind, for it seemed to feel about it with its muffled arms in a groping and random fashion. Turning half away from him, it became suddenly conscious of the bed he had just left, and darted towards it, and bent over and felt the pillows in a way which made Parkins shudder as he had never in his life thought it possible. In a very few moments it seemed to know that the bed was empty, and then, moving forward into the area of light and facing the window, it showed for the first time what manner of thing it was.

Parkins, who very much dislikes being questioned about it, did once describe something of it in my hearing, and I gathered that what he chiefly remembers about it is a horrible, an intensely horrible, face *of crumpled linen*. What expression he read upon it he could not or would not tell, but that the fear of it went nigh to maddening him is certain.

But he was not at leisure to watch it for long. With formidable quickness it moved into the middle of the room, and, as it groped and waved, one corner of its draperies swept across Parkins's face. He could not—though he knew how perilous a sound was—he could not keep back a cry of disgust, and this gave the searcher an instant clue. It leapt towards him upon the instant, and the next moment he was half-way through the window backwards, uttering cry upon cry at the utmost pitch of his voice, and the linen face was thrust close into his own. At this, almost the last possible second, deliverance came, as you will have guessed: the Colonel burst the door open, and was just in time to see the dreaful group at the window. When he reached the figures only one was left. Parkins sank forward into the room in a faint, and before him on the floor lay a tumbled heap of bed-clothes.

Colonel Wilson asked no questions, but busied himself in keeping everyone else out of the room and in getting Parkins back to his bed; and himself, wrapped in a rug, occupied the other bed for the rest of the night. Early on the next day Rogers arrived, more welcome than he would have been a day before, and the three of them held a very long consultation in the Professor's room. At the end of it the Colonel left the hotel door carrying a small object between his finger and thumb, which he cast as far into the sea as a very brawny arm could send it. Later on the smoke of a burning ascended from the back premises of the Globe.

Exactly what explanation was patched up for the staff and visitors at the hotel I must confess I do not recollect. The Professor was somehow cleared of the ready suspicion of delirium tremens, and the hotel of the reputation of a troubled house.

There is not much question as to what would have happened to Parkins if the Colonel had not intervened when he did. He would either have fallen out of the window or else lost his wits. But it is not so evident what more the creature that came in answer to the whistle could have done than frighten. There seemed to be absolutely nothing material about it save the bed-clothes of which it had made itself a body. The Colonel, who remembered a not very dissimilar occurrence in India, was of opinion that if Parkins had closed with it it could really have done very little, and that its one power was that of frightening. The whole thing, he said, served to confirm his opinion of the Church of Rome.

There is really nothing more to tell, but, as you may imagine, the Professor's views on certain points are less clear cut than they used to be. His nerves, too, have suffered: he cannot even now see a surplice hanging on a door quite unmoved, and the spectacle of a scarecrow in a field late on a winter afternoon has cost him more than one sleepless night.

1904

Mr Humphreys and His Inheritance

About fifteen years ago, on a date late in August or early in September, a train drew up at Wilsthorpe, a country station in eastern England. Out of it stepped (with other passengers) a rather tall and reasonably good-looking young man, carrying a hand bag and some papers tied up in a packet.

He was expecting to be met, one would say, from the way in which he looked about him: and he was, as obviously, expected. The stationmaster ran forward a step or two, and then, seeming to recollect himself, turned and beckoned to a stout and consequential person with a short round beard who was scanning the train with some appearance of bewilderment. "Mr Cooper," he called out, "Mr Cooper, I think this is your gentleman"; and then, to the passenger who had just alighted, "Mr Humphreys, sir? Glad to bid you welcome to Wilsthorpe. There's a cart from the Hall for your luggage, and here's Mr Cooper, what I think you know." Mr Cooper had hurried up, and now raised his hat and shook hands. "Very pleased, I'm sure," he said, "to give the echo to Mr Palmer's kind words. I should have been the first to render expression to them but for the face not being familiar to me, Mr Humphreys. May your residence among us be marked as a red-letter day, sir." "Thank you very much, Mr Cooper," said Humphreys, "for your good wishes, and Mr Palmer also. I do hope very much that this change of—er—tenancy—which you must all regret, I am sure—will not be to the detriment of those with whom I shall be brought in contact." He stopped, feeling that the words were not fitting themselves together in the happiest way, and Mr Cooper cut in. "Oh you may rest satisfied of that, Mr Humphreys. I'll take it upon myself to assure you, sir, that a warm welcome awaits you on all sides. And as to any change of propriety turning out detrimental to the neighbourhood, well, your late uncle——" and here Mr Cooper also stopped, possibly in obedience to an inner monitor, possibly because Mr Palmer, clearing his throat loudly, asked Humphreys for his ticket. The two men left the little station, and—at Humphreys' suggestion—decided to walk to Mr Cooper's house, where luncheon was awaiting them.

The relation in which these personages stood to each other can be explained in a very few lines. Humphreys had inherited—quite unexpectedly—a property from an uncle: neither the property nor the uncle had he ever seen. He was alone in the world—a man of good ability and kindly nature, whose employment in a government office for the last four or five years had not gone far to fit him for the life of a country gentleman. He was studious and rather diffident, and had few out-of-door pursuits except golf and gardening. Today he had come down for the first time to visit Wilsthorpe and confer with Mr Cooper the bailiff as to the matters which needed immediate attention. It may be asked how this came to be his first visit? Ought he not in decency to have attended his uncle's funeral? The answer is not far to seek: he had been abroad at the time of the death, and his address had not been at once procurable. So he had put off coming to Wilsthorpe till he heard that all things were ready for him. And now we find him arrived at Mr Cooper's comfortable house, facing the parsonage, and having just shaken hands with the smiling Mrs and Miss Cooper.

During the minutes that preceded the announcement of luncheon the party settled themselves on elaborate chairs in the drawing-room, Humphreys, for his part, perspiring quietly in the consciousness that stock was being taken of him.

"I was just saying to Mr Humphreys, my dear," said Mr Cooper, "that I hope and trust that his residence among us here in Wilsthorpe will be marked as a red-letter day."

"Yes indeed, I'm sure," said Mrs Cooper heartily, "and many, many of them."

Miss Cooper murmured words to the same effect, and Humphreys attempted a pleasantry about painting the whole calendar red, which, though greeted with shrill laughter, was evidently not fully understood. At this point they proceeded to luncheon.

"Do you know this part of the country at all, Mr Humphreys?" said Mrs Cooper after a short interval. This was a better opening.

"No, I'm sorry to say I do *not*," said Humphreys. "It seems very pleasant, what I could see of it coming down in the train."

"Oh it *is* a pleasant part. Really, I sometimes say I don't know a nicer district for the country; and the people round, too: such a quantity always going on. But I'm afraid you've come a little late for some of the better garden parties, Mr Humphreys."

"I suppose I have; dear me, what a pity!" said Humphreys with a gleam of relief; and then, feeling that something more could be got out of this topic, "But after all, you see, Mrs Cooper, even if I could have been here earlier, I should have been cut off from them, should I not? My poor uncle's recent death, you know——"

"Oh dear, Mr Humphreys, to be sure, what a dreadful thing of me to say!" (And Mr and Miss Cooper seconded the proposition inarticulately.) "What must you have thought? I *am* so sorry: you must really forgive me."

"Not at all Mrs Cooper, I assure you. I can't honestly assert that my uncle's death was a great grief to me, for I had never seen him. All I meant was that I supposed I shouldn't be expected to take part for some little time in festivities of that kind."

"Now really it's very kind of you to take it in that way, Mr Humphreys, isn't it George? And you *do* forgive me? But only fancy! You never saw poor old Mr Wilson!"

"Never in my life; nor did I ever have a letter from him. But, by the way, you have something to forgive *me* for. I've never thanked you except by letter for all the trouble you've taken to find people to look after me at the Hall."

"Oh I'm sure that was nothing, Mr Humphreys; but I really do think that you'll find them give satisfaction. The man and his wife whom we've got for the butler and housekeeper we've known for a number of years: such a nice respectable couple, and Mr Cooper I'm sure can answer for the men in the stables and gardens."

"Yes, Mr Humphreys, they're a good lot. The head gardener's the only one who's stopped on from Mr Wilson's time. The major part of the employees, as you no doubt saw by the will, received legacies from the old gentleman and retired from their posts, and as the wife says, your housekeeper and butler are calculated to render you every satisfaction."

"So everything, Mr Humphreys, is ready for you to step in this very day, according to what I understood you to wish," said Mrs Cooper. "Everything, that is, except company, and there I'm afraid you'll find yourself quite at a standstill. Only we did understand it was your intention to move in at once. If not I'm sure you know we should have been only too pleased for you to stay here."

"I'm quite sure you would, Mrs Cooper, and I'm very grateful to you. But I thought I had really better make the plunge at once. I'm accustomed to living alone, and there will be quite enough to occupy my evenings—looking over papers and books and so on—for some time to come. I thought if Mr Cooper could spare the time this afternoon to go over the house and grounds with me——"

"Certainly, certainly Mr Humphreys. My time is your own, up to any hour you please——"

"Till dinner-time, father, you mean," said Miss Cooper. "Don't forget we're going over to the Brasnetts'. And have you got all the garden keys?"

"Are you a great gardener, Miss Cooper?" said Mr Humphreys. "I wish you would tell me what I'm to expect at the Hall."

"Oh I don't know about a *great* gardener, Mr Humphreys: I'm very fond of flowers—but the Hall garden might be made quite lovely, I often say. It's very old-fashioned as it is: and a great deal of shrubbery. There's an old temple, besides, and a maze."

"Really? Have you explored it ever?"

"No-o," said Miss Cooper drawing in her lips and shaking her head. "I've often longed to try, but old Mr Wilson always kept it locked. He wouldn't even let Lady Wardrop into it. (She lives near here, at Bentley, you know, and she's a *great* gardener, if you like.) That's why I asked father if he had all the keys."

"I see: well, I must evidently look into that, and show you over it when I've learnt the way."

"Oh thank you so much, Mr Humphreys! Now I shall have the laugh of Miss Foster (that's our rector's daughter, you know—they're away on their holiday now—such nice people). We always had a joke between us which should be the first to get into the maze."

"I think the garden keys must be up at the house," said Mr Cooper, who had been looking over a large bunch. "There is a number there in the library. Now, Mr Humphreys, if you're prepared, we might bid goodbye to these ladies and set forward on our little tour of exploration."

As they came out of Mr Cooper's front gate, Humphreys had to run the gauntlet—not of an organized demonstration, but of a good deal of touching of hats and careful contemplation from the men and women who had gathered in somewhat unusual numbers in the village street. He had further to exchange some remarks with the wife of the lodge-keeper as they passed the park gates, and with the lodge-keeper himself, who was attending to the park road. I cannot, however, spare the time to report the progress fully. As they traversed the half-mile or so between the lodge and the house, Humphreys took occasion to ask his companion some question which brought up the topic of his late uncle, and it did not take long before Mr Cooper was embarked upon a disquisition.

"It is singular to think, as the wife was saying just now, that you should never have seen the old gentleman. And yet—you won't misunderstand me, Mr Humphreys, I feel confident, when I say that in my opinion there would have been but little congeniality betwixt yourself and him. Not that I have a word to say in deprecation—not a single word. I can tell you what he was," said Mr Cooper, pulling up suddenly and fixing Humphreys with his eye. "Can tell you what he was in a nutshell, as the saying goes. He was a complete, thorough, valentudinarian. That describes him to a T. That's what he was, sir, a complete valentudinarian. No participation in what went on around him. I did venture, I think, to send you a few words of cutting from our local paper which I took the occasion to contribute on his decease. If I recollect myself aright such is very much the ghist of them. But don't, Mr Humphreys," continued Cooper, tapping him impressively on the chest, "don't you run away with the impression that I wish to say aught but what is most creditable—*most* creditable—of your respected uncle and my late employer. Upright, Mr Humphreys, open as the day; liberal to all in his dealings. He had the heart to feel and the hand to accommodate. But there it was: there was the stumbling-block—his unfortunate health—or as I might more truly phrase it, his *want* of health."

"Yes, poor man. Did he suffer from any special disorder before his last illness—which I take it was little more than old age?"

"Just that, Mr Humphreys—just that. The flash flickering slowly away in the pan," said Cooper with what he considered an appropriate gesture, "—the golden bowl gradually ceasing to vibrate. But as to your other question I should return a negative answer. General absence of vitality? yes: special complaint? no, unless you reckon a nasty cough he had with him. Why, here we are pretty much at the house. A handsome mansion Mr Humphreys, don't you consider?"

It deserved the epithet on the whole: but it was oddly proportioned—a very tall red-brick house with a plain parapet concealing the roof almost entirely. It gave the impression of a town house set down in the country; there was a basement, and a rather imposing flight of steps leading up to the front door. It seemed also, owing to its height, to desiderate wings, but there were none. The stables and other offices were concealed by trees. Humphreys guessed its probable date at 1770 or thereabouts.

The mature couple who had been engaged to act as butler and cook-housekeeper were waiting inside the front door, and opened it as their new master approached. Their name, Humphreys already knew, was Calton; of their appearance and manner he formed a favourable impression in the few minutes' talk he had with them. It was agreed that he should go through the plate and the cellar next day with Mr Calton, and that Mrs C. should have a talk with him about linen, bedding, and so on—what there was, and what there ought to be. Then he and Cooper, dismissing the Caltons for the present, began their view of the house. Its topography is not of importance to this story. The large rooms on the ground floor were satisfactory, especially the library, which was as large as the dining-room and had three tall windows facing east. The bedroom prepared for Humphreys was immediately above it. There were many pleasant, and a few really interesting, old pictures. None of the furniture was new, and hardly any of the books were later than the seventies. After hearing of and seeing the few changes his uncle had made in the house, and contemplating a shiny portrait of him which adorned the drawing-room, Humphreys was forced to agree with Cooper that in all probability there would have been little to attract him in his predecessor. It made him rather sad that he could not be sorry *(dolebat se dolere non posse)* for the man who, whether with or without some feeling of kindliness towards his unknown nephew, had contributed so much to his well-being; for he felt that Wilsthorpe was a place in which he could be happy, and especially happy, it might be, in its library.

And now it was time to go over the garden: the empty stables could wait, and so could the laundry. So to the garden they addressed themselves, and it was soon evident that Miss Cooper had been right in thinking that there were possibilities. Also that Mr Cooper had done well in keeping on the gardener. The deceased Mr Wilson might not have, indeed plainly had not, been imbued with the latest views on gardening, but whatever had been done here had been done under the eye of a knowledgeable man, and the equipment and stock were excellent. Cooper was delighted with the pleasure Humphreys showed, and with the suggestions he let fall from time to time. "I can see," he said, "that you've found your meatear here, Mr Humphreys: you'll make this place a regular signosier before very many seasons have passed over our heads. I wish Clutterham had been here—that's the head gardener—and here he would have been of course, as I told you, but for his son's being horse doover with a fever, poor fellow! I should like him to have heard how the place strikes you."

"Yes, you told me he couldn't be here today, and I was very sorry to hear the reason, but it will be time enough tomorrow. What is that white building on the mound at the end of the grass ride? Is it the temple Miss Cooper mentioned?"

"That it is, Mr Humphreys—the Temple of Friendship. Constructed of marble brought out of Italy for the purpose by your late uncle's grandfather. Would it interest you perhaps to take a turn there? You get a very sweet prospect of the park."

The general lines of the temple were those of the Sibyl's Temple at Tivoli, helped out by a dome, only the whole was a good deal smaller. Some ancient sepulchral reliefs were built into the wall and about it all was a pleasant flavour of the grand tour. Cooper produced the key and with some difficulty opened the heavy door. Inside there was a handsome ceiling, but little furniture. Most of the floor was occupied by a pile of thick circular blocks of stone, each of which had a single letter deeply cut on its slightly convex upper surface. "What is the meaning of these?" Humphreys inquired.

"Meaning? Well, all things we're told have their purpose Mr Humphreys, and I suppose these blocks have had theirs as well as another. But what that purpose is or was [Mr Cooper assumed a didactic attitude here] I for one should be at a loss to point out to you, sir. All I know of them—and it's summed up in a very few words—is just this: that they're stated to have been removed by your late uncle at a period before I entered on the scene, from the maze. That, Mr Humphreys, is——"

"Oh, the maze!" exclaimed Humphreys. "I'd forgotten that: we must have a look at it. Where is it?"

Cooper drew him to the door of the temple and pointed with his stick. "Guide your eye," he said (somewhat in the manner of the second Elder in Handel's *Susanna*—

> Far to the west direct your straining eyes
> Where yon tall holm-tree rises to the skies.)

"Guide your eye by my stick here, and follow out the line directly opposite to the spot where we're standing now, and I'll engage, Mr Humphreys, that you'll catch the archway over the entrance. You'll see it just at the end of the walk answering to the one that leads up to this very building. Did you think of going there at once? because if that be the case, I must go to the house and procure the key. If you would walk on there, I'll rejoin you in a few moments' time."

Accordingly Humphreys strolled down the ride leading to the temple, past the garden-front of the house, and up the turfy approach to the archway which Cooper had pointed out to him. He was surprised to find that the whole maze was surrounded by a high wall and that the archway was provided with a padlocked iron gate; but then he remembered that Miss Cooper had spoken of his uncle's objection to letting anyone enter this part of the garden. He was now at the gate, and still Cooper came not. For a few minutes he occupied himself in reading the motto cut over the entrance—*Secretum meum mihi et filiis domus meae*—and in trying to recollect the source of it. Then he became impatient, and considered the possibility of scaling the wall. This was clearly not worth while; it might have been done if he had been wearing an older suit: or could the padlock—a very old one—be forced? No, apparently not: and yet, as he gave a final irritated kick at the gate, something gave way, and the lock fell at his feet. He pushed the gate open, inconveniencing a number of nettles as he did so, and stepped into the enclosure.

It was a yew maze of circular form and the hedges, long untrimmed, had grown out and upwards to a most unorthodox breadth and height. The walks, too, were next door to impassable. Only by entirely disregarding scratches, nettle-stings, and wet could Humphreys force his way along them; but at any rate this condition of things, he reflected, would make it easier for him to find his way out again, for he left a very visible track. So far as he could remember he had never been in a maze before, nor did it seem to him now that he had missed much. The dankness and darkness and smell of crushed goosegrass and nettles were anything but cheerful. Still, it did not seem to be a very intricate specimen of its kind. Here he was (by the way, was that Cooper arrived at last? No) very nearly at the heart of it without having taken much thought as to what path he was following. Ah, there at last was the centre, easily gained. And there was something to reward him.

His first impression was that the central ornament was a sundial, but when he had switched away some portion of the thick growth of brambles and bindweed that had formed over it, he saw that it was a less ordinary decoration. A stone column about four feet high and on the top of it a metal globe—copper, to judge by the green patina—engraved, and finely engraved, too, with figures in outline, and letters. That was what Humphreys saw, and a brief glance at the figures convinced him that it was one of those mysterious things called celestial globes, from which, one would suppose, no one ever yet derived any information about the heavens. However, it was too dark—at least in the maze—for him to examine this curiosity at all closely, and besides, he now heard Cooper's voice, and sounds as of an elephant in the jungle. Humphreys called to him to follow the track he had beaten out, and soon Cooper emerged panting into the central circle. He was full of apologies for his delay; he had not been able, after all, to find the key. "But there!" he said, "you've penetrated into the heart of the mystery unaided and unannealed, as the saying goes. Well! I suppose it's a matter of thirty to forty years since any human foot has trod these precincts. Certain it is that I've never set foot in them before. Well, well, what's the old proverb about angels fearing to tread? It's proved true once again in this case." Humphreys' acquaintance with Cooper, though it had been short, was sufficient to assure him that there was no guile in this allusion, and he forbore the obvious remark, merely suggesting that it was fully time to get back to the house for a late cup of tea and to release Cooper for his evening engagement. They left the maze accordingly, experiencing wellnigh the same ease in retracing their path as they had in coming in.

"Have you any idea," Humphreys asked, as they went towards the house, "why my uncle kept that place so carefully locked?"

Cooper pulled up, and Humphreys felt that he must be on the brink of a revelation.

"I should merely be deceiving you, Mr Humphreys, and that to no good purpose, if I laid claim to possess any information whatsoever on that topic. When I first entered upon my duties here some eighteen years back that maze was word for word in the condition you see it now, and the one and only occasion on which the question ever arose within my knowledge was that of which my girl made mention in your hearing.

Lady Wardrop—I've not a word to say against her—wrote applying for admission to the maze. Your uncle showed me the note—a most civil note—everything that could be expected from such a quarter. 'Cooper,' he said, 'I wish you'd reply to that note on my behalf.' 'Certainly Mr Wilson,' I said, for I was quite inured to acting as his secretary, 'what answer shall I return to it?' 'Well,' he said, 'give Lady Wardrop my compliments and tell her that if ever that portion of the grounds is taken in hand I shall be happy to give her the first opportunity of viewing it, but that it has been shut up now for a number of years and I shall be grateful to her if she kindly won't press the matter.' That, Mr Humphreys, was your good uncle's last word on the subject, and I don't think I can add anything to it. Unless," added Cooper after a pause, "it might be just this: that, so far as I could form a judgment, he had a dislike (as people often will for one reason or another) to the memory of his grandfather, who, as I mentioned to you, had that maze laid out. A man of peculiar teenets, Mr Humphreys, and a great traveller. You'll have the opportunity, on the coming Sabbath, of seeing the tablet to him in our little parish church; put up it was some long time after his death."

"Oh? I should have expected a man who had such a taste for building to have designed a mausoleum for himself."

"Well, I've never noticed anything of the kind you mention; and in fact, come to think of it, I'm not at all sure that his resting-place is within our boundaries at all: that he lays in the vault I'm pretty confident is not the case. Curious now, that I shouldn't be in a position to inform you on that heading! Still, after all, we can't say, can we Mr Humphreys, that it's a point of crucial importance where the pore mortal coils are bestowed?"

At this point they entered the house, and Cooper's speculations were interrupted.

Tea was laid in the library, where Mr Cooper fell upon subjects appropriate to the scene. "A fine collection of books! One of the finest, I've understood from connoisseurs, in this part of the country; splendid plates, too, in some of these works. I recollect your uncle showing me one with views of foreign towns—most absorbing it was: got up in first-rate style. And another all done by hand, with the ink as fresh as if it had been laid on yesterday, and yet he told me it was the work of some old monk hundreds of years back. I've always taken a keen interest in literature myself. Hardly anything to my mind can compare with a good hour's reading after a hard day's work; far better than wasting the whole evening at a friend's house—and that reminds me, to be sure. I shall be getting into trouble with the wife if I don't make the best of my way home and get ready to squander away one of these same evenings! I must be off, Mr Humphreys."

"And that reminds *me*," said Humphreys, "if I'm to show Miss Cooper the maze tomorrow, we must have it cleared out a bit. Could you say a word about that to the proper person?"

"Why to be sure. A couple of men with scythes could cut out a track tomorrow morning. I'll leave word as I pass the lodge, and I'll tell them what'll save you the trouble, perhaps, Mr Humphreys, of having to go up and extract them yourself: that they'd better have some sticks or a tape to mark out their way with as they go on."

"A very good idea—yes, do that; and I'll expect Mrs and Miss Cooper in the afternoon, and yourself about half-past ten in the morning."

"It'll be a pleasure I'm sure both to them and to myself, Mr Humphreys. Good night!"

Humphreys dined at eight. But for the fact that it was his first evening, and that Calton was evidently inclined for occasional conversation, he would have finished the novel he had bought for his journey. As it was, he had to listen and reply to some of Calton's impressions of the neighbourhood and the season: the latter, it appeared, was seasonable, and the former had changed considerably—and not altogether for the worse—since Carlton's boyhood (which had been spent there). The village shop in particular had greatly improved since the year 1870. It was now possible to procure there pretty much anything you liked in reason: which was a conveniency, because suppose anythink was required of a suddent (and he had known such things before now) he, Calton, could step down there (supposing the shop to be still open) and order it in, without he borrered it of the Rectory, whereas in earlier days it would have been useless to pursue such a course in respect of anything but candles or soap or treacle or perhaps a penny child's picture-book, and nine times out of ten it'd be something more in the nature of a bottle of whisky *you'd* be requiring, leastways—— On the whole Humphreys thought he would be prepared with a book in future.

The library was the obvious place for the after-dinner hours. Candle in hand and pipe in mouth, he moved round the room for some time taking stock of the titles of the books. He had all the predisposition to take interest in an old library, and there was every opportunity for him here to make systematic acquaintance with one, for he had learned from Cooper that there was no catalogue save the very superficial one made for purposes of probate. The drawing up of a *catalogue raisonné* would be a delicious occupation for winter. There were probably treasures to be found, too: even manuscripts if Cooper might be trusted.

As he pursued his round the sense came upon him (as it does upon most of us in similar places) of the extreme unreadableness of a great portion of the collection. "Editions of classics and Fathers, and Picart's

Religious Ceremonies, and the *Harleian Miscellany,* I suppose are all very well, but who is ever going to read Tostatus Abulensis, or Pineda on Job, or a book like this?" He picked out a small quarto, loose in the binding, and from which the lettered label had fallen off; and observing that coffee was waiting for him, retired to a chair. Eventually he opened the book. It will be observed that his condemnation of it rested wholly on external grounds: for all he knew it might have been a collection of unique plays, but undeniably the outside was blank and forbidding. As a matter of fact, it was a collection of sermons or meditations, and mutilated at that, for the first sheet was gone. It seemed to belong to the latter end of the seventeenth century. He turned over the pages till his eye was caught by a marginal note: *"A Parable of this Unhappy Condition,"* and he thought he would see what aptitudes the author might have for imaginative composition.

"I have heard or read," so ran the passage, "whether in the way of *Parable* or true *Relation* I leave my Reader to judge, of a Man who like *Theseus* in the *Attick Tale* should adventure himself, into a *Labyrinth* or *Maze:* and such a one indeed as was not laid out in the Fashion of our *Topiary* artists of this Age, but of a wide compass, in which moreover such unknown Pitfalls and Snares, nay, such ill omened Inhabitants were commonly thought to lurk as could only be encountered at the Hazard of one's very life. Now you may be sure that in such a Case the Disswasions of Friends were not wanting. 'Consider of such-an-one' says a Brother 'how he went the way you wot of, and was never seen more.' 'Or of such another' says the Mother 'that adventured himself but a little way in, and from that day forth is so troubled in his Wits that he cannot tell what he saw, nor hath passed one good Night.' 'And have you never heard' cries a Neighbour 'of what Faces have been seen to look out over the *Palisadoes* and betwixt the Bars of the Gate?' But all would not do: the Man was set upon his Purpose: for it seems it was the common fireside Talk of that Country that at the Heart and Centre of this *Labyrinth* there was a Jewel of such Price and Rarity that would enrich the Finder thereof for his life: and this should be his by right that could persever to come at it. What then? *Quid multa?* The Adventurer pass'd the Gates and for a whole day's space his Friends without had no news of him, except it might be by some indistinct Cries heard afar off in the Night, such as made them turn in their restless Beds and sweat for very Fear, not doubting but that their Son and Brother had put one more to the *Catalogue* of those unfortunates that had suffer'd shipwreck on that Voyage. So the next day they went with weeping Tears to the Clark of the Parish to order the Bell to be toll'd. And their Way took them hard by the gate of the *Labyrinth:* which they would have hastened by, from the Horrour they had of it, but that they caught sight of a sudden of a

Man's Body lying in the Roadway, and going up to it (with what Antici-
pations may be easily figured) found it to be him whom they reckoned as
lost: and not dead, though he were in a Swound most like death. They
then who had gone forth as Mourners came back rejoycing and set to by
all means to revive their Prodigal. Who being come to himself and
hearing of their Anxieties and their Errand of that Morning, 'Ay' says he
'you may as well finish what you were about: for, for all I have brought
back the Jewel (which he shew'd them, and 'twas indeed a rare Piece) I
have brought back that with it that will leave me neither Rest at Night
nor Pleasure by Day.' Whereupon they were instant with him to learn
his Meaning, and where his Company should be that went so sore
against his Stomach. 'O' says he ' 'tis here in my Breast: I cannot flee
from it, do what I may.' So it needed no Wizard to help them to a guess
that it was the Recollection of what he had seen that troubled him so
wonderfully. But they could get no more of him for a long Time but by
Fits and Starts. However at long and at last they made shift to collect
somewhat of this kind: that at first, while the Sun was bright, he went
merrily on, and without any Difficulty reached the Heart of the *Labyrinth* and got the Jewel, and so set out on his Way back rejoycing: but as
the Night fell, *wherein all the Beasts of the Forest do move,* he begun to
be sensible of some Creature keeping Pace with him and, as he thought,
peering and looking upon him from the next Alley to that he was in; and
that when he should stop, this Companion should stop also, which put
him in some Disorder of his Spirits. And indeed as the Darkness in-
creas'd, it seemed to him that there was more than one, and, it might be,
even a whole Band of such Followers: at least so he judg'd by the Rustling and Cracking that they kept among the Thickets; besides that
there would be at a Time a Sound of Whispering, which seem'd to
import a Conference among them. But in regard of who they were or
what Form they were of, he would not be persuaded to say what he
thought. Upon his Hearers asking him what the Cries were which they
heard in the Night (as was observ'd above) he gave them this Account:
That about Midnight (so far as he could judge) he heard his Name call'd
from a long way off, and he would have been sworn it was his Brother
that so call'd him. So he stood still and hilloo'd at the Pitch of his Voice,
and he suppos'd that the *Echo*, or the Noyse of his Shouting, disguis'd
for the Moment any lesser sound; because, when there fell a Stillness
again, he distinguish'd a Trampling (not loud) of running Feet coming
very close behind him, wherewith he was so daunted that himself set off
to run, and that he continued till the dawn broke. Sometimes when his
Breath fail'd him, he would cast himself flat on his Face, and hope that
his Pursuers might over-run him in the darkness, but at such a Time they
would regularly make a Pause, and he could hear them pant and snuff as

it had been a Hound at Fault: which wrought in him so extream an Horrour of mind, that he would be forc'd to betake himself again to turning and doubling, if by any Means he might throw them off the Scent. And, as if this Exertion was in itself not terrible enough, he had before him the constant Fear of falling into some Pit or Trap, of which he had heard and indeed seen with his own Eyes that there were several, some at the sides and other in the midst, of the Alleys. So that in fine (he said) a more dreadful Night was never spent by Mortal Creature than that he had endur'd in that *Labyrinth,* and not that Jewel which he had in his Wallet nor the richest that was ever brought out of the *Indies* could be a sufficient Recompence to him for the Pains he had suffered.

"I will spare to set down the further Recital of this Man's Troubles, inasmuch as I am confident my Reader's Intelligence will hit the *Parallel* I desire to draw. For is not this Jewel a just Emblem of the Satisfaction which a Man may bring back with him from a Course of this World's Pleasures? and will not the *Labyrinth* serve for an Image of the World itself wherein such a Treasure (if we may believe the common Voice) is stored up?"

At about this point Humphreys thought that a little Patience would be an agreeable change, and that the writer's "improvement" of his Parable might be left to itself. So he put the book back in its former place, wondering as he did so whether his uncle had ever stumbled across that passage; and if so whether it had worked on his fancy so much as to make him dislike the idea of a maze, and determine to shut up the one in the garden. Not long afterwards he went to bed.

The next day brought a morning's hard work with Mr Cooper who, if exuberant in language, had the business of the estate at his fingers' ends. He was very breezy this morning, Mr Cooper was: had not forgotten the order to clear out the maze—the work was going on at that moment: his girl was on the tentacles of expectation about it. He also hoped that Humphreys had slept the sleep of the just and that we should be favoured with a continuance of this congenial weather. At luncheon he enlarged on the pictures in the dining-room and pointed out the portrait of the constructor of the temple and the maze. Humphreys examined this with considerable interest. It was the work of an Italian, and had been painted when old Mr Wilson was visiting Rome as a young man. (There was, indeed, a view of the Colosseum in the background.) A pale thin face and large eyes were the characteristic features. In the hand was a partially unfolded roll of paper on which could be distinguished the plan of a circular building, very probably the temple, and also part of that of a labyrinth. Humphreys got up on a chair to examine it, but it was not painted with sufficient clearness to be worth copying. It suggested to him however that he might as well make a plan of his own maze and hang it in the hall for the use of visitors.

This determination of his was confirmed that same afternoon; for when Mrs and Miss Cooper arrived, eager to be inducted into the maze, he found that he was wholly unable to lead them to the centre. The gardeners had removed the guide-marks they had been using, and even Clutterham, when summoned to assist, was as helpless as the rest. "The point is, you see, Mr Wilson—I should say 'Umphreys—these mazes is purposely constructed so much alike, with a view to mislead. Still, if you'll foller me, I think I can put you right. I'll just put my 'at down 'ere as a starting-point." He stumped off and after five minutes brought the party safe to the hat again. "Now that's a very peculiar thing," he said, with a sheepish laugh. "I made sure I'd left that 'at just over against a bramble-bush and you can see for yourself there ain't no bramble-bush not in this walk at all. If you'll allow me, Mr Humphreys—that's the name, ain't it, sir?—I'll just call one of the men in to mark the place like."

William Crack arrived in answer to repeated shouts. He had some difficulty in making his way to the party. First he was seen or heard in an inside alley, then—almost at the same moment—in an outer one. However, he joined them at last and was first consulted without effect and then stationed by the hat, which Clutterham still considered it necessary to leave on the ground. In spite of this strategy, they spent the best part of three-quarters of an hour in quite fruitless wanderings, and Humphreys was obliged at last, seeing how tired Mrs Cooper was becoming, to suggest a retreat to tea, with profuse apologies to Miss Cooper. "At any rate you've won your bet with Miss Foster," he said; "you have been inside the maze, and I promise you the first thing I do shall be to make a proper plan of it with the lines marked out for you to go by." "That's what's wanted, sir," said Clutterham, "someone to draw out a plan and keep it by them. It might be very awkward you see anyone getting into that place and a shower of rain come on and them not able to find their way out again; it might be hours before they could be got out, without you'd permit of me makin' a short cut to the middle: what my meanin' is, takin' down a couple of trees in each 'edge in a straight line so as you could git a clear view right through. Of course that'd do away with it as a maze, but I don't know as you'd approve of that."

"No, I won't have that done yet: I'll make a plan first and let you have a copy. Later on if we find occasion I'll think of what you say."

Humphreys was vexed and ashamed at the fiasco of the afternoon and could not be satisfied without making another effort that evening to reach the centre of the maze. His irritation was increased by finding it without a single false step. He had thoughts of beginning his plan at once; but the light was fading, and he felt that by the time he had got the necessary materials together, work would be impossible.

Next morning accordingly, carrying a drawing-board, pencils, compasses, cartridge paper, and so forth (some of which had been borrowed from the Coopers and some found in the library cupboards), he went to the middle of the maze (again without any hesitation) and set out his materials. He was however delayed in making a start. The brambles and weeds that had obscured the column and globe were now all cleared away and it was for the first time possible to see clearly what these were like. The column was featureless, resembling those on which sundials are usually placed. Not so the globe. I have said that it was finely engraved with figures and inscriptions and that on a first glance Humphreys had taken it for a celestial globe: but he soon found that it did not answer to his recollection of such things. One feature seemed familiar: a winged serpent—*Draco*—encircled it about the place which, on a terrestrial globe, is occupied by the equator: but on the other hand, a good part of the upper hemisphere was covered by the outspread wings of a large figure whose head was concealed by a ring at the pole or summit of the whole. Around the place of the head the words *princeps tenebrarum* could be deciphered. In the lower hemisphere there was a space hatched all over with cross-lines and marked as *umbra mortis*. Near it was a range of mountains and among them a valley with flames rising from it. This was lettered (will you be surprised to learn it?) *vallis filiorum Hinnom*. Above and below *Draco* were outlined various figures not unlike the pictures of the ordinary constellations, but not the same. Thus, a nude man with a raised club was described not as *Hercules* but as *Cain*. Another, plunged up to his middle in earth and stretching out despairing arms, was *Chore* not *Ophiuchus*, and a third, hung by his hair to a snaky tree, was *Absolon*. Near the last a man in long robes and high cap standing in a circle and addressing two shaggy demons who hovered outside was described as *Hostanes magus* (a character unfamiliar to Humphreys). The scheme of the whole, indeed, seemed to be an assemblage of the patriarchs of evil, perhaps not uninfluenced by a study of Dante. Humphreys thought it an unusual exhibition of his great-grandfather's taste but reflected that he had probably picked it up in Italy and had never taken the trouble to examine it closely: certainly, had he set much store by it, he would not have exposed it to wind and weather. He tapped the metal; it seemed hollow and not very thick, and, turning from it, addressed himself to his plan. After half an hour's work he found it was impossible to get on without using a clue. So he procured a roll of twine from Clutterham, and laid it out along the alleys from the entrance to the centre, tying the end to the ring at the top of the globe. This expedient helped him to set out a rough plan before luncheon, and in the afternoon he was able to draw it in more neatly. Towards tea-time Mr Cooper joined him and was much interested in his progress. "Now this——" said Mr Cooper laying his hand on the globe, and then drawing it away hastily. "Whew! Holds the heat, doesn't it, to a surprising degree Mr Humphreys. I suppose this metal—copper, isn't it?—would be an insulator or conductor, or whatever they call it."

"The sun has been pretty strong this afternoon," said Humphreys, evading the scientific point, "but I didn't notice the globe had got hot. No—it doesn't seem very hot to me," he added.

"Odd," said Mr Cooper. "Now I can't hardly bear my hand on it. Something in the difference of temperament between us, I suppose. I dare say you're a chilly subject, Mr Humphreys: I'm not: and there's where the distinction lies. All this summer I've slept, if you'll believe me, practically *in statu quo,* and had my morning tub as cold as I could get it. Day out and day in—let me assist you with that string."

"It's all right, thanks; but if you'll collect some of these pencils and things that are lying about I shall be much obliged. Now I think we've got everything, and we might get back to the house."

They left the maze, Humphreys rolling up the clue as they went. The night was rainy.

Most unfortunately it turned out that, whether by Cooper's fault or not, the plan had been the one thing forgotten the evening before. As was to be expected, it was ruined by the wet. There was nothing for it but to begin again (the job would not be a long one this time). The clue therefore was put in place once more and a fresh start made. But Humphreys had not done much before an interruption came in the shape of Calton with a telegram. His late chief in London wanted to consult him. Only a brief interview was wanted, but the summons was urgent. This was annoying, yet it was not really upsetting. There was a train available in half an hour, and unless things went very cross he could be back, possibly by five o'clock, certainly by eight. He gave the plan to Calton to take to the house, but it was not worth while to remove the clue.

All went as he had hoped. He spent a rather exciting evening in the library, for he lighted tonight upon a cupboard where some of the rarer books were kept. When he went up to bed he was glad to find that the servant had remembered to leave his curtains undrawn and his windows open. He put down his light and went to the window which commanded a view of the garden and the park. It was a brilliant moonlight night. In a few weeks' time the sonorous winds of autumn would break up all this calm, but now the distant woods were in a deep stillness. The slopes of the lawns were shining with dew: the colours of some of the flowers could almost be guessed. The light of the moon just caught the cornice of the temple and the curve of its leaden dome, and Humphreys had to own that so seen these conceits of a past age have a real beauty. In short, the light, the perfume of the woods, and the absolute quiet called up such kind old associations in his mind that he went on ruminating them for a long long time. As he turned from the window he felt he had never seen anything more complete of its sort. The one feature that struck him with a sense of incongruity was a small Irish yew, thin and black, which stood out like an outpost of the shrubbery through which the maze was approached. That, he thought, might as well be away: the wonder was that anyone should have thought it would look well in that position.

However, next morning, in the press of answering letters and going over books with Mr Cooper, the Irish yew was forgotten. One letter, by the way, arrived this day which has to be mentioned. It was from that Lady Wardrop whom Miss Cooper had mentioned and it renewed the application which she had addressed to Mr Wilson. She pleaded in the first place that she was about to publish a Book of Mazes and earnestly desired to include the plan of the Wilsthorpe Maze, and also that it would be a great kindness if Mr Humphreys could let her see it (if at all) at an early date, since she would soon have to go abroad for the winter months. Her house at Bentley was not far distant, so Humphreys was able to send a note by hand to her suggesting the very next day or the day after for her visit; it may be said at once that the messenger brought back a most grateful answer, to the effect that the morrow would suit her admirably.

The only other event of the day was that the plan of the maze was successfully finished.

This night again was fair and brilliant and calm, and Humphreys lingered almost as long at his window. The Irish yew came to his mind again as he was on the point of drawing his curtains: but either he had been misled by a shadow the night before or else the shrub was not really so obtrusive as he had fancied. Anyhow he saw no reason for interfering with it. What he *would* do away with, however, was a clump of dark growth which had usurped a place against the house wall and was threatening to obscure one of the lower range of windows. It did not look as if it could possibly be worth keeping; he fancied it dank and unhealthy, little as he could see of it.

Next day (it was a Friday—he had arrived at Wilsthorpe on a Monday) Lady Wardrop came over in her car soon after luncheon. She was a stout elderly person, very full of talk of all sorts and particularly inclined to make herself agreeable to Humphreys, who had gratified her very much by his ready granting of her request. They made a thorough exploration of the place together and Lady Wardrop's opinion of her host obviously rose sky-high when she found that he really knew something of gardening. She entered enthusiastically into all his plans for improvement, but agreed that it would be a vandalism to interfere with the characteristic laying-out of the ground near the house. With the temple she was particularly delighted and, said she, "Do you know, Mr Humphreys, I think your bailiff must be right about those lettered blocks of stone. One of my mazes (I'm sorry to say the stupid people have destroyed it now—it was at a place in Hampshire) had the track marked out in that way. They were tiles there but lettered just like yours, and the letters taken in the right order formed an inscription—what it was I forget—something about Theseus and Ariadne. I have a copy of it as well as the plan of the maze where it was. How people can do such things! I shall never forgive you if you injure *your* maze. Do you know, they're becoming very uncommon? Almost every year I hear of one being grubbed up. Now do let's get straight to it: or if you're too busy, I know my way there perfectly, and I'm not afraid of getting lost in it: I know too much about mazes for that. Though I remember missing my lunch—not so very long ago either—through getting entangled in the one at Busbury. Well, of course, if you *can* manage to come with me, that will be all the nicer."

After this confident prelude justice would seem to require that Lady Wardrop should have been hopelessly muddled by the Wilsthorpe maze. Nothing of that kind happened: yet it is to be doubted whether she got all the enjoyment from her new specimen that she expected. She was interested—keenly interested—to be sure, and pointed out to Humphreys a series of little depressions in the ground which she thought marked the places of the lettered blocks. She told him, too, what other mazes resembled his most closely in arrangement, and explained how it was usually possible to date a maze to within twenty years by means of its plan. This one, she already knew, must be about as old as 1780 and its features were just what might be expected. The globe, furthermore, completely absorbed her. It was unique in her experience, and she pored over it for long. "I should like a rubbing of that," she said, "if it could possibly be made—yes, I am sure you would be most kind about it, Mr Humphreys, but I trust you won't attempt it on my account, I do indeed; I shouldn't like to take any liberties here. I have the feeling that it might be resented. Now, confess," she went on, turning and facing Humphreys, "don't you feel—haven't you felt ever since you came in here— that a watch is being kept on us and that if we overstepped the mark in any way there would be a—well, a pounce? No? *I* do—and I don't care how soon we are outside the gate.

"After all," she said, when they were once more on their way to the house, "it may have been only the airlessness and the dull heat of that place that pressed on my brain. Still, I'll take back one thing I said. I'm not sure that I shan't forgive you after all if I find next spring that that maze has been grubbed up."

"Whether or no that's done, you shall have the plan, Lady Wardrop. I have made one, and no later than tonight I can trace you a copy."

"Admirable: a pencil tracing will be all I want, with an indication of the scale. I can easily have it brought into line with the rest of my plates. Many, many thanks."

"Very well, you shall have that tomorrow. I wish you could help me to a solution of my block-puzzle."

"What, those stones in the summerhouse? That *is* a puzzle; they are in no sort of order? Of course not. But the men who put them down must have had some directions—perhaps you'll find a paper about it among your uncle's things. If not, you'll have to call in somebody who's an expert in cyphers."

"Advise me about something else, please," said Humphreys. "That bush-thing under the library window: you would have that away, wouldn't you?"

"Which? That? Oh I think not," said Lady Wardrop. "I can't see it very well from this distance, but it's not unsightly."

"Perhaps you're right; only looking out of my window just above it last night, I thought it took up too much room. It doesn't seem to, as one sees it from here, certainly. Very well, I'll leave it alone for a bit."

Tea was the next business, soon after which Lady Wardrop drove off; but half-way down the drive she stopped the car and beckoned to Humphreys, who was still on the front-door steps. He ran to glean her parting words, which were: "It just occurs to me, it might be worth your while to look at the underside of those stones. They *must* have been numbered, mustn't they? *Good*-bye again. Home, please."

The main occupation of this evening at any rate was settled. The tracing of the plan for Lady Wardrop and the careful collation of it with the original meant a couple of hours' work at least. Accordingly, soon after nine Humphreys had his materials put out in the library and began. It was a still stuffy evening; windows had to stand open and he had more than one grisly encounter with a bat. These unnerving episodes made him keep the tail of his eye on the window. Once or twice it was a question whether there was—not a bat, but something more considerable—that had a mind to join him. How unpleasant it would be if someone had slipped noiselessly over the sill, and was crouching on the floor!

The tracing of the plan was done: it remained to compare it with the original and to see whether any paths had been wrongly closed or left open. With one finger on each paper he traced out the course that must be followed from the entrance. There were one or two slight mistakes, but here, near the centre, was a bad confusion, probably due to the entry of the second or third bat. Before correcting the copy he followed out carefully the last turnings of the path on the original. These at least were right; they led without a hitch to the middle space. Here was a feature which need not be repeated on the copy—an ugly black spot about the size of a shilling. Ink? No. It resembled a hole, but how should a hole be there? He stared at it with tired eyes: the work of tracing had been very laborious and he was drowsy and oppressed. But surely this was a very odd hole. It seemed to go not only through the paper but through the table on which it lay. Yes, and through the floor below that, down, and still down, even into infinite depths. He craned over it utterly bewildered. Just as, when you were a child, you may have pored over a square inch of counterpane until it became a landscape with wooded hills, and perhaps even churches and houses, and you lost all thought of the true size of yourself and it, so this hole seemed to Humphreys for the moment the only thing in the world. For some reason it was hateful to him from the first, but he had gazed at it for some moments before any feeling of anxiety came upon him; and then it did come, stronger and stronger—a horror lest something might emerge from it, and a really agonizing conviction that a terror was on its way, from the sight of which he would not be able to escape. Oh yes, far, far down there was a movement, and the movement was upwards—towards the surface. Nearer and nearer it came, and it was of a blackish-grey colour with more than one dark hole. It took shape as a face—a human face—a *burnt* human face: and with the odious writhings of a wasp creeping out of a rotten apple there clambered forth an appearance of a form, waving black arms prepared to clasp the head that was bending over them. With a convulsion of despair Humphreys threw himself back, struck his head against a hanging lamp, and fell.

There was concussion of the brain, shock to the system, and a long confinement to bed. The doctor was badly puzzled, not by the symptoms, but by a request which Humphreys made to him as soon as he was able to say anything. "I wish you would open the ball in the maze." "Hardly room enough there, I should have thought," was the best answer he could summon up; "but it's more in your way than mine: my dancing days are over." At which Humphreys muttered and turned over to sleep, and the doctor intimated to the nurses that the patient was not out of the wood yet. When he was better able to express his views, Humphreys made his meaning clear, and received a promise that the thing should be done at once. He was so anxious to learn the result that the doctor, who seemed a little pensive next morning, saw that more harm than good would be done by saving up his report. "Well," he said, "I am afraid the ball is done for; the metal must have worn thin I

suppose. Anyhow it went all to bits with the first blow of the chisel."
"Well? go on, do!" said Humphreys impatiently. "Oh, you want to know
what we found in it, of course. Well, it was half full of stuff like ashes."
"Ashes? What did you make of them?" "I haven't thoroughly examined
them yet; there's hardly been time: but Cooper's made up his mind—I
dare say from something I said—that it's a case of cremation. Now don't
excite yourself, my good sir: yes, I must allow I think he's probably
right."

The maze is gone, and Lady Wardrop has forgiven Humphreys; in
fact I believe he married her niece. She was right, too, in her conjecture
that the stones in the temple were numbered. There had been a numeral
painted on the bottom of each. Some few of these had rubbed off, but
enough remained to enable Humphreys to reconstruct the inscription. It
ran thus:

PENETRANS AD INTERIORA MORTIS.

Grateful as Humphreys was to the memory of his uncle, he could not
quite forgive him for having burnt the journals and letters of the James
Wilson who had gifted Wilsthorpe with the maze and the temple. As to
the circumstances of that ancestor's death and burial no tradition survived; but his will, which was almost the only record of him accessible,
assigned an unusually generous legacy to a servant who bore an Italian
name.

Mr Cooper's view is that, humanly speaking, all these many solemn
events have a meaning for us, if our limited intelligence permitted of our
disintegrating it, while Mr Calton has been reminded of an aunt now
gone from us, who about the year 1866 had been lost for upwards of an
hour and a half in the maze at Covent Gardens, or it might be Hampton
Court.

One of the oddest things in the whole series of transactions is that the
book which contained the Parable has entirely disappeared. Humphreys
has never been able to find it since he copied out the passage to send to
Lady Wardrop.   1911

COUNT MAGNUS

By what means the papers out of which I have made a connected story
came into my hands is the last point which the reader will learn from
these pages. But it is necessary to prefix to my extracts from them a
statement of the form in which I possess them.

They consist, then, partly of a series of collections for a book of travels, such a volume as was a common product of the forties and fifties. Horace Marryat's *Journal of a Residence in Jutland and the Danish Isles* is a fair specimen of the class to which I allude. These books usually treated of some unfamiliar district on the Continent. They were illustrated with woodcuts or steel plates. They gave details of hotel accommodation, and of means of communication, such as we now expect to find in any well-regulated guidebook, and they dealt largely in reported conversations with intelligent foreigners, racy innkeepers and garrulous peasants. In a word, they were chatty.

Begun with the idea of furnishing material for such a book, my papers as they progressed assumed the character of a record of one single personal experience, and this record was continued up to the very eve, almost, of its termination.

The writer was a Mr Wraxall. For my knowledge of him I have to depend entirely on the evidence his writings afford, and from these I deduce that he was a man past middle age, possessed of some private means, and very much alone in the world. He had, it seems, no settled abode in England, but was a denizen of hotels and boarding-houses. It is probable that he entertained the idea of settling down at some future time which never came; and I think it also likely that the Pantechnicon fire in the early seventies must have destroyed a great deal that would have thrown light on his antecedents, for he refers once or twice to property of his that was warehoused at that establishment.

It is further apparent that Mr Wraxall had published a book, and that it treated of a holiday he had once taken in Brittany. More than this I cannot say about his work, because a diligent search in bibliographical works has convinced me that it must have appeared either anonymously or under a pseudonym.

As to his character, it is not difficult to form some superficial opinion. He must have been an intelligent and cultivated man. It seems that he was near being a Fellow of his college at Oxford—Brasenose, as I judge from the Calendar. His besetting fault was pretty clearly that of over-inquisitiveness, possibly a good fault in a traveller, certainly a fault for which this traveller paid dearly enough in the end.

On what proved to be his last expedition, he was plotting another book. Scandinavia, a region not widely known to Englishmen forty years ago, had struck him as an interesting field. He must have lighted on some old books of Swedish history or memoirs, and the idea had struck him that there was room for a book descriptive of travel in Sweden, interspersed with episodes from the history of some of the great Swedish families. He procured letters of introduction, therefore, to some persons of quality in Sweden, and set out thither in the early summer of 1863.

Of his travels in the North there is no need to speak, nor of his residence of some weeks in Stockholm. I need only mention that some *savant* resident there put him on the track of an important collection of family papers belonging to the proprietors of an ancient manor-house in Vestergothland, and obtained for him permission to examine them.

The manor-house, or *herrgård*, in question is to be called Råbäck (pronounced something like Roebeck), though that is not its name. It is one of the best buildings of its kind in all the country, and the picture of it in Dahlenberg's *Suecia antiqua et moderna*, engraved in 1694, shows it very much as the tourist may see it today. It was built soon after 1600, and is, roughly speaking, very much like an English house of that period in respect of material—red-brick with stone facings—and style. The man who built it was a scion of the great house of De la Gardie, and his descendants possess it still. De la Gardie is the name by which I will designate them when mention of them becomes necessary.

They received Mr Wraxall with great kindness and courtesy, and pressed him to stay in the house as long as his researches lasted. But, preferring to be independent, and mistrusting his powers of conversing in Swedish, he settled himself at the village inn, which turned out quite sufficiently comfortable, at any rate during the summer months. This arrangement would entail a short walk daily to and from the manor-house of something under a mile. The house itself stood in a park, and was protected—we should say grown up—with large old timber. Near it you found the walled garden, and then entered a close wood fringing one of the small lakes with which the whole country is pitted. Then came the wall of the demesne, and you climbed a steep knoll—a knob of rock lightly covered with soil—and on the top of this stood the church, fenced in with tall dark trees. It was a curious building to English eyes. The nave and aisles were low, and filled with pews and galleries. In the western gallery stood the handsome old organ, gaily painted, and with silver pipes. The ceiling was flat, and had been adorned by a seventeenth-century artist with a strange and hideous "Last Judgement," full of lurid flames, falling cities, burning ships, crying souls, and brown and smiling demons. Handsome brass coronae hung from the roof; the pulpit was like a doll's-house, covered with little painted wooden cherubs and saints; a stand with three hour-glasses was hinged to the preacher's desk. Such sights as these may be seen in many a church in Sweden now, but what distinguished this one was an addition to the original building. At the eastern end of the north aisle the builder of the manor-house had erected a mausoleum for himself and his family. It was a largish eight-sided building, lighted by a series of oval windows, and it had a domed roof, topped by a kind of pumpkin-shaped object rising into a spire, a form in which Swedish architects greatly delighted. The roof was of copper externally, and was painted black, while the walls, in common with those of the church, were staringly white. To this mausoleum there was no access from the church. It had a portal and steps of its own on the northern side.

Past the churchyard the path to the village goes, and not more than three or four minutes bring you to the inn door.

On the first day of his stay at Råbäck Mr Wraxall found the church door open, and made those notes of the interior which I have epitomized. Into the mausoleum, however, he could not make his way. He could by looking through the keyhole just descry that there were fine marble effigies and sarcophagi of copper, and a wealth of armorial ornament, which made him very anxious to spend some time in investigation.

The papers he had come to examine at the manor-house proved to be of just the kind he wanted for his book. There were family correspondence, journals, and account-books of the earliest owners of the estate, very carefully kept and clearly written, full of amusing and picturesque detail. The first De la Gardie appeared in them as a strong and capable man. Shortly after the building of the mansion there had been a period of distress in the district, and the peasants had risen and attacked several châteaux and done some damage. The owner of Råbäck took a leading part in suppressing the trouble, and there was reference to executions of ringleaders and severe punishments inflicted with no sparing hand.

The portrait of this Magnus de la Gardie was one of the best in the house, and Mr Wraxall studied it with no little interest after his day's work. He gives no detailed description of it, but I gather that the face impressed him rather by its power than by its beauty or goodness; in fact, he writes that Count Magnus was an almost phenomenally ugly man.

On this day Mr Wraxall took his supper with the family, and walked back in the late but still bright evening.

"I must remember," he writes, "to ask the sexton if he can let me into the mausoleum at the church. He evidently has access to it himself, for I saw him tonight standing on the steps, and, as I thought, locking or unlocking the door."

I find that early on the following day Mr Wraxall had some conversation with his landlord. His setting it down at such length as he does surprised me at first; but I soon realized that the papers I was reading were, at least in their beginning, the materials for the book he was meditating, and that it was to have been one of those quasi-journalistic productions which admit of the introduction of an admixture of conversational matter.

His object, he says, was to find out whether any traditions of Count Magnus de la Gardie lingered on in the scenes of that gentleman's activity, and whether the popular estimate of him were favourable or not. He found that the Count was decidedly not a favourite. If his tenants came late to their work on the days which they owed to him as Lord of the Manor, they were set on the wooden horse, or flogged and branded in the manor-house yard. One or two cases there were of men who had occupied lands which encroached on the lord's domain, and whose houses had been mysteriously burnt on a winter's night, with the whole family inside. But what seemed to dwell on the innkeeper's mind most—for he returned to the subject more than once—was that the Count had been on the Black Pilgrimage, and had brought something or someone back with him.

You will naturally inquire, as Mr Wraxall did, what the Black Pilgrimage may have been. But your curiosity on the point must remain unsatisfied for the time being, just as his did. The landlord was evidently unwilling to give a full answer, or indeed any answer, on the point, and, being called out for a moment, trotted off with obvious alacrity, only putting his head in at the door a few minutes afterwards to say that he was called away to Skara, and should not be back till evening.

So Mr Wraxall had to go unsatisfied to his day's work at the manorhouse. The papers on which he was just then engaged soon put his thoughts into another channel, for he had to occupy himself with glancing over the correspondence between Sophia Albertina in Stockholm and her married cousin Ulrica Leonora at Råbäck in the years 1705–10. The letters were of exceptional interest from the light they threw upon the culture of that period in Sweden, as anyone can testify who has read the full edition of them in the publications of the Swedish Historical Manuscripts Commission.

In the afternoon he had done with these, and after returning the boxes in which they were kept to their places on the shelf, he proceeded, very naturally, to take down some of the volumes nearest to them, in order to determine which of them had best be his principal subject of investigation next day. The shelf he had hit upon was occupied mostly by a collection of account-books in the writing of the first Count Magnus. But one among them was not an account-book, but a book of alchemical and other tracts in another sixteenth-century hand. Not being very familiar with alchemical literature, Mr Wraxall spends much space which he might have spared in setting out the names and beginnings of the various treatises: The book of the Phoenix, book of the Thirty Words, book of the Toad, book of Miriam, Turba philosophorum, and so forth; and then he announces with a good deal of circumstance his delight at finding, on a leaf originally left blank near the middle of the book, some writing of Count Magnus himself headed "Liber nigrae peregrinationis." It is true that only a few lines were written, but there was quite enough to show that the landlord had that morning been referring to a belief at least as old as the time of Count Magnus, and probably shared by him. This is the English of what was written:

"If any man desires to obtain a long life, if he would obtain a faithful messenger and see the blood of his enemies, it is necessary that he should first go into the city of Chorazin, and there salute the prince . . ." Here there was an erasure of one word, not very thoroughly done, so that Mr Wraxall felt pretty sure that he was right in reading it as *aëris* ("of the air"). But there was no more of the text copied, only a line in Latin: *"Quaere reliqua hujus materiei inter secretiora"* (See the rest of this matter among the more private things).

It could not be denied that this threw a rather lurid light upon the tastes and beliefs of the Count; but to Mr Wraxall, separated from him by nearly three centuries, the thought that he might have added to his general forcefulness alchemy, and to alchemy something like magic, only made him a more picturesque figure; and when, after a rather prolonged contemplation of his picture in the hall, Mr Wraxall set out on his homeward way, his mind was full of the thought of Count Magnus. He had no eyes for his surroundings, no perception of the evening scents of the woods or the evening light on the lake; and when all of a sudden he pulled up short, he was astonished to find himself already at the gate of the churchyard, and within a few minutes of his dinner. His eyes fell on the mausoleum.

"Ah," he said, "Count Magnus, there you are. I should dearly like to see you."

"Like many solitary men," he writes, "I have a habit of talking to myself aloud; and, unlike some of the Greek and Latin particles, I do not expect an answer. Certainly, and perhaps fortunately in this case, there was neither voice nor any that regarded: only the woman who, I suppose, was cleaning up the church, dropped some metallic object on the floor, whose clang startled me. Count Magnus, I think, sleeps sound enough."

That same evening the landlord of the inn, who had heard Mr Wraxall say that he wished to see the clerk or deacon (as he would be called in Sweden) of the parish, introduced him to that official in the inn parlour. A visit to the De la Gardie tomb-house was soon arranged for the next day, and a little general conversation ensued.

Mr Wraxall, remembering that one function of Scandinavian deacons is to teach candidates for Confirmation, thought he would refresh his own memory on a Biblical point.

"Can you tell me," he said, "anything about Chorazin?"

The deacon seemed startled, but readily reminded him how that village had once been denounced.

"To be sure," said Mr Wraxall; "it is, I suppose, quite a ruin now?"

"So I expect," replied the deacon. "I have heard some of our old priests say that Antichrist is to be born there; and there are tales—"

"Ah! what tales are those?" Mr Wraxall put in.

"Tales, I was going to say, which I have forgotten," said the deacon; and soon after that he said good night.

The landlord was now alone, and at Mr Wraxall's mercy; and that inquirer was not inclined to spare him.

"Herr Nielsen," he said, "I have found out something about the Black Pilgrimage. You may as well tell me what you know. What did the Count bring back with him?"

Swedes are habitually slow, perhaps, in answering, or perhaps the landlord was an exception. I am not sure; but Mr Wraxall notes that the landlord spent at least one minute in looking at him before he said anything at all. Then he came close up to his guest, and with a good deal of effort he spoke:

"Mr Wraxall, I can tell you this one little tale, and no more—not any more. You must not ask anything when I have done. In my grandfather's time—that is, ninety-two years ago—there were two men who said: 'The Count is dead; we do not care for him. We will go tonight and have a free hunt in his wood'—the long wood on the hill that you have seen behind Råbäck. Well, those that heard them say this, they said: 'No, do not go; we are sure you will meet with persons walking who should not be walking. They should be resting, not walking.' These men laughed. There were no forest-men to keep the wood, because no one wished to hunt there. The family were not here at the house. These men could do what they wished.

"Very well, they go to the wood that night. My grandfather was sitting here in this room. It was the summer, and a light night. With the window open, he could see out to the wood, and hear.

"So he sat there, and two or three men with him, and they listened. At first they hear nothing at all; then they hear someone—you know how far away it is—they hear someone scream, just as if the most inside part of his soul was twisted out of him. All of them in the room caught hold of each other, and they sat so for three-quarters of an hour. Then they hear someone else, only about three hundred ells off. They hear him laugh out loud: it was not one of those two men that laughed, and, indeed, they have all of them said that it was not any man at all. After that they hear a great door shut.

"Then, when it was just light with the sun, they all went to the priest. They said to him:

" 'Father, put on your gown and your ruff, and come to bury these men, Anders Bjornsen and Hans Thorbjorn.'

"You understand that they were sure these men were dead. So they went to the wood—my grandfather never forgot this. He said they were all like so many dead men themselves. The priest, too, he was in a white fear. He said when they came to him:

" 'I heard one cry in the night, and I heard one laugh afterwards. If I cannot forget that, I shall not be able to sleep again.'

"So they went to the wood, and they found these men on the edge of the wood. Hans Thorbjorn was standing with his back against a tree, and all the time he was pushing with his hands—pushing something away from him which was not there. So he was not dead. And they led him away, and took him to the house at Nykjoping, and he died before the winter; but he went on pushing with his hands. Also Anders Bjornsen was there; but he was dead. And I tell you this about Anders Bjornsen, that he was once a beautiful man, but now his face was not there, because the flesh of it was sucked away off the bones. You understand that? My grandfather did not forget that. And they laid him on the bier which they brought, and they put a cloth over his head, and the priest walked before; and they began to sing the psalm for the dead as well as they could. So, as they were singing the end of the first verse, one fell down, who was carrying the head of the bier, and the others looked back, and they saw that the cloth had fallen off, and the eyes of Anders Bjornsen were looking up, because there was nothing to close over them. And this they could not bear. Therefore the priest laid the cloth upon him, and sent for a spade, and they buried him in that place."

The next day Mr Wraxall records that the deacon called for him soon after his breakfast, and took him to the church and mausoleum. He noticed that the key of the latter was hung on a nail just by the pulpit, and it occurred to him that, as the church door seemed to be left unlocked as a rule, it would not be difficult for him to pay a second and more private visit to the monuments if there proved to be more of interest among them than could be digested at first. The building, when he entered it, he found not unimposing. The monuments, mostly large erections of the seventeenth and eighteenth centuries, were dignified if luxuriant, and the epitaphs and heraldry were copious. The central space of the domed room was occupied by three copper sarcophagi, covered with finely-engraved ornament. Two of them had, as is commonly the case in Denmark and Sweden, a large metal crucifix on the lid. The third, that of Count Magnus, as it appeared, had, instead of that, a full-length effigy engraved upon it, and round the edge were several bands of similar ornament representing various scenes. One was a battle, with cannon belching out smoke, and walled towns, and troops of pikemen. Another showed an execution. In a third, among trees, was a man running at full speed, with flying hair and outstretched hands. After him followed a strange form; it would be hard to say whether the artist had intended it for a man, and was unable to give the requisite similitude, or whether it was intentionally made as monstrous as it looked. In view of the skill with which the rest of the drawing was done, Mr Wraxall felt inclined to adopt the latter idea. The figure was unduly short, and was for the most part muffled in a hooded garment which swept the ground. The only part of the form which projected from that shelter was not shaped like any hand or arm. Mr Wraxall compares it to the tentacle of a devil-fish, and continues: "On seeing this, I said to myself, 'This, then, which is evidently an allegorical representation of some kind—a fiend pursuing a hunted soul—may be the origin of the story of Count Magnus and his mysterious companion. Let us see how the huntsman is pictured: doubtless it will be a demon blowing his horn.' " But, as it turned out, there was no such sensational figure, only the semblance of a cloaked man on a hillock, who stood leaning on a stick, and watching the hunt with an interest which the engraver had tried to express in his attitude.

Mr Wraxall noted the finely-worked and massive steel padlocks—three in number—which secured the sarcophagus. One of them, he saw, was detached, and lay on the pavement. And then, unwilling to delay the deacon longer or to waste his own working-time, he made his way onward to the manor-house.

"It is curious," he notes, "how on retracing a familiar path one's thoughts engross one to the absolute exclusion of surrounding objects. Tonight, for the second time, I had entirely failed to notice where I was going (I had planned a private visit to the tomb-house to copy the epitaphs), when I suddenly, as it were, awoke to consciousness, and found myself (as before) turning in at the churchyard gate, and, I believe, singing or chanting some such words as, 'Are you awake, Count Magnus? Are you asleep, Count Magnus?' and then something more which I have failed to recollect. It seemed to me that I must have been behaving in this nonsensical way for some time."

He found the key of the mausoleum where he had expected to find it, and copied the greater part of what he wanted; in fact, he stayed until the light began to fail him.

"I must have been wrong," he writes, "in saying that one of the padlocks of my Count's sarcophagus was unfastened; I see tonight that two are loose. I picked both up, and laid them carefully on the window-ledge, after trying unsuccessfully to close them. The remaining one is still firm, and, though I take it to be a spring lock, I cannot guess how it is opened. Had I succeeded in undoing it, I am almost afraid I should have taken the liberty of opening the sarcophagus. It is strange, the interest I feel in the personality of this, I fear, somewhat ferocious and grim old noble."

The day following was, as it turned out, the last of Mr Wraxall's stay at Råbäck. He received letters connected with certain investments which made it desirable that he should return to England; his work among the papers was practically done, and travelling was slow. He decided, therefore, to make his farewells, put some finishing touches to his notes, and be off.

These finishing touches and farewells, as it turned out, took more time than he had expected. The hospitable family insisted on his staying to dine with them—they dined at three—and it was verging on half-past six before he was outside the iron gates of Råbäck. He dwelt on every step of his walk by the lake, determined to saturate himself, now that he trod it for the last time, in the sentiment of the place and hour. And when he reached the summit of the churchyard knoll, he lingered for many minutes, gazing at the limitless prospect of woods near and distant, all dark beneath a sky of liquid green. When at last he turned to go, the thought struck him that surely he must bid farewell to Count Magnus as well as the rest of the De la Gardies. The church was but twenty yards away, and he knew where the key of the mausoleum hung. It was not long before he was standing over the great copper coffin, and, as usual, talking to himself aloud. "You may have been a bit of a rascal in your time, Magnus," he was saying, "but for all that I should like to see you, or, rather—"

"Just at that instant," he says, "I felt a blow on my foot. Hastily enough I drew it back, and something fell on the pavement with a clash. It was the third, the last of the three padlocks which had fastened the sarcophagus. I stooped to pick it up, and—Heaven is my witness that I am writing only the bare truth—before I had raised myself there was a sound of metal hinges creaking, and I distinctly saw the lid shifting upwards. I may have behaved like a coward, but I could not for my life stay for one moment. I was outside that dreadful building in less time than I can write—almost as quickly as I could have said—the words; and what frightens me yet more, I could not turn the key in the lock. As I sit here in my room noting these facts, I ask myself (it was not twenty minutes ago) whether that noise of creaking metal continued, and I cannot tell whether it did or not. I only know that there was something more than I have written that alarmed me, but whether it was sound or sight I am not able to remember. What is this that I have done?"

Poor Mr Wraxall! He set out on his journey to England on the next day, as he had planned, and he reached England in safety; and yet, as I gather from his changed hand and inconsequent jottings, a broken man. One of several small notebooks that have come to me with his papers gives, not a key to, but a kind of inkling of, his experiences. Much of his journey was made by canal-boat, and I find not less than six painful attempts to enumerate and describe his fellow-passengers. The entries are of this kind:

24. Pastor of village in Skåne. Usual black coat and soft black hat.
25. Commercial traveller from Stockholm going to Trollhättan. Black cloak, brown hat.
26. Man in long black cloak, broad-leafed hat, very old-fashioned.

This entry is lined out, and a note added: "Perhaps identical with No. 13. Have not yet seen his face." On referring to No. 13, I find that he is a Roman priest in a cassock.

The net result of the reckoning is always the same. Twenty-eight people appear in the enumeration, one being always a man in a long black cloak and broad hat, and the other a "short figure in dark cloak and hood." On the other hand, it is always noted that only twenty-six passengers appear at meals, and that the man in the cloak is perhaps absent, and the short figure is certainly absent.

On reaching England, it appears that Mr Wraxall landed at Harwich, and that he resolved at once to put himself out of the reach of some person or persons whom he never specifies, but whom he had evidently come to regard as his pursuers. Accordingly he took a vehicle—it was a closed fly—not trusting the railway, and drove across country to the village of Belchamp St Paul. It was about nine o'clock on a moonlight August night when he neared the place. He was sitting forward, and looking out of the window at the fields and thickets—there was little else to be seen—racing past him. Suddenly he came to a cross-road. At the corner two figures were standing motionless; both were in dark cloaks; the taller one wore a hat, the shorter a hood. He had no time to see their faces, nor did they make any motion that he could discern. Yet the horse shied violently and broke into a gallop, and Mr Wraxall sank back into his seat in something like desperation. He had seen them before.

Arrived at Belchamp St Paul, he was fortunate enough to find a decent furnished lodging, and for the next twenty-four hours he lived, comparatively speaking, in peace. His last notes were written on this day. They are too disjointed and ejaculatory to be given here in full, but the substance of them is clear enough. He is expecting a visit from his pursuers—how or when he knows not—and his constant cry is "What has he done?" and "Is there no hope?" Doctors, he knows, would call him mad, policemen would laugh at him. The parson is away. What can he do but lock his door and cry to God?

People still remembered last year at Belchamp St Paul how a strange gentleman came one evening in August years back; and how the next morning but one he was found dead, and there was an inquest; and the jury that viewed the body fainted, seven of 'em did, and none of 'em wouldn't speak to what they see, and the verdict was visitation of God; and how the people as kep' the 'ouse moved out that same week, and went away from that part. But they do not, I think, know that any glimmer of light has ever been thrown, or could be thrown, on the mystery. It so happened that last year the little house came into my hands as part of a legacy. It had stood empty since 1863, and there seemed no prospect of letting it; so I had it pulled down, and the papers of which I have given you an abstract were found in a forgotten cupboard under the window in the best bedroom.   1904

EDITH WHARTON

MISS MARY PASK

I

It was not till the following spring that I plucked up courage to tell Mrs. Bridgeworth what had happened to me that night at Morgat.

In the first place, Mrs. Bridgeworth was in America; and after the night in question I lingered on abroad for several months—not for pleasure, God knows, but because of a nervous collapse supposed to be the result of having taken up my work again too soon after my touch of fever in Egypt. But, in any case, if I had been door to door with Grace Bridgeworth I could not have spoken of the affair before, to her or to anyone else; not till I had been rest-cured and built up again at one of those wonderful Swiss sanatoria where they clean the cobwebs out of you. I could not even have written to her—not to save my life. The happenings of that night had to be overlaid with layer upon layer of time and forgetfulness before I could tolerate any return to them.

The beginning was idiotically simple; just the sudden reflex of a New England conscience acting on an enfeebled constitution. I had been painting in Brittany, in lovely but uncertain autumn weather, one day all blue and silver, the next shrieking gales or driving fog. There is a rough little whitewashed inn out on the Pointe du Raz, swarmed over by tourists in summer but a sea-washed solitude in autumn; and there I was staying and trying to do waves, when someone said: "You ought to go over to Cape something else, beyond Morgat."

I went, and had a silver-and-blue day there; and on the way back the name of Morgat set up an unexpected association of ideas: Morgat—Grace Bridgeworth—Grace's sister, Mary Pask—"You know my darling Mary has a little place now near Morgat; if you ever go to Brittany do go to see her. She lives such a lonely life—it makes me so unhappy."

That was the way it came about. I had known Mrs. Bridgeworth well for years, but had only a hazy intermittent acquaintance with Mary Pask, her older and unmarried sister. Grace and she were greatly attached to each other, I knew; it had been Grace's chief sorrow, when she married my old friend Horace Bridgeworth, and went to live in New York, that Mary, from whom she had never before been separated, obstinately lingered on in Europe, where the two sisters had been traveling since their mother's death. I never quite understood why Mary Pask refused to join Grace in America. Grace said it was because she was "too artistic"— but, knowing the elder Miss Pask, and the extremely elementary nature of her interest in art, I wondered whether it were not rather because she disliked Horace Bridgeworth. There was a third alternative—more conceivable if one knew Horace—and that was that she may have liked him too much. But that again became untenable (at least I supposed it did) when one knew Miss Pask: Miss Pask with her round flushed face, her innocent bulging eyes, her old-maidish flat decorated with art-tidies, and her vague and timid philanthropy. Aspire to Horace—!

Well, it was all rather puzzling, or would have been if it had been interesting enough to be worth puzzling over. But it was not. Mary Pask was like hundreds of other dowdy old maids, cheerful derelicts content with their innumerable little substitutes for living. Even Grace would not have interested me particularly if she hadn't happened to marry one of my oldest friends, and to be kind to his friends. She was a handsome, capable and rather dull woman, absorbed in her husband and children, and without an ounce of imagination; and between her attachment to her sister and Mary Pask's worship of her there lay the inevitable gulf between the feelings of the sentimentally unemployed and those whose affections are satisfied. But a close intimacy had linked the two sisters before Grace's marriage, and Grace was one of the sweet conscientious women who go on using the language of devotion about people whom they live happily without seeing; so that when she said: "You know it's years since Mary and I have been together—not since little Molly was born. If only she'd come to America! Just think . . . Molly is six, and has never seen her darling auntie. . . ." When she said this, and added: "If you go to Brittany promise me you'll look up my Mary," I was moved in that dim depth of one where unnecessary obligations are contracted.

And so it came about that, on that silver-and-blue afternoon, the idea "Morgat—Mary Pask—to please Grace" suddenly unlocked the sense of duty in me. Very well: I would chuck a few things into my bag, do my day's painting, go to see Miss Pask when the light faded, and spend the night at the inn at Morgat. To this end I ordered a rickety one-horse vehicle to await me at the inn when I got back from my painting, and in it I started out toward sunset to hunt for Mary Pask. . . .

As suddenly as a pair of hands clapped over one's eyes, the sea fog shut down on us. A minute before we had been driving over a wide bare upland, our backs turned to a sunset that crimsoned the road ahead; now the densest night enveloped us. No one had been able to tell me exactly where Miss Pask lived; but I thought it likely that I should find out at the fishers' hamlet toward which we were trying to make our way. And I was right . . . an old man in a doorway said: Yes—over the next rise, and then down a lane to the left that led to the sea; the American lady who always used to dress in white. Oh, *he* knew . . . near the *Baie des Trépassés.*

"Yes; but how can we see to find it? I don't know the place," grumbled the reluctant boy who was driving me.

"You will when we get there," I remarked.

"Yes—and the horse foundered meantime! I can't risk it, sir; I'll get into trouble with the *patron.*"

Finally an opportune argument induced him to get out and lead the stumbling horse, and we continued on our way. We seemed to crawl on for a long time through a wet blackness impenetrable to the glimmer of our only lamp. But now and then the pall lifted or its folds divided; and then our feeble light would drag out of the night some perfectly commonplace object—a white gate, a cow's staring face, a heap of roadside stones—made portentous and incredible by being thus detached from its setting, capriciously thrust at us, and as suddenly withdrawn. After each of these projections the darkness grew three times as thick; and the sense I had had for some time of descending a gradual slope now became that of scrambling down a precipice. I jumped out hurriedly and joined my young driver at the horse's head.

"I can't go on—I won't, sir!" he whimpered.

"Why, see, there's a light over there—just ahead!"

The veil swayed aside, and we beheld two faintly illuminated squares in a low mass that was surely the front of a house.

"Get me as far as that—then you can go back if you like."

The veil dropped again; but the boy had seen the lights and took heart. Certainly there was a house ahead of us; and certainly it must be Miss Pask's, since there could hardly be two in such a desert. Besides, the old man in the hamlet had said: "Near the sea"; and those endless modulations of the ocean's voice, so familiar in every corner of the Breton land that one gets to measure distances by them rather than by visual means, had told me for some time past that we must be making for the shore. The boy continued to lead the horse on without making any answer. The fog had shut in more closely than ever, and our lamp merely showed us the big round drops of wet on the horse's shaggy quarters.

The boy stopped with a jerk. "There's no house—we're going straight down to the sea."

"But you saw those lights, didn't you?"

"I thought I did. But where are they now? The fog's thinner again. Look—I can make out trees ahead. But there are no lights any more."

"Perhaps the people have gone to bed," I suggested jocosely.

"Then hadn't we better turn back, sir?"

"What—two yards from the gate?"

The boy was silent: certainly there was a gate ahead, and presumably, behind the dripping trees, some sort of dwelling. Unless there was just a field and the sea . . . the sea whose hungry voice I heard asking and asking, close below us. No wonder the place was called the Bay of the Dead! But what could have induced the rosy benevolent Mary Pask to come and bury herself there? Of course the boy wouldn't wait for me . . . I knew that . . . the *Baie des Trépassés* indeed! The sea whined down there as if it were feeding time, and the Furies, its keepers, had forgotten it. . . .

There *was* the gate! My hand had struck against it. I felt along to the latch, undid it, and brushed between wet bushes to the house front. Not a candle glint anywhere. If the house were indeed Miss Pask's, she certainly kept early hours. . . .

II

Night and fog were now one, and the darkness as thick as a blanket. I felt vainly about for a bell. At last my hand came in contact with a knocker and I lifted it. The clatter with which it fell sent a prolonged echo through the silence; but for a minute or two nothing else happened.

"There's no one there, I tell you!" the boy called impatiently from the gate.

But there was. I had heard no steps inside, but presently a bolt shot back, and an old woman in a peasant's cap pushed her head out. She had set her candle down on a table behind her, so that her face, aureoled with lacy wings, was in obscurity; but I knew she was old by the stoop of her shoulders and her fumbling movements. The candlelight, which made her invisible, fell full on my face, and she looked at me.

"This is Miss Mary Pask's house?"

"Yes, sir." Her voice—a very old voice—was pleasant enough, unsurprised and even friendly.

"I'll tell her," she added, shuffling off.

"Do you think she'll see me?" I threw after her.

"Oh, why not? The idea!" she almost chuckled. As she retreated I saw that she was wrapped in a shawl and had a cotton umbrella under her arm. Obviously she was going out—perhaps going home for the night. I wondered if Mary Pask lived all alone in her hermitage.

The old woman disappeared with the candle and I was left in total darkness. After an interval I heard a door shut at the back of the house and then a slow clumping of aged *sabots* along the flags outside. The old woman had evidently picked up her *sabots* in the kitchen and left the house. I wondered if she had told Miss Pask of my presence before going, or whether she had just left me there, the butt of some grim practical joke of her own. Certainly there was no sound within doors. The footsteps died out, I heard a gate click—then complete silence closed in again like the fog.

"I wonder—" I began within myself; and at that moment a smothered memory struggled abruptly to the surface of my languid mind.

"But she's *dead*—Mary Pask is *dead!*" I almost screamed it aloud in my amazement.

It was incredible, the tricks my memory had played on me since my fever! I had known for nearly a year that Mary Pask was dead—had died suddenly the previous autumn—and though I had been thinking of her almost continuously for the last two or three days it was only now that the forgotten fact of her death suddenly burst up again to consciousness.

Dead! But hadn't I found Grace Bridgeworth in tears and crepe the very day I had gone to bid her good-bye before sailing for Egypt? Hadn't she laid the cable before my eyes, her own streaming with tears while I read: "Sister died suddenly this morning requested burial in garden of house particulars by letter"—with the signature of the American Consul at Brest, a friend of Bridgeworth's I seemed to recall? I could see the very words of the message printed on the darkness before me.

As I stood there I was a good deal more disturbed by the discovery of the gap in my memory than by the fact of being alone in a pitch-dark house, either empty or else inhabited by strangers. Once before of late I had noted this queer temporary blotting-out of some well-known fact; and here was a second instance of it. Decidedly, I wasn't as well over my illness as the doctors had told me. . . . Well, I would get back to Morgat and lie up there for a day or two, doing nothing, just eating and sleeping. . . .

In my self-absorption I had lost my bearings, and no longer remembered where the door was. I felt in every pocket in turn for a match—but since the doctors had made me give up smoking, why should I have found one?

The failure to find a match increased my sense of irritated helplessness, and I was groping clumsily about the hall among the angles of unseen furniture when a light slanted along the rough-cast wall of the stairs. I followed its direction, and on the landing above me I saw a figure in white shading a candle with one hand and looking down. A chill ran along my spine, for the figure bore a strange resemblance to that of Mary Pask as I used to know her.

"Oh, it's *you!*" she exclaimed in the cracked twittering voice which was at one moment like an old woman's quaver, at another like a boy's falsetto. She came shuffling down in her baggy white garments, with her usual clumsy swaying movements; but I noticed that her steps on the wooden stairs were soundless. Well—they would be, naturally!

I stood without a word, gazing up at the strange vision above me, and saying to myself: "There's nothing there, nothing whatever. It's your digestion, or your eyes, or some damned thing wrong with you some-where—"

But there was the candle, at any rate; and as it drew nearer, and lit up the place about me, I turned and caught hold of the doorlatch. For, remember, I had seen the cable, and Grace in crepe. . . .

"Why, what's the matter? I assure you, you don't disturb me!" the white figure twittered; adding, with a faint laugh: "I don't have so many visitors nowadays—"

She had reached the hall, and stood before me, lifting her candle shakily and peering up into my face. "You haven't changed—not as much as I should have thought. But I have, haven't I?" She appealed to me with another laugh; and abruptly she laid her hand on my arm. I looked down at the hand, and thought to myself: *"That* can't deceive me."

I have always been a noticer of hands. The key to character that other people seek in the eyes, the mouth, the modeling of the skull, I find in the curve of the nails, the cut of the finger tips, the way the palm, rosy or sallow, smooth or seamed, swells up from its base. I remembered Mary Pask's hand vividly because it was so like a caricature of herself; round, puffy, pink, yet prematurely old and useless. And there, unmistakably, it lay on my sleeve: but changed and shriveled—somehow like one of those pale freckled toadstools that the least touch resolves to dust . . . Well—to dust? Of course . . .

I looked at the soft wrinkled fingers, with their foolish little oval finger tips that used to be so innocently and naturally pink, and now were blue under the yellowing nails—and my flesh rose in ridges of fear.

"Come in, come in," she fluted, cocking her white untidy head on one side and rolling her bulging blue eyes at me. The horrible thing was that she still practiced the same arts, all the childish wiles of a clumsy caper-ing coquetry. I felt her pull on my sleeve and it drew me in her wake like a steel cable.

The room she led me into was—well, "unchanged" is the term gener-ally used in such cases. For as a rule, after people die, things are tidied up, furniture is sold, remembrances are dispatched to the family. But some morbid piety (or Grace's instructions, perhaps) had kept this room looking exactly as I supposed it had in Miss Pask's lifetime. I wasn't in the mood for noting details; but in the faint dabble of moving candle-light I was half aware of bedraggled cushions, odds and ends of copper pots, and a jar holding a faded branch of some late-flowering shrub. A real Mary Pask "interior"!

The white figure flitted spectrally to the chimney piece, lit two more candles, and set down the third on a table. I hadn't supposed I was superstitious—but those three candles! Hardly knowing what I did, I hurriedly bent and blew one out. Her laugh sounded behind me.

"Three candles—you still mind that sort of thing? I've got beyond all that, you know," she chuckled. "Such a comfort . . . such a sense of freedom. . . ." A fresh shiver joined the others already coursing over me.

"Come and sit down by me," she entreated, sinking to a sofa. "It's such an age since I've seen a living being!"

Her choice of terms was certainly strange, and as she leaned back on the white slippery sofa and beckoned me with one of those unburied hands my impulse was to turn and run. But her old face, hovering there in the candlelight, with the unnaturally red cheeks like varnished apples and the blue eyes swimming in vague kindliness, seemed to appeal to me against my cowardice, to remind me that, dead or alive, Mary Pask would never harm a fly.

"Do sit down!" she repeated, and I took the other corner of the sofa.

"It's so wonderfully good of you—I suppose Grace asked you to come?" She laughed again—her conversation had always been punctuated by rambling laughter. "It's an event—quite an event! I've had so few visitors since my death, you see."

Another bucketful of cold water ran over me; but I looked at her resolutely, and again the innocence of her face disarmed me.

I cleared my throat and spoke—with a huge panting effort, as if I had been heaving up a gravestone. "You live here alone?" I brought out.

"Ah, I'm glad to hear your voice—I still remember voices, though I hear so few," she murmured dreamily. "Yes—I live here alone. The old woman you saw goes away at night. She won't stay after dark . . . she says she can't. Isn't it funny? But it doesn't matter; I like the darkness." She leaned to me with one of her irrelevant smiles. "The dead," she said, "naturally get used to it."

Once more I cleared my throat; but nothing followed.

She continued to gaze at me with confidential blinks. "And Grace? Tell me all about my darling. I wish I could have seen her again . . . just once." Her laugh came out grotesquely. "When she got the news of my death—were you with her? Was she terribly upset?"

I stumbled to my feet with a meaningless stammer. I couldn't answer—I couldn't go on looking at her.

"Ah, I see . . . it's too painful," she acquiesced, her eyes brimming, and she turned her shaking head away.

"But after all . . . I'm glad she was so sorry. . . . It's what I've been longing to be told, and hardly hoped for. Grace forgets. . . ." She stood up too and flitted across the room, wavering nearer and nearer to the door.

"Thank God," I thought, "she's going."

"Do you know this place by daylight?" she asked abruptly.

I shook my head.

"It's very beautiful. But you wouldn't have seen *me* then. You'd have had to take your choice between me and the landscape. I hate the light—it makes my head ache. And so I sleep all day. I was just waking up when you came." She smiled at me with an increasing air of confidence. "Do you know where I usually sleep? Down below there—in the garden!" Her laugh shrilled out again. "There's a shady corner down at the bottom where the sun never bothers one. Sometimes I sleep there till the stars come out."

The phrase about the garden, in the consul's cable, came back to me and I thought: "After all, it's not such an unhappy state. I wonder if she isn't better off than when she was alive?"

Perhaps she was—but I was sure I wasn't, in her company. And her way of sidling nearer to the door made me distinctly want to reach it before she did. In a rush of cowardice I strode ahead of her—but a second later she had the latch in her hand and was leaning against the panels, her long white raiment hanging about her like graveclothes. She drooped her head a little sideways and peered at me under her lashless lids.

"You're not going?" she reproached me.

I dived down in vain for my missing voice, and silently signed that I was.

"Going—going away? Altogether?" Her eyes were still fixed on me, and I saw two tears gather in their corners and run down over the red glistening circles on her cheeks. "Oh, but you mustn't," she said gently. "I'm too lonely. . . ."

I stammered something inarticulate, my eyes on the blue-nailed hand that grasped the latch. Suddenly the window behind us crashed open, and a gust of wind, surging in out of the blackness, extinguished the candle on the nearest chimney corner. I glanced back nervously to see if the other candle were going out too.

"You don't like the noise of the wind? I do. It's all I have to talk to. People don't like me much since I've been dead. Queer, isn't it? The peasants are so superstitious. At times I'm really lonely. . . ." Her voice cracked in a last effort at laughter, and she swayed toward me, one hand still on the latch.

"Lonely, lonely! If you *knew* how lonely! It was a lie when I told you I wasn't! And now you come, and your face looks friendly . . . and you say you're going to leave me! No—no—no—you shan't! Or else, why did you come? It's cruel . . . I used to think I knew what loneliness was . . . after Grace married, you know. Grace thought she was always thinking of me, but she wasn't. She called me 'darling,' but she was thinking of her husband and children. I said to myself then: 'You couldn't be lonelier if you were dead.' But I know better now. . . . There's been no loneliness like this last year's . . . none! And sometimes I sit here and think: 'If a man came along someday and took a fancy to you?' " She gave another wavering cackle. "Well, such things *have* happened, you know, even after youth's gone . . . a man who'd had his troubles too. But no one came till tonight . . . and now you say you're going!" Suddenly she flung herself toward me. "Oh, stay with me, stay with me . . . just tonight. . . . It's so sweet and quiet here. . . . No one need know . . . no one will ever come and trouble us."

I ought to have shut the window when the first gust came. I might have known there would soon be another, fiercer one. It came now, slamming back the loose-hinged lattice, filling the room with the noise of the sea and with wet swirls of fog, and dashing the other candle to the floor. The light went out, and I stood there—we stood there—lost to each other in the roaring coiling darkness. My heart seemed to stop beating; I had to fetch up my breath with great heaves that covered me with sweat. The door—the door—well, I knew I had been facing it when the candle went. Something white and wraithlike seemed to melt and crumple up before me in the night, and avoiding the spot where it had sunk away I stumbled around it in a wide circle, got the latch in my hand, caught my foot in a scarf or sleeve, trailing loose and invisible, and freed myself with a jerk from this last obstacle. I had the door open now. As I got into the hall I heard a whimper from the blackness behind me; but I scrambled on to the hall door, dragged it open and bolted out into the night. I slammed the door on that pitiful low whimper, and the fog and wind enveloped me in healing arms.

III

When I was well enough to trust myself to think about it all again I found that a very little thinking got my temperature up, and my heart hammering in my throat. No use . . . I simply couldn't stand it . . . for I'd seen Grace Bridgeworth in crepe, weeping over the cable, and yet I'd sat and talked with her sister, on the same sofa—her sister who'd been dead a year!

The circle was a vicious one; I couldn't break through it. The fact that I was down with fever the next morning might have explained it; yet I couldn't get away from the clinging reality of the vision. Supposing it *was* a ghost I had been talking to, and not a mere projection of my fever? Supposing something survived of Mary Pask—enough to cry out to me the unuttered loneliness of a lifetime, to express at last what the living woman had always had to keep dumb and hidden? The thought moved me curiously—in my weakness I lay and wept over it. No end of women were like that, I supposed, and perhaps, after death, if they got their chance they tried to use it. . . . Old tales and legends floated through my mind; the bride of Corinth, the medieval vampire—but what names to attach to the plaintive image of Mary Pask!

My weak mind wandered in and out among these visions and conjectures, and the longer I lived with them the more convinced I became that something *which had been Mary Pask* had talked with me that night. . . . I made up my mind, when I was up again, to drive back to the place (in broad daylight, this time), to hunt out the grave in the garden—that "shady corner where the sun never bothers one"—and appease the poor ghost with a few flowers. But the doctors decided otherwise; and perhaps my weak will unknowingly abetted them. At any rate, I yielded to their insistence that I should be driven straight from my hotel to the train for Paris, and thence shipped, like a piece of luggage, to the Swiss sanatorium they had in view for me. Of course I meant to come back when I was patched up again . . . and meanwhile, more and more tenderly, but more intermittently, my thoughts went back from my snow mountain to that wailing autumn night above the *Baie des Trépassés,* and the revelation of the dead Mary Pask who was so much more real to me than ever the living one had been.

IV

After all, why should I tell Grace Bridgeworth—ever? I had had a glimpse of things that were really no business of hers. If the revelation had been vouchsafed to me, ought I not to bury it in those deepest depths where the inexplicable and the unforgettable sleep together? And besides, what interest could there be to a woman like Grace in a tale she could neither understand nor believe in? She would just set me down as "queer"—and enough people had done that already. My first object, when I finally did get back to New York, was to convince everybody of my complete return to mental and physical soundness; and into this scheme of evidence my experience with Mary Pask did not seem to fit. All things considered, I would hold my tongue.

But after a while the thought of the grave began to trouble me. I wondered if Grace had ever had a proper gravestone put on it. The queer neglected look of the house gave me the idea that perhaps she had done nothing—had brushed the whole matter aside, to be attended to when she next went abroad. "Grace forgets," I heard the poor ghost quaver. . . . No, decidedly, there could be no harm in putting (tactfully) just that one question about the care of the grave; the more so as I was beginning to reproach myself for not having gone back to see with my own eyes how it was kept. . . .

Grace and Horace welcomed me with all their old friendliness, and I soon slipped into the habit of dropping in on them for a meal when I thought they were likely to be alone. Nevertheless my opportunity didn't come at once—I had to wait for some weeks. And then one evening, when Horace was dining out and I sat alone with Grace, my glance lit on a photograph of her sister—an old faded photograph which seemed to meet my eyes reproachfully.

"By the way, Grace," I began with a jerk, "I don't believe I ever told you: I went down to that little place of . . . of your sister's the day before I had that bad relapse."

At once her face lit up emotionally. "No, you never told me. How sweet of you to go!" The ready tears overbrimmed her eyes. "I'm *so* glad you did." She lowered her voice and added softly: "And did you see her?"

The question sent one of my old shudders over me. I looked with amazement at Mrs. Bridgeworth's plump face, smiling at me through a veil of painless tears. "I do reproach myself more and more about darling Mary," she added tremulously. "But tell me—tell me everything."

There was a knot in my throat; I felt almost as comfortable as I had in Mary Pask's own presence. Yet I had never before noticed anything uncanny about Grace Bridgeworth. I forced my voice up to my lips.

"Everything? Oh, I can't—" I tried to smile.

"But you did see her?"

I managed to nod, still smiling.

Her face grew suddenly haggard—yes, haggard! "And the change was so dreadful that you can't speak of it? Tell me—was that it?"

I shook my head. After all, what had shocked me was that the change was so slight—that between being dead and alive there seemed after all to be so little difference, except that of a mysterious increase in reality. But Grace's eyes were still searching me insistently. "You must tell me," she reiterated. "I know I ought to have gone there long ago—"

"Yes; perhaps you ought." I hesitated. "To see about the grave, at least. . . ."

She sat silent, her eyes still on my face. Her tears had stopped, but her look of solicitude slowly grew into a stare of something like terror. Hesitatingly, almost reluctantly, she stretched out her hand and laid it on mine for an instant. "Dear old friend—" she began.

"Unfortunately," I interrupted, "I couldn't get back myself to see the grave . . . because I was taken ill the next day."

"Yes, yes; of course. I know." She paused. "Are you *sure* you went there at all?" she asked abruptly.

"Sure? Good Lord—" It was my turn to stare. "Do you suspect me of not being quite right yet?" I suggested with an uneasy laugh.

"No—no . . . of course not . . . but I don't understand."

"Understand what? I went into the house . . . I saw everything, in fact, *but* her grave. . . ."

"Her grave?" Grace jumped up, clasping her hands on her breast and darting away from me. At the other end of the room she stood and gazed, and then moved slowly back.

"Then, after all—I wonder?" She held her eyes on me, half fearful and half reassured. "Could it be simply that you never heard?"

"Never heard?"

"But it was in all the papers! Don't you ever read them? I meant to write . . . I thought I *had* written . . . but I said: 'At any rate he'll see it in the papers.' . . . You know I'm always lazy about letters. . . ."

"See what in the papers?"

"Why, that she *didn't* die. . . . She isn't dead! There isn't any grave, my dear man! It was only a cataleptic trance . . . an extraordinary case, the doctors say. . . . But didn't she tell you all about it—if you say you saw her?" She burst into half-hysterical laughter: "Surely she must have told you that she wasn't dead?"

"No," I said slowly, "she didn't tell me that."

We talked about it together for a long time after that—talked on till Horace came back from his men's dinner, after midnight. Grace insisted on going in and out of the whole subject, over and over again. As she kept repeating, it was certainly the only time that poor Mary had ever been in the papers. But though I sat and listened patiently I couldn't get up any real interest in what she said. I felt I should never again be interested in Mary Pask, or in anything concerning her.   1925

THE LOOKING GLASS

I

Mrs. Attlee had never been able to understand why there was any harm in giving people a little encouragement when they needed it.

Sitting back in her comfortable armchair by the fire, her working days over, and her muscular masseuse's hands lying swollen and powerless on her knee, she was at leisure to turn the problem over, and ponder it as there had never been time to do before.

Mrs. Attlee was so infirm now that, when her widowed daughter-in-law was away for the day, her granddaughter Moyra Attlee had to stay with her until the kitchen girl had prepared the cold supper, and could come in and sit in the parlor.

"You'd be surprised, you know, my dear, to find how discouraged the grand people get, in those big houses with all the help, and the silver dinner plates, and a bell always handy if the fire wants poking, or the pet dog asks for a drink. . . . And what'd a masseuse be good for, if she didn't jolly up their minds a little along with their muscles?—as Dr. Welbridge used to say to me many a time, when he'd given me a difficult patient. And he always gave me the most difficult," she added proudly.

She paused, aware (for even now little escaped her) that Moyra had ceased to listen, but accepting the fact resignedly, as she did most things in the slow decline of her days.

"It's a fine afternoon," she reflected, "and likely she's fidgety because there's a new movie on; or that young fellow's fixed it up to get back earlier from New York. . . ."

She relapsed into silence, following her thoughts; but presently, as happens with old people, they came to the surface again.

"And I hope I'm a good Catholic, as I said to Father Divott the other day, and at peace with heaven, if ever I was took suddenly—but no matter what happens I've got to risk my punishment for the wrong I did to Mrs. Clingsland, because as long as I've never repented it there's no use telling Father Divott about it. Is there?"

Mrs. Attlee heaved an introspective sigh. Like many humble persons of her kind and creed, she had a vague idea that a sin unrevealed was, as far as the consequences went, a sin uncommitted; and this conviction had often helped her in the difficult task of reconciling doctrine and practice.

II

Moyra Attlee interrupted her listless stare down the empty Sunday street of the New Jersey suburb, and turned an astonished glance on her grandmother.

"Mrs. Clingsland? A wrong you did to Mrs. Clingsland?"

Hitherto she had lent an inattentive ear to her grandmother's ramblings; the talk of old people seemed to be a language hardly worth learning. But it was not always so with Mrs. Attlee's. Her activities among the rich had ceased before the first symptoms of the financial depression; but her tenacious memory was stored with pictures of the luxurious days of which her granddaughter's generation, even in a wider world, knew only by hearsay. Mrs. Attlee had a gift for evoking in a few

words scenes of half-understood opulence and leisure, like a guide leading a stranger through the gallery of a palace in the twilight, and now
and then lifting a lamp to a shimmering Rembrandt or a jeweled Ru-
bens; and it was particularly when she mentioned Mrs. Clingsland that
Moyra caught these dazzling glimpses. Mrs. Clingsland had always been
something more than a name to the Attlee family. They knew (though
they did not know why) that it was through her help that Grandmother
Attlee had been able, years ago, to buy the little house at Montclair, with
a patch of garden behind it, where, all through the depression, she had
held out, thanks to fortunate investments made on the advice of Mrs.
Clingsland's great friend, the banker.

"She had so many friends, and they were all high-up people, you
understand. Many's the time she'd say to me: 'Cora' (think of the loveliness of her calling me Cora), 'Cora, I'm going to buy some Golden Flyer
shares on Mr. Stoner's advice; Mr. Stoner of the National Union Bank,
you know. He's getting me in on the ground floor, as they say, and if you
want to step in with me, why come along. There's nothing too good for
you, in my opinion,' she used to say. And, as it turned out, those shares
have kept their head above water all through the bad years, and now I
think they'll see me through, and be there when I'm gone, to help out
you children."

Today Moyra Attlee heard the revered name with a new interest. The
phrase: "The wrong I did to Mrs. Clingsland," had struck through her
listlessness, rousing her to sudden curiosity. What could her grandmother mean by saying she had done a wrong to the benefactress whose
bounties she was never tired of recording? Moyra believed her grandmother to be a very good woman—certainly she had been wonderfully
generous in all her dealings with her children and grandchildren; and it
seemed incredible that, if there had been one grave lapse in her life, it
should have taken the form of an injury to Mrs. Clingsland. True, whatever the lapse was, she seemed to have made peace with herself about it;
yet it was clear that its being unconfessed lurked disquietingly in the
back of her mind.

"How can you say you ever did harm to a friend like Mrs. Clingsland,
Gran?"

Mrs. Attlee's eyes grew sharp behind her spectacles, and she fixed
them half distrustfully on the girl's face. But in a moment she seemed to
recover herself. "Not harm, I don't say; I'll never think I harmed her.
Bless you, it wasn't to harm her I'd ever have lifted a finger. All I wanted
was to help. But when you try to help too many people at once, the devil
sometimes takes note of it. You see, there's quotas nowadays for everything, doing good included, my darling."

Moyra made an impatient movement. She did not care to hear her grandmother philosophize. "Well—but you said you did a wrong to Mrs. Clingsland."

Mrs. Attlee's sharp eyes seemed to draw back behind a mist of age. She sat silent, her hands lying heavily over one another in their tragic uselessness.

"What would *you* have done, I wonder," she began suddenly, "if you'd ha' come in on her that morning, and seen her laying in her lovely great bed, with the lace a yard deep on the sheets, and her face buried in the pillows, so I knew she was crying? Would you have opened your bag same as usual, and got out your cocoanut cream and talcum powder, and the nail polishers, and all the rest of it, and waited there like a statue till she turned over to you; or'd you have gone up to her, and turned her softly round, like you would a baby, and said to her: 'Now, my dear, I guess you can tell Cora Attlee what's the trouble'? Well, that's what I did, anyhow; and there she was, with her face streaming with tears, and looking like a martyred saint on an altar, and when I said to her: 'Come, now, you tell me, and it'll help you,' she just sobbed out: 'Nothing can ever help me, now I've lost it.'"

"'Lost what?' I said, thinking first of her boy, the Lord help me, though I'd heard him whistling on the stairs as I went up; but she said: 'My beauty, Cora—I saw it suddenly slipping out of the door from me this morning'.... Well, at that I had to laugh, and half angrily too. 'Your beauty,' I said to her, 'and is that all? And me that thought it was your husband, or your son—or your fortune even. If it's only your beauty, can't I give it back to you with these hands of mine? But what are you saying to me about beauty, with that seraph's face looking up at me this minute?' I said to her, for she angered me as if she'd been blaspheming."

"Well, was it true?" Moyra broke in, impatient and yet curious.

"True that she'd lost her beauty?" Mrs. Attlee paused to consider. "Do you know how it is, sometimes when you're doing a bit of fine darning, sitting by the window in the afternoon; and one minute it's full daylight, and your needle seems to find the way of itself; and the next minute you say: 'Is it my eyes?' because the work seems blurred; and presently you see it's the daylight going, stealing away, softlike, from your corner, though there's plenty left overhead. Well—it was that way with her...."

But Moyra had never done fine darning, or strained her eyes in fading light, and she intervened again, more impatiently: "Well, what did she do?"

Mrs. Attlee once more reflected. "Why, she made me tell her every morning that it wasn't true; and every morning she believed me a little less. And she asked everybody in the house, beginning with her husband, poor man—him so bewildered when you asked him anything outside of his business, or his club or his horses, and never noticing any difference in her looks since the day he'd led her home as his bride, twenty years before, maybe. . . .

"But there—nothing he could have said, if he'd had the wit to say it, would have made any difference. From the day she saw the first little line around her eyes she thought of herself as an old woman, and the thought never left her for more than a few minutes at a time. Oh, when she was dressed up, and laughing, and receiving company, then I don't say the faith in her beauty wouldn't come back to her, and go to her head like champagne; but it wore off quicker than champagne, and I've seen her run upstairs with the foot of a girl, and then, before she'd tossed off her finery, sit down in a heap in front of one of her big looking glasses—it was looking glasses everywhere in her room—and stare and stare till the tears ran down over her powder."

"Oh, well, I suppose it's always hateful growing old," said Moyra, her indifference returning.

Mrs. Attlee smiled retrospectively. "How can I say that, when my own old age has been made so peaceful by all her goodness to me?"

Moyra stood up with a shrug. "And yet you tell me you acted wrong to her. How am I to know what you mean?"

Her grandmother made no answer. She closed her eyes, and leaned her head against the little cushion behind her neck. Her lips seemed to murmur, but no words came. Moyra reflected that she was probably falling asleep, and that when she woke she would not remember what she had been about to reveal.

"It's not much fun sitting here all this time, if you can't even keep awake long enough to tell me what you mean about Mrs. Clingsland," she grumbled.

Mrs. Attlee roused herself with a start.

III

Well (she began) you know what happened in the war—I mean, the way all the fine ladies, and the poor shabby ones too, took to running to the mediums and the clairvoyants, or whatever the stylish folk call 'em. The women had to have news of their men; and they were made to pay high enough for it. . . . Oh, the stories I used to hear—and the price paid wasn't only money, either! There was a fair lot of swindlers and black-mailers in the business, there was. I'd sooner have trusted a gypsy at a fair . . . but the women just *had* to go to them.

Well, my dear, I'd always had a way of seeing things; from the cradle, even. I don't mean reading the tea leaves, or dealing the cards; that's for the kitchen. No, no; I mean, feeling there's things about you, behind you, whispering over your shoulder. . . . Once my mother, on the Connemara hills, saw the leprechauns at dusk; and she said they smelt fine and high, too. . . . Well, when I used to go from one grand house to another, to give my massage and face treatment, I got more and more sorry for those poor wretches that the soothsaying swindlers were dragging the money out of for a pack of lies; and one day I couldn't stand it any longer, and though I knew the Church was against it, when I saw one lady nearly crazy, because for months she'd had no news of her boy at the front, I said to her: "If you'll come over to my place tomorrow, I might have a word for you." And the wonder of it was that I *had!* For that night I dreamt a message came saying there was good news for her, and the next day, sure enough, she had a cable, telling her her son had escaped from a German camp. . . .

After that the ladies came in flocks—in flocks fairly . . . you're too young to remember, child; but your mother could tell you. Only she wouldn't, because after a bit the priest got wind of it, and then it had to stop . . . so she won't even talk of it any more. But I always said: how could I help it? For I *did* see things, and hear things, at that time. . . . And of course the ladies were supposed to come just for the face treatment . . . and was I to blame if I kept hearing those messages for them, poor souls, or seeing things they wanted me to see?

It's no matter now, for I made it all straight with Father Divott years ago; and now nobody comes after me any more, as you can see for yourself. And all I ask is to be left alone in my chair. . . .

But with Mrs. Clingsland—well, that was different. To begin with, she was the patient I liked best. There was nothing she wouldn't do for you, if ever for a minute you could get her to stop thinking of herself . . . and that's saying a good deal, for a rich lady. Money's an armor, you see; and there's few cracks in it. But Mrs. Clingsland was a loving nature, if only anybody'd shown her how to love. . . . Oh, dear, and wouldn't she have been surprised if you'd told her that! Her that thought she was living up to her chin in love and love-making. But as soon as the lines began to come about her eyes, she didn't believe in it any more. And she had to be always hunting for new people to tell her she was as beautiful as ever; because she wore the others out, forever asking them: "Don't you think I'm beginning to go off a little?"—till finally fewer and fewer came to the house, and as far as a poor masseuse like me can judge, I didn't much fancy the looks of those that did; and I saw Mrs. Clingsland didn't either.

But there was the children, you'll say. I know, I know! And she did love her children in a way; only it wasn't their way. The girl, who was a good bit the eldest, took after her father: a plain face and plain words. Dogs and horses and athletics. With her mother she was cold and scared;

so her mother was cold and scared with her. The boy was delicate when he was little, so she could curl him up, and put him into black velvet pants, like that boy in the book—little Lord Something. But when his long legs grew out of the pants, and they sent him to school, she said he wasn't her own little cuddly baby any more; and it riles a growing boy to hear himself talked about like that.

She had good friends left, of course; mostly elderly ladies they were, of her own age (for she *was* elderly now; the change had come), who used to drop in often for a gossip; but, bless your heart, they weren't much help, for what she wanted, and couldn't do without, was the gaze of men struck dumb by her beauty. And that was what she couldn't get any longer, except she paid for it. And even so—!

For, you see, she was too quick and clever to be humbugged long by the kind that tried to get things out of her. How she used to laugh at the old double-chinners trotting round to the nightclubs with their boy friends! She laughed at old ladies in love; and yet she couldn't bear to be out of love, though she knew she was getting to be an old lady herself.

Well, I remember one day another patient of mine, who'd never had much looks beyond what you can buy in Fifth Avenue, laughing at me about Mrs. Clingsland, about her dread of old age, and her craze for admiration—and as I listened, I suddenly thought: "Why, we don't either of us know anything about what a beautiful woman suffers when she loses her beauty. For you and me, and thousands like us, beginning to grow old is like going from a bright warm room to one a little less warm and bright; but to a beauty like Mrs. Clingsland it's like being pushed out of an illuminated ballroom, all flowers and chandeliers, into the winter night and the snow." And I had to bite the words back, not to say them to my patient. . . .

IV

Mrs. Clingsland brightened up a little when her own son grew up and went to college. She used to go over and see him now and again; or he'd come home for the holidays. And he used to take her out for lunch, or to dance at those cabaret places; and when the headwaiters took her for his sweetheart she'd talk about it for a week. But one day a hall porter said: "Better hurry up, mister. There's your mother waiting for you over there, looking clean fagged out"; and after that she didn't go round with him so much.

For a time she used to get some comfort out of telling me about her early triumphs; and I used to listen patiently, because I knew it was safer for her to talk to me than to the flatterers who were beginning to get round her.

You mustn't think of her, though, as an unkind woman. She was friendly to her husband, and friendly to her children; but they meant less and less to her. What she wanted was a looking glass to stare into; and when her own people took enough notice of her to serve as looking glasses, which wasn't often, she didn't much fancy what she saw there. I think this was about the worst time of her life. She lost a tooth; she began to dye her hair; she went into retirement to have her face lifted, and then got frightened, and came out again looking like a ghost, with a pouch under one eye, where they'd begun the treatment. . . .

I began to be really worried about her then. She got sour and bitter toward everybody, and I seemed to be the only person she could talk out to. She used to keep me by for hours, always paying for the appointments she made me miss, and going over the same thing again and again; how when she was young and came into a ballroom, or a restaurant or a theatre, everybody stopped what they were doing to turn and look at her—even the actors on the stage did, she said; and it was the truth, I dare say. But that was over. . . .

Well, what could I say to her? She'd heard it all often enough. But there were people prowling about in the background that I didn't like the look of; people, you understand, who live on weak women that can't grow old. One day she showed me a love letter. She said she didn't know the man who'd sent it; but she knew about him. He was a Count Somebody; a foreigner. He'd had adventures. Trouble in his own country, I guess. . . . She laughed and tore the letter up. Another came from him, and I saw that too—but I didn't see her tear it up.

"Oh, I know what he's after," she said. "Those kind of men are always looking out for silly old women with money. . . . Ah," says she, "it was different in old times. I remember one day I'd gone into a florist's to buy some violets, and I saw a young fellow there; well, maybe he was a little younger than me—but I looked like a girl still. And when he saw me he just stopped short with what he was saying to the florist, and his face turned so white I thought he was going to faint. I bought my violets; and as I went out a violet dropped from the bunch, and I saw him stoop and pick it up, and hide it away as if it had been money he'd stolen. . . . Well," she says, "a few days after that I met him at a dinner, and it turned out he was the son of a friend of mine, a woman older than myself, who'd married abroad. He'd been brought up in England, and had just come to New York to take up a job there. . . ."

She lay back with her eyes closed, and a quiet smile on her poor tormented face. "I didn't know it then, but I suppose that was the only time I've ever been in love. . . ." For a while she didn't say anything more, and I noticed the tears beginning to roll down her cheeks. "Tell me about it, now do, you poor soul," I says; for I thought, this is better for her than fandangoing with that oily count whose letter she hasn't torn up.

"There's so little to tell," she said. "We met only four or five times—and then Harry went down on the 'Titanic.' "

"Mercy," says I, "and was it all those years ago?"

"The years don't make any difference, Cora," she says. "The way he looked at me I know no one ever worshiped me as he did."

"And did he tell you so?" I went on, humoring her; though I felt kind of guilty toward her husband.

"Some things don't have to be told," says she, with the smile of a bride. "If only he hadn't died, Cora. . . . It's the sorrowing for him that's made me old before my time." (Before her time! And her well over fifty.)

Well, a day or two after that I got a shock. Coming out of Mrs. Clingsland's front door as I was going into it I met a woman I'd know among a million if I was to meet her again in hell—where I will, I know, if I don't mind my steps. . . . You see, Moyra, though I broke years ago with all that crystal-reading, and table-rapping, and what the Church forbids, I was mixed up in it for a time (till Father Divott ordered me to stop), and I knew, by sight at any rate, most of the big mediums and their touts. And this woman on the doorstep was a tout, one of the worst and most notorious in New York; I knew cases where she'd sucked people dry selling them the news they wanted, like she was selling them a forbidden drug. And all of a sudden it came to me that I'd heard it said that she kept a foreign count, who was sucking *her* dry—and I gave one jump home to my own place, and sat down there to think it over.

I saw well enough what was going to happen. Either she'd persuade my poor lady that the count was mad over her beauty, and get a hold over her that way; or else—and this was worse—she'd make Mrs. Clingsland talk, and get at the story of the poor young man called Harry, who was drowned, and bring her messages from him; and that might go on forever, and bring in more money than the count. . . .

Well, Moyra, could I help it? I was so sorry for her, you see. I could see she was sick and fading away, and her will weaker than it used to be; and if I was to save her from those gangsters I had to do it right away, and make it straight with my conscience afterward—if I could. . . .

V

I don't believe I ever did such hard thinking as I did that night. For what was I after doing? Something that was against my Church and against my own principles; and if ever I got found out, it was all up with me—me, with my thirty years' name of being the best masseuse in New York, and none honester, nor more respectable!

Well, then, I says to myself, what'll happen if that woman gets hold of Mrs. Clingsland? Why, one way or another, she'll bleed her white, and then leave her without help or comfort. I'd seen households where that had happened, and I wasn't going to let it happen to my poor lady. What I was after was to make her believe in herself again, so that she'd be in a kindlier mind toward others . . . and by the next day I'd thought my plan out, and set it going.

It wasn't so easy, neither; and I sometimes wonder at my nerve. I'd figured it out that the other woman would have to work the stunt of the young man who was drowned, because I was pretty sure Mrs. Clingsland, at the last minute, would shy away from the count. Well, then, thinks I, I'll work the same stunt myself—but how?

You see, dearie, those big people, when they talk and write to each other, they use lovely words we ain't used to; and I was afraid if I began to bring messages to her, I'd word them wrong, and she'd suspect something. I knew I could work it the first day or the second; but after that I wasn't so sure. But there was no time to lose, and when I went back to her next morning I said: "A queer thing happened to me last night. I guess it was the way you spoke to me about that gentleman—the one on the 'Titanic.' Making me see him as clear as if he was in the room with us—" and at that I had her sitting up in bed with her great eyes burning into me like gimlets. "Oh, Cora, perhaps he *is!* Oh, tell me quickly what happened!"

"Well, when I was laying in my bed last night something came to me from him. I knew at once it was from him; it was a word he was telling me to bring you. . . ."

I had to wait then, she was crying so hard, before she could listen to me again; and when I went on she hung on to me, saving the word, as if I'd been her Saviour. The poor woman!

The message I'd hit on for that first day was easy enough. I said he'd told me to tell her he'd always loved her. It went down her throat like honey, and she just lay there and tasted it. But after a while she lifted up her head. "Then why didn't he tell me so?" says she.

"Ah," says I, "I'll have to try to reach him again, and ask him that." And that day she fairly drove me off on my other jobs, for fear I'd be late getting home, and too tired to hear him if he came again. "And he *will* come, Cora; I know he will! And you must be ready for him, and write down everything. I want every word written down the minute he says it, for fear you'll forget a single one."

Well, that was a new difficulty. Writing wasn't ever my strong point; and when it came to finding the words for a young gentleman in love who'd gone down on the "Titanic," you might as well have asked me to write a Chinese dictionary. Not that I couldn't imagine how he'd have felt; but I didn't for Mary's grace know how to say it for him.

But it's wonderful, as Father Divott says, how Providence sometimes seems to be listening behind the door. That night when I got home I found a message from a patient, asking me to go to see a poor young fellow she'd befriended when she was better off—he'd been her children's tutor, I believe—who was down and out, and dying in a miserable rooming house down here at Montclair. Well, I went; and I saw at once why he hadn't kept this job, or any other job. Poor fellow, it was the drink; and now he was dying of it. It was a pretty bad story, but there's only a bit of it belongs to what I'm telling you.

He was a highly educated gentleman, and as quick as a flash; and before I'd half explained, he told me what to say, and wrote out the message for me. I remember it now. "He was so blinded by your beauty that he couldn't speak—and when he saw you the next time, at that dinner, in your bare shoulders and your pearls, he felt farther away from you than ever. And he walked the streets till morning, and then went home, and wrote you a letter; but he didn't dare to send it after all."

This time Mrs. Clingsland swallowed it down like champagne. Blinded by her beauty; struck dumb by love of her! Oh, but that's what she'd been thirsting and hungering for all these years. Only, once it had begun, she had to have more of it, and always more . . . and my job didn't get any easier.

Luckily, though, I had that young fellow to help me; and after a while, when I'd given him a hint of what it was all about, he got as much interested as I was, and began to fret for me the days I didn't come.

But, my, what questions she asked. "Tell him, if it's true that I took his breath away that first evening at dinner, to describe to you how I was dressed. They must remember things like that even in the other world, don't you think so? And you say he noticed my pearls?"

Luckily she'd described that dress to me so often that I had no difficulty about telling the young man what to say—and so it went on, and it went on, and one way or another I managed each time to have an answer that satisfied her. But one day, after Harry'd sent her a particularly lovely message from the Over There (as those people call it) she burst into tears and cried out: "Oh, why did he never say things like that to me when we were together?"

That was a poser, as they say; I couldn't imagine why he hadn't. Of course I knew it was all wrong and immoral, anyway; but, poor thing, I don't see who it can hurt to help the love-making between a sick woman and a ghost. And I'd taken care to say a Novena against Father Divott finding me out.

Well, I told the poor young man what she wanted to know, and he said: "Oh, you can tell her an evil influence came between them. Someone who was jealous, and worked against him—here, give me a pencil, and I'll write it out. . . ." and he pushed out his hot twitching hand for the paper.

That message fairly made her face burn with joy. "I knew it—I always knew it!" She flung her thin arms about me, and kissed me. "Tell me again, Cora, how he said I looked the first day he saw me. . . ."

"Why, you must have looked as you look now," says I to her, "for there's twenty years fallen from your face." And so there was.

What helped me to keep on was that she'd grown so much gentler and quieter. Less impatient with the people who waited on her, more understanding with the daughter and Mr. Clingsland. There was a different atmosphere in the house. And sometimes she'd say: "Cora, there must be poor souls in trouble, with nobody to hold out a hand to them; and I want you to come to me when you run across anybody like that." So I used to keep that poor young fellow well looked after, and cheered up with little dainties. And you'll never make me believe there was anything wrong in that—or in letting Mrs. Clingsland help me out with the new roof on this house, either.

But there was a day when I found her sitting up in bed when I came in, with two red spots on her thin cheeks. And all the peace had gone out of her poor face. "Why, Mrs. Clingsland, my dear, what's the matter?" But I could see well enough what it was. Somebody's been undermining her belief in spirit communications, or whatever they call them, and she'd been crying herself into a fever, thinking I'd made up all I'd told her. "How do I know you're a medium, anyhow," she flung out at me with pitiful furious eyes, "and not taking advantage of me with all this stuff every morning?"

Well, the queer thing was that I took offense at that, not because I was afraid of being found out, but because—heaven help us!—I'd somehow come to believe in that young man Harry and his love-making, and it made me angry to be treated as a fraud. But I kept my temper and my tongue, and went on with the message as if I hadn't heard her; and she was ashamed to say any more to me. The quarrel between us lasted a week; and then one day, poor soul, she said, whimpering like a drug taker: "Cora, I can't get on without the messages you bring me. The ones I get through other people don't sound like Harry—and yours do."

I was so sorry for her then that I had hard work not to cry with her; but I kept my head, and answered quietly: "Mrs. Clingsland, I've been going against my Church, and risking my immortal soul, to get those messages through to you; and if you've found others that can help you, so much the better for me, and I'll go and make my peace with Heaven this very evening," I said.

"But the other messages don't help me, and I don't want to disbelieve in you," she sobbed out. "Only lying awake all night and turning things over, I get so miserable. I shall die if you can't prove to me that it's really Harry speaking to you."

I began to pack up my things. "I can't prove that, I'm afraid," I says in a cold voice, turning away my head so she wouldn't see the tears running down my cheeks.

"Oh, but you must, Cora, or I shall die!" she entreated me; and she looked as if she would, the poor soul.

"How can I prove it to you?" I answered. For all my pity for her, I still resented the way she'd spoken; and I thought how glad I'd be to get the whole business off my soul that very night in the confessional.

She opened her great eyes and looked up at me; and I seemed to see the wraith of her young beauty looking out of them. "There's only one way," she whispered.

"Well," I said, still offended, "what's the way?"

"You must ask him to repeat to you that letter he wrote, and didn't dare send to me. I'll know instantly then if you're in communication with him, and if you are I'll never doubt you any more."

Well, I sat down and gave a laugh. "You think it's as easy as that to talk with the dead, do you?"

"I think he'll know I'm dying too, and have pity on me, and do as I ask." I said nothing more, but packed up my things and went away.

VI

That letter seemed to me a mountain in my path; and the poor young man, when I told him, thought so too. "Ah, that's too difficult," he said. But he told me he'd think it over, and do his best—and I was to come back the next day if I could. "If only I knew more about her—or about *him*. It's damn difficult, making love for a dead man to a woman you've never seen," says he with his little cracked laugh. I couldn't deny that it was; but I knew he'd do what he could, and I could see that the difficulty of it somehow spurred him on, while me it only cast down.

So I went back to his room the next evening; and as I climbed the stairs I felt one of those sudden warnings that sometimes used to take me by the throat.

"It's as cold as ice on these stairs," I thought, "and I'll wager there's no one made up the fire in his room since morning." But it wasn't really the cold I was afraid of; I could tell there was worse than that waiting for me.

I pushed open the door and went in. "Well," says I, as cheerful as I could, "I've got a pint of champagne and a thermos of hot soup for you; but before you get them you've got to tell me—"

He laid there in his bed as if he didn't see me, though his eyes were open; and when I spoke to him he didn't answer. I tried to laugh. "Mercy!" I says, "are you so sleepy you can't even look round to see the champagne? Hasn't that slut of a woman been in to 'tend to the stove for you? The room's as cold as death—" I says, and at the word I stopped short. He neither moved nor spoke; and I felt that the cold came from him, and not from the empty stove. I took hold of his hand, and held the cracked looking glass to his lips; and I knew he was gone to his Maker. I drew his lids down, and fell on my knees beside the bed. "You shan't go without a prayer, you poor fellow," I whispered to him, pulling out my beads.

But though my heart was full of mourning I dursn't pray for long, for I knew I ought to call the people of the house. So I just muttered a prayer for the dead, and then got to my feet again. But before calling in anybody I took a quick look around; for I said to myself it would be better not to leave about any of those bits he'd written down for me. In the shock of finding the poor young man gone I'd clean forgotten all about the letter; but I looked among his few books and papers for anything about the spirit messages, and found nothing. After that I turned back for a last look at him, and a last blessing; and then it was, fallen on the floor and half under the bed, I saw a sheet of paper scribbled over in pencil in his weak writing. I picked it up, and, holy Mother, it was the letter! I hid it away quick in my bag, and I stooped down and kissed him. And then I called the people in.

Well, I mourned the poor young man like a son, and I had a busy day arranging things, and settling about the funeral with the lady that used to befriend him. And with all there was to do I never went near Mrs. Clingsland nor so much as thought of her, that day or the next; and the day after that there was a frantic message, asking what had happened, and saying she was very ill, and I was to come quick, no matter how much else I had to do.

I didn't more than half believe in the illness; I've been about too long among the rich not to be pretty well used to their scares and fusses. But I knew Mrs. Clingsland was just pining to find out if I'd got the letter, and that my only chance of keeping my hold over her was to have it ready in my bag when I went back. And if I didn't keep my hold over her, I knew what slimy hands were waiting in the dark to pull her down.

Well, the labor I had copying out that letter was so great that I didn't hardly notice what was in it; and if I thought about it at all, it was only to wonder if it wasn't worded too plainlike, and if there oughtn't to have been more long words in it, coming from a gentleman to his lady. So with one thing and another I wasn't any too easy in my mind when I appeared again at Mrs. Clingsland's; and if ever I wished myself out of a dangerous job, my dear, I can tell you that was the day. . . .

I went up to her room, the poor lady, and found her in bed, and tossing about, her eyes blazing, and her face full of all the wrinkles I'd worked so hard to rub out of it; and the sight of her softened my heart. After all, I thought, these people don't know what real trouble is; but they've manufactured something so like it that it's about as bad as the genuine thing.

"Well," she said in a fever, "well, Cora—the letter? Have you brought me the letter?"

I pulled it out of my bag, and handed it to her; and then I sat down and waited, my heart in my boots. I waited a long time, looking away from her; you couldn't stare at a lady who was reading a message from her sweetheart, could you?

I waited a long time; she must have read the letter very slowly, and then reread it. Once she sighed, ever so softly; and once she said: "Oh, Harry, no, no—how foolish" . . . and laughed a little under her breath. Then she was still again for so long that at last I turned my head and took a stealthy look at her. And there she lay on her pillows, the hair waving over them, the letter clasped tight in her hands, and her face smoothed out the way it was years before, when I first knew her. Yes—those few words had done more for her than all my labor.

"Well—?" said I, smiling a little at her.

"Oh, Cora—now at last he's spoken to me, really spoken." And the tears were running down her young cheeks.

I couldn't hardly keep back my own, the heart was so light in me. "And now you'll believe in me, I hope, ma'am, won't you?"

"I was mad ever to doubt you, Cora. . . ." She lifted the letter to her breast, and slipped it in among her laces. "How did you manage to get it, you darling, you?"

Dear me, thinks I, and what if she asks me to get her another one like it, and then another? I waited a moment, and then I spoke very gravely. "It's not an easy thing, ma'am, coaxing a letter like that from the dead." And suddenly, with a start, I saw that I'd spoken the truth. It *was* from the dead that I'd got it.

"No, Cora; I can well believe it. But this is a treasure I can live on for years. Only you must tell me how I can repay you. . . . In a hundred years I could never do enough for you," she says.

Well, that word went to my heart; but for a minute I didn't know how to answer. For it was true I'd risked my soul, and that was something she couldn't pay me for; but then maybe I'd saved hers, in getting her away from those foul people, so the whole business was more of a puzzle to me than ever. But then I had a thought that made me easier.

"Well, ma'am, the day before yesterday I was with a young man about the age of—of your Harry; a poor young man, without health or hope, lying sick in a mean rooming house. I used to go there and see him sometimes—"

Mrs. Clingsland sat up in bed in a flutter of pity. "Oh, Cora, how dreadful! Why did you never tell me? You must hire a better room for him at once. Has he a doctor? Has he a nurse? Quick—give me my checkbook!"

"Thank you, ma'am. But he don't need no nurse nor no doctor; and he's in a room underground by now. All I wanted to ask you for," said I at length, though I knew I might have got a king's ransom from her, "is money enough to have a few masses said for his soul—because maybe there's no one else to do it."

I had hard work making her believe there was no end to the masses you could say for a hundred dollars; but somehow it's comforted me ever since that I took no more from her that day. I saw to it that Father Divott said the masses and got a good bit of the money; so he was a sort of accomplice too, though he never knew it.   1935

ELIZABETH TAYLOR

Poor Girl

Miss Chasty's first pupil was a flirtatious little boy. At seven years, he was alarmingly precocious and sometimes she thought that he despised his childhood, regarding it as a waiting time which he used only as a rehearsal for adult life. He was already more sophisticated than his young governess and disturbed her with his air of dalliance, the mockery with which he set about his lessons, the preposterous conversations he led her into, guiding her skillfully away from work, confusing her with bizarre conjectures and irreverent ideas, so that she would clasp her hands tightly under the plush table-cloth and pray that his father would not choose such a moment to observe her teaching, coming in abruptly as he sometimes did and signalling to her to continue her lesson.

At those times, his son's eyes were especially lively, fixed cruelly upon his governess as he listened, smiling faintly, to her faltering voice, measuring her timidity. He would answer her questions correctly, but significantly, as if he knew that by his aptitude he rescued her from dismissal. There were many governesses waiting employment, he implied—and this was so at the beginning of the century. He underlined her good fortune at having a pupil who could so easily learn, could display the results of her teaching to such advantage for the benefit of the rather sombre, pompous figure seated at the window. When his father, apparently satisfied, had left them without a word, the boy's manner changed. He seemed fatigued and too absent-minded to reply to any more questions.

"Hilary!" she would say sharply. "Are you attending to me?" Her sharpness and her foolishness amused him, coming as he knew they did from the tension of the last ten minutes.

"Why, my dear girl, of course."

"You must address me by my name."

"Certainly, dear Florence."

"Miss Chasty."

His lips might shape the words, which he was too weary to say.

Sometimes, when she was correcting his sums, he would come round the table to stand beside her, leaning against her heavily, looking closely at her face, not at his book, breathing steadily down his nose so that tendrils of hair wavered on her neck and against her cheeks. His stillness, his concentration on her and his too heavy leaning, worried her. She felt something experimental in his attitude, as if he were not leaning against her at all, but against someone in the future. "He is only a baby," she reminded herself, but she would try to shift from him, feeling a vague distaste. She would blush, as if he were a grown man, and her heart could be heard beating quickly. He was aware of this and would take up the corrected book and move back to his place.

Once he proposed to her and she had the feeling that it was a proposal-rehearsal and that he was making use of her, as an actor might ask her to hear his lines.

"You must go on with your work," she said.

"I can shade in a map and talk as well."

"Then talk sensibly."

"You think I am too young, I daresay; but you could wait for me to grow up. I can do that quickly enough."

"You are far from grown-up at the moment."

"You only say these things because you think that governesses ought to. I suppose you don't know *how* governesses go on, because you have never been one until now, and you were too poor to have one of your own when you were young."

"That is impertinent, Hilary."

"You once told me that your father couldn't afford one."

"Which is a different way of putting it."

"I shouldn't have thought they cost so much." He had a way of just making a remark, of breathing it so gently that it was scarcely said, and might conveniently be ignored.

He was a dandified little boy. His smooth hair was like a silk cap, combed straight from the crown to a level line above his topaz eyes. His sailor-suits were spotless. The usual boldness changed to an agonised fussiness if his serge sleeve brushed against chalk or if he should slip on the grassy terrace and stain his clothes with green. On their afternoon walks he took no risks and Florence, who had younger brothers, urged him in vain to climb a tree or jump across puddles. At first, she thought him intimidated by his mother or nurse; but soon she realised that his mother entirely indulged him and the nurse had her thoughts all bent upon the new baby: his fussiness was just another part of his grown-upness come too soon.

The house was comfortable, although to Florence rather too sealed-up and overheated after her own damp and draughty home. Her work was not hard and her loneliness only what she had expected. Cut off from the kitchen by her education, she lacked the feuds and camaraderie, gossip and cups of tea, which made life more interesting for the domestic staff. None of the maids—coming to light the lamp at dusk or laying the schoolroom-table for tea—ever presumed beyond a remark or two about the weather.

One late afternoon, she and Hilary returned from their walk and found the lamps already lit. Florence went to her room to tidy herself before tea. When she came down to the schoolroom, Hilary was already there, sitting on the window-seat and staring out over the park as his father did. The room was bright and warm and a maid had put a white cloth over the plush one and was beginning to lay the table.

The air was full of a heavy scent, dry and musky. To Florence, it smelt quite unlike the eau de cologne she sometimes sprinkled on her handkerchief, when she had a headache and she disapproved so much that she returned the maid's greeting coldly and bade Hilary open the window.

"Open the window, dear girl?" he said. "We shall catch our very deaths."

"You will do as I ask and remember in future how to address me."

She was angry with the maid—who now seemed to her an immoral creature—and angry to be humiliated before her.

"But why?" asked Hilary.

"I don't approve of my schoolroom being turned into a scented bower." She kept her back to the room and was trembling, for she had never rebuked a servant before.

"I approve of it," Hilary said, sniffing loudly.

"I think it's lovely," the maid said. "I noticed it as soon as I opened the door."

"Is this some joke, Hilary?" Florence asked when the maid had gone.

"No. What?"

"This smell in the room?"

"No. You smell of it most, anyhow." He put his nose to her sleeve and breathed deeply.

It seemed to Florence that this was so, that her clothes had caught the perfume among their folds. She lifted her palms to her face, then went to the window and leant out into the air as far as she could.

"Shall I pour out the tea, dear girl?"

"Yes, please."

She took her place at the table abstractedly, and as she drank her tea she stared about the room, frowning. When Hilary's mother looked in, as she often did at this time, Florence stood up in a startled way.

"Good-evening, Mrs Wilson. Hilary, put a chair for your mamma."

"Don't let me disturb you."

Mrs Wilson sank into the rocking-chair by the fire and gently tipped to and fro.

"Have you finished your tea, darling boy?" she asked. "Are you going to read me a story from your book? Oh, there is Lady scratching at the door. Let her in for mamma."

Hilary opened the door and a balding old pug-dog with blood-shot eyes waddled in.

"Come, Lady! Beautiful one. Come to mistress! What is wrong with her, poor pet lamb?"

The bitch had stopped just inside the room and lifted her head and howled. "What has frightened her, then? Come, beauty! Coax her with a sponge-cake, Hilary."

She reached forward to the table to take the dish and doing so noticed Florence's empty tea-cup. On the rim was a crimson smear, like the imprint of a lip. She gave a sponge-finger to Hilary, who tried to quieten the pug, then she leaned back in her chair and studied Florence again as she had studied her when she had engaged her a few weeks earlier. The girl's looks were appropriate enough, appropriate to a clergyman's daughter and a governess. Her square chin looked resolute, her green eyes innocent, her dress was modest and unbecoming. Yet Mrs Wilson could detect an excitability, even feverishness, which she had not noticed before and she wondered if she had mistaken guardedness for innocence and deceit for modesty.

She was reaching this conclusion—rocking back and forth—when she saw Florence's hand stretch out and turn the cup round in its saucer so that the red stain was out of sight.

"What is wrong with Lady?" Hilary asked, for the dog would not be pacified with sponge-fingers, but kept making barking advances further into the room, then growling in retreat.

"Perhaps she is crying at the new moon," said Florence and she went to the window and drew back the curtain. As she moved, her skirts rustled. "If she has silk underwear as well!" Mrs Wilson thought. She had clearly heard the sound of taffetas and she imagined the drab, shiny alpaca dress concealing frivolity and wantonness.

"Open the door, Hilary!" she said. "I will take Lady away. Vernon shall give her a run in the park. I think a quiet read for Hilary and then an early bed-time, Miss Chasty. He looks pale this evening."

"Yes, Mrs Wilson." Florence stood respectfully by the table, hiding the cup.

"The hypocrisy!" Mrs Wilson thought and she trembled as she crossed the landing and went downstairs.

She hesitated to tell her husband of her uneasiness, knowing his susceptibilities to women whom his conscience taught him to deplore. Hidden below the apparent urbanity of their married life were old unhappiness—little acts of treachery and disloyalty which pained her to remember, bruises upon her peace of mind and her pride: letters found, a pretty maid dismissed, an actress who had blackmailed him. As he read the Lesson in church, looking so perfectly upright and honourable a man, she sometimes thought of his escapades; but not with bitterness or cynicism, only with pain at her memories and a whisper of fear about the future. For some time she had been spared those whispers and had hoped that their marriage had at last achieved its calm. To speak of Florence as she must might both arouse his curiosity and revive the past. Nevertheless, she had her duty to her son to fulfil and her own anger to appease and she opened the Library door very determinedly.

"Oliver, I am sorry to interrupt your work, but I must speak to you."

He put down the *Strand* magazine quite happily, aware that she was not a sarcastic woman.

Oliver and his son were extraordinarily alike. "As soon as Hilary has grown a moustache we shall not know them apart," Mrs Wilson often said, and her husband liked this little joke which made him feel more youthful. He did not know that she added a silent prayer—"O God, please do not let him *be* like him, though."

"You seem troubled, Louise." His voice was rich and authoritative. He enjoyed setting to rights her little domestic flurries and waited indulgently to hear of some tradesman's misdemeanour or servant's laziness.

"Yes, I am troubled about Miss Chasty."

"Little Miss Mouse? I was rather troubled myself. I noticed two spelling-faults in Hilary's botany essay, which she claimed to have corrected. I said nothing before the boy; but I shall acquaint her with it when the opportunity arises."

"Do you often go to the schoolroom, then?"

"From time to time. I like to be sure that our choice was wise."

"It was not. It was misguided *and* unwise."

"All young people seem slip-shod nowadays."

"She is more than slip-shod. I believe she should go. I think she is quite brazen. Oh yes, I should have laughed at that myself if it had been said to me an hour ago, but I have just come from the schoolroom and it occurs to me that now she has settled down and feels more secure—since you pass over her mistakes—she is beginning to take advantage of your leniency and to show herself in her true colours. I felt a sinister atmosphere up there and I am quite upset and exhausted by it. I went up to hear Hilary's reading. They were finishing tea and the room was full of the most overpowering scent—*her* scent. It was disgusting."

"Unpleasant?"

"No, not at all. But upsetting."

"Disturbing?"

She would not look at him or reply, hearing no more indulgence or condescension in his voice, but the quality of warming interest.

"And then I saw her tea-cup and there was a mark on it—a red smear where her lips had touched it. She did not know I saw it and as soon as she noticed it herself she turned it round, away from me. She is an immoral woman and has come into our house to teach our son."

"I have never noticed a trace of artificiality in her looks. It seemed to me that she was rather colourless."

"She has been sly. This evening she looked quite different, quite flushed and excitable. I know that she had rouged her lips or painted them, or whatever those women do." Her eyes filled with tears.

"I shall observe her for a day or two," Oliver said, trying to keep anticipation from his voice.

"I should like her to go at once."

"Never act rashly. She is entitled to a quarter's notice unless there is definite blame. We could make ourselves very foolish if you have been mistaken. Oh, I know that you are sure; but it has been known for you to misjudge others. I shall take stock of her and decide if she is suitable. She is still Miss Mouse to me and I cannot think otherwise until I see the evidence with my own eyes."

"There was something else as well," Mrs Wilson said wretchedly.

"And what was that?"

"I should rather not say." She had changed her mind about further accusations. Silk underwear would prove, she guessed, too inflammatory.

"I shall go up ostensibly to mention Hilary's spelling-faults." He could not go fast enough and stood up at once.

"But Hilary will be in bed."

"I could not mention the spelling-faults if he were not."

"Shall I come with you?"

"My dear Louise, why should you? It would look very strange—a deputation about two spelling-faults."

"Then don't be long, will you? I hope you won't be long."

He went to the schoolroom, but there was no one there. Hilary's story-book lay closed upon the table and Miss Chasty's sewing was folded neatly. As he was standing there looking about him and sniffing hard, a maid came in with a tray of crockery.

"Has Master Hilary gone to bed?" he asked, feeling rather foolish and confused.

The only scent in the air was a distinct smell—even a haze—of cigarette smoke.

"Yes, sir."

"And Miss Chasty—where is she?"

"She went to bed, too, sir."

"Is she unwell?"

"She spoke of a chronic head, sir."

The maid stacked the cups and saucers in the cupboard and went out. Nothing was wrong with the room apart from the smell of smoke and Mr Wilson went downstairs. His wife was waiting in the hall. She looked up expectantly, in some relief at seeing him so soon.

"Nothing," he said dramatically. "She has gone to bed with a headache. No wonder she looked feverish."

"You noticed the scent."

"There was none," he said. "No trace. Nothing. Just imagination, dear Louise. I thought that it must be so."

He went to the library and took up his magazine again, but he was too disturbed to read and thought with impatience of the following day.

Florence could not sleep. She had gone to her room, not with a headache but to escape conversations until she had faced her predicament alone. This she was doing, lying on the honeycomb quilt which, since maids do not wait on governesses, had not been turned down.

The schoolroom this evening seemed to have been wreathed about with a strange miasma; the innocent nature of the place polluted in a way which she could not understand or have explained. Something new, it seemed, had entered the room which had not belonged to her or become a part of her—the scent had clung about her clothes; the stained cup was her cup, and her handkerchief with which she had rubbed it clean was still reddened; and, finally, as she had stared in the mirror, trying to re-establish her personality, the affected little laugh which startled her had come from herself. It had driven her from the room.

"I cannot explain the inexplicable," she thought wearily and began to prepare herself for bed. Home-sickness hit her like a blow on the head. "Whatever they do to me, I have always my home," she promised herself. But she could not think who "they" might be; for no one in this house had threatened her. Mrs Wilson had done no more than irritate her with her commonplace fussing over Hilary and her dog, and Florence was prepared to overcome much more than irritations. Mr Wilson's pomposity, his constant watch on her work, intimidated her, but she knew that all who must earn their living must have fears lest their work should not seem worth the payment. Hilary was easy to manage; she had quickly seen that she could always deflect him from rebelliousness by opening a new subject for conversation; any idea would be a counter-attraction to naughtiness; he wanted her to sharpen his wits upon. "And is that all that teaching is, or should be?" she had wondered. The servants had been good to her, realising that she would demand nothing of them. She had suffered great loneliness, but had foreseen it as part of her position. Now she felt fear nudging it away. "I am not lonely any more," she thought. "I am not alone any more. And I have lost something." She said her prayers; then, sitting up in bed, kept the candle alight while she brushed her hair and read the Bible.

"Perhaps I have lost my reason," she suddenly thought, resting her fingers on her place in the Psalms. She lifted her head and saw her shadow stretch up the powdery, rose-sprinkled wall. "Now can I keep *that* secret?" she wondered. "When there is no one to help me to do it? Only those who are watching to see it happen."

She was not afraid in her bedroom as she had been in the schoolroom, but her perplexed mind found no replies to its questions. She blew out the candle and tried to fall asleep but lay and cried for a long time, and yearned to be at home again and comforted in her mother's arms.

In the morning she met kind enquiries. Nurse was so full of solicitude that Florence felt guilty. "I came up with a warm drink and put my head round the door but you were in the land of Nod so I drank it myself. I should take a grey powder; or I could mix you a gargle. There are a lot of throats about."

"I am quite better this morning," said Florence and she felt calmer as she sat down at the schoolroom-table with Hilary. "Yet it was all true," her reason whispered. "The morning hasn't altered that."

"You have been crying," said Hilary. "Your eyes are red."

"Sometimes people's eyes are red from other causes—headaches and colds." She smiled brightly.

"And sometimes from crying, as I said. I should think *usually* from crying."

"Page fifty-one," she said, locking her hands together in her lap.

"Very well." He opened the book, pressed down the pages and lowered his nose to them, breathing the smell of print. "He is utterly sensuous," she thought. "He extracts every pleasure, every sensation, down to the most trivial."

They seemed imprisoned in the schoolroom, by the silence of the rest of the house and by the rain outside. Her calm began to break up into frustration and she put her hands behind her chair and pressed them against the hot mesh of the fireguard to steady herself. As she did so, she felt a curious derangement of both mind and body; of desire unsettling her once sluggish, peaceful nature, desire horribly defined, though without direction.

"I have soon finished those," said Hilary, bringing his sums and placing them before her. She glanced at her palms which were criss-crossed deep with crimson where she had pressed them against the fireguard, then she took up her pen and dipped it into the red ink.

"Don't lean against me, Hilary," she said.

"I love the scent so much."

It had returned, musky, enveloping, varying as she moved. She ticked the sums quickly, thinking that she would set Hilary more work and escape for a moment to calm herself—change her clothes or cleanse herself in the rain. Hearing Mr Wilson's footsteps along the passage, she knew that her escape was cut off and raised wild-looking eyes as he came in. He mistook panic for passion, thought that by opening the door suddenly he had caught her out and laid bare her secret, her pathetic adoration.

"Good-morning," he said musically and made his way to the window-seat. "Don't let me disturb you." He said this without irony, although he thought: "So it is that way the wind blows! Poor creature!" He had never found it difficult to imagine that women were in love with him.

"I will hear your verbs," Florence told Hilary, and opened the French Grammar as if she did not know them herself. Her eyes—from so much crying—were a pale and brilliant green, and as the scent drifted in Oliver's direction and he turned to her, she looked fully at him.

"Ah, the still waters!" he thought and stood up suddenly. *"Ils vont,"* he corrected Hilary and touched his shoulders as he passed. "Are you attending to Miss Chasty?"

"Is she attending to me?" Hilary murmured. The risk was worth taking, for neither heard. His father appeared to be sleep-walking and Florence deliberately closed her eyes, as if looking down were not enough to blur the outlines of her desire.

"I find it difficult," Oliver said to his wife, "to reconcile your remarks about Miss Chasty with the young woman herself. I have just come from the schoolroom and she was engaged in nothing more immoral than teaching French verbs—that not very well, incidentally."

"But can you *explain* what I have told you?"

"I can't do that," he said gaily. For who can explain a jealous woman's fancies? he implied.

He began to spend more time in the schoolroom; from surveillance, he said. Miss Chasty, though not outwardly of an amorous nature, was still not what he had at first supposed. A suppressed wantonness hovered beneath her primness. She was the ideal governess in his eyes—irreproachable, yet not unapproachable. As she was so conveniently installed, he could take his time in divining the extent of her willingness; especially as he was growing older and the game was beginning to be worth more than the triumph of winning it. To his wife, he upheld Florence, saw nothing wrong save in her scholarship, which needed to be looked into—the explanation for his more frequent visits to the schoolroom. He laughed teasingly at Louise's fancies.

The schoolroom indeed became a focal point of the house—the

stronghold of Mr Wilson's desire and his wife's jealousy.

"We are never alone," said Hilary. "Either Papa or Mamma is here. Perhaps they wonder if you are good enough for me."

"Hilary!" His father had heard the last sentence as he opened the door and the first as he hovered outside listening. "I doubt if my ears deceived me. You will go to your room while you think of a suitable apology and I think of an ample punishment."

"Shall I take my history book with me or shall I just waste time?"

"I have indicated how to spend your time."

"That won't take long enough," said Hilary beneath his breath as he closed the door.

"Meanwhile, I apologise for him," said his father. He did not go to his customary place by the window, but came to the hearth-rug where Florence stood behind her chair. "We have indulged him too much and he has been too much with adults. Have there been other occasions?"

"No, indeed, sir."

"You find him tractable?"

"Oh, yes."

"And are you happy in your position?"

"Yes."

As the dreaded, the now so familiar scent began to wreathe about the room, she stepped back from him and began to speak rapidly, as urgently as if she were dying and must make some explanation while she could. "Perhaps, after all, Hilary is right and you do wonder about my competence—and if I can give him all he should have. Perhaps a man would teach him more . . ."

She began to feel a curious infraction of the room and of her personality, seemed to lose the true Florence, and the room lightened as if the season had been changed.

"You are mistaken," he was saying. "Have I ever given you any hint that we were not satisfied?"

Her timidity had quite dissolved and he was shocked by the sudden boldness of her glance.

"No, no hint," she said smiling. As she moved, he heard the silken swish of her clothes.

"I should rather give you a hint of how well pleased I am."

"Then why don't you?" she asked.

She leaned back against the chimney-piece and looped about her fingers a long necklace of glittering green beads. "Where did these come from?" she wondered. She could not remember ever having seen them before, but she could not pursue her bewilderment, for the necklace felt familiar to her hands, much more familiar than the rest of the room.

"*When* shall I?" he was insisting. "This evening, perhaps? when Hilary is in bed?"

"Then who is *he*, if Hilary is to be in bed?" she wondered. She glanced at him and smiled again. "You are extraordinarily alike," she said. "You and Hilary." "But Hilary is a little boy," she reminded herself. "It is silly to confuse the two."

"We must discuss Hilary's progress," he said, his voice so burdened with meaning that she began to laugh at him.

"Indeed we must," she agreed.

"Your necklace is the colour of your eyes." He took it from her finger and leaned forward, as if to kiss her. Hearing footsteps in the passage she moved sharply aside, the necklace broke and the beads were scattered over the floor.

"Why is Hilary in the garden at this hour?" Mrs Wilson asked. Her husband and the governess were on their knees, gathering up the beads.

"Miss Chasty's necklace broke," her husband said. She had heard that submissive tone before: his voice lacked authority only when he was caught out in some infidelity.

"I was asking about Hilary. I have just seen him running in the shrubbery without a coat."

"He was sent to his room for being impertinent to Miss Chasty."

"Please fetch him at once," Mrs Wilson told Florence. Her voice always gained in authority what her husband's lacked.

Florence hurried from the room, still holding a handful of beads. She felt badly shaken—as if she had been brought to the edge of some experience which had then retreated beyond her grasp.

"He was told to stay in his room," Mr Wilson said feebly.

"Why did her beads break?"

"She was fidgeting with them. I think she was nervous. I was making it rather apparent to her that I regarded Hilary's insubordination as proof of too much leniency on her part."

"I didn't know that she had such a necklace. It is the showiest trash that I have ever seen."

"We cannot blame her for the cheapness of her trinkets. It is rather pathetic."

"There is nothing pathetic about her. We will continue this in the morning-room and *they* can continue their lessons, which are, after all, her reason for being here."

"Oh, they are gone," said Hilary. His cheeks were pink from the cold outside.

"Why did you not stay in your bedroom as you were told?"

"I had nothing to do. I thought of my apology before I got there. It was: 'I am sorry, dear girl, that I spoke too near the point.' "

"You could have spent longer and thought of a real apology."

"Look how long Papa spent and he did not even think of a punishment, which is a much easier thing."

Several times during the evening Mr Wilson said: "But you cannot dismiss the girl because her beads break."

"There have been other things and will be more," his wife replied.

So that there should not be more that evening, he did not move from the drawing-room where he sat watching her doing her wool-work. For the same reason, Florence left the schoolroom early. She went out and walked rather nervously in the park, feeling remorseful, astonished and upset.

"Did you mend your necklace?" Hilary asked her in the morning.

"I lost the beads."

"But my poor girl, they must be somewhere."

She thought: "There is no reason to suppose that I shall get back what I never had in the first place."

"Have you got a headache?"

"Yes. Go on with your work, Hilary."

"Is it from losing the beads?"

"No."

"Have you a great deal of jewellery I have not seen yet?"

She did not answer and he went on: "You still have your brooch with your grandmother's plaited hair in it. Was it cut off her head when she was dead?"

"Your *work*, Hilary."

"I shudder to think of chopping it off a corpse. You could have some of my hair, now, while I am living." He fingered it with admiration, regarded a sum aloofly, and jotted down its answer. "Could I cut some of yours?" he asked, bringing his book to be corrected. He whistled softly, close to her, and the tendrils of hair round her ears were gently blown about.

"It is ungentlemanly to whistle," she said.

"My sums are always right. It shows how I can chatter and subtract at the same time. Any governess would be annoyed by that. I suppose your brothers never whistle."

"Never."

"Are they to be clergymen like your father?"

"It is what we hope for one of them."

"I am to be a famous judge. When you read about me, will you say: 'And to think I might have been his wife if I had not been so self-willed'?"

"No, but I hope that I shall feel proud that once I taught you."

"You sound doubtful."

He took his book back to the table. "We are having a quiet morning," he remarked. "No one has visited us. Poor Miss Chasty, it is a pity about the necklace," he murmured, as he took up his pencil again.

Evenings were dangerous to her. "He said he would come," she told herself, "and I allowed him to say so. On what compulsion did I?"

Fearfully, she spent her lonely hours out in the dark garden or in her cold and candlelit bedroom. He was under his wife's vigilance and Florence did not know that he dared not leave the drawing-room. But the vigilance relaxed, as it does: his carelessness returned and steady rain and bitter cold drove Florence to warm her chilblains at the schoolroom fire.

Her relationship with Mrs Wilson had changed. A wary hostility took the place of meekness, and when Mrs Wilson came to the schoolroom at tea-times, Florence stood up defiantly and cast a look round the room as if to say: "Find what you can. There is nothing here." Mrs Wilson's suspicious ways increased her rebelliousness. "I have done nothing wrong," she told herself. But in her bedroom at night: "*I* have done nothing wrong," she would think.

"They have quite deserted us," Hilary said from time to time. "They have realised you are worth your weight in gold, dear girl; or perhaps I made it clear to my father that in this room he is an interloper."

"Hilary!"

"You want to put yourself in the right in case that door opens suddenly as it has been doing lately. There, you see! Good-evening, Mamma. I was just saying that I have scarcely seen you all day." He drew forward her chair and held the cushion behind her until she leaned back.

"I have been resting."

"Are you ill, Mamma?"

"I have a headache."

"I will stroke it for you, dear lady."

He stood behind her chair and began to smooth her forehead. "Or shall I read to you?" he asked, soon tiring of his task. "Or play the musical-box?"

"No, nothing more, thank you."

Mrs Wilson looked about her, at the tea-cups, then at Florence. Sometimes it seemed to her that her husband was right and that she was growing fanciful. The innocent appearance of the room lulled her and she closed her eyes for a while, rocking gently in her chair.

"I dozed off," she said when she awoke. The table was cleared and Florence and Hilary sat playing chess, whispering so that they should not disturb her.

"It made a domestic scene for us," said Hilary. "Often Miss Chasty and I feel that we are left too much in solitary bliss."

The two women smiled and Mrs Wilson shook her head. "You have too old a head on your shoulders," she said. "What will they say of you when you go to school?"

"What shall I say of *them?*" he asked bravely, but he lowered his eyes and kept them lowered. When his mother had gone, he asked Florence: "Did you go to school?"

"Yes."

"Were you unhappy there?"

"No. I was homesick at first."

"If I don't like it, there will be no point in my staying," he said hurriedly. "I can learn anywhere and I don't particularly want the corners knocked off, as my father once spoke of it. I shouldn't like to play cricket and all those childish games. Only to do boxing and draw blood," he added, with sudden bravado. He laughed excitedly and clenched his fists.

"You would never be good at boxing if you lost your temper."

"I suppose your brothers told you that. They don't sound very manly to me. They would be afraid of a good fight and the sight of blood, I daresay."

"Yes, I daresay. It is bedtime."

He was whipped up by the excitement he had created from his fears.

"Chess is a woman's game," he said and upset the board. He took the cushion from the rocking-chair and kicked it inexpertly across the room. "I should have thought the door would have opened then," he said. "But as my father doesn't appear to send me to my room, I will go there of my own accord. It wouldn't have been a punishment at bedtime in any case. When I am a judge I shall be better at punishments than he is."

When he had gone, Florence picked up the cushion and the chessboard. "I am no good at punishments, either," she thought. She tidied the room, made up the fire, then sat down in the rocking-chair, thinking of all the lonely schoolroom evenings of her future. She bent her head over her needlework—the beaded sachet for her mother's birthday present. When she looked up she thought the lamp was smoking and she went to the table and turned down the wick. Then she noticed that the smoke was wreathing upwards from near the fireplace, forming rings which drifted towards the ceiling and were lost in a haze. She could hear a woman's voice humming softly and the floorboards creaked as if someone were treading up and down the room impatiently.

She felt in herself a sense of burning impatience and anticipation and watching the door opening found herself thinking: "If it is not he, I cannot bear it."

He closed the door quietly. "She has gone to bed," he said in a lowered voice. "For days I dared not come. She has watched me at every moment. At last, this evening, she gave way to a headache. Were you expecting me?"

"Yes."

"And once I called you Miss Mouse! And you are still Miss Mouse when I see you about the garden, or at luncheon."

"In this room I can be myself. It belongs to us."

"And not to Hilary as well—ever?" he asked her in amusement.

She gave him a quick and puzzled glance.

"Let no one intrude," he said hastily. "It is our room, just as you say."

She had turned the lamp too low and it began to splutter. "Firelight is good enough for us," he said, putting the light out altogether.

When he kissed her, she felt an enormous sense of disappointment, almost as if he were the wrong person embracing her in the dark. His arch masterfulness merely bored her. "A long wait for so little," she thought.

He, however, found her entirely seductive. She responded with a sensuous languor, unruffled and at ease like the most perfect hostess.

"Where did you practise this, Miss Mouse?" he asked her. But he did not wait for the reply, fancying that he heard a step on the landing. When his wife opened the door, he was trying desperately to light a taper at the fire. His hand was trembling, and when at last, in the terribly silent room, the flame crept up the spill it simply served to show Florence's disarray which, like a sleep-walker, she had not noticed or put right.

She did not see Hilary again, except as a blurred little figure at the schoolroom window—blurred because of her tear-swollen eyes.

She was driven away in the carriage, although Mr Wilson had suggested the station fly. "Let us keep her disgrace and her tearfulness to ourselves," he begged, although he was exhausted by the repetitious burden of his wife's grief.

"*Her* disgrace!"

"My mistake, I have said, was in not taking your accusations about her seriously. I see now that I was in some way bewitched—yes, bewitched is what it was—acting against my judgment; nay, my very nature. I am astonished that anyone so seemingly meek could have cast such a spell upon me."

Poor Florence turned her head aside as Williams, the coachman, came to fetch her little trunk and the basket-work holdall. Then she put on her cloak, and prepared herself to go downstairs, fearful lest she should meet anyone on the way. Yet her thoughts were even more on her journey's end; for what, she wondered, could she tell her father and how expect him to understand what she could not understand herself?

Her head was bent as she crossed the landing and she hurried past the schoolroom door. At the turn of the staircase she pressed back against the wall to allow someone to pass. She heard laughter and then up the stairs came a young woman and a little girl. The child was clinging to the woman's arm and coaxing her, as sometimes Hilary had tried to coax Florence. "After lessons," the woman said firmly, but gaily. She looked ahead, smiling to herself. Her clothes were unlike anything that Florence had ever seen. Later, when she tried to describe them to her mother, she could only remember the shortness of a tunic which scarcely covered the knees, a hat like a helmet drawn down over eyes intensely green and matching the long necklace of glass beads which swung on her flat bosom. As she came up the stairs and drew near to Florence, she was humming softly against the child's pleading; silk rustled against her silken legs and all of the staircase, as Florence quickly descended, was full of fragrance.

In the darkness of the hall a man was watching the two go round the bend of the stairs. The woman must have looked back, for Florence saw him lift his hand in a secretive gesture of understanding.

"It is Hilary, not his father!" she thought. But the figure turned before she could be sure and went into the library.

Outside on the drive Williams was waiting with her luggage stowed away in the carriage. When she had settled herself, she looked up at the schoolroom window and saw Hilary standing there rather forlornly and she could almost imagine him saying: "My poor dear girl; so you were not good enough for me, after all?"

"When does the new governess arrive?" she asked Williams in a casual voice, which hoped to conceal both pride and grief.

"There's nothing fixed as far as I have heard," he said.

They drove out into the lane.

"When will it be *her* time?" Florence wondered. "I am glad that I saw her before I left."

"We are sorry to see you going, Miss." He had heard that the maids were sorry, for she had given them no trouble.

"Thank you, Williams."

As they went on towards the station, she leaned back and looked at the familiar places where she had walked with Hilary. "I know what I shall tell my father now," she thought, and she felt peaceful and meek as though beginning to be convalescent after a long illness.   1958

OLIVER ONIONS

THE BECKONING FAIR ONE

I

The three or four "To Let" boards had stood within the low paling as long as the inhabitants of the little triangular "Square" could remember, and if they had ever been vertical it was a very long time ago. They now overhung the palings each at its own angle, and resembled nothing so much as a row of wooden choppers, ever in the act of falling upon some passer-by, yet never cutting off a tenant for the old house from the stream of his fellows. Not that there was ever any great "stream" through the square; the stream passed a furlong and more away, beyond the intricacy of tenements and alleys and byways that had sprung up since the old house had been built, hemming it in completely; and probably the house itself was only suffered to stand pending the falling-in of a lease or two, when doubtless a clearance would be made of the whole neighbourhood.

It was of bloomy old red brick, and built into its walls were the crowns and clasped hands and other insignia of insurance companies long since defunct. The children of the secluded square had swung upon the low gate at the end of the entrance-alley until little more than the solid top bar of it remained, and the alley itself ran past boarded basement windows on which tramps had chalked their cryptic marks. The path was washed and worn uneven by the spilling of water from the eaves of the encroaching next house, and cats and dogs had made the approach their own. The chances of a tenant did not seem such as to warrant the keeping of the "To Let" boards in a state of legibility and repair, and as a matter of fact they were not so kept.

For six months Oleron had passed the old place twice a day or oftener, on his way from his lodgings to the room, ten minutes' walk away, he had taken to work in; and for six months no hatchet-like notice-board had fallen across his path. This might have been due to the fact that he usually took the other side of the square. But he chanced one morning to take the side that ran past the broken gate and the rain-worn entrance alley, and to pause before one of the inclined boards. The board bore, besides the agent's name, the announcement, written apparently about the time of Oleron's own early youth, that the key was to be had at Number Six.

Now Oleron was already paying, for his separate bedroom and work-room, more than an author who, without private means, habitually disregards his public, can afford; and he was paying in addition a small rent for the storage of the greater part of his grandmother's furniture. Moreover, it invariably happened that the book he wished to read in bed was at his working-quarters half a mile or more away, while the note or letter he had sudden need of during the day was as likely as not to be in the pocket of another coat hanging behind his bedroom door. And there were other inconveniences in having a divided domicile. Therefore Oleron, brought suddenly up by the hatchet-like notice-board, looked first down through some scanty privet-bushes at the boarded basement windows, then up at the blank and grimy windows of the first floor, and so up to the second floor and the flat stone coping of the leads. He stood for a minute thumbing his lean and shaven jaw; then, with another glance at the board, he walked slowly across the square to Number Six.

He knocked, and waited for two or three minutes, but, although the door stood open, received no answer. He was knocking again when a long-nosed man in shirt-sleeves appeared.

"I was arsking a blessing on our food," he said in severe explanation.

Oleron asked if he might have the key of the old house; and the long-nosed man withdrew again.

Oleron waited for another five minutes on the step; then the man, appearing again and masticating some of the food of which he had spoken, announced that the key was lost.

"But you won't want it," he said. "The entrance door isn't closed, and a push'll open any of the others. I'm a agent for it, if you're thinking of taking it——"

Oleron recrossed the square, descended the two steps at the broken gate, passed along the alley, and turned in at the old wide doorway. To the right, immediately within the door, steps descended to the roomy cellars, and the staircase before him had a carved rail, and was broad and handsome and filthy. Oleron ascended it, avoiding contact with the rail and wall, and stopped at the first landing. A door facing him had been boarded up, but he pushed at that on his right hand, and an insecure bolt or staple yielded. He entered the empty first floor.

He spent a quarter of an hour in the place, and then came out again. Without mounting higher, he descended and recrossed the square to the house of the man who had lost the key.

"Can you tell me how much the rent is?" he asked.

The man mentioned a figure, the comparative lowness of which seemed accounted for by the character of the neighbourhood and the abominable state of unrepair of the place.

"Would it be possible to rent a single floor?"

The long-nosed man did not know; they might. . . .

"Who are they?"

The man gave Oleron the name of a firm of lawyers in Lincoln's Inn.

"You might mention my name—Barrett," he added.

Pressure of work prevented Oleron from going down to Lincoln's Inn that afternoon, but he went on the morrow, and was instantly offered the whole house as a purchase for fifty pounds down, the remainder of the purchase-money to remain on mortgage. It took him half an hour to disabuse the lawyer's mind of the idea that he wished anything more of the place than to rent a single floor of it. This made certain hums and haws of a difference, and the lawyer was by no means certain that it lay within his power to do as Oleron suggested; but it was finally extracted from him that, provided the notice-boards were allowed to remain up, and that, provided it was agreed that in the event of the whole house letting, the arrangement should terminate automatically without further notice, something might be done. That the old place should suddenly let over his head seemed to Oleron the slightest of risks to take, and he promised a decision within a week. On the morrow he visited the house again, went through it from top to bottom, and then went home to his lodgings to take a bath.

He was immensely taken with that portion of the house he had already determined should be his own. Scraped clean and repainted, and with that old furniture of Oleron's grandmother's, it ought to be entirely charming. He went to the storage warehouse to refresh his memory of his half-forgotten belongings, and to take the measurements; and thence he went to a decorator's. He was very busy with his regular work, and could have wished that the notice-board had caught his attention either a few months earlier or else later in the year; but the quickest way would be to suspend work entirely until after his removal. . . .

A fortnight later his first floor was painted throughout in a tender, elder-flower white, the paint was dry, and Oleron was in the middle of his installation. He was animated, delighted; and he rubbed his hands as he polished and made disposals of his grandmother's effects—the tall lattice-paned china cupboard with its Derby and Mason and Spode, the large folding Sheraton table, the long, low bookshelves (he had had two of them "copied"), the chairs, the Sheffield candlesticks, the riveted rose-bowls. These things he set against his newly painted elder-white walls—walls of wood panelled in the happiest proportions, and moulded and coffered to the low-seated window-recesses in a mood of gaiety and rest that the builders of rooms no longer know. The ceilings were lofty, and faintly painted with an old pattern of stars; even the tapering mouldings of his iron fireplace were as delicately designed as jewellery; and Oleron walked about rubbing his hands, frequently stopping for the mere pleasure of the glimpses from white room to white room. . . .

"Charming, charming!" he said to himself. "I wonder what Elsie Bengough will think of this!"

He bought a bolt and a Yale lock for his door, and shut off his quarters from the rest of the house. If he now wanted to read in bed, his book could be had for stepping into the next room. All the time, he thought how exceedingly lucky he was to get the place. He put up a hat-rack in the little square hall, and hung up his hats and caps and coats; and passers through the small triangular square late at night, looking up over the little serried row of wooden "To Let" hatchets, could see the light within Oleron's red blinds, or else the sudden darkening of one blind and the illumination of another, as Oleron, candlestick in hand, passed from room to room, making final settlings of his furniture, or preparing to resume the work that his removal had interrupted.

II

As far as the chief business of his life—his writing—was concerned, Paul Oleron treated the world a good deal better than he was treated by it; but he seldom took the trouble to strike a balance, or to compute how far, at forty-four years of age, he was behind his points on the handicap. To have done so wouldn't have altered matters, and it might have depressed Oleron. He had chosen his path, and was committed to it beyond possibility of withdrawal. Perhaps he had chosen it in the days when he had been easily swayed by something a little disinterested, a little generous, a little noble; and had he ever thought of questioning himself he would still have held to it that a life without nobility and generosity and disinterestedness was no life for him. Only quite recently, and rarely, had he even vaguely suspected that there was more in it than this; but it was no good anticipating the day when, he supposed, he would reach that maximum point of his powers beyond which he must inevitably decline, and be left face to face with the question whether it would not have profited him better to have ruled his life by less exigent ideals.

In the meantime, his removal into the old house with the insurance marks built into its brick merely interrupted *Romilly Bishop* at the fifteenth chapter.

As this tall man with the lean, ascetic face moved about his new abode, arranging, changing, altering, hardly yet into his working-stride again, he gave the impression of almost spinster-like precision and nicety. For twenty years past, in a score of lodgings, garrets, flats, and rooms furnished and unfurnished, he had been accustomed to do many things for himself, and he had discovered that it saves time and temper to be methodical. He had arranged with the wife of the long-nosed Barrett, a stout Welsh woman with a falsetto voice, the Merionethshire accent of which long residence in London had not perceptibly modified, to come across the square each morning to prepare his breakfast, and also to "turn the place out" on Saturday mornings; and for the rest, he even welcomed a little housework as a relaxation from the strain of writing.

His kitchen, together with the adjoining strip of an apartment into which a modern bath had been fitted, overlooked the alley at the side of the house; and at one end of it was a large closet with a door, and a square sliding hatch in the upper part of the door. This had been a powder-closet, and through the hatch the elaborately dressed head had been thrust to receive the click and puff of the powder-pistol. Oleron puzzled a little over this closet; then, as its use occurred to him, he smiled faintly, a little moved, he knew not by what. . . . He would have to put it to a very different purpose from its original one; it would probably have to serve as his larder. . . . It was in this closet that he made a discovery. The back of it was shelved, and, rummaging on an upper shelf that ran deeply into the wall, Oleron found a couple of mushroom-shaped old wooden wig-stands. He did not know how they had come to be there. Doubtless the painters had turned them up somewhere or other, and had put them there. But his five rooms, as a whole, were short of cupboard and closet-room; and it was only by the exercise of some ingenuity that he was able to find places for the bestowal of his household linen, his boxes, and his seldom-used but not-to-be-destroyed accumulation of papers.

It was in early spring that Oleron entered on his tenancy, and he was anxious to have *Romilly* ready for publication in the coming autumn. Nevertheless, he did not intend to force its production. Should it demand longer in the doing, so much the worse; he realised its importance, its crucial importance, in his artistic development, and it must have its own length and time. In the workroom he had recently left he had been making excellent progress; *Romilly* had begun, as the saying is, to speak and act of herself; and he did not doubt she would continue to do so the moment the distraction of his removal was over. This distraction was almost over; he told himself it was time he pulled himself together again; and on a March morning he went out, returned again with two great bunches of yellow daffodils, placed one bunch on his mantelpiece between the Sheffield sticks and the other on the table before him, and took out the half-completed manuscript of *Romilly Bishop*.

But before beginning work he went to a small rosewood cabinet and took from a drawer his cheque-book and pass-book. He totted them up, and his monk-like face grew thoughtful. His installation had cost him more than he had intended it should, and his balance was rather less than fifty pounds, with no immediate prospect of more.

"Hm! I'd forgotten rugs and chintz curtains and so forth mounted up so," said Oleron. "But it would have been a pity to spoil the place for the want of ten pounds or so. . . . Well, *Romilly* simply *must* be out for the autumn, that's all. So here goes——"

He drew his papers towards him.

But he worked badly; or, rather, he did not work at all. The square outside had its own noises, frequent and new, and Oleron could only hope that he would speedily become accustomed to these. First came hawkers, with their carts and cries; at midday the children, returning from school, trooped into the square and swung on Oleron's gate; and when the children had departed again for afternoon school, an itinerant musician with a mandoline posted himself beneath Oleron's window and began to strum. This was a not unpleasant distraction, and Oleron, pushing up his window, threw the man a penny. Then he returned to his table again. . . .

But it was no good. He came to himself, at long intervals, to find that he had been looking about his room and wondering how it had formerly been furnished—whether a settee in buttercup or petunia satin had stood under the farther window, whether from the centre moulding of the light lofty ceiling had depended a glimmering crystal chandelier, or where the tambour-frame or the picquet-table had stood. . . . No, it was no good; he had far better be frankly doing nothing than getting fruit-lessly tired; and he decided that he would take a walk, but, chancing to sit down for a moment, dozed in his chair instead.

"This won't do," he yawned when he awoke at half-past four in the afternoon; "I must do better than this tomorrow——"

And he felt so deliciously lazy that for some minutes he even contemplated the breach of an appointment he had for the evening.

The next morning he sat down to work without even permitting himself to answer one of his three letters—two of them tradesmen's accounts, the third a note from Miss Bengough, forwarded from his old address. It was a jolly day of white and blue, with a gay noisy wind and a subtle turn in the colour of growing things; and over and over again, once or twice a minute, his room became suddenly light and then subdued again, as the shining white clouds rolled north-eastwards over the square. The soft fitful illumination was reflected in the polished surface of the table and even in the footworn old floor; and the morning noises had begun again.

Oleron made a pattern of dots on the paper before him, and then broke off to move the jar of daffodils exactly opposite the centre of a creamy panel. Then he wrote a sentence that ran continuously for a couple of lines, after which it broke off into notes and jottings. For a time he succeeded in persuading himself that in making these memoranda he was really working; then he rose and began to pace his room. As he did so, he was struck by an idea. It was that the place might possibly be a little better for more positive colour. It was, perhaps, a thought *too* pale—mild and sweet as a kind old face, but a little devitalised, even wan. . . . Yes, decidedly it would bear a robuster note—more and richer flowers, and possibly some warm and gay stuff for cushions for the window-seats. . . .

"Of course, I really can't afford it," he muttered, as he went for a two-foot and began to measure the width of the window recesses. . . .

In stooping to measure a recess, his attitude suddenly changed to one of interest and attention. Presently he rose again, rubbing his hands with gentle glee.

"Oho, oho!" he said. "These look to me very much like window-boxes, nailed up. We must look into this! Yes, those are boxes, or I'm . . . oho, this is an adventure!"

On that wall of his sitting-room there were two windows (the third was in another corner), and, beyond the open bedroom door, on the same wall, was another. The seats of all had been painted, repainted, and painted again; and Oleron's investigating finger had barely detected the old nailheads beneath the paint. Under the ledge over which he stooped an old keyhole also had been puttied up. Oleron took out his penknife.

He worked carefully for five minutes, and then went into the kitchen for a hammer and chisel. Driving the chisel cautiously under the seat, he started the whole lid slightly. Again using the penknife, he cut along the hinged edge and outward along the ends; and then he fetched a wedge and a wooden mallet.

"Now for our little mystery——" he said.

The sound of the mallet on the wedge seemed, in that sweet and pale apartment, somehow a little brutal—nay, even shocking. The panelling rang and rattled and vibrated to the blows like a sounding-board. The whole house seemed to echo; from the roomy cellarage to the garrets above a flock of echoes seemed to awake; and the sound got a little on Oleron's nerves. All at once he paused, fetched a duster, and muffled the mallet. . . . When the edge was sufficiently raised he put his fingers under it and lifted. The paint flaked and starred a little; the rusty old nails squeaked and grunted; and the lid came up, laying open the box beneath. Oleron looked into it. Save for a couple of inches of scurf and mould and old cobwebs it was empty.

"No treasure there," said Oleron, a little amused that he should have fancied there might have been. *"Romilly* will still have to be out by the autumn. Let's have a look at the others."

He turned to the second window.

The raising of the two remaining seats occupied him until well into the afternoon. That of the bedroom, like the first, was empty; but from the second seat of his sitting-room he drew out something yielding and folded and furred over an inch thick with dust. He carried the object into the kitchen, and having swept it over a bucket, took a duster to it.

It was some sort of a large bag, of an ancient frieze-like material, and when unfolded it occupied the greater part of the small kitchen floor. In shape it was an irregular, a very irregular, triangle, and it had a couple of wide flaps, with the remains of straps and buckles. The patch that had been uppermost in the folding was of a faded yellowish brown; but the rest of it was of shades of crimson that varied according to the exposure of the parts of it.

"Now whatever can that have been?" Oleron mused as he stood surveying it. . . . "I give it up. Whatever it is, it's settled my work for to-day, I'm afraid—"

He folded the object up carelessly and thrust it into a corner of the kitchen; then, taking pans and brushes and an old knife, he returned to the sitting-room and began to scrape and to wash and to line with paper his newly discovered receptacles. When he had finished, he put his spare boots and books and papers into them; and he closed the lids again, amused with his little adventure, but also a little anxious for the hour to come when he should settle fairly down to his work again.

III

It piqued Oleron a little that his friend, Miss Bengough, should dismiss with a glance the place he himself had found so singularly winning. Indeed she scarcely lifted her eyes to it. But then she had always been more or less like that—a little indifferent to the graces of life, careless of appearances, and perhaps a shade more herself when she ate biscuits from a paper bag than when she dined with greater observance of the convenances. She was an unattached journalist of thirty-four, large, showy, fair as butter, pink as a dog-rose, reminding one of a florist's picked specimen bloom, and given to sudden and ample movements and moist and explosive utterances. She "pulled a better living out of the pool" (as she expressed it) than Oleron did; and by cunningly disguised puffs of drapers and haberdashers she "pulled" also the greater part of her very varied wardrobe. She left small whirlwinds of air behind her when she moved, in which her veils and scarves fluttered and spun.

Oleron heard the flurry of her skirts on his staircase and her single loud knock at his door when he had been a month in his new abode. Her garments brought in the outer air, and she flung a bundle of ladies' journals down on a chair.

"Don't knock off for me," she said across a mouthful of large-headed hatpins as she removed her hat and veil. "I didn't know whether you were straight yet, so I've brought some sandwiches for lunch. You've got coffee, I suppose?—No, don't get up—I'll find the kitchen——"

"Oh, that's all right, I'll clear these things away. To tell the truth, I'm rather glad to be interrupted," said Oleron.

He gathered his work together and put it away. She was already in the kitchen; he heard the running of water into the kettle. He joined her, and ten minutes later followed her back to the sitting-room with the coffee and sandwiches on a tray. They sat down, with the tray on a small table between them.

"Well, what do you think of the new place?" Oleron asked as she poured out coffee.

"Hm! . . . Anybody'd think you were going to get married, Paul."

He laughed.

"Oh no. But it's an improvement on some of them, isn't it?"

"Is it? I suppose it is; I don't know. I liked the last place, in spite of the black ceiling and no watertap. How's *Romilly?*"

Oleron thumbed his chin.

"Hm! I'm rather ashamed to tell you. The fact is, I've not got on very well with it. But it will be all right on the night, as you used to say."

"Stuck?"

"Rather stuck."

"Got any of it you care to read to me? . . ."

Oleron had long been in the habit of reading portions of his work to Miss Bengough occasionally. Her comments were always quick and practical, sometimes directly useful, sometimes indirectly suggestive. She, in return for his confidence, always kept all mention of her own work sedulously from him. His, she said, was "real work"; hers merely filled space, not always even grammatically.

"I'm afraid there isn't," Oleron replied, still meditatively dry-shaving his chin. Then he added, with a little burst of candour, "The fact is, Elsie, I've not written—not actually written—very much more of it— *any* more of it, in fact. But, of course, that doesn't mean I haven't progressed. I've progressed, in one sense, rather alarmingly. I'm now thinking of reconstructing the whole thing."

Miss Bengough gave a gasp. "Reconstructing!"

"Making Romilly herself a different type of woman. Somehow, I've begun to feel that I'm not getting the most out of her. As she stands, I've certainly lost interest in her to some extent."

"But—but——" Miss Bengough protested, "you had her so real, so *living*, Paul!"

Oleron smiled faintly. He had been quite prepared for Miss Bengough's disapproval. He wasn't surprised that she liked Romilly as she at present existed; she would. Whether she realised it or not, there was much of herself in his fictitious creation. Naturally Romilly would seem "real," "living," to her. . . .

"But are you really serious, Paul?" Miss Bengough asked presently, with a round-eyed stare.

"Quite serious."

"You're really going to scrap those fifteen chapters?"

"I didn't exactly say that."

"That fine, rich love-scene?"

"I should only do it reluctantly, and for the sake of something I thought better."

"And that beautiful, *beau*tiful description of Romilly on the shore?"

"It wouldn't necessarily be wasted," he said a little uneasily.

But Miss Bengough made a large and windy gesture, and then let him have it.

"Really, you are *too* trying!" she broke out. "I do wish sometimes you'd remember you're human, and live in a world! You know I'd be the *last* to wish you to lower your standard one inch, but it wouldn't be lowering it to bring it within human comprehension. Oh, you're sometimes altogether too godlike! . . . Why, it would be a wicked, criminal waste of your powers to destroy those fifteen chapters! Look at it reasonably, now. You've been working for nearly twenty years; you've now got what you've been working for almost within your grasp; your affairs are at a most critical stage (oh, don't tell me; I know you're about at the end of your money); and here you are, deliberately proposing to withdraw a thing that will probably make your name, and to substitute for it something that ten to one nobody on earth will ever want to read—and small blame to them! Really, you try my patience!"

Oleron had shaken his head slowly as she had talked. It was an old story between them. The noisy, able, practical journalist was an admirable friend—up to a certain point; beyond that . . . well, each of us knows that point beyond which we stand alone. Elsie Bengough sometimes said that had she had one-tenth part of Oleron's genius there were few things she could not have done—thus making that genius a quantitatively divisible thing, a sort of ingredient, to be added to or to be subtracted from in the admixture of his work. That it was a qualitative thing, essential, indivisible, informing, passed her comprehension. Their spirits parted company at that point. Oleron knew it. She did not appear to know it.

"Yes, yes, yes," he said a little wearily, by-and-by, "practically you're quite right, entirely right, and I haven't a word to say. If I could only turn *Romilly* over to you you'd make an enormous success of her. But that can't be, and I, for my part, am seriously doubting whether she's worth my while. You know what that means."

"What does it mean?" she demanded bluntly.

"Well," he said, smiling wanly, "what *does* it mean when you're convinced a thing isn't worth doing? You simply don't do it."

Miss Bengough's eyes swept the ceiling for assistance against this impossible man.

"What utter rubbish!" she broke out at last. "Why, when I saw you last you were simply oozing *Romilly;* you were turning her off at the rate of four chapters a week; if you hadn't moved you'd have had her three-parts done by now. What on earth possessed you to move right in the middle of your most important work?"

Oleron tried to put her off with a recital of inconveniences, but she wouldn't have it. Perhaps in her heart she partly suspected the reason. He was simply mortally weary of the narrow circumstances of his life. He had had twenty years of it—twenty years of garrets and roof-chambers and dingy flats and shabby lodgings, and he was tired of dinginess and shabbiness. The reward was as far off as ever—or if it was not, he no longer cared as once he would have cared to put out his hand and take it. It is all very well to tell a man who is at the point of exhaustion that only another effort is required of him; if he cannot make it he is as far off as ever. . . .

"Anyway," Oleron summed up, "I'm happier here than I've been for a long time. That's some sort of a justification."

"And doing no work," said Miss Bengough pointedly.

At that a trifling petulance that had been gathering in Oleron came to a head.

"And why should I do nothing but work?" he demanded. "How much happier am I for it? I don't say I don't love my work—when it's done; but I hate doing it. Sometimes it's an intolerable burden that I simply long to be rid of. Once in many weeks it has a moment, one moment, of glow and thrill for me; I remember the days when it was all glow and thrill; and now I'm forty-four, and it's becoming drudgery. Nobody wants it; I'm ceasing to want it myself; and if any ordinary sensible man were to ask me whether I didn't think I was a fool to go on, I think I should agree that I was."

Miss Bengough's comely pink face was serious.

"But you knew all that, many, many years ago, Paul—and still you chose it," she said in a low voice.

"Well, and how should I have known?" he demanded. "I didn't know. I was told so. My heart, if you like, told me so, and I thought I knew. Youth always thinks it knows; then one day it discovers that it is nearly fifty——"

"Forty-four, Paul——"

"—forty-four, then—and it finds that the glamour isn't in front, but behind. Yes, I knew and chose, if *that's* knowing and choosing . . . but it's a costly choice we're called on to make when we're young!"

Miss Bengough's eyes were on the floor. Without moving them she said, "You're not regretting it, Paul?"

"Am I not?" he took her up. "Upon my word, I've lately thought I am! What *do* I get in return for it all?"

"You know what you get," she replied.

He might have known from her tone what else he could have had for the holding up of a finger—herself. She knew, but could not tell him, that he could have done no better thing for himself. Had he, any time these ten years, asked her to marry him, she would have replied quietly, "Very well; when?" He had never thought of it. . . .

"Yours is the real work," she continued quietly. "Without you we jackals couldn't exist. You and a few like you hold everything upon your shoulders."

For a minute there was a silence. Then it occurred to Oleron that this was common vulgar grumbling. It was not his habit. Suddenly he rose and began to stack cups and plates on the tray.

"Sorry you catch me like this, Elsie," he said, with a little laugh. . . . "No, I'll take them out; then we'll go for a walk, if you like. . . ."

He carried out the tray, and then began to show Miss Bengough round his flat. She made few comments. In the kitchen she asked what an old faded square of reddish frieze was, that Mrs. Barrett used as a cushion for her wooden chair.

"That? I should be glad if you could tell *me* what it is," Oleron replied as he unfolded the bag and related the story of its finding in the window-seat.

"I think I know what it is," said Miss Bengough. "It's been used to wrap up a harp before putting it into its case."

"By Jove, that's probably just what it was," said Oleron. "I could make neither head nor tail of it. . . ."

They finished the tour of the flat, and returned to the sitting-room.

"And who lives in the rest of the house?" Miss Bengough asked.

"I dare say a tramp sleeps in the cellar occasionally. Nobody else."

"Hm! . . . Well, I'll tell you what I think about it, if you like."

"I should like."

"You'll never work here."

"Oh?" said Oleron quickly. "Why not?"

"You'll never finish *Romilly* here. Why, I don't know, but you won't. I know it. You'll have to leave before you get on with that book."

He mused for a moment, and then said:

"Isn't that a little—prejudiced, Elsie?"

"Perfectly ridiculous. As an argument it hasn't a leg to stand on. But there it is," she replied, her mouth once more full of the large-headed hat pins.

Oleron was reaching down his hat and coat. He laughed.

"I can only hope you're entirely wrong," he said, "for I shall be in a serious mess if *Romilly* isn't out in the autumn."

IV

As Oleron sat by his fire that evening, pondering Miss Bengough's prognostication that difficulties awaited him in his work, he came to the conclusion that it would have been far better had she kept her beliefs to herself. No man does a thing better for having his confidence damped at the outset, and to speak of difficulties is in a sense to make them. Speech itself becomes a deterrent act, to which other discouragements accrete until the very event of which warning is given is as likely as not to come to pass. He heartily confounded her. An influence hostile to the completion of *Romilly* had been born.

And in some illogical, dogmatic way women seem to have, she had attached this antagonistic influence to his new abode. Was ever anything so absurd! "You'll never finish *Romilly* here." . . . Why not? Was this her idea of the luxury that saps the springs of action and brings a man down to indolence and dropping out of the race? The place was well enough—it was entirely charming, for that matter—but it was not so demoralising as all that! No; Elsie had missed the mark that time. . . .

He moved his chair to look round the room that smiled, positively smiled, in the firelight. He too smiled, as if pity was to be entertained for a maligned apartment. Even that slight lack of robust colour he had remarked was not noticeable in the soft glow. The drawn chintz curtains—they had a flowered and trellised pattern, with baskets and oaten pipes—fell in long quiet folds to the window-seats; the rows of bindings in old bookcases took the light richly; the last trace of sallowness had gone with the daylight; and, if the truth must be told, it had been Elsie herself who had seemed a little out of the picture.

That reflection struck him a little, and presently he returned to it. Yes, the room had, quite accidentally, done Miss Bengough a disservice that afternoon. It had, in some subtle but unmistakable way, placed her, marked a contrast of qualities. Assuming for the sake of argument the slightly ridiculous proposition that the room in which Oleron sat *was* characterised by a certain sparsity and lack of vigour; so much the worse for Miss Bengough; she certainly erred on the side of redundancy and general muchness. And if one must contrast abstract qualities, Oleron inclined to the austere in taste. . . .

Yes, here Oleron had made a distinct discovery; he wondered he had not made it before. He pictured Miss Bengough again as she had appeared that afternoon—large, showy, moistly pink, with that quality of the prize bloom exuding, as it were, from her; and instantly she suffered in his thought. He even recognised now that he had noticed something odd at the time, and that unconsciously his attitude, even while she had been there, had been one of criticism. The mechanism of her was a little obvious; her melting humidity was the result of analysable processes; and behind her there had seemed to lurk some dim shape emblematic of mortality. He had never, during the ten years of their intimacy, dreamed for a moment of asking her to marry him; none the less, he now felt for the first time a thankfulness that he had not done so. . . .

Then, suddenly and swiftly, his face flamed that he should be thinking thus of his friend. What! Elsie Bengough, with whom he had spent weeks and weeks of afternoons—she, the good chum, on whose help he would have counted had all the rest of the world failed him—she, whose loyalty to him would not, he knew, swerve as long as there was breath in her—Elsie to be even in thought dissected thus! He was an ingrate and a cad. . . .

Had she been there in that moment he would have abased himself before her.

For ten minutes and more he sat, still gazing into the fire, with that humiliating red fading slowly from his cheeks. All was still within and without, save for a tiny musical tinkling that came from his kitchen—the dripping of water from an imperfectly turned-off tap into the vessel beneath it. Mechanically he began to beat with his fingers to the faintly heard falling of the drops; the tiny regular movement seemed to hasten that shameful withdrawal from his face. He grew cool once more; and when he resumed his meditation he was all unconscious that he took it up again at the same point. . . .

It was not only her florid superfluity of build that he had approached in the attitude of criticism; he was conscious also of the wide differences between her mind and his own. He felt no thankfulness that up to a certain point their natures had ever run companionably side by side; he was now full of questions beyond that point. Their intellects diverged;

there was no denying it; and, looking back, he was inclined to doubt whether there had been any real coincidence. True, he had read his writings to her and she had appeared to speak comprehendingly and to the point; but what can a man do who, having assumed that another sees as he does, is suddenly brought up sharp by something that falsifies and discredits all that has gone before? He doubted all now. . . . It did for a moment occur to him that the man who demands of a friend more than can be given to him is in danger of losing that friend, but he put the thought aside.

Again he ceased to think, and again moved his finger to the distant dripping of the tap. . . .

And now (he resumed by-and-by), if these things were true of Elsie Bengough, they were also true of the creation of which she was the prototype—Romilly Bishop. And since he could say of Romilly what for very shame he could not say of Elsie, he gave his thoughts rein. He did so in that smiling, fire-lighted room, to the accompaniment of the faintly heard tap.

There was no longer any doubt about it; he hated the central character of his novel. Even as he had described her physically she overpowered the senses; she was coarse-fibred, over-coloured, rank. It became true the moment he formulated his thought; Gulliver had described the Brobdingnagian maids-of-honour thus: and mentally and spiritually she corresponded—was unsensitive, limited, common. The model (he closed his eyes for a moment)—the model stuck out through fifteen vulgar and blatant chapters to such a pitch that, without seeing the reason, he had been unable to begin the sixteenth. He marvelled that it had only just dawned upon him.

And *this* was to have been his Beatrice, his vision! As Elsie she was to have gone into the furnace of his art, and she was to have come out the Woman all men desire! Her thoughts were to have been culled from his own finest, her form from his dearest dreams, and her setting wherever he could find one fit for her worth. He had brooded long before making the attempt; then one day he had felt her stir within him as a mother feels a quickening, and he had begun to write; and so he had added chapter to chapter. . . .

And those fifteen sodden chapters were what he had produced!

Again he sat, softly moving his finger. . . .

Then he bestirred himself.

She must go, all fifteen chapters of her. That was settled. For what was to take her place his mind was a blank; but one thing at a time; a man is not excused from taking the wrong course because the right one is not immediately revealed to him. Better would come if it was to come; in the meantime——

He rose, fetched the fifteen chapters, and read them over before he should drop them into the fire.

But instead of putting them into the fire he let them fall from his hand. He became conscious of the dripping of the tap again. It had a tinkling gamut of four or five notes, on which it rang irregular changes, and it was foolishly sweet and dulcimer-like. In his mind Oleron could see the gathering of each drop, its little tremble on the lip of the tap, and the tiny percussion of its fall "Plink—plunk," minimised almost to inaudibility. Following the lowest note there seemed to be a brief phrase, irregularly repeated; and presently Oleron found himself waiting for the recurrence of this phrase. It was quite pretty. . . .

But it did not conduce to wakefulness, and Oleron dozed over his fire.

When he awoke again the fire had burned low and the flames of the candles were licking the rims of the Sheffield sticks. Sluggishly he rose, yawned, went his nightly round of door-locks, and window-fastenings, and passed into his bedroom. Soon, he slept soundly.

But a curious little sequel followed on the morrow. Mrs. Barrett usually tapped, not at his door, but at the wooden wall beyond which lay Oleron's bed; and then Oleron rose, put on his dressing-gown, and admitted her. He was not conscious that as he did so that morning he hummed an air; but Mrs. Barrett lingered with her hand on the doorknob and her face a little averted and smiling.

"De-ar me!" her soft falsetto rose. "But that will be a very o-ald tune, Mr. Oleron! I will not have heard it this for-ty years!"

"What tune?" Oleron asked.

"The tune, indeed, that you was humming, sir."

Oleron had his thumb in the flap of a letter. It remained there.

"*I* was humming? . . . Sing it, Mrs. Barrett."

Mrs. Barrett prut-prutted.

"I have no voice for singing, Mr. Oleron; it was Ann Pugh was the singer of our family; but the tune will be very o-ald, and it is called 'The Beckoning Fair One.' "

"Try to sing it," said Oleron, his thumb still in the envelope; and Mrs. Barrett, with much dimpling and confusion, hummed the air.

"They do say it was sung to a harp, Mr. Oleron, and it will be very o-ald," she concluded.

"And *I* was singing that?"

"Indeed you was. I would not be likely to tell you lies."

With a "Very well—let me have breakfast," Oleron opened his letter; but the trifling circumstance struck him as more odd than he would have admitted to himself. The phrase he had hummed had been that which he had associated with the falling from the tap on the evening before.

V

Even more curious than that the commonplace dripping of an ordinary water-tap should have tallied so closely with an actually existing air was another result it had, namely, that it awakened, or seemed to awaken, in Oleron an abnormal sensitiveness to other noises of the old house. It has been remarked that silence obtains its fullest and most impressive quality when it is broken by some minute sound; and, truth to tell, the place was never still. Perhaps the mildness of the spring air operated on its torpid old timbers; perhaps Oleron's fires caused it to stretch its old anatomy; and certainly a whole world of insect life bored and burrowed in its baulks and joists. At any rate Oleron had only to sit quiet in his chair and to wait for a minute or two in order to become aware of such a change in the auditory scale as comes upon a man who, conceiving the mid-summer woods to be motionless and still, all at once finds his ear sharpened to the crepitation of a myriad insects.

And he smiled to think of man's arbitrary distinction between that which has life and that which has not. Here, quite apart from such recognisable sounds as the scampering of mice, the falling of plaster behind his panelling, and the popping of purses or coffins from his fire, was a whole house talking to him had he but known its language. Beams settled with a tired sigh into their old mortices; creatures ticked in the walls; joints cracked, boards complained; with no palpable stirring of the air window-sashes changed their positions with a soft knock in their frames. And whether the place had life in this sense or not, it had at all events a winsome personality. It needed but an hour of musing for Oleron to conceive the idea that, as his own body stood in friendly relation to his soul, so, by an extension and an attenuation, his habitation might fantastically be supposed to stand in some relation to himself. He even amused himself with the farfetched fancy that he might so identify himself with the place that some future tenant, taking possession, might regard it as in a sense haunted. It would be rather a joke if he, a perfectly harmless author, with nothing on his mind worse than a novel he had discovered he must begin again, should turn out to be laying the foundation of a future ghost! . . .

In proportion, however, as he felt this growing attachment to the fabric of his abode, Elsie Bengough, from being merely unattracted, began to show a dislike of the place that was more and more marked. And she did not scruple to speak of her aversion.

"It doesn't belong to today at all, and for you especially it's bad," she said with decision. "You're only too ready to let go your hold on actual things and to slip into apathy; *you* ought to be in a place with concrete floors and a patent gas-meter and a tradesman's lift. And it would do you all the good in the world if you had a job that made you scramble and rub elbows with your fellow-men. Now, if I could get you a job, for, say, two or three days a week, one that would allow you heaps of time for your proper work—would you take it?"

Somehow, Oleron resented a little being diagnosed like this. He thanked Miss Bengough, but without a smile.

"Thank you, but I don't think so. After all each of us has his own life to live," he could not refrain from adding.

"His own life to live! . . . How long is it since you were out, Paul?"

"About two hours."

"I don't mean to buy stamps or to post a letter. How long is it since you had anything like a stretch?"

"Oh, some little time perhaps. I don't know."

"Since I was here last?"

"I haven't been out much."

"And has *Romilly* progressed much better for your being cooped up?"

"I think she has. I'm laying the foundations of her. I shall begin the actual writing presently."

It seemed as if Miss Bengough had forgotten their tussle about the first *Romilly*. She frowned, turned half away, and then quickly turned again.

"Ah! . . . So you've still got that ridiculous idea in your head?"

"If you mean," said Oleron slowly, "that I've discarded the old *Romilly,* and am at work on a new one, you're right. I have still got that idea in my head."

Something uncordial in his tone struck her; but she was a fighter. His own absurd sensitiveness hardened her. She gave a "Pshaw!" of impatience.

"Where is the old one?" she demanded abruptly.

"Why?" asked Oleron.

"I want to see it. I want to show some of it to you. I want, if you're not wool-gathering entirely, to bring you back to your senses."

This time it was he who turned his back. But when he turned round again he spoke more gently.

"It's no good, Elsie. I'm responsible for the way I go, and you must allow me to go it—even if it should seem wrong to you. Believe me, I am giving thought to it. . . . The manuscript, I was on the point of burning it, but I didn't. It's in that window-seat, if you must see it."

Miss Bengough crossed quickly to the window-seat, and lifted the lid. Suddenly she gave a little exclamation, and put the back of her hand to her mouth. She spoke over her shoulder:

"You ought to knock those nails in, Paul," she said.

He strode to her side.

"What? What is it? What's the matter?" he asked. "I did knock them in—or, rather, pulled them out."

"You left enough to scratch with," she replied, showing her hand. From the upper wrist to the knuckle of the little finger a welling red wound showed.

"Good gracious?" Oleron ejaculated. . . . "Here, come to the bathroom and bathe it quickly——"

He hurried her to the bathroom, turned on warm water, and bathed and cleansed the bad gash. Then, still holding the hand, he turned cold water on it, uttering broken phrases of astonishment and concern.

"Good Lord, how did that happen! As far as I knew I'd . . . is this water too cold? Does that hurt? I can't imagine how on earth . . . there; that'll do——"

"No—one moment longer—I can bear it," she murmured, her eyes closed. . . .

Presently he led her back to the sitting room and bound the hand in one of his handkerchiefs; but his face did not lose its expression of perplexity. He had spent half a day in opening and making serviceable the three window-boxes, and he could not conceive how he had come to leave an inch and a half of rusty nail standing in the wood. He himself had opened the lids of each of them a dozen times and had not noticed any nail; but there it was. . . .

"It shall come out now, at all events," he muttered, as he went for a pair of pincers. And he made no mistake about it that time.

Elsie Bengough had sunk into a chair, and her face was rather white; but in her hand was the manuscript of *Romilly*. She had not finished with *Romilly* yet. Presently she returned to the charge.

"Oh, Paul, it will be the greatest mistake you ever, *ever* made if you do not publish this!" she said.

He hung his head, genuinely distressed. He couldn't get that incident of the nail out of his head, and *Romilly* occupied a second place in his thoughts for the moment. But still she insisted; and when presently he spoke it was almost as if he asked her pardon for something.

"What can I say, Elsie? I can only hope that when you see the new version, you'll see how right I am. And if in spite of all you *don't* like her, well . . ." he made a hopeless gesture. "Don't you see that I *must* be guided by my own lights?"

She was silent.

"Come, Elsie," he said gently. "We've got along well so far; don't let us split on this."

The last words had hardly passed his lips before he regretted them.

She had been nursing her injured hand, with her eyes once more closed; but her lips and lids quivered simultaneously. Her voice shook as she spoke.

"I can't help saying it, Paul, but you are so greatly changed."

"Hush, Elsie," he murmured soothingly; "you've had a shock; rest for a while. How could I change?"

"I don't know, but you are. You've not been yourself ever since you came here. I wish you'd never seen the place. It's stopped your work, it's making you into a person I hardly know, and it's made me horribly anxious about you. . . . Oh, how my hand is beginning to throb!"

"Poor child!" he murmured. "Will you let me take you to a doctor and have it properly dressed?"

"No—I shall be all right presently—I'll keep it raised——"

She put her elbow on the back of her chair, and the bandaged hand rested lightly on his shoulder.

At that touch an entirely new anxiety stirred suddenly within him. Hundreds of times previously, on their jaunts and excursions, she had slipped her hand within his arm as she might have slipped it into the arm of a brother, and he had accepted the little affectionate gesture as a brother might have accepted it. But now, for the first time, there rushed into his mind a hundred startling questions. Her eyes were still closed, and her head had fallen pathetically back; and there was a lost and ineffable smile on her parted lips. The truth broke in upon him. Good God! . . . And he had never divined it!

And stranger than all was that, now that he did see that she was lost in love of him, there came to him, not sorrow and humility and abasement, but something else that he struggled in vain against—something entirely strange and new, that, had he analyzed it, he would have found to be petulance and irritation and resentment and ungentleness. The sudden selfish prompting mastered him before he was aware. He all but gave it words. What was she doing there at all? Why was she not getting on with her own work? Why was she here interfering with his? Who had given her this guardianship over him that lately she had put forward so assertively? "Changed?" It was she, not himself, who had changed. . . .

But by the time she had opened her eyes again he had overcome his resentment sufficiently to speak gently, albeit with reserve.

"I wish you would let me take you to a doctor."

She rose.

"No, thank you, Paul," she said. "I'll go now. If I need a dressing I'll get one; take the other hand, please. Good-bye——"

He did not attempt to detain her. He walked with her to the foot of the stairs. Half-way along the narrow alley she turned.

"It would be a long way to come if you happened not to be in," she said; "I'll send you a postcard the next time."

At the gate she turned again.

"Leave here, Paul," she said, with a mournful look. "Everything's wrong with this house."

Then she was gone.

Oleron returned to his room. He crossed straight to the window-box. He opened the lid and stood long looking at it. Then he closed it again and turned away.

"That's rather frightening," he muttered. "It's simply not possible that I should not have removed that nail. . . ."

VI

Oleron knew very well what Elsie had meant when she had said that her next visit would be preceded by a postcard. She, too, had realized that at last, at last he knew—knew, and didn't want her. It gave him a miserable, pitiful pang, therefore, when she came again within a week, knocking at the door unannounced. She spoke from the landing; she did not intend to stay, she said; and he had to press her before she would so much as enter.

Her excuse for calling was that she had heard of an inquiry for short stories that he might be wise to follow up. He thanked her. Then, her business over, she seemed anxious to get away again. Oleron did not seek to detain her; even he saw through the pretext of the stories; and he accompanied her down the stairs.

But Elsie Bengough had no luck whatever in that house. A second accident befell her. Half-way down the staircase there was the sharp sound of splintering wood, and she checked a loud cry. Oleron knew the woodwork to be old, but he himself had ascended and descended frequently enough without mishap. . . .

Elsie had put her foot through one of the stairs.

He sprang to her side in alarm.

"Oh, I say! My poor girl!"

She laughed hysterically.

"It's my weight—I know I'm getting fat——"

"Keep still—let me clear these splinters away," he muttered between his teeth.

She continued to laugh and sob that it was her weight—she was getting fat——

He thrust downwards at the broken boards. The extrication was no easy matter, and her torn boot showed him how badly the foot and ankle within it must be abraded.

"Good God—good God!" he muttered over and over again.

"I shall be too heavy for anything soon," she sobbed and laughed.

But she refused to reascend and to examine her hurt.

"No, let me go quickly—let me go quickly," she repeated.

"But it's a frightful gash!"

"No—not so bad—let me get away quickly—I'm—I'm not wanted."

At her words, that she was not wanted, his head dropped as if she had given him a buffet.

"Elsie!" he choked, brokenly and shocked.

But she too made a quick gesture, as if she put something violently aside.

"Oh, Paul, not *that*—not *you*—of course I do mean that too in a sense—oh, you know what I mean! . . . But if the other can't be, spare me this now! I—I wouldn't have come, but—but oh, I did, I *did* try to keep away!"

It was intolerable, heartbreaking; but what could he do—what could he say? He did not love her. . . .

"Let me go—I'm not wanted—let me take away what's left of me—"

"Dear Elsie—you are very dear to me——"

But again she made the gesture, as of putting something violently aside.

"No, not that—not anything less—don't offer me anything less—leave me a little pride——"

"Let me get my hat and coat—let me take you to a doctor," he muttered.

But she refused. She refused even the support of his arm. She gave another unsteady laugh.

"I'm sorry I broke your stairs, Paul. . . . You will go and see about the short stories, won't you?"

He groaned.

"Then if you won't see a doctor, will you go across the square and let Mrs. Barrett look at you? Look, there's Barrett passing now——"

The long-nosed Barrett was looking curiously down the alley, but as Oleron was about to call him he made off without a word. Elsie seemed anxious for nothing so much as to be clear of the place, and finally promised to go straight to a doctor, but insisted on going alone.

"Good-bye," she said.

And Oleron watched her until she was past the hatchet-like "To Let" boards, as if he feared that even they might fall upon her and maim her.

That night Oleron did not dine. He had far too much on his mind. He walked from room to room of his flat, as if he could have walked away from Elsie Bengough's haunting cry that still rang in his ears. "I'm not wanted—don't offer me anything less—let me take away what's left of me——"

Oh, if he could only have persuaded himself that he loved her!

He walked until twilight fell, then, without lighting candles, he stirred up the fire and flung himself into a chair.

Poor, poor Elsie! . . .

But even while his heart ached for her, it was out of the question. If only he had known! If only he had used common observation! But those walks, those sisterly takings of the arm—what a fool he had been! . . . Well, it was too late now. It was she, not he, who must now act—act by keeping away. He would help her all he could. He himself would not sit in her presence. If she came, he would hurry her out again as fast as he could. . . . Poor, poor Elsie!

His room grew dark; the fire burned dead; and he continued to sit, wincing from time to time as a fresh tortured phrase rang again in his ears.

Then suddenly, he knew not why, he found himself anxious for her in a new sense—uneasy about her personal safety. A horrible fancy that even then she might be looking over an embankment down into dark water, that she might even now be glancing up at the hook on the door, took him. Women had been known to do those things. . . . Then there would be an inquest, and he himself would be called upon to identify her, and would be asked how she had come by an ill-healed wound on the hand and a bad abrasion of the ankle. Barrett would say that he had seen her leaving his house. . . .

Then he recognized that his thoughts were morbid. By an effort of will he put them aside, and sat for a while listening to the faint creakings and tickings and rappings within his panelling. . . .

If only he could have married her! . . . But he couldn't. Her face had risen before him again as he had seen it on the stairs, drawn with pain and ugly and swollen with tears. Ugly—yes, positively blubbered; if tears were women's weapons, as they were said to be, such tears were weapons turning against themselves . . . suicide again. . . .

Then all at once he found himself attentively considering her two accidents.

Extraordinary they had been, both of them. He *could not* have left that old nail standing in the wood; why, he had fetched tools specially from the kitchen; and he was convinced that that step that had broken beneath her weight had been as sound as the others. It was inexplicable. If these things could happen, anything could happen. There was not a beam nor a jamb in the place that might not fall without warning, not a plank that might not crash inwards, not a nail that might not become a dagger. The whole place was full of life even now; as he sat there in the dark he heard its crowds of noises as if the house had been one great microphone. . . .

Only half conscious that he did so, he had been sitting for some time identifying these noises, attributing to each crack or creak or knock its material cause; but there was one noise which, again not fully conscious of the omission, he had not sought to account for. It had last come some minutes ago; it came again now—a sort of soft sweeping rustle that seemed to hold an almost inaudible minute crackling. For half a minute or so it had Oleron's attention; then his heavy thoughts were of Elsie Bengough again.

He was nearer to loving her in that moment than he had ever been. He thought how to some men their loved ones were but the dearer for those poor mortal blemishes that tell us we are but sojourners on earth, with a common fate not far distant that makes it hardly worth while to do anything but love for the time remaining. Strangling sobs, blearing tears, bodies buffeted by sickness, hearts and minds callous and hard with the rubs of the world—how little love there would be were these things a barrier to love! In that sense he did love Elsie Bengough. What her happiness had never moved in him her sorrow almost awoke. . . .

Suddenly his meditation went. His ear had once more become conscious of that soft and repeated noise—the long sweep with the almost inaudible crackle in it. Again and again it came, with a curious insistence and urgency. It quickened a little as he became increasingly attentive . . . it seemed to Oleron that it grew louder. . . .

All at once he started bolt upright in his chair, tense and listening. The silky rustle came again; he was trying to attach it to something. . . .

The next moment he had leapt to his feet, unnerved and terrified. His chair hung poised for a moment, and then went over, setting the fire-irons clattering as it fell. There was only one noise in the world like that which had caused him to spring thus to his feet. . . .

The next time it came Oleron felt behind him at the empty air with his hand, and backed slowly until he found himself against the wall.

"God in Heaven!" The ejaculation broke from Oleron's lips. The sound had ceased.

The next moment he had given a high cry.

"What is it? What's there? *Who's* there?"

A sound of scuttling caused his knees to bend under him for a moment; but that, he knew, was a mouse. That was not something that his stomach turned sick and his mind reeled to entertain. That other sound, the like of which was not in the world, had now entirely ceased; and again he called. . . .

He called and continued to call; and then another terror, a terror of the sound of his own voice, seized him. He did not dare to call again. His shaking hand went to his pocket for a match, but found none. He thought there might be matches on the mantelpiece——

He worked his way to the mantelpiece round a little recess, without for a moment leaving the wall. Then his hand encountered the mantelpiece, and groped along it. A box of matches fell to the hearth. He could just see them in the firelight, but his hand could not pick them up until he had cornered them inside the fender.

Then he rose and struck a light.

The room was as usual. He struck a second match. A candle stood on the table. He lighted it, and the flame sank for a moment and then burned up clear. Again he looked round.

There was nothing.

There was nothing; but there had been something, and might still be something. Formerly, Oleron had smiled at the fantastic thought that, by a merging and interplay of identities between himself and his beautiful room, he might be preparing a ghost for the future; it had not occurred to him *that there might have been a similar merging and coalescence in the past.* Yet with this staggering impossibility he was now face to face. Something did persist in the house; it had a tenant other than himself; and that tenant, whatsoever or whosoever, had appalled Oleron's soul by producing the sound of a woman brushing her hair.

VII

Without quite knowing how he came to be there Oleron found himself striding over the loose board he had temporarily placed on the step broken by Miss Bengough. He was hatless, and descending the stairs. Not until later did there return to him a hazy memory that he had left the candle burning on the table, had opened the door no wider than was necessary to allow the passage of his body, and had sidled out, closing the door softly behind him. At the foot of the stairs another shock awaited him. Something dashed with a flurry up from the disused cellars and disappeared out of the door. It was only a cat, but Oleron gave a childish sob.

He passed out of the gate, and stood for a moment under the "To Let" boards, plucking foolishly at his lip and looking up at the glimmer of light behind one of his red blinds. Then, still looking over his shoulder, he moved stumblingly up the square. There was a small public-house round the corner; Oleron had never entered it; but he entered it now, and put down a shilling that missed the counter by inches.

"B—b—bran—brandy," he said, and then stooped to look for the shilling.

He had the little sawdusted bar to himself; what company there was—carters and labourers and the small tradesmen of the neighborhood—was gathered in the farther compartment, beyond the space where the white-haired landlady moved among her taps and bottles. Oleron sat down on a hardwood settee with a perforated seat, drank half his brandy, and then, thinking he might as well drink it as spill it, finished it.

Then he fell to wondering which of the men whose voices he heard across the public-house would undertake the removal of his effects on the morrow.

In the meantime he ordered more brandy.

For he did not intend to go back to that room where he had left the candle burning. Oh no! He couldn't have faced even the entry and the staircase with the broken step—certainly not that pith-white, fascinating room. He would go back for the present to his old arrangement, of workroom and separate sleeping-quarters; he would go to his old landlady at once—presently—when he had finished his brandy—and see if she could put him up for the night. His glass was empty now. . . .

He rose, had it refilled, and sat down again.

And if anybody asked his reason for removing again? Oh, he had reason enough—reason enough! Nails that put themselves back into wood again and gashed people's hands, steps that broke when you trod on them, and women who came into a man's place and brushed their hair in the dark, were reasons enough! He was querulous and injured about it all. He had taken the place for himself, not for invisible women to brush their hair in; that lawyer fellow in Lincoln's Inn should be told so, too, before many hours were out; it was outrageous, letting people in for agreements like that!

A cut-glass partition divided the compartment where Oleron sat from the space where the white-haired landlady moved; but it stopped seven or eight inches above the level of the counter. There was no partition at the further bar. Presently Oleron, raising his eyes, saw that faces were watching him through the aperture. The faces disappeared when he looked at them.

He moved to a corner where he could not be seen from the other bar; but this brought him into line with the white-haired landlady.

She knew him by sight—had doubtless seen him passing and repassing; and presently she made a remark on the weather. Oleron did not know what he replied, but it sufficed to call forth the further remark that the winter had been a bad one for influenza, but that the spring weather seemed to be coming at last. . . . Even this slight contact with the commonplace steadied Oleron a little; an idle, nascent wonder whether the landlady brushed her hair every night, and, if so, whether it gave out

those little electric cracklings, was shut down with a snap; and Oleron
was better. . . .

With his next glass of brandy he was all for going back to his flat. Not
go back? Indeed, he would go back! They should very soon see whether
he was to be turned out of his place like that! He began to wonder why
he was doing the rather unusual thing he was doing at that moment,
unusual for him—sitting hatless, drinking brandy, in a public-house.
Suppose he were to tell the white-haired landlady all about it—to tell her
that a caller had scratched her hand on a nail, had later had the bad luck
to put her foot through a rotten stair, and that he himself, in an old
house full of squeaks and creaks and whispers, had heard a minute noise
and had bolted from it in fright—what would she think of him? That he
was mad, of course. . . . Pshaw! The real truth of the matter was that he
hadn't been doing enough work to occupy him. He had been dreaming
his days away, filling his head with a lot of moonshine about a new
Romilly (as if the old one was not good enough), and now he was
surprised that the devil should enter an empty head!

Yes, he would go back. He would take a walk in the air first—he
hadn't walked enough lately—and then he would take himself in hand,
settle the hash of that sixteenth chapter of *Romilly* (fancy, he had
actually been fool enough to think of destroying fifteen chapters!) and
thenceforward he would remember that he had obligations to his fellow
men and work to do in the world. There was the matter in a nutshell.

He finished his brandy and went out.

He had walked for some time before any other bearing of the matter
than that on himself occurred to him. At first, the fresh air had increased
the heady effect of the brandy he had drunk; but afterwards his mind
grew clearer than it had been since morning. And the clearer it grew, the
less final did his boastful self-assurances become, and the firmer his
conviction that, when all explanations had been made, there remained
something that could not be explained. His hysteria of an hour before
had passed; he grew steadily calmer; but the disquieting conviction remained. A deep fear took possession of him. It was a fear for Elsie.

For something in his place was inimical to her safety. Of themselves,
her two accidents might not have persuaded him of this; but she herself
had said it. *"I'm not wanted here. . . ."* And she had declared that there
was something wrong with the place. She had seen it before he had.
Well and good. One thing stood out clearly: namely, that if this was so,
she must be kept away for quite another reason than that which had so
confounded and humiliated Oleron. Luckily she had expressed her intention of staying away; she must be held to that intention. He must see
to it.

And he must see to it all the more that he now saw his first example, never to set foot in the place again, was absurd. People did not do that kind of thing. With Elsie made secure, he could not with any respect to himself suffer himself to be turned out by a shadow, nor even by a danger merely because it was a danger. He had to live somewhere, and he would live there. He must return.

He mastered the faint chill of fear that came with the decision, and turned in his walk abruptly. Should fear grow on him again he would, perhaps, take one more glass of brandy. . . .

But by the time he reached the short street that led to the square he was too late for more brandy. The little public-house was still lighted, but closed, and one or two men were standing talking on the kerb. Oleron noticed that a sudden silence fell on them as he passed, and he noticed further that the long-nosed Barrett, whom he passed a little lower down, did not return his good-night. He turned in at the broken gate, hesitated merely an instant in the alley, and then mounted his stairs again.

Only an inch of candle remained in the Sheffield stick, and Oleron did not light another one. Deliberately he forced himself to take it up and to make the tour of his five rooms before retiring. It was as he returned from the kitchen across his little hall that he noticed that a letter lay on the floor. He carried it into his sitting-room, and glanced at the envelope before opening it.

It was unstamped, and had been put into the door by hand. Its handwriting was clumsy, and it ran from beginning to end without comma or period. Oleron read the first line, turned to the signature, and then finished the letter.

It was from the man Barrett, and it informed Oleron that he, Barrett, would be obliged if Mr. Oleron would make other arrangements for the preparing of his breakfasts and the cleaning-out of his place. The sting lay in the tail, that is to say, the postscript. This consisted of a text of Scripture. It embodied an allusion that could only be to Elsie Bengough. . . .

A seldom-seen frown had cut deeply into Oleron's brow. So! That was it! Very well; they would see about that on the morrow. . . . For the rest, this seemed merely another reason why Elsie should keep away. . . .

Then his suppressed rage broke out. . . .

The foul-minded lot! The devil himself could not have given a leer at anything that had ever passed between Paul Oleron and Elsie Bengough, yet this nosing rascal must be prying and talking! . . .

Oleron crumpled the paper up, held it in the candle flame, and then ground the ashes under his heel.

One useful purpose, however, the letter had served: it had created in

Oleron a wrathful blaze that effectually banished pale shadows. Nevertheless, one other puzzling circumstance was to close the day. As he undressed, he chanced to glance at his bed. The coverlets bore an impress as if somebody had lain on them. Oleron could not remember that he himself had lain down during the day—off-hand, he would have said that certainly he had not; but after all he could not be positive. His indignation for Elsie, acting possibly with the residue of the brandy in him, excluded all other considerations; and he put out his candle, lay down, and passed immediately into a deep and dreamless sleep, which, in the absence of Mrs. Barrett's morning call, lasted almost once round the clock.

VIII

To the man who pays heed to that voice within him which warns him that twilight and danger are settling over his soul, terror is apt to appear an absolute thing, against which his heart must be safeguarded in a twink unless there is to take place an alteration in the whole range and scale of his nature. Mercifully, he has never far to look for safeguards. Of the immediate and small and common and momentary things of life, of usages and observances and modes and conventions, he builds up fortifications against the powers of darkness. He is even content that, not terror only, but joy also, should for working purposes be placed in the category of the absolute things; and the last treason he will commit will be that breaking down of terms and limits that strikes, not at one man, but at the welfare of the souls of all.

In his own person, Oleron began to commit this treason. He began to commit it by admitting the inexplicable and horrible to an increasing familiarity. He did it insensibly, unconsciously, by a neglect of the things that he now regarded it as an impertinence in Elsie Bengough to have prescribed. Two months before, the words "a haunted house," applied to his lovely bemusing dwelling, would have chilled his marrow; now, his scale of sensation becoming depressed, he could ask "Haunted by what?" and remain unconscious that horror, when it can be proved to be relative, by so much loses its proper quality. He was setting aside the landmarks. Mists and confusion had begun to enwrap him.

And he was conscious of nothing so much as of a voracious inquisitiveness. He wanted *to know*. He was resolved to know. Nothing but the knowledge would satisfy him; and craftily he cast about for means whereby he might attain it.

He might have spared his craft. The matter was the easiest imaginable. As in time past he had known, in his writing, moments when his thoughts had seemed to rise of themselves and to embody themselves in words not to be altered afterwards, so now the questions he put himself seemed to be answered even in the moment of their asking. There was exhilaration in the swift, easy processes. He had known no such joy in his own power since the days when his writing had been a daily freshness and a delight to him. It was almost as if the course he must pursue was being dictated to him.

And the first thing he must do, of course, was to define the problem. He defined it in terms of mathematics. Granted that he had not the place to himself; granted that the old house had inexpressibly caught and engaged his spirit; granted that, by virtue of the common denominator of the place, this unknown co-tenant stood in some relation to himself: what next? Clearly, the nature of the other numerator must be ascertained.

And how? Ordinarily this would not have seemed simple, but to Oleron it was now pellucidly clear. The key, *of course,* lay in his half-written novel—or rather, in both *Romillys,* the old and the proposed new one.

A little while before Oleron would have thought himself mad to have embraced such an opinion; now he accepted the dizzying hypothesis without a quiver.

He began to examine the first and second *Romilly*s.

From the moment of his doing so the thing advanced by leaps and bounds. Swiftly he reviewed the history of the *Romilly* of the fifteen chapters. He remembered clearly now that he had found her insufficient on the very first morning on which he had sat down to work in his new place. Other instances of his aversion leaped up to confirm his obscure investigation. There had come the night when he had hardly forborne to throw the whole thing into the fire; and the next morning he had begun the planning of the new *Romilly.* It had been on that morning that Mrs. Barrett, overhearing him humming a brief phrase that the dripping of a tap the night before had suggested, had informed him that he was singing some air he had never in his life heard before, called "The Beckoning Fair One." . . .

The Beckoning Fair One! . . .

With scarcely a pause in thought he continued:

The first *Romilly* having been definitely thrown over, the second had instantly fastened herself upon him, clamouring for birth in his brain. He even fancied now, looking back, that there had been something like passion, hate almost, in the supplanting, and that more than once a stray thought given to his discarded creation had—(it was astonishing how credible Oleron found the almost unthinkable idea)—had offended the supplanter.

Yet that a malignancy almost homicidal should be extended to his fiction's poor mortal prototype. . . .

In spite of his inuring to a scale in which the horrible was now a thing to be fingered and turned this way and that, a "Good God!" broke from Oleron.

This intrusion of the first *Romilly*'s prototype into his thought again was a factor that for the moment brought his inquiry into the nature of his problem to a termination; the mere thought of Elsie was fatal to anything abstract. For another thing, he could not yet think of that letter of Barrett's, nor of a little scene that had followed it, without a mounting of colour and a quick contraction of the brow. For, wisely or not, he had had that argument out at once. Striding across the square on the following morning, he had bearded Barrett on his own doorstep. Coming back again a few minutes later, he had been strongly of opinion that he had only made matters worse. The man had been vagueness itself. He had not been able to be either challenged or browbeaten into anything more definite than a muttered farrago in which the words "Certain things . . . Mrs. Barrett . . . respectable house . . . if the cap fits . . . proceedings that shall be nameless," had been constantly repeated.

"Not that I make any charge——" he had concluded.

"Charge!" Oleron had cried.

"I 'ave my idears of things, as I don't doubt you 'ave yours——"

"Ideas—mine!" Oleron had cried wrathfully, immediately dropping his voice as heads had appeared at windows of the square. "Look you here, my man; you've an unwholesome mind, which probably you can't help, but a tongue which you can help, and shall! If there is a breath of this repeated . . ."

"I'll not be talked to on my own doorstep like this by anybody, . . ." Barrett had blustered. . . .

"You shall, and I'm doing it . . ."

"Don't you forget there's a Gawd above all, Who 'as said . . ."

"You're a low scandalmonger! . . ."

And so forth, continuing badly what was already badly begun. Oleron had returned wrathfully to his own house, and thenceforward, looking out of his windows, had seen Barrett's face at odd times, lifting blinds or peering round curtains, as if he sought to put himself in possession of Heaven knew what evidence, in case it should be required of him.

The unfortunate occurrence made certain minor differences in Oleron's domestic arrangements. Barrett's tongue, he gathered, had already been busy; he was looked at askance by the dwellers of the square; and he judged it better, until he should be able to obtain other help, to make his purchases of provisions a little farther afield rather than at the small shops of the immediate neighborhood. For the rest, house-keeping was no new thing to him, and he would resume his old bachelor habits. . . .

Besides, he was deep in certain rather abstruse investigations, in which it was better that he should not be disturbed.

He was looking out of his window one midday rather tired, not very well, and glad that it was not very likely he would have to stir out of doors, when he saw Elsie Bengough crossing the square towards his house. The weather had broken; it was a raw and gusty day; and she had to force her way against the wind that set her ample skirts bellying about her opulent figure and her veil spinning and streaming behind her.

Oleron acted swiftly and instinctively. Seizing his hat, he sprang to the door and descended the stairs at a run. A sort of panic had seized him. She must be prevented from setting foot in the place. As he ran along the alley he was conscious that his eyes went up to the eaves as if something drew them. He did not know that a slate might not accidentally fall. . . .

He met her at the gate, and spoke with curious volubleness.

"This is really too bad, Elsie! Just as I'm urgently called away! I'm afraid it can't be helped though, and that you'll have to think me an inhospitable beast." He poured it out just as it came into his head.

She asked if he was going to town.

"Yes, yes—to town," he replied. "I've got to call on—on Chambers. You know Chambers, don't you? No, I remember you don't; a big man you once saw me with. . . . I ought to have gone yesterday, and—" this he felt to be a brilliant effort—"and he's going out of town this afternoon. To Brighton. I had a letter from him this morning."

He took her arm and led her up the square. She had to remind him that his way to town lay in the other direction.

"Of course—how stupid of me!" he said, with a little loud laugh. "I'm so used to going the other way with you—of course; it's the other way to the bus. Will you come along with me? I am so awfully sorry it's hap-pened like this. . . ."

They took the street to the bus terminus.

This time Elsie bore no signs of having gone through interior strug-gles. If she detected anything unusual in his manner she made no com-ment, and he, seeing her calm, began to talk less recklessly through silences. By the time they reached the bus terminus, nobody, seeing the pallid-faced man without an overcoat and the large ample-skirted girl at his side, would have supposed that one of them was ready to sink on his knees for thankfulness that he had, as he believed, saved the other from a wildly unthinkable danger.

They mounted to the top of the bus, Oleron protesting that he should not miss his overcoat, and that he found the day, if anything, rather oppressively hot. They sat down on a front seat.

Now that this meeting was forced upon him, he had something else to say that would make demands upon his tact. It had been on his mind for some time, and was, indeed, peculiarly difficult to put. He revolved it for some minutes, and then, remembering the success of his story of a sudden call to town, cut the knot of his difficulty with another lie.

"I'm thinking of going away for a little while, Elsie," he said.

She merely said, "Oh?"

"Somewhere for a change. I need a change. I think I shall go to-morrow, or the day after. Yes, to-morrow, I think."

"Yes," she replied.

"I don't quite know how long I shall be," he continued. "I shall have to let you know when I am back."

"Yes, let me know," she replied in an even tone.

The tone was, for her, suspiciously even. He was a little uneasy.

"You don't ask me where I'm going," he said, with a little cumbrous effort to rally her.

She was looking straight before her, past the bus-driver.

"I know," she said.

He was startled. "How, you know?"

"You're not going anywhere," she replied.

He found not a word to say. It was a minute or so before she continued, in the same controlled voice she had employed from the start.

"You're not going anywhere. You weren't going out this morning. You only came out because I appeared; don't behave as if we were strangers, Paul."

A flush of pink had mounted to his cheeks. He noticed that the wind had given her the pink of early rhubarb. Still he found nothing to say.

"Of course, you ought to go away," she continued. "I don't know whether you look at yourself often in the glass, but you're rather notice-able. Several people have turned to look at you this morning. So, of course, you ought to go away. But you won't, and I know why."

He shivered, coughed a little, and then broke silence.

"Then if you know, there's no use in continuing this discussion," he said curtly.

"Not for me, perhaps, but there is for you," she replied. "Shall I tell you what I know?"

"No," he said in a voice slightly raised.

"No?" she asked, her round eyes earnestly on him.

"No."

Again he was getting out of patience with her; again he was conscious of the strain. Her devotion and fidelity and love plagued him; she was

only humiliating both herself and him. It would have been bad enough
had he ever, by word or deed, given her cause for thus fastening herself
on him . . . but there; that was the worst of that kind of life for a woman.
Women such as she, business women, in and out of offices all the time,
always, whether they realised it or not, made comradeship a cover for
something else. They accepted the unconventional status, came and
went freely, as men did, were honestly taken by men at their own valua-
tion—and then it turned out to be the other thing after all, and they
went and fell in love. No wonder there was gossip in shops and squares
and public-houses! In a sense the gossipers were in the right of it. Independent, yet not efficient; with some of womanhood's graces forgone,
and yet with all the woman's hunger and need; half sophisticated, yet
not wise; Oleron was tired of it all. . . .

And it was time he told her so.

"I suppose," he said tremblingly, looking down between his knees, "I
suppose the real trouble is in the life women who earn their own living
are obliged to lead."

He could not tell in what sense she took the lame generality; she
merely replied, "I suppose so."

"It can't be helped," he continued, "but you do sacrifice a good deal."

She agreed: a good deal; and then she added after a moment, "What,
for instance?"

"You may or may not be gradually attaining a new status, but you're in
a false position to-day."

It was very likely, she said; she hadn't thought of it much in that
light——

"And," he continued desperately, "you're bound to suffer. Your most
innocent acts are misunderstood; motives you never dreamed of are
attributed to you; and in the end it comes to"—he hesitated a moment
and then took the plunge,—"to the sidelong look and the leer."

She took his meaning with perfect ease. She merely shivered a little as
she pronounced the name.

"Barrett?"

His silence told her the rest.

Anything further that was to be said must come from her. It came as
the bus stopped at a stage and fresh passengers mounted the stairs.

"You'd better get down here and go back, Paul," she said. "I understand perfectly—perfectly. It isn't Barrett. You'd be able to deal with
Barrett. It's merely convenient for you to say it's Barrett. I know what it
is . . . but you said I wasn't to tell you that. Very well. But before you go
let me tell you why I came up this morning."

In a dull tone he asked her why. Again she looked straight before her
as she replied:

"I came to force your hand. Things couldn't go on as they have been going, you know; and now that's all over."

"All over," he repeated stupidly.

"All over. I want you now to consider yourself, as far as I'm concerned, perfectly free. I make only one reservation."

He hardly had the spirit to ask her what that was.

"If *I* merely need *you*," she said, "please don't give that a thought; that's nothing; I shan't come near for that. But," she dropped her voice, "if *you're* in need of *me*, Paul—I shall know if you are, *and you will be*—then I shall come at no matter what cost. You understand that?"

He could only groan.

"So that's understood," she concluded. "And I think that's all. Now go back. I should advise you to walk back, for you're shivering—good-bye——"

She gave him a cold hand, and he descended. He turned on the edge of the kerb as the bus started again. For the first time in all the years he had known her she parted from him with no smile and no wave of her long arm.

IX

He stood on the kerb plunged in misery, looking after her as long as she remained in sight; but almost instantly with her disappearance he felt the heaviness lift a little from his spirit. She had given him his liberty; true, there was a sense in which he had never parted with it, but now was no time for splitting hairs; he was free to act, and all was clear ahead. Swiftly the sense of lightness grew on him: it became a positive rejoicing in his liberty; and before he was half-way home he had decided what must be done next.

The vicar of the parish in which his dwelling was situated lived within ten minutes of the square. To his house Oleron turned his steps. It was necessary that he should have all the information he could get about this old house with the insurance marks and the sloping "To Let" boards, and the vicar was the person most likely to be able to furnish it. This last preliminary out of the way, and—aha! Oleron chuckled—things might be expected to happen!

But he gained less information than he had hoped for. The house, the vicar said, was old—but there needed no vicar to tell Oleron that; it was reputed (Oleron pricked up his ears) to be haunted—but there were few old houses about which some such rumour did not circulate among the ignorant; and the deplorable lack of Faith of the modern world, the vicar thought, did not tend to dissipate these superstitions. For the rest, his manner was the soothing manner of one who prefers not to make statements without knowing how they will be taken by his hearer. Oleron smiled as he perceived this.

"You may leave my nerves out of the question," he said. "How long has the place been empty?"

"A dozen years, I should say," the vicar replied.

"And the last tenant—did you know him—or her?" Oleron was conscious of a tingling of his nerves as he offered the vicar the alternative of sex.

"Him," said the vicar. "A man. If I remember rightly, his name was Madley; an artist. He was a great recluse; seldom went out of the place, and"—the vicar hesitated and then broke into a little gush of candour—"and since you appear to have come for this information, and since it is better that the truth should be told than that garbled versions should get about, I don't mind saying that this man Madley died there, under somewhat unusual circumstances. It was ascertained at the post-mortem that there was not a particle of food in his stomach, although he was found to be not without money. And his frame was simply worn out. Suicide was spoken of, but you'll agree with me that deliberate starvation is, to say the least, an uncommon form of suicide. An open verdict was returned."

"Ah!" said Oleron. . . . "Does there happen to be any comprehensive history of this parish?"

"No; partial ones only. I myself am not guiltless of having made a number of notes on its purely ecclesiastical history, its registers and so forth, which I shall be happy to show you if you would care to see them; but it is a large parish, I have only one curate, and my leisure, as you will readily understand . . ."

The extent of the parish and the scantiness of the vicar's leisure occupied the remainder of the interview, and Oleron thanked the vicar, took his leave, and walked slowly home.

He walked slowly for a reason, twice turning away from the house within a stone's-throw of the gate and taking another turn of twenty minutes or so. He had a very ticklish piece of work now before him; it required the greatest mental concentration; it was nothing less than to bring his mind, if he might, into such a state of unpreoccupation and receptivity that he should see the place as he had seen it on that morning when, his removal accomplished, he had sat down to begin the sixteenth chapter of the first *Romilly*.

For, could he recapture that first impression, he now hoped for far more from it. Formerly, he had carried no end of mental lumber. Before the influence of the place had been able to find him out at all, it had had the inertia of those dreary chapters to overcome. No results had shown. The process had been one of slow saturation, charging, filling up to a brim. But now he was light, unburdened, rid at last both of that *Romilly* and of her prototype. Now for the new unknown, coy, jealous, bewitching, Beckoning Fair! . . .

At half-past two of the afternoon he put his key into the Yale lock, entered, and closed the door behind him. . . .

His fantastic attempt was instantly and astonishingly successful. He could have shouted with triumph as he entered the room; it was as if he had *escaped* into it. Once more, as in the days when his writing had had a daily freshness and wonder and promise for him, he was conscious of that new ease and mastery and exhilaration and release. The air of the place seemed to hold more oxygen; as if his own specific gravity had changed, his very tread seemed less ponderable. The flowers in the bowls, the fair proportions of the meadowsweet-coloured panels and mouldings, the polished floor, and the lofty and faintly starred ceiling, fairly laughed their welcome. Oleron actually laughed back, and spoke aloud.

"Oh, you're pretty, pretty!" he flattered it.

Then he lay down on his couch.

He spent that afternoon as a convalescent who expected a dear visitor might have spent it—in a delicious vacancy, smiling now and then as if in his sleep, and ever lifting drowsy and contented eyes to his alluring surroundings. He lay thus until darkness came, and, with darkness, the nocturnal noises of the old house. . . .

But if he waited for any specific happening, he waited in vain.

He waited similarly in vain on the morrow, maintaining, though with less ease, that sensitised-late-like condition of his mind. Nothing occurred to give it an impression. Whatever it was which he so patiently wooed, it seemed to be both shy and exacting.

Then on the third day he thought he understood. A look of gentle drollery and cunning came into his eyes, and he chuckled.

"Oho, oho! . . . Well, if the wind sits in *that* quarter we must see what else there is to be done. What is there, now? . . . No, I won't send for Elsie; we don't need a wheel to break the butterfly on; we won't go to those lengths, my butterfly. . . ."

He was standing musing, thumbing his lean jaw, looking aslant; suddenly he crossed to his hall, took down his hat, and went out.

"My lady is coquettish, is she? Well, we'll see what a little neglect will do," he chuckled as he went down the stairs.

He sought a railway station, got into a train, and spent the rest of the day in the country. Oh, yes: Oleron thought *he* was the man to deal with Fair Ones who beckoned, and invited, and then took refuge in shyness and hanging back!

He did not return until after eleven that night.

"Now, my Fair Beckoner!" he murmured as he walked along the alley and felt in his pocket for his keys. . . .

Inside his flat, he was perfectly composed, perfectly deliberate, exceedingly careful not to give himself away. As if to intimate that he intended to retire immediately, he lighted only a single candle; and as he set out with it on his nightly round he affected to yawn. He went first into his kitchen. There was a full moon, and a lozenge of moonlight, almost peacock-blue by contrast with his candle-frame, lay on the floor. The window was uncurtained, and he could see the reflection of the candle, and, faintly, that of his own face, as he moved about. The door of the powder-closet stood a little ajar, and he closed it before sitting down to remove his boots on the chair with the cushion made of the folded harp-bag. From the kitchen he passed to the bathroom. There, another slant of blue moonlight cut the windowsill and lay across the pipes on the wall. He visited his seldom-used study, and stood for a moment gazing at the silvered roofs across the square. Then, walking straight through his sitting-room, his stockinged feet making no noise, he entered his bedroom and put the candle on the chest of drawers. His face all this time wore no expression save that of tiredness. He had never been wilier nor more alert.

His small bedroom fireplace was opposite the chest of drawers on which the mirror stood, and his bed and the window occupied the remaining sides of the room. Oleron drew down his blind, took off his coat, and then stooped to get his slippers from under the bed.

He could have given no reason for the conviction, but that the manifestation that for two days had been withheld was close at hand he never for an instant doubted. Nor, though he could not form the faintest guess of the shape it might take, did he experience fear. Startling or surprising it might be; he was prepared for that; but that was all; his scale of sensation had become depressed. His hand moved this way and that under the bed in search of his slippers. . . .

But for all his caution and method and preparedness, his heart all at once gave a leap and a pause that was almost horrid. His hand had found the slippers, but he was still on his knees; save for this circumstance he would have fallen. The bed was a low one; the groping for the slippers accounted for the turn of his head to one side; and he was careful to keep the attitude until he had partly recovered his self-possession. When presently he rose there was a drop of blood on his lower lip where he had caught at it with his teeth, and his watch had jerked out of the pocket of his waistcoat and was dangling at the end of its short leather guard. . . .

Then, before the watch had ceased its little oscillation, he was himself again.

In the middle of his mantelpiece there stood a picture, a portrait of his grandmother; he placed himself before this picture, so that he could see in the glass of it the steady flame of the candle that burned behind him on the chest of drawers. He could see also in the picture-glass the little glancings of light from the bevels and facets of the objects about the mirror and candle. But he could see more. These twinklings and reflections and re-reflections did not change their position; but there was one gleam that had motion. It was fainter than the rest, and it moved up and down through the air. It was the reflection of the candle on Oleron's black vulcanite comb, and each of its downward movements was accompanied by a silky and crackling rustle.

Oleron, watching what went on in the glass of his grandmother's portrait, continued to play his part. He felt for his dangling watch and began slowly to wind it up. Then, for a moment ceasing to watch, he began to empty his trousers pockets and to place methodically in a little row on the mantelpiece the pennies and halfpennies he took from them. The sweeping, minutely electric noise filled the whole bedroom, and had Oleron altered his point of observation he could have brought the dim gleam of the moving comb so into position that it would almost have outlined his grandmother's head.

Any other head of which it might have been following the outline was invisible.

Oleron finished the emptying of his pockets; then, under cover of another simulated yawn, not so much summoning his resolution as overmastered by an exorbitant curiosity, he swung suddenly round. That which was being combed was still not to be seen, but the comb did not stop. It had altered its angle a little, and had moved a little to the left. It was passing, in fairly regular sweeps, from a point rather more than five feet from the ground, in a direction roughly vertical, to another point a few inches below the level of the chest of drawers.

Oleron continued to act to admiration. He walked to his little washstand in the corner, poured out water, and began to wash his hands. He removed his waistcoat, and continued his preparations for bed. The combing did not cease, and he stood for a moment in thought. Again his eyes twinkled. The next was very cunning——

"Hm! . . . *I think I'll read for a quarter of an hour,*" he said aloud. . . .

He passed out of the room.

He was away a couple of minutes; when he returned again the room was suddenly quiet. He glanced at the chest of drawers; the comb lay still, between the collar he had removed and a pair of gloves. Without hesitation Oleron put out his hand and picked it up. It was an ordinary eighteen-penny comb, taken from a card in a chemist's shop, of a substance of a definite specific gravity, and no more capable of rebellion against the Laws by which it existed than are the worlds that keep their orbits through the void. Oleron put it down again; then he glanced at the bundle of papers he held in his hand. What he had gone to fetch had been the fifteen chapters of the original *Romilly*.

"Hm!" he muttered as he threw the manuscript into a chair. . . . "As I thought. . . . She's just blindly, ragingly, murderously jealous."

On the night after that, and on the following night, and for many nights and days, so many that he began to be uncertain about the count of them, Oleron, courting, cajoling, neglecting, threatening, beseeching, eaten out with unappeased curiosity and regardless that his life was becoming one consuming passion and desire, continued his search for the unknown co-numerator of his abode.

X

As time went on, it came to pass that few except the postman mounted Oleron's stairs; and since men who do not write letters receive few, even the postman's tread became so infrequent that it was not heard more than once or twice a week. There came a letter from Oleron's publishers, asking when they might expect to receive the manuscript of his new book; he delayed for some days to answer it, and finally forgot it. A second letter came, which also he failed to answer. He received no third.

The weather grew bright and warm. The privet bushes among the chopper-like notice-boards flowered, and in the streets where Oleron did his shopping the baskets of flower-women lined the kerbs. Oleron purchased flowers daily; his room clamoured for flowers, fresh and continually renewed; and Oleron did not stint its demands. Nevertheless, the necessity for going out to buy them began to irk him more and more, and it was with a greater and ever greater sense of relief that he returned home again. He began to be conscious that again his scale of sensation had suffered a subtle change—a change that was not restoration to its former capacity, but an extension and enlarging that once more included terror. It admitted it in an entirely new form. *Lux orco, tenebræ Jovi.* The name of this terror was agoraphobia. Oleron had begun to dread air and space and the horror that might pounce upon the unguarded back.

Presently he so contrived it that his food and flowers were delivered daily at his door. He rubbed his hands when he had hit upon this expedient. That was better! Now he could please himself whether he went out or not. . . .

Quickly he was confirmed in his choice. It became his pleasure to remain immured.

But he was not happy—or, if he was, his happiness took an extraordinary turn. He fretted discontentedly, could sometimes have wept for mere weakness and misery; and yet he was dimly conscious that he would not have exchanged his sadness for all the noisy mirth of the world outside. And speaking of noise: noise, much noise, now caused him the acutest discomfort. It was hardly more to be endured than that new-born fear that kept him, on the increasingly rare occasions when he did go out, sidling close to walls and feeling friendly railings with his hand. He moved from room to room softly and in slippers, and sometimes stood for many seconds closing a door so gently that not a sound broke the stillness that was in itself a delight. Sunday now became an intolerable day to him, for, since the coming of the fine weather, there had begun to assemble in the square under his windows each Sunday morning certain members of the sect to which the long-nosed Barrett adhered. These came with a great drum and large brass-bellied instruments; men and women uplifted anguished voices, struggling with their God; and Barrett himself, with upraised face and closed eyes and working brows, prayed that the sound of his voice might penetrate the ears of all unbelievers— as it certainly did Oleron's. One day, in the middle of one of these rhapsodies, Oleron sprang to his blind and pulled it down, and heard as he did so, his own name made the object of a fresh torrent of outpouring.

And sometimes, but not as expecting a reply, Oleron stood still and called softly. Once or twice he called "Romilly!" and then waited; but more often his whispering did not take the shape of a name.

There was one spot in particular of his abode that he began to haunt with increasing persistency. This was just within the opening of his bedroom door. He had discovered one day that by opening every door in his place (always excepting the outer one, which he only opened unwillingly) and by placing himself on this particular spot, he could actually see to a greater or less extent into each of his five rooms without changing his position. He could see the whole of his sitting-room, all of his bedroom except the part hidden by the open door, and glimpses of his kitchen, bathroom, and of his rarely used study. He was often in this place, breathless and with his finger on his lip. One day, as he stood there, he suddenly found himself wondering whether this Madley, of whom the vicar had spoken, had ever discovered the strategic importance of the bedroom entry.

Light, moreover, now caused him greater disquietude than did darkness. Direct sunlight, of which, as the sun passed daily round the house, each of his rooms had now its share, was like a flame in his brain; and even diffused light was a dull and numbing ache. He began, at successive hours of the day, one after another, to lower his crimson blinds. He made short and daring excursions in order to do this; but he was ever careful to leave his retreat open, in case he should have sudden need of it. Presently this lowering of the blinds had become a daily methodical exercise, and his rooms, when he had been his round, had the blood-red half-light of a photographer's dark-room.

One day, as he drew down the blind of his little study and backed in good order out of the room again, he broke into a soft laugh.

"*That* bilks Mr. Barrett!" he said; and the baffling of Barrett continued to afford him mirth for an hour.

But on another day, soon after, he had a fright that left him trembling also for an hour. He had seized the cord to darken the window over the seat in which he had found the harp-bag, and was standing with his back well protected in the embrasure, when he thought he saw the tail of a black-and-white check skirt disappear round the corner of the house. He could not be sure—had he run to the window of the other wall, which was blinded, the skirt must have been already past—but he was *almost* sure that it was Elsie. He listened in an agony of suspense for her tread on the stairs. . . .

But no tread came, and after three or four minutes he drew a long breath of relief.

"By Jove, but that would have compromised me horribly!" he muttered. . . .

And he continued to mutter from time to time, "Horribly compromising . . . *no* woman would stand that . . . not *any* kind of woman . . . oh, compromising in the extreme!"

Yet he was not happy. He could not have assigned the cause of the fits of quiet weeping which took him sometimes; they came and went, like the fitful illumination of the clouds that travelled over the square; and perhaps, after all, if he was not happy, he was not unhappy. Before he could be unhappy something must have been withdrawn, and nothing had been granted. He was waiting for that granting, in that flower-laden, frightfully enticing apartment of his, with the pith-white walls tinged and subdued by the crimson blinds to a blood-like gloom.

He paid no heed to it that his stock of money was running perilously low, nor that he had ceased to work. Ceased to work? He had not ceased to work. They knew very little about it who supposed that Oleron had ceased to work! He was in truth only now beginning to work. He was preparing such a work . . . such a work . . . such a Mistress was a-making in the gestation of his Art . . . let him but get this period of probation and poignant waiting over and men should see. . . . How *should* men know her, this Fair One of Oleron's, until Oleron himself knew her? Lovely radiant creations are not thrown off like How-d'ye-do's. The men to whom it is committed to father them must weep wretched tears, as Oleron did, must swell with vain presumptuous hopes, as Oleron did, must pursue, as Oleron pursued, the capricious, fair, mocking, slippery, eager Spirit that, ever eluding, ever sees to it that the chase does not slacken. Let Oleron but hunt this Huntress a little longer . . . he would have her sparkling and panting in his arms yet. . . . Oh no: they were very far from the truth who supposed that Oleron had ceased to work!

And if all else was falling away from Oleron, gladly he was letting it go. So do we all when our Fair Ones beckon. Quite at the beginning we wink, and promise ourselves that we will put Her Ladyship through her paces, neglect her for a day, turn her own jealous wiles against her, flout and ignore her when she comes wheedling; perhaps there lurks within us all the time a heartless sprite who is never fooled; but in the end all falls away. She beckons, beckons, and all goes. . . .

And so Oleron kept his strategic post within the frame of his bedroom door, and watched, and waited, and smiled, with his finger on his lips. . . . It was his duteous service, his worship, his troth-plighting, all that he had ever known of Love. And when he found himself, as he now and then did, hating the dead man Madley, and wishing that he had never lived, he felt that that, too, was an acceptable service. . . .

But, as he thus prepared himself, as it were, for a Marriage, and moped and chafed more and more that the Bride made no sign, he made a discovery that he ought to have made weeks before.

It was through a thought of the dead Madley that he made it. Since that night when he had thought in his greenness that a little studied neglect would bring the lovely Beckoner to her knees, and had made use of her own jealousy to banish her, he had not set eyes on those fifteen discarded chapters of *Romilly*. He had thrown them back into the window-seat, forgotten their very existence. But his own jealousy of Madley put him in mind of hers of her jilted rival of flesh and blood, and he remembered them. . . . Fool that he had been! Had he, then, expected his Desire to manifest herself while there still existed the evidence of his divided allegiance? What, and she with a passion so fierce and centred that it had not hesitated at the destruction, twice attempted, of her rival? Fool that he had been! . . .

But if *that* was all the pledge and sacrifice she required she should have it—ah, yes, and quickly!

He took the manuscript from the window-seat, and brought it to the fire.

He kept his fire always burning now; the warmth brought out the last vestige of odour of the flowers with which his room was banked. He did not know what time it was; long since he had allowed his clock to run down—it had seemed a foolish measurer of time in regard to the stupendous things that were happening to Oleron; but he knew it was late. He took the *Romilly* manuscript and knelt before the fire.

But he had not finished removing the fastening that held the sheets together before he suddenly gave a start, turned his head over his shoul-

der, and listened intently. The sound he had heard had not been loud—
it had been, indeed, no more than a tap, twice or thrice repeated—but it
had filled Oleron with alarm. His face grew dark as it came again.

He heard a voice outside on his landing.

"Paul! . . . Paul! . . ."

It was Elsie's voice.

"Paul! . . . I know you're in . . . I want to see you. . . ."

He cursed her under his breath, but kept perfectly still. He did not
intend to admit her.

"Paul! . . . You're in trouble. . . . I believe you're in danger . . . at least
come to the door! . . ."

Oleron smothered a low laugh. It somehow amused him that she, in
such danger herself, should talk to him of *his* danger! . . . Well, if she
was, serve her right; she knew, or said she knew, all about it. . . .

"Paul! . . . Paul! . . ."

"*Paul! . . . Paul! . . .*" He mimicked her under his breath.

"Oh, Paul, it's *horrible! . . .*"

Horrible was it? thought Oleron. Then let her get away. . . .

"I only want to help you, Paul. . . . I didn't promise not to come if you
needed me. . . ."

He was impervious to the pitiful sob that interrupted the low cry. The
devil take the woman! Should he shout to her to go away and not come
back? No: let her call and knock and sob. She had a gift for sobbing; she
mustn't think her sobs would move him. They irritated him, so that he
set his teeth and shook his fist at her, but that was all. Let her sob.

"*Paul! . . . Paul! . . .*"

With his teeth hard set, he dropped the first page of *Romilly* into the
fire. Then he began to drop the rest in, sheet by sheet.

For many minutes the calling behind his door continued; then suddenly it ceased. He heard the sound of feet slowly descending the stairs.
He listened for the noise of a fall or a cry or the crash of a piece of the
handrail of the upper landing; but none of these things came. She was
spared. Apparently her rival suffered her to crawl abject and beaten
away. Oleron heard the passing of her steps under his window; then she
was gone.

He dropped the last page into the fire, and then, with a low laugh rose.
He looked fondly round his room.

"Lucky to get away like that," he remarked. "She wouldn't have got
away if I'd given her as much as a word or a look! What devils these
women are! . . . But no; I oughtn't to say that; one of 'em showed
forbearance. . . ."

Who showed forbearance? And what was forborne? Ah, Oleron
knew! . . . Contempt, no doubt, had been at the bottom of it, but that

didn't matter: the pestering creature had been allowed to go unharmed. Yes, she was lucky; Oleron hoped she knew it. . . .

And now, now, now for his reward!

Oleron crossed the room. All his doors were open; his eyes shone as he placed himself within that of his bedroom.

Fool that he had been, not to think of destroying the manuscript sooner! . . .

How, in a houseful of shadows, should he know his own Shadow? How, in a houseful of noises, distinguish the summons he felt to be at hand? Ah, trust him! He would know! The place was full of a jugglery of dim lights. The blind at his elbow that allowed the light of a street lamp to struggle vaguely through—the glimpse of greeny blue moonlight seen through the distant kitchen door—the sulky glow of the fire under the black ashes of the burnt manuscript—the glimmering of the tulips and the moon-daisies and narcissi in the bowls and jugs and jars—these did not so trick and bewilder his eyes that he would not know his Own! It was he, not she, who had been delaying the shadowy Bridal; he hung his head for a moment in mute acknowledgment; then he bent his eyes on the deceiving, puzzling gloom again. He would have called her name had he known it—but now he would not ask her to share even a name with the other. . . .

His own face, within the frame of the door, glimmered white as the narcissi in the darkness. . . .

A shadow, light as fleece, seemed to take shape in the kitchen (the time had been when Oleron would have said that a cloud had passed over the unseen moon). The low illumination on the blind at his elbow grew dimmer (the time had been when Oleron would have concluded that the lamplighter going his rounds had turned low the flame of the lamp). The fire settled, letting down the black and charred papers; a flower fell from a bowl, and lay indistinct upon the floor; all was still; and then a stray draught moved through the old house, passing before Oleron's face. . . .

Suddenly, inclining his head, he withdrew a little from the door-jamb. The wandering draught caused the door to move a little on its hinges. Oleron trembled violently, stood for a moment longer, and then, putting his hand out to the knob, softly drew the door to, sat down on the nearest chair, and waited, as a man might await the calling of his name that should summon him to some weighty, high and privy Audience. . . .

XI

One knows not whether there can be human compassion for anæmia of the soul. When the pitch of Life is dropped, and the spirit is so put over and reversed that that only is horrible which before was sweet and worldly and of the day, the human relation disappears. The sane soul turns appalled away, lest not merely itself, but sanity should suffer. We are not gods. We cannot drive out devils. We must see selfishly to it that devils do not enter into ourselves.

And this we must do even though Love so transfuse us that we may well deem our nature to be half divine. We shall but speak of honour and duty in vain. The letter dropped within the dark door will lie unregarded, or, if regarded for a brief instant between two unspeakable lapses, left and forgotten again. The telegram will be undelivered, nor will the whistling messenger (wiselier guided than he knows to whistle) be conscious as he walks away of the drawn blind that is pushed aside an inch by a finger and then fearfully replaced again. No: let the miserable wrestle with his own shadows; let him, if indeed he be so mad, clip and strain and enfold and couch the succubus; but let him do so in a house into which not an air of Heaven penetrates, nor a bright finger of the sun pierces the filthy twilight. The lost must remain lost. Humanity has other business to attend to.

For the handwriting of the two letters that Oleron, stealing noiselessly one June day into his kitchen to rid his sitting-room of an armful of fætid and decaying flowers, had seen on the floor within his door, had had no more meaning for him than if it had belonged to some dim and far-away dream. And at the beating of the telegraph-boy upon the door, within a few feet of the bed where he lay, he had gnashed his teeth and stopped his ears. He had pictured the lad standing there, just beyond his partition, among packets of provisions and bundles of dead and dying flowers. For his outer landing was littered with these. Oleron had feared to open his door to take them in. After a week, the errand lads had reported that there must be some mistake about the order, and had left no more. Inside, in the red twilight, the old flowers turned brown and fell and decayed where they lay.

Gradually his power was draining away. The Abomination fastened on Oleron's power. The steady sapping sometimes left him for many hours of prostration gazing vacantly up at his red-tinged ceiling, idly suffering such fancies as came of themselves to have their way with him. Even the strongest of his memories had no more than a precarious hold upon his attention. Sometimes a flitting half-memory, of a novel to be written, a novel it was important that he should write, tantalised him for a space before vanishing again; and sometimes whole novels, perfect, splendid, established to endure, rose magically before him. And sometimes the memories were absurdly remote and trivial, of garrets he had inhabited and lodgings that had sheltered him, and so forth. Oleron had known a good deal about such things in his time, but all that was now past. He

had at last found a place which he did not intend to leave until they
fetched him out—a place that some might have thought a little on the
green-sick side, that others might have considered to be a little too
redolent of long-dead and morbid things for a living man to be mewed
up in, but ah, so irresistible, with such an authority of its own, with such
an associate of its own, and a place of such delights when once a man had
ceased to struggle against its inexorable will! A novel? Somebody ought
to write a novel about a place like that! There must be lots to write about
in a place like that if one could but get to the bottom of it! It had
probably already been painted, by a man called Madley who had lived
there . . . but Oleron had not known this Madley—had a strong feeling
that he wouldn't have liked him—would rather he had lived somewhere
else—really couldn't stand the fellow—hated him, Madley, in fact.
(Aha! That was a joke!) He seriously doubted whether the man had led
the life he ought; Oleron was in two minds sometimes whether he
wouldn't tell that long-nosed guardian of the public morals across the
way about him; but probably he knew, and had made his praying hul-
labaloos for him also. That was his line. Why, Oleron himself had had a
dust-up with him about something or other . . . some girl or other . . .
Elsie Bengough her name was, he remembered. . . .

Oleron had moments of deep uneasiness about this Elsie Bengough.
Or rather, he was not so much uneasy about her as restless about the
things she did. Chief of these was the way in which she persisted in
thrusting herself into his thoughts; and, whenever he was quick enough,
he sent her packing the moment she made her appearance there. The
truth was that she was not merely a bore; she had always been that; it had
now come to the pitch when her very presence in his fancy was inimical
to the full enjoyment of certain experiences. . . . She had no tact; really
ought to have known that people are not at home to the thoughts of
everybody all the time; ought in mere politeness to have allowed him
certain seasons quite to himself; and was monstrously ignorant of things
if she did not know, as she appeared not to know, that there were certain
special hours when a man's veins ran with fire and daring and power, in
which . . . well, in which he had a reasonable right to treat folk as he had
treated that prying Barrett—to shut them out completely. . . . But no, up
she popped: the thought of her, and ruined all. Bright towering fabrics,
by the side of which even those perfect, magical novels of which he
dreamed were dun and grey, vanished utterly at her intrusion. It was as if
a fog should suddenly quench some fair-beaming star, as if at the threshold of some golden portal prepared for Oleron a pit should suddenly
gape, as if a bat-like shadow should turn the growing dawn to mirk and
darkness again. . . . Therefore, Oleron strove to stifle even the nascent
thought of her.

Nevertheless, there came an occasion on which this woman Bengough absolutely refused to be suppressed. Oleron could not have told exactly when this happened; he only knew by the glimmer of the street lamp on his blind that it was some time during the night, and that for some time she had not presented herself.

He had no warning, none, of her coming; she just came—was there. Strive as he would, he could not shake off the thought of her nor the image of her face. She haunted him.

But for her to come at *that* moment of all moments! . . . Really, it was past belief! How *she* could endure it, Oleron could not conceive! Actually, to look on, as it were, at the triumph of a Rival. . . . Good God! It was monstrous! tact—reticence—he had never credited her with an overwhelming amount of either: but he had never attributed mere—oh, there was no word for it! Monstrous—monstrous! Did she intend thenceforward. . . . Good God! To look on! . . .

Oleron felt the blood rush up to the roots of his hair with anger against her.

"Damnation take her!" he choked. . . .

But the next moment his heat and resentment had changed to a cold sweat of cowering fear. Panic-stricken, he strove to comprehend what he had done. For though he knew not what, he knew he had done something, something fatal, irreparable, blasting. Anger he had felt, but not *this* blaze of ire that suddenly flooded the twilight of his consciousness with a white infernal light. *That* appalling flash was not his—not his *that* open rift of bright and searing Hell—not his, not his! His had been the hand of a child, preparing a puny blow; but what was *this other* horrific hand that was drawn back to strike in the same place? Had *he* set that in motion? Had *he* provided the spark that had touched off the whole accumulated power of that formidable and relentless place? He did not know. He only knew that that poor igniting particle in himself was blown out, that—— Oh, impossible!—a clinging kiss (how else to express it?) had changed on his very lips to a gnashing and a removal, and that for very pity of the awful odds he must cry out to her against whom he had lately raged to guard herself . . . guard herself. . . .

"*Look out!*" he shrieked aloud. . . .

The revulsion was instant. As if a cold slow billow had broken over him, he came to to find that he was lying in his bed, that the mist and horror that had for so long enwrapped him had departed, that he was Paul Oleron, and that he was sick, naked, helpless, and unutterably abandoned and alone. His faculties, though weak, answered at last to his calls upon them; and he knew that it must have been a hideous nightmare that had left him sweating and shaking thus.

Yes, he was himself, Paul Oleron, a tired novelist, already past the summit of his best work, and slipping downhill again empty-handed from it all. He had struck short in his life's aim. He had tried too much, had over-estimated his strength, and was a failure, a failure. . . .

It all came to him in the single word, enwrapped and complete; it needed no sequential thought; he was a failure. He had missed. . . .

And he had missed not one happiness, but two. He had missed the ease of this world, which men love, and he had missed also that other shining prize for which men forgo ease, the snatching and holding and triumphant bearing up aloft of which is the only justification of the mad adventurer who hazards the enterprise. And there was no second attempt. Fate has no morrow. Oleron's morrow must be to sit down to profitless, ill-done, unrequired work again, and so on the morrow after that, and the morrow after that, and as many morrows as there might be. . . .

He lay there, weakly yet sanely considering it. . . .

And since the whole attempt had failed, it was hardly worth while to consider whether a little might not be saved from the general wreck. No good would ever come of that half-finished novel. He had intended that it should appear in the autumn; was under contract that it should appear; no matter; it was better to pay forfeit to his publishers than to waste what days were left. He was spent; age was not far off; and paths of wisdom and sadness were the properest for the remainder of the journey. . . .

If only he had chosen the wife, the child, the faithful friend at the fireside, and let them follow an *ignis fatuus* that list! . . .

In the meantime it began to puzzle him exceedingly why he should be so weak, that his room should smell so overpoweringly of decaying vegetable matter, and that his hand, chancing to stray to his face in the darkness, should encounter a beard.

"Most extraordinary!" he began to mutter to himself. "Have I been ill? Am I ill now? And if so, why have they left me alone? . . . Extraordinary! . . ."

He thought he heard a sound from the kitchen or bathroom. He rose a little on his pillow, and listened. . . . Ah! He was not alone, then! It certainly would have been extraordinary if they had left him ill and alone— Alone? Oh no. He would be looked after. He wouldn't be left, ill, to shift for himself. If everybody else had forsaken him, he could trust Elsie Bengough, the dearest chum he had, for that . . . bless her faithful heart!

But suddenly a short, stifled, spluttering cry rang sharply out:

"Paul!"

It came from the kitchen.

And in the same moment it flashed upon Oleron, he knew not how, that two, three, five, he knew not how many minutes before, another sound, unmarked at the time but suddenly transfixing his attention now, had striven to reach his intelligence. This sound had been the slight touch of metal on metal—just such a sound as Oleron made when he put his key into the lock.

"Hallo! . . . Who's that?" he called sharply from his bed.

He had no answer.

He called again. "Hallo! . . . Who's there? . . . Who is it?"

This time he was sure he heard noises, soft and heavy, in the kitchen.

"This is a queer thing altogether," he muttered. "By Jove, I'm as weak as a kitten too. . . . Hallo, there! Somebody called, didn't they? . . . Elsie! Is that you? . . ."

Then he began to knock with his hand on the wall at the side of his bed.

"Elsie! . . . Elsie! . . . You called, didn't you? . . . Please come here, whoever it is! . . ."

There was a sound as of a closing door, and then silence. Oleron began to get rather alarmed.

"It may be a nurse," he muttered; "Elsie'd have to get me a nurse, of course. She'd sit with me as long as she could spare the time, brave lass, and she'd get a nurse for the rest. . . . But it was awfully like her voice. . . . Elsie, or whoever it is! . . . I can't make this out at all. I must go and see what's the matter. . . ."

He put one leg out of bed. Feeling its feebleness, he reached with his hand for the additional support of the wall. . . .

But before putting out the other leg he stopped and considered, picking at his new-found beard. He was suddenly wondering whether he *dared* go into the kitchen. It was such a frightfully long way; no man knew what horror might not leap and huddle on his shoulders if he went so far; when a man has an overmastering impulse to get back into bed he ought to take heed of the warning and obey it. Besides, why should he go? What was there to go for? If it was that Bengough creature again, let her look after herself; Oleron was not going to have things cramp themselves on his defenceless back for the sake of such a spoilsport as *she!* . . . If she was in, let her let herself out again, and the sooner the better for her! Oleron simply couldn't be bothered. He had his work to do. On the morrow, he must set about the writing of a novel with a heroine so winsome, capricious, adorable, jealous, wicked, beautiful, inflaming, and altogether evil, that men should stand amazed. She was coming over him now; he knew by the alteration of the very air of the room when she was near him; and that soft thrill of bliss that had begun to stir in him never came unless she was beckoning, beckoning. . . .

He let go the wall and fell back into bed again as—oh, unthinkable!—the other half of that kiss that a gnash had interrupted was placed (how else convey it?) on his lips, robbing him of very breath. . . .

XII

In the bright June sunlight a crowd filled the square, and looked up at the windows of the old house with the antique insurance marks in its walls of red brick and the agents' notice-boards hanging like wooden choppers over the paling. Two constables stood at the broken gate of the narrow entrance-alley, keeping folk back. The women kept to the outskirts of the throng, moving now and then as if to see the drawn red blinds of the old house from a new angle, and talking in whispers. The children were in the houses, behind closed doors.

A long-nosed man had a little group about him, and he was telling some story over and over again; and another man, little and fat and wide-eyed, sought to capture the long-nosed man's audience with some relation in which a key figured.

". . . and it was revealed to me that there'd been something that very afternoon," the long-nosed man was saying. "I was standing there, where Constable Saunders is—or rather, I was passing about my business, when they came out. There was no deceiving me, oh, no deceiving *me! I* saw her face. . . ."

"What was it like, Mr. Barrett?" a man asked.

"It was like hers whom our Lord said to, 'Woman, doth any man accuse thee?'—white as paper, and no mistake! Don't tell *me!* . . . And so I walks straight across to Mrs. Barrett, and 'Jane,' I says, 'this must stop, and stop at once; we are commanded to avoid evil,' I says, 'and it must come to an end now; let him get help elsewhere.' And she says to me, 'John,' she says, 'it's four-and-sixpence a week'—them was her words. 'Jane,' I says, 'if it was forty-six thousand pounds it should stop' . . . and from that day to this she hasn't set foot inside that gate."

There was a short silence: then,

"Did Mrs. Barrett ever . . . *see* anythink, like?" somebody vaguely inquired.

Barrett turned austerely on the speaker.

"What Mrs. Barrett saw and Mrs. Barrett didn't see shall not pass these lips; even as it is written, keep thy tongue from speaking evil," he said.

Another man spoke.

"He was pretty near canned up in the *Waggon and Horses* that night, weren't he, Jim?"

"Yes, 'e 'adn't 'alf copped it. . . ."

"Not standing treat much, neither; he was in the bar, all on his own. . . ."

"So 'e was; we talked about it. . . ."

The fat, scared-eyed man made another attempt.

"She got the key off of me—she 'ad the number of it—she came into my shop of a Tuesday evening. . . ."

Nobody heeded him.

"Shut your heads," a heavy labourer commented gruffly, "she hasn't been found yet. 'Ere's the inspectors; we shall know more in a bit."

Two inspectors had come up and were talking to the constables who guarded the gate. The little fat man ran eagerly forward, saying that she had bought the key of him. "I remember the number, because of it's being three one's and three three's—III333!" he exclaimed excitedly.

An inspector put him aside.

"Nobody's been in?" he asked of one of the constables.

"No, sir."

"Then you, Brackley, come with us; you, Smith, keep the gate. There's a squad on its way."

The two inspectors and the constable passed down the alley and entered the house. They mounted the wide carved staircase.

"This don't look as if he'd been out much lately," one of the inspectors muttered as he kicked aside a litter of dead leaves and paper that lay outside Oleron's door. "I don't think we need knock—break a pane, Brackley."

The door had two glazed panels; there was a sound of shattered glass; and Brackley put his hand through the hole his elbow had made and drew back the latch.

"Faugh!" . . . choked one of the inspectors as they entered. "Let some light and air in, quick. It stinks like a hearse——"

The assembly out in the square saw the red blinds go up and the windows of the old house flung open.

"That's better," said one of the inspectors, putting his head out of a window and drawing a deep breath. . . . "That seems to be the bedroom in there; will you go in, Simms, while I go over the rest? . . ."

They had drawn up the bedroom blind also, and the waxy-white, emaciated man on the bed had made a blinker of his hand against the torturing flood of brightness. Nor could he believe that his hearing was not playing tricks with him, for there were two policemen in his room, bending over him and asking where "she" was. He shook his head.

"This woman Bengough . . . goes by the name of Miss Elsie Bengough . . . d'ye hear? Where is she? . . . No good, Brackley; get him up; be careful with him; I'll just shove *my* head out of the window, I think. . . ."

The other inspector had been through Oleron's study and had found nothing, and was now in the kitchen, kicking aside an ankle-deep mass of vegetable refuse that cumbered the floor. The kitchen window had no blind, and was overshadowed by the blank end of the house across the alley. The kitchen appeared to be empty.

But the inspector, kicking aside the dead flowers, noticed that a shuffling track that was not of his making had been swept to a cupboard in the corner. In the upper part of the door of the cupboard was a square panel that looked as if it slid on runners. The door itself was closed.

The inspector advanced, put out his hand to the little knob, and slid the hatch along its groove.

Then he took an involuntary step back again.

Framed in the aperture, and falling forward a little before it jammed again in its frame, was something that resembled a large lumpy pudding, done up in a pudding-bag of faded browny red frieze.

"Ah!" said the inspector.

To close the hatch again he would have had to thrust that pudding back with his hand; and somehow he did not quite like the idea of touching it. Instead, he turned the handle of the cupboard itself. There was weight behind it, so much weight that, after opening the door three or four inches and peering inside, he had to put his shoulder to it in order to close it again. In closing it he left sticking out, a few inches from the floor, a triangle of black-and-white check skirt.

He went into the small hall.

"All right!" he called.

They had got Oleron into his clothes. He still used his hands as blinkers, and his brain was very confused. A number of things were happening that he couldn't understand. He couldn't understand the extraordinary mess of dead flowers there seemed to be everywhere; he couldn't understand why there should be police officers in his room; he couldn't understand why one of these should be sent for a four-wheeler and a stretcher; and he couldn't understand what heavy article they seemed to be moving about in the kitchen—his kitchen. . . .

"What's the matter?" he muttered sleepily. . . .

Then he heard a murmur in the square, and the stopping of a four-wheeler outside. A police officer was at his elbow again, and Oleron wondered why, when he whispered something to him, he should run off a string of words—something about "used in evidence against you." They had lifted him to his feet, and were assisting him towards the door. . . .

No, Oleron couldn't understand it at all.

They got him down the stairs and along the alley. Oleron was aware of confused angry shoutings; he gathered that a number of people wanted to lynch somebody or other. Then his attention became fixed on a little fat frightened-eyed man who appeared to be making a statement that an officer was taking down in a notebook.

"I'd seen her with him . . . they was often together . . . she came into my shop and said it was for him . . . I thought it was all right . . . III333 the number was," the man was saying.

The people seemed to be very angry; many police were keeping them back; but one of the inspectors had a voice that Oleron thought quite kind and friendly. He was telling somebody to get somebody else into the cab before something or other was brought out; and Oleron noticed that a four-wheeler was drawn up at the gate. It appeared that it was himself who was to be put into it; and as they lifted him up he saw that the inspector tried to stand between him and something that stood behind the cab, but was not quick enough to prevent Oleron seeing that this something was a hooded stretcher. The angry voices sounded like a sea; something hard, like a stone, hit the back of the cab; and the inspector followed Oleron in and stood with his back to the window nearer the side where the people were. The door they had put Oleron in at remained open, apparently till the other inspector should come; and through the opening Oleron had a glimpse of the hatchet-like "To Let" boards among the privet-trees. One of them said that the key was at Number Six. . . .

Suddenly the raging of voices was hushed. Along the entrance-alley shuffling steps were heard, and the other inspector appeared at the cab door.

"Right away," he said to the driver.

He entered, fastened the door after him, and blocked up the second window with his back. Between the two inspectors Oleron slept peacefully. The cab moved down the square, the other vehicle went up the hill. The mortuary lay that way.   1911

"SAKI" (H. H. MUNRO)

The Open Window

"My aunt will be down presently, Mr. Nuttel," said a very self-possessed young lady of fifteen; "in the meantime you must try and put up with me."

Framton Nuttel endeavoured to say the correct something which should duly flatter the niece of the moment without unduly discounting the aunt that was to come. Privately he doubted more than ever whether these formal visits on a succession of total strangers would do much towards helping the nerve cure which he was supposed to be undergoing.

"I know how it will be," his sister had said when he was preparing to migrate to this rural retreat; "you will bury yourself down there and not speak to a living soul, and your nerves will be worse than ever from moping. I shall just give you letters of introduction to all the people I know there. Some of them, as far as I can remember, were quite nice."

Framton wondered whether Mrs. Sappleton, the lady to whom he was presenting one of the letters of introduction, came into the nice division.

"Do you know many of the people round here?" asked the niece, when she judged that they had had sufficient silent communion.

"Hardly a soul," said Framton. "My sister was staying here, at the rectory, you know, some four years ago, and she gave me letters of introduction to some of the people here."

He made the last statement in a tone of distinct regret.

"Then you know practically nothing about my aunt?" pursued the self-possessed young lady.

"Only her name and address," admitted the caller. He was wondering whether Mrs. Sappleton was in the married or widowed state. An indefinable something about the room seemed to suggest masculine habitation.

"Her great tragedy happened just three years ago," said the child; "that would be since your sister's time."

"Her tragedy?" asked Framton; somehow in this restful country spot tragedies seemed out of place.

"You may wonder why we keep that window wide open on an October afternoon," said the niece, indicating a large French window that opened on to a lawn.

"It is quite warm for the time of the year," said Framton; "but has that window got anything to do with the tragedy?"

"Out through that window, three years ago to a day, her husband and her two young brothers went off for their day's shooting. They never came back. In crossing the moor to their favorite snipe-shooting ground they were all three engulfed in a treacherous piece of bog. It had been that dreadful wet summer, you know, and places that were safe in other years gave way suddenly without warning. Their bodies were never recovered. That was the dreadful part of it." Here the child's voice lost its self-possessed note and became falteringly human. "Poor aunt always thinks that they will come back some day, they and the little brown spaniel that was lost with them, and walk in at that window just as they used to do. That is why the window is kept open every evening till it is quite dusk. Poor dear aunt, she has often told me how they went out, her husband with his white waterproof coat over his arm, and Ronnie, her youngest brother, singing 'Bertie, why do you bound?' as he always did to tease her, because she said it got on her nerves. Do you know, sometimes on still, quiet evenings like this, I almost get a creepy feeling that they will all walk in through that window——"

She broke off with a little shudder. It was a relief to Framton when the aunt bustled into the room with a whirl of apologies for being late in making her appearance.

"I hope Vera has been amusing you?" she said.

"She has been very interesting," said Framton.

"I hope you don't mind the open window," said Mrs. Sappleton briskly; "my husband and brothers will be home directly from shooting, and they always come in this way. They've been out for snipe in the marshes to-day, so they'll make a fine mess over my poor carpets. So like you menfolks, isn't it?"

She rattled on cheerfully about the shooting and the scarcity of birds, and the prospects for duck in the winter. To Framton it was all purely horrible. He made a desperate but only partially successful effort to turn the talk on to a less ghastly topic; he was conscious that his hostess was giving him only a fragment of her attention, and her eyes were constantly straying past him to the open window and the lawn beyond. It was certainly an unfortunate coincidence that he should have paid his visit on this tragic anniversary.

"The doctors agree in ordering me complete rest, an absence of mental excitement, and avoidance of anything in the nature of violent physical exercise," announced Framton, who labored under the tolerably wide-spread delusion that total strangers and chance acquaintances are hungry for the least detail of one's ailments and infirmities, their cause and cure. "On the matter of diet they are not so much in agreement," he continued.

"No?" said Mrs. Sappleton, in a voice which only replaced a yawn at the last moment. Then she suddenly brightened into alert attention— but not to what Framton was saying.

"Here they are at last!" she cried. "Just in time for tea, and don't they look as if they were muddy up to the eyes!"

Framton shivered slightly and turned toward the niece with a look intended to convey sympathetic comprehension. The child was staring out through the open window with dazed horror in her eyes. In a chill shock of nameless fear Framton swung round in his seat and looked in the same direction.

In the deepening twilight three figures were walking across the lawn towards the window; they all carried guns under their arms, and one of them was additionally burdened with a white coat hung over his shoulders. A tired brown spaniel kept close at their heels. Noiselessly they neared the house, and then a hoarse young voice chanted out of the dusk: "I said, Bertie, why do you bound?"

Framton grabbed wildly at his stick and hat; the hall-door, the gravel-drive, and the front gate were dimly noted stages in his headlong retreat. A cyclist coming along the road had to run into the hedge to avoid imminent collision.

"Here we are, my dear," said the bearer of the white mackintosh, coming in through the window; "fairly muddy, but most of it's dry. Who was that who bolted out as we came up?"

"A most extraordinary man, a Mr. Nuttel," said Mrs. Sappleton; "could only talk about his illness, and dashed off without a word of good-bye or apology when you arrived. One would think he had seen a ghost."

"I expect it was the spaniel," said the niece calmly; "he told me he had a horror of dogs. He was once hunted into a cemetery somewhere on the banks of the Ganges by a pack of pariah dogs, and had to spend the night in a newly dug grave with the creatures snarling and grinning and foaming just above him. Enough to make anyone lose their nerve."

Romance at short notice was her specialty. 1914

ELIZABETH BOWEN

Hand in Glove

Jasmine Lodge was favourably set on a residential, prettily-wooded hill-side in the south of Ireland, overlooking a river and, still better, the roofs of a lively garrison town. Around 1904, which was the flowering period of the Miss Trevors, girls could not have had a more auspicious home—the neighbourhood spun merrily round the military. Ethel and Elsie, a spirited pair, garnered the full advantage—no ball, hop, picnic, lawn tennis, croquet or boating party was complete without them; in winter, though they could not afford to hunt, they trimly bicycled to all meets, and on frosty evenings, with their guitars, set off to *soirées,* snug inside their cab in their fur-tipped capes.

They possessed an aunt, a Mrs Varley de Grey, *née* Elysia Trevor, a formerly notable local belle, who, drawn back again in her widowhood to what had been the scene of her early triumphs, occupied a back bedroom in Jasmine Lodge. Mrs Varley de Grey had had no luck: her splashing match, in its time the talk of two kingdoms, had ended up in disaster—the well-born captain in a cavalry regiment having gone so far as to blow out his brains in India, leaving behind him nothing but her and debts. Mrs Varley de Grey had returned from India with nothing but seven large trunks crammed with recent finery; and she also had been impaired by shock. This had taken place while Ethel and Elsie, whose father had married late, were still unborn—so it was that, for as long as the girls recalled, their aunt had been the sole drawback to Jasmine Lodge. Their parents had orphaned them, somewhat thoughtlessly, by simultaneously dying of scarlet fever when Ethel was just out and Elsie soon to be—they were therefore left lacking a chaperone and, with their gift for putting everything to some use, propped the aunt up in order that she might play that role. Only when her peculiarities became too marked did they feel it necessary to withdraw her: by that time, however, all the surrounding ladies could be said to compete for the honour of taking into society the sought-after Miss Trevors. From then on, no more was seen or heard of Mrs Varley de Grey. ("Oh, just a trifle unwell, but nothing much!") She remained upstairs, at the back: when the girls were giving one of their little parties, or a couple of officers came to call, the key of her room would be turned in the outer lock.

The girls hung Chinese lanterns from the creepered veranda, and would sit lightly strumming on their guitars. Not less fascinating was their badinage, accompanied by a daring flash of the eyes. They were known as the clever Miss Trevors, not because of any taint of dogmatism or book-learning—no, when a gentleman cried, "Those girls have brains!" he meant it wholly in admiration—but because of their accomplishments, ingenuity and agility. They took leading parts in theatricals, lent spirit to numbers of drawing-room games, were naughty mimics, and sang duets. Nor did their fingers lag behind their wits—they constructed lampshades, crêpe paper flowers and picturesque hats; and, above all, varied their dresses marvellously—no one could beat them for ideas, nipping, slashing or fitting. Once more allowing nothing to go to waste, they had remodelled the trousseau out of their aunt's trunks, causing sad old tulles and tarlatans, satins and *moiré* taffetas, to appear to have come from Paris only today. They re-stitched spangles, pressed ruffles crisp, and revived many a corsage of squashed silk roses. They went somewhat softly about that task, for the trunks were all stored in the attic immediately over the back room.

They wore their clothes well. "A pin on either of those two would look smart!" declared other girls. All that they were short of was evening gloves—they had two pairs each, which they had been compelled to buy. *What* could have become of Mrs Varley de Grey's presumably sumptuous numbers of this item, they were unable to fathom, and it was too bad. Had gloves been overlooked in her rush from India?—or, were they here, in that *one* trunk the Trevors could not get at? All other locks had yielded to pulls or pickings, or the sisters found key to fit them, or they had used the tool-box; but this last stronghold defied them. In that sad little soiled silk sack, always on her person, Mrs Varley de Grey, they became convinced, hoarded the operative keys, along with some frippery rings and brooches—all true emeralds, pearls and diamonds having been long ago, as they knew, sold. Such contrariety on their aunt's part irked them—meanwhile, gaieties bore hard on their existing gloves. Last thing at nights when they came in, last thing in the evenings before they went out, they would manfully dab away at the fingertips. So, it must be admitted that a long whiff of benzine pursued them as they whirled round the ballroom floor.

They were tall and handsome—nothing so soft as pretty, but in those days it was a vocation to be a handsome girl; many of the best marriages had been made by such. They carried themselves imposingly, had good busts and shoulders, waists firm under the whalebone, and straight

backs. Their features were striking, their colouring high; low on their
foreheads bounced dark mops of curls. Ethel was, perhaps, the dominant
one, but both girls were pronounced to be full of character.

Whom, and still more when, did they mean to marry? They had
already seen regiments out and in; for quite a number of years, it began
to seem, bets in the neighborhood had been running high. Sympathetic
spy-glasses were trained on the conspicuous gateway to Jasmine Lodge;
each new cavalier was noted. The only trouble might be, their promoters
claimed, that the clever Trevors were always so surrounded that they had
not a moment in which to turn or choose. Or otherwise, could it possibly
be that the admiration aroused by Ethel and Elsie, and their now institu-
tional place in the local scene, scared out more tender feeling from the
masculine breast? It came to be felt, and perhaps by the girls themselves,
that, having lingered so long and so puzzlingly, it was up to them to
bring off (like their aunt) a *coup*. Society around this garrison town had
long plumed itself upon its romantic record; summer and winter, Cupid
shot his darts. Lush scenery, the oblivion of all things else bred by the
steamy climate, and perpetual gallivanting—all were conducive. Ethel's
and Elsie's names, it could be presumed, were by now murmured wherever the Union Jack flew. Nevertheless, it was time they should decide.

Ethel's decision took place late one spring. She set her cap at the
second son of an English marquess. Lord Fred had come on a visit, for
the fishing, to a mansion some miles down the river from Jasmine Lodge.
He first made his appearance, with the rest of the house party, at one of
the more resplendent military balls, and was understood to be a man-
about-town. The civilian glint of his pince-nez, at once serene and su-
perb, instantaneously wrought, with his great name, on Ethel's heart.
She beheld him, and the assembled audience, with approbation, looked
on at the moment so big with fate. The truth, it appeared in a flash, was
that Ethel, though so condescending with her charms, had not from the
first been destined to love a soldier; and that here, after long attrition,
her answer was. Lord Fred was, by all, at once signed over to her. For his
part, he responded to her attentions quite gladly, though in a somewhat
dazed way. If he did not so often dance with her—indeed, how could he,
for she was much besought?—he could at least be perceived to gaze. At a
swiftly organized river picnic, the next evening, he by consent fell to
Ethel's lot—she had spent the foregoing morning snipping and tacking
at a remaining muslin of Mrs Varley de Grey's, a very fresh forget-me-
not-dotted pattern. The muslin did not survive the evening out, for
when the moon should have risen, rain poured into the boats. Ethel's
good-humoured drollery carried all before it, and Lord Fred wrapped his
blazer around her form.

Next day, more rain; and all felt flat. At Jasmine Lodge, the expectant deck chairs had to be hurried in from the garden, and the small close rooms, with their greeneried windows and plentiful bric-à-brac, gave out a stuffy, resentful, indoor smell. The maid was out; Elsie was lying down with a migraine; so it devolved on Ethel to carry up Mrs Varley de Grey's tea—the invalid set very great store by tea, and her manifestations by door rattlings, sobs and mutters were apt to become disturbing if it did not appear. Ethel, with the not particularly dainty tray, accordingly entered the back room, this afternoon rendered dark by its outlook into a dripping uphill wood. The aunt, her visage draped in a cobweb shawl, was as usual sitting up in bed. *"Aha,"* she at once cried, screwing one eye up and glittering round at Ethel with the other, "so what's all this in the wind today?"

Ethel, as she lodged the meal on the bed, shrugged her shoulders, saying: "I'm in a hurry."

"No doubt you are. The question is, will you get him?"

"Oh, drink your tea!" snapped Ethel, her colour rising.

The old wretch responded by popping a lump of sugar into her cheek, and sucking at it while she fixed her wink on her niece. She then observed: *"I* could tell you a thing or two!"

"We've had enough of *your* fabrications, Auntie."

"Fabrications!" croaked Mrs Varley de Grey. "And who's been the fabricator, I'd like to ask? Who's so nifty with the scissors and needle? Who's been going a-hunting in my clothes?"

"Oh, what a fib!" exclaimed Ethel, turning her eyes up. "Those old musty miserable bundles of things of yours—would Elsie or I consider laying a finger on them?"

Mrs Varley de Grey replied, as she sometimes did, by heaving up and throwing the tray at Ethel. Nought, therefore, but cast-off kitchen china nowadays was ever exposed to risk; and the young woman, not trying to gather the debris up, statuesquely, thoughtfully stood with her arms folded, watching tea steam rise from the carpet. Today, the effort required seemed to have been too much for Aunt Elysia, who collapsed on her pillows, faintly blue in the face. "Rats in the attic," she muttered. *"I've* heard them, rats in the attic! Now where's my tea?"

"You've had it," said Ethel, turning to leave the room. However, she paused to study a photograph in a tarnished, elaborate silver frame. "Really quite an Adonis, poor Uncle Harry.—From the first glance, you say, he never looked back?"

"My lovely tea," said her aunt, beginning to sob.

As Ethel slowly put down the photograph, her eyes could be seen to calculate, her mouth hardened and a reflective cast came over her brow.

Step by step, once more she approached the bed, and, as she did so, altered her tune. She suggested, in a beguiling tone: "You said you could tell me a thing or two . . . ?"

Time went on; Lord Fred, though forever promising, still failed to come quite within Ethel's grasp. Ground gained one hour seemed to be lost the next—it seemed, for example, that things went better for Ethel in the afternoons, in the open air, than at the dressier evening functions. It was when she swept down on him in full plumage that Lord Fred seemed to contract. Could it be that he feared his passions?—she hardly thought so. Or, did her complexion not light up well? When there was a question of dancing, he came so late that her programme already was black with other names, whereupon he would heave a gallant sigh. When they did take the floor together, he held her so far at arm's length, and with his face turned so far away, that when she wished to address him she had to shout—she told herself this must be the London style, but it piqued her, naturally. Next morning, all would be as it was before, with nobody so completely assiduous as Lord Fred—but, through it all, he still never came to the point. And worse, the days of his visit were running out; he would soon be back in the heart of the London Season. "Will you ever get him, Ethel, now, do you think?" Elsie asked, with trying solicitude, and no doubt the neighborhood wondered also.

She conjured up all her fascinations. But was something further needed, to do the trick?

It was now that she began to frequent her aunt.

In that dank little back room looking into the hill, proud Ethel humbled herself, to prise out the secret. Sessions were close and long. Elsie, in mystification outside the door, heard the dotty voice of their relative rising, falling, with, now and then, blood-curdling little knowing laughs. Mrs Varley de Grey was back in the golden days. Always, though, of a sudden it would break off, drop back into pleas, whimpers, and jagged breathing. No doctor, though she constantly asked for one, had for years been allowed to visit Mrs Varley de Grey—the girls saw no reason for that expense, or for the interference which might follow. Aunt's affliction, they swore, was confined to the head; all she required was quiet, and that she got. Knowing, however, how gossip spreads, they would let no servant near her for more than a minute or two, and then with one of themselves on watch at the door. They had much to bear from the foetid state of her room.

"You don't think you'll kill her, Ethel?" the out-of-it Elsie asked. "Forever sitting on top of her, as you now do. Can it be healthy, egging her on to talk? What's this attraction, all of a sudden?—whatever's this which has sprung up between you two? She and you are becoming quite hand-in-glove."

Elsie merely remarked this, and soon forgot: she had her own fish to fry. It was Ethel who had cause to recall the words—for, the afternoon of the very day they were spoken, Aunt Elysia whizzed off on another track, screamed for what was impossible and, upon being thwarted, went into a seizure unknown before. The worst of it was, at the outset her mind cleared—she pushed her shawl back, reared up her unkempt grey head and looked at Ethel, unblinkingly studied Ethel, with a lucid accumulation of years of hate. "You fool of a gawk," she said, and with such contempt! "Coming running to me to know how to trap a man. Could *you* learn, if it was from Venus herself? Wait till I show you beauty.— Bring down those trunks!"

"Oh, Auntie."

"Bring them down, I say. I'm about to dress myself up."

"Oh, but I cannot; they're heavy; I'm single-handed."

"Heavy?—they came here heavy. But there've been rats in the attic.—*I* saw you, swishing downstairs in my *eau-de-nil!*"

"Oh, you dreamed that!"

"Through the crack of the door.—Let me up, then. Let us go where they are, and look—we shall soon see!" Aunt Elysia threw back the bedclothes and began to get up. "Let's take a look," she said, "at the rats' work." She set out to totter towards the door.

"Oh, but you're not fit!" Ethel protested.

"And when did a doctor say so?" There was a swaying: Ethel caught her in time and, not gently, lugged her back to the bed—and Ethel's mind the whole of this time was whirling, for tonight was the night upon which all hung. Lord Fred's last local appearance was to be, like his first, at a ball: tomorrow he left for London. So it must be tonight, at this ball, or never! How was it that Ethel felt so strangely, wildly confident of the outcome? It was time to begin on her coiffure, lay out her dress. Oh, tonight she would shine as never before! She flung back the bedclothes over the helpless form, heard a clock strike, and hastily turned to go.

"I will be quits with you," said the voice behind her.

Ethel, in a kimono, hair half done, was in her own room, in front of the open glove drawer, when Elsie came in—home from a tennis party. Elsie acted oddly; she went at once to the drawer and buried her nose in it. "Oh, my goodness," she cried, "it's all too true, and it's awful!"

"What is?" Ethel carelessly asked.

"Ethel dear, would you ever face it out if I were to tell you a certain rumour I heard today at the party as to Lord Fred?"

Ethel turned from her sister, took up the heated tongs and applied more crimps to her natural curliness. She said: "Certainly; spit it out."

"Since childhood, he's recoiled from the breath of benzine. He wilts away when it enters the very room!"

"Who says that's so?"

"He confided it to his hostess, who is now spitefully putting it around the country."

Ethel bit her lip and put down the tongs, while Elsie sorrowfully concluded: "And your gloves stink, Ethel, as I'm sure do mine." Elsie then thought it wiser to slip away.

In a minute more, however, she was back, and this time with a still more peculiar air. She demanded: "In what state did you leave Auntie? She was sounding so very quiet that I peeped in, and *I* don't care for the looks of her now at all!" Ethel swore, but consented to take a look. She stayed in there in the back room, with Elsie biting her thumb-nail outside the door, for what seemed an ominous length of time—when she did emerge, she looked greenish, but held her head high. The sisters' eyes met. Ethel said, stonily: "Dozing."

"You're certain she's *not . . . ?* She *couldn't* ever be—you know?"

"Dozing, I tell you." Ethel stared Elsie out.

"If she *was* gone," quavered the frailer sister, "just think of it—why, we'd never get to the ball!—And a ball that everything hangs on," she ended up, with a scared but conspiratorial glance at Ethel.

"Reassure yourself. Didn't you hear me say?"

As she spoke Ethel, chiefly from habit, locked her late aunt's door on the outside. The act caused a sort of secret jingle to be heard from inside her fist, and Elsie asked: "What's that you've got hold of, now?" "Just a few little keys and trinkets she made me keep," replied Ethel, disclosing the small bag she had found where she'd looked for it, under the dead one's pillow. "Scurry on now, Elsie, or you'll never be dressed. Care to make use of my tongs, while they're so splendidly hot?"

Alone at last, Ethel drew in a breath, and, with a gesture of resolution, retied her kimono sash tightly over her corset. She shook the key from the bag and regarded it, murmuring, "Providential!," then gave a glance upward, towards where the attics were. The late spring sun had set, but an apricot afterglow, not unlike the light cast by a Chinese lantern, crept through the upper storey of Jasmine Lodge. The cessation of all those rustlings, tappings, whimpers and moans from inside Mrs Varley de Grey's room had set up an unfamiliar, somewhat unnerving hush. Not till a whiff of singeing hair announced that Elsie was well employed did Ethel set out on the quest which held all her hopes. Success was imperative—she *must* have gloves. Gloves, gloves . . .

Soundlessly, she set foot on the attic stairs.

Under the skylight, she had to suppress a shriek, for a rat—yes, of all things!—leaped at her out of an empty hatbox; and the rodent gave her a wink before it darted away. Now Ethel and Elsie knew for a certain fact that there never *had* been rats in Jasmine Lodge. However, she continued to steel her nerves, and to push her way to the one inviolate trunk.

All Mrs Varley de Grey's other Indian luggage gaped and yawned at Ethel, void, showing its linings, on end or toppling, forming a barricade around the object of her search—she pushed, pitched and pulled, scowling as the dust flew into her hair. But the last trunk, when it came into view and reach, still had something select and bridal about it: on top, the initials E. V. de G. stared out, quite luminous in a frightening way—for indeed how dusky the attic was! Shadows not only multiplied in the corners but seemed to finger their way up the sloping roof. Silence pierced up through the floor from that room below—and, worst, Ethel had the sensation of being watched by that pair of fixed eyes she had not stayed to close. She glanced this way, that way, backward over her shoulder. But, Lord Fred was at stake!—she knelt down and got to work with the key.

This trunk had two neat brass locks, one left, one right, along the front of the lid. Ethel, after fumbling, opened the first—then, so great was her hurry to know what might be within that she could not wait but slipped her hand in under the lifted corner. She pulled out one pricelessly lacy tip of what must be a bride-veil, and gave a quick laugh—must not this be an omen? She pulled again, but the stuff resisted, almost as though it were being grasped from inside the trunk—she let go, and either her eyes deceived her or the lace began to be drawn back slowly, in again, inch by inch. What was odder was, that the spotless fingertip of a white kid glove appeared for a moment, as though exploring its way out, then withdrew.

Ethel's heart stood still—but she turned to the other lock. Was a giddy attack overcoming her?—for, as she gazed, the entire lid of the trunk seemed to bulge upward, heave and strain, so that the E. V. de G. upon it rippled.

Untouched by the key in her trembling hand, the second lock tore itself open.

She recoiled, while the lid slowly rose—of its own accord.

She should have fled. But oh, how she craved what lay there exposed!—layer upon layer, wrapped in transparent paper, of elbow-length, magnolia-pure white gloves, bedded on the inert folds of the veil. "Lord Fred," thought Ethel, "now you're within my grasp!"

That was her last thought, nor was the grasp to be hers. Down on her knees again, breathless with lust and joy, Ethel flung herself forward on to that sea of kid, scrabbling and seizing. The glove she had seen before was now, however, readier for its purpose. At first it merely pounced after Ethel's fingers, as though making mock of their greedy course; but the hand within it was all the time filling out . . . With one snowy flash through the dusk, the glove clutched Ethel's front hair, tangled itself in her black curls, and dragged her head down. She began to choke among the sachets and tissue—then the glove let go, hurled her back, and made its leap at her throat.

It was a marvel that anything so dainty should be so strong. So great, so convulsive was the swell of the force that, during the strangling of Ethel, the seams of the glove split.

In any case, the glove would have been too small for her.

The shrieks of Elsie, upon the attic threshold, began only when all other sounds had died down . . . The ultimate spark of the once-famous cleverness of the Miss Trevors appeared in Elsie's extrication of herself from this awkward mess—for, who was to credit how Ethel came by her end? The sisters' reputation for warmth of heart was to stand the survivor in good stead—for, could those affections nursed in Jasmine Lodge, extending so freely even to the unwell aunt, have culminated in Elsie's setting on Ethel? No. In the end, the matter was hushed up—which is to say, is still talked about even now. Ethel Trevor and Mrs Varley de Grey were interred in the same grave, as everyone understood that they would have wished. What conversation took place under the earth, one does not know.

1952

The Demon Lover

Towards the end of her day in London Mrs Drover went round to her shut-up house to look for several things she wanted to take away. Some belonged to herself, some to her family, who were by now used to their country life. It was late August; it had been a steamy, showery day: at the moment the trees down the pavement glittered in an escape of humid yellow afternoon sun. Against the next batch of clouds, already piling up ink-dark, broken chimneys and parapets stood out. In her once familiar street, as in any unused channel, an unfamiliar queerness had silted up; a cat wove itself in and out of railings, but no human eye watched Mrs Drover's return. Shifting some parcels under her arm, she slowly forced round her latchkey in an unwilling lock, then gave the door, which had warped, a push with her knee. Dead air came out to meet her as she went in.

The staircase window having been boarded up, no light came down into the hall. But one door, she could just see, stood ajar, so she went quickly through into the room and unshuttered the big window in there. Now the prosaic woman, looking about her, was more perplexed than she knew by everything that she saw, by traces of her long former habit of life—the yellow smokestain up the white marble mantelpiece, the ring left by a vase on the top of the escritoire; the bruise in the wallpaper where, on the door being thrown open widely, the china handle had always hit the wall. The piano, having gone away to be stored, had left what looked like claw marks on its part of the parquet. Though not much dust had seeped in, each object wore a film of another kind; and, the only ventilation being the chimney, the whole drawing-room smelled of the cold hearth. Mrs Drover put down her parcels on the escritoire and left the room to proceed upstairs; the things she wanted were in a bedroom chest.

She had been anxious to see how the house was—the part-time care-taker she shared with some neighbours was away this week on his holi-day, known to be not yet back. At the best of times he did not look in often, and she was never sure that she trusted him. There were some cracks in the structure, left by the last bombing, on which she was anxious to keep an eye. Not that one could do anything—

A shaft of refracted daylight now lay across the hall. She stopped dead and stared at the hall table—on this lay a letter addressed to her.

She thought first—then the caretaker *must* be back. All the same, who, seeing the house shuttered, would have dropped a letter in at the box? It was not a circular, it was not a bill. And the post office redirected, to the address in the country, everything for her that came through the post. The caretaker (even if he *were* back) did not know she was due in London today—her call here had been planned to be a surprise—so his negligence in the manner of this letter, leaving it to wait in the dusk and the dust, annoyed her. Annoyed, she picked up the letter, which bore no stamp. But it cannot be important, or they would know . . . She took the letter rapidly upstairs with her, without a stop to look at the writing till she reached what had been her bedroom, where she let in light. The room looked over the garden and other gardens: the sun had gone in; as the clouds sharpened and lowered, the trees and rank lawns seemed already to smoke with dark. Her reluctance to look again at the letter came from the fact that she felt intruded upon—and by someone con-temptuous of her ways. However, in the tenseness preceding the fall of rain she read it: it was a few lines.

Dear Kathleen: You will not have forgotten that today is our anniversary, and the day we said. The years have gone by at once slowly and fast. In view of the fact that nothing has changed, I shall rely upon you to keep your promise. I was sorry to see you leave London, but was satisfied that you would be back in time. You may expect me, therefore, at the hour arranged. Until then . . . K.

Mrs Drover looked for the date: it was today's. She dropped the letter on to the bed-springs, then picked it up to see the writing again—her lips, beneath the remains of lipstick, beginning to go white. She felt so much the change in her own face that she went to the mirror, polished a clear patch in it and looked at once urgently and stealthily in. She was confronted by a woman of forty-four, with eyes starting out under a hat-brim that had been rather carelessly pulled down. She had not put on any more powder since she left the shop where she ate her solitary tea. The pearls her husband had given her on their marriage hung loose round her now rather thinner throat, slipping in the V of the pink wool jumper her sister knitted last autumn as they sat round the fire. Mrs Drover's most normal expression was one of controlled worry, but of assent. Since the birth of the third of her little boys, attended by a quite serious illness, she had had an intermittent muscular flicker to the left of her mouth, but in spite of this she could always sustain a manner that was at once energetic and calm.

Turning from her own face as precipitately as she had gone to meet it, she went to the chest where the things were, unlocked it, threw up the lid and knelt to search. But as rain began to come crashing down she could not keep from looking over her shoulder at the stripped bed on which the letter lay. Behind the blanket of rain the clock of the church that still stood struck six—with rapidly heightening apprehension she counted each of the slow strokes. "The hour arranged . . . My God," she said, *"what* hour? How should I . . . ? After twenty-five years . . ."

The young girl talking to the soldier in the garden had not ever completely seen his face. It was dark; they were saying goodbye under a tree. Now and then—for it felt, from not seeing him at this intense moment, as though she had never seen him at all—she verified his presence for these few moments longer by putting out a hand, which he each time pressed, without very much kindness, and painfully, on to one of the breast buttons of his uniform. That cut of the button on the palm of her hand was, principally, what she was to carry away. This was so near the end of a leave from France that she could only wish him already gone. It was August 1916. Being not kissed, being drawn away from and looked at intimidated Kathleen till she imagined spectral glitters in the place of his eyes. Turning away and looking back up the lawn she saw, through branches of trees, the drawing-room window alight: she caught a breath for the moment when she could go running back there into the safe arms of her mother and sister, and cry: "What shall I do, what shall I do? He has gone."

Hearing her catch her breath, her fiancé said, without feeling: "Cold?"

"You're going away such a long way."

"Not so far as you think."

"I don't understand?"

"You don't have to," he said. "You will. You know what we said."

"But that was—suppose you—I mean, suppose."

"I shall be with you," he said, "sooner or later. You won't forget that. You need do nothing but wait."

Only a little more than a minute later she was free to run up the silent lawn. Looking in through the window at her mother and sister, who did not for the moment perceive her, she already felt that unnatural promise drive down between her and the rest of all human kind. No other way of having given herself could have made her feel so apart, lost and forsworn. She could not have plighted a more sinister troth.

Kathleen behaved well when, some months later, her fiancé was reported missing, presumed killed. Her family not only supported her but were able to praise her courage without stint because they could not regret, as a husband for her, the man they knew almost nothing about. They hoped she would, in a year or two, console herself—and had it been only a question of consolation things might have gone much straighter ahead. But her trouble, behind just a little grief, was a complete dislocation from everything. She did not reject other lovers, for these failed to appear: for years she failed to attract men—and with the approach of her thirties she became natural enough to share her family's anxiousness on this score. She began to put herself out, to wonder; and at thirty-two she was very greatly relieved to find herself being courted by William Drover. She married him, and the two of them settled down in this quiet, arboreal part of Kensington: in this house the years piled up, her children were born, and they all lived till they were driven out by the bombs of the next war. Her movements as Mrs Drover were circumscribed, and she dismissed any idea that they were still watched.

As things were—dead or living the letter-writer sent her only a threat. Unable, for some minutes, to go on kneeling with her back exposed to the empty room, Mrs Drover rose from the chest to sit on an upright chair whose back was firmly against the wall. The desuetude of her former bedroom, her married London home's whole air of being a cracked cup from which memory, with its reassuring power, had either evaporated or leaked away, made a crisis—and at just this crisis the letter-writer had, knowledgeably, struck. The hollowness of the house this evening cancelled years on years of voices, habits and steps. Through the shut windows she only heard rain fall on the roofs around. To rally herself, she said she was in a mood—and, for two or three seconds shutting her eyes, told herself that she had imagined the letter. But she opened them—there it lay on the bed.

On the supernatural side of the letter's entrance she was not permitting her mind to dwell. Who, in London, knew she meant to call at the house today? Evidently, however, this had been known. The caretaker, *had* he come back, had had no cause to expect her: he would have taken the letter in his pocket, to forward it, at his own time, through the post. There was no other sign that the caretaker had been in—but, if not? Letters dropped in at doors of deserted houses do not fly or walk to tables in halls. They do not sit on the dust of empty tables with the air of certainty that they will be found. There is needed some human hand— but nobody but the caretaker had a key. Under circumstances she did not care to consider, a house can be entered without a key. It was possible that she was not alone now. She might be being waited for, downstairs. Waited for—until when? Until "the hour arranged." At least that was not six o'clock: six had struck.

She rose from the chair and went over and locked the door.

The thing was, to get out. To fly? No, not that: she had to catch her train. As a woman whose utter dependability was the keystone of her family life she was not willing to return to the country, to her husband, her little boys and her sister, without the objects she had come up to fetch. Resuming work at the chest she set about making up a number of parcels in a rapid, fumbling-decisive way. These, with her shopping parcels, would be too much to carry; these meant a taxi—at the thought of the taxi her heart went up and her normal breathing resumed. I will ring up the taxi now; the taxi cannot come too soon: I shall hear the taxi out there running its engine, till I walk calmly down to it through the hall. I'll ring up—But no: the telephone is cut off . . . She tugged at a knot she had tied wrong.

The idea of flight . . . He was never kind to me, not really. I don't remember him kind at all. Mother said he never considered me. He was set on me, that was what it was—not love. Not love, not meaning a person well. What did he do, to make me promise like that? I can't remember—But she found that she could.

She remembered with such dreadful acuteness that the twenty-five years since then dissolved like smoke and she instinctively looked for the weal left by the button on the palm of her hand. She remembered not only all that he said and did but the complete suspension of *her* existence during that August week. I was not myself—they all told me so at the time. She remembered—but with one white burning blank as where acid has dropped on a photograph: *under no conditions* could she remember his face.

So, wherever he may be waiting, I shall not know him. You have no time to run from a face you do not expect.

The thing was to get to the taxi before any clock struck what could be the hour. She would slip down the street and round the side of the square to where the square gave on the main road. She would return in the taxi, safe, to her own door, and bring the solid driver into the house with her to pick up the parcels from room to room. The idea of the taxi driver made her decisive, bold: she unlocked her door, went to the top of the staircase and listened down.

She heard nothing—but while she was hearing nothing the *passé* air of the staircase was disturbed by a draught that travelled up to her face. It emanated from the basement: down there a door or window was being opened by someone who chose this moment to leave the house.

The rain had stopped; the pavements steamily shone as Mrs Drover let herself out by inches from her own front door into the empty street. The unoccupied houses opposite continued to meet her look with their damaged stare. Making towards the thoroughfare and the taxi, she tried not to keep looking behind. Indeed, the silence was so intense—one of those creeks of London silence exaggerated this summer by the damage of war—that no tread could have gained on hers unheard. Where her street debouched on the square where people went on living, she grew conscious of, and checked, her unnatural pace. Across the open end of the square two buses impassively passed each other: women, a perambulator, cyclists, a man wheeling a barrow signalized, once again, the ordinary flow of life. At the square's most populous corner should be— and was—the short taxi rank. This evening, only one taxi—but this, although it presented its blank rump, appeared already to be alertly waiting for her. Indeed, without looking round the driver started his engine as she panted up from behind and put her hand on the door. As she did so, the clock struck seven. The taxi faced the main road: to make the trip back to her house it would have to turn—she had settled back on the seat and the taxi *had* turned before she, surprised by its knowing movement, recollected that she had not "said where." She leaned forward to scratch at the glass panel that divided the driver's head from her own.

The driver braked to what was almost a stop, turned round and slid the glass panel back: the jolt of this flung Mrs Drover forward till her face was almost into the glass. Through the aperture driver and passenger, not six inches between them, remained for an eternity eye to eye. Mrs Drover's mouth hung open for some seconds before she could issue her first scream. After that she continued to scream freely and to beat with her gloved hands on the glass all round as the taxi, accelerating without mercy, made off with her into the hinterland of deserted streets.

1941

THE CAT JUMPS

After the Bentley murder, Rose Hill stood empty two years. Lawns mounted to meadows; white paint peeled from the balconies; the sun, looking more constantly, less fearfully in than sightseers' eyes through the naked windows, bleached the floral wallpapers. The week after the execution Harold Bentley's legatees had placed the house on the books of the principal agents, London and local. But though sunny, up to date, and convenient, though so delightfully situated over the Thames valley (above flood level), within easy reach of a golfcourse, Rose Hill, while frequently viewed, remained unpurchased. Dreadful associations apart, the privacy of the place had been violated; with its terraced garden, lily pond and pergola cheerfully rose-encrusted, the public had been made too familiar. On the domestic scene too many eyes had burnt the impress of their horror. Moreover, that pearly bathroom, that bedroom with wide outlook over a loop of the Thames . . . *"The Rose Hill Horror"*: headlines flashed up at the very sound of the name. "Oh, *no*, dear!" many wives had exclaimed, drawing their husbands hurriedly from the gate. "Come away!" they had urged crumpling the agent's order to view as though the house were advancing upon them. And husbands came away—with a backward glance at the garage. Funny to think a chap who was hanged had kept his car there.

The Harold Wrights, however, were not deterred. They had light, bright, shadowless, thoroughly disinfected minds. They believed that they disbelieved in most things but were unprejudiced; they enjoyed frank discussions. They dreaded nothing but inhibitions: they had no inhibitions. They were pious agnostics, earnest for social reform; they explained everything to their children, and were annoyed to find their children could not sleep at nights because they thought there was a complex under the bed. They knew all crime to be pathological, and read their murders only in scientific books. They had Vita glass put into all their windows. No family, in fact, could have been more unlike the mistaken Harold Bentleys.

Rose Hill, from the first glance, suited the Wrights admirably. They were in search of a cheerful week-end house with a nice atmosphere, where their friends could join them for frank discussions, and their own and their friends' children "run wild" during the summer months. Harold Wright, who had a good head, got the agent to knock six hundred off the quoted price of the house. "That unfortunate affair," he murmured. Jocelyn commended his inspiration. Otherwise, they did not give the Bentleys another thought.

The Wrights had the floral wallpapers all stripped off and the walls cream-washed; they removed some disagreeably thick pink shades from the electricity and had the paint renewed inside and out. (The front of the house was bracketed over with balconies, like an overmantel.) Their bedroom mantelpiece, stained by the late Mrs Bentley's cosmetics, had to be scrubbed with chemicals. Also, they had removed from the rock-garden Mrs Bentley's little dog's memorial tablet, with a quotation on it from *Indian Love Lyrics*. Jocelyn Wright, looking into the unfortunate bath—*the* bath, so square and opulent, with its surround of nacreous tiles—said, laughing lightly, she supposed anyone *else* would have had that bath changed. "Not that that would be possible," she added; "the bath's built in . . . I've always wanted a built-in bath."

Harold and Jocelyn turned from the bath to look down at the cheerful river shimmering under a spring haze. All the way down the slope cherry trees were in blossom. Life should be simplified for the Wrights; they were fortunate in their mentality.

After an experimental week-end, without guests or children, only one thing troubled them: a resolute stuffiness, upstairs and down—due, presumably, to the house's having been so long shut up—a smell of unsavoury habitation, of rich cigarette smoke stale in the folds of unaired curtains, of scent spilled on unbrushed carpets, an alcoholic smell—persistent in their perhaps too sensitive nostrils after days of airing, doors and windows open, in rooms drenched thoroughly with sun and wind. They told each other it came from the parquet; they didn't like it, somehow. They had the parquet taken up—at great expense—and put down plain oak floors.

In their practical way, the Wrights now set out to expel, live out, live down, almost (had the word had place in their vocabulary) to "lay" the Bentleys. Deferred by trouble over the parquet, their occupation of Rose Hill, which should have dated from mid-April, did not begin till the end of May. Throughout a week, Jocelyn had motored from town daily, so that the final installation of themselves and the children was able to coincide with their first week-end party—they asked down five of their friends to warm the house.

That first Friday, everything was auspicious; afternoon sky blue as the garden irises; later, a full moon pendent over the river; a night so warm that, after midnight, their enlightened friends, in pyjamas, could run on the blanched lawns in a state of high though rational excitement. Jane, Jacob and Janet, their admirably spaced-out children, kept awake by the moonlight, hailed their elders out of the nursery skylight. Jocelyn waved to them: they never had been repressed.

The girl Muriel Barker was found looking up the terraces at the house a shade doubtfully. "You know," she said, "I do rather wonder they don't feel . . . *sometimes* . . . you know what I mean?"

"No," replied her companion, a young scientist.

Muriel sighed. "No one would mind if it had been just a short sharp shooting. But it was so . . . prolonged. It went on all over the house. Do you remember?" she said timidly.

"No," replied Mr Cartaret. "It didn't interest me."

"Oh, nor me either!" agreed Muriel quickly, but added: "How he must have hated her . . ."

The scientist, sleepy, yawned frankly and referred her to Krafft Ebing. But Muriel went to bed with *Alice in Wonderland;* she went to sleep with the lights on. She was not, as Jocelyn realized later, the sort of girl to have asked at all.

Next morning was overcast; in the afternoon it rained, suddenly and heavily—interrupting, for some, tennis, for others, a pleasant discussion, in a punt, on marriage under the Soviet. Defeated, they all rushed in. Jocelyn went round from room to room, shutting tightly the rain-lashed casements along the front of the house. These continued to rattle; the balconies creaked. An early dusk set in; an oppressive, almost visible moisture, up from the darkening river, pressed on the panes like a presence and slid through the house. The party gathered in the library, round an expansive but thinly burning fire. Harold circulated photographs of modern architecture; they discussed these tendencies. Then Mrs Monkhouse, sniffing, exclaimed: "Who uses 'Trèfle Incarnat'?"

"Now, *who* ever would—" her hostess began scornfully. Then from the hall came a howl, scuffle, a thin shriek. They sat too still; in the dusky library Mr Cartaret laughed out loud. Harold Wright, indignantly throwing open the door, revealed Jane and Jacob rolling at the foot of the stairs, biting each other, their faces dark with uninhibited passion. Bumping alternate heads against the foot of the banisters, they shrieked in concert.

"Extraordinary," said Harold; "they've never done that before. They have always understood each other so well."

"I wouldn't do that," advised Jocelyn, raising her voice slightly; "you'll hurt your teeth. Other teeth won't grow at once, you know."

"You should let them find that out for themselves," disapproved Edward Cartaret, taking up the *New Statesman*. Harold, in perplexity, shut the door on his children, who soon stunned each other to silence.

Meanwhile, Sara and Talbot Monkhouse, Muriel Barker and Theodora Smith, had drawn together over the fire in a tight little knot.

Their voices twanged with excitement. By that shock, just now, something seemed to have been released. Even Cartaret gave them half his attention. They were discussing *crime passionnel*.

"Of course, if that's what they really *want* to discuss . . ." thought Jocelyn. But it did seem unfortunate. Partly from an innocent desire to annoy her visitors, partly because the room felt awful—you would have thought fifty people had been there for a week—she went across and opened one of the windows, admitting a pounce of damp wind. They all turned, startled, to hear rain crash on the lead of an upstairs balcony. Muriel's voice was left in forlorn solo: "Dragged herself . . . whining 'Harold' . . ."

Harold Wright looked remarkably conscious. Jocelyn said brightly, "Whatever *are* you talking about?" But, unfortunately, Harold, on almost the same breath, suggested: "Let's leave that family alone, shall we?" Their friends all felt they might not be asked again. Though they did feel, plaintively, that they had been being natural. However, they disowned Muriel, who, getting up abruptly, said she thought she'd like to go for a walk in the rain before dinner. Nobody accompanied her.

Later, overtaking Mrs Monkhouse on the stairs, Muriel confided: absolutely, she could not stand Edward Cartaret. She could hardly bear to be in the room with him. He seemed so . . . cruel. Cold-blooded? No, she meant cruel. Sara Monkhouse, going into Jocelyn's room for a chat (at her entrance Jocelyn started violently), told Jocelyn that Muriel could not stand Edward, could hardly bear to be in a room with him. "Pity," said Jocelyn. "I had thought they might do for each other." Jocelyn and Sara agreed that Muriel was unrealized: what she ought to have was a baby. But when Sara, dressing, told Talbot Monkhouse that Muriel could not stand Edward, and Talbot said Muriel was unrealized, Sara was furious. The Monkhouses, who never did quarrel, quarrelled bitterly, and were late for dinner. They would have been later if the meal itself had not been delayed by an outburst of sex antagonism between the nice Jacksons, a couple imported from London to run the house. Mrs Jackson, putting everything in the oven, had locked herself into her room.

"Curious," said Harold; "the Jacksons' relations to each other always seemed so modern. They have the most intelligent discussions."

Theodora said she had been re-reading Shakespeare—this brought them point-blank up against *Othello*. Harold, with Titanic force, wrenched round the conversation to relativity: about this no one seemed to have anything to say but Edward Cartaret. And Muriel, who by some mischance had again been placed beside him, sat deathly, turning down her dark-rimmed eyes. In fact, on the intelligent sharp-featured faces all round the table something—perhaps simply a clearness—seemed to be lacking, as though these were wax faces for one fatal instant exposed to a furnace. Voices came out from some dark interiority; in each conversational interchange a mutual vote of no confidence was implicit. You would have said that each personality had been attacked by some kind of decomposition.

"No moon tonight," complained Sara Monkhouse. Never mind, they would have a cosy evening; they would play paper games, Jocelyn promised.

"If you can see," said Harold. "Something seems to be going wrong with the light."

Did Harold think so? They had all noticed the light seemed to be losing quality, as though a film, smoke-like, were creeping over the bulbs. The light, thinning, darkening, seemed to contract round each lamp into a blurred aura. They had noticed, but, each with a proper dread of his own subjectivity, had not spoken.

"Funny stuff, electricity," Harold said.

Mr Cartaret could not agree with him.

Though it was late, though they yawned and would not play paper games, they were reluctant to go to bed. You would have supposed a delightful evening. Jocelyn was not gratified.

The library stools, rugs and divans were strewn with Krafft Ebing, Freud, Forel, Weiniger and the heterosexual volume of Havelock Ellis. (Harold had thought it right to install his reference library; his friends hated to discuss without basis.) The volumes were pressed open with paper-knives and small pieces of modern statuary; stooping from one to another, purposeful as a bee, Edward Cartaret read extracts aloud to Harold, to Talbot Monkhouse, and to Theodora Smith, who stitched *gros point* with resolution. At the far end of the library under a sallow drip from a group of electric candles, Mrs Monkhouse and Miss Barker shared an ottoman, spines pressed rigid against the wall. Tensely one spoke, one listened.

"And these," thought Jocelyn, leaning back with her eyes shut between the two groups, "are the friends I liked to have in my life. Pellucid, sane . . ."

It was remarkable how much Muriel knew. Sara, very much shocked, edged up till their thighs touched. You would have thought the Harold Bentleys had been Muriel's relatives. Surely, Sara attempted, in one's large, bright world one did not think of these things? Practically, they did not exist! Surely Muriel should not . . . But Muriel looked at her strangely.

"Did you know," she said, "that one of Mrs Bentley's hands was found in the library?"

Sara, smiling a little awkwardly, licked her lip. "Oh," she said.

"But the fingers were in the dining-room. He began there."

"Why isn't he in Broadmoor?"

"That defence failed. He didn't really subscribe to it. He said having done what he wanted was worth anything."

"Oh!"

"Yes, he was nearly lynched . . . She dragged herself upstairs. She couldn't lock any doors—naturally. One maid—her maid—got shut into the house with them: he'd sent all the others away. For a long time everything seemed so quiet: the maid crept out and saw Harold Bentley sitting half way upstairs, finishing a cigarette. All the lights were full on. He nodded to her and dropped the cigarette through the banisters. Then she saw the . . . the state of the hall. He went upstairs after Mrs Bentley, saying: 'Lucinda!' He looked into room after room, whistling: then he said *'Here we are,'* and shut a door after him.

"The maid fainted. When she came to, it was still going on, upstairs . . . Harold Bentley had locked all the garden doors; there were locks even on the french windows. The maid couldn't get out. Everything she touched was . . . sticky. At last she broke a pane and got through. As she ran down the garden—the lights were on all over the house—she saw Harold Bentley moving about in the bathroom. She fell right over the edge of a terrace and one of the tradesmen picked her up next day.

"Doesn't it seem odd, Sara, to think of Jocelyn in that bath?"

Finishing her recital, Muriel turned on Sara an ecstatic and brooding look that made her almost beautiful. Sara fumbled with a cigarette; match after match failed her. "Muriel, *you* ought to see a specialist."

Muriel held out her hand for a cigarette. "He put her heart in her hat-box. He said it belonged in there."

"You had no right to come here. It was most unfair on Jocelyn. Most . . . indelicate."

Muriel, to whom the word was, properly, unfamiliar, eyed incredulously Sara's lips.

"How dared you come?"

"I thought I might like it. I thought I ought to fulfil myself. I'd never had any experience of these things."

"Muriel . . ."

"Besides, I wanted to meet Edward Cartaret. Several people said we were made for each other. Now, of course, I shall never marry. Look what comes of it . . . I must say, Sara, I wouldn't be you or Jocelyn. Shut up all night with a man all alone—I don't know how you dare sleep. I've arranged to sleep with Theodora, and we shall barricade the door. I noticed something about Edward Cartaret the moment I arrived: a kind of insane glitter. He is utterly pathological. He's got instruments in his room, in that black bag. Yes, I looked. Did you notice the way he went on and on about cutting up that cat, and the way Talbot and Harold listened?"

Sara, looking furtively round the room, saw Mr Cartaret making passes over the head of Theodora Smith with a paper-knife. Both appeared to laugh heartily, but in silence.

"Here we are," said Harold, showing his teeth, smiling.

He stood over Muriel with a siphon in one hand, glass in the other.

At this point Jocelyn, rising, said she, for one, intended to go to bed.

Jocelyn's bedroom curtains swelled a little over the noisy window. The room was stuffy and—insupportable, so that she did not know where to turn. The house, fingered outwardly by the wind that dragged unceasingly past the walls, was, within, a solid silence: silence heavy as flesh. Jocelyn dropped her wrap to the floor, then watched how its feathered edges crept a little. A draught came in, under her bathroom door.

Jocelyn turned away in despair and hostility from the strained, pale woman looking at her from her oblong glass. She said aloud, "There *is* no fear"; then, within herself, heard this taken up: "But the death fear, that one is not there to relate! If the spirit, dismembered in agony, dies before the body! If the spirit, in the whole knowledge of its dissolution, drags from chamber to chamber, drops from plane to plane of awareness (as from knife to knife down an oubliette), shedding, receiving agony! Till, long afterwards, death, with its little pain, is established in the indifferent body." There was no comfort: death (now at every turn and instant claiming her) was, in its every possible manifestation, violent death: ultimately, she was to be given up to terror.

Undressing, shocked by the iteration of her reflected movements, she flung a towel over the glass. With what desperate eyes of appeal, at Sara's door, she and Sara had looked at each other, clung with their looks—and parted. She could have sworn she heard Sara's bolt slide softly to. But what then, subsequently, of Talbot? And what—she eyed her own bolt, so bright (and, for the late Mrs Bentley, so ineffective)—what of Harold?

"It's atavistic!" she said aloud, in the dark-lit room, and, kicking her slippers away, got into bed. She took *Erewhon* from the rack, but lay rigid, listening. As though snatched by a movement, the towel slipped from the mirror beyond her bed-end. She faced the two eyes of an animal in extremity, eyes black, mindless. The clock struck two: she had been waiting an hour.

On the floor, her feathered wrap shivered again all over. She heard the other door of the bathroom very stealthily open, then shut. Harold moved in softly, heavily, knocked against the side of the bath, and stood still. He was quietly whistling.

"Why didn't I understand? He must always have hated me. It's tonight he's been waiting for . . . *He wanted this house.* His look, as we went upstairs . . ."

She shrieked: "Harold!"

Harold, so softly whistling, remained behind the imperturbable door, remained quite still . . . "He's *listening* for me . . ." One pinpoint of hope at the tunnel end: to get to Sara, to Theodora, to Muriel. Unmasked, incautious, with a long tearing sound of displaced air, Jocelyn leapt from the bed to the door.

But her door had been locked from the outside.

With a strange rueful smile, like an actress, Jocelyn, skirting the foot of the two beds, approached the door of the bathroom. "At least I have still . . . my feet.' For for some time the heavy body of Mrs Bentley, tenacious of life, had been dragging itself from room to room. *"Harold!"* she said to the silence, face close to the door.

The door opened on Harold, looking more dreadfully at her than she had imagined. With a quick, vague movement he roused himself from his meditation. Therein he had assumed the entire burden of Harold Bentley. Forces he did not know of assembling darkly, he had faced for untold ages the imperturbable door to his wife's room. She would be there, densely, smotheringly there. She lay like a great cat, always, over the mouth of his life.

The Harolds, superimposed on each other, stood searching the bedroom strangely. Taking a step forward, shutting the door behind him: "Here we are," said Harold.

Jocelyn went down heavily. Harold watched.

Harold Wright was appalled. Jocelyn had fainted: Jocelyn never had fainted before. He shook, he fanned, he applied restoratives. His perplexed thoughts fled to Sara—oh, Sara certainly. "Hi!" he cried, "Sara!" and successively fled from each to each of the locked doors. There was no way out.

Across the passage a door throbbed to the maniac drumming of Sara Monkhouse. She had been locked in. For Talbot, agonized with solicitude, it was equally impossible to emerge from his dressing-room. Further down the passage, Edward Cartaret, interested by this nocturnal manifestation, wrenched and rattled his door-handle in vain.

Muriel, on her silent way through the house to Theodora's bedroom, had turned all the keys on the outside, impartially. She did not know which door might be Edward Cartaret's. Muriel was a woman who took no chances.   1934

W. F. HARVEY

THE CLOCK

I liked your description of the people at the *pension*. I can just picture
that rather sinister Miss Cornelius, with her toupee and clinking ban-
gles. I don't wonder you felt frightened that night when you found her
sleep-walking in the corridor. But after all, why shouldn't she sleep-walk?
As to the movements of the furniture in the lounge on the Sunday, you
are, I suppose, in an earthquake zone, though an earthquake seems too
big an explanation for the ringing of that little handbell on the mantelpiece. It's rather as if our parlourmaid—another new one!—were to call
a stray elephant to account for the teapot we found broken yesterday.
You have at least escaped the eternal problem of maids in Italy.

Yes, my dear, I most certainly believe you. I have never had experiences quite like yours, but your mention of Miss Cornelius has reminded
me of something rather similar that happened nearly twenty years ago,
soon after I left school. I was staying with my aunt in Hampstead. You
remember her, I expect; or, if not her, the poodle, Monsieur, that she
used to make perform such pathetic tricks. There was another guest,
whom I had never met before, a Mrs Caleb. She lived in Lewes and had
been staying with my aunt for about a fortnight, recuperating after a
series of domestic upheavals, which had culminated in her two servants
leaving her at an hour's notice, without any reason, according to Mrs
Caleb; but I wondered. I had never seen the maids; I had seen Mrs
Caleb and, frankly, I disliked her. She left the same sort of impression on
me as I gather your Miss Cornelius leaves on you—something queer and
secretive; underground, if you can use the expression, rather than under-
hand. And I could feel in my body that she did not like me.

It was summer. Joan Denton—you remember her; her husband was
killed in Gallipoli—had suggested that I should go down to spend the
day with her. Her people had rented a little cottage some three miles out
of Lewes. We arranged a day. It was gloriously fine for a wonder, and I
had planned to leave that stuffy old Hampstead house before the old

ladies were astir. But Mrs Caleb waylaid me in the hall, just as I was going out.

"I wonder," she said, "I wonder if you could do me a small favour. If you *do* have any time to spare in Lewes—only if you do—would you be so kind as to call at my house? I left a little travelling-clock there in the hurry of parting. If it's not in the drawing-room, it will be in my bedroom or in one of the maids' bedrooms. I know I lent it to the cook, who was a poor riser, but I can't remember if she returned it. Would it be too much to ask? The house has been locked up for twelve days, but everything is in order. I have the keys here; the large one is for the garden gate, the small one for the front door."

I could only accept, and she proceeded to tell me how I could find Ash Grove House.

"You will feel quite like a burglar," she said. "But mind, it's only if you have time to spare."

As a matter of fact I found myself glad of any excuse to kill time. Poor old Joan had been taken suddenly ill in the night—they feared appendicitis—and though her people were very kind and asked me to stay to lunch, I could see that I should only be in the way, and made Mrs. Caleb's commission an excuse for an early departure.

I found Ash Grove without difficulty. It was a medium-sized red-brick house, standing by itself in a high walled garden that bounded a narrow lane. A flagged path led from the gate to the front door, in front of which grew, not an ash, but a monkey-puzzle, that must have made the rooms unnecessarily gloomy. The side door, as I expected, was locked. The dining-room and drawing-room lay on either side of the hall and, as the windows of both were shuttered, I left the hall door open, and in the dim light looked round hurriedly for the clock, which, from what Mrs Caleb had said, I hardly expected to find in either of the downstairs rooms. It was neither on table nor mantelpiece. The rest of the furniture was carefully covered over with white dust-sheets. Then I went upstairs. But, before doing so, I closed the front door. I did in fact feel rather like a burglar, and I thought that if anyone did happen to see the front door open, I might have difficulty in explaining things. Happily the upstairs windows were not shuttered. I made a hurried search of the principal bedrooms. They had been left in apple-pie order; nothing was out of place; but there was no sign of Mrs Caleb's clock. The impression that the house gave me—you know the sense of personality that a house conveys—was neither pleasing nor displeasing, but it was stuffy, stuffy from the absence of fresh air, with an additional stuffiness added, that seemed to come out from the hangings and quilts and antimacassars. The corridor, on to which the bedrooms I had examined opened, com-

municated with a smaller wing, an older part of the house, I imagined,
which contained a box-room and the maids' sleeping-quarters. The last
door that I unlocked—(I should say that the doors of all the rooms were
locked, and relocked by me after I had glanced inside them)—contained
the object of my search. Mrs Caleb's travelling-clock was on the mantelpiece, ticking away merrily.

That was how I thought of it at first. And then for the first time I
realised that there was something wrong. The clock had no business to
be ticking. The house had been shut up for twelve days. No one had
come in to air it or to light fires. I remember how Mrs Caleb had told my
aunt that if she left the keys with a neighbour, she was never sure who
might get hold of them. And yet the clock was going. I wondered if some
vibration had set the mechanism in motion, and pulled out my watch to
see the time. It was five minutes to one. The clock on the mantelpiece
said four minutes to the hour. Then, without quite knowing why, I shut
the door on to the landing, locked myself in, and again looked round the
room. Nothing was out of place. The only thing that might have called
for remark was that there appeared to be a slight indentation on the
pillow and the bed; but the mattress was a feather mattress, and you
know how difficult it is to make them perfectly smooth. You won't need
to be told that I gave a hurried glance under the bed—do you remember
your supposed burglar in Number Six at St Ursula's?—and then, and
much more reluctantly, opened the doors of two horribly capacious cupboards, both happily empty, except for a framed text with its face to the
wall. By this time I really was frightened. The clock went ticking on. I
had a horrible feeling that an alarm might go off at any moment, and the
thought of being in that empty house was almost too much for me.
However, I made an attempt to pull myself together. It might after all be
a fourteen-day clock. If it were, then it would be almost run down. I
could roughly find out how long the clock had been going by winding it
up. I hesitated to put the matter to the test; but the uncertainty was too
much for me. I took it out of its case and began to wind. I had scarcely
turned the winding-screw twice when it stopped. The clock clearly was
not running down; the hands had been set in motion probably only an
hour or two before. I felt cold and faint and, going to the window, threw
up the sash, letting in the sweet, live air of the garden. I knew now that
the house was queer, horribly queer. Could someone be living in the
house? Was someone else in the house now? I thought that I had been in
all the rooms, but had I? I had only just opened the bathroom door, and
I had certainly not opened any cupboards, except those in the room in
which I was. Then, as I stood by the open window, wondering what I
should do next and feeling that I just couldn't go down that corridor into
the darkened hall to fumble at the latch of the front door with I don't

know what behind me, I heard a noise. It was very faint at first, and seemed to be coming from the stairs. It was a curious noise—not the noise of anyone climbing up the stairs, but—you will laugh if this letter reaches you by a morning post—of something hopping up the stairs, like a very big bird would hop. I heard it on the landing; it stopped. Then there was a curious scratching noise against one of the bedroom doors, the sort of noise you can make with the nail of your little finger scratching polished wood. Whatever it was, was coming slowly down the corridor, scratching at the doors as it went. I could stand it no longer. Nightmare pictures of locked doors opening filled my brain. I took up the clock wrapped it in my macintosh and dropped it out of the window on to a flower-bed. Then I managed to crawl out of the window and, getting a grip of the sill, "successfully negotiated," as the journalists would say, "a twelve-foot drop." So much for our much abused Gym at St Ursula's. Picking up the mackintosh, I ran round to the front door and locked it. Then I felt I could breathe, but not until I was on the far side of the gate in the garden wall did I feel safe.

Then I remembered that the bedroom window was open. What was I to do? Wild horses wouldn't have dragged me into that house again unaccompanied. I made up my mind to go to the police-station and tell them everything. I should be laughed at, of course, and they might easily refuse to believe my story of Mrs Caleb's commission. I had actually begun to walk down the lane in the direction of the town, when I chanced to look back at the house. The window that I had left open was shut.

No, my dear, I didn't see any face or anything dreadful like that . . . and, of course, it may have shut by itself. It was an ordinary sash-window, and you know they are often difficult to keep open.

And the rest? Why, there's really nothing more to tell. I didn't even see Mrs Caleb again. She had had some sort of fainting fit just before lunch-time, my aunt informed me on my return, and had had to go to bed. Next morning I travelled down to Cornwall to join mother and the children. I thought I had forgotten all about it, but when three years later Uncle Charles suggested giving me a travelling-clock for a twenty-first birthday present, I was foolish enough to prefer the alternative that he offered, a collected edition of the works of Thomas Carlyle.

1928

SHIRLEY JACKSON

The Tooth

The bus was waiting, panting heavily at the curb in front of the small bus station, its great blue-and-silver bulk glittering in the moonlight. There were only a few people interested in the bus, and at that time of night no one passing on the sidewalk: the one movie theatre in town had finished its show and closed its doors an hour before, and all the movie patrons had been to the drugstore for ice cream and gone on home; now the drugstore was closed and dark, another silent doorway in the long midnight street. The only town lights were the street lights, the lights in the all-night lunchstand across the street, and the one remaining counter lamp in the bus station where the girl sat in the ticket office with her hat and coat on, only waiting for the New York bus to leave before she went home to bed.

Standing on the sidewalk next to the open door of the bus, Clara Spencer held her husband's arm nervously. "I feel so funny," she said.

"Are you all right?" he asked. "Do you think I ought to go with you?"

"No, of course not," she said. "I'll be all right." It was hard for her to talk because of her swollen jaw; she kept a handkerchief pressed to her face and held hard to her husband. "Are you sure *you*'ll be all right?" she asked. "I'll be back tomorrow night at the latest. Or else I'll call."

"Everything will be fine," he said heartily. "By tomorrow noon it'll all be gone. Tell the dentist if there's anything wrong I can come right down."

"I feel so funny," she said. "Light-headed, and sort of dizzy."

"That's because of the dope," he said. "All that codeine, and the whisky, and nothing to eat all day."

She giggled nervously. "I couldn't comb my hair, my hand shook so. I'm glad it's dark."

"Try to sleep in the bus," he said. "Did you take a sleeping pill?"

"Yes," she said. They were waiting for the bus driver to finish his cup of coffee in the lunchstand; they could see him through the glass window, sitting at the counter, taking his time. "I feel so *funny,*" she said.

298

"You know, Clara," he made his voice very weighty, as though if he spoke more seriously his words would carry more conviction and be therefore more comforting, "you know, I'm glad you're going down to New York to have Zimmerman take care of this. I'd never forgive myself if it turned out to be something serious and I let you go to this butcher up here."

"It's just a *toothache,*" Clara said uneasily, "nothing very serious about a *toothache.*"

"You can't tell," he said. "It might be abscessed or something; I'm sure he'll have to pull it."

"Don't even talk like that," she said, and shivered.

"Well, it looks pretty bad," he said soberly, as before. "Your face so swollen, and all. Don't you worry."

"I'm not worrying," she said. "I just feel as if I were all tooth. Nothing else."

The bus driver got up from the stool and walked over to pay his check. Clara moved toward the bus, and her husband said, "Take your time, you've got plenty of time."

"I just feel funny," Clara said.

"Listen," her husband said, "that tooth's been bothering you off and on for years; at least six or seven times since I've known you you've had trouble with that tooth. It's about time something was done. You had a toothache on our honeymoon," he finished accusingly.

"Did I?" Clara said. "You know," she went on, and laughed, "I was in such a hurry I didn't dress properly. I have on old stockings and I just dumped everything into my good pocketbook."

"Are you sure you have enough money?" he said.

"Almost twenty-five dollars," Clara said. "I'll be home tomorrow."

"Wire if you need more," he said. The bus driver appeared in the doorway of the lunchroom. "Don't worry," he said.

"Listen," Clara said suddenly, "are you *sure* you'll be all right? Mrs. Lang will be over in the morning in time to make breakfast, and Johnny doesn't need to go to school if things are too mixed up."

"I know," he said.

"Mrs. Lang," she said, checking on her fingers. "I called Mrs. Lang, I left the grocery order on the kitchen table, you can have the cold tongue for lunch and in case I don't get back Mrs. Lang will give you dinner. The cleaner ought to come about four o'clock, I won't be back so give him your brown suit and it doesn't matter if you forget but be sure to empty the pockets."

"Wire if you need more money," he said. "Or call. I'll stay home tomorrow so you can call at home."

"Mrs. Lang will take care of the baby," she said.

"Or you can wire," he said.

The bus driver came across the street and stood by the entrance to the bus.

"Okay?" the bus driver said.

"Good-bye," Clara said to her husband.

"You'll feel all right tomorrow," her husband said. "It's only a tooth-ache."

"I'm fine," Clara said. "Don't you worry." She got on the bus and then stopped, with the bus driver waiting behind her. "Milkman," she said to her husband. "Leave a note telling him we want eggs."

"I will," her husband said. "Good-bye."

"Good-bye," Clara said. She moved on into the bus and behind her the driver swung into his seat. The bus was nearly empty and she went far back and sat down at the window outside which her husband waited. "Good-bye," she said to him through the glass, "take care of yourself."

"Good-bye," he said, waving violently.

The bus stirred, groaned, and pulled itself forward. Clara turned her head to wave good-bye once more and then lay back against the heavy soft seat. Good Lord, she thought, what a thing to do! Outside, the familiar street slipped past, strange and dark and seen, unexpectedly, from the unique station of a person leaving town, going away on a bus. It isn't as though it's the first time I've ever been to New York, Clara thought indignantly, it's the whisky and the codeine and the sleeping pill and the toothache. She checked hastily to see if her codeine tablets were in her pocketbook; they had been standing, along with the aspirin and a glass of water, on the dining-room sideboard, but somewhere in the lunatic flight from her home she must have picked them up, because they were in her pocketbook now, along with the twenty-odd dollars and her compact and comb and lipstick. She could tell from the feel of the lipstick that she had brought the old, nearly finished one, not the new one that was a darker shade and had cost two-fifty. There was a run in her stocking and a hole in the toe that she never noticed at home wearing her old comfortable shoes, but which was now suddenly and disagreeably apparent inside her best walking shoes. Well, she thought, I can buy new stockings in New York tomorrow, after the tooth is fixed, after everything's all right. She put her tongue cautiously on the tooth and was rewarded with a split-second crash of pain.

The bus stopped at a red light and the driver got out of his seat and came back toward her. "Forgot to get your ticket before," he said.

"I guess I was a little rushed at the last minute," she said. She found the ticket in her coat pocket and gave it to him. "When do we get to New York?" she asked.

"Five-fifteen," he said. "Plenty of time for breakfast. One-way ticket?"

"I'm coming back by train," she said, without seeing why she had to tell him, except that it was late at night and people isolated together in some strange prison like a bus had to be more friendly and communicative than at other times.

"Me, I'm coming back by bus," he said, and they both laughed, she painfully because of her swollen face. When he went back to his seat far away at the front of the bus she lay back peacefully against the seat. She could feel the sleeping pill pulling at her; the throb of the toothache was distant now, and mingled with the movement of the bus, a steady beat like her heartbeat which she could hear louder and louder, going on through the night. She put her head back and her feet up, discreetly covered with her skirt, and fell asleep without saying good-bye to the town.

She opened her eyes once and they were moving almost silently through the darkness. Her tooth was pulsing steadily and she turned her cheek against the cool back of the seat in weary resignation. There was a thin line of lights along the ceiling of the bus and no other light. Far ahead of her in the bus she could see the other people sitting; the driver, so far away as to be only a tiny figure at the end of a telescope, was straight at the wheel, seemingly awake. She fell back into her fantastic sleep.

She woke up later because the bus had stopped, the end of that silent motion through the darkness so positive a shock that it woke her stunned, and it was a minute before the ache began again. People were moving along the aisle of the bus and the driver, turning around, said, "Fifteen minutes." She got up and followed everyone else out, all but her eyes still asleep, her feet moving without awareness. They were stopped beside an all-night restaurant, lonely and lighted on the vacant road. Inside, it was warm and busy and full of people. She saw a seat at the end of the counter and sat down, not aware that she had fallen asleep again when someone sat down next to her and touched her arm. When she looked around foggily he said, "Traveling far?"

"Yes," she said.

He was wearing a blue suit and he looked tall; she could not focus her eyes to see any more.

"You want coffee?" he asked.

She nodded and he pointed to the counter in front of her where a cup of coffee sat steaming.

"Drink it quickly," he said.

She sipped at it delicately; she may have put her face down and tasted it without lifting the cup. The strange man was talking.

"Even farther than Samarkand," he was saying, "and the waves ringing on the shore like bells."

"Okay, folks," the bus driver said, and she gulped quickly at the coffee, drank enough to get her back into the bus.

When she sat down in her seat again the strange man sat down beside her. It was so dark in the bus that the lights from the restaurant were unbearably glaring and she closed her eyes. When her eyes were shut, before she fell asleep, she was closed in alone with the toothache.

"The flutes play all night," the strange man said, "and the stars are as big as the moon and the moon is as big as a lake."

As the bus started up again they slipped back into the darkness and only the thin thread of lights along the ceiling of the bus held them together, brought the back of the bus where she sat along with the front of the bus where the driver sat and the people sitting there so far away from her. The lights tied them together and the strange man next to her was saying, "Nothing to do all day but lie under the trees."

Inside the bus, traveling on, she was nothing; she was passing the trees and the occasional sleeping houses, and she was in the bus but she was between here and there, joined tenuously to the bus driver by a thread of lights, being carried along without effort of her own.

"My name is Jim," the strange man said.

She was so deeply asleep that she stirred uneasily without knowledge, her forehead against the window, the darkness moving along beside her.

Then again that numbing shock, and, driven awake, she said, frightened, "What's happened?"

"It's all right," the strange man—Jim—said immediately. "Come along."

She followed him out of the bus, into the same restaurant, seemingly, but when she started to sit down at the same seat at the end of the counter he took her hand and led her to a table. "Go and wash your face," he said. "Come back here afterward."

She went into the ladies' room and there was a girl standing there powdering her nose. Without turning around the girl said, "Cost's a nickel. Leave the door fixed so's the next one won't have to pay."

The door was wedged so it would not close, with half a match folder in the lock. She left it the same way and went back to the table where Jim was sitting.

"What do you want?" she said, and he pointed to another cup of coffee and a sandwich. "Go ahead," he said.

While she was eating her sandwich she heard his voice, musical and soft, "And while we were sailing past the island we heard a voice calling us. . . ."

Back in the bus Jim said, "Put your head on my shoulder now, and go to sleep."

"I'm all right," she said.

"No," Jim said. "Before, your head was rattling against the window."

Once more she slept, and once more the bus stopped and she woke frightened, and Jim brought her again to a restaurant and more coffee. Her tooth came alive then, and with one hand pressing her cheek she searched through the pockets of her coat and then through her pocketbook until she found the little bottle of codeine pills and she took two while Jim watched her.

She was finishing her coffee when she heard the sound of the bus motor and she started up suddenly, hurrying, and with Jim holding her arm she fled back into the dark shelter of her seat. The bus was moving forward when she realized that she had left her bottle of codeine pills sitting on the table in the restaurant and now she was at the mercy of her tooth. For a minute she stared back at the lights of the restaurant through the bus window and then she put her head on Jim's shoulder and he was saying as she fell asleep, "The sand is so white it looks like snow, but it's hot, even at night it's hot under your feet."

Then they stopped for the last time, and Jim brought her out of the bus and they stood for a minute in New York together. A woman passing them in the station said to the man following her with suitcases, "We're just on time, it's five-fifteen."

"I'm going to the dentist," she said to Jim.

"I know," he said. "I'll watch out for you."

He went away, although she did not see him go. She thought to watch for his blue suit going through the door, but there was nothing.

I ought to have thanked him, she thought stupidly, and went slowly into the station restaurant, where she ordered coffee again. The counter man looked at her with the worn sympathy of one who has spent a long night watching people get off and on buses. "Sleepy?" he asked.

"Yes," she said.

She discovered after a while that the bus station joined Pennsylvania Terminal and she was able to get into the main waiting-room and find a seat on one of the benches by the time she fell asleep again.

Then someone shook her rudely by the shoulder and said, "What train you taking, lady, it's nearly seven." She sat up and saw her pocketbook on her lap, her feet neatly crossed, a clock glaring into her face. She said, "Thank you," and got up and walked blindly past the benches and got on to the escalator. Someone got on immediately behind her and touched her arm; she turned and it was Jim. "The grass is so green and so soft," he said, smiling, "and the water of the river is so cool."

She stared at him tiredly. When the escalator reached the top she stepped off and started to walk to the street she saw ahead. Jim came along beside her and his voice went on, "The sky is bluer than anything you've ever seen, and the songs. . . ."

She stepped quickly away from him and thought that people were looking at her as they passed. She stood on the corner waiting for the light to change and Jim came swiftly up to her and then away. "Look," he said as he passed, and he held out a handful of pearls.

Across the street there was a restaurant, just opening. She went in and sat down at a table, and a waitress was standing beside her frowning. "You was asleep," the waitress said accusingly.

"I'm very sorry," she said. It was morning. "Poached eggs and coffee, please."

It was a quarter to eight when she left the restaurant, and she thought, if I take a bus, and go straight downtown now, I can sit in the drugstore across the street from the dentist's office and have more coffee until about eight-thirty and then go into the dentist's when it opens and he can take me first.

The buses were beginning to fill up; she got into the first bus that came along and could not find a seat. She wanted to go to Twenty-third Street, and got a seat just as they were passing Twenty-sixth Street; when she woke she was so far downtown that it took her nearly half-an-hour to find a bus and get back to Twenty-third.

At the corner of Twenty-third Street, while she was waiting for the light to change, she was caught up in a crowd of people, and when they crossed the street and separated to go different directions someone fell into step beside her. For a minute she walked on without looking up, staring resentfully at the sidewalk, her tooth burning her, and then she looked up, but there was no blue suit among the people pressing by on either side.

When she turned into the office building where her dentist was, it was still very early morning. The doorman in the office building was freshly shaven and his hair was combed; he held the door open briskly, as at five o'clock he would be sluggish, his hair faintly out of place. She went in through the door with a feeling of achievement; she had come successfully from one place to another, and this was the end of her journey and her objective.

The clean white nurse sat at the desk in the office; her eyes took in the swollen cheek, the tired shoulders, and she said, "You poor thing, you look worn out."

"I have a toothache." The nurse half-smiled, as though she were still waiting for the day when someone would come in and say, "My feet hurt." She stood up into the professional sunlight. "Come right in," she said. "We won't make you wait."

There was sunlight on the headrest of the dentist's chair, on the round white table, on the drill bending its smooth chromium head. The dentist smiled with the same tolerance as the nurse; perhaps all human ailments were contained in the teeth, and he could fix them if people would only come to him in time. The nurse said smoothly, "I'll get her file, doctor. We thought we'd better bring her right in."

She felt, while they were taking an X-ray, that there was nothing in her head to stop the malicious eye of the camera, as though the camera would look through her and photograph the nails in the wall next to her, or the dentist's cuff buttons, or the small thin bones of the dentist's instruments; the dentist said, "Extraction," regretfully to the nurse, and the nurse said, "Yes, doctor, I'll call them right away."

Her tooth, which had brought her here unerringly, seemed now the only part of her to have any identity. It seemed to have had its picture taken without her; it was the important creature which must be recorded and examined and gratified; she was only its unwilling vehicle, and only as such was she of interest to the dentist and the nurse, only as the bearer of her tooth was she worth their immediate and practised attention. The dentist handed her a slip of paper with the picture of a full set of teeth drawn on it; her living tooth was checked with a black mark, and across the top of the paper was written "Lower molar; extraction."

"Take this slip," the dentist said, "and go right up to the address on this card; it's a surgeon dentist. They'll take care of you there."

"What will they do?" she said. Not the question she wanted to ask, not: What about me? or, How far down do the roots go?

"They'll take that tooth out," the dentist said testily, turning away. "Should have been done years ago."

I've stayed too long, she thought, he's tired of my tooth. She got up out of the dentist chair and said, "Thank you. Good-bye."

"Good-bye," the dentist said. At the last minute he smiled at her, showing her his full white teeth, all in perfect control.

"Are you all right? Does it bother you too much?" the nurse asked.

"I'm all right."

"I can give you some codeine tablets," the nurse said. "We'd rather you didn't take anything right now, of course, but I think I could let you have them if the tooth is really bad."

"No," she said, remembering her little bottle of codeine pills on the table of a restaurant between here and there. "No, it doesn't bother me too much."

"Well," the nurse said, "good luck."

She went down the stairs and out past the doorman; in the fifteen minutes she had been upstairs he had lost a little of his pristine morning-ness, and his bow was just a fraction smaller than before.

"Taxi?" he asked, and, remembering the bus down to Twenty-third Street, she said, "Yes."

Just as the doorman came back from the curb, bowing to the taxi he seemed to believe he had invented, she thought a hand waved to her from the crowd across the street.

She read the address on the card the dentist had given her and re-peated it carefully to the taxi driver. With the card and the little slip of paper with "Lower molar" written on it and her tooth identified so clearly, she sat without moving, her hands still around the papers, her eyes almost closed. She thought she must have been asleep again when the taxi stopped suddenly, and the driver, reaching around to open the door, said, "Here we are, lady." He looked at her curiously.

"I'm going to have a tooth pulled," she said.

"Jesus," the taxi driver said. She paid him and he said, "Good luck," as he slammed the door.

This was a strange building, the entrance flanked by medical signs carved in stone; the doorman here was faintly professional, as though he were competent to prescribe if she did not care to go any farther. She went past him, going straight ahead until an elevator opened its door to her. In the elevator she showed the elevator man the card and he said, "Seventh floor."

She had to back up in the elevator for a nurse to wheel in an old lady in a wheel chair. The old lady was calm and restful, sitting there in the elevator with a rug over her knees; she said, "Nice day" to the elevator operator and he said, "Good to see the sun," and then the old lady lay back in her chair and the nurse straightened the rug around her knees and said, "Now we're not going to worry," and the old lady said irritably, "Who's worrying?"

They got out at the fourth floor. The elevator went on up and then the operator said, "Seven," and the elevator stopped and the door opened.

"Straight down the hall and to your left," the operator said.

There were closed doors on either side of the hall. Some of them said "DDS," some of them said "Clinic," some of them said "X-Ray." One of them, looking wholesome and friendly and somehow most compre-hensible, said "Ladies." Then she turned to the left and found a door with the name on the card and she opened it and went in. There was a nurse sitting behind a glass window, almost as in a bank, and potted palms in tubs in the corners of the waiting room, and new magazines and comfortable chairs. The nurse behind the glass window said, "Yes?" as though you had overdrawn your account with the dentist and were two teeth in arrears.

She handed her slip of paper through the glass window and the nurse looked at it and said, "Lower molar, yes. They called about you. Will you come right in, please? Through the door to your left."

Into the vault? she almost said, and then silently opened the door and went in. Another nurse was waiting, and she smiled and turned, expecting to be followed, with no visible doubt about her right to lead.

There was another X-ray, and the nurse told another nurse: "Lower molar," and the other nurse said, "Come this way, please."

There were labyrinths and passages, seeming to lead into the heart of the office building, and she was put, finally, in a cubicle where there was a couch with a pillow and a wash-basin and a chair.

"Wait here," the nurse said. "Relax if you can."

"I'll probably go to sleep," she said.

"Fine," the nurse said. "You won't have to wait long."

She waited probably, for over an hour, although she spent the time half-sleeping, waking only when someone passed the door; occasionally the nurse looked in and smiled, once she said, "Won't have to wait much longer." Then, suddenly, the nurse was back, no longer smiling, no longer the good hostess, but efficient and hurried. "Come along," she said, and moved purposefully out of the little room into the hallways again.

Then, quickly, more quickly than she was able to see, she was sitting in the chair and there was a towel around her head and a towel under her chin and the nurse was leaning a hand on her shoulder.

"Will it hurt?" she asked.

"No," the nurse said, smiling. "You know it won't hurt, don't you?"

"Yes," she said.

The dentist came in and smiled down on her from over her head. "Well," he said.

"Will it hurt?" she said.

"Now," he said cheerfully, "we couldn't stay in business if we hurt people." All the time he talked he was busying himself with metal hidden under a towel, and great machinery being wheeled in almost silently behind her. "We couldn't stay in business at all," he said. "All you've got to worry about is telling us all your secrets while you're asleep. Want to watch out for that, you know. Lower molar?" he said to the nurse.

"Lower molar, doctor," she said.

Then they put the metal-tasting rubber mask over her face and the dentist said, "You know," two or three times absentmindedly while she could still see him over the mask. The nurse said "Relax your hands, dear," and after a long time she felt her fingers relaxing.

First of all things get so far away, she thought, remember this. And remember the metallic sound and taste of all of it. And the outrage.

And then the whirling music, the ringing confusedly loud music that went on and on, around and around, and she was running as fast as she could down a long horribly clear hallway with doors on both sides and at the end of the hallway was Jim, holding out his hands and laughing, and calling something she could never hear because of the loud music, and she was running and then she said, "I'm not afraid," and someone from the door next to her took her arm and pulled her through and the world widened alarmingly until it would never stop and then it stopped with the head of the dentist looking down at her and the window dropped into place in front of her and the nurse was holding her arm.

"Why did you pull me back?" she said, and her mouth was full of blood. "I wanted to go on."

"I didn't pull you," the nurse said, but the dentist said, "She's not out of it yet."

She began to cry without moving and felt the tears rolling down her face and the nurse wiped them off with a towel. There was no blood anywhere around except in her mouth; everything was as clean as before. The dentist was gone, suddenly, and the nurse put out her arm and helped her out of the chair. "Did I talk?" she asked suddenly, anxiously. "Did I say anything?"

"You said, 'I'm not afraid,' " the nurse said soothingly. "Just as you were coming out of it."

"No," she said, stopping to pull at the arm around her. "Did I *say* anything? Did I say where he is?"

"You didn't say *anything*," the nurse said. "The doctor was only teasing you."

"Where's my tooth?" she asked suddenly, and the nurse laughed and said, "All gone. Never bother you again."

She was back in the cubicle, and she lay down on the couch and cried, and the nurse brought her whisky in a paper cup and set it on the edge of the wash-basin.

"God has given me blood to drink," she said to the nurse, and the nurse said, "Don't rinse your mouth or it won't clot."

After a long time the nurse came back and said to her from the doorway, smiling, "I see you're awake again."

"Why?" she said.

"You've been asleep," the nurse said. "I didn't want to wake you."

She sat up; she was dizzy and it seemed that she had been in the cubicle all her life.

"Do you want to come along now?" the nurse said, all kindness again. She held out the same arm, strong enough to guide any wavering footstep; this time they went back through the long corridor to where the nurse sat behind the bank window.

"All through?" this nurse said brightly. "Sit down a minute, then." She indicated a chair next to the glass window, and turned away to write busily. "Do not rinse your mouth for two hours," she said, without turning around. "Take a laxative tonight, take two aspirin if there is any pain. If there is much pain or excessive bleeding, notify this office at once. All right?" she said, and smiled brightly again.

There was a new little slip of paper; this one said, "Extraction," and underneath, "Do not rinse mouth. Take mild laxative. Two aspirin for pain. If pain is excessive or any hemorrhage occurs, notify office."

"Good-bye," the nurse said pleasantly.

"Good-bye," she said.

With the little slip of paper in her hand, she went out through the glass door and, still almost asleep, turned the corner and started down the hall. When she opened her eyes a little and saw that it was a long hall with doorways on either side, she stopped and then saw the door marked "Ladies" and went in. Inside there was a vast room with windows and wicker chairs and glaring white tiles and glittering silver faucets; there were four or five women around the wash-basins, combing their hair, putting on lipstick. She went directly to the nearest of the three wash-basins, took a paper towel, dropped her pocketbook and the little slip of paper on the floor next to her, and fumbled with the faucets, soaking the towel until it was dripping. Then she slapped it against her face violently. Her eyes cleared and she felt fresher, so she soaked the paper again and rubbed her face with it. She felt out blindly for another paper towel, and the woman next to her handed her one, with a laugh she could hear, although she could not see for the water in her eyes. She heard one of the women say, "Where we going for lunch?" and another one say, "Just downstairs, prob'ly. Old fool says I gotta be back in half-an-hour."

Then she realized that at the wash-basin she was in the way of the women in a hurry so she dried her face quickly. It was when she stepped a little aside to let someone else get to the basin and stood up and glanced into the mirror that she realized with a slight stinging shock that she had no idea which face was hers.

She looked into the mirror as though into a group of strangers, all staring at her or around her; no one was familiar in the group, no one smiled at her or looked at her with recognition; you'd think my own face would know me, she thought, with a queer numbness in her throat. There was a creamy chinless face with bright blond hair, and a sharp-looking face under a red veiled hat, and a colorless anxious face with brown hair pulled straight back, and a square rosy face under a square haircut, and two or three more faces pushing close to the mirror, moving, regarding themselves. Perhaps it's not a mirror, she thought, maybe it's a window and I'm looking straight through at women washing on the other side. But there were women combing their hair and consulting the mirror; the group was on her side, and she thought, I hope I'm not the blonde, and lifted her hand and put it on her cheek.

She was the pale anxious one with the hair pulled back and when she realized it she was indignant and moved hurriedly back through the crowd of women, thinking, It isn't fair, why don't I have any color in my face? There were some pretty faces there, why didn't I take one of those? I didn't have time, she told herself sullenly, they didn't give me time to think, I could have had one of the nice faces, even the blonde would be better.

She backed up and sat down in one of the wicker chairs. It's mean, she was thinking. She put her hand up and felt her hair; it was loosened after her sleep but that was definitely the way she wore it, pulled straight back all around and fastened at the back of her neck with a wide tight barrette. Like a schoolgirl, she thought, only—remembering the pale face in the mirror—only I'm older than that. She unfastened the barrette with difficulty and brought it around where she could look at it. Her hair fell softly around her face; it was warm and reached to her shoulders. The barrette was silver; engraved on it was the name, "Clara."

"Clara," she said aloud. *"Clara?"* Two of the women leaving the room smiled back at her over their shoulders; almost all the women were leaving now, correctly combed and lipsticked, hurrying out talking together. In the space of a second, like birds leaving a tree, they all were gone and she sat alone in the room. She dropped the barrette into the ashstand next to her chair; the ashstand was deep and metal, and the barrette made a satisfactory clang falling down. Her hair down on her shoulders, she opened her pocketbook, and began to take things out, setting them on her lap as she did so. Handkerchief, plain, white, uninitialled. Compact, square and brown tortoise-shell plastic, with a powder compartment and a rouge compartment; the rouge compartment had obviously never been used, although the powder cake was half-gone. That's why I'm so pale, she thought, and set the compact down. Lipstick, a rose shade, almost finished. A comb, an opened package of cigarettes and a package of matches, a change purse, and a wallet. The change purse was red imitation leather with a zipper across the top; she opened it and dumped the money out into her hand. Nickels, dimes, pennies, a quarter. Ninety-seven cents. Can't go far on that, she thought, and opened the brown leather wallet; there was money in it but she looked first for papers and found nothing. The only thing in the wallet was money. She counted it; there were nineteen dollars. I can go a little farther on *that,* she thought.

There was nothing else in the pocketbook. No keys—shouldn't I have keys? she wondered—no papers, no address book, no identification. The pocketbook itself was imitation leather, light grey, and she looked down and discovered that she was wearing a dark grey flannel suit and a salmon pink blouse with a ruffle around the neck. Her shoes were black and stout with moderate heels and they had laces, one of which was untied. She was wearing beige stockings and there was a ragged tear in the right knee and a great ragged run going down her leg and ending in a hole in the toe which she could feel inside her shoe. She was wearing a pin on the lapel of her suit which, when she turned it around to look at it, was a blue plastic letter C. She took the pin off and dropped it into the ashstand, and it made a sort of clatter at the bottom, with a metallic clang when it landed on the barrette. Her hands were small, with stubby fingers and no nail polish; she wore a thin gold wedding ring on her left hand and no other jewelry.

Sitting alone in the ladies' room in the wicker chair, she thought, The least I can do is get rid of these stockings. Since no one was around she took off her shoes and stripped away the stockings with a feeling of relief when her toe was released from the hole. Hide them, she thought: the paper towel wastebasket. When she stood up she got a better sight of herself in the mirror; it was worse than she had thought: the grey suit bagged in the seat, her legs were bony, and her shoulders sagged. I look fifty, she thought; and then, consulting the face, but I can't be more than thirty. Her hair hung down untidily around the pale face and with sudden anger she fumbled in the pocketbook and found the lipstick; she drew an emphatic rosy mouth on the pale face, realizing as she did so that she was not very expert at it, and with the red mouth the face looking at her seemed somehow better to her, so she opened the compact and put on pink cheeks with the rouge. The cheeks were uneven and patent, and the red mouth glaring, but at least the face was no longer pale and anxious.

She put the stockings into the wastebasket and went bare-legged out into the hall again, and purposefully to the elevator. The elevator operator said, "Down?" when he saw her and she stepped in and the elevator carried her silently downstairs. She went back past the grave professional doorman and out into the street where people were passing, and she stood in front of the building and waited. After a few minutes Jim came out of a crowd of people passing and came over to her and took her hand.

Somewhere between here and there was her bottle of codeine pills, upstairs on the floor of the ladies' room she had left a little slip of paper headed "Extraction"; seven floors below, oblivious of the people who stepped sharply along the sidewalk, not noticing their occasional curious glances, her hand in Jim's and her hair down on her shoulders, she ran barefoot through hot sand.   1948

V. S. PRITCHETT

A Story of Don Juan

It is said that on one night of his life Don Juan slept alone, though I think the point has been disputed. Returning to Seville in the spring he was held up, some hours' ride from the city, by the floods of the Quadalquiver, a river as dirty as an old lion after the rains, and was obliged to stay at the *finca* of the Quintero family. The doorway, the walls, the windows of the house were hung with the black and violet draperies of mourning when he arrived there. God rest her soul (the peasants said), the lady of the house was dead. She had been dead a year. The young Quintero was a widower. Nevertheless Quintero took him in and even smiled to see a gallant spattered and drooping in the rain like a sodden cockerel. There was malice in that smile, for Quintero was mad with loneliness and grief; the man who had possessed and discarded all women, was received by a man demented because he had lost only one.

"My house is yours," said Quintero, speaking the formula. There was bewilderment in his eyes; those who grieve do not find the world and its people either real or believable. Irony inflects the voices of mourners, and there was malice, too, in Quintero's further greetings; for grief appears to put one at an advantage, the advantage (in Quintero's case) being the macabre one that he could receive Juan now without that fear, that terror which Juan brought to the husbands of Seville. It was perfect, Quintero thought, that for once in his life Juan should have arrived at an empty house.

There was not even (as Juan quickly ascertained) a maid, for Quintero was served only by a manservant, being unable any longer to bear the sight of women. This servant dried Don Juan's clothes and in an hour or two brought in a bad dinner, food which stamped up and down in the stomach like people waiting for a coach in the cold. Quintero was torturing his body as well as his mind, and as the familiar pains arrived they agonized him and set him off about his wife. Grief had also made Quintero an actor. His eyes had that hollow, taper-haunted dusk of the theatre as he spoke of the beautiful girl. He dwelled upon their courtship, on details of her beauty and temperament, and how he had rushed her from the church to the marriage bed like a man racing a tray of diamonds through the streets into the safety of a bank vault. The presence of Don Juan turned every man into an artist when he was telling his own love story—one had to tantalize and surpass the great seducer—and Quintero, rolling it all off in the grand manner, could not resist telling that his bride had died on her marriage night.

"Man!" cried Don Juan. He started straight off on stories of his own. But Quintero hardly listened; he had returned to the state of exhaustion and emptiness which is natural to grief. As Juan talked, the madman followed his own thoughts like an actor preparing and mumbling the next entrance; and the thought he had had when Juan had first appeared at his door returned to him: that Juan must be a monster to make a man feel triumphant that his own wife was dead. Half-listening, and indigestion aiding, Quintero felt within himself the total hatred of all the husbands of Seville for this diabolical man. And as Quintero brooded upon this it occurred to him that it was probably not a chance that he had it in his power to effect the most curious revenge on behalf of the husbands of Seville.

The decision was made. The wine being finished Quintero called for his manservant and gave orders to change Don Juan's room.

"For," said Quintero drily, "his Excellency's visit is an honour and I cannot allow one who has slept in the most delicately scented room in Spain to pass the night in a chamber which stinks to heaven of goat."

"The closed room?" said the manservant, astonished that the room which still held the great dynastic marriage bed and which had not been used more than half a dozen times by his master since the lady's death— and then only at the full moon when his frenzy was worst—was to be given to a stranger.

Yet to this room Quintero led his guest and there parted from him with eyes so sparkling with ill-intention that Juan, who was sensitive to this kind of point, understood perfectly that the cat was being let into the cage only because the bird had long ago flown out. The humiliation was unpleasant. Juan saw the night stretching before him like a desert.

What a bed to lie in: so wide, so unutterably vacant, so malignantly inopportune! June took off his clothes, snuffed the lamp wick. He lay down conscious that on either side of him lay wastes of sheet, draughty and uninhabited except by the nomadic bug. A desert. To move an arm one inch to the side, to push out a leg, however cautiously, was to enter desolation. For miles and miles the foot might probe, the fingers or the knee explore a friendless Antarctica. Yet to lie rigid and still was to have a foretaste of the grave. And here, too, he was frustrated: for though the wine kept him yawning, that awful food romped in his stomach, jolting him back from the edge of sleep the moment he got there.

There is an art in sleeping alone in a double bed but, naturally, this art was unknown to Juan; he had to learn it. The difficulty is easily solved. If you cannot sleep on one side of the bed, you move over and try the other. Two hours or more must have passed before this occurred to Juan. Sullen-headed he advanced into the desert and the night air lying chill between the sheets flapped, and made him shiver. He stretched out his arm and crawled towards the opposite pillow. Mother of God, the coldness, the more than virgin frigidity of linen! Juan put down his head and, drawing up his knees, he shivered. Soon, he supposed, he would be warm again, but in the meantime, ice could not have been colder. It was unbelievable.

Ice was the word for that pillow and those sheets. Ice. Was he ill? Had the rain chilled him that his teeth must chatter like this and his legs tremble? Far from getting warmer he found the cold growing. Now it was on his forehead and his cheeks, like arms of ice on his body, like legs of ice upon his legs. Suddenly in superstition he got up on his hands and stared down at the pillow in the darkness, threw back the bed-clothes and looked down upon the sheet; his breath was hot, yet blowing against his cheeks was a breath colder than the grave, his shoulders and body were hot, yet limbs of snow were drawing him down; and just as he would have shouted his appalled suspicion, lips like wet ice unfolded upon his own and he sank down to a kiss, unmistakably a kiss, which froze him like a winter.

In his own room Quintero lay listening. His mad eyes were exalted and his ears were waiting. He was waiting for the scream of horror. He knew the apparition. There would be a scream, a tumble, hands fighting for the light, fists knocking at the door. And Quintero had locked the door. But when no scream came, Quintero lay talking to himself, remembering the night the apparition had first come to him and had made him speechless and left him choked and stiff. It would be even better if there were no scream! Quintero lay awake through the night building castle after castle of triumphant revenge and receiving, as he did so, the ovations of the husbands of Seville. "The stallion is gelded!" At an early hour Quintero unlocked the door and waited downstairs impatiently. He was a wreck after a night like that.

Juan came down at last. He was (Quintero observed) pale. Or was he pale?

"Did you sleep well?" Quintero asked furtively.

"Very well," Juan replied.

"I do not sleep well in strange beds myself," Quintero insinuated. Juan smiled and replied that he was more used to strange beds than his own. Quintero scowled.

"I reproach myself: the bed was large," he said. But the large, Juan said, were necessarily as familiar to him as the strange. Quintero bit his nails. Some noise had been heard in the night—something like a scream, a disturbance. The manservant had noticed it also. Juan answered him that disturbances in the night had indeed bothered him at the beginning of his career, but now he took them in his stride. Quintero dug his nails into the palms of his hands. He brought out the trump.

"I am afraid," Quintero said, "it was a cold bed. You must have *frozen.*"

"I am never cold for long," Juan said, and, unconsciously anticipating the manner of a poem that was to be written in his memory two centuries later, declaimed: "The blood of Don Juan is hot, for the sun is the blood of Don Juan."

Quintero watched. His eyes jumped like flies to every movement of his guest. He watched him drink his coffee. He watched him tighten the stirrups of his horse. He watched Juan vault into the saddle. Don Juan was humming and when he went off was singing, was singing in that intolerable tenor of his which was like a cock crow in the olive groves.

Quintero went into the house and rubbed his unshaven chin. Then he went out again to the road where the figure of Don Juan was now only a small smoke of dust between the eucalyptus trees. Quintero went up to the room where Juan had slept and stared at it with accusations and suspicions. He called the manservant.

"I shall sleep here tonight," Quintero said.

The manservant answered carefully. Quintero was mad again and the moon was still only in its first quarter. The man watched his master during the day looking towards Seville. It was too warm after the rains, the country steamed like a laundry.

And then, when the night came, Quintero laughed at his doubts. He went up to the room and as he undressed he thought of the assurance of those ice-cold lips, those icicle fingers and those icy arms. She had not come last night; oh what fidelity! To think, he would say in his remorse to the ghost, that malice had so disordered him that he had been base and credulous to use the dead for a trick.

Tears were in his eyes as he lay down and for some time he dared not turn on his side and stretch out his hand to touch what, in his disorder, he had been willing to betray. He loathed his heart. He craved—yet how could he hope for it now?—the miracle of recognition and forgiveness. It was this craving which moved him at last. His hands went out. And they were met.

The hands, the arms, the lips moved out of their invisibility and soundlessness towards him. They touched him, they clasped him, they drew him down, but—what was this? He gave a shout, he fought to get

away, kicked out and swore; and so the manservant found him wrestling
with the sheets, striking out with fists and knees, roaring that he was in
hell. Those hands, those lips, those limbs, he screamed, were *burning*
him. They were of ice no more. They were of fire.   1950

MURIEL SPARK

THE PORTOBELLO ROAD

One day in my young youth at high summer, lolling with my lovely companions upon a haystack, I found a needle. Already and privately for some years I had been guessing that I was set apart from the common run, but this of the needle attested the fact to my whole public: George, Kathleen and Skinny. I sucked my thumb, for when I had thrust my idle hand deep into the hay, the thumb was where the needle had stuck.

When everyone had recovered George said, "She put in her thumb and pulled out a plum." Then away we were into our merciless hacking-hecking laughter again.

The needle had gone fairly deep into the thumby cushion and a small red river flowed and spread from this tiny puncture. So that nothing of our joy should lag, George put in quickly,

"Mind your bloody thumb on my shirt."

Then hac-hec-hoo, we shrieked into the hot Borderland afternoon. Really I should not care to be so young of heart again. That is my thought every time I turn over my old papers and come across the photograph. Skinny, Kathleen and myself are in the photo atop the haystack. Skinny had just finished analysing the inwards of my find.

"It couldn't have been done by brains. You haven't much brains but you're a lucky wee thing."

Everyone agreed that the needle betokened extraordinary luck. As it was becoming a serious conversation, George said,

"I'll take a photo."

I wrapped my hanky round my thumb and got myself organised. George pointed up from his camera and shouted,

"Look, there's a mouse!"

Kathleen screamed and I screamed although I think we knew there was no mouse. But this gave us an extra session of squalling hee-hoo's. Finally we three composed ourselves for George's picture. We look lovely and it was a great day at the time, but I would not care for it all over again. From that day I was known as Needle.

One Saturday in recent years I was mooching down the Portobello Road, threading among the crowds of marketers on the narrow pavement when I saw a woman. She had a haggard, careworn, wealthy look, thin but for the breasts forced-up high like a pigeon's. I had not seen her for nearly five years. How changed she was! But I recognised Kathleen, my friend; her features had already begun to sink and protrude in the way that mouths and noses do in people destined always to be old for their years. When I had last seen her, nearly five years ago, Kathleen, barely thirty, had said,

"I've lost all my looks, it's in the family. All the women are handsome as girls, but we go off early, we go brown and nosey."

I stood silently among the people, watching. As you will see, I wasn't in a position to speak to Kathleen. I saw her shoving in her avid manner from stall to stall. She was always fond of antique jewellery and of bargains. I wondered that I had not seen her before in the Portobello Road on my Saturday morning ambles. Her long stiff-crooked fingers pounced to select a jade ring from amongst the jumble of brooches and pendants, onyx, moonstone and gold, set out on the stall.

"What do you think of this?" she said.

I saw then who was with her. I had been half-conscious of the huge man following several paces behind her, and now I noticed him.

"It looks all right," he said. "How much is it?"

"How much is it?" Kathleen asked the vendor.

I took a good look at this man accompanying Kathleen. It was her husband. The beard was unfamiliar, but I recognised beneath it his enormous mouth, the bright sensuous lips, the large brown eyes forever brimming with pathos.

It was not for me to speak to Kathleen, but I had a sudden inspiration which caused me to say quietly,

"Hallo, George."

The giant of a man turned round to face the direction of my face. There were so many people—but at length he saw me.

"Hallo, George," I said again.

Kathleen had started to haggle with the stall-owner, in her old way, over the price of the jade ring. George continued to stare at me, his big mouth slightly parted so that I could see a wide slit of red lips and white teeth between the fair grassy growths of beard and moustache.

"My God!" he said.

"What's the matter?" said Kathleen.

"Hallo, George!" I said again, quite loud this time, and cheerfully.

"Look!" said George. "Look who's there, over beside the fruit stall."

Kathleen looked but didn't see.

"Who is it?" she said impatiently.

"It's Needle," he said. "She said 'Hallo, George.' "

"Needle," said Kathleen. "Who do you mean? You don't mean our old friend *Needle* who—"

"Yes. There she is. My God!"

He looked very ill, although when I had said "Hallo, George" I had spoken friendly enough.

"I don't see anyone faintly resembling poor Needle," said Kathleen looking at him. She was worried.

George pointed straight at me. "Look *there.* I tell you that is Needle."

"You're ill, George. Heavens, you must be seeing things. Come on home. Needle isn't there. You know as well as I do, Needle is dead."

I must explain that I departed this life nearly five years ago. But I did not altogether depart this world. There were those odd things still to be done which one's executors can never do properly. Papers to be looked over, even after the executors have torn them up. Lots of business except, of course, on Sundays and Holidays of Obligation, plenty to take an interest in for the time being. I take my recreation on Saturday mornings. If it is a wet Saturday I wander up and down the substantial lanes of Woolworth's as I did when I was young and visible. There is a pleasurable spread of objects on the counters which I now perceive and exploit with a certain detachment, since it suits with my condition of life. Creams, toothpastes, combs and hankies, cotton gloves, flimsy flowering scarves, writing-paper and crayons, ice-cream cones and orangeade, screwdrivers, boxes of tacks, tins of paint, of glue, of marmalade; I always liked them but far more now that I have no need of any. When Saturdays are fine I go instead to the Portobello Road where formerly I would jaunt with Kathleen in our grown-up days. The barrow-loads do not change much, of apples and rayon vests in common blues and low-taste mauve, of silver plate, trays and teapots long since changed hands from the bygone citizens to dealers, from shops to the new flats and breakable homes, and then over to the barrow-stalls and the dealers again: Georgian spoons, rings, ear-rings of turquoise and opal set in the butterfly pattern of true-lovers' knot, patch-boxes with miniature paintings of ladies on ivory, snuff-boxes of silver with Scotch pebbles inset.

Sometimes as occasion arises on a Saturday morning, my friend Kathleen, who is a Catholic, has a Mass said for my soul, and then I am in attendance, as it were, at the church. But most Saturdays I take my delight among the solemn crowds with their aimless purposes, their eternal life not far away, who push past the counters and stalls, who handle, buy, steal, touch, desire and ogle the merchandise. I hear the tinkling tills, I hear the jangle of loose change and tongues and children wanting to hold and have.

That is how I came to be in the Portobello Road that Saturday morning when I saw George and Kathleen. I would not have spoken had I not been inspired to it. Indeed it's one of the things I can't do now—to speak out, unless inspired. And most extraordinary, on that morning as I spoke, a degree of visibility set in. I suppose from poor George's point of view it was like seeing a ghost when he saw me standing by the fruit barrow repeating in so friendly a manner, "Hallo, George!"

We were bound for the south. When our education, what we could get of it from the north, was thought to be finished, one by one we were sent or sent for to London. John Skinner, whom we called Skinny, went to study more archaeology, George to join his uncle's tobacco farm, Kathleen to stay with her rich connections and to potter intermittently in the Mayfair hat shop which one of them owned. A little later I also went to London to see life, for it was my ambition to write about life, which first I had to see.

"We four must stick together," George said very often in that yearning way of his. He was always desperately afraid of neglect. We four looked likely to shift off in different directions and George did not trust the other three of us not to forget all about him. More and more as the time came for him to depart for his uncle's tobacco farm in Africa he said,

"We four must keep in touch."

And before he left he told each of us anxiously,

"I'll write regularly, once a month. We must keep together for the sake of the old times." He had three prints taken from the negative of that photo on the haystack, wrote on the back of them "George took this the day that Needle found the needle" and gave us a copy each. I think we all wished he could become a bit more callous.

During my lifetime I was a drifter, nothing organised. It was difficult for my friends to follow the logic of my life. By the normal reckonings I should have come to starvation and ruin, which I never did. Of course, I did not live to write about life as I wanted to do. Possibly that is why I am inspired to do so now in these peculiar circumstances.

I taught in a private school in Kensington for almost three months, very small children. I didn't know what to do with them but I was kept fairly busy escorting incontinent little boys to the lavatory and telling the little girls to use their handkerchiefs. After that I lived a winter holiday in London on my small capital, and when that had run out I found a diamond bracelet in the cinema for which I received a reward of fifty pounds. When it was used up I got a job with a publicity man, writing speeches for absorbed industrialists, in which the dictionary of quotations came in very useful. So it went on. I got engaged to Skinny, but shortly after that I was left a small legacy, enough to keep me for six months. This somehow decided me that I didn't love Skinny so I gave him back the ring.

But it was through Skinny that I went to Africa. He was engaged with a party of researchers to investigate King Solomon's mines, that series of ancient workings ranging from the ancient port of Ophir, now called Beira, across Portuguese East Africa and Southern Rhodesia to the mighty jungle-city of Zimbabwe whose temple walls still stand by the approach to an ancient and sacred mountain, where the rubble of that civilisation scatters itself over the surrounding Rhodesian waste. I accompanied the party as a sort of secretary. Skinny vouched for me, he paid my fare, he sympathised by his action with my inconsequential life although when he spoke of it he disapproved. A life like mine annoys most people; they go to their jobs every day, attend to things, give orders, pummel typewriters, and get two or three weeks off every year, and it vexes them to see someone else not bothering to do these things and yet getting away with it, not starving, being lucky as they call it. Skinny, when I had broken off our engagement, lectured me about this, but still he took me to Africa knowing I should probably leave his unit within a few months.

We were there a few weeks before we began enquiring for George, who was farming about four hundred miles away to the north. We had not told him of our plans.

"If we tell George to expect us in his part of the world he'll come rushing to pester us the first week. After all, we're going on business," Skinny had said.

Before we left Kathleen told us, "Give George my love and tell him not to send frantic cables every time I don't answer his letters right away. Tell him I'm busy in the hat shop and being presented. You would think he hadn't another friend in the world the way he carries on."

We had settled first at Fort Victoria, our nearest place of access to the Zimbabwe ruins. There we made enquiries about George. It was clear he hadn't many friends. The older settlers were the most tolerant about the half-caste woman he was living with, as we found, but they were furious about his methods of raising tobacco which we learned were most unprofessional and in some mysterious way disloyal to the whites. We could never discover how it was that George's style of tobacco farming gave the blacks opinions about themselves, but that's what the older settlers claimed. The newer immigrants thought he was unsociable and, of course, his living with that nig made visiting impossible.

I must say I was myself a bit off-put by this news about the brown woman. I was brought up in a university town to which came Indian,

African and Asiatic students in a variety of tints and hues. I was brought up to avoid them for reasons connected with local reputation and God's ordinances. You cannot easily go against what you were brought up to do unless you are a rebel by nature.

Anyhow, we visited George eventually, taking advantage of the offer of transport from some people bound north in search of game. He had heard of our arrival in Rhodesia and though he was glad, almost relieved, to see us he pursued a policy of sullenness for the first hour.

"We wanted to give you a surprise, George."

"How were we to know that you'd get to hear of our arrival, George? News here must travel faster than light, George."

"We did hope to give you a surprise, George."

At last he said, "Well, I must say it's good to see you. All we need now is Kathleen. We four simply must stick together. You find when you're in a place like this, there's nothing like old friends."

He showed us his drying sheds. He showed us a paddock where he was experimenting with a horse and a zebra mare, attempting to mate them. They were frolicking happily, but not together. They passed each other in their private play time and again, but without acknowledgment and without resentment.

"It's been done before," George said. "It makes a fine strong beast, more intelligent than a mule and sturdier than a horse. But I'm not having any success with this pair, they won't look at each other."

After a while, he said, "Come in for a drink and meet Matilda."

She was dark brown, with a subservient hollow chest and round shoulders, a gawky woman, very snappy with the house-boys. We said pleasant things as we drank on the stoep before dinner, but we found George difficult. For some reason he began to rail at me for breaking off my engagement to Skinny, saying what a dirty trick it was after all those good times in the old days. I diverted attention to Matilda. I supposed, I said, she knew this part of the country well?

"No," said she, "I been a-shellitered my life. I not put out to working. Me nothing to go from place to place is allowed like dirty girls does." In her speech she gave every syllable equal stress.

George explained, "Her father was a white magistrate in Natal. She had a sheltered upbringing, different from the other coloureds, you realise."

"Man, me no black-eyed Susan," said Matilda, "no, no."

On the whole, George treated her as a servant. She was about four months advanced in pregnancy, but he made her get up and fetch for him, many times. Soap: that was one of the things Matilda had to fetch. George made his own bath soap, showed it proudly, gave us the recipe which I did not trouble to remember; I was fond of nice soaps during my lifetime and George's smelt of brilliantine and looked likely to soil one's skin.

"D'yo brahn?" Matilda asked me.

George said, "She is asking if you go brown in the sun."

"No, I go freckled."

"I got sister-in-law go freckles."

She never spoke another word to Skinny nor to me, and we never saw her again.

Some months later I said to Skinny,

"I'm fed up with being a camp-follower."

He was not surprised that I was leaving his unit, but he hated my way of expressing it. He gave me a Presbyterian look.

"Don't talk like that. Are you going back to England or staying?"

"Staying, for a while."

"Well, don't wander too far off."

I was able to live on the fee I got for writing a gossip column in a local weekly, which wasn't my idea of writing about life, of course. I made friends, more than I could cope with, after I left Skinny's exclusive little band of archaeologists. I had the attractions of being newly out from England and of wanting to see life. Of the countless young men and go-ahead families who purred me along the Rhodesian roads, hundred after hundred miles, I only kept up with one family when I returned to my native land. I think that was because they were the most representative, they stood for all the rest: people in those parts are very typical of each other, as one group of standing stones in that wilderness is like the next.

I met George once more in a hotel in Bulawayo. We drank highballs and spoke of war. Skinny's party were just then deciding whether to remain in the country or return home. They had reached an exciting part of their research, and whenever I got a chance to visit Zimbabwe he would take me for a moonlight walk in the ruined temple and try to make me see phantom Phoenicians flitting ahead of us, or along the walls. I had half a mind to marry Skinny; perhaps, I thought, when his studies were finished. The impending war was in our bones: so I remarked to George as we sat drinking highballs on the hotel stoep in the hard bright sunny July winter of that year.

George was inquisitive about my relations with Skinny. He tried to pump me for about half an hour and when at last I said, "You are becoming aggressive, George," he stopped. He became quite pathetic. He said, "War or no war I'm clearing out of this."

"It's the heat does it," I said.

"I'm clearing out in any case. I've lost a fortune in tobacco. My uncle is making a fuss. It's the other bloody planters; once you get the wrong side of them you're finished in this wide land."

"What about Matilda?" I asked.

He said, "She'll be all right. She's got hundreds of relatives."

I had already heard about the baby girl. Coal black, by repute, with George's features. And another on the way, they said.

"What about the child?"

He didn't say anything to that. He ordered more highballs and when they arrived he swizzled his for a long time with a stick. "Why didn't you ask me to your twenty-first?" he said then.

"I didn't have anything special, no party, George. We had a quiet drink among ourselves, George, just Skinny and the old professors and two of the wives and me, George."

"You didn't ask me to your twenty-first," he said. "Kathleen writes to me regularly."

This wasn't true. Kathleen sent me letters fairly often in which she said, "Don't tell George I wrote to you as he will be expecting word from me and I can't be bothered actually."

"But you," said George, "don't seem to have any sense of old friendships, you and Skinny."

"Oh, George!" I said.

"Remember the times we had," George said. "We used to have times." His large brown eyes began to water.

"I'll have to be getting along," I said.

"Please don't go. Don't leave me just yet. I've something to tell you."

"Something nice?" I laid on an eager smile. All responses to George had to be overdone.

"You don't know how lucky you are," George said.

"How?" I said. Sometimes I got tired of being called lucky by everybody. There were times when, privately practising my writings about life, I knew the bitter side of my fortune. When I failed again and again to reproduce life in some satisfactory and perfect form, I was the more imprisoned, for all my carefree living, within my craving for this satisfaction. Sometimes, in my impotence and need I secreted a venom which infected all my life for days on end and which spurted out indiscriminately on Skinny or on anyone who crossed my path.

"You aren't bound by anyone," George said. "You come and go as you please. Something always turns up for you. You're free, and you don't know your luck."

"You're a damn sight more free than I am," I said sharply. "You've got your rich uncle."

"He's losing interest in me," George said. "He's had enough."

"Oh well, you're young yet. What was it you wanted to tell me?"

"A secret," George said. "Remember we used to have those secrets."

"Oh, yes we did."

"Did you ever tell any of mine?"

"Oh no, George." In reality, I couldn't remember any particular secret out of the dozens we must have exchanged from our schooldays onwards.

"Well, this is a secret, mind. Promise not to tell."

"Promise."

"I'm married."

"Married, George! Oh, who to?"

"Matilda."

"How dreadful!" I spoke before I could think, but he agreed with me.

"Yes, it's awful, but what could I do?"

"You might have asked my advice," I said pompously.

"I'm two years older than you are. I don't ask advice from you, Needle, little beast."

"Don't ask for sympathy then."

"A nice friend you are," he said, "I must say after all these years."

"Poor George!" I said.

"There are three white men to one white woman in this country," said George. "An isolated planter doesn't see a white woman and if he sees one she doesn't see him. What could I do? I needed the woman."

I was nearly sick. One, because of my Scottish upbringing. Two, because of my horror of corny phrases like "I needed the woman," which George repeated twice again.

"And Matilda got tough," said George, "after you and Skinny came to visit us. She had some friends at the Mission, and she packed up and went to them."

"You should have let her go," I said.

"I went after her," George said. "She insisted on being married, so I married her."

"That's not a proper secret, then," I said. "The news of a mixed marriage soon gets about."

"I took care of that," George said. "Crazy as I was, I took her to the Congo and married her there. She promised to keep quiet about it."

"Well, you can't clear off and leave her now, surely," I said.

"I'm going to get out of this place. I can't stand the woman and I can't stand the country. I didn't realise what it would be like. Two years of the country and three months of my wife has been enough."

"Will you get a divorce?"

"No, Matilda's Catholic. She won't divorce."

George was fairly getting through the highballs, and I wasn't far behind him. His brown eyes floated shiny and liquid as he told me how he had written to tell his uncle of his plight, "Except, of course, I didn't say we were married, that would have been too much for him. He's a prejudiced hardened old colonial. I only said I'd had a child by a coloured woman and was expecting another, and he perfectly understood. He came at once by plane a few weeks ago. He's made a settlement on her, providing she keeps her mouth shut about her association with me."

"Will she do that?"

"Oh, yes, or she won't get the money."

"But as your wife she has a claim on you, in any case."

"If she claimed as my wife she'd get far less. Matilda knows what she's doing, greedy bitch she is. She'll keep her mouth shut."

"Only, you won't be able to marry again, will you, George?"

"Not unless she dies," he said. "And she's as strong as a trek ox."

"Well, I'm sorry, George," I said.

"Good of you to say so," he said. "But I can see by your chin that you disapprove of me. Even my old uncle understood."

"Oh, George, I quite understand. You were lonely, I suppose."

"You didn't even ask me to your twenty-first. If you and Skinny had been nicer to me, I would never have lost my head and married the woman, never."

"You didn't ask me to your wedding," I said.

"You're a catty bissom, Needle, not like what you were in the old times when you used to tell us your wee stories."

"I'll have to be getting along," I said.

"Mind you keep the secret," George said.

"Can't I tell Skinny? He would be very sorry for you, George."

"You mustn't tell anyone. Keep it a secret. Promise."

"Promise," I said. I understood that he wished to enforce some sort of bond between us with this secret, and I thought, "Oh well, I suppose he's lonely. Keeping his secret won't do any harm."

I returned to England with Skinny's party just before the war.

I did not see George again till just before my death, five years ago.

After the war Skinny returned to his studies. He had two more exams, over a period of eighteen months, and I thought I might marry him when the exams were over.

"You might do worse than Skinny," Kathleen used to say to me on our Saturday morning excursions to the antique shops and the junk stalls.

She too was getting on in years. The remainder of our families in Scotland were hinting that it was time we settled down with husbands. Kathleen was a little younger than me, but looked much older. She knew her chances were diminishing but at that time I did not think she cared very much. As for myself, the main attraction of marrying Skinny was his prospective expeditions to Mesopotamia. My desire to marry him had to be stimulated by the continual reading of books about Babylon and Assyria; perhaps Skinny felt this, because he supplied the books and even started instructing me in the art of deciphering cuneiform tablets.

Kathleen was more interested in marriage than I thought. Like me, she had racketed around a good deal during the war; she had actually been engaged to an officer in the U.S. navy, who was killed. Now she kept an antique shop near Lambeth, was doing very nicely, lived in a Chelsea square, but for all that she must have wanted to be married and have children. She would stop and look into all the prams which the mothers had left outside shops or area gates.

"The poet Swinburne used to do that," I told her once.

"Really? Did he want children of his own?"

"I shouldn't think so. He simply liked babies."

Before Skinny's final exam he fell ill and was sent to a sanatorium in Switzerland.

"You're fortunate after all not to be married to him," Kathleen said. "You might have caught T.B."

I was fortunate, I was lucky . . . so everyone kept telling me on different occasions. Although it annoyed me to hear, I knew they were right, but in a way that was different from what they meant. It took me very small effort to make a living; book reviews, odd jobs for Kathleen, a few months with the publicity man again, still getting up speeches about literature, art, and life for industrial tycoons. I was waiting to write about life and it seemed to me that the good fortune lay in this, whenever it should be. And until then I was assured of my charmed life, the necessities of existence always coming my way and I with far more leisure than anyone else. I thought of my type of luck after I became a Catholic and was being confirmed. The Bishop touches the candidate on the cheek, a symbolic reminder of the sufferings a Christian is supposed to undertake. I thought, how lucky, what a feathery symbol to stand for the hellish violence of its true meaning.

I visited Skinny twice in the two years that he was in the sanatorium. He was almost cured, and expected to be home within a few months. I told Kathleen after my last visit.

"Maybe I'll marry Skinny when he's well again."

"Make it definite, Needle, and not so much of the maybe. You don't know when you're well off," she said.

This was five years ago, in the last year of my life. Kathleen and I had become very close friends. We met several times each week, and after our Saturday morning excursions in the Portobello Road very often I would accompany Kathleen to her aunt's house in Kent for a long week-end.

One day in the June of that year I met Kathleen specially for lunch because she had phoned me to say she had news.

"Guess who came into the shop this afternoon," she said.

"Who?"

"George."

We had half imagined George was dead. We had received no letters in the past ten years. Early in the war we had heard rumours of his keeping a night club in Durban, but nothing after that. We could have made enquiries if we had felt moved to do so.

At one time, when we discussed him, Kathleen had said,

"I ought to get in touch with poor George. But then I think he would write back. He would demand a regular correspondence again."

"We four must stick together," I mimicked.

"I can visualise his reproachful limpid orbs," Kathleen said.

Skinny said, "He's probably gone native. With his coffee concubine and a dozen mahogany kids."

"Perhaps he's dead," Kathleen said.

I did not speak of George's marriage, nor of any of his confidences in the hotel at Bulawayo. As the years passed we ceased to mention him except in passing, as someone more or less dead so far as we were concerned.

Kathleen was excited about George's turning up. She had forgotten her impatience with him in former days; she said,

"It was so wonderful to see old George. He seems to need a friend, feels neglected, out of touch with things."

"He needs mothering, I suppose."

Kathleen didn't notice the malice. She declared, "That's exactly the case with George. It always has been, I can see it now."

She seemed ready to come to any rapid new and happy conclusion about George. In the course of the morning he had told her of his wartime night club in Durban, his game-shooting expeditions since. It was clear he had not mentioned Matilda. He had put on weight, Kathleen told me, but he could carry it.

I was curious to see this version of George, but I was leaving for Scotland next day and did not see him till September of that year, just before my death.

While I was in Scotland I gathered from Kathleen's letters that she was seeing George very frequently, finding enjoyable company in him, looking after him. "You'll be surprised to see how he has developed."

Apparently he would hang round Kathleen in her shop most days, "it makes him feel useful" as she maternally expressed it. He had an old relative in Kent whom he visited at week-ends; this old lady lived a few miles from Kathleen's aunt, which made it easy for them to travel down together on Saturdays, and go for long country walks.

"You'll see such a difference in George," Kathleen said on my return to London in September. I was to meet him that night, a Saturday. Kathleen's aunt was abroad, the maid on holiday, and I was to keep Kathleen company in the empty house.

George had left London for Kent a few days earlier. "He's actually helping with the harvest down there!" Kathleen told me lovingly.

Kathleen and I planned to travel down together, but on that Saturday she was unexpectedly delayed in London on some business. It was arranged that I should go ahead of her in the early afternoon to see to the provisions for our party; Kathleen had invited George to dinner at her aunt's house that night.

"I should be with you by seven," she said. "Sure you won't mind the empty house? I hate arriving at empty houses, myself."

I said no, I liked an empty house.

So I did, when I got there. I had never found the house more likeable. A large Georgian vicarage in about eight acres, most of the rooms shut and sheeted, there being only one servant. I discovered that I wouldn't need to go shopping, Kathleen's aunt had left many and delicate supplies with notes attached to them: "Eat this up please do, see also fridge" and "A treat for three hungry people see also 2 bttles beaune for yr party on back kn table." It was like a treasure hunt as I followed clue after clue through the cool silent domestic quarters. A house in which there are no people—but with all the signs of tenancy—can be a most tranquil good place. People take up space in a house out of proportion to their size. On my previous visits I had seen the rooms overflowing as it seemed, with Kathleen, her aunt, and the little fat maidservant; they were always on the move. As I wandered through that part of the house which was in use, opening windows to let in the pale yellow air of September, I was not conscious that I, Needle, was taking up any space at all, I might have been a ghost.

The only thing to be fetched was the milk. I waited till after four when the milking should be done, then set off for the farm which lay across two fields at the back of the orchard. There, when the byreman was handing me the bottle, I saw George.

"Hallo, George," I said.

"Needle! What are you doing here?" he said.

"Fetching milk," I said.

"So am I. Well, it's good to see you, I must say."

As we paid the farm-hand, George said, "I'll walk back with you part of the way. But I mustn't stop, my old cousin's without any milk for her tea. How's Kathleen?"

"She was kept in London. She's coming on later, about seven, she expects."

We had reached the end of the first field. George's way led to the left and on to the main road.

"We'll see you tonight, then?" I said.

"Yes, and talk about old times."

"Grand," I said.

But George got over the stile with me.

"Look here," he said. "I'd like to talk to you, Needle."

"We'll talk tonight, George. Better not keep your cousin waiting for the milk." I found myself speaking to him almost as if he were a child.

"No, I want to talk to you alone. This is a good opportunity."

We began to cross the second field. I had been hoping to have the house to myself for a couple more hours and I was rather petulant.

"See," he said suddenly, "that haystack."

"Yes," I said absently.

"Let's sit there and talk. I'd like to see you up on a haystack again. I still keep that photo. Remember that time when—"

"I found the needle," I said very quickly, to get it over.

But I was glad to rest. The stack had been broken up, but we managed to find a nest in it. I buried my bottle of milk in the hay for coolness. George placed his carefully at the foot of the stack.

"My old cousin is terribly vague, poor soul. A bit hazy in her head. She hasn't the least sense of time. If I tell her I've only been gone ten minutes she'll believe it."

I giggled, and looked at him. His face had grown much larger, his lips full, wide and with a ripe colour that is strange in a man. His brown eyes were abounding as before with some inarticulate plea.

"So you're going to marry Skinny after all these years?"

"I really don't know, George."

"You played him up properly."

"It isn't for you to judge. I have my own reasons for what I do."

"Don't get sharp," he said, "I was only funning." To prove it, he lifted a tuft of hay and brushed my face with it.

"D'you know," he said next, "I didn't think you and Skinny treated me very decently in Rhodesia."

"Well, we were busy, George. And we were younger then, we had a lot to do and see. After all, we could see you any other time, George."

"A touch of selfishness," he said.

"I'll have to be getting along, George." I made to get down from the stack.

He pulled me back. "Wait, I've got something to tell you."

"O.K., George, tell me."

"First promise not to tell Kathleen. She wants it kept a secret so that she can tell you herself."

"All right. Promise."

"I'm going to marry Kathleen."

"But you're already married."

Sometimes I heard news of Matilda from the one Rhodesian family with whom I still kept up. They referred to her as "George's Dark Lady" and of course they did not know he was married to her. She had apparently made a good thing out of George, they said, for she minced around all tarted up, never did a stroke of work, and was always unsettling the respectable coloured girls in their neighbourhood. According to accounts, she was a living example of the folly of behaving as George did.

"I married Matilda in the Congo," George was saying.

"It would still be bigamy," I said.

He was furious when I used that word bigamy. He lifted a handful of hay as if he would throw it in my face, but controlling himself meanwhile he fanned it at me playfully.

"I'm not sure that the Congo marriage was valid," he continued. "Anyway, as far as I'm concerned, it isn't."

"You can't do a thing like that," I said.

"I need Kathleen. She's been decent to me. I think we were always meant for each other, me and Kathleen."

"I'll have to be going," I said.

But he put his knee over my ankles, so that I couldn't move. I sat still and gazed into space.

He tickled my face with a wisp of hay.

"Smile up, Needle," he said; "let's talk like old times."

"Well?"

"No one knows about my marriage to Matilda except you and me."

"And Matilda," I said.

"She'll hold her tongue so long as she gets her payments. My uncle left an annuity for the purpose, his lawyers see to it."

"Let me go, George."

"You promised to keep it a secret," he said, "you promised."

"Yes, I promised."

"And now that you're going to marry Skinny, we'll be properly coupled off as we should have been years ago. We should have been—but youth!—our youth got in the way, didn't it?"

"Life got in the way," I said.

"But everything's going to be all right now. You'll keep my secret, won't you? You promised." He had released my feet. I edged a little further from him.

I said, "If Kathleen intends to marry you, I shall tell her that you're already married."

"You wouldn't do a dirty trick like that, Needle? You're going to be happy with Skinny, you wouldn't stand in the way of my—"

"I must, Kathleen's my best friend," I said swiftly.

He looked as if he would murder me and he did. He stuffed hay into my mouth until it could hold no more, kneeling on my body to keep it still, holding both my wrists tight in his huge left hand. I saw the red full lines of his mouth and the white slit of his teeth last thing on earth. Not another soul passed by as he pressed my body into the stack, as he made a deep nest for me, tearing up the hay to make a groove the length of my corpse, and finally pulling the warm dry stuff in a mound over this concealment, so natural-looking in a broken haystack. Then George climbed down, took up his bottle of milk, and went his way. I suppose that was why he looked so unwell when I stood, nearly five years later, by the barrow in the Portobello Road and said in easy tones, "Hallo, George!"

The Haystack Murder was one of the notorious crimes of that year.

My friends said, "A girl who had everything to live for."

After a search that lasted twenty hours, when my body was found, the evening papers said, " 'Needle' is found: in haystack!"

Kathleen, speaking from that Catholic point of view which takes some getting used to, said, "She was at Confession only the day before she died—wasn't she lucky?"

The poor byre-hand who sold us the milk was grilled for hour after hour by the local police, and later by Scotland Yard. So was George. He admitted walking as far as the haystack with me, but he denied lingering there.

"You hadn't seen your friend for ten years?" the Inspector asked him.

"That's right," said George.

"And you didn't stop to have a chat?"

"No. We'd arranged to meet later at dinner. My cousin was waiting for the milk, I couldn't stop."

The old soul, his cousin, swore that he hadn't been gone more than ten minutes in all, and she believed it to the day of her death a few months later. There was the microscopic evidence of hay on George's jacket, of course, but the same evidence was on every man's jacket in the district that fine harvest year. Unfortunately, the byreman's hands were

even brawnier and mightier than George's. The marks on my wrists had
been done by such hands, so the laboratory charts indicated when my
post-mortem was all completed. But the wrist-marks weren't enough to
pin down the crime to either man. If I hadn't been wearing my long-
sleeved cardigan, it was said, the bruises might have matched up properly with someone's fingers.

Kathleen, to prove that George had absolutely no motive, told the
police that she was engaged to him. George thought this a little foolish.
They checked up on his life in Africa, right back to his living with
Matilda. But the marriage didn't come out—who would think of looking
up registers in the Congo? Not that this would have proved any motive
for murder. All the same, George was relieved when the enquiries were
over without the marriage to Matilda being disclosed. He was able to
have his nervous breakdown at the same time as Kathleen had hers, and
they recovered together and got married, long after the police had
shifted their enquiries to an Air Force camp five miles from Kathleen's
aunt's home. Only a lot of excitement and drinks came of those investigations. The Haystack Murder was one of the unsolved crimes that year.

Shortly afterwards the byre-hand emigrated to Canada to start afresh,
with the help of Skinny who felt sorry for him.

After seeing George taken away home by Kathleen that Saturday in
the Portobello Road, I thought that perhaps I might be seeing more of
him in similar circumstances. The next Saturday I looked out for him,
and at last there he was, without Kathleen, half-worried, half-hopeful.

I dashed his hopes. I said, "Hallo, George!"

He looked in my direction, rooted in the midst of the flowing market-
mongers in that convivial street. I thought to myself, "He looks as if he
had a mouthful of hay." It was the new bristly maize-coloured beard and
moustache surrounding his great mouth which suggested the thought,
gay and lyrical as life.

"Hallo, George!" I said again.

I might have been inspired to say more on that agreeable morning,
but he didn't wait. He was away down a side street and along another
street and down one more, zig-zag, as far and as devious as he could take
himself from the Portobello Road.

Nevertheless he was back again next week. Poor Kathleen had
brought him in her car. She left it at the top of the street, and got out
with him, holding him tight by the arm. It grieved me to see Kathleen
ignoring the spread of scintillations on the stalls. I had myself seen a
charming Battersea box quite to her taste, also a pair of enamelled silver
earrings. But she took no notice of these wares, clinging close to George,
and, poor Kathleen—I hate to say how she looked.

And George was haggard. His eyes seemed to have got smaller as if he had been recently in pain. He advanced up the road with Kathleen on his arm, letting himself lurch from side to side with his wife bobbing beside him, as the crowds asserted their rights of way.

"Oh, George!" I said. "You don't look at all well, George."

"Look!" said George. "Over there by the hardware barrow. That's Needle."

Kathleen was crying. "Come back home, dear," she said.

"Oh, you don't look well, George!" I said.

They took him to a nursing home. He was fairly quiet, except on Saturday mornings when they had a hard time of it to keep him indoors and away from the Portobello Road.

But a couple of months later he did escape. It was a Monday.

They searched for him in the Portobello Road, but actually he had gone off to Kent to the village near the scene of the Haystack Murder. There he went to the police and gave himself up, but they could tell from the way he was talking that there was something wrong with the man.

"I saw Needle in the Portobello Road three Saturdays running," he explained, "and they put me in a private ward but I got away while the nurses were seeing to the new patient. You remember the murder of Needle—well, I did it. Now you know the truth, and that will keep bloody Needle's mouth shut."

Dozens of poor mad fellows confess to every murder. The police obtained an ambulance to take him back to the nursing home. He wasn't there long. Kathleen gave up her shop and devoted herself to looking after him at home. But she found that the Saturday mornings were a strain. He insisted on going to see me in the Portobello Road and would come back to insist that he'd murdered Needle. Once he tried to tell her something about Matilda, but Kathleen was so kind and solicitous, I don't think he had the courage to remember what he had to say.

Skinny had always been rather reserved with George since the murder. But he was kind to Kathleen. It was he who persuaded them to emigrate to Canada so that George should be well out of reach of the Portobello Road.

George has recovered somewhat in Canada but of course he will never be the old George again, as Kathleen writes to Skinny. "That Haystack tragedy did for George," she writes, "I feel sorrier for George sometimes than I am for poor Needle. But I do often have Masses said for Needle's soul."

I doubt if George will ever see me again in the Portobello Road. He broods much over the crumpled snapshot he took of us on the haystack.

Kathleen does not like the photograph, I don't wonder. For my part, I consider it quite a jolly snap, but I don't think we were any of us so lovely as we look in it, gazing blatantly over the ripe cornfields, Skinny with his humorous expression, I secure in my difference from the rest, Kathleen with her head prettily perched on her hand, each reflecting fearlessly in the face of George's camera the glory of the world, as if it would never pass.   1956

ELIZABETH JANE HOWARD

THREE MILES UP

There was absolutely nothing like it.

An unoriginal conclusion, and one that he had drawn a hundred times during the last fortnight. Clifford would make some subtle and intelligent comparison, but he, John, could only continue to repeat that it was quite unlike anything else. It had been Clifford's idea, which, considering Clifford, was surprising. When you looked at him, you would not suppose him capable of it. However, John reflected, he had been ill, some sort of breakdown these clever people went in for, and that might account for his uncharacteristic idea of hiring a boat and travelling on canals. On the whole, John had to admit, it was a good idea. He had never been on a canal in his life, although he had been in almost every kind of boat, and thought he knew a good deal about them; so much indeed, that he had embarked on the venture in a light-hearted, almost a patronizing manner. But it was not nearly as simple as he had imagined. Clifford, of course, knew nothing about boats; but he had admitted that almost everything had gone wrong with a kind of devilish versatility which had almost frightened him. However, that was all over, and John, who had learned painfully all about the boat and her engine, felt that the former at least had run her gamut of disaster. They had run out of food, out of petrol, and out of water; had dropped their windlass into the deepest lock, and, more humiliating, their boathook into a side-pond. The head had come off the hammer. They had been disturbed for one whole night by a curious rustling in the cabin, like a rat in a paper bag, when there was no paper, and, so far as they knew, no rat. The battery had failed and had had to be re-charged. Clifford had put his elbow through an already cracked window in the cabin. A large piece of rope had wound itself round the propeller with a malignant intensity which required three men and half a morning to unravel. And so on, until now there was really nothing left to go wrong, unless one of them drowned, and surely it was impossible to drown in a canal.

"I suppose one might easily drown in a lock?" he asked aloud.

"We must be careful not to fall into one," Clifford replied.

"What?" John steered with fierce concentration, and never heard anything people said to him for the first time, almost on principle.

"I said we must be careful not to fall *into* a lock."

"Oh. Well there aren't any more now until after the Junction. Anyway, we haven't yet, so there's really no reason why we should start now. I only wanted to know whether we'd drown if we did."

"Sharon might."

"What?"

"Sharon might."

"Better warn her then. She seems agile enough." His concentrated frown returned, and he settled down again to the wheel. John didn't mind where they went, or what happened, so long as he handled the boat, and all things considered, he handled her remarkably well. Clifford planned and John steered: and until two days ago they had both quarrelled and argued over a smoking and unusually temperamental primus. Which reminded Clifford of Sharon. Her advent and the weather were really their two unadulterated strokes of good fortune. There had been no rain, and Sharon had, as it were, dropped from the blue on to the boat, where she speedily restored domestic order, stimulated evening conversation, and touched the whole venture with her attractive being: the requisite number of miles each day were achieved, the boat behaved herself, and admirable meals were steadily and regularly prepared. She had, in fact, identified herself with the journey, without making the slightest effort to control it: a talent which many women were supposed in theory to possess, when, in fact, Clifford reflected gloomily, most of them were bored with the whole thing, or tried to dominate it.

Her advent was a remarkable, almost a miraculous piece of luck. He had, after a particularly ill-fed day, and their failure to dine at a small hotel, desperately telephoned all the women he knew who seemed in the least suitable (and they were surprisingly few), with no success. They had spent a miserable evening, John determined to argue about everything, and he, Clifford, refusing to speak; until, both in a fine state of emotional tension, they had turned in for the night. While John snored, Clifford had lain distraught, his resentment and despair circling round John and then touching his own smallest and most random thoughts; until his mind found no refuge and he was left, divided from it, hostile and afraid, watching it in terror racing on in the dark like some malignant machine utterly out of his control.

The next day things had proved no better between them, and they had continued throughout the morning in a silence which was only occasionally and elaborately broken. They had tied up for lunch beside a wood, which hung heavy and magnificent over the canal. There was a small clearing beside which John then proposed to moor, but Clifford failed to achieve the considerable leap necessary to stop the boat; and they had drifted helplessly past it. John flung him a line, but it was not until the boat was secured, and they were safely in the cabin, that the storm had broken. John, in attempting to light the primus, spilt a quantity of paraffin on Clifford's bunk. Instantly all his despair of the previous evening had contracted. He hated John so much that he could have murdered him. They both lost their tempers, and for the ensuing hour and a half had conducted a blazing quarrel, which, even at the time, secretly horrified them both in its intensity.

It had finally ended with John striding out of the cabin, there being no more to say. He had returned almost at once, however.

"I say, Clifford. Come and look at this."

"At what?"

"Outside, on the bank."

For some unknown reason Clifford did get up and did look. Lying face downwards quite still on the ground, with her arms clasping the trunk of a large tree, was a girl.

"How long has she been there?"

"She's asleep."

"She can't have been asleep all the time. She must have heard some of what we said."

"Anyway, who is she? What is she doing here?"

Clifford looked at her again. She was wearing a dark twill shirt and dark trousers, and her hair hung over her face, so that it was almost invisible. "I don't know. I suppose she's alive?"

John jumped cautiously ashore. "Yes, she's alive all right. Funny way to lie."

"Well, it's none of our business anyway. Anyone can lie on a bank if they want to."

"Yes, but she must have come in the middle of our row, and it does seem queer to stay, and then go to sleep."

"Extraordinary," said Clifford wearily. Nothing was really extraordinary, he felt, nothing. "Are we moving on?"

"Let's eat first. I'll do it."

"Oh, I'll do it."

The girl stirred, unclasped her arms, and sat up. They had all stared at each other for a moment, the girl slowly pushing the hair from her forehead. Then she had said: "If you will give me a meal, I'll cook it."

Afterwards they had left her to wash up, and walked about the wood, while Clifford suggested to John that they ask the girl to join them. "I'm sure she'd come," he said. "She didn't seem at all clear about what she was doing."

"We can't just pick somebody up out of a wood," said John, scandalized.

"Where do you suggest we pick them up? If we don't have someone, this holiday will be a failure."

"We don't know anything about her."

"I can't see that that matters very much. She seems to cook well. We can at least ask her."

"All right. Ask her then. She won't come."

When they returned to the boat, she had finished the washing up, and was sitting on the floor of the cockpit, with her arms stretched behind her head. Clifford asked her; and she accepted as though she had known them a long time and they were simply inviting her to tea.

"Well, but look here," said John, thoroughly taken aback. "What about your things?"

"My things?" she looked inquiringly and a little defensively from one to the other.

"Clothes and so on. Or haven't you got any? Are you a gipsy or something? Where do you come from?"

"I am not a gipsy," she began patiently; when Clifford, thoroughly embarrassed and ashamed, interrupted her.

"Really, it's none of our business who you are, and there is absolutely no need for us to ask you anything. I'm very glad you will come with us, although I feel we should warn you that we are new to this life, and anything might happen."

"No need to warn me," she said and smiled gratefully at him.

After that, they both felt bound to ask her nothing; John because he was afraid of being made to look foolish by Clifford, and Clifford because he had stopped John.

"Good Lord, we shall never get rid of her; and she'll fuss about condensation," John had muttered aggressively as he started the engine. But she was very young, and did not fuss about anything. She had told them her name, and settled down, immediately and easily: gentle, assured and unselfconscious to a degree remarkable in one so young. They were never sure how much she had overheard them, for she gave no sign of having heard anything. A friendly but uncommunicative creature.

The map on the engine box started to flap, and immediately John asked, "Where are we?"

"I haven't been watching, I'm afraid. Wait a minute."

"We just passed under a railway bridge," John said helpfully.

"Right. Yes. About four miles from the Junction, I think. What is the time?"

"Five-thirty."

"Which way are we going when we get to the Junction?"

"We haven't time for the big loop. I must be back in London by the 15th."

"The alternative is to go up as far as the basin, and then simply turn round and come back, and who wants to do that?"

"Well, we'll know the route then. It'll be much easier coming back."

Clifford did not reply. He was not attracted by the route being easier, and he wanted to complete his original plan.

"Let us wait till we get there." Sharon appeared with tea and marmalade sandwiches.

"All right, let's wait." Clifford was relieved.

"It will be almost dark by six-thirty. I think we ought to have a plan," John said. "Thank you, Sharon."

"Have tea first." She curled herself on to the floor with her back to the cabin doors and a mug in her hands.

They were passing rows of little houses with gardens that backed on to the canal. They were long narrow strips, streaked with cinder paths, and crowded with vegetables and chicken huts, fruit trees and perambulators; sometimes ending with fat white ducks, and sometimes in a tiny patch of grass with a bench on it.

"Would you rather keep ducks or sit on a bench?" asked Clifford.

"Keep ducks," said John promptly. "More useful. Sharon wouldn't mind which she did. Would you, Sharon?" He liked saying her name, Clifford noticed. "You could be happy anywhere, couldn't you?" He seemed to be presenting her with the widest possible choice.

"I might *be* anywhere," she answered after a moment's thought.

"Well you happen to be on a canal, and very nice for us."

"In a wood, and then on a canal," she replied contentedly, bending her smooth dark head over her mug.

"Going to be fine tomorrow," said John. He was always a little embarrassed at any mention of how they found her and his subsequent rudeness.

"Yes. I like it when the whole sky is so red and burning and it begins to be cold."

"*Are* you cold?" said John, wanting to worry about it: but she tucked her dark shirt into her trousers and answered composedly:

"Oh no. I am never cold."

They drank their tea in a comfortable silence. Clifford started to read his map, and then said they were almost on to another sheet. "New country," he said with satisfaction. "I've never been here before."

"You make it sound like an exploration; doesn't he, Sharon?" said John.

"Is that a bad thing?" She collected the mugs. "I am going to put these away. You will call me if I am wanted for anything." And she went into the cabin again.

There was a second's pause, a minute tribute to her departure; and, lighting cigarettes, they settled down to stare at the long silent stretch of water ahead.

John thought about Sharon. He thought rather desperately that really they still knew nothing about her, and that when they went back to London, they would, in all probability, never see her again. Perhaps Clifford would fall in love with her, and she would naturally reciprocate, because she was so young and Clifford was reputed to be so fascinating and intelligent, and because women were always foolish and loved the wrong man. He thought all these things with equal intensity, glanced cautiously at Clifford, and supposed he was thinking about her; then wondered what she would be like in London, clad in anything else but her dark trousers and shirt. The engine coughed; and he turned to it in relief.

Clifford was making frantic calculations of time and distance; stretching their time, and diminishing the distance, and groaning that with the utmost optimism they could not be made to fit. He was interrupted by John swearing at the engine, and then for no particular reason he remembered Sharon, and reflected with pleasure how easily she left the mind when she was not present, how she neither obsessed nor possessed one in her absence, but was charming to see.

The sun had almost set when they reached the Junction, and John slowed down to neutral while they made up their minds. To the left was the straight cut which involved the longer journey originally planned; and curving away to the right was the short arm which John advocated. The canal was fringed with rushes, and there was one small cottage with no light in it. Clifford went into the cabin to tell Sharon where they were, and then, as they drifted slowly in the middle of the Junction, John suddenly shouted: "Clifford! What's the third turning?"

"There are only two." Clifford reappeared. "Sharon is busy with dinner."

"No, look. Surely that is another cut."

Clifford stared ahead. "Can't see it."

"Just to the right of the cottage. Look. It's not so dark as all that."

Then Clifford saw it very plainly. It seemed to wind away from the cottage on a fairly steep curve, and the rushes surrounding it from anything but the closest view were taller than the rest.

"Have another look at the map. I'll reverse for a bit."

"Found it. It's just another turn. Probably been abandoned," said Clifford eventually.

The boat had swung round; and now they could see the continuance of the curve dully gleaming ahead, and banked by reeds.

"Well, what shall we do?"

"Getting dark. Let's go up a little way, and moor. Nice quiet mooring."

"With some nice quiet mudbanks," said John grimly. "Nobody uses that."

"How do you know?"

"Well, look at it. All those rushes, and it's sure to be thick with weed."

"Don't go up it then. But we shall go aground if we drift about like this."

"*I* don't mind going up it," said John doggedly. "What about Sharon?"

"What about her?"

"Tell her about it."

"We've found a third turning," Clifford called above the noise of the primus through the cabin door.

"One you had not expected?"

"Yes. It looks very wild. We were thinking of going up it."

"Didn't you say you wanted to explore?" she smiled at him.

"You are quite ready to try it? I warn you we shall probably run hard aground. Look out for bumps with the primus."

"I am quite ready, and I am quite sure we shan't run aground," she answered with charming confidence in their skill.

They moved slowly forward in the dusk. Why they did not run aground, Clifford could not imagine: John really was damned good at it. The canal wound and wound, and the reeds grew not only thick on each bank, but in clumps across the canal. The light drained out of the sky into the water and slowly drowned there; the trees and the banks became heavy and black.

Clifford began to clear things away from the heavy dew which had begun to rise. After two journeys he remained in the cabin, while John crawled on, alone. Once, on a bend, John thought he saw a range of hills ahead with lights on them, but when he was round the curve, and had time to look again he could see no hills: only a dark indeterminate waste of country stretched ahead.

He was beginning to consider the necessity of mooring, when they came to a bridge; and shortly after, he saw a dark mass which he took to be houses. When the boat had crawled for another fifty yards or so, he stopped the engine, and drifted in absolute silence to the bank. The houses, about half a dozen of them, were much nearer than he had at first imagined, but there were no lights to be seen. Distance is always deceptive in the dark, he thought, and jumped ashore with a bow line. When, a few minutes later, he took a sounding with the boathook, the water proved unexpectedly deep; and he concluded that they had by incredible good fortune moored at the village wharf. He made everything fast, and joined the others in the cabin with mixed feelings of pride and resentment; that he should have achieved so much under such difficult conditions, and that they (by "they" he meant Clifford) should have contributed so little towards the achievement. He found Clifford reading Bradshaw's *Guide to the Canals and Navigable Rivers* in one corner, and Sharon, with her hair pushed back behind her ears, bending over the primus with a knife. Her ears are pale, exactly the colour of her face, he thought; wanted to touch them; then felt horribly ashamed, and hated Clifford.

"Let's have a look at Bradshaw," he said, as though he had not noticed Clifford reading it.

But Clifford handed him the book in the most friendly manner, remarking that he couldn't see where they were. "In fact you have surpassed yourself with your brilliant navigation. We seem to be miles from anywhere."

"What about your famous ordnance?"

"It's not on any sheet I have. The new one I thought we should use only covers the loop we planned. There is precisely three quarters of a mile of this canal shown on the present sheet and then we run off the map. I suppose there must once have been trade here, but I cannot imagine what, or where."

"I expect things change," said Sharon. "Here is the meal."

"How can you see to cook?" asked John eyeing his plate ravenously.

"There is a candle."

"Yes, but we've selfishly appropriated that."

"Should I need more light?" she asked, and looked troubled.

"There's no should about it. I just don't know how you do it, that's all. Chips exactly the right colour, and you never drop anything. It's marvellous."

She smiled a little uncertainly at him and lit another candle. "Luck, probably," she said, and set it on the table.

They ate their meal, and John told them about the mooring. "Some sort of village. I think we're moored at the wharf. I couldn't find any rings without the torch, so I've used the anchor." This small shaft was intended for Clifford, who had dropped the spare torch-battery in the washing-up bowl, and forgotten to buy another. But it was only a small shaft, and immediately afterwards John felt much better. His aggression slowly left him, and he felt nothing but peaceful and well-fed affection for the other two.

"Extraordinary cut off this is," he remarked over coffee.

"It is very pleasant in here. Warm, and extremely full of us."

"Yes. I know. A quiet village, though, you must admit."

"I shall believe in your village when I see it."

"Then you would believe it?"

"No he wouldn't, Sharon. Not if he didn't want to, and couldn't find it on the map. That map!"

The conversation turned again to their remoteness, and to how cut off one liked to be and at what point it ceased to be desirable; to boats, telephones, and, finally, canals: which, Clifford maintained, possessed the perfect proportions of urbanity and solitude.

Hours later, when they had turned in for the night, Clifford reviewed the conversation, together with others they had had, and remembered with surprise how little Sharon had actually said. She listened to everything and occasionally, when they appealed to her, made some small composed remark which was oddly at variance with their passionate interest. "She has an elusive quality of freshness about her," he thought, "which is neither naive nor stupid nor dull, and she invokes no responsibility. She does not want us to know what she was, or why we found her as we did, and curiously, I, at least, do not want to know. She is what women ought to be," he concluded with sudden pleasure; and slept.

He woke the next morning to find it very late, and stretched out his hand to wake John.

"We've all overslept. Look at the time."

"Good Lord! Better wake Sharon."

Sharon lay between them on the floor, which they had ceded her because, oddly enough, it was the widest and most comfortable bed. She seemed profoundly asleep, but at the mention of her name sat up immediately, and rose, almost as though she had not been asleep at all.

The morning routine, which, involving the clothing of three people and shaving of two of them, was necessarily a long and complicated business, began. Sharon boiled water, and Clifford, grumbling gently, hoisted himself out of his bunk and repaired with a steaming jug to the cockpit. He put the jug on a seat, lifted the canvas awning, and leaned out. It was absolutely grey and still; a little white mist hung over the canal, and the country stretched out desolate and unkempt on every side with no sign of a living creature. The village, he thought suddenly: John's village: and was possessed of a perilous uncertainty and fear. I am getting worse, he thought, this holiday is doing me no good. I am mad. I imagined that he said we moored by a village wharf. For several seconds he stood gripping the gunwale, and searching desperately for anything, huts, a clump of trees, which could in the darkness have been mistaken for a village. But there was nothing near the boat except tall rank rushes which did not move at all. Then, when his suspense was becoming unbearable, John joined him with another steaming jug of water.

"We shan't get anywhere at this rate," he began; and then . . . "Hullo! Where's my village?"

"I was wondering that," said Clifford. He could almost have wept with relief, and quickly began to shave, deeply ashamed of his private panic.

"Can't understand it," John was saying. It was no joke, Clifford decided, as he listened to his hearty puzzled ruminations.

At breakfast John continued to speculate upon what he had or had not seen, and Sharon listened intently while she filled the coffee pot and cut bread. Once or twice she met Clifford's eye with a glance of discreet amusement.

"I must be mad, or else the whole place is haunted," finished John comfortably. These two possibilities seemed to relieve him of any further anxiety in the matter, as he ate a huge breakfast and set about greasing the engine.

"Well," said Clifford, when he was alone with Sharon. "What do you make of that?"

"It is easy to be deceived in such matters," she answered perfunctorily.

"Evidently. Still, John is an unlikely candidate you must admit. Here, I'll help you dry."

"Oh no. It is what I am here for."

"Not entirely, I hope."

"Not entirely." She smiled and relinquished the cloth.

John eventually announced that they were ready to start. Clifford, who had assumed that they were to recover their journey, was surprised, and a little alarmed, to find John intent upon continuing it. He seemed undeterred by the state of the canal, which, as Clifford immediately pointed out, rendered navigation both arduous and unrewarding. He announced that the harder it was, the more he liked it, adding very firmly that "anyway we must see what happens."

"We shan't have time to do anything else."

"Thought you wanted to explore."

"I do, but . . . what do you think, Sharon?"

"I think John will have to be a very good navigator to manage that." She indicated the rush and weed-ridden reach before them. "Do you think it's possible?"

"Of course it's possible. I'll probably need some help though."

"I'll help you," she said.

So on they went.

They made incredibly slow progress. John enjoys showing off his powers to her, thought Clifford, half amused, half exasperated, as he struggled for the fourth time in an hour to scrape weeds off the propeller.

Sharon eventually retired to cook lunch.

"Surprising amount of water here," John said suddenly.

"Oh?"

"Well, I mean, with all this weed and stuff, you'd expect the canal to have silted up. I'm sure nobody uses it."

"The whole thing is extraordinary."

"Is it too late in the year for birds?" asked Clifford later.

"No, I don't think so. Why?"

"I haven't heard one, have you?"

"Haven't noticed, I'm afraid. There's someone anyway. First sign of life."

An old man stood near the bank watching them. He was dressed in corduroy and wore a straw hat.

"Good morning," shouted John, as they drew nearer.

He made no reply, but inclined his head slightly. He seemed very old. He was leaning on a scythe, and as they drew almost level with him, he turned away and began slowly cutting rushes. A pile of them lay neatly stacked beside him.

"Where does this canal go? Is there a village further on?" Clifford and John asked simultaneously. He seemed not to hear, and as they chugged steadily past, Clifford was about to suggest that they stop and ask again, when he called after them: "Three miles up you'll find the village. Three miles up that is," and turned away to his rushes again.

"Well, now we know something, anyway," said John.

"We don't even know what the village is called."

"Soon find out. Only three miles."

"Three miles!" said Clifford darkly. "That might mean anything."

"Do you want to turn back?"

"Oh no, not now. I want to see this village now. My curiosity is thoroughly aroused."

"Shouldn't think there'll be anything to see. Never been in such a wild spot. Look at it."

Clifford looked at it. Half wilderness, half marsh, dank and grey and still, with single trees bare of their leaves; clumps of hawthorn that might once have been hedge, sparse and sharp with berries; and, in the distance, hills and an occasional wood: these were all one could see, beyond the lines of rushes which edged the canal winding ahead.

They stopped for a lengthy meal, which Sharon described as lunch and tea together, it being so late; and then, appalled at how little daylight was left, continued.

"We've hardly been any distance at all," said John forlornly. "Good thing there were no locks. I shouldn't think they'd have worked if there were."

"*Much* more than three miles," he said, about two hours later. Darkness was descending and it was becoming very cold.

"Better stop," said Clifford.

"Not yet. I'm determined to reach that village."

"Dinner is ready," said Sharon sadly. "It will be cold."

"Let's stop."

"You have your meal. I'll call if I want you."

Sharon looked at them, and Clifford shrugged his shoulders. "Come on. I will. I'm tired of this."

They shut the cabin doors. John could hear the pleasant clatter of their meal, and just as he was coming to the end of the decent interval which he felt must elapse before he gave in, they passed under a bridge, the first of the day, and, clutching at any straw, he immediately assumed that it prefaced the village. "I think we're nearly there," he called.

Clifford opened the door. "The village?"

"No, a bridge. Can't be far now."

"You're mad, John. It's pitch dark."

"You can see the bridge though."

"Yes. Why not moor under it?"

"Too late. Can't turn round in this light, and she's not good at reversing. Must be nearly there. You go back, I don't need you."

Clifford shut the door again. He was beginning to feel irritated with John behaving in this childish manner and showing off to impress Sharon. It was amusing in the morning, but really he was carrying it a bit far. Let him manage the thing himself then. When, a few minutes later, John shouted that they had reached the sought after village, Clifford merely pulled back the little curtain over a cabin window, rubbed the condensation, and remarked that he could see nothing. "No light at least."

"He is happy anyhow," said Sharon peaceably.

"Going to have a look round," said John, slamming the cabin doors and blowing his nose.

"Surely you'll eat first?"

"If you've left anything. My God it's cold! It's *unnaturally* cold."

"We won't be held responsible if he dies of exposure will we?" said Clifford.

She looked at him, hesitated a moment, but did not reply, and placed a steaming plate in front of John. She doesn't want us to quarrel, Clifford thought, and with an effort of friendliness he asked: "What does to-night's village look like?"

"Much the same. Only one or two houses you know. But the old man called it a village." He seemed uncommunicative; Clifford thought he was sulking. But after eating the meal, he suddenly announced, almost apologetically, "I don't think I shall walk round. I'm absolutely worn out. You go if you like. I shall start turning in."

"All right. I'll have a look. You've had a hard day."

Clifford pulled on a coat and went outside. It was, as John said, incredibly cold and almost overwhelmingly silent. The clouds hung very low over the boat, and mist was rising everywhere from the ground, but he could dimly discern the black huddle of cottages lying on a little slope above the bank against which the boat was moored. He did actually set foot on shore, but his shoe sank immediately into a marshy hole. He withdrew it, and changed his mind. The prospect of groping round those dark and silent houses became suddenly distasteful, and he joined the others with the excuse that it was too cold and that he also was tired.

A little later, he lay half conscious in a kind of restless trance, with John sleeping heavily opposite him. His mind seemed full of foreboding, fear of something unknown and intangible: he thought of them lying in warmth on the cold secret canal with desolate miles of water behind and probably beyond; the old man and the silent houses; John, cut off and asleep, and Sharon, who lay on the floor beside him. Immediately he was filled with a sudden and most violent desire for her, even to touch her, for her to know that he was awake.

"Sharon," he whispered; "Sharon, Sharon," and stretched down his fingers to her in the dark.

Instantly her hand was in his, each smooth and separate finger warmly clasped. She did not move or speak, but his relief was indescribable and for a long while he lay in an ecstasy of delight and peace, until his mind slipped imperceptibly with her fingers into oblivion.

When he woke he found John absent and Sharon standing over the primus. "He's outside," she said.

"Have I overslept again?"

"It is late. I am boiling water for you now."

"We'd better try and get some supplies this morning."

"There is no village," she said, in a matter of fact tone.

"What?"

"John says not. But we have enough food, if you don't mind this queer milk from a tin."

"No, I don't mind," he replied, watching her affectionately. "It doesn't really surprise me," he added after a moment.

"The village?"

"No village. Yesterday I should have minded awfully. Is that you, do you think?"

"Perhaps."

"It doesn't surprise you about the village at all, does it? Do you love me?"

She glanced at him quickly, a little shocked, and said quietly: "Don't you know?" then added: "It doesn't surprise me."

John seemed very disturbed. "I don't like it," he kept saying as they shaved. "Can't understand it at all. I could have sworn there were houses last night. You saw them didn't you?"

"Yes."

"Well, don't you think it's very odd?"

"I do."

"Everything looks the same as yesterday morning. I don't like it."

"It's an adventure you must admit."

"Yes, but I've had enough of it. I suggest we turn back."

Sharon suddenly appeared, and, seeing her, Clifford knew that he did not want to go back. He remembered her saying: "Didn't you say you wanted to explore?" She would think him weak-hearted if they turned back all those dreary miles with nothing to show for it. At breakfast, he exerted himself in persuading John to the same opinion. John finally agreed to one more day, but, in turn, extracted a promise that they would then go back whatever happened. Clifford agreed to this, and Sharon for some inexplicable reason laughed at them both. So that eventually they prepared to set off in an atmosphere of general good humour.

Sharon began to fill the water tank with their four-gallon can. It seemed too heavy for her, and John dropped the starter and leapt to her assistance.

She let him take the can and held the funnel for him. Together they watched the rich even stream of water disappear.

"You shouldn't try to do that," he said. "You'll hurt yourself."

"Gipsies do it," she said.

"I'm awfully sorry about that. You know I am."

"I should not have minded if you had thought I was a gipsy."

"I do like you," he said, not looking at her. "I do like you. You won't disappear altogether when this is over, will you?"

"You probably won't find I'll disappear for good," she replied comfortingly.

"Come on," shouted Clifford.

It's all right for *him* to talk to her, John thought, as he struggled to swing the starter. He just doesn't like me doing it; and he wished, as he had begun often to do, that Clifford was not there.

They had spasmodic engine trouble in the morning, which slowed them down; and the consequent halts, with the difficulty they experienced of mooring anywhere (the banks seemed nothing but marsh), were depressing and cold. Their good spirits evaporated: by lunch-time John was plainly irritable and frightened, and Clifford had begun to hate the grey silent land on either side, with the woods and hills which remained so consistently distant. They both wanted to give it up by then, but John felt bound to stick to his promise, and Clifford was secretly sure that Sharon wished to continue.

While she was preparing another late lunch, they saw a small boy who stood on what once had been the towpath watching them. He was bare-headed, wore corduroy, and had no shoes. He held a long reed, the end of which he chewed as he stared at them.

"Ask him where we are," said John; and Clifford asked.

He took the reed out of his mouth, but did not reply.

"Where do you live then?" asked Clifford as they drew almost level with him.

"I told you. Three miles up," he said; and then he gave a sudden little shriek of fear, dropped the reed, and turned to run down the bank the way they had come. Once he looked back, stumbled and fell, picked himself up sobbing, and ran faster. Sharon had appeared with lunch a moment before, and together they listened to his gasping cries growing fainter and fainter, until he had run himself out of their sight.

"What on earth frightened him?" said Clifford.

"I don't know. Unless it was Sharon popping out of the cabin like that."

"Nonsense. But he was a very frightened little boy. And, I say, do you realize . . ."

"He was a very foolish little boy," Sharon interrupted. She was angry, Clifford noticed with surprise, really angry, white and trembling, and with a curious expression which he did not like.

"We might have got something out of him," said John sadly.

"Too late now," Sharon said. She had quite recovered herself.

They saw no one else. They journeyed on throughout the afternoon; it grew colder, and at the same time more and more airless and still. When the light began to fail, Sharon disappeared as usual to the cabin. The canal became more tortuous, and John asked Clifford to help him with the turns. Clifford complied unwillingly; he did not want to leave Sharon, but as it had been he who had insisted on their continuing, he could hardly refuse. The turns were nerve wracking, as the canal was very narrow and the light grew worse and worse.

"All right if we stop soon?" asked John eventually.

"Stop now if you like."

"Well, we'll try and find a tree to tie up to. This swamp is awful. Can't think how that child ran."

"That child . . ." began Clifford anxiously; but John, who had been equally unnerved by the incident, and did not want to think about it, interrupted. "Is there a tree ahead anywhere?"

"Can't see one. There's a hell of a bend coming though. Almost back on itself. Better slow a bit more."

"Can't. We're right down as it is."

They crawled round, clinging to the outside bank, which seemed always to approach them, its rushes to rub against their bows, although the wheel was hard over. John grunted with relief, and they both stared ahead for the next turn.

They were presented with the most terrible spectacle. The canal immediately broadened, until no longer a canal but a sheet, an infinity, of water stretched ahead; oily, silent, and still, as far as the eye could see, with no country edging it, nothing but water to the low grey sky above it. John had almost immediately cut out the engine, and now he tried desperately to start it again, in order to turn round. Clifford instinctively glanced behind them. He saw no canal at all, no inlet, but grasping and close to the stern of the boat, the reeds and rushes of a marshy waste closing in behind them. He stumbled to the cabin doors and pulled them open. It was very neat and tidy in there, but empty. Only one stern door of the cabin was free of its catch, and it flapped irregularly backwards and forwards with their movements in the boat.

There was no sign of Sharon at all. 1975

MARGHANITA LASKI

The Tower

*The road begins to rise in a series of gentle curves, passing through pleas-
ing groves of olives and vines. 5 km. on the left is the fork for Florence. To
the right may be seen the Tower of Sacrifice (470 steps) built in 1535 by
Niccolo di Ferramano; superstitious fear left the tower intact when, in
1549, the surrounding village was completely destroyed . . .*

Triumphantly Caroline lifted her finger from the fine italic type.
There was nothing to mar the success of this afternoon. Not only had
she taken the car out alone for the first time, driving unerringly on the
right-hand side of the road, but what she had achieved was not a simple
drive but a cultural excursion. She had taken the Italian guide-book
Neville was always urging on her, and hesitantly, haltingly, she had
managed to piece out enough of the language to choose a route that took
in four well-thought-of frescoes, two universally-admired campaniles,
and one wooden crucifix in a village church quite a long way from the
main road. It was not, after all, such a bad thing that a British Council
meeting had kept Neville in Florence. True, he was certain to know all
about the campaniles and the frescoes, but there was just a chance that
he hadn't discovered the crucifix, and how gratifying if she could, at last,
have something of her own to contribute to his constantly accumulating
hoard of culture.

But could she add still more? There was at least another hour of
daylight, and it wouldn't take more than thirty-five minutes to get back
to the flat in Florence. Perhaps there would just be time to add this
tower to her dutiful collection? What was it called? She bent to the
guide-book again, carefully tracing the text with her finger to be sure she
was translating it correctly, word by word.

But this time her moving finger stopped abruptly at the name of
Niccolo di Ferramano. There had risen in her mind a picture—no, not a
picture, a portrait—of a thin white face with deep-set black eyes that
stared intently into hers. Why a portrait? she asked, and then she remembered.

It had been about three months ago, just after they were married, when Neville had first brought her to Florence. He himself had already lived there for two years, and during that time had been at least as concerned to accumulate Tuscan culture for himself as to disseminate English culture to the Italians. What more natural than that he should wish to share—perhaps even to show off—his discoveries to his young wife?

Caroline had come out to Italy with the idea that when she had worked through one or two galleries and made a few trips—say to Assisi and Siena—she would have done her duty as a British Council wife, and could then settle down to examining the Florentine shops, which everyone had told her were too marvellous for words. But Neville had been contemptuous of her programme. "You can see the stuff in the galleries at any time," he had said, "but I'd like you to start with the pieces that the ordinary tourist doesn't see," and of course Caroline couldn't possibly let herself be classed as an ordinary tourist. She had been proud to accompany Neville to castles and palaces privately owned to which his work gave him entry, and there to gaze with what she hoped was pleasure on the undiscovered Raphael, the Titian that had hung on the same wall ever since it was painted, the Giotto fresco under which the family that had originally commissioned it still said their prayers.

It had been on one of these pilgrimages that she had seen the face of the young man with the black eyes. They had made a long slow drive over narrow ill-made roads and at last had come to a castle on the top of a hill. The family was, to Neville's disappointment, away, but the housekeeper remembered him and led them to a long gallery lined with five centuries of family portraits.

Though she could not have admitted it even to herself, Caroline had become almost anaesthetized to Italian art. Dutifully she had followed Neville along the gallery, listening politely while in his light well-bred voice he had told her intimate anecdotes of history, and involuntarily she had let her eyes wander round the room, glancing anywhere but at the particular portrait of Neville's immediate dissertation.

It was thus that her eye was caught by a face on the other side of the room, and forgetting what was due to politeness she caught her husband's arm and demanded, "Neville, who's that girl over there?"

But he was pleased with her. He said, "Ah, I'm glad you picked that one out. It's generally thought to be the best thing in the collection—a Bronzino, of course," and they went over to look at it.

The picture was painted in rich pale colours, a green curtain, a blue dress, a young face with calm brown eyes under plaits of honey-gold hair. Caroline read out the name under the picture—*Giovanna di Ferramano, 1531–1549.* That was the year the village was destroyed, she remem-

bered now, sitting in the car by the roadside, but then she had exclaimed, "Neville, she was only eighteen when she died."

"They married young in those days," Neville commented, and Caroline said in surprise, "Oh, was she married?" It had been the radiantly
virginal character of the face that had caught at her inattention.

"Yes, she was married," Neville answered, and added, "Look at the
portrait beside her. It's Bronzino again. What do you think of it?"

And this was when Caroline had seen the pale young man. There were
no clear light colours in this picture. There was only the whiteness of the
face, the blackness of the eyes, the hair, the clothes, and the glint of gold
letters on the pile of books on which the young man rested his hand.
Underneath this picture was written *Portrait of an Unknown Gentleman.*

"Do you mean he's her husband?" Caroline asked. "Surely they'd
know if he was, instead of calling him an Unknown Gentleman?"

"He's Niccolo di Ferramano all right," said Neville. "I've seen another portrait of him somewhere, and it's not a face one would forget,
but," he added reluctantly, because he hated to admit ignorance,
"there's apparently some queer scandal about him, and though they
don't turn his picture out, they won't even mention his name. Last time
I was here, the old Count himself took me through the gallery. I asked
him about little Giovanna and her husband." He laughed uneasily.
"Mind you, my Italian was far from perfect at that time, but it was
horribly clear that I shouldn't have asked." "But what did he *say?*"
Caroline demanded. "I've tried to remember," said Neville. "For some
reason it stuck in my mind. He said either 'She was lost' or 'She was
damned,' but which word it was I can never be sure. The portrait of
Niccolo he just ignored altogether."

"What was wrong with Niccolo, I wonder?" mused Caroline, and
Neville answered, "I don't know but I can guess. Do you notice the
lettering on those books up there, under his hand? It's all in Hebrew or
Arabic. Undoubtedly the unmentionable Niccolo dabbled in Black
Magic."

Caroline shivered. "I don't like him," she said. "Let's look at Giovanna again," and they had moved back to the first portrait, and Neville
had said casually, "Do you know, she's rather like you."

"I've just got time to look at the tower," Caroline now said aloud, and
she put the guide-book back in the pigeon-hole under the dashboard,
and drove carefully along the gentle curves until she came to the fork for
Florence on the left.

On the top of a little hill to the right stood a tall round tower. There
was no other building in sight. In a land where every available piece of
ground is cultivated, there was no cultivated ground around this tower.

On the left was the fork for Florence: on the right a rough track led up to the top of the hill.

Caroline knew that she wanted to take the fork to the left, to Florence and home and Neville and—said an urgent voice inside her—for safety. This voice so much shocked her that she got out of the car and began to trudge up the dusty track towards the tower.

After all, I may not come this way again, she argued; it seems silly to miss the chance of seeing it when I've already got a reason for being interested. I'm only just going to have a quick look—and she glanced at the setting sun, telling herself that she would indeed have to be quick if she were to get back to Florence before dark.

And now she had climbed the hill and was standing in front of the tower. It was built of narrow red bricks, and only thin slits pierced its surface right up to the top where Caroline could see some kind of narrow platform encircling it. Before her was an arched doorway. I'm just going to have a quick look, she assured herself again, and then she walked in.

She was in an empty room with a low arched ceiling. A narrow stone staircase clung to the wall and circled round the room to disappear through a hole in the ceiling.

"There ought to be a wonderful view at the top," said Caroline firmly to herself, and she laid her hand on the rusty rail and started to climb, and as she climbed, she counted.

"—thirty-nine, forty, forty-one," she said, and with the forty-first step she came through the ceiling and saw over her head, far far above, the deep blue evening sky, a small circle of blue framed in a narrowing shaft round which the narrow staircase spiralled. There was no inner wall; only the rusty railing protected the climber on the inside.

"—eighty-three, eighty-four—" counted Caroline. The sky above her was losing its colour and she wondered why the narrow slit windows in the wall had all been so placed that they spiralled round the staircase too high for anyone climbing it to see through them.

"It's getting dark very quickly," said Caroline at the hundred-and-fiftieth step. "I know what the tower is like now. It would be much more sensible to give up and go home."

At the two-hundred-and-sixty-ninth step, her hand, moving forward on the railing, met only empty space. For an interminable second she shivered, pressing back to the hard brick on the other side. Then hesitantly she groped forwards, upwards, and at last her fingers met the rusty rail again, and again she climbed.

But now the breaks in the rail became more and more frequent. Sometimes she had to climb several steps with her left shoulder pressed tightly to the brick wall before her searching hand could find the tenuous rusty comfort again.

At the three-hundred-and-seventy-fifth step, the rail, as her moving hand clutched it, crumpled away under her fingers. "I'd better just go by the wall," she told herself, and now her left hand traced the rough brick as she climbed up and up.

"Four-hundred-and-twenty-two, four-hundred-and-twenty-three," counted Caroline with part of her brain. "I really ought to go down now," said another part, "I wish—oh, I want to go down now—" but she could not. "It would be so silly to give up," she told herself, desperately trying to rationalize what drove her on. "Just because one's afraid—" and then she had to stifle that thought too, and there was nothing left in her brain but the steadily mounting tally of the steps.

"—four-hundred-and-seventy!" said Caroline aloud with explosive relief, and then she stopped abruptly because the steps had stopped too. There was nothing ahead but a piece of broken railing barring her way, and the sky, drained now of all its colour, was still some twenty feet above her head.

"But how idiotic," she said to the air. "The whole thing's absolutely pointless," and then the fingers of her left hand, exploring the wall beside her, met not brick but wood.

She turned to see what it was, and there in the wall, level with the top step, was a small wooden door. "So it does go somewhere after all," she said, and she fumbled with the rusty handle. The door pushed open and she stepped through.

She was on a narrow stone platform about a yard wide. It seemed to encircle the tower. The platform sloped downwards away from the tower and its stones were smooth and very shiny—and this was all she noticed before she looked beyond the stones and down.

She was immeasurably, unbelievably high and alone and the ground below was a world away. It was not credible, not possible that she should be so far from the ground. All her being was suddenly absorbed in the single impulse to hurl herself from the sloping platform. "I cannot go down any other way," she said, and then she heard what she said and stepped back, frenziedly clutching the soft rotten wood of the doorway with hands sodden with sweat. There is no other way, said the voice in her brain, there is no other way.

"This is vertigo," said Caroline. "I've only got to close my eyes and keep still for a minute and it will pass off. It's bound to pass off. I've never had it before but I know what it is and it's vertigo." She closed her eyes and kept very still and felt the cold sweat running down her body.

"I should be all right now," she said at last, and carefully she stepped back through the doorway on to the four-hundred-and-seventieth step and pulled the door shut before her. She looked up at the sky, swiftly darkening with night. Then, for the first time, she looked down into the shaft of the tower, down to the narrow unprotected staircase spiralling round and round and round, and disappearing into the dark. She said— she screamed—"I can't go down."

She stood still on the top step, staring downwards, and slowly the last light faded from the tower. She could not move. It was not possible that she should dare to go down, step by step down the unprotected stairs into the dark below. It would be much easier to fall, said the voice in her head, to take one step to the left and fall and it would all be over. You cannot climb down.

She began to cry, shuddering with the pain of her sobs. It could not be true that she had brought herself to this peril, that there could be no safety for her unless she could climb down the menacing stairs. The reality *must* be that she was safe at home with Neville—but this was the reality and here were the stairs; at last she stopped crying and said "Now I shall go down."

"One!" she counted and, her right hand tearing at the brick wall, she moved first one and then the other foot down to the second step. "Two!" she counted, and then she thought of the depth below her and stood still, stupefied with terror. The stone beneath her feet, the brick against her hand were too frail protections for her exposed body. They could not save her from the voice that repeated that it would be easier to fall. Abruptly she sat down on the step.

"Two," she counted again, and spreading both her hands tightly against the step on each side of her, she swung her body off the second step, down on to the third. "Three," she counted, then "four" then "five," pressing closer and closer into the wall, away from the empty drop on the other side.

At the twenty-first step she said, "I think I can do it now." She slid her right hand up the rough wall and slowly stood upright. Then with the other hand she reached for the railing it was now too dark to see, but it was not there.

For timeless time she stood there, knowing nothing but fear. "Twenty-one," she said, "twenty-one," over and over again, but she could not step on to the twenty-second stair.

Something brushed her face. She knew it was a bat, not a hand, that touched her but still it was horror beyond conceivable horror, and it was this horror, without any sense of moving from dread to safety, that at last impelled her down the stairs.

"Twenty-three, twenty-four, twenty-five—" she counted, and around her the air was full of whispering skin-stretched wings. If one of them should touch her again, she must fall. "Twenty-six, twenty-seven, twenty-eight—" The skin of her right hand was torn and hot with blood, for she would never lift it from the wall, only press it slowly down and force her rigid legs to move from the knowledge of each step to the peril of the next.

So Caroline came down the dark tower. She could not think. She could know nothing but fear. Only her brain remorselessly recorded the tally. "Five-hundred-and-one," it counted, "five-hundred-and-two—and three—and four—"

1955

ANN BRIDGE

THE BUICK SALOON

To Mrs James St George Bernard Bowlby it seemed almost providential that she should recover from the series of illnesses which had perforce kept her in England, at the precise moment when Bowlby was promoted from being No. 2 to being No. 1 in the Grand Oriental Bank in Peking. Her improved health and his improved circumstances made it obvious that now at last she should join him, and she wrote to suggest it. Bowlby, of course, agreed, and out she came. He went down to meet her in Shanghai, but business having called him farther still, to Hong Kong, Mrs Bowlby proceeded to Peking alone, and took up her quarters in the big, ugly, grey-brick house over the bank in Legation Street. She tried, as many managers' wives had tried before her, to do her best with the solid mahogany and green leather furniture provided by the bank, wondering the while how Bowlby, so dependent always on the feminine touch on his life and surroundings, had endured the lesser solidities of the sub-manager's house alone for so long. She bought silks and black-wood and scroll paintings. She also bought a car. "You'll need a car, and you'd better have a saloon, because of the dust," Bowlby had said.

People who come to Peking without motors of their own seldom buy new ones. There are always second-hand cars going, from many sources; the leavings of transferred diplomatists, the jetsam of financial ventures, the sediment of conferences. So one morning Mrs Bowlby went down with Thompson, the new No. 2 in the bank, to Maxon's garage in the Nan Shih Tzu to choose her car. After much conversation with the Canadian manager they pitched on a Buick saloon. It was a Buick of the type which is practically standard in the Far East, and had been entirely repainted outside, a respectable dark blue; the inside had been newly done up in a pleasant soft grey which appealed to Mrs Bowlby. The manager was loud in its praises. The suspension was excellent. ("You want that on these roads, Mrs Bowlby.") The driver and his colleague sat outside. ("Much better, Mr Thompson. If these fellows have been eating garlic—they shouldn't, but do—") Thompson knew they did, and agreed heartily. Mrs Bowlby, new to such transactions, wanted to know whom the car had belonged to. The manager was firmly vague. This was not a commission sale—he had bought the car when the owner left. Very good people—"from the Quarter." This fully satisfied Thompson, who knew that only Europeans live (above the rose, anyhow) in the Legation Quarter of Peking.

So the Buick saloon was bought. Thompson, having heard at the club that the late Grand Oriental chauffeur drank petrol, did not re-engage him with the rest of the servants according to custom, but secured instead for Mrs Bowlby the chauffeur of a departing manager of the Banque Franco-Belge. By the time Bowlby returned from Hong Kong the chauffeur and his colleagues had been fitted out with khaki livery for winter, with white for summer—in either case with trim gold cuff-and-hat-bands—and Mrs Bowlby, in her blue saloon, had settled down to pay her calls.

In Peking the newcomer calls first; a curious and discouraging system. It is an ordeal even to the hardened. Mrs Bowlby was not hardened; she was a small, shy, frail woman, who wore grey by preference, and looked grey—eyes, hair, and skin. She had no idea of asserting herself; if she had things in her—subtleties, delicacies—she did not wear them outside; she did not impose herself. She hated the calls. But as she was also extremely conscientious, day after day, trying to fortify herself by the sight of the two khaki-and-gold figures in front of her exhaling their possible garlic to the outer air beyond the glass partition, she called. She called on the diplomats' wives in the Quarter; she called on "the Salt" (officials of the Salt Gabelle); she called on the Customs—English, Italian, American, and French; she called on the Posts—French, Italian, American, and English. The annual displacement of pasteboard in Peking must amount to many tons, and in this useful work Mrs Bowlby, alone in the grey interior of her car, faithfully took her share. She carried with her a little list on which, with the help of her Number One Boy (as much a permanent fixture in the bank house, almost, as the doors and windows), she had written out the styles, titles and addresses of the ladies she wished to visit. The late chauffeur of the Banque Franco-Belge spoke excellent French; so did Mrs Bowlby—it was one of her few accomplishments; but as no Chinese can or will master European names, the Europeans needs must learn and use the peculiar versions current among them. "Ta Ch'in chai T'ai-t'ai, Turkuo-fu," read out Mrs Bowlby when she wished to call on the wife of the German minister. "Oui, Madame!" said Shwang. "Péi T'ai-t'ai, Kung Hsien Hutung," read out Mrs Bowlby when visiting Mrs Bray, the doctor's wife; but when she wished to call on

Mrs Bennett, the wife of the commandant of the English Guard, and Mrs Baines, chaplain's wife, she found that they were both Péi T'ai-t'ai too—which led to confusion.

It began towards the end of the first week. Possibly it was her absorption in the lists and the Chinese names that prevented her from noticing it sooner, but at the end of that week Mrs Bowlby would have sworn that she heard French spoken beside her as she drove about. Once, a little later, as she was driving down the rue Marco Polo to fetch her husband from the club, a voice said: "C'est lui!" in an underbreath, eagerly—or so she thought. The windows were lowered, and Mrs Bowlby put it down to the servants in front. But it persisted. More than once she thought she heard a soft sigh. "Nerves!" thought Mrs Bowlby—her nerves were always a menace, and Peking, she knew, was bad for them.

She went on saying "nerves" for two or three more days; then, one afternoon, she changed her mind. She was driving along the Ta Chiang an Chieh, the great thoroughfare running east and west outside the Legation Quarter, where the trams ring and clang past the scarlet walls and golden roofs of the Forbidden City, and long lines of camels, coming in with coal from the country as they have come for centuries, cross the road between the Dodges and Daimlers of the new China. It was a soft, brilliant afternoon in April, and the cinder track along the Glacis of the Quarter was thronged with riders; polo had begun, and as the car neared Hatamen Street she caught a glimpse of the white and scarlet figures through the drifting dust on her right. At the corner of the Hatamen the car stopped; a string of camels was passing up to the great gateway, and she had to wait.

She sat back in the car, glad of the pause; she was unusually moved by the loveliness of the day, by the beauty and strangeness of the scene, by the whole magic of spring in Peking. She was going later to watch the polo, a terrifying game; she wished Jim didn't play. Suddenly, across her idle thoughts, a voice beside her spoke clearly: "Au revoir!" it said, "mon très-cher. Ne tombes pas, je t'en prie." And as the car moved forward behind the last of the camels, soft and unmistakable there came a sigh, and the words "Ce polo! Quel sport affreux! Dieu, que je le déteste!" in a passionate undertone.

"That *wasn't* the chauffeur!" was what Mrs Bowlby found herself saying. The front windows were up. And besides, that low, rather husky voice, the cultivated and clear accent, could not be confounded for a moment with Shwang's guttural French. And besides, what chauffeur would talk like that? The thing was ridiculous. "And it *wasn't* nerves this time," said Mrs Bowlby, her thoughts running this way and that round the phenomenon. "She did say it." "Then it was she who said: 'C'est lui!' before—" she said almost triumphantly, a moment later.

Curiously, though she was puzzled and startled, she realized presently that she was not in the least frightened. That someone with a beautiful voice should speak French in her car was absurd and impossible, but it wasn't alarming. In her timid way Mrs Bowlby rather prided herself on her common sense, and as she shopped and called she considered this extraordinary occurrence from all the common sense points of view that she could think of, but it remained a baffling and obstinate fact. Before her drive was over she found herself wishing simply to hear the voice again. It was ridiculous, but she did. And she had her wish. As the car turned into Legation Street an hour later she saw that it was too late to go to the polo; the last chukka was over, and the players were leaving the ground, over which dust still hung in the low brilliant light, in cars and rickshaws. As she passed the gate the voice spoke again—almost in front of her, this time, as though the speaker were leaning forward to the window. "Le voilà!" it said—and then, quite loudly, "Jacques!" Mrs Bowlby almost leaned out of the window herself, to look for whoever was being summoned—as she sat back, conscious of her folly, she heard again beside her, quite low: "Il ne m'a pas vue."

There was no mistake about it. It was broad daylight; there she was in her car, bowling along Legation Street—past the Belgian bank, past the German Legation; rickshaws skimming in front of her, Madame de Réan bowing to her. And just as clear and certain as all these things had been this woman's voice, calling to "Jacques," whoever he was—terrified lest he should fall at polo, hating the game for his sake. What a lovely voice it was! Who was she, Mrs Bowlby wondered, and what and who was Jacques? "Mon très-cher!" she had called him—a delicious expression. It belonged to the day and the place—it was near to her own mood as she had sat at the corner of the Hatamen and noticed the spring, and hated the polo too for Jim's sake. She would have liked to call Jim "mon très-cher," only he would have been so surprised.

The thought of Bowlby brought her up with a round turn. What would he say to this affair? Instantly, though she prolonged the discussion with herself for form's sake, she knew that she was not going to tell him. Not yet, anyhow. Bowlby had not been very satisfied with her choice of a car as it was—he said it was too big and too expensive to run. Besides, there was the question of her nerves. If he failed to hear the voice too she would be in a terribly difficult position. But there was more to it than that. She had a faint sense that she had been eavesdropping, however involuntarily. She had no right to give away even a voice which said "mon très-cher" in that tone.

This feeling grew upon her in the days that followed. The voice that haunted the Buick became of almost daily occurrence, furnishing a curious secret background to her social routine of calls and "At Homes." It

spoke always in French, always to or about "Jacques"—a person, whoever he was, greatly loved. Sometimes it was clear to Mrs Bowlby that
she was hearing only half of a conversation between the two, as one does
at the telephone. The man's voice she never heard, but, as at the telephone, she could often guess at what he said. Much of the speech was
trivial enough; arrangements for meetings at lunches, at the polo; for
week-end parties at Pao-ma-chang in the temple of this person or that.
This was more eerie than anything else to Mrs Bowlby—the hearing of
plans concerned with people she knew, "Alors, dimanche prochain, chez
les Milne." Meeting "les Milne" soon after, she would stare at them
uneasily, as though by looking long enough she might find about them
some trace of the presence which was more familiar to her than their
own. Her voice was making ghosts of the living. But whether plans, or
snatches of talk about people or ponies, there came always, sooner or
later, the undernote of tenderness, now hesitant, now frank—the close
concern, the monopolizing happiness of a woman in love.

It puzzled Mrs Bowlby that the car should only register, as it were, the
woman's voice. But then the whole affair bristled with puzzles. Why did
Bowlby hear nothing? For he did not—she would have realized her
worst fears if she *had* told him. She remembered always the first time
that the voice spoke when he was with her. They were going to a Thé
Dansant at the Peking Hotel, a farewell party for some minister. As the
car swung out of the Jade Canal Road, past the policemen who stand
with fixed bayonets at the edge of the Glacis, the voice began suddenly,
as it so often did, in French: "Then I leave thee now—thou wilt send
back the car?" And as they lurched across the tramlines towards the
huge European building and pulled up, it went on: "But tonight, one
will dance, *n'est-ce pas?*"

"Goodness, what a crowd!" said Bowlby. "This is going to be simply
awful. Don't let's stay long. Will half an hour be enough, do you think?"

Mrs Bowlby stared at him without answering. Was it possible? She
nearly gave herself away in the shock of astonishment. "What's the
matter?" said Bowlby. "What are you looking at?"

Bowlby had not heard a word!

She noticed other things. There were certain places where the voice
"came through," so to speak, more clearly and regularly than elsewhere.
Intermittent fragments, sometimes unintelligible, occurred anywhere.
But she came to know where to expect to hear most. Near the polo
ground, for instance, which she hardly ever passed without hearing some
expression of anxiety or pride. She often went to the polo, for Jim was a
keen and brilliant player; but it was a horror while he played, and this
feeling was a sort of link, it seemed to her, between her and her unseen
companion. More and more, too, she heard it near the Hatamen and the

hu-t'ungs or alleys to the east of it. Mrs Bowlby liked the East City. It lies rather in a backwater, between the crowded noisy thoroughfare of Hatamen Street, with its trams, dust, cars, and camels, and the silent angle of the Tartar Wall, rising above the low one-story houses. A good many Europeans live there, and she was always glad when a call took her that way, through the narrow hu-t'ungs where the car lurched over heaps of rubbish or skidded in the deep dust, and rickshaws pulled aside into gateways to let her pass. Many of these lanes end vaguely in big open spaces, where pigs root among the refuse and little boys wander about, singing long monotonous songs with a curious jerky rhythm in their high nasal voices. Sometimes, as she waited before a scarlet door, a flute-player out of sight would begin to play, and the thin sweet melody filled the sunny air between the blank grey walls. Flowering trees showed here and there above them; coppersmiths plied their trade on the steps of carved marble gateways; dogs and beggars sunned themselves under the white and scarlet walls of temple courtyards. Here, more than anywhere else, the voice spoke clearly, freely, continuously, the rounded French syllables falling on the air from nowhere, now high, light, and merry, with teasing words and inflection, now sinking into low murmurs of rapturous happiness. At such times Mrs Bowlby sat wholly absorbed in listening, drawn by the lovely voice into a world not her own and held fascinated by the spell of this passionate adventure. Happy as she was with Bowlby, her life with him had never known anything like this. He had never wanted, and she had never dared to use, the endearments lavished by the late owner of the Buick saloon on her Jacques.

She heard enough to follow the course of the affair pretty closely. They met when they could in public, but somewhere in the Chinese City there was clearly a meeting-place of their own—"notre petit asile." And gradually this haven began to take shape in Mrs Bowlby's mind. Joyous references were made to various features of it. Tomorrow they would drink tea on the stone table under "our great white pine." There was the fishpond shaped like a shamrock where one of the goldfish died—"pourtant en Irlande cela porte bonheur, le trèfle, n'est-ce pas?" The parapet of this pond broke away and had to be repaired, and "Jacques" made some sort of inscription in the damp mortar, for the voice thrilled softly one day as it murmured: "Maintenant il se lit là pour toujours, ton amour!" And all through that enchanted spring, first the lilac bushes perfumed the hours spent beneath the pine, and then the acacias that stood in a square round the shamrock pond. Still more that life and hers seemed to Mrs Bowlby strangely mingled; her own lilacs bloomed and scented the courtyard behind the grey bank building, and one day as they drove to lunch in the British Legation she drew Jim's attention to the scent of the acacias, which drowned the whole compound in perfume. But Bowlby said, with a sort of shiver, that he hated the smell; and he swore at the chauffeur in French, which he spoke even better than his wife.

The desire grew on Mrs Bowlby to know more of her pair, who and what they were and how their story ended. But it seemed wholly impossible to find out. Her reticences made her quite unequal to setting anyone on to question the people at the garage again. And then one day, accidentally, the clue was given to her. She had been calling at one of the houses in the French Legation; the two house servants, in blue and silver gowns, stood respectfully on the steps; her footman held open the door of the car for her. As she seated herself the voice said in a clear tone of command: "Deux cent trente, Por Hua Shan Hut'ung!" Acting on an impulse which surprised her, Mrs Bowlby repeated the order: "Deux cent trente, Por Hua Shan Hut'ung," she said. Shwang's colleague bowed and shut the door. But she caught sight, as she spoke, of the faces of the two servants on the steps. Was it imagination? Surely not. She would have sworn that a flicker of some emotion—surprise, and recollection—had appeared for a moment on their sealed and impassive countenances. In Peking the servants in Legation houses are commonly handed on from employer to employer, like the furniture, and the fact struck on her with sudden conviction—they had heard those words before!

Her heart rose with excitement as the car swung out of the compound into Legation Street. Where was it going? She had no idea where the Por Hua Shan Hut'ung was. Was she about to get a stage nearer to the solution of the mystery at last? At the Hatamen the Buick turned south along the Glacis. So far so good. They left the Hatamen, bumped into the Suchow Hut'ung, followed on down the Tung Tsung Pu Hut'ung right into the heart of the East City. Her breath came fast. It must be right. Now they were skirting the edge of one of the rubbish-strewn open spaces, and the East Wall rose close ahead of them. They turned left, parallel with it; turned right again towards it; stopped. Shwang beckoned to a pancake-seller who was rolling out his wares in a doorway, and a colloquy in Chinese ensued. They went on slowly then, down a lane between high walls which ended at the Wall's very foot, and pulled up some hundred yards short of it before a high scarlet door, whose rows of golden knobs in fives betokened the former dwelling of some Chinese of rank.

It was only when Liu came to open the door and held out his cotton-gloved hand for her cards that Mrs Bowlby realized that she had no idea what she was going to do. She could not call on a voice! She summoned Shwang, Liu's French was not his strong point. "Ask," she said to Shwang, "who lives here—the T'ai-t'ai's name." Shwang rang the bell. There was a long pause. Shwang rang again. There came a sound of shuffling feet inside; creaking on its hinges the door opened, and the head of an old Chinaman, thinly bearded and topped with a little black cap, appeared in the crack. A conversation followed, and then Shwang returned to the car.

"The house is empty," he said. "Ask him who lived there last," said Mrs Bowlby. Another and longer conversation followed, but at last Shwang came to the window with the information that a foreign T'ai-t'ai, "Fa-kuo T'ai-t'ai" (French lady), he thought, had lived there, but she had gone away. With that Mrs Bowlby had to be content. It was something. It might be much. The car had moved on towards the Wall, seeking a place to turn, when an idea struck her. Telling Shwang to wait, she got out, and glanced along the foot of the Wall in both directions. Yes! Some two hundred yards from where she stood one of those huge ramps, used in former times to ride or drive up on to the summit of the Wall, descended into the dusty strip of waste land at its foot. She hurried towards it, nervously, picking her way between the rough fallen lumps of stone and heaps of rubbish; she was afraid that the servants would regard her action as strange, and that when she reached the foot of the ramp she might not be able to get up it. Since Boxer times the top of the Tartar Wall is forbidden as a promenade, save for a short trip just above the Legation Quarter, and the ramps are stoutly closed at the foot, theoretically. But in China theory and practice do not always correspond, Mrs Bowlby knew; and as she hurried, she hoped.

Her hope was justified. Though a solid wooden barrier closed the foot of the ramp, a few feet higher up a little bolt-hole, large enough to admit a goat or a small man, had been picked away in the masonry of the parapet. Mrs Bowlby scrambled through and found herself on the cobbled slope of the ramp; panting a little, she walked up it on to the Wall. The great flagged top, broad enough for two motor-lorries to drive abreast, stretched away to left and right; a thick undergrowth of thorny bushes had sprung up between the flags, and through them wound a little path, manifestly used by goats and goat-herds. Below her Peking lay spread out—a city turned by the trees which grow in every courtyard into the semblance of a green wood, out of which rose the immense golden roofs of the Forbidden City; beyond it, far away, the faint mauve line of the Western Hills hung on the sky.

But Mrs Bowlby had no eyes for the unparalleled view. Peeping cautiously through the battlements she located the Buick saloon, shining incongruously neat and modern in its squalid and deserted surroundings; by it she took her bearings, and moved with a beating heart along the little path between the thorns. Hoopoes flew out in front of her, calling their sweet note, and perched again, raising and lowering their crests; she never heeded them, nor her torn silk stockings. Now she was above the car; yes, there was the lane up which they had come, and the wall beyond it was the wall of that house! She could see the doorkeeper, doll-like below her, still standing in his scarlet doorway, watching the car curiously. The garden wall stretched up close to the foot of the City Wall itself, so that, as she came abreast of it, the whole compound—the house, with its manifold courtyards, and the formal garden—lay spread out at her feet with the minute perfection of a child's toy farm on the floor.

Mrs Bowlby stood looking down at it. A dream-like sense of unreality came over her, greater than any yet caused even by her impossible voice. A magnificent white pine, trunk and branches gleaming as if white-washed among its dark needles, rose out of the garden, and below it stood a round stone table among groups of lilacs. Just as the voice had described it! Close by, separated from the pine garden by a wall pierced with a fan-shaped doorway, was another with a goldfish pond like a shamrock, and round it stood a square pleached alley of acacias. Flowers in great tubs bloomed everywhere. Here was the very setting of her lovers' secret idyll; silent, sunny, sweet, it lay under the brooding protection of the Tartar Wall. Here she was indeed near to the heart of her mystery, Mrs Bowlby felt, as she leaned on the stone parapet, looking down at the deserted garden. A strange fancy came to her that she would have liked to bring Jim here, and people it once again. But she and Jim, she reflected with a little sigh, were staid married people, with no need of a secret haven hidden away in the East City. And with the thought of Jim the claims of everyday life reasserted themselves. She must go—and with a last glance at the garden she hastened back to the car.

During the next day or so Mrs Bowlby brooded over her new discovery and all that had led to it. Everything—the place where the address had been given by the voice, the flicker of recognition on the faces of the servants at the house in the French Legation, that fact of the doorkeeper in the East City having mentioned a Fa-kuo T'ai-t'ai as his late employer—pointed to one thing, that the former owner of the Buick saloon had lived in the house where she had first called on that momentous afternoon. More than ever, the thing took hold of her—having penetrated the secret of the voice so far, she felt that she must follow it further yet. Timid or not, she must brace herself to ask some questions.

At a dinner a few nights later she found herself seated next to Mr van Adam. Mr van Adam was an elderly American, the doyen of Peking society, who had seen everything and known everyone since before Boxer days—a walking memory and a mine of social information. Mrs Bowlby determined to apply to him. She displayed unwonted craft. She spoke of Legation compounds in general and of the French compound in particular; she praised the garden of the house where she had called.

And then: "Who lived there before the Vernets came?" she asked, and waited eagerly for the answer. Mr van Adam eyed her a little curiously, she thought, but replied that it was a certain Count d'Ardennes. "Was he married?" Mrs Bowlby next inquired. Oh, yes, he was married right enough—but the usual reminiscent flow of anecdote seemed to fail Mr van Adam in this case. Struggling against a vague sense of difficulty, of a hitch somewhere, Mrs Bowlby pushed on nevertheless to an inquiry as to what the Countess d'Ardennes was like. "A siren!" Mr van Adam replied briefly—adding, "Lovely creature, though, as ever stepped."

He edged away rather from the subject, or so it seemed to Mrs Bowlby, but she nerved herself to another question—"Had they a car?" Mr van Adam fairly stared at that; then he broke into a laugh. "Car? Why, yes—she went everywhere in a yellow Buick—we used to call it 'the canary.' " The talk drifted off on to cars in general, and Mrs Bowlby let it drift; she was revolving in her mind the form of her last question. Her curiosity must look odd, she reflected nervously; it was all more difficult, somehow, than she had expected. Her craft was failing her— she could not think of a good excuse for further questions that would not run the risk of betraying her secret. There must have been a scandal— there *would* have been, of course; but Mrs Bowlby was not of the order of women who in Peking ask coolly at the dinner-table: "And what was *her* scandal?" At dessert, in desperation, she put it hurriedly, badly: "When did the d'Ardennes leave?"

Mr van Adam paused before he answered: "Oh, going on for a year ago, now. She was ill, they said—looked it, anyway—and went back to France. He was transferred to Bangkok soon after, but I don't know if she's gone out to him again. The East didn't suit her." "Oh, poor thing!" murmured Mrs Bowlby, softly and sincerely, her heart full of pity for the woman with the lovely voice and the lovely name, whose failing health had severed her from her Jacques. Not even love such as hers could control this wretched feeble body, reflected Mrs Bowlby, whom few places suited. The ladies rose, and too absorbed in her reflections to pay any further attention to Mr van Adam, she rose and went with them.

At this stage Mrs Bowlby went to Pei-t'ai-ho for the summer. Peking, with a temperature of over 100 degrees in the shade, is no place for delicate women in July and August. Cars are not allowed on the sandy roads of the pleasant straggling seaside resort, and missionaries and diplomatists alike are obliged to fall back on rickshaws and donkeys as a means of locomotion. So the Buick saloon was left in Peking with Jim, who came down for long weekends as often as he could. Thus separated from her car, and in changed surroundings, Mrs Bowlby endeavoured to take stock of the whole affair dispassionately. Get away from it she could not. Bathing, idling on the hot sunny beach, walking through the green paths bordered with maize and kaoliang, sitting out in the blessedly cool dark after dinner, she found herself as much absorbed as ever in this personality whose secret life she so strangely shared. Curiously enough, she felt no wish to ask any more questions of any one. With her knowledge of Madame d'Ardennes's name the sense of eavesdropping had returned in full force. One thing struck her as a little odd: that if there *had* been a scandal she should not have heard of it—in Peking, where scandals were innumerable, and treated with startling openness and frank disregard. Perhaps she had been mistaken, though, in Mr van Adam's attitude, and there had not been one. Or—the illumination came to her belated and suddenly—hadn't Mr van Adam's son in the Customs, who went home last year, been called Jack? He had! and Mrs Bowlby shuddered at the thought of her clumsiness. She could not have chosen a worse person for her inquiries.

Another thing, at Pei-t'ai-ho, she realized with a certain astonishment—that she had not been perceptibly shocked by this intrigue. Mrs Bowlby had always believed herself to hold thoroughly conventional British views on marriage; the late owner of the Buick saloon clearly had not, yet Mrs Bowlby had never thought of censuring her. She had even been a little resentful of Mr van Adam's calling her a "siren." Sirens were cold-hearted creatures, who lured men frivolously to their doom; her voice was not the voice of a siren. Mrs Bowlby was all on the side of her voice. Didn't such love justify itself, argued Mrs Bowlby, awake at last to her own moral failure to condemn another, or very nearly? Perhaps, she caught herself thinking, if people knew as much about all love-affairs as she knew about this one, they would be less censorious.

Mrs Bowlby stayed late at Pei-t'ai-ho, well on into September, till the breezes blew chilly off the sea, the green paths had faded to a dusty yellow, and the maize and kaoliang were being cut. When she returned to Peking she was at once very busy—calling begins all over again after the seaside holiday, and she spent hours in the Buick saloon leaving cards. The voice was with her again, as before. But something had overshadowed the blissful happiness of the spring days; there was an undertone of distress, of foreboding, often in the conversations. What exactly caused it she could not make out. But it increased, and one day half-way through October, driving in the East City, the voice dropped away into a burst of passionate sobbing. This distressed Mrs Bowlby extraordinarily. It was a strange and terrible thing to sit in the car with those low, heart-broken sounds at her side. She almost put out her arms to take and comfort the unhappy creature—but there was only empty air, and the empty seat, with her bag, her book, and her little calling list. Obeying one of those sudden impulses which the voice alone seemed to call out in her, she abandoned her calls and told Shwang to drive to the Por Hua Shan Hut'ung. As they neared it the sobs beside her ceased, and murmured apologies for being *un peu énervée* followed.

When she reached the house Mrs Bowlby got out, and again climbed the ramp on to the Tartar Wall. The thorns and bushes between the battlements were brown and sere, and no hoopoes flew and fluted among them. She reached the spot where she could look down into the gardens. The lilacs were bare now, as her own were; the tubs of flowers were gone, and heaps of leaves had drifted round the feet of the acacias—only the white pine stood up, stately and untouched by the general decay. A deep melancholy took hold of Mrs Bowlby; already shaken by the sobs in the car, the desolation of this deserted autumn garden weighed with an intense oppression on her spirit. She turned away, slowly, and slowly descended to the Buick. The sense of impending misfortune had seized on her too; something, she vaguely felt, had come to an end in that garden.

As she was about to get into the car another impulse moved her. She felt an overmastering desire to enter that garden and see its features from close at hand. The oppression still hung over her, and she felt that a visit to the garden might in some way resolve it. She looked in her purse and found a five-dollar note. Handing it to the startled Shwang, "Give that," said Mrs Bowlby, "to the k'ai-men-ti, and tell him I wish to walk in the garden of that house." Shwang bowed; rang the bell; conversed; Mrs Bowlby waited, trembling with impatience, till the clinching argument of the note was at last produced, and the old man whom she had seen before beckoned to her to enter.

She followed him through several courtyards. It was a rambling Chinese house, little modernized; the blind paper lattice of the windows looked blankly on to the miniature lakes and rocky landscapes in the open courts. Finally they passed through a round doorway into the garden below the Tartar Wall, and bowing, the old custodian stood aside to let her walk alone.

Before her rose the white pine, and she strolled towards it, and sitting down on a marble bench beside the round stone table, gazed about her. Beautiful even in its decay, melancholy, serene, the garden lay under the battlements which cut the pale autumn sky behind her. And here the owner of the voice had sat, hidden and secure, her lover beside her! A sudden burst of tears surprised Mrs Bowlby. Cruel life, she thought, which parts dear lovers. Had *she* too sat here alone? A sharp unexpected sense of her own solitude drove Mrs Bowlby up from her seat. This visit was a mistake; her oppression was not lightened; to have sat in this place seemed somehow to have involved herself in the disaster and misery of that parted pair. She wandered on, through the fan-shaped doorway, and came to a halt beside the goldfish pond. Staring at it through her tears, she noticed the repair to the coping of which the voice had spoken, where "Jacques" had made an inscription in the damp mortar. She moved round to the place where it still showed white against the grey surface, murmuring, "Maintenant il se lit là pour toujours, ton amour!"—the phrase of the voice had stayed rooted in her mind. Stooping down, she read the inscription, scratched out neatly and carefully with a penknife in the fine plaster:

> Douce sépulture, mon coeur dans ton coeur,
> Doux paradis, mon âme dans ton âme.

And below two sets of initials:

A. de A.
de
J. St G. B. B.

The verse touched Mrs Bowlby to fresh tears, and it was actually a moment or two before she focused her attention on the initials. When she did, she started back as though a serpent had stung her, and shut her eyes and stood still. Then with a curious blind movement she opened her bag and took out one of her own cards, and laid it on the coping beside the inscription, as if to compare them. *Mrs J. St G. B. Bowlby*—the fine black letters stared up at her, uncompromising and clear, from the white oblong, beside the capitals cut in the plaster. There could be no mistake. Her mystery was solved at last, but it seemed as if she could not take it in. "Jim?" murmured Mrs Bowlby to herself, as if puzzled—and then "Jacques?" Slowly, while she stood there, all the connections and verifications unrolled themselves backwards in her mind with devastating certainty and force. Her sentiment, her intuition on the wall had been terribly right—something *had* come to an end in that garden that day. Standing by the shamrock pond, with the first waves of an engulfing desolation sweeping over her, hardly conscious of her words, she whispered: "Pourtant cela porte bonheur, le trèfle, n'est-ce pas?"

And with that second question from the voice she seemed at last to wake from the sort of stupor in which she had stood. Intolerable! She must hear no more. Passing back, almost running, into the pine garden, she beckoned to the old k'ai-men-ti to take her out. He led her again, bowing, through the courtyards to the great gateway. Through the open red and gold doors she saw the Buick saloon, dark and shiny, standing as she had so often, and with what pleasure, seen it stand before how many doors? She stopped and looked round her almost wildly—behind her the garden, before her the Buick! Liu caught sight of her, and flew to hold open the door. But Mrs Bowlby did not get in. She made Shwang call a rickshaw, and when it came ordered him to direct the coolie to take her to the bank house. Shwang, exercising the respectful supervision which Chinese servants are wont to bestow on their employers, reminded her that she was to go to the polo to pick up the lao-yé, Bowlby. Before his astonished eyes his mistress shuddered visibly from head to foot. "The bank! The bank!" she repeated, with a sort of desperate impatience.

Standing before his scarlet door, lighting his little black and silver pipe, the old k'ai-men-ti watched them go. First the rickshaw, with a small drooping grey figure in it, lurched down the dusty hu-t'ung, and after it, empty, bumped the Buick saloon.   1936

PENELOPE FITZGERALD

The Axe

. . . You will recall that when the planned redundancies became necessary as the result of the discouraging trading figures shown by this small firm—in contrast, so I gather from the Company reports, with several of your other enterprises—you personally deputed to me the task of "speaking" to those who were to be asked to leave. It was suggested to me that if they were asked to resign in order to avoid the unpleasantness of being given their cards, it might be unnecessary for the firm to offer any compensation. Having glanced personally through my staff sheets, you underlined the names of four people, the first being that of my clerical assistant, W. S. Singlebury. Your actual words to me were that he seemed fairly old and could probably be frightened into taking a powder. You were speaking to me in your "democratic" style.

From this point on I feel able to write more freely, it being well understood, at office-managerial level, that you do not read more than the first two sentences of any given report. You believe that anything which cannot be put into two sentences is not worth attending to, a piece of wisdom which you usually attribute to the late Lord Beaverbrook.

As I question whether you have ever seen Singlebury, with whom this report is mainly concerned, it may be helpful to describe him. He worked for the Company for many more years than myself, and his attendance record was excellent. On Mondays, Wednesdays and Fridays, he wore a blue suit and a green knitted garment with a front zip. On Tuesdays and Thursdays he wore a pair of grey trousers of man-made material which he called "my flannels," and a fawn cardigan. The cardigan was omitted in summer. He had, however, one distinguishing feature, very light blue eyes, with a defensive expression, as though apologizing for something which he felt guilty about, but could not put right. The fact is that he was getting old. Getting old is, of course, a crime of which we grow more guilty every day.

Singlebury had no wife or dependants, and was by no means a communicative man. His room is, or was, a kind of cubby-hole adjoining mine—you have to go through it to get into my room—and it was always kept very neat. About his "things" he did show some mild emotion. They had to be ranged in a certain pattern in respect to his in and out trays, and Singlebury stayed behind for two or three minutes every evening to do this. He also managed to retain every year the complimentary desk calendar sent to us by Dino's, the Italian café on the corner. Singlebury was in fact the only one of my personnel who was always quite certain of the date. To this too his attitude was apologetic. His phrase was, "I'm afraid it's Tuesday."

His work, as was freely admitted, was his life, but the nature of his duties—though they included the post-book and the addressograph—were rather hard to define, having grown round him with the years. I can only say that after he left, I was surprised myself to discover how much he had had to do.

Oddly connected in my mind with the matter of the redundancies is the irritation of the damp in the office this summer and the peculiar smell (not the ordinary smell of damp), emphasized by the sudden appearance of representatives of a firm of damp eliminators who had not been sent for by me, nor is there any record of my having done so. These people simply vanished at the end of the day and have not returned. Another firm, to whom I applied as a result of frequent complaints by the female staff, have answered my letters but have so far failed to call.

Singlebury remained unaffected by the smell. Joining, very much against his usual habit, in one of the too frequent discussions of the subject, he said that he knew what it was; it was the smell of disappointment. For an awkward moment I thought he must have found out by some means that he was going to be asked to go, but he went on to explain that in 1942 the whole building had been requisitioned by the Admiralty and that relatives had been allowed to wait or queue there in the hope of getting news of those missing at sea. The repeated disappointment of these women, Singlebury said, must have permeated the building like a corrosive gas. All this was very unlike him. I make it a point not to encourage anything morbid. Singlebury was quite insistent, and added, as though by way of proof, that the lino in the corridors was Admiralty issue and had not been renewed since 1942 either. I was astonished to realize that he had been working in the building for so many years before the present tenancy. I realized that he must be considerably older than he had given us to understand. This, of course, will mean that there are wrong entries on his cards.

The actual notification to the redundant staff passed off rather better, in a way, than I had anticipated. By that time everyone in the office seemed inexplicably conversant with the details, and several of them in fact had gone far beyond their terms of reference, young Patel, for instance, who openly admits that he will be leaving us as soon as he can get a better job, taking me aside and telling me that to such a man as Singlebury dismissal would be like death. Dismissal is not the right word, I said. But death is, Patel replied. Singlebury himself, however, took it very quietly. Even when I raised the question of the Company's Early Retirement pension scheme, which I could not pretend was over-generous, he said very little. He was generally felt to be in a state of shock. The two girls whom you asked me to speak to were quite unaffected, having already found themselves employment as hostesses at the Dolphinarium near here. Mrs. Horrocks, of Filing, on the other hand, *did* protest, and was so offensive on the question of severance pay that I was obliged to agree to refer it to a higher level. I consider this as one of the hardest day's work that I have ever done for the Company.

Just before his month's notice (if we are to call it that) was up, Singlebury, to my great surprise, asked me to come home with him one evening for a meal. In all the past years the idea of his having a home, still less asking anyone back to it, had never arisen, and I did not at all want to go there now. I felt sure, too, that he would want to reopen the matter of compensation, and only a quite unjustified feeling of guilt made me accept. We took an Underground together after work, travelling in the late rush-hour to Clapham North, and walked some distance in the rain. His place, when we eventually got to it, seemed particularly inconvenient, the entrance being through a small cleaner's shop. It consisted of one room and a shared toilet on the half-landing. The room itself was tidy, arranged, so it struck me, much on the lines of his cubby-hole, but the window was shut and it was oppressively stuffy. This is where I bury myself, said Singlebury.

There were no cooking arrangements and he left me there while he went down to fetch us something ready to eat from the Steakorama next to the cleaners. In his absence I took the opportunity to examine his room, though of course not in an inquisitive or prying manner. I was struck by the fact that none of his small store of stationery had been brought home from the office. He returned with two steaks wrapped in aluminum foil, evidently a special treat in my honour, and afterwards he went out on to the landing and made cocoa, a drink which I had not tasted for more than thirty years. The evening dragged rather. In the course of conversation it turned out that Singlebury was fond of reading. There were in fact several issues of a colour-printed encyclopaedia which he had been collecting as it came out, but unfortunately it had ceased publication after the seventh part. Reading is my hobby, he said. I pointed out that a hobby was rather something that one did with one's hands or in the open air—a relief from the work of the brain. Oh, I don't accept that distinction, Singlebury said. The mind and the body are the same. Well, one cannot deny the connection, I replied. Fear, for example, releases adrenalin, which directly affects the nerves. I don't mean connection, I mean identity, Singlebury said, the mind is the blood. Nonsense, I said, you might just as well tell me that the blood is the mind. It stands to reason that the blood can't think.

I was right, after all, in thinking that he would refer to the matter of the redundancy. This was not until he was seeing me off at the bus-stop, when for a moment he turned his grey, exposed-looking face away from me and said that he did not see how he could manage if he really had to go. He stood there like someone who has "tried to give satisfaction"—he even used this phrase, saying that if the expression were not redolent of a bygone age, he would like to feel he had given satisfaction. Fortunately we had not long to wait for the 45 bus.

At the expiry of the month the staff gave a small tea-party for those who were leaving. I cannot describe this occasion as a success.

The following Monday I missed Singlebury as a familiar presence and also, as mentioned above, because I had never quite realized how much work he had been taking upon himself. As a direct consequence of losing him I found myself having to stay late—not altogether unwillingly, since although following general instructions I have discouraged overtime, the extra pay in my own case would be instrumental in making ends meet. Meanwhile Singlebury's desk had not been cleared—that is, of the trays, pencil-sharpener and complimentary calendar which were, of course, office property. The feeling that he would come back—not like Mrs Horrocks, who has rung up and called round incessantly—but simply come back to work out of habit and through not knowing what else to do, was very strong, without being openly mentioned. I myself half expected and dreaded it, and I had mentally prepared two or three lines of argument in order to persuade him, if he *did* come, not to try it again. Nothing happened, however, and on the Thursday I personally removed the "things" from the cubby-hole into my own room.

Meanwhile in order to dispel certain quite unfounded rumours I thought it best to issue a notice for general circulation, pointing out that if Mr Singlebury should turn out to have taken any unwise step, and if in consequence any inquiry should be necessary, we should be the first to hear about it from the police. I dictated this to our only permanent typist, who immediately said, oh, he would never do that. He would never cause any unpleasantness like bringing police into the place, he'd do all he could to avoid that. I did not encourage any further discussion, but I asked my wife, who is very used to social work, to call round at Singlebury's place in Clapham North and find out how he was. She did not have very much luck. The people in the cleaner's shop knew, or thought they knew, that he was away, but they had not been sufficiently interested to ask where he was going.

On Friday young Patel said he would be leaving, as the damp and the smell were affecting his health. The damp is certainly not drying out in this seasonably warm weather.

I also, as you know, received another invitation on the Friday, at very short notice, in fact no notice at all; I was told to come to your house in Suffolk Park Gardens that evening for drinks. I was not unduly elated, having been asked once before after I had done rather an awkward small job for you. In our Company, justice has not only not to be done, but it must be seen not to be done. The food was quite nice; it came from your Caterers Grade 3. I spent most of the evening talking to Ted Hollow, one of the area sales-managers. I did not expect to be introduced to your wife, nor was I. Towards the end of the evening you spoke to me for three minutes in the small room with a green marble floor and matching wallpaper leading to the ground-floor toilets. You asked me if everything was all right, to which I replied, all right for whom? You said that nobody's fault was nobody's funeral. I said that I had tried to give satisfaction. Passing on towards the washbasins, you told me with seeming cordiality to be careful and watch it when I had had mixed drinks.

I would describe my feeling at this point as resentment, and I cannot identify exactly the moment when it passed into unease. I do know that I was acutely uneasy as I crossed the hall and saw two of your domestic staff, a man and a woman, holding my coat, which I had left in the lobby, and apparently trying to brush it. Your domestic staff all appear to be of foreign extraction and I personally feel sorry for them and do not grudge them a smile at the oddly assorted guests. Then I saw they were not smiling at my coat but that they seemed to be examining their fingers and looking at me earnestly and silently, and the collar or shoulders of my coat was covered with blood. As I came up to them, although they were still both absolutely silent, the illusion or impression passed, and I put on my coat and left the house in what I hope was a normal manner.

I now come to the present time. The feeling of uneasiness which I have described as making itself felt in your house has not diminished during this past weekend, and partly to take my mind off it and partly for the reasons I have given, I decided to work overtime again tonight, Monday the 23rd. This was in spite of the fact that the damp smell had become almost a stench, as of something putrid, which must have affected my nerves to some extent, because when I went out to get something to eat at Dino's I left the lights on, both in my own office, and in the entrance hall. I mean that for the first time since I began to work for the Company I left them on deliberately. As I walked to the corner I looked back and saw the two solitary lights looking somewhat forlorn in contrast to the glitter of the Arab-American Mutual Loan Corporation opposite. After my meal I felt absolutely reluctant to go back to the building, and wished then that I had not given way to the impulse to leave the lights on, but since I had done so and they must be turned off, I had no choice.

As I stood in the empty hallway I could hear the numerous creakings, settlings and faint tickings of an old building, possibly associated with the plumbing system. The lifts for reasons of economy do not operate after 6.30 P.M., so I began to walk up the stairs. After one flight I felt a strong creeping tension in the nerves of the back such as any of us feel when there is danger from behind; one might say that the body was thinking for itself on these occasions. I did not look round, but simply continued upwards as rapidly as I could. At the third floor I paused, and could hear footsteps coming patiently up behind me. This was not a surprise; I had been expecting them all evening.

Just at the door of my own office, or rather of the cubby-hole, for I have to pass through that, I turned, and saw at the end of the dim corridor what I had also expected, Singlebury, advancing towards me with his unmistakable shuffling step. My first reaction was a kind of bewilderment as to why he, who had been such an excellent timekeeper, so regular day by day, should become a creature of the night. He was wearing the blue suit. This I could make out by its familiar outline, but it was not till he came halfway down the corridor towards me, and reached the patch of light falling through the window from the street, that I saw that he was not himself—I mean that his head was nodding or rather swivelling irregularly from side to side. It crossed my mind that Singlebury was drunk. I had never known him drunk or indeed seen him take anything to drink, even at the office Christmas party, but one cannot estimate the effect that trouble will have upon a man. I began to think what steps I should take in this situation. I turned on the light in his cubby-hole as I went through and waited at the entrance of my own office. As he appeared in the outer doorway I saw that I had not been correct about the reason for the odd movement of the head. The throat was cut from ear to ear so that the head was nearly severed from the shoulders. It was this which had given the impression of nodding, or rather, lolling. As he walked into his cubby-hole Singlebury raised both hands and tried to steady the head as though conscious that something was wrong. The eyes were thickly filmed over, as one sees in the carcasses in a butcher's shop.

I shut and locked my door, and not wishing to give way to nausea, or to lose all control of myself, I sat down at my desk. My work was waiting for me as I had left it—it was the file on the matter of the damp elimination—and, there not being anything else to do, I tried to look through it.

On the other side of the door I could hear Singlebury sit down also, and then try the drawers of the table, evidently looking for the "things" without which he could not start work. After the drawers had been tried, one after another, several times, there was almost total silence.

The present position is that I am locked in my office and would not, no matter what you offered me, indeed I could not, go out through the cubby-hole and pass what is sitting at the desk. The early cleaners will not be here for seven hours and forty-five minutes. I have passed the time so far as best I could in writing this report. One consideration strikes me. If what I have next door is a visitant which should not be walking but buried in the earth, then its wound cannot bleed, and there will be no stream of blood moving slowly under the whole width of the communicating door. However I am sitting at the moment with my back to the door, so that, without turning round, I have no means of telling whether it has done so or not.   1975

JOHN CHEEVER

TORCH SONG

After Jack Lorey had known Joan Harris in New York for a few years, he began to think of her as the Widow. She always wore black, and he was always given the feeling, by a curious disorder in her apartment, that the undertakers had just left. This impression did not stem from malice on his part, for he was fond of Joan. They came from the same city in Ohio and had reached New York at about the same time in the middle thirties. They were the same age, and during their first summer in the city they used to meet after work and drink Martinis in places like the Brevoort and Charles', and have dinner and play checkers at the Lafayette.

Joan went to a school for models when she settled in the city, but it turned out that she photographed badly, so after spending six weeks learning how to walk with a book on her head she got a job as a hostess in a Longchamps. For the rest of the summer she stood by the hatrack, bathed in an intense pink light and the string music of heartbreak, swinging her mane of dark hair and her black skirt as she moved forward to greet the customers. She was then a big, handsome girl with a wonderful voice, and her face, her whole presence, always seemed infused with a gentle and healthy pleasure at her surroundings, whatever they were. She was innocently and incorrigibly convivial, and would get out of bed and dress at three in the morning if someone called her and asked her to come out for a drink, as Jack often did. In the fall, she got some kind of freshman executive job in a department store. They saw less and less of each other and then for quite a while stopped seeing each other altogether. Jack was living with a girl he had met at a party, and it never occurred to him to wonder what had become of Joan.

Jack's girl had some friends in Pennsylvania, and in the spring and summer of his second year in town he often went there with her for weekends. All of this—the shared apartment in the Village, the illicit relationship, the Friday-night train to a country house—was what he had imagined life in New York to be, and he was intensely happy. He was returning to New York with his girl one Sunday night on the Lehigh line. It was one of those trains that move slowly across the face of New Jersey, bringing back to the city hundreds of people, like the victims of an immense and strenuous picnic, whose faces are blazing and whose muscles are lame. Jack and his girl, like most of the other passengers, were overburdened with vegetables and flowers. When the train stopped in Pennsylvania Station, they moved with the crowd along the platform, toward the escalator. As they were passing the wide, lighted windows of the diner, Jack turned his head and saw Joan. It was the first time he had seen her since Thanksgiving, or since Christmas. He couldn't remember.

Joan was with a man who had obviously passed out. His head was in his arms on the table, and an overturned highball glass was near one of his elbows. Joan was shaking his shoulders gently and speaking to him. She seemed to be vaguely troubled, vaguely amused. The waiters had cleared off all the other tables and were standing around Joan, waiting for her to resurrect her escort. It troubled Jack to see in these straits a girl who reminded him of the trees and the lawns of his home town, but there was nothing he could do to help. Joan continued to shake the man's shoulders, and the crowd pressed Jack past one after another of the diner's windows, past the malodorous kitchen, and up the escalator.

He saw Joan again, later that summer, when he was having dinner in a Village restaurant. He was with a new girl, a Southerner. There were many Southern girls in the city that year. Jack and his belle had wandered into the restaurant because it was convenient, but the food was terrible and the place was lighted with candles. Halfway through dinner, Jack noticed Joan on the other side of the room, and when he had finished eating, he crossed the room and spoke to her. She was with a tall man who was wearing a monocle. He stood, bowed stiffly from the waist, and said to Jack, "We are very pleased to meet you." Then he excused himself and headed for the toilet. "He's a count, he's a Swedish count," Joan said. "He's on the radio, Friday afternoons at four-fifteen. Isn't it exciting?" She seemed to be delighted with the count and the terrible restaurant.

Sometime the next winter, Jack moved from the Village to an apartment in the East Thirties. He was crossing Park Avenue one cold morning on his way to the office when he noticed, in the crowd, a woman he had met a few times at Joan's apartment. He spoke to her and asked about his friend. "Haven't you heard?" she said. She pulled a long face. "Perhaps I'd better tell you. Perhaps you can help." She and Jack had breakfast in a drugstore on Madison Avenue and she unburdened herself of the story.

The count had a program called "The Songs of the Fiords," or something like that, and he sang Swedish folk songs. Everyone suspected him of being a fake, but that didn't bother Joan. He had met her at a party and, sensing a soft touch, had moved in with her the following night. About a week later, he complained of pains in his back and said he must have some morphine. Then he needed morphine all the time. If he didn't get morphine, he was abusive and violent. Joan began to deal with those doctors and druggists who peddle dope, and when they wouldn't supply her, she went to the bottom of the city. Her friends were afraid she would be found some morning stuffed in a drain. She got pregnant. She had an abortion. The count left her and moved to a flea bag near Times Square, but she was so impressed by then with his helplessness, so afraid that he would die without her, that she followed him there and shared his room and continued to buy his narcotics. He abandoned her again, and Joan waited a week for him to return before she went back to her place and her friends in the Village.

It shocked Jack to think of the innocent girl from Ohio having lived with a brutal dope addict and traded with criminals, and when he got to his office that morning, he telephoned her and made a date for dinner that night. He met her at Charles'. When she came into the bar, she seemed as wholesome and calm as ever. Her voice was sweet, and re-minded him of elms, of lawns, of those glass arrangements that used to be hung from porch ceilings to tinkle in the summer wind. She told him about the count. She spoke of him charitably and with no trace of bitterness, as if her voice, her disposition, were incapable of registering anything beyond simple affection and pleasure. Her walk, when she moved ahead of him toward their table, was light and graceful. She ate a large dinner and talked enthusiastically about her job. They went to a movie and said goodbye in front of her apartment house.

That winter, Jack met a girl he decided to marry. Their engagement was announced in January and they planned to marry in July. In the spring, he received, in his office mail, an invitation to cocktails at Joan's. It was for a Saturday when his fiancée was going to Massachusetts to visit her parents, and when the time came and he had nothing better to do, he took a bus to the Village. Joan had the same apartment. It was a walk-up. You rang the bell above the mailbox in the vestibule and were answered with a death rattle in the lock. Joan lived on the third floor. Her calling card was in a slot in the mailbox, and above her name was written the name Hugh Bascomb.

Jack climbed the two flights of carpeted stairs, and when he reached Joan's apartment, she was standing by the open door in a black dress. After she greeted Jack, she took his arm and guided him across the room. "I want you to meet Hugh, Jack," she said.

Hugh was a big man with a red face and pale-blue eyes. His manner was courtly and his eyes were inflamed with drink. Jack talked with him for a little while and then went over to speak to someone he knew, who was standing by the mantelpiece. He noticed then, for the first time, the indescribable disorder of Joan's apartment. The books were in their shelves and the furniture was reasonably good, but the place was all wrong, somehow. It was as if things had been put in place without thought or real interest, and for the first time, too, he had the impression that there had been a death there recently.

As Jack moved around the room, he felt that he had met the ten or twelve guests at other parties. There was a woman executive with a fancy hat, a man who could imitate Roosevelt, a grim couple whose play was in rehearsal, and a newspaperman who kept turning on the radio for news of the Spanish Civil War. Jack drank Martinis and talked with the woman in the fancy hat. He looked out of the window at the back yards and the ailanthus trees and heard, in the distance, thunder exploding off the cliffs of the Hudson.

Hugh Bascomb got very drunk. He began to spill liquor, as if drinking, for him, were a kind of jolly slaughter and he enjoyed the bloodshed and the mess. He spilled whiskey from a bottle. He spilled a drink on his shirt and then tipped over someone else's drink. The party was not quiet, but Hugh's hoarse voice began to dominate the others. He attacked a photographer who was sitting in a corner explaining camera techniques to a homely woman. "What did you come to the party for if all you wanted to do was to sit there and stare at your shoes?" Hugh shouted. "What did you come for? Why don't you stay at home?"

The photographer didn't know what to say. He was not staring at his shoes. Joan moved lightly to Hugh's side. "Please don't get into a fight now, darling," she said. "Not this afternoon."

"Shut up," he said. "Let me alone. Mind your own business." He lost his balance, and in struggling to steady himself he tipped over a lamp.

"Oh, your lovely lamp, Joan," a woman sighed.

"Lamps!" Hugh roared. He threw his arms into the air and worked them around his head as if he were bludgeoning himself. "Lamps. Glasses. Cigarette boxes. Dishes. They're killing me. They're killing me, for Christ's sake. Let's all go up to the mountains and hunt and fish and live like men, for Christ's sake."

People were scattering as if a rain had begun to fall in the room. It had, as a matter of fact, begun to rain outside. Someone offered Jack a ride uptown, and he jumped at the chance. Joan stood at the door, saying goodbye to her routed friends. Her voice remained soft, and her manner, unlike that of those Christian women who in the face of disaster can summon new and formidable sources of composure, seemed genuinely simple. She appeared to be oblivious of the raging drunk at her back, who was pacing up and down, grinding glass into the rug, and haranguing one of the survivors of the party with a story of how he, Hugh, had once gone without food for three weeks.

In July, Jack was married in an orchard in Duxbury, and he and his wife went to West Chop for a few weeks. When they returned to town, their apartment was cluttered with presents, including a dozen after-dinner coffee cups from Joan. His wife sent her the required note, but they did nothing else.

Late in the summer, Joan telephoned Jack at his office and asked if he wouldn't bring his wife to see her; she named an evening the following week. He felt guilty about not having called her, and accepted the invitation. This made his wife angry. She was an ambitious girl who liked a social life that offered rewards, and she went unwillingly to Joan's Village apartment with him.

Written above Joan's name on the mailbox was the name Franz Denzel. Jack and his wife climbed the stairs and were met by Joan at the open door. They went into her apartment and found themselves among a group of people for whom Jack, at least, was unable to find any bearings.

Franz Denzel was a middle-aged German. His face was pinched with bitterness or illness. He greeted Jack and his wife with that elaborate and clever politeness that is intended to make guests feel that they have come too early or too late. He insisted sharply upon Jack's sitting in the chair in which he himself had been sitting, and then went and sat on a radiator. There were five other Germans sitting around the room, drinking coffee. In a corner was another American couple, who looked uncomfortable. Joan passed Jack and his wife small cups of coffee with whipped cream. "These cups belonged to Franz's mother," she said. "Aren't they lovely? They were the only things he took from Germany when he escaped from the Nazis."

Franz turned to Jack and said, "Perhaps you will give us your opinion on the American educational system. That is what we were discussing when you arrived."

Before Jack could speak, one of the German guests opened an attack on the American educational system. The other Germans joined in, and went on from there to describe every vulgarity that had impressed them in American life and to contrast German and American culture generally. Where, they asked one another passionately, could you find in America anything like the Mitropa dining cars, the Black Forest, the pictures in Munich, the music in Bayreuth? Franz and his friends began speaking in German. Neither Jack nor his wife nor Joan could understand German, and the other American couple had not opened their mouths since they were introduced. Joan went happily around the room, filling everyone's cup with coffee, as if the music of a foreign language were enough to make an evening for her.

Jack drank five cups of coffee. He was desperately uncomfortable. Joan went into the kitchen while the Germans were laughing at their German jokes, and he hoped she would return with some drinks, but when she came back, it was with a tray of ice cream and mulberries.

"Isn't this pleasant?" Franz asked, speaking in English again.

Joan collected the coffee cups, and as she was about to take them back to the kitchen, Franz stopped her.

"Isn't one of those cups chipped?"

"No, darling," Joan said. "I never let the maid touch them. I wash them myself."

"What's that?" he asked, pointing at the rim of one of the cups.

"That's the cup that's always been chipped, darling. It was chipped when you unpacked it. You noticed it then."

"These things were perfect when they arrived in this country," he said.

Joan went into the kitchen and he followed her.

Jack tried to make conversation with the Germans. From the kitchen there was the sound of a blow and a cry. Franz returned and began to eat his mulberries greedily. Joan came back with her dish of ice cream. Her voice was gentle. Her tears, if she had been crying, had dried as quickly as the tears of a child. Jack and his wife finished their ice cream and made their escape. The wasted and unnerving evening enraged Jack's wife, and he supposed that he would never see Joan again.

Jack's wife got pregnant early in the fall, and she seized on all the prerogatives of an expectant mother. She took long naps, ate canned peaches in the middle of the night, and talked about the rudimentary kidney. She chose to see only other couples who were expecting children, and the parties that she and Jack gave were temperate. The baby, a boy, was born in May, and Jack was very proud and happy. The first party he and his wife went to after her convalescence was the wedding of a girl whose family Jack had known in Ohio.

The wedding was at St. James's, and afterward there was a big reception at the River Club. There was an orchestra dressed like Hungarians, and a lot of champagne and Scotch. Toward the end of the afternoon, Jack was walking down a dim corridor when he heard Joan's voice. "Please don't, darling," she was saying. "You'll break my arm. *Please* don't, darling." She was being pressed against the wall by a man who seemed to be twisting her arm. As soon as they saw Jack, the struggle stopped. All three of them were intensely embarrassed. Joan's face was wet and she made an effort to smile through her tears at Jack. He said hello and went on without stopping. When he returned, she and the man had disappeared.

When Jack's son was less than two years old, his wife flew with the baby to Nevada to get a divorce. Jack gave her the apartment and all its furnishings and took a room in a hotel near Grand Central. His wife got her decree in due course, and the story was in the newspapers. Jack had a telephone call from Joan a few days later.

"I'm awfully sorry to hear about your divorce, Jack," she said. "She seemed like *such* a nice girl. But that wasn't what I called you about. I want your help, and I wondered if you could come down to my place tonight around six. It's something I don't want to talk about over the phone."

He went obediently to the Village that night and climbed the stairs. Her apartment was a mess. The pictures and the curtains were down and the books were in boxes. "You moving, Joan?" he asked.

"That's what I wanted to see you about, Jack. First, I'll give you a drink." She made two Old-Fashioneds. "I'm being evicted, Jack," she said. "I'm being evicted because I'm an immoral woman. The couple who have the apartment downstairs—they're charming people, I've always thought—have told the real-estate agent that I'm a drunk and a prostitute and all kinds of things. Isn't that fantastic? This real-estate agent has always been so nice to me that I didn't think he'd believe them, but he's canceled my lease, and if I make any trouble, he's threatened to take the matter up with the store, and I don't want to lose my job. This nice real-estate agent won't even talk with me any more. When I go over to the office, the receptionist leers at me as if I were some kind of dreadful woman. Of course, there have been a lot of men here and we sometimes are noisy, but I can't be expected to go to bed at ten every night. Can I? Well, the agent who manages this building has apparently told all the other agents in the neighborhood that I'm an immoral and drunken woman, and none of them will give me an apartment. I went in to talk with one man—he seemed to be such a nice old gentleman—and he made me an indecent proposal. Isn't it fantastic? I have to be out of here on Thursday and I'm literally being turned out into the street."

Joan seemed as serene and innocent as ever while she described this scourge of agents and neighbors. Jack listened carefully for some sign of indignation or bitterness or even urgency in her recital, but there was none. He was reminded of a torch song, of one of those forlorn and touching ballads that had been sung neither for him nor for her but for their older brothers and sisters by Marion Harris. Joan seemed to be singing her wrongs.

"They've made my life miserable," she went on quietly. "If I keep the radio on after ten o'clock, they telephone the agent in the morning and tell him I had some kind of orgy here. One night when Philip—I don't think you've met Philip; he's in the Royal Air Force; he's gone back to England—one night when Philip and some other people were here, they called the police. The police came bursting in the door and talked to me as if I were I don't know what and then looked in the bedroom. If they think there's a man up here after midnight, they call me on the telephone and say all kinds of disgusting things. Of course, I can put my furniture into storage and go to a hotel, I guess. I guess a hotel will take a woman with my kind of reputation, but I thought perhaps you might know of an apartment. I thought—"

It angered Jack to think of this big, splendid girl's being persecuted by her neighbors, and he said he would do what he could. He asked her to have dinner with him, but she said she was busy.

Having nothing better to do, Jack decided to walk uptown to his hotel. It was a hot night. The sky was overcast. On his way, he saw a parade in a dark side street off Broadway near Madison Square. All the buildings in the neighborhood were dark. It was so dark that he could not see the placards the marchers carried until he came to a street light. Their signs urged the entry of the United States into the war, and each platoon represented a nation that had been subjugated by the Axis powers. They marched up Broadway, as he watched, to no music, to no sound but their own steps on the rough cobbles. It was for the most part an army of elderly men and women—Poles, Norwegians, Danes, Jews, Chinese. A few idle people like himself lined the sidewalks, and the marchers passed between them with all the self-consciousness of enemy prisoners. There were children among them dressed in the costumes in which they had, for the newsreels, presented the Mayor with a package of tea, a petition, a protest, a constitution, a check, or a pair of tickets. They hobbled through the darkness of the loft neighborhood like a mortified and destroyed people, toward Greeley Square.

In the morning, Jack put the problem of finding an apartment for Joan up to his secretary. She started phoning real-estate agents, and by afternoon she had found a couple of available apartments in the West Twenties. Joan called Jack the next day to say that she had taken one of the apartments and to thank him.

Jack didn't see Joan again until the following summer. It was a Sunday evening; he had left a cocktail party in a Washington Square apartment and had decided to walk a few blocks up Fifth Avenue before he took a bus. As he was passing the Brevoort, Joan called to him. She was with a man at one of the tables on the sidewalk. She looked cool and fresh, and the man appeared to be respectable. His name, it turned out, was Pete

Bristol. He invited Jack to sit down and join in a celebration. Germany had invaded Russia that weekend, and Joan and Pete were drinking champagne to celebrate Russia's changed position in the war. The three of them drank champagne until it got dark. They had dinner and drank champagne with their dinner. They drank more champagne afterward and then went over to the Lafayette and then to two or three other places. Joan had always been tireless in her gentle way. She hated to see the night end, and it was after three o'clock when Jack stumbled into his apartment. The following morning he woke up haggard and sick, and with no recollection of the last hour or so of the previous evening. His suit was soiled and he had lost his hat. He didn't get to his office until eleven. Joan had already called him twice, and she called him again soon after he got in. There was no hoarseness at all in her voice. She said that she had to see him, and he agreed to meet her for lunch in a seafood restaurant in the Fifties.

He was standing at the bar when she breezed in, looking as though she had taken no part in that calamitous night. The advice she wanted concerned selling her jewelry. Her grandmother had left her some jewelry, and she wanted to raise money on it but didn't know where to go. She took some rings and bracelets out of her purse and showed them to Jack. He said that he didn't know anything about jewelry but that he could lend her some money. "Oh, I couldn't borrow money from you, Jack," she said. "You see, I want to get the money for Pete. I want to help him. He wants to open an advertising agency, and he needs quite a lot to begin with." Jack didn't press her to accept his offer of a loan after that, and the project wasn't mentioned again during lunch.

He next heard about Joan from a young doctor who was a friend of theirs. "Have you seen Joan recently?" the doctor asked Jack one evening when they were having dinner together. He said no. "I gave her a checkup last week," the doctor said, "and while she's been through enough to kill the average mortal—and you'll never know what she's been through—she still has the constitution of a virtuous and healthy woman. Did you hear about the last one? She sold her jewelry to put him into some kind of business, and as soon as he got the money, he left her for another girl, who had a car—a convertible."

Jack was drafted into the Army in the spring of 1942. He was kept at Fort Dix for nearly a month, and during this time he came to New York in the evening whenever he could get permission. Those nights had for him the intense keenness of a reprieve, a sensation that was heightened by the fact that on the train in from Trenton women would often press upon him dog-eared copies of *Life* and half-eaten boxes of candy, as though the brown clothes he wore were surely cerements. He telephoned Joan from Pennsylvania Station one night. "Come right over,

Jack," she said. "Come right over. I want you to meet Ralph."

She was living in that place in the West Twenties that Jack had found
for her. The neighborhood was a slum. Ash cans stood in front of her
house, and an old woman was there picking out bits of refuse and gar-
bage and stuffing them into a perambulator. The house in which Joan's
apartment was located was shabby, but the apartment itself seemed
familiar. The furniture was the same. Joan was the same big, easygoing
girl. "I'm so glad you called me," she said. "It's so good to see you. I'll
make you a drink. I was having one myself. Ralph ought to be here by
now. He promised to take me to dinner." Jack offered to take her to
Cavanagh's, but she said that Ralph might come while she was out. "If
he doesn't come by nine, I'm going to make myself a sandwich. I'm not
really hungry."

Jack talked about the Army. She talked about the store. She had been
working in the same place for—how long was it? He didn't know. He
had never seen her at her desk and he couldn't imagine what she did.
"I'm terribly sorry Ralph isn't here," she said. "I'm sure you'd like him.
He's not a young man. He's a heart specialist who loves to play the
viola." She turned on some lights, for the summer sky had got dark. "He
had this dreadful wife on Riverside Drive and four ungrateful children.
He—"

The noise of an air-raid siren, lugubrious and seeming to spring from
pain, as if all the misery and indecision in the city had been given a voice,
cut her off. Other sirens, in distant neighborhoods, sounded, until the
dark air was full of their noise. "Let me fix you another drink before I
have to turn out the lights," Joan said, and took his glass. She brought
the drink back to him and snapped off the lights. They went to the
windows, and, as children watch a thunderstorm, they watched the city
darken. All the lights nearby went out but one. Air-raid wardens had
begun to sound their whistles in the street. From a distant yard came a
hoarse shriek of anger. "Put out your lights, you Fascists!" a woman
screamed. "Put out your lights, you Nazi Fascist Germans. Turn out
your lights. Turn out your lights." The last light went off. They went
away from the window and sat in the lightless room.

In the darkness, Joan began to talk about her departed lovers, and
from what she said Jack gathered that they had all had a hard time. Nils,
the suspect count, was dead. Hugh Bascomb, the drunk, had joined the
Merchant Marine and was missing in the North Atlantic. Franz, the
German, had taken poison the night the Nazis bombed Warsaw. "We
listened to the news on the radio," Joan said, "and then he went back to
his hotel and took poison. The maid found him dead in the bathroom
the next morning." When Jack asked her about the one who was going
to open an advertising agency, she seemed at first to have forgotten him.

"Oh, Pete," she said after a pause. "Well, he was always very sick, you know. He was supposed to go to Saranac, but he kept putting it off and putting it off and—" She stopped talking when she heard steps on the stairs, hoping, he supposed, that it was Ralph, but whoever it was turned at the landing and continued to the top of the house. "I wish Ralph would come," she said, with a sigh. "I want you to meet him." Jack asked her again to go out, but she refused, and when the all-clear sounded, he said goodbye.

Jack was shipped from Dix to an infantry training camp in the Carolinas and from there to an infantry division stationed in Georgia. He had been in Georgia three months when he married a girl from the Augusta boarding-house aristocracy. A year or so later, he crossed the continent in a day coach and thought sententiously that the last he might see of the country he loved was the desert towns like Barstow, that the last he might hear of it was the ringing of the trolleys on the Bay Bridge. He was sent into the Pacific and returned to the United States twenty months later, uninjured and apparently unchanged. As soon as he received his furlough, he went to Augusta. He presented his wife with the souvenirs he had brought from the islands, quarreled violently with her and all her family, and, after making arrangements for her to get an Arkansas divorce, left for New York.

Jack was discharged from the Army at a camp in the East a few months later. He took a vacation and then went back to the job he had left in 1942. He seemed to have picked up his life at approximately the moment when it had been interrupted by the war. In time, everything came to look and feel the same. He saw most of his old friends. Only two of the men he knew had been killed in the war. He didn't call Joan, but he met her one winter afternoon on a crosstown bus.

Her fresh face, her black clothes, and her soft voice instantly destroyed the sense—if he had ever had such a sense—that anything had changed or intervened since their last meeting, three or four years ago. She asked him up for cocktails and he went to her apartment the next Saturday afternoon. Her room and her guests reminded him of the parties she had given when she had first come to New York. There was a woman with a fancy hat, an elderly doctor, and a man who stayed close to the radio, listening for news from the Balkans. Jack wondered which of the men belonged to Joan and decided on an Englishman who kept coughing into a handkerchief that he pulled out of his sleeve. Jack was right. "Isn't Stephen brilliant?" Joan asked him a little later, when they were alone in a corner. "He knows more about the Polynesians than anyone else in the world."

Jack had returned not only to his old job but to his old salary. Since living costs had doubled and since he was paying alimony to two wives, he had to draw on his savings. He took another job, which promised more money, but it didn't last long and he found himself out of work. This didn't bother him at all. He still had money in the bank, and anyhow it was easy to borrow from friends. His indifference was the consequence not of lassitude or despair but rather of an excess of hope. He had the feeling that he had only recently come to New York from Ohio. The sense that he was very young and that the best years of his life still lay before him was an illusion that he could not seem to escape. There was all the time in the world. He was living in hotels then, moving from one to another every five days.

In the spring, Jack moved to a furnished room in the badlands west of Central Park. He was running out of money. Then, when he began to feel that a job was a desperate necessity, he got sick. At first, he seemed to have only a bad cold, but he was unable to shake it and he began to run a fever and to cough blood. The fever kept him drowsy most of the time, but he roused himself occasionally and went out to a cafeteria for a meal. He felt sure that none of his friends knew where he was, and he was glad of this. He hadn't counted on Joan.

Late one morning, he heard her speaking in the hall with his landlady. A few moments later, she knocked on his door. He was lying on the bed in a pair of pants and a soiled pajama top, and he didn't answer. She knocked again and walked in. "I've been looking everywhere for you, Jack," she said. She spoke softly. "When I found out that you were in a place like this I thought you must be broke or sick. I stopped at the bank and got some money, in case you're broke. I've brought you some Scotch. I thought a little drink wouldn't do you any harm. Want a little drink?"

Joan's dress was black. Her voice was low and serene. She sat in a chair beside his bed as if she had been coming there every day to nurse him. Her features had coarsened, he thought, but there were still very few lines in her face. She was heavier. She was nearly fat. She was wearing black cotton gloves. She got two glasses and poured Scotch into them. He drank his whiskey greedily. "I didn't get to bed until three last night," she said. Her voice had once before reminded him of a gentle and despairing song, but now, perhaps because he was sick, her mildness, the mourning she wore, her stealthy grace, made him uneasy. "It was one of those nights," she said. "We went to the theater. Afterward, someone asked us up to his place. I don't know who he was. It was one of those places. They're so strange. There were some meat-eating plants and a collection of Chinese snuff bottles. Why do people collect Chinese snuff bottles? We all autographed a lampshade, as I remember, but I can't remember much."

Jack tried to sit up in bed, as if there were some need to defend himself, and then fell back again, against the pillows. "How did you find me, Joan?" he asked.

"It was simple," she said. "I called that hotel. The one you were staying in. They gave me this address. My secretary got the telephone number. Have another little drink."

"You know, you've never come to a place of mine before—never," he said. "Why did you come now?"

"Why did I come, darling?" she asked. "What a question! I've known you for thirty years. You're the oldest friend I have in New York. Remember that night in the Village when it snowed and we stayed up until morning and drank whiskey sours for breakfast? That doesn't seem like twelve years ago. And that night—"

"I don't like to have you see me in a place like this," he said earnestly. He touched his face and felt his beard.

"And all the people who used to imitate Roosevelt," she said, as if she had not heard him, as if she were deaf. "And that place on Staten Island where we all used to go for dinner when Henry had a car. Poor Henry. He bought a place in Connecticut and went out there by himself one weekend. He fell asleep with a lighted cigarette and the house, the barn, everything burned. Ethel took the children out to California." She poured more Scotch into his glass and handed it to him. She lighted a cigarette and put it between his lips. The intimacy of this gesture, which made it seem not only as if he were deathly ill but as if he were her lover, troubled him.

"As soon as I'm better," he said, "I'll take a room at a good hotel. I'll call you then. It was nice of you to come."

"Oh, don't be ashamed of this room, Jack," she said. "Rooms never bother me. It doesn't seem to matter to me where I am. Stanley had a filthy room in Chelsea. At least, other people told me it was filthy. I never noticed it. Rats used to eat the food I brought him. He used to have to hang the food from the ceiling, from the light chain."

"I'll call you as soon as I'm better," Jack said. "I think I can sleep now if I'm left alone. I seem to need a lot of sleep."

"You really *are* sick, darling," she said. "You must have a fever." She sat on the edge of his bed and put a hand on his forehead.

"How is that Englishman, Joan?" he asked. "Do you still see him?"

"What Englishman?" she said.

"You know. I met him at your house. He kept a handkerchief up his sleeve. He coughed all the time. You know the one I mean."

"You must be thinking of someone else," she said. "I haven't had an Englishman at my place since the war. Of course, I can't remember everyone." She turned and, taking one of his hands, linked her fingers in his.

"He's dead, isn't he?" Jack said. "That Englishman's dead." He pushed her off the bed, and got up himself. "Get out," he said.

"You're sick, darling," she said. "I can't leave you alone here."

"Get out," he said again, and when she didn't move, he shouted, "What kind of an obscenity are you that you can smell sickness and death the way you do?"

"You poor darling."

"Does it make you feel young to watch the dying?" he shouted. "Is that the lewdness that keeps you young? Is that why you dress like a crow? Oh, I know there's nothing I can say that will hurt you. I know there's nothing filthy or corrupt or depraved or brutish or base that the others haven't tried, but this time you're wrong. I'm not ready. My life isn't ending. My life's beginning. There are wonderful years ahead of me. There are, there are wonderful, wonderful, wonderful years ahead of me, and when they're over, when it's time, then I'll call you. Then, as an old friend, I'll call you and give you whatever dirty pleasure you take in watching the dying, but until then, you and your ugly and misshapen forms will leave me alone."

She finished her drink and looked at her watch. "I guess I'd better show up at the office," she said. "I'll see you later. I'll come back tonight. You'll feel better then, you poor darling." She closed the door after her, and he heard her light step on the stairs.

Jack emptied the whiskey bottle into the sink. He began to dress. He stuffed his dirty clothes into a bag. He was trembling and crying with sickness and fear. He could see the blue sky from his window, and in his fear it seemed miraculous that the sky should be blue, that the white clouds should remind him of snow, that from the sidewalk he could hear the shrill voices of children shrieking, "I'm the king of the mountain, I'm the king of the mountain, I'm the king of the mountain." He emptied the ashtray containing his nail parings and cigarette butts into the toilet, and swept the floor with a shirt, so that there would be no trace of his life, of his body, when that lewd and searching shape of death came there to find him in the evening.   1947

The Music Teacher

It all seemed to have been arranged—Seton sensed this when he opened the door of his house that evening and walked down the hall into the living room. It all seemed to have been set with as much care as, in an earlier period of his life, he had known girls to devote to the flowers, the candles, and the records for the phonograph. This scene was not arranged for his pleasure, nor was it arranged for anything so simple as reproach. "Hello," he said loudly and cheerfully. Sobbing and moaning rent the air. In the middle of the small living room stood an ironing board. One of his shirts was draped over it, and his wife, Jessica, wiped away a tear as she ironed. Near the piano stood Jocelin, the baby. Jocelin was howling. Sitting in a chair near her little sister was Millicent, his oldest daughter, sobbing and holding in her hands the pieces of a broken doll. Phyllis, the middle child, was on her hands and knees, prying the stuffing out of an armchair with a beer-can opener. Clouds of smoke from what smelled like a burning leg of lamb drifted out of the open kitchen door into the living room.

He could not believe that they had passed the day in such disorder. It must all have been planned, arranged—including the conflagration in the oven—for the moment of his homecoming. He even thought he saw a look of inner tranquility on his wife's harassed face as she glanced around the room and admired the effectiveness of the scene. He felt routed but not despairing and, standing on the threshold, he made a quick estimate of his remaining forces and settled on a kiss as his first move; but as he approached the ironing board his wife waved him away, saying, "Don't come near me. You'll catch my cold. I have a *terrible* cold." He then got Phyllis away from the armchair, promised to mend Millicent's doll, and carried the baby into the bathroom and changed her diapers. From the kitchen came loud oaths as Jessica fought her way through the clouds of smoke and took the meat out of the stove.

It was burned. So was almost everything else—the rolls, the potatoes, and the frozen apple tart. There were cinders in Seton's mouth and a great heaviness in his heart as he looked past the plates of spoiled food to Jessica's face, once gifted with wit and passion but now dark and lost to him. After supper he helped with the dishes and read to the children, and the purity of their interest in what he read and did, the power of trust in their love, seemed to make the taste of burned meat sad as well as bitter. The smell of smoke stayed in the air long after everyone but Seton had gone to bed. He sat alone in the living room, recounting his problems to himself. He had been married ten years, and Jessica still seemed to him to possess an unusual loveliness of person and nature, but in the last year or two something grave and mysterious had come between them. The burned roast was not unusual; it was routine. She burned the chops, she burned the hamburgers, she even burned the turkey at Thanksgiving, and she seemed to burn the food deliberately, as if it was a means of expressing her resentment toward him. It was not rebellion against drudgery. Cleaning women and mechanical appliances—the lightening of her burden—made no difference. It was not, he thought, even resentment. It was like some subterranean sea change, some sexual campaign or revolution stirring—unknown perhaps to her—beneath the shining and common appearance of things.

He did not want to leave Jessica, but how much longer could he cope with the tearful children, the dark looks, the smoky and chaotic house? It was not discord that he resisted but a threat to the most healthy and precious part of his self-esteem. To be long-suffering under the circumstances seemed to him indecent. What could he do? Change, motion, openings seemed to be what he and Jessica needed, and it was perhaps an indication of his limitations that, in trying to devise some way of extending his marriage, the only thing he could think of was to take Jessica to dinner in a restaurant where they had often gone ten years ago, when they were lovers. But even this, he knew, would not be simple. A point-blank invitation would only get him a point-blank, bitter refusal. He would have to be wary. He would have to surprise and disarm her.

This was in the early autumn. The days were clear. The yellow leaves were falling everywhere. From all the windows of the house and through the glass panes in the front door, one saw them coming down. Seton waited for two or three days. He waited for an unusually fine day, and then he called Jessica from his office, in the middle of the morning. There was a cleaning woman at the house, he knew. Millicent and Phyllis would be in school, and Jocelin would be asleep. Jessica would not have too much to do. She might even be idle and reflective. He called her and told her—he did not invite her—to come to town and to have dinner with him. She hesitated; she said it would be difficult to find someone to stay with the children; and finally she succumbed. He even seemed to hear in her voice when she agreed to come a trace of the gentle tenderness he adored.

It was a year since they had done anything like dining together in a restaurant, and when he left his office that night and turned away from the direction of the station he was conscious of the mountainous and deadening accrual of habit that burdened their relationship. Too many circles had been drawn around his life, he thought; but how easy it was to overstep them. The restaurant where he went to wait for her was modest and good—polished, starched, smelling of fresh bread and sauces, and in a charming state of readiness when he reached it that evening. The hat-check girl remembered him, and he remembered the exuberance with which he had come down the flight of steps into the bar when he was younger. How wonderful everything smelled. The bartender had just come on duty, freshly shaved and in a white coat. Everything seemed cordial and ceremonious. Every surface was shining, and the light that fell onto his shoulders was the light that had fallen there ten years ago. When the headwaiter stopped to say good evening, Seton asked to have a bottle of wine—*their* wine—iced. The door into the night was the door he used to watch in order to see Jessica come in with snow in her hair, to see her come in with a new dress and new shoes, to see her come in with good news, worries, apologies for being late. He could remember the way she glanced at the bar to see if he was there, the way she stopped to speak with the hat-check girl, and then lightly crossed the floor to put her hand in his and to join lightly and gracefully in his pleasure for the rest of the night.

Then he heard a child crying. He turned toward the door in time to see Jessica enter. She carried the crying baby against her shoulder. Phyllis and Millicent followed in their worn snowsuits. It was still early in the evening, and the restaurant was not crowded. This entrance, this tableau, was not as spectacular as it would have been an hour later, but it was—for Seton, at least—powerful enough. As Jessica stood in the doorway with a sobbing child in her arms and one on each side of her, the sense was not that she had come to meet her husband and, through some breakdown in arrangements, had been forced to bring the children; the sense was that she had come to make a public accusation of the man who had wronged her. She did not point her finger at him, but the significance of the group was dramatic and accusatory.

Seton went to them at once. It was not the kind of restaurant one brought children to, but the hat-check girl was kindly and helped Millicent and Phyllis out of their snowsuits. Seton took Jocelin in his arms, and she stopped crying.

"The baby-sitter couldn't come," Jessica said, but she hardly met his eyes, and she turned away when he kissed her. They were taken to a table at the back of the place. Jocelin upset a bowl of olives, and the meal was as gloomy and chaotic as the burned supper at home. The children fell asleep on the drive back, and Seton could see that he had failed—failed or been outwitted again. He wondered, for the first time, if he was dealing not with the shadows and mysteries of Jessica's sex but with plain fractiousness.

He tried again, along the same lines; he asked the Thompsons for cocktails one Saturday afternoon. He could tell that they didn't want to come. They were going to the Carmignoles'—everyone was going to the Carmignoles'—and it was a year or more since the Setons had entertained; their house had suffered a kind of social infamy. The Thompsons came only out of friendship, and they came only for one drink. They were an attractive couple, and Jack Thompson seemed to enjoy a tender mastery over his wife that Seton envied. He had told Jessica the Thompsons were coming. She had said nothing. She was not in the living room when they arrived, but she appeared a few minutes later, carrying a laundry basket full of wash, and when Seton asked her if she wouldn't have a drink, she said that she didn't have time. The Thompsons could see that he was in trouble, but they could not stay to help him—they would be late at the Carmignoles'. But when Lucy Thompson had got into the car, Jack came back to the door and spoke to Seton so forcefully—so clearly out of friendship and sympathy—that Seton hung on his words. He said that he could see what was going on, and that Seton should have a hobby—a specific hobby: he should take piano lessons. There was a lady named Miss Deming and he should see her. She would help. Then he waved goodbye and went down to his car. This advice did not seem in any way strange to Seton. He was desperate and tired, and where was the sense in life? When he returned to the living room, Phyllis was attacking the chair again with the beer-can opener. Her excuse was that she had lost a quarter in the upholstery. Jocelin and Millicent were crying. Jessica had begun to burn the evening meal.

They had burned veal on Sunday, burned meat loaf on Monday, and on Tuesday the meat was so burned that Seton couldn't guess what it was. He thought of Miss Deming, and decided she might be a jolly trollop who consoled the men of the neighborhood under the guise of giving music lessons. But when he telephoned, her voice was the voice of a crone. He said that Jack Thompson had given him her name, and she said for him to come the next evening at seven o'clock. As he left his house after supper on Wednesday, he thought that there was at least some therapy in getting out of the place and absorbing himself in something besides his domestic and business worries. Miss Deming lived on Bellevue Avenue, on the other side of town. The house numbers were difficult to see, and Seton parked his car at the curb and walked, looking for the number of her house.

It was an evening in the fall. Bellevue Avenue was one of those back streets of frame houses that are irreproachable in their demeanor, their effect, but that are ornamented, through some caprice, with little minarets and curtains of wooden beading, like a mistaken or at least a mysterious nod to the faraway mosques and harems of bloody Islam. This paradox gave the place its charm. The street was declining, but it was declining gracefully; its decay was luxuriant, and in the back yards roses bloomed in profusion, and cardinals sang in the fir trees. A few householders were still raking their lawns. Seton had been raised on just such a street, and he was charmed to stumble on this fragment of his past. The sun was setting—there was a show of red light at the foot of the street—and at the sight of this he felt a pang in his stomach as keen as hunger, but it was not hunger, it was simple aspiration. Oh to lead an illustrious life!

Miss Deming's house had no porch, and may have needed paint more than the others, although he could not tell for sure, now that the light had begun to fade. A sign on the door said: KNOCK AND COME IN. He stepped into a small hallway, with a staircase and a wooden hatrack. In a farther room he saw a man as old as himself bent over the piano keys. "You're early," Miss Deming called out. "Please sit down and wait."

She spoke with such deep resignation, such weariness, that the tone of her voice seemed to imply to Seton that what he waited for would be disgusting and painful. He sat down on a bench, under the hatrack. He was uncomfortable. His hands sweated, and he felt painfully large for the house, the bench, the situation. How mysterious was this life, he thought, where his wife had hidden her charms and he was planning to study the piano. His discomfort got so intense that he thought for a moment of fleeing. He could step out of the door, into Bellevue Avenue, and never come back again. A memory of the confusion at home kept him where he was. Then the thought of waiting as a mode of eternity attacked him. How much time one spent waiting in dentists' and doctors' anterooms, waiting for trains, for planes, waiting in front of telephone booths and in restaurants. It seemed that he had wasted the best of his life in waiting, and that by contracting to wait for piano lessons he might throw away the few vivid years that were left to him. Again he thought of escaping, but at that moment the lesson in the other room came to an end. "You've not been practicing enough," he heard Miss Deming say crossly. "You have to practice an hour a day, without exception, or else you'll simply be wasting my time." Her pupil came through the little hall with his coat collar turned up so that Seton couldn't see his face. "Next," she said.

The little room with the upright piano in it was more cluttered than the hall. Miss Deming hardly looked up when he came in. She was a small woman. Her brown hair was streaked with gray, braided, and pinned to her head in a sparse coronet. She sat on an inflated cushion, with her hands folded in her lap, and moved her lips now and then with distaste, as if something galled her. Seton blundered onto the little piano stool. "I've never taken piano lessons," he said. "I once took cornet lessons. I rented a cornet when I was in high school—"

"We'll forget about that," she said. She pointed out middle C and asked him to play a scale. His fingers, in the bright light from the music rack, looked enormous and naked. He struggled with his scale. Once or twice, she rapped his knuckles with a pencil; once or twice, she manipulated his fingers with hers, and he had a vision of her life as a nightmare of clean hands, dirty hands, hairy hands, limp and muscular hands, and he decided that this might account for her feeling of distaste. Halfway through the lesson, Seton dropped his hands into his lap. His irresolution only made her impatient, and she placed his hands back on the keys. He wanted to smile, but on the wall above the piano there was a large sign that forbade this. His shirt was wet when the lesson ended.

"Please bring the exact change when you come again. Put the money in the vase on the desk," she said. "Next." Seton and the next pupil passed each other in the doorway, but the stranger averted his face.

The end of the ordeal elated Seton, and as he stepped out into the darkness of Bellevue Avenue he had a pleasant and silly image of himself as a pianist. He wondered if these simple pleasures were what Jack Thompson had meant. The children were in bed when he got home, and he sat down to practice. Miss Deming had given him a two-handed finger drill with a little melody, and he went over this again and again for an hour. He practiced every day, including Sunday, and sincerely hoped when he went for his second lesson that she would compliment him by giving him something more difficult, but she spent the hour criticizing his phrasing and fingering, and told him to practice the drill for another week. He thought that at least after his third lesson he would have a change, but he went home with the same drill.

Jessica neither encouraged him nor complained. She seemed mystified by this turn of events. The music got on her nerves, and he could see where it would. The simple drill, with its melody, impressed itself even onto the memories of his daughters. It seemed to become a part of all their lives, as unwelcome as an infection, and as pestilential. It drifted through Seton's mind all during the business day, and at any sudden turn of feeling—pain or surprise—the melody would swell and come to the front of his consciousness. Seton had never known that this drudgery, this harrying of the mind, was a part of mastering the piano. Now in the evening after supper when he sat down to practice, Jessica hastily left the room and went upstairs. She seemed intimidated by the music, or perhaps afraid. His own relationship to the drill was oppressive and unclear. Taking a late train one evening and walking up from the station past the Thompsons', he heard the same pestilential drill coming through the walls of their house. Jack must be practicing. There was nothing very strange about this, but when he passed the Carmignoles' and heard the drill again, he wondered if it was not his own memory that made it ring in his ears. The night was dark, and with his sense of reality thus shaken, he stood on his own doorstep thinking that the world changed more swiftly than one could perceive—died and renewed itself—and that he moved through the events of his life with no more comprehension than a naked swimmer.

Jessica had not burned the meat that night. She had kept a decent supper for him in the oven, and she served it to him with a timidity that made him wonder if she was not about to return to him as his wife. After supper, he read to the children and then rolled back his shirtsleeves and sat down at the piano. As Jessica was preparing to leave the room, she turned and spoke to him. Her manner was pleading, and this made her eyes seem larger and darker, and deepened her natural pallor. "I don't like to interfere," she said softly, "and I know I don't know anything about music, but I wonder if you couldn't ask her—your teacher—if she couldn't give you something else to practice. That exercise is on my mind so. I hear it all day. If she could give you a new piece—"

"I know what you mean," he said. "I'll ask her."

By his fifth lesson, the days had grown much shorter and there was no longer any fiery sunset at the foot of Bellevue Avenue to remind him of his high hopes, his longings. He knocked, and stepped into the little house, and noticed at once the smell of cigarette smoke. He took off his hat and coat and went into the living room, but Miss Deming was not on her cushion. He called her, and she answered from the kitchen and opened the door onto a scene that astonished him. Two young men sat at the kitchen table, smoking and drinking beer. Their dark hair gleamed with oil and was swept back in wings. They wore motorcycle boots and red hunting shirts, and their manners seemed developed, to a fine point, for the expression of lawless youth. "We'll be waiting for you, lover," one of them said loudly as she closed the door after her, and as she came toward Seton he saw a look of pleasure on her face—of lightness and self-esteem—fade, and the return of her habitually galled look.

"My boys," she said, and sighed.

"Are they neighbors?" Seton asked.

"Oh, no. They come from New York. They come up and spend the night sometimes. I help them when I can, poor things. They're like sons to me."

"It must be nice for them," Seton said.

"Please commence," she said. All the feeling had left her voice.

"My wife wanted to know if I couldn't have something different—a new piece."

"They always do," she said wearily.

"Something a little less repetitious," Seton said.

"None of the gentlemen who come here have ever complained about my methods. If you're not satisfied, you don't have to come. Of course, Mr. Purvis went too far. Mrs. Purvis is still in the sanatorium, but I don't think the fault is mine. You want to bring her to her knees, don't you? Isn't that what you're here for? Please commence."

Seton began to play, but with more than his usual clumsiness. The unholy old woman's remarks had stunned him. What had he got into? Was he guilty? Had his instinct to flee when he first entered the house been the one he should have followed? Had he, by condoning the stuffiness of the place, committed himself to some kind of obscenity, some kind of witchcraft? Had he agreed to hold over a lovely woman the subtle threat of madness? The old crone spoke softly now and, he thought, wickedly. "Play the melody lightly, lightly, lightly," she said. "That is how it will do its work."

He went on playing, borne along on an unthinking devotion to consecutiveness, for if he protested, as he knew he should, he would only authenticate the nightmare. His head and his fingers worked with perfect independence of his feelings, and while one part of him was full of shock, alarm, and self-reproach, his fingers went on producing the insidious melody. From the kitchen he could hear deep laughter, the pouring of beer, the shuffle of motorcycle boots. Perhaps because she wanted to rejoin her friends—her boys—she cut the lesson short, and Seton's relief was euphoric.

He had to ask himself again and again if she had really said what he thought he heard her say, and it seemed so improbable that he wanted to stop and talk with Jack Thompson about it, until he realized that he could not mention what had happened; he would not be able to put it into words. This darkness where men and women struggled pitilessly for supremacy and withered crones practiced witchcraft was not the world where he made his life. The old lady seemed to inhabit some barrier reef of consciousness, some gray moment after waking that would be demolished by the light of day.

Jessica was in the living room when he got home, and as he put his music on the rack he saw a look of dread in her face. "Did she give you a piece?" she asked. "Did she give you something besides that drill?"

"Not this time," he said. "I guess I'm not ready. Perhaps next time."

"Are you going to practice now?"

"I might."

"Oh, not tonight, darling! Please not tonight! Please, please, *please* not tonight, my love!" and she was on her knees.

The restoration of Seton's happiness—and it returned to them both with a rush—left him oddly self-righteous about how it had come about, and when he thought of Miss Deming he thought of her with contempt and disgust. Caught up in a whirl of palatable suppers and lovemaking, he didn't go near the piano. He washed his hands of her methods. He had chosen to forget the whole thing. But when Wednesday night came around again, he got up to go there at the usual time and say goodbye. He could have telephoned her. Jessica was uneasy about his going back, but he explained that it was merely to end the arrangement, and kissed her, and went out.

It was a dark night. The Turkish shapes of Bellevue Avenue were dimly lighted. Someone was burning leaves. He knocked on Miss Deming's door and stepped into the little hall. The house was dark. The only light came through the windows from the street. "Miss Deming," he called. "Miss Deming?" He called her name three times. The chair beside the piano bench was empty, but he could feel the old lady's touch on everything in the place. She was not there—that is, she did not answer his voice—but she seemed to be standing in the door to the kitchen, standing on the stairs, standing in the dark at the end of the hall; and a light sound he heard from upstairs seemed to be her footfall.

He went home, and he hadn't been there half an hour when the police came and asked him to come with them. He went outside—he didn't want the children to hear—and he made the natural mistake of protesting, since, after all, was he not a most law-abiding man? Had he not always paid for his morning paper, obeyed the traffic lights, bathed daily, prayed weekly, kept his tax affairs in order, and paid his bills on the tenth of the month? There was not, in the broad landscape of his past, a trace, a hint of illegality. What did the police want with him? They wouldn't say, but they insisted that he come with them, and finally he got into the patrol car with them and drove to the other side of town, across some railroad tracks, to a dead-end place, a dump, where there were some other policemen. It was a scene for violence—bare, ugly, hidden away from any house, and with no one to hear her cries for help. She lay on the crossroads, like a witch. Her neck was broken, and her clothes were still disordered from her struggle with the great powers of death. They asked if he knew her, and he said yes. Had he ever seen any young men around her house, they asked, and he said no. His name and address had been found in a notebook on her desk, and he explained that she had been his piano teacher. They were satisfied with this explanation, and they let him go.   1959

A. S. BYATT

The July Ghost

"I think I must move out of where I'm living," he said. "I have this problem with my landlady."

He picked a long, bright hair off the back of her dress, so deftly that the act seemed simply considerate. He had been skilful at balancing glass, plate, and cutlery, too. He had a look of dignified misery, like a dejected hawk. She was interested.

"What sort of problem? Amatory, financial, or domestic?"

"None of those, really. Well, not financial."

He turned the hair on his finger, examining it intently, not meeting her eye.

"Not financial. Can you tell me? I might know somewhere you could stay. I know a lot of people."

"You would." He smiled shyly. "It's not an easy problem to describe. There's just the two of us. I occupy the attics. Mostly."

He came to a stop. He was obviously reserved and secretive. But he was telling her something. This is usually attractive.

"Mostly?" Encouraging him.

"Oh, it's not like *that*. Well, not . . . Shall we sit down?"

They moved across the party, which was a big party, on a hot day. He stopped and found a bottle and filled her glass. He had not needed to ask what she was drinking. They sat side by side on a sofa: he admired the brilliant poppies bold on her emerald dress, and her pretty sandals. She had come to London for the summer to work in the British Museum. She could really have managed with microfilm in Tucson for what little manuscript research was needed, but there was a dragging love affair to end. There is an age at which, however desperately happy one is in stolen moments, days, or weekends with one's married professor, one either prises him loose or cuts and runs. She had had a stab at both, and now considered she had successfully cut and run.

So it was nice to be immediately appreciated. Problems are capable of solution. She said as much to him, turning her soft face to his ravaged one, swinging the long bright hair. It had begun a year ago, he told her in a rush, at another party actually; he had met this woman, the landlady in question, and had made, not immediately, a kind of *faux pas*, he now saw, and she had been very decent, all things considered, and so . . .

He had said, "I think I must move out of where I'm living." He had been quite wild, had nearly not come to the party, but could not go on drinking alone. The woman had considered him coolly and asked, "Why?" One could not, he said, go on in a place where one had once been blissfully happy, and was now miserable, however convenient the place. Convenient, that was, for work, and friends, and things that seemed, as he mentioned them, ashy and insubstantial compared to the memory and the hope of opening the door and finding Anne outside it, laughing and breathless, waiting to be told what he had read, or thought, or eaten, or felt that day. Someone I loved left, he told the woman. Reticent on that occasion too, he bit back the flurry of sentences about the total unexpectedness of it, the arriving back and finding only an envelope on a clean table, and spaces in the bookshelves, the record stack, the kitchen cupboard. It must have been planned for weeks, she must have been thinking it out while he rolled on her, while she poured wine for him, while . . . No, no. Vituperation is undignified and in this case what he felt was lower and worse than rage: just pure, child-like loss. "One ought not to mind places," he said to the woman. "But one does," she had said. "I know."

She had suggested to him that he could come and be her lodger, then; she had, she said, a lot of spare space going to waste, and her husband wasn't there much. "We've not had a lot to say to each other, lately." He could be quite self-contained, there was a kitchen and bathroom in the attics; she wouldn't bother him. There was a large garden. It was possibly this that decided him: it was very hot, central London, the time of year when a man feels he would give anything to live in a room opening on to grass and trees, not a high flat in a dusty street. And if Anne came back, the door would be locked and mortice-locked. He could stop thinking about Anne coming back. That was a decisive move: Anne thought he wasn't decisive. He would live without Anne.

For some weeks after he moved in he had seen very little of the woman. They met on the stairs, and once she came up, on a hot Sunday, to tell him he must feel free to use the garden. He had offered to do some weeding and mowing and she had accepted. That was the weekend her husband came back, driving furiously up to the front door, running in, and calling in the empty hall, "Imogen, Imogen!" To which she had replied, uncharacteristically, by screaming hysterically. There was nothing in her husband, Noel's, appearance to warrant this reaction; their lodger, peering over the banister at the sound, had seen their upturned faces in the stairwell and watched hers settle into its usual prim and placid expression as he did so. Seeing Noel, a balding, fluffy-templed, stooping thirty-five or so, shabby corduroy suit, cotton polo neck, he realized he was now able to guess her age, as he had not been. She was a very neat woman, faded blonde, her hair in a knot on the back of her head, her legs long and slender, her eyes downcast. Mild was not quite the right word for her, though. She explained then that she had screamed because Noel had come home unexpectedly and startled her: she was sorry. It seemed a reasonable explanation. The extraordinary vehemence of the screaming was probably an echo in the stairwell. Noel seemed wholly downcast by it, all the same.

He had kept out of the way, that weekend, taking the stairs two at a time and lightly, feeling a little aggrieved, looking out of his kitchen window into the lovely, overgrown garden, that they were lurking indoors, wasting all the summer sun. At Sunday lunch-time he had heard the husband, Noel, shouting on the stairs.

"I can't go on, if you go on like that. I've done my best, I've tried to get through. Nothing will shift you, will it, you won't *try*, will you, you just go on and on. Well, I have my life to live, you can't throw a life away . . . can you?"

He had crept out again on to the dark upper landing and seen her standing, half-way down the stairs, quite still, watching Noel wave his arms and roar, or almost roar, with a look of impassive patience, as though this nuisance must pass off. Noel swallowed and gasped; he turned his face up to her and said plaintively,

"You do see I can't stand it? I'll be in touch, shall I? You must want . . . you must need . . . you must . . . ."

She didn't speak.

"If you need anything, you know where to get me."

"Yes."

"Oh, well . . . ." said Noel, and went to the door. She watched him, from the stairs, until it was shut, and then came up again, step by step, as though it was an effort, a little, and went on coming past her bedroom, to his landing, to come in and ask him, entirely naturally, please to use the garden if he wanted to, and please not to mind marital rows. She was sure he understood . . . things were difficult . . . Noel wouldn't be back for some time. He was a journalist: his work took him away a lot. Just as well. She committed herself to the "just as well." She was a very economical speaker.

So he took to sitting in the garden. It was a lovely place: a huge, hidden, walled south London garden, with old fruit trees at the end, a wildly waving disorderly buddleia, curving beds full of old roses, and a lawn of overgrown, dense rye-grass. Over the wall at the foot was the Common, with a footpath running behind all the gardens. She came out to the shed and helped him to assemble and oil the lawnmower, standing on the little path under the apple branches while he cut an experimental serpentine across her hay. Over the wall came the high sound of children's voices, and the thunk and thud of a football. He asked her how to raise the blades: he was not mechanically minded.

"The children get quite noisy," she said. "And dogs. I hope they don't bother you. There aren't many safe places for children, round here."

He replied truthfully that he never heard sounds that didn't concern him, when he was concentrating. When he'd got the lawn into shape, he was going to sit on it and do a lot of reading, try to get his mind in trim again, to write a paper on Hardy's poems, on their curiously archaic vocabulary.

"It isn't very far to the road on the other side, really," she said. "It just seems to be. The Common is an illusion of space, really. Just a spur of brambles and gorse-bushes and bits of football pitch between two fast four-laned main roads. I hate London commons."

"There's a lovely smell, though, from the gorse and the wet grass. It's a pleasant illusion."

"No illusions are pleasant," she said, decisively, and went in. He wondered what she did with her time: apart from little shopping expeditions she seemed to be always in the house. He was sure that when he'd met her she'd been introduced as having some profession: vaguely literary, vaguely academic, like everyone he knew. Perhaps she wrote poetry in her north-facing living-room. He had no idea what it would be like. Women generally wrote emotional poetry, much nicer than men, as Kingsley Amis has stated, but she seemed, despite her placid stillness, too spare and too fierce—grim?—for that. He remembered the screaming. Perhaps she wrote Plath-like chants of violence. He didn't think that quite fitted the bill, either. Perhaps she was a freelance radio journalist. He didn't bother to ask anyone who might be a common acquaintance. During the whole year, he explained to the American at the party, he hadn't actually *discussed* her with anyone. Of course he wouldn't, she agreed vaguely and warmly. She knew he wouldn't. He didn't see why he shouldn't, in fact, but went on, for the time, with his narrative.

They had got to know each other a little better over the next few weeks, at least on the level of borrowing tea, or even sharing pots of it. The weather had got hotter. He had found an old-fashioned deck-chair, with faded striped canvas, in the shed, and had brushed it over and brought it out on to his mown lawn, where he sat writing a little, reading a little, getting up and pulling up a tuft of couch grass. He had been wrong about the children not bothering him: there was a succession of incursions by all sizes of children looking for all sizes of balls, which bounced to his feet, or crashed in the shrubs, or vanished in the herbaceous border, black and white footballs, beach-balls with concentric circles of primary colours, acid yellow tennis balls. The children came over the wall: black faces, brown faces, floppy long hair, shaven heads, respectable dotted sun-hats and camouflaged cotton army hats from Milletts. They came over easily, as though they were used to it, sandals, training shoes, a few bare toes, grubby sunburned legs, cotton skirts, jeans, football shorts. Sometimes, perched on the top, they saw him and gestured at the balls; one or two asked permission. Sometimes he threw a ball back, but was apt to knock down a few knobby little unripe apples or pears. There was a gate in the wall, under the fringing trees, which he once tried to open, spending time on rusty bolts only to discover that the lock was new and secure, and the key not in it.

The boy sitting in the tree did not seem to be looking for a ball. He was in a fork of the tree nearest the gate, swinging his legs, doing something to a knot in a frayed end of rope that was attached to the branch he sat on. He wore blue jeans and training shoes, and a brilliant tee shirt, striped in the colours of the spectrum, arranged in the right order, which the man on the grass found visually pleasing. He had rather long blond hair, falling over his eyes, so that his face was obscured.

"Hey, you. Do you think you ought to be up there? It might not be safe."

The boy looked up, grinned, and vanished monkey-like over the wall. He had a nice, frank grin, friendly, not cheeky.

He was there again, the next day, leaning back in the crook of the tree, arms crossed. He had on the same shirt and jeans. The man watched him, expecting him to move again, but he sat, immobile, smiling down pleasantly, and then staring up at the sky. The man read a little, looked up, saw him still there, and said.

"Have you lost anything?"

The child did not reply: after a moment he climbed down a little, swung along the branch hand over hand, dropped to the ground, raised an arm in salute, and was up over the usual route over the wall.

Two days later he was lying on his stomach on the edge of the lawn, out of the shade, this time in a white tee shirt with a pattern of blue ships and water-lines on it, his bare feet and legs stretched in the sun. He was chewing a grass stem, and studying the earth, as though watching for insects. The man said "Hi, there," and the boy looked up, met his look with intensely blue eyes under long lashes, smiled with the same complete warmth and openness, and returned his look to the earth.

He felt reluctant to inform on the boy, who seemed so harmless and considerate: but when he met him walking out of the kitchen door, spoke to him, and got no answer but the gentle smile before the boy ran off towards the wall, he wondered if he should speak to his landlady. So he asked her, did she mind the children coming in the garden. She said no, children must look for balls, that was part of being children. He persisted—they sat there, too, and he had met one coming out of the house. He hadn't seemed to be doing any harm, the boy, but you couldn't tell. He thought she should know.

He was probably a friend of her son's, she said. She looked at him kindly and explained. Her son had run off the Common with some other children, two years ago, in the summer, in July, and had been killed on the road. More or less instantly, she had added drily, as though calculating that just *enough* information would preclude the need for further questions. He said he was sorry, very sorry, feeling to blame, which was ridiculous, and a little injured, because he had not known about her son, and might inadvertently have made a fool of himself with some casual reference whose ignorance would be embarrassing.

What was the boy like, she said. The one in the house? "I don't—talk to his friends. I find it painful. It could be Timmy, or Martin. They might have lost something, or want . . ."

He described the boy. Blond, about ten at a guess, he was not very good at children's ages, very blue eyes, slightly built, with a rainbow-striped tee shirt and blue jeans, mostly though not always—oh, and those football practice shoes, black and green. And the other tee shirt, with the ships and wavy lines. And an extraordinarily nice smile. A really *warm* smile. A nice-looking boy.

He was used to her being silent. But this silence went on and on and on. She was just staring into the garden. After a time, she said, in her precise conversational tone,

"The only thing I want, the only thing I want at all in this world, is to see that boy."

She stared at the garden and he stared with her, until the grass began to dance with empty light, and the edges of the shrubbery wavered. For a brief moment he shared the strain of not seeing the boy. Then she gave a little sigh, sat down, neatly, as always, and passed out at his feet.

After this she became, for her, voluble. He didn't move after she fainted, but sat patiently by her, until she stirred and sat up; then he fetched her some water, and would have gone away, but she talked.

"I'm too rational to see ghosts, I'm not someone who would see anything there was to see, I don't believe in an after-life. I don't see how anyone can, I always found a kind of satisfaction for myself in the idea that one just came to an end, to a sliced-off stop. But that was myself; I didn't think *he*—not *he*—I thought ghosts were what people *wanted* to see, or were afraid to see . . . and after he died, and best hope I had, it sounds silly, was that I would go mad enough so that instead of waiting every day for him to come home from school and rattle the letter-box I might actually have the illusion of seeing or hearing him come in. Because I can't stop my body and mind waiting, every day, every day, I can't let go. And his bedroom, sometimes at night I go in, I think I might just for a moment forget he *wasn't* in there sleeping, I think I would pay almost anything—anything at all—for a moment of seeing him like I used to. In his pyjamas, with his—his—his hair . . . ruffled, and, his . . . you said, his . . . that *smile*.

"When it happened, they got Noel, and Noel came in and shouted my name, like he did the other day, that's why I screamed, because it—seemed the same—and then they said, he is dead, and I thought coolly, *is* dead, that will go on and on and on till the end of time, it's a continuous present tense, one thinks the most ridiculous things, there I was thinking about grammar, the verb to be, when it ends to be dead . . . And then I came out into the garden, and I half saw, in my mind's eye, a kind of ghost of his face, just the eyes and hair, coming towards me—like every day waiting for him to come home, the way you think of your son, with such pleasure, when he's—not there—and I—I thought—no, I won't *see* him, because he is dead, and I won't dream about him because he is dead, I'll be rational and practical and continue to live because one must, and there was Noel . . .

"I got it wrong, you see, I was so *sensible,* and then I was so shocked because I couldn't get to want anything—I couldn't *talk* to Noel—I—I—made Noel take away, destroy, all the photos, I—didn't dream, you can will not to dream, I didn't . . . visit a grave, flowers, there isn't any point. I was so sensible. Only my body wouldn't stop waiting and all it wants is to—see that boy. *That* boy. That boy you—saw."

He did not say that he might have seen another boy, maybe even a boy who had been given the tee shirts and jeans afterwards. He did not say, though the idea crossed his mind, that maybe what he had seen was some kind of impression from her terrible desire to see a boy where nothing was. The boy had had nothing terrible, no aura of pain about him: he had been, his memory insisted, such a pleasant, courteous, self-contained boy, with his own purposes. And in fact the woman herself almost immediately raised the possibility that what he had seen was what she desired to see, a kind of mix-up of radio waves, like when you overheard police messages on the radio, or got BBC 1 on a switch that said ITV. She was thinking fast, and went on almost immediately to say that perhaps his sense of loss, his loss of Anne, which was what had led her to feel she could bear his presence in her house, was what had brought them—dare she say—near enough, for their wavelengths, to mingle, perhaps, had made him susceptible . . . You mean, he had said, we are a kind of emotional vacuum, between us, that must be filled. Something like that, she had said, and had added, "But I don't believe in ghosts."

Anne, he thought, could not be a ghost, because she was elsewhere, with someone else, doing for someone else those little things she had done so gaily for him, tasty little suppers, bits of research, a sudden vase of unusual flowers, a new bold shirt, unlike his own cautious taste, but suiting him, suiting him. In a sense, Anne was worse lost because voluntarily absent, an absence that could not be loved because love was at an end, for Anne.

"I don't suppose you will, now," the woman was saying. "I think talking would probably stop any—mixing of messages, if that's what it is, don't you? But—if—*if* he comes again"—and here for the first time her eyes were full of tears—"if—you must promise, you will *tell* me, you must promise."

He had promised, easily enough, because he was fairly sure she was right, the boy would not be seen again. But the next day he was on the lawn, nearer than ever, sitting on the grass beside the deck-chair, his arms clasping his bent, warm brown knees, the thick, pale hair glittering in the sun. He was wearing a football shirt, this time, Chelsea's colours. Sitting down in the deck-chair, the man could have put out a hand and touched him, but did not: it was not, it seemed, a possible gesture to make. But the boy looked up and smiled, with a pleasant complicity, as though they now understood each other very well. The man tried speech: he said, "It's nice to see you again," and the boy nodded acknowledgement of this remark, without speaking himself. This was the beginning of communication between them, or what the man supposed to be communication. He did not think of fetching the woman. He became aware that he was in some strange way *enjoying the boy's company*. His pleasant stillness—and he sat there all morning, occasionally lying back on the grass, occasionally staring thoughtfully at the house—

was calming and comfortable. The man did quite a lot of work—wrote about three reasonable pages on Hardy's original air-blue gown—and looked up now and then to make sure the boy was still there and happy.

He went to report to the woman—as he had after all promised to do—that evening. She had obviously been waiting and hoping—her unnatural calm had given way to agitated pacing, and her eyes were dark and deeper in. At this point in the story he found in himself a necessity to bowdlerize for the sympathetic American, as he had indeed already begun to do. He had mentioned only a child who had "seemed like" the woman's lost son, and he now ceased to mention the child at all, as an actor in the story, with the result that what the American woman heard was a tale of how he, the man, had become increasingly involved in the woman's solitary grief, how their two losses had become a kind of *folie à deux* from which he could not extricate himself. What follows is not what he told the American girl, though it may be clear at which points the bowdlerized version coincided with what he really believed to have happened. There was a sense he could not at first analyse that it was improper to talk about the boy—not because he might not be believed; that did not come into it; but because something dreadful might happen.
"He sat on the lawn all morning. In a football shirt."
"Chelsea?"
"Chelsea."
"What did he do? Does he look happy? Did he speak?" Her desire to know was terrible.
"He doesn't speak. He didn't move much. He seemed—very calm. He stayed a long time."
"This is terrible. This is ludicrous. There *is no boy.*"
"No. But I saw him."
"Why you?"
"I don't know." A pause. "I do *like* him."
"He is—was—a most likeable boy."

Some days later he saw the boy running along the landing in the evening, wearing what might have been pyjamas, in peacock towelling, or might have been a track suit. Pyjamas, the woman stated confidently, when he told her: his new pyjamas. With white ribbed cuffs, weren't they? and a white polo neck? He corroborated this, watching her cry— she cried more easily now—finding her anxiety and disturbance very hard to bear. But it never occurred to him that it was possible to break his promise to tell her when he saw the boy. That was another curious imperative from some undefined authority.

They discussed clothes. If there were ghosts, how could they appear in clothes long burned, or rotted, or worn away by other people? You could imagine, they agreed, that something of a person might linger—as the Tibetans and others believe the soul lingers near the body before setting out on its long journey. But clothes? And in this case so many clothes? I must be seeing your memories, he told her, and she nodded fiercely, compressing her lips, agreeing that this was likely, adding, "I am too rational to go mad, so I seem to be putting it on you."

He tried a joke. "That isn't very kind to me, to infer that madness comes more easily to me."

"No, sensitivity. I am insensible. I was always a bit like that, and this made it worse. I am the *last* person to see any ghost that was trying to haunt me."

"We agreed it was your memories I saw."

"Yes. We agree. That's rational. As rational as we can be, considering."

All the same, the brilliance of the boy's blue regard, his gravely smiling salutation in the garden next morning, did not seem like anyone's tortured memories of earlier happiness. The man spoke to him directly then:

"Is there anything I can *do* for you? Anything you want? Can I help you?"

The boy seemed to puzzle about this for a while, inclining his head as though hearing was difficult. Then he nodded, quickly and perhaps urgently, turned, and ran into the house, looking back to make sure he was followed. The man entered the living-room through the french windows, behind the running boy, who stopped for a moment in the centre of the room, with the man blinking behind him at the sudden transition from sunlight to comparative dark. The woman was sitting in an armchair, looking at nothing there. She often sat like that. She looked up, across the boy, at the man, and the boy, his face for the first time anxious, met the man's eyes again, asking, before he went out into the garden.

"What is it? What is it? Have you seen him again? Why are you . . .?"

"He came in here. He went—out through the door."

"I didn't see him."

"No."

"Did he—oh, this is so *silly*—did he see me?"

He could not remember. He told the only truth he knew.

"He brought me in here."

"Oh, what can I do, what am I going to *do?* If I killed myself—I have thought of that—but the idea that I should be with him is an illusion I . . . this silly situation is the nearest I shall ever get. To him. He was *in here with me?*"

"Yes."

And she was crying again. Out in the garden he could see the boy, swinging agile on the apple branch.

He was not quite sure, looking back, when he had thought he had realized what the boy had wanted him to do. This was also at the party, his worst piece of what he called bowdlerization, though in some sense it was clearly the opposite of bowdlerization. He told the American girl that he had come to the conclusion that it was the woman herself who had wanted it, though there was in fact, throughout, no sign of her wanting anything except to see the boy, as she said. The boy, bolder and more frequent, had appeared several nights running on the landing, wandering in and out of bathrooms and bedrooms, restlessly, a little agitated, questing almost, until it had "come to" the man that what he required was to be re-engendered, for him, the man, to give to his mother another child, into which he could peacefully vanish. The idea was so clear that it was like another imperative, though he did not have the courage to ask the child to confirm it. Possibly this was out of delicacy—the child was too young to be talked to about sex. Possibly there were other reasons. Possibly he was mistaken: the situation was making him hysterical, he felt action of some kind was required and must be possible. He could not spend the rest of the summer, the rest of his life, describing non-existent tee shirts and blond smiles.

He could think of no sensible way of embarking on his venture, so in the end simply walked into her bedroom one night. She was lying there, reading; when she saw him her instinctive gesture was to hide, not her bare arms and throat, but her book. She seemed, in fact, quite surprised to see his pyjamaed figure, and, after she had recovered her coolness, brought out the book definitely and laid it on the bedspread.

"My new taste in illegitimate literature. I keep them in a box under the bed."

Ena Twigg, Medium. The Infinite Hive. The Spirit World. Is There Life After Death?

"Pathetic," she proffered.

He sat down delicately on the bed.

"Please, don't grieve so. Please, let yourself be comforted. Please . . ."

He put an arm round her. She shuddered. He pulled her closer. He asked why she had had only the one son, and she seemed to understand the purport of his question, for she tried, angular and chilly, to lean on him a little, she became apparently compliant. "No real reason," she assured him, no material reason. Just her husband's profession and lack of inclination: that covered it.

"Perhaps," he suggested, "if she would be comforted a little, perhaps she could hope, perhaps . . ."

For comfort then, she said, dolefully, and lay back, pushing Ena Twigg off the bed with one fierce gesture, then lying placidly. He got in beside her, put his arms round her, kissed her cold cheek, thought of Anne, of what was never to be again. Come on, he said to the woman, you must live, you must try to live, let us hold each other for comfort.

She hissed at him "Don't *talk*" between clenched teeth, so he stroked her lightly, over her nightdress, breasts and buttocks and long stiff legs, composed like an effigy on an Elizabethan tomb. She allowed this, trembling slightly, and then trembling violently: he took this to be a sign of some mixture of pleasure and pain, of the return of life to stone. He put a hand between her legs and she moved them heavily apart; he heaved himself over her and pushed, unsuccessfully. She was contorted and locked tight: frigid, he thought grimly, was not the word. *Rigor mortis*, his mind said to him, before she began to scream.

He was ridiculously cross about this. He jumped away and said quite rudely "Shut up," and then ungraciously "I'm sorry." She stopped screaming as suddenly as she had begun and made one of her painstaking economical explanations.

"Sex and death don't go. I can't afford to let go of my grip on myself. I hoped. What you hoped. It was a bad idea. I apologize."

"Oh, never mind," he said and rushed out again on to the landing, feeling foolish and almost in tears for warm, lovely Anne.

The child was on the landing, waiting. When the man saw him, he looked questioning, and then turned his face against the wall and leant there, rigid, his shoulders hunched, his hair hiding his expression. There was a similarity between woman and child. The man felt, for the first time, almost uncharitable towards the boy, and then felt something else.

"Look, I'm sorry. I tried. I did try. Please turn around."

Uncompromising, rigid, clenched back view.

"Oh well," said the man, and went into his bedroom.

So now, he said to the American woman at the party, I feel a fool, I feel embarrassed, I feel we are hurting, not helping each other, I feel it isn't a refuge. Of course you feel that, she said, of course you're right—it was temporarily necessary, it helped both of you, but you've got to live your life. Yes, he said, I've done my best, I've tried to get through, I have my life to live. Look, she said, I want to help, I really do, I have these wonderful friends I'm renting this flat from, why don't you come, just for a few days, just for a break, why don't you? They're real sympathetic people, you'd like them, I like them, you could get your emotions kind of straightened out. She'd probably be glad to see the back of you, she must feel as bad as you do, she's got to relate to her situation in her own way in the end. We all have.

He said he would think about it. He knew he had elected to tell the sympathetic American because he had sensed she would be—would offer—a way out. He had to get out. He took her home from the party and went back to his house and landlady without seeing her into her flat. They both knew that this reticence was promising—that he hadn't come in then, because he meant to come later. Her warmth and readiness were like sunshine, she was open. He did not know what to say to the woman.

In fact, she made it easy for him: she asked, briskly, if he now found it perhaps uncomfortable to stay, and he replied that he had felt he should move on, he was of so little use . . . Very well, she had agreed, and had added crisply that it had to be better for everyone if "all this" came to an end. He remembered the firmness with which she had told him that no illusions were pleasant. She was strong: too strong for her own good. It would take years to wear away that stony, closed, simply surviving insensibility. It was not his job. He would go. All the same, he felt bad.

He got out his suitcases and put some things in them. He went down to the garden, nervously, and put away the deck-chair. The garden was empty. There were no voices over the wall. The silence was thick and deadening. He wondered, knowing he would not see the boy again, if anyone else would do so, or if, now he was gone, no one would describe a tee shirt, a sandal, a smile, seen, remembered, or desired. He went slowly up to his room again.

The boy was sitting on his suitcase, arms crossed, face frowning and serious. He held the man's look for a long moment, and then the man went and sat on his bed. The boy continued to sit. The man found himself speaking.

"You do see I have to go? I've tried to get through. I can't get through. I'm no use to you, am I?"

The boy remained immobile, his head on one side, considering. The man stood up and walked towards him.

"Please. Let me go. What are we, in this house? A man and a woman and a child, and none of us can get through. You can't want that?"

He went as close as he dared. He had, he thought, the intention of putting his hand on or through the child. But could not bring himself to feel there was no boy. So he stood, and repeated,

"I can't get through. Do you want me to stay?"

Upon which, as he stood helplessly there, the boy turned on him again the brilliant, open, confiding, beautiful desired smile. 1982

PHILIP GRAHAM

ANCIENT MUSIC

That night Mr. and Mrs. Michaels cheated at Scrabble. He asked for a glass of water, and when she left the room he flipped through the dictionary, looking for words beginning with the letter *z*. In the kitchen, Mrs. Michaels could hear the pages turning, and when she came back he was counting up his fifty-eight points for *zooid*. "What's that?" she asked, thinking to trap him. But he peered at her as if she were far away, her ignorance barely bridgeable. "Any organism capable of a separate existence, of course," he said. Mrs. Michaels kept quiet. She didn't even complain when all she could manage was surrounding a vowel already on the board with her only consonants, for *rat*. "What's the score?" she asked, and while Mr. Michaels touched the tip of his pencil to the numbered columns, she quickly palmed two of her four *a*'s and returned them to the box where she chose her new letters. Mr. Michaels heard more clicks and scrapes than there should have been, but he kept his head lowered until his wife was done, when he announced, "You're still ahead." But at the end of the game their scores were tied, the first time they could ever remember this happening. Each filled with guilty knowledge, they were both grateful neither of them had won.

"Well, Mr. Michaels," she said, this formal name having long ago transformed into tenderness, "I think that's enough for one night, don't you?"

"Yes, I suppose," he replied, but she was already walking up the stairs, leaving the lights for him. He checked the rooms on the first floor, leaving the kitchen for last. He pressed the refrigerator door to make sure it was closed and then he looked out the window at the backyard. He could see in the porch light the yellow-green buds of the trees hovering tentatively, feeling the pull of the branch and the pull of the wind as well. He flicked off the light switch and slowly walked up to the bedroom.

Mrs. Michaels heard her husband's careful footsteps. Standing naked in the lamplight, weary of her body, she quickly pulled her nightgown over her head. When he opened the bedroom door she glanced at him as if she were hiding a secret behind her back. He didn't notice and rolled up one of her sleeves and tickled her elbow. "This is where all your pretty wrinkles began, Mrs. Michaels, all those years of leaning on the table," he said, and then kissed it, forgiving her this irrevocable mistake.

"You were always wrinkled," she whispered in his ear, "I can't remember a time when you weren't," and at this fib he led her down to the bed where they slowly twisted the blankets beneath them. His hands against her back called up for her a darkened room forty years ago when the blinds, lit by the lamp outside, had swayed as they both had on the bed. Her knees rocking against his echoed for him an ancient summer, when they had floated on a raft so far from shore no one could have seen what they were doing. But their eyes always opened to the present, to each other's aged faces. Soon she felt a warm release, a small reminder of distant, stronger evenings. Her thin breasts brushing against the sheets, she remembered a greeting card he had sent her long ago, how its pale, printed flowers had only hinted at his darker passion. "Oh, Mr. Michaels," she cried, "oh, Mr. Michaels!"

Later, she listened to him breathing quietly beside her, the room around them absolutely black, and she imagined she was lying in a field. Above her, clouds shaped like words passed by—a long white list of first names. Her husband's was somewhere among them and she waited for its approach, though the sky grew darker and she fell asleep.

When Mr. Michaels died in the early morning, he floated up through the bedsheets to the ceiling, then slowly into the attic, the old suitcases and rolled-up rugs barely visible in the dark. Finally his eyes breached the roof and the shingles receded as he quickly drifted up in the air. But the long view of the surrounding town and the distant horizon, the sun still hidden, made him dizzy. There wasn't any place he wanted to be but home, so he imagined his feet were weighted, each toe fat, each foot heavy. He slowly fell and thought of where he wanted his feet to take him: to the kitchen for the breakfast smell of butter melting into toast, then to the living room to feel the serrated edges of the rare domestic issues of his stamp collection. As he thought of the thick lenses of his glasses on the night table, his feet slipped through the bedroom ceiling, his entire form descending in the air to the carpeted floor. There he stared at his still body and waited for his wife to wake up. It wasn't until she opened her eyes that he realized what she saw—his quiet figure, its absence of breath easily discovered as she placed her palm against his nostrils. Then she slowly moved her hand down to his chest and held it there for a very long time, her face pressed against his shoulders. Only when she sat up could he see her smeared and silent tears.

Mrs. Michaels closed her eyes. She didn't want to see the room or anything in it. She groped for the door to the hallway, and even if her eyes had been open she wouldn't have seen her husband, hovering and arms wide to embrace her, as she passed through him. At the stairs she stopped and looked down at the light slanting through the living room curtains. "This is an ordinary day," she said aloud. "The sun is up. Nothing has happened." But when she looked back past the bedroom doorway, her husband's motionless figure silently refuted her.

His body was soon carried from the house by strangers and driven off. Mr. Michaels stood by the window, the sunlight passing through him as he watched the vanishing car. He waved good-bye and his hand passed through the glass pane, near where a fly was resting. He pulled his hand back inside and trapped it, easily. But the fly continued rubbing its thin legs together, unaware of his enveloping, invisible hand. It flew through his fingers to a lampshade. He followed and captured it and again it escaped in contented and unpredictable flight. While he chased the fly about the house with an anger and frustration that almost convinced him he was alive, his wife remained upstairs, silent before the unmade bed.

The phone rang through the day, interrupted by Mrs. Michaels' long and sad conversations. The children began to arrive—the only son, the three daughters. Unseen, Mr. Michaels examined them closely. They looked old, and he felt that he was a child and they were his parents. He couldn't bear this, but when he closed his eyes he saw right through his transparent lids. He quickly glided away to the laundry room—the quietest part of the house—and slid through the curved metal door of the hamper and hid. He settled among the soiled clothes and listened to the murmur of familiar voices that pulled at him like fingers. When the house was empty, the family far away at his wake and then funeral, he came out to practice his new existence and he sat for hours in the wing chair, balancing his elbows so they wouldn't sink down into the upholstered arms.

After the funeral everyone returned to the house for a farewell lunch. The large families of his children crowded the rooms and mingled with the neighbors and friends. No one was aware of him. He listened but soon grew depressed because he couldn't recognize himself in their stories. He didn't remember any roller-coaster ride or repairing a bicycle. He wandered off and found himself following his great-grandchildren— two boys—who were walking uncertainly away from the adults. He stared at their strange, tiny faces, but he still couldn't recall their names. They babbled in an almost-English that they seemed to understand as they circled each other. One tottered and, off-balance, grabbed at the other and they both fell. Mr. Michaels fell too, in sympathy, but at their cries the boys were swept up by their mothers and he sat alone. He stayed there and watched his wife. She insisted on organizing every-thing—the sandwiches, the passing of cold beer, the requests for coffee. Only when she paused did he see the frantic look in her eyes. He re-turned to the hamper and stared for hours at a sock curled in on itself.

Mrs. Michaels overlooked the slow departure of friends and family. Sally, her oldest daughter, offered to stay a few days but was thanked and refused. Sally herself was a grandmother and she looked so old Mrs. Michaels couldn't wait for her to leave. When she was finally alone she closed the curtains to hide her own reflection. Then she walked to the laundry room. She stood before the hamper and opened it. Out spilled the clothes and her husband, though she didn't see his confused, invisi-ble tumbling. Instead, she separated his clothes from hers, determined not to wash them and erase his smell, his stains. She carried them to the bedroom and hung his shirts and pants in the closet, folded and settled his underwear and socks in the dresser. When she closed the doors, she felt that somehow she was holding him inside.

Mr. Michaels quickly discovered death has no sleep, and day and night became for him a turning of light and dark. At night, while his wife slept alone, he sat awake in a chair downstairs. He missed dreams and invented his own from the sounds outside. When he heard the hiss of a car passing in the street he became its driver, chased by something swift and unseen. In the summer heat the moths tapping against the windows were the footsteps of someone whose arrival he constantly awaited. During the day he wandered in the house, trying to avoid his wife, for though he was the ghost, her sorrow was haunting *him.* She read paragraphs aloud from the newspaper and then stopped, embar-rassed at the sight of his empty chair. All the while he was pacing across the room, but he had long given up responding. At these moments he felt a tug at his shoulders, as if he were connected to strings. He realized he belonged somewhere else and he had only to let himself float up and he would find it, but something always held him back.

One evening Mrs. Michaels set the table for two as she prepared dinner—minute steaks, rice boiled in chicken broth, buttered broccoli. But no one arrived for the meal by the time she filled the plates and sat alone to eat. Mr. Michaels hesitated at first, then he sat down at his place. He pretended he could lift a knife and fork and picked at his untouched portions. Beyond hunger, he watched her. A pressure to rise pulled at his shoulders. It's time to leave, he thought, and his feet rose.

Mrs. Michaels' sorrow suddenly seized her and she pushed back from the table and leapt up. She quickly left the kitchen and searched in the rooms for her dead husband, as if it were all a trick and he were only hiding. She peered into the closets, the hangers screeching against the metal poles as she pushed them aside. She bent down to stare at the cool dark under the beds. She didn't know he was behind her, drawn by her search, his shoulders no longer tingling. He hoped he *could* be found, that somehow they both would find him in a corner with dust on his fingers, and a slight smile on his ashamed face. But finally, in the basement, coming out from a pile of deserted furniture, she said to no one, "He's dead." Though he was still poking about in a warped armoire, he silently agreed.

Because she knew he wasn't there, Mrs. Michaels could see her husband more clearly in the space he had abandoned, and she no longer called to or searched for him. Instead, she noticed his absence beside her in the morning, the blankets smooth on his side of the bed. She remembered how he would pretend to be still asleep so she could wash up before him and she rose with pleasure and walked to the bathroom. Next to her hovered Mr. Michaels, who, unable to know her thoughts, saw only her satisfaction and felt more than invisible: forgotten. He watched her morning ritual for the first time, as she washed her face and pressed soapy fingers into the wrinkles with determination, as she combed her thin gray hair carefully, the curls twisting as they slipped through the dark plastic teeth. A strand fell to the floor and Mr. Michaels wished he could catch it. But it was yet another small, private moment of his wife's that had passed him invisibly all his life and that now, in death, couldn't be held. And when she began to pull up her nightgown to sit on the toilet, he had to look away.

After dressing, Mrs. Michaels walked downstairs, remembering her husband by the lack of his morning cough, by not hearing him humming while he opened and closed the drawers and closet door. In the kitchen she filled the cereal bowl with flakes of bran, poking among them and counting the number of raisins. Her unhappy husband counted along with her, amazed at the deftness of her fingers, yet lonely as she poured the milk into the bowl and smiled at his empty place.

When his wife left to go to the market, Mr. Michaels called to the closing door, "Please, come back!" but she didn't hear. He was afraid to follow, certain that he'd float away in the wind outside, and when she returned he attended her movements even more closely. In the evening, as Mrs. Michaels sat in the tub's cloudy water and carefully untangled the hair under her arms after sponging off the soap, she felt a chill of wind on her back while her husband attempted to knead her stiff shoulders with his invisible fingers.

One night in bed Mrs. Michaels' hands began to travel, palms lingering at the rise of hips. Her fingers probed, tentatively, to a distant past. Eyes closed, she saw her husband much younger, his hair still thick and dark. Mr. Michaels, hovering in bed beside her, watched her hands moving with grace and he couldn't turn away and grant her this private act. Instead, he floated over and drifted gently down upon her. He tried to move his airy body in the ways he thought she was imagining while her hands called up memories of his elbows by her arms, his lips at her forehead. When her body finally shook and settled, he remained over her, a transparent blanket in the dark. Then she pulled up the covers and he curled into the folds. He could hear the leaves falling in the wind outside and he imagined they were words he whispered to his wife, to which she responded by half-turning, her thin legs against him. In her unsettled sleep she dreamt she was a child chasing something she couldn't see, growing older with every stride she took. Yet for him, always awake, the darkness was now a kind of sleep, her rustlings under the blanket a kind of dream.

He rose in the middle of the night and glided to the window, where the furious whistling of the wind surged against the glass. He watched the brown twisting leaves scuttle over the black lawn, and when his wife rose from the bed, drawn as well to the wind, he imagined that she knew he was beside the window. Slowly, awkwardly at first, she hummed along with the insistent, then muted flourishes outside and he joined her, trying with his transparent voice to harmonize. In their own ways they followed the turns of an ancient music, Mrs. Michaels in her white nightgown, accompanied by her lover, her invisible husband.   1985

NOTES ON THE AUTHORS

ELIZABETH BOWEN (1899–1973) was born in Dublin and lived principally in County Cork and in London. She is the author of a number of
novels, the best-known of which are perhaps *The Death of the Heart* and
The Heat of the Day. A number of her supernatural stories were inspired
by the dislocations and the darkness of the Blitz.

ANN BRIDGE (Lady Mary Dolling Sanders O'Malley) (1899–1974) was
born in Bridgend, Surrey, England. She spent much of her childhood in
northern Italy and traveled extensively as an adult. Her works include
Peking Picnic, a novel, and *The Song in the House*, a collection of
stories.

A. S. BYATT (b. 1936) was born in Sheffield, England, and educated at
Newnham College, Cambridge. She has been a lecturer and critic and
has written several works of fiction. Her novel *Possession* won the
Booker Prize in 1990.

JOHN CHEEVER (1912–1982) published a great many short stories in *The
New Yorker* over a prolific career. Although best-known as a short story
writer, he wrote a number of memorable novels, including *The Wapshot
Chronicle* and *Bullet Park*. He won the Pulitzer Prize for fiction in
1978.

PENELOPE FITZGERALD (b. 1916) was born in Lincoln, England. She
started writing relatively late in life. Her biographies include *Edward
Burne-Jones* (1975), *The Knox Brothers* (1977), and *Charlotte Mew and
Her Friends* (1984); her novels include *The Golden Child* (1977), *The
Bookshop* (1978), *Offshore* (1979), *Human Voices* (1980), and *At Fred-
die's* (1982).

PHILIP GRAHAM (b. 1951) was born in Brooklyn, New York. He holds
degrees in creative writing from Sarah Lawrence College and The City
College of New York. An NEA grant recipient, Graham principally

writes prose poems and stories, but has also written memoirs and a forthcoming novel.

W(ILLIAM) F(RYER) HARVEY (1885–1937) was born near Leeds, England. His first collection of stories, *The Beast with Five Fingers, and Other Tales,* was followed by *Midnight House, and Other Tales,* and *The Arm of Mrs. Egan, and Other Stories,* among others.

ELIZABETH JANE HOWARD (b. 1923) was born in London. She has published a number of works of fiction, including the novels *After Julius* and *Something in Disguise*, and a collection of short stories, *Mr. Wrong.*

SHIRLEY JACKSON (1916–1965) wrote novels and stories of psychological suspense and the supernatural, including one of the few significant full-length ghost novels, *The Haunting of Hill House.* She also wrote humorous books of domestic life, such as *Life Among the Savages* and *Raising Demons,* as well as children's books.

HENRY JAMES (1843–1916) was born in New York, the son of a philosopher and theologian, Henry James Senior, and the brother of the distinguished philosopher William James. After dropping out of Harvard Law School, he settled in Europe in 1875. Most of his writing life was spent in England. His work includes novels, travel sketches, plays, and critical essays, and over one hundred short stories. He had a lifelong interest in the supernatural, as did his brother William, who was a pioneer in the field of scientific psychical research. Henry James's novella *The Turn of the Screw* is widely acknowledged to be a masterpiece of supernatural fiction. He was at work on a supernatural novel at the time of his death.

M(ONTAGUE) R(HODES) JAMES (1862–1936) served as provost of King's College, Cambridge, and of Eton. A brilliant academic—linguist, paleographer, medievalist, biblical scholar—he devoted little time or attention to the work that today secures his reputation as perhaps the best-loved writer of ghost stories in the language. He published *Ghost Stories of an Antiquary* in 1904, and *More Ghost Stories of an Antiquary* in 1911.

MARGHANITA LASKI (1915–1988) was born in London. She was a novelist, critic, and editor, writing both under her own name and under the pseudonym Sarah Russell. Her works include the horror novel *The Victorian Chaise Longue,* which appeared in 1953.

OLIVER ONIONS (1873–1961) was born in Bradford, England. His novels and short stories often have a historical setting. Among his works are *The Story of Ragged Robyn, The Compleat Bachelor,* and a collection of supernatural stories, *Widdershins.*

v(ICTOR) s(AWDON) PRITCHETT (b. 1900) was born in Ipswich, England. He has had a long and extremely versatile career. He was a journalist for the *Christian Science Monitor* in Ireland and Spain before settling in London. His short story collections include *The Spanish Virgin, You Make Your Own Life,* and *It May Never Happen.*

"SAKI" (Hector Hugh Munro) (1870–1916) was born in Burma and raised in North Devon, England. He was a member of the military police in Burma before embarking on a literary career. He was a journalist and satirist as well as a short story writer and novelist.

MURIEL SPARK (b. 1918) was born and educated in Edinburgh. She lived in Central Africa for several years and worked in the British Foreign Office before becoming an editor, poet, and fiction writer. Among her novels are *The Prime of Miss Jean Brodie, The Girls of Slender Means,* and *The Mandelbaum Gate.*

ELIZABETH TAYLOR (1912–1975), English writer, wrote a number of novels of middle-class life, but she is perhaps best known for her short fiction, collected in *Hester Lilly* and *A Dedicated Man,* among others.

EDITH WHARTON (1862–1937) was born in New York, to a wealthy and distinguished family. Much of her work satirizes upper-class society. Her works include the novels *The House of Mirth, The Age of Innocence,* and *The Custom of the Country,* and the novella *Ethan Frome.* She was the first woman to receive the Pulitzer Prize for fiction.

COPYRIGHT ACKNOWLEDGMENTS